# EVELINA

# EVELINA,

## OR, A YOUNG LADY'S ENTRANCE INTO THE WORLD.

### IN A SERIES OF LETTERS.

Frances Burney

*edited by Susan Kubica Howard*

broadview literary texts

**Canadian Cataloguing in Publication Data**
Burney, Fanny, 1752-1840
        Evelina, or, A young lady's entrance into the world

(Broadview literary texts)
Includes bibliographical references.
ISBN 1-55111-237-X
I. Howard, Susan Kubica, 1958-  .    II. Title.    III. Title: Young lady's entrance into the world.    IV. Series.


PR3316.A4E87 2000        823'.6        C00-931202-1


Broadview Press Ltd., is an independent, international publishing house, incorporated in 1985.


North America:
P.O. Box 1243, Peterborough, Ontario, Canada K9J 7H5
3576 California Road, Orchard Park, NY 14127
TEL: (705) 743-8990; FAX: (705) 743-8353;
E-MAIL: customerservice@broadviewpress.com

United Kingdom:
Turpin Distribution Services Ltd.,
Blackhorse Rd., Letchworth, Hertfordshire SG6 1HN
TEL: (1462) 672555; FAX (1462) 480947; E-MAIL: turpin@rsc.org

Australia:
St. Clair Press, P.O. Box 287, Rozelle, NSW 2039
TEL: (02) 818-1942; FAX: (02) 418-1923

www.broadviewpress.com

Broadview Press gratefully acknowledges the financial support of the Book Publishing Industry Development Program, Ministry of Canadian Heritage, Government of Canada.

Broadview Press is grateful to Professor Eugene Benson for advice on editorial matters for the Broadview Literary Texts series.

Text design and composition by George Kirkpatrick

PRINTED IN CANADA

*For Amy and Ben*

*Mortimer inv.t et delin.*    *Walker sculp.t*

Evelina helping Madame Duval from the ditch, frontispiece to
volume II of *Evelina* (4th. ed., 1779), by John Mortimer.
Princeton University Library.

# Contents

Acknowledgements • 9

Introduction • 11

Frances Burney: A Brief Chronology • 79

A Note on the Text • 82

*Evelina* • 87

Introduction to Appendices • 555

Appendix A: Contemporary Reviews
1. *London Review* (February 1778) • 559
2. *Monthly Review* (April 1778) • 559
3. *Westminster Magazine* (June 1778) • 559
4. *Gentleman's Magazine* (September 1778) • 559
5. *Critical Review* (September 1778) • 560

Appendix B: Works on Family
1. George Savile, Marquis of Halifax, *The Lady's New-Year's-Gift* • 563
2. William Fleetwood, *The Relative Duties of Parents and Children, Husbands and Wives, Masters and Servants* • 569
3. Sarah, Duchess of Marlborough, "Correspondence with her Granddaughter, Diana, Duchess of Bedford, 1732-35" • 580
4. Samuel Richardson, *Letters Written To and For Particular Friends, on the Most Important Occasions* • 584
5. [John Hill], *On the Management and Education of Children* • 600
6. Samuel Richardson, *A Collection of the Moral and Instructive Sentiments, Maxims, Cautions, and Reflexions, Contained in the Histories of* PAMELA, CLARISSA, *and* SIR CHARLES GRANDISON • 601

7. James Nelson, *An Essay on the Government of Children* • 611
8. Eliza Haywood, *The Female Spectator* • 613
9. Lady Sarah Pennington, *An Unfortunate Mother's Advice to Her Absent Daughters* • 621
10. "Portia" [pseud.], *The Polite Lady* • 627
11. Hester Mulso Chapone, *Letters on the Improvement of the Mind* • 630
12. Clara Reeve, *Plans of Education* • 631
13. Mrs. Bonhote, *The Parental Monitor* • 638
14. Thomas Gisborne, *An Enquiry into the Duties of the Female Sex* • 639
15. Maria Edgeworth and Richard Lovell Edgeworth, *Practical Education* • 642
16. Francis Burney D'Arblay, *Memoirs of Doctor Burney* • 644

Appendix C: Works on Comedy
1. Anon., *Pasquil's Jests, Mixed with Mother Bunches Merriments* • 649
2. Joseph Addison, *The Spectator* • 650
3. Anon., *Scoggin's Jests* • 658
4. [John Mottley], *Joe Miller's Jest Book* • 660
5. [Corbyn Morris], *An Essay Towards Fixing the True Standards of Wit, Humour, Raillery, Satire, and Ridicule* • 662
6. Eliza Haywood, *The Female Spectator* • 664
7. Jane Collier, *An Essay on the Art of Ingeniously Tormenting* • 666
8. Christopher Anstey, *The New Bath Guide* • 669
9. [James Quin], *Quin's Jests* • 676
10. Anon., *An Essay on Laughter* • 679
11. William Hazlitt, *Lectures on the English Comic Writers* • 682

Select Bibliography • 687

# Acknowledgements

The goodwill and efforts of many people contributed to the publishing of this edition. I offer my heartfelt thanks to them all, and especially:

The staff at Duquesne University's Gumberg Library, in particular Kathy Julius, head of the Interlibrary Loan Office, who worked diligently to fill my many orders for primary works.

The administration, faculty, and staff of Duquesne University, especially the English Department and its Chair, Dr. Ronald Arnett, for funding a sabbatical and a research assistant, for the reduction of my teaching load, for covering travel costs to the 1998 ASECS conference at which I presented part of the introduction, and for photocopying.

Research Assistant Kathryn Pivak, who handled many tasks relating to the production of this project, from photocopying to word processing, proofreading to researching illustrations, conscientiously and competently, with an admirable sense of dedication and generosity of spirit. Without her fine efforts this project could not have been completed in a timely manner.

Students in my classes at Duquesne University who helped me to work through my focus.

Tim Johnson, Curator of Special Collections at the University of Minnesota at Minneapolis library for generously lending the second edition of *Evelina* to Duquesne for me to read there.

Princeton University Library, Department of Rare Books and Special Collections, for permission to use Mortimer's 1779 engraving of Evelina helping Madame Duval from the ditch as the frontispiece for this edition.

Scholars whose work on Burney, on issues of family, on comic theory and women's comedy have informed my own views; editors of past editions of *Evelina* from whose introductions, annotations, and textual notes I have benefited immeasurably.

The readers, editorial staff, and president of Broadview Press.

My children, Ben and Amy, for their patience, fortitude, and good-humor; my friends and family, particularly my parents, Helen and Walter Kubica, my sister, Sandy Kubica, and my brother, John Kubica, and my friends Kathy and Mark Stall and Maryann Porch for their generous, constant support.

# Introduction

## I. *Evelina*: Genesis, Composition, Publication, and Reception

In a conversation with Sir Walter Scott in 1826, Frances Burney d'Arblay shared the "real history of Evelina's *Entrance into the World*" (*Memoirs* II 122), which she later recorded in her *Memoirs of Dr. Burney* (1832). This history reveals that though as a shy child of eight, Frances Burney could neither read nor write, by age ten she was writing her own stories secretly on scraps of paper. In order to enjoy the privacy of her writings, and so that she should not be chastised for such frivolous labor when there was so much to be done in a busy household, she told only her sister Susanna about her writing. And, too, as she notes in the preface to her fourth and final novel, *The Wanderer*, she could not avoid being "impressed ... with ideas that fastened degradation to this class of composition" (8); it is this feeling that she is doing something wrong in writing fiction that causes the struggle the adolescent Burney feels, a struggle that results, on her fifteenth birthday, with only her sister Susanna as a witness, in Burney burning all of her writings in a bonfire in the garden in an effort to "extinguish for ever in their ashes her scribbling propensity" (*Memoirs* II 125). Included in the works destroyed was the draft of a novel, *The History of Caroline Evelyn*, and it was the fate of Caroline's infant daughter, Evelina, that Burney pondered in the years after the bonfire, especially the situation of "the unequal birth by which she hung suspended between the elegant connexions of her mother, and the vulgar ones of her grandmother" (125-26). She recalls in the preface to *The Wanderer*, that "in defiance of every self-effort, Evelina struggled herself into life" (8). According to Burney, the whole of *Evelina* was written in her head before she wrote any of it down; composing the novel was not difficult, then, but finding the opportunity to get it down on paper was, since she needed to do it in secret, and in the few moments she could spare from helping her father, a well-known musician and teacher, with his scholarly work. As her father notes, "'her first work ... was written by stealth, in a closet up two pair of stairs, that was appropriated to the younger children as a play room'" (qtd. in *Memoirs* II 168-69). Given this, her statement in the letter "To the Authors of the Monthly and Critical Reviews" that prefaces *Evelina* that the novel was simply "the trifling production of a few idle hours" belies the difficulty of Burney's situation and the diligence which the novel's composition required.

Burney composed *Evelina* in secrecy as she had written her juvenalia in secrecy, out of a need to have this private creative outlet. But her secrecy may also have been a result of her being a member of an intellectual family in which novel writing may have been associated with the degradation the fifteen-year-old Burney had connected with the endeavor. Her father's library, after all, included only one novel, Henry Fielding's *Amelia*. She may have feared her father's disapproval, especially as, Margaret Anne Doody points out, Burney made it a practice to keep "each matter of importance secret from her father" (*Frances Burney* 25). Doody also conjectures that Burney's struggle with her writing is a struggle against the intensity of her involvement with it, and that this is what made her uncomfortable enough with it to actually burn all of her work in an effort to get herself to quit such an addictive pasttime.

As her story took shape on the page, Burney began to desire its publication and shared her hopes for the novel with her siblings. She copied the manuscript in a "feigned hand" for a number of reasons: her handwriting was known by publishers of her father's work, since she was his secretary, and she did not want to imperil the respected Burney name with an effort that might be judged negatively. In addition, Burney notes in her "Preface" to *Evelina* that the novel as a genre, having passed out of the hands of the greats – Fielding, Richardson, Sterne and Smollett – was in a state of limbo, its reputation poised between the respect commanded by the relatively few classic works and the suspect nature of those abundant popular novels written for circulating libraries. Despite the respected work of such women novelists as Charlotte Lennox or Sarah Fielding, unless a woman expressly wrote out of financial need, her literary endeavors were usually viewed as a blight upon her character, which explains Burney's publishing the novel anonymously. As Judy Simons points out, "to remain respectable, respectable women needed to retain their privacy" (19). Copying the novel, which also involved some revision,[1] was as difficult a task as the original composing had been. Burney writes in her Journal for 1777, that "the fear of Discovery, or of suspicion in the House, made the Copying extremely laborious to me; for, in the Day Time, I could only take odd moments, so that I was obliged to sit up the greatest part of many Nights, in order to get it ready" (*EJL* II 231-32).

In an unsigned letter, Burney offered the first two volumes of the novel to James Dodsley, a well-known publisher in the fashionable West End of London, hoping he'd publish those two volumes immediately and the "sequel" the next year. When Dodsley refused to look at the novel because it was anonymous, Burney and her sister Susanna and brother Charles decided to try a publisher in the city, Thomas Lowndes of Fleet Street. On 25 December 1776, Burney wrote to Lowndes:

> I have in my possession a M: S. novel, which has never yet been seen but by myself; I am desirous of having the 2 first volumes printed immediately, – and the publication of the rest, shall depend wholly on their success. (*EJL* II 213)

Lowndes readily agreed to read the manuscript, despite its being anonymous; Burney's younger brother, Charles, disguised to look much older, carried the manuscript of the first volume to Lowndes with an accompanying letter that explained that "The plan of the first Volume, is the Introduction of a well educated, but inexperienced young woman into public company, and a round of the most fashionable Spring Diversions of London" (*EJL* II 215); the letter went on to note that such a

---

1   FB notes in a letter to her publisher, Thomas Lowndes, dated 11 November 1777, that she took "pains to Copy & Correct [*Evelina*] ... for the Press" (*The Early Journals and Letters of Fanny Burney* II 288).

plan "has not before been executed, though it seems a fair field open for the Novelist, as it offers a fund inexhaustible for Conversation, observations, and probable Incidents" (*EJL* II 215). And, in a 17 January 1777 letter to Lowndes accompanying the second volume, sent to him at his request shortly after he had finished the first volume, Burney notes of the action of this volume: "The Heroine, as you will find, descending into a lower circle, now partakes of a round of Summer *Diversions*, which, though of an inferior cast to those of the Spring, are not less productive of Incidents for a Novel" (*EJL* II 216).

After having read the two volumes, Lowndes suggested that its author finish the novel and "publish it compleat. I'm sure it will be your interest as well as the Booksellers, you may well add One Volume to these, & I shall more eagerly print it" (*EJL* II 216-17).[1] Burney responded by indicating that her original plan had been to publish the two completed volumes and to "have *felt the pulse* of the public, before I had proceeded" with the next two projected volumes. She concludes: "I yield, however, to your Experience in these matters, & will defer the publication, till the Work is completed ..." (*EJL* II 217). In her Journal, however, she complains of Lowndes' advice:

Now this man, knowing nothing of my situation, supposed, in all probability, that I could seat myself quietly at my Bureau, & write on with all expedition & ease, till the work was finished: but so different was the case, that I had hardly Time to write half a page in a Day; & niether my Health, nor inclination, would allow me to continue my *Nocturnal* scribling for so long a Time as to write first, &

---

1 In a 5 September 1782 letter to FB's father, Dr. Charles Burney, questioning why FB had not chosen him to publish her second novel, *Cecilia*, Lowndes recalls that "'In Respect to *Evelina*, the two first volumes were sent to get my opinion; I answered that the Author had Ability, and if the *Marybone* scene was abridged, and the City Visits lessened, the Work would appear more lively; and if the Author would write a third Volume, replete with Modern Characters, I should be glad to see it when finished. About six months afterwards the whole was brought by a plain-dressed young Gentleman, who did not chuse to mention the Author. I named a sum, which was accepted and paid, and he afterwards said the Writer was contented with it'" (qtd. in Mackinnon [3]).

then Copy, a whole volume. I was, therefore, obliged to give the attempt & affair entirely over for the present. (*EJL* II 232)

In fact, Lars E. Troide, the editor of Burney's *Early Journals and Letters*, notes that Burney used the pretense of writing letters to her sister Susanna while visiting her friend and mentor, Samuel Crisp, as a cover to composing volume three of *Evelina* (*EJL* II 219 n.8).

By September 1777, Burney had composed and copied the third volume of *Evelina*, and written to Lowndes asking whether he still wished to see it; he wrote back two months later requesting she send him the third volume. Her cousin Edward Francisco Burney acted as her courier this time, since her brother Charles was at college. Before Burney sent the third volume, she told her father she was working on a novel, though she gave him no specific details about it, not even its title, and was relieved, she notes in her Journal, with his disinterest which allowed her to continue her efforts toward publication in "total secresy and silence" (*EJL* II 233). Lowndes quickly wrote back saying that he thought the third volume "better than 1 & 2d If you please I'll give you Twenty Guineas for the Manuscript and without loss of time put it to Press" (*EJL* II 287). Burney's remembrance of her response to Lowndes' offer in her *Memoirs of Dr. Burney* was that she "accepted with alacrity, and boundless surprise at [the offer's] magnificence" (*Memoirs* II 132), but her initial response to Lowndes, apparent in a letter dated 11 November 1777, registers dismay at the price he was willing to pay for the copyright: "though it was originally written merely for amusement, I should not have taken the pains to Copy & Correct it for the Press, had I imagined that 10 Guineas a Volume would have been more than its worth" (*EJL* II 288).[1] In business-like terms, she suggests he reconsider or she will show the manuscript to a "Gentleman who is much more experienced in authorship

---

1   As Joyce Hemlow and other critics note, FB's remembrance in the *Memoirs* of the incidents of forty years before sometimes contradicts information in the letters and journal entries dating from that period (*History* 87).

business than myself, & [will] … abide by his Decision" (288). Apparently, Lowndes' terms were finally accepted, though Burney notes in her *Memoirs of Dr. Burney* that with the publication of the third edition of the novel in 1779 Lowndes sent Burney another £10, making the price he paid for the copyright for *Evelina* to Burney ultimately £30 (*Memoirs* II 151).[1]

Once Burney had accepted his terms, Lowndes hurried the novel to press. He apparently sent Burney no proofs of the first edition, but a "printed copy, … in sheets" from which she was to prepare a list of *Errata* was sent by Lowndes to Gregg's Coffee House in Covent Garden c/o Mr. Grafton; Burney did not receive this package until 7 January 1778 (Dobson xiii). Though she quickly prepared a list of corrections, Lowndes did not incorporate them into the text, instead placing the *Errata* at the beginning of the first volume. It wasn't until the second edition that Burney would actually see the bulk of these corrections incorporated into the text, as well as more substantive alterations. (For further discussion of Burney's revision of *Evelina*, see "A Note on the Text" which follows this introduction.)

The first edition of *Evelina, or, A Young Lady's Entrance into the World*,[2] in three volumes, was published Thursday 29 January 1778 and available at "seven shillings and sixpence sewed, or

---

1    This is the generally accepted view with regard to the amount Lowndes paid FB for *Evelina*, though recent Burney biographer Kate Chisholm contends that FB's "ruse worked. Lowndes evidently realised that he had a bestseller on his hands, and that thirty guineas was a bargain price" (43), which implies that Lowndes paid FB the £30 up front to publish *Evelina*. While contemporaries of Lowndes did not fault him for not having guessed at *Evelina's* potential, his colleagues in the trade were apparently very critical of his unwillingness to share the wealth with FB as the popularity of the novel grew. Mr. Bowen, a bookseller in Brighton, in conversation with Mrs. Thrale, reputedly remarked "'O, ma'am, what a Book thrown away was that! – all the Trade cry shame on Lowndes…. [N]ot, ma'am, that I expected he could have known its worth, because that's out of the question, – but when its profits told him what it was, it's quite scandalous that he should have done nothing! – quite ungentleman like indeed'" (qtd. in Gallagher 227 n.49). His poor treatment explains FB's decision to look elsewhere for a publisher of her subsequent novels, though at the time she expressed her satisfaction with the price paid. In her Journal for 1778, she writes that her father was "*enraged* that Lowndes gave no more for the M.S. – but *I* was satisfied, – & that sufficed" (*EJL* III 54).

2    The title was changed to *Evelina, or The History of a Young Lady's Entrance into the World* with the publication of the third edition in 1779.

nine shillings bound" (*EJL* III 1 n.1). Burney only became aware of this "from hearing the … advertisement read, accidentally, aloud at breakfast-time," by her stepmother (*Memoirs* II 132). A few months followed in which her authorship remained unknown, though the novel began to catch on. She nursed her father through a fever, and then came down with it herself and had to leave London for the country home of Samuel Crisp, a family friend, where she recuperated. Six months after the novel's publication, Burney's father stumbled on the truth of its authorship; he read, and admired it, confiding in his daughter Susanna that "'Upon my soul I think it the best Novel I know excepting Fieldings, – &, in some respects, *better* than his!'" (qtd. in Chisholm 56). Burney's stepmother, usually a difficult person to please, also approved of *Evelina*, and it won favor with influential people in society. Mrs. Cholmondeley, influential in literary and social circles, was the "'*first* person who publicly praised & recommended Evelina among the Wits,'" according to Samuel Johnson (*EJL* III 222); she introduced the novel to such intellectual and aesthetic heavyweights as Edmund Burke, who read it in a night; Joshua Reynolds, who did the same; and Johnson, who told the influential literary hostess, Hester Thrale, about it. After discovering the secret of its authorship, Thrale invited Burney to her home at Streatham and helped to solidify Burney's place in the literary world of London.

So the novel entered popular culture through its influential readers who promoted it privately and publicly, to the point where it was the "universal topic;" its phrases were repeated in polite conversation and its characters' gestures were appropriated for mimicry and amusement at social gatherings. Chisholm notes that "the diaries and letters of the time are filled with references to 'Madame French', the 'Holborn Beau' (Mr. Smith) and the 'old sea dog' (Captain Mirvan)" (58). Mrs. Cholmondeley could not resist Madame Duval's "Ma fois." Johnson particularly liked "'The Holbourn Beau,'" according to Mrs. Thrale, who noted: "'He has got those incomparable Brangtons quite by heart, and he recited scene after scene of their squabbles, and selfishness, and forwardness, till he quite shook his sides with laughter'" (*Memoirs* II 155). Johnson felt that the novel's "'comic humour of character ... owes its effect to contrast; for without Lord Orville, and Mr. Villars, and that melancholy and gentleman-like half-starved Scotchman, poor Macartney, the Branghtons, and the Duvals, would be less than nothing; for vulgarity, in its own unshadowed glare, is only disgusting'" (qtd. in *Memoirs* II 155-56). In conversation with Dr. Burney, Mrs. Thrale declared of *Evelina* that "'there's a vast deal of humour and entertainment in it ... there's a great deal of human *Life* in this Book, & of the Manners of the present time. It's writ by somebody that knows *the top & the bottom – the highest and lowest* of Mankind'" (*EJL* III 35 n.12) – though once Burney's authorship was known, Thrale was more reserved in her praise of *Evelina*, referring to it in her diary as "'flimzy'" compared to works by Fielding, Richardson, Lennox, Smollett, and Rousseau (*EJL* III 36 n.12). Other contemporary readers found fault with the novel's "use of colloquial language and depiction of low-life characters" (Chisholm 62). The violence of several scenes disconcerted some readers, but entertained others: Dr. Burney and Samuel Crisp both found Lovel too harshly dealt with by Captain Mirvan and the monkey (*EJL* III 28-29; 178-79), but Mrs. Thrale and Dr. Johnson were amused by Captain Mirvan's practical jokes.

Literary reviews were also predominantly positive, though there were aspects that the five reviews published within the first year after the novel's appearance did criticize. While Burney confesses in her Journal of 1778 that she awaited the critics' reviews of *Evelina* with "fear and fidgets.... I have very little doubt but I shall be horribly mauled" (*EJL* III 13), her novel fared well, especially as compared to other novels of the time. William Kenrick of the *London Review*, as early as February 1778, distinguished *Evelina* from contemporary novels for its "stile, character and incident." The *Monthly Review* in April 1778 pronounced *Evelina* "one of the most sprightly, entertaining, and agreeable productions of this kind ...", especially noting the "great variety of natural incidents," the diversity in characterization, and easy style, though criticizing the unrealistic depiction of Captain Mirvan.[1] The *Westminster Magazine* in June 1778 in a brief review deemed the novel "useful and entertaining" and recommends it to young men and women. The *Gentleman's Magazine* for September 1778 stated that *Evelina* "will afford a pleasing, innocent amusement, exhibiting, in an easy style, many such characters as occur in the world...." And finally, also in September 1778, the *Critical Review* devoted two and one-quarter pages to *Evelina*, again distinguishing it from other contemporary novels and placing it firmly in the house of Richardson, both in its strengths – "moral and literary" – and its weaknesses. The reviewer found it a "well written," "amusing and instructive novel," but criticized it for its dependence on upper class characters when the readers of novels invariably belong to the "middle ranks of life."[2]

Initially, Burney was "extremely satisfied with what was said" in the earliest reviews, but in later years, as she awaited reviews of her third novel, *Camilla*, she had occasion to note in a letter of 8 November 1796, that while the positive reviews of *Evelina* did not hurt the novel, they were not responsible for its success:

> Evelina made its way all by itself: it was well spoken of, indeed, in all the Reviews, compared with general Novels; but it was undistinguished by any quotation, & only put in the Monthly Catalogue, & only allowed a short single paragraph. It was circulated only by the general public, till it reached through that unbiassed medium, Dr. Johnson – and thence it wanted no patron. (*The Journals and Letters of Fanny Burney* III 222)

By July, 1778, the 500 copies printed of the first edition were

---

1   FB wrote in her Diary, 28 May 1780, that "'the more I see of sea-captains, the less reason I have to be ashamed of Captain Mirvan; for they have all so irresistibly a propensity to wanton mischief, to roasting beaux and detesting old women, that I quite rejoice I showed the book to no one ere printed, lest I should have been prevailed upon to soften his character'" (qtd. in L.B. Seeley, *Fanny Burney and Her Friends* [London: Seeley and Co., 1895], 71).
2   See Appendix A for the full text of the above reviews.

sold out (Chisholm 47);[1] 1779 saw four more editions (one of them pirated); indeed, proof that the novel "continues to sell in a most wonderful manner," according to Burney, was the fact that the fourth edition, with an imprint date of 1779, though not actually published until February 1780, included "Cuts, designed by Mortimer just before he Died, & executed by Hall & Bartolozzi" as well as Walker, for which Lowndes reportedly paid more than he did for the copyright for the novel itself (*EJL* III 264).[2] The novel's popularity was also apparent in the fact that it was translated into German, Dutch, and French and published in America, all before the end of the century (Chisholm 47).

After her phenomenal success with *Evelina*, Burney went on to become a respected figure in the literary milieu of eighteenth-century London; to write three more novels – none of them published anonymously, now that her literary reputation was secured and could not damage her family's name – in addition to a number of tragedies, comedies, and prose works; to marry happily and to raise a family.

## II. *Evelina*: Family and Comedy

The subtitle of Burney's novel, "A Young Lady's Entrance into the World," emphasizes Evelina's movement into the public sphere of society. In its most literal sense, this focus is played out in the many social encounters Evelina experiences against a variety of public backdrops, both fashionable and common. But in its deepest sense, the novel's understanding of "society" is Rousseau's: "'the earliest of all societies, and the only natural one, is the family'" (qtd. in Gottlieb 232). Evelina's entrance

---

1   FB was under the impression that the first edition's run was 800, but Dobson notes that in an unpublished letter from Lowndes to Dr. Burney, Lowndes indicates the first edition's run had been 500, which, he told FB's sister Charlotte, was "'the common number for a novel'" (xiii n.1). Hemlow concludes that for the first three editions, between 2300-2500 copies of the novel were printed (*JL* III 206 n.5).

2   Dobson writes that Lowndes paid "seventy-three pounds, or just forty-three more than he had given for the copyright of the novel" (xviii); Dobson is here including the £10 Lowndes gave Burney after the publication of the third edition in 1779, bringing the total amount paid for the copyright of *Evelina* to £30.

into society, then, can also be seen as her introduction to several of the various manifestations of family in the world. In the course of the novel, she embraces and is enveloped by a number of different families as she searches for a suitable family to which she may belong.

While the nuclear family – a husband, wife and their children – was the predominant family structure in eighteenth-century England,[1] contemporary dictionaries defined "family" in several ways: as the nuclear family; as the "household," which could include along with the nuclear family, servants, lodgers, companions, and visitors typically unrelated to the members of the nuclear family by blood or marriage; and as kin, who, bound by blood or marriage, did not necessarily live together (Gottlieb 7; Flandrin 4-6). The way a family was structured depended on a number of factors, including economic situation, class, and household location. Upper class households, for instance, with their numerous servants as well as guests, were usually larger than those of the poor, which tended to be simple nuclear families (Houlbrooke 24; Gottlieb 13). Many middle class urban households took in lodgers, since it was less likely the household would contain extended kin, people living in cities often having come from homes in the country, leaving family connections behind (Earle 217). Many nuclear families were incomplete since families often sent their children away from home when they were as young as eight or nine. Working class families did this out of economic necessity. Their children went off to become servants, apprentices, or companions in more affluent homes (Gottlieb 7-11); and the upper classes sent their children to friends or wealthier kin with a number of motives in mind: to give them greater experience of the world; to provide polish – this was especially true for children growing up in the country (Gillis *World* 9-10) – ; to allow for advantages and opportunities in careers or marriage; or, as a last resort when their own parenting skills had failed. While the benefits to children and families alike were generally great, and the children so treated typically found a comfortable place in the

---

1  See for instance Houlbrooke 18, Rendall 4, Laslett *Family Life* 13, and Durston 1.

new families they joined (Gillis *World* 10), for some, indeed, the new life was more attractive than the old and they succumbed to what Thomas Gisborne, in *An Enquiry into the Duties of the Female Sex* (1797), termed a dissatisfaction "with the calm occupations and enjoyments of the family fireside" (see Appendix B).

## The Family in the Conduct Books

Evelina's movement between different households and in different capacities – from Berry Hill, to Howard Grove, to London; as ward, guest, and companion – exemplifies the fluid nature of the household at this time, and the fact that one's role within one household might not resemble one's role in another (O'Day 94, Gottlieb 14; Anderson 30). Within the nuclear family, however, it was necessary for each individual to play his or her prescribed role.[1] Conduct books of the time indicate that it was the father's role to command his family with authority as well as love, and the mother's role to nurture and protect her children, as well as to obey her husband.[2] Children were to obey both parents, according to such progressive writers as John Locke in *Two Treatises* (1693) and William Fleetwood in *The Relative Duties of Parents and Children* ... (1705), but ultimately, it was the father's word that held sway in a family. This patriarchal structure, in which the father controlled all members of the household, from his wife and children to his servants and

---

1 Gottlieb 259. In *Family Fortunes: Men and Women of the English Middle Class, 1780-1850*, Davidoff and Hall note that "the expectations and responsibilities surrounding all family relationships were to some extent mutable. They were most strongly enforced within the inner core of husband and wife, parents and children and siblings, radiating outwards to aunts and uncles, nieces and nephews, grandparents and cousins" (354-55).

2 See in particular the excerpts from John Hill's *On the Management and Education of Children* (1754) and James Nelson's *An Essay on the Government of Children* (1756) in Appendix B. The objective of most Conduct Books was the reformation of manners through stories which recounted the punishment of vice and the reward of virtue. Many dealt with family relationships and stressed the need for children to obey their parents. They were usually addressed to the educated middle classes, with many specifically concerned with the moral and social education of young women.

visitors, enacted a parent-child relationship on an extended scale.[1] Richard Allestree's *The Whole Duty of Man*, first published in 1658 but influential well into the eighteenth century, represents a popular view that regardless of parents' "infirmities," children must not "despise or contemn them, either in outward behaviour, or so much as inwardly in our hearts," but "reverence and respect" them. He notes that these same duties are owed "brethren" and relations.[2] While Allestree means by parents "natural" or biological parents, the "parents of our flesh," his contemporary, Thomas Cobbett, in *A Fruitful and Useful Discourse touching the honour due from children wherein both the respective duties of children to parents and of parents to children are cleared from scripture* ... expands the definition of parents to include "all superiours," in years, parts, or law.[3]

William Fleetwood, writing fifty years later in *The Relative Duties of Parents and Children, Husbands and Wives, Masters and Servants* (1705) continues Cobbett's dictate that children should honor father and mother equally, but concedes that when one can only please one parent, it is the father whose authority reigns supreme since he is superior to the mother "both in Natural Strength, in Wisdom, and by God's appointment." Children owe their parents "Love, Respect, or Honour, Obedience, and Support of all kinds, whenever they stand in need of it." Parents, too, have responsibilities in this relationship, since all relationships imply mutual obligations. The law gives parents much power over children but assumes that parents' natural affection for their children will guide their actions; if parents

---

1   While this would seem a negative situation for women, Linda Gordon sees this paternalistic structure as one which women could benefit from since its hierarchical structure, while giving men the ultimate control, forced them to delegate responsibilities, which allowed women certain authority over their daughters and young sons, resulting in a close bond between mother and children which would aid the women as they faced old age ("Family Violence, Feminism, and Social Control," in *Rethinking the Family*, Ed. Barrie Thorne and Marilyn Yalom, ([Boston: Northeastern University Press, 1992], 272). Margaret Ezell, in *The Patriarch's Wife*, views this involvement of mothers in their children's lives as a "'recognizable' pattern of matriarchy" ([Chapel Hill: University of North Carolina Press, 1987], 33).
2   (London: Griffith, Farran, Okeden, and Welsh, 1889), 174, 184.
3   (London: John Rothwell, 1656), 2.

are cruel to their children the law will intervene, and, indeed, children who are abused by their parents "should implore assistance in such case." No one, Fleetwood assures the reader, will view children who seek assistance from the Magistrate as disobedient or undutiful, though the occasion must be just and the provocation great. In fact, Fleetwood goes so far as to write that parents' "barbarous usage cancell[s] ... the bond of Nature, and [leaves children] ... under no other Obligation to their Parents, than to Strangers" (see Appendix B).

Parents who did not play their roles satisfactorily – who did not maintain, protect, and educate their children, as the law compelled them to[1] – Defoe calls "unnatural" and as such, they are undeserving of "returns to Affection from their Children." In *The Family Instructor* (1715), Defoe notes that in situations where parental neglect has resulted in a dysfunctional household in which all, but especially the children, are suffering, extended family and friends can help parents to learn how to correct their problems for the benefit of the family and the community.[2] Samuel Richardson, in both *Familiar Letters on Important Occasions* (1741) and *A Collection of the Moral And Instructive Sentiments ... Contained in the Histories of Pamela, Clarissa, and Sir Charles Grandison* (1755), is essentially in agreement with Defoe. A parent is not "morose and sour, and hard to be pleased, but mild, indulgent, kind, and such an one as would rather govern by persuasion, than force" (*Col.*) (see Appendix B). In all cases parents have the right to control their children, but should act reasonably. "Tyranny in *all shapes* is odious; but *Fathers* and *Mothers* who are tyrants can have no bowels."[3] He balances these remarks with the assertion that a child's duty to her parents remains despite a change in her situation or fortune, and applauds the daughter whose "high

---

1 See William Blackstone's *Commentaries on the Laws of England* I 446.
2 (Oxford: Thomas Tegg, 1841), 201.
3 *A Collection of the Moral and Instructive Sentiments.* (Delmar, New York: Scholars' Facsimiles and Reprints, 1980) 206. Ian Bell, in *Literature and Crime in Augustan England* (London: Routledge, 1991) 16, makes the point that while fathers had authority to punish their children under the law, the image of the father as absolute monarch received little support from conduct books.

degree of understanding and discretion [allows her to mingle] ... reverence with her love to a Parent, who has talents visibly inferior to her own" (*Col.*).

Also writing at mid-century, James Nelson, in *An Essay on the Government of Children* (1756), essentially agrees with Richardson that parents need to have reasonable dominion over their children. Nelson's goal is to produce children who are innocent, tractable, orderly, and courteous; they should be reasonable and not overly passionate. Like Defoe, he bemoans the fact that most people don't know how to parent children. Nelson recommends that both mother and father should raise their children because the "mother's sweetness" and the "father's authority" need to be blended. Like those conduct book writers before him, he stresses the need for parents to present a consolidated front to their children (see Appendix B).

In later eighteenth-century tracts, the goal of affective parent/child relationships is emphatically present: Mrs. Bonhote's *The Parental Monitor* (1796) remarks on "How pleasant and soothing [it is] ... to have a set of tender and sincere friends in our nearest and dearest relatives!" (55). She advocates tolerating and never exposing the frailties of those closest to us if we would like to be treated similarly; the ties of nature should also be the ties of the heart. Thomas Gisborne, in *An Enquiry into the Duties of the Female Sex* (1797), also stresses the affectionate relationship between parent and child, and the good communication between them that results from mutual sympathy.[1]

## The Family in Literature

Representations of the family in imaginative literature of the period – principally fiction and drama – of course vary, but seem to emphasize two prevailing perspectives on family relations: on the one hand, the reader/audience is propelled into a sympathetic relationship with the child victims of dysfunctional families; on the other, the reader/audience is urged to celebrate what Fielding often in his work refers to as the "family of

---

1  Excerpts from these two texts appear in Appendix B.

love" in its victory over the harshness of society. At times the two perspectives play out in one work.

By mid century the family as depicted in the novel seems to be predominantly a negative force in a child's life.[1] The lesson Robinson Crusoe learned in Defoe's 1718 novel that disobeying one's father led to grave consequences has been replaced by the plight of Richardson's Clarissa, whose attempts to honor the commands of her parents contribute to her death. While conduct books throughout the century generally privilege the parental perspective, novelists of the period are more likely to present a sympathetic portrait of the individual having to negotiate the often unreasonable demands of family in an attempt to find a sustaining, viable family structure. Fathers in these novels seem intent on maintaining control over their offspring and resort to unseemly methods, usually involving threats regarding inheritance, to assert their socially sanctioned power and maintain that control.[2] Mothers are inept, bowing to the greater power of their brutish spouses, sacrificing their children in their attempts to maintain a serene exterior to family relations. Or the situation is reversed, and it is the mother who controls, albeit poorly, the affairs of the family, sacrificing the family to her own appetites, and the father who is ineffective or absent.[3] Siblings are in competition for their parents' attention, if not their love, and for the ultimate prize, the family inheritance. These relationships capture one side of the conduct books' emphasis on parental authority and children's obedience, but

---

1 Pierre Fauchery argues that while "'the canonical function of kinship is in principle tutelary ... [in the eighteenth-century novel] the family makes itself wholly a negation.'" And Ronald Paulson contends that the eighteenth-century fictional family does not nurture the individual, nor does it "'socialize the child acceptably'" (qtd. in Flanders 114, 120).

2 Grandfathers appear on occasion in an equally harsh light, if we think of the treatment Smollett's Roderick Random receives at the hands of his grandfather, whose insensitive actions destroy his family (*The Adventures of Roderick Random* [1748]).

3 The titular heroines of Defoe's early eighteenth-century novels *Moll Flanders* (1722) and *Roxana* (1724) are two such women who allow their own needs to supersede their maternal duties and the happiness and well-being of the children to whom they give birth. The story of Flavia in Eliza Haywood's *The Female Spectator* (1744–46) illustrates the near-tragic consequences of a mother whose love of gallantry overwhelms her maternal feelings and responsibilities.

ignore the admonition that the authority be rational and moderate, and that affection be its guide.

While novels and dramas of the period continued to treat audiences to the machinations of the stock characters of Restoration comedies – libertine husbands, rakes, unmotherly mothers, tyrannical fathers – the actions of these characters, T. G. A. Nelson contends, are no longer harmless; instead, they hold serious consequences for their innocent victims, and it is toward these victims that the audience's sympathies glide.[1] Mandeville's prose work, *The Virgin Unmasked* (1709), for instance, gives a very negative portrait of the rakish Dorante, a precursor to Burney's Sir John Belmont, who as husband and father is irresponsible and heartless, refusing to acknowledge his child as his own.

As a balance to the sentimental leanings of the depictions of the young victims of the family's tyranny in these works, Nelson finds that novelists and dramatists include many of the "traditional jests and critiques" (234) of the family prevalent in Restoration drama, though these jokes simply serve as comic relief; they do not carry the emotional weight of the play or novel (189). This can be said as well of the novels that depict an alternative vision of the family, especially Henry Fielding's comic novels, which, while they have their share of comic types and scenes, seriously explore the affective mode of family relationships. The resolutions of Fielding's novels exemplify this view of family: for instance, after experiencing harsh treatment within the family in which he has been raised, Tom Jones finds happiness with his wife Sophia in the relative isolation of a country estate, far from the distractions and temptations of London life. The final emphasis in *Tom Jones*, then, is on the couple, the infant nuclear family, rather than on the extended family. The love between the married couple is shown to be affectionate and exclusive, and promises to avoid the dysfunctionality of most other family relationships in the novel.

---

1    *Children, Parents, and The Rise of the Novel* (Newark, DE: University of Delaware Press, 1995), 51.

## Non-Fiction Accounts of Family Life

In general, accounts of family relations in diaries written by both parents and children during this period present the family in a positive light.[1] These accounts make clear that parents wished to spend more time with their families in pleasurable activities. The nuclear family was an intimate unit, its intimacy reflected in the more informal modes of address used by family members with one another[2] and in the portraits of family groups after 1750 which show the family at play, enjoying entertaining pursuits usually in a natural setting, rather than posed formally inside a house (Plumb 67). In general, these portraits depict the nuclear family rather than the larger household or extended family.[3] The many portraits of mothers with their children during this period attest to the particular intimacy shared by mothers and children; this bond was viewed as a natural one since wives and children also shared the same status under the law and within the patriarchal household (Gottlieb 173). While indulgent, loving fathers were also commonplace, and a special bond was created between father and oldest son through the demands of primogeniture (at least among the wealthy),[4] it was believed that a mother's love was naturally stronger than a father's for their children. Indeed, a mother

---

1  Some researchers, including Stone, Gillis, and Trumbach, argue that the eighteenth century saw a movement toward greater parental affection for children, while others, such as Casey, Pollock, Macfarlane, and Abbott argue that no such change was necessary since parents have always, throughout time, loved and nurtured their children (to the extent that their circumstances allowed).

2  Spierenburg writes that between 1500 and 1820 "conjugal life among the European elite was transformed"; evidence for the increasing intimacy and decreasing hierarchization within the nuclear family can be found in the movement away from formality in form of address between spouses. "'My lord husband'" is replaced by the husband's name (245).

3  See for example: George Romney's "The Leigh Family" (1768); Johann Zoffany's "Music Party of the Sharp Family on the Thames" (1781); and George Keating's "Georgiana, Duchess of Devonshire with her Daughter" (1787).

4  Toni Bowers, *The Politics of Motherhood: British Writing and Culture 1680-1760* (New York: Cambridge University Press, 1996), 163; Houlbrooke 135, 180, 186. The strength of the bond between father and daughter often depended on the degree to which the daughter was obedient, especially with regard to the choice of a marriage partner.

who did not show affection toward her child was deemed a monster. Such is the view in a mid-seventeenth-century pamphlet entitled *The Unnatural GrandMother, or A True Relation of a Most Barbarous Murther*, which records the details of a woman's murder of her young granddaughter, and condemns the grandmother (who had also at one time attempted to kill her own daughter). As if completely baffled by such an action, the writer asks "What shall we think of this unnaturall Grand-Mother? That in stead of nourishing, and cherishing that which come at first from her own Loines, she so unwoman like and unnaturally hath now destroyed."[1]

The growing concern with good manners and civilized behavior within social discourse in the eighteenth century extended to the private sphere of the family, with the result that violent acts and words were less tolerated on the domestic front, between husband and wife especially, but also between parents and children (Houlbrooke 30). Diaries reveal parents who are affectionate toward their children, who expect obedience from their children but use corporal discipline rarely and alternative forms of discipline with moderation, who recognize the independent natures of their children and do not wish to break their spirits.[2] In contrast, parenting practices in eighteenth-century France, before the 1789 French Revolution, were much stricter than in England. There, parents were expected to have complete control over their children while they were financially responsible for them, and children of all ages were expected to show obedience and respect to their parents. This strict parental control extended to choosing a marriage partner for their children: according to Paris law during the mid- to late-eighteenth century parental consent was necessary for sons and daughters under twenty-five to marry. Daughters especially were strictly supervised and parents tried to exercise more control over daughters than sons.[3]

---

1 (London: Thomas Higgins, 1659), 5.
2 See Linda Pollock's *Forgotten Children: Parent-Child Relations from 1500-1900* for additional eighteenth-century diary entries which comment upon family relations.
3 David Garrioch, *Neighborhood and Community in Paris, 1740-90* (New York: Cambridge University Press, 1986), 67; James Traer, *Marriage and the Family in Eighteenth-Century France* (Ithaca: Cornell University Press, 1980).

## Relationships with Extended Kin

The roles of extended kin were usually somewhat distinct from the roles of members of the nuclear family and varied widely depending on the degree of intimacy or usefulness of the relationship. The strength of these ties between kin depended on a number of considerations, including emotional, geographical, and genealogical distance, and class affiliation. Kin were motivated to help one another by a sense of duty, by affection, or by expectation of benefit. Attitudes toward helping kin varied from individual to individual. There were the generous kin who took their obligations seriously and reached out to help kin in need, taking to heart the belief that kin have a right to expect "to be made easy" by their kindred who can do so without hurting themselves (Richardson *Col.*). But there were also those like Richardson's popular mid-century heroine, Pamela, who gives her father a lengthy list of reasons for why he should not employ their poor relations to help him on Mr. B's farm. Or like the seventeenth-century diarist Samuel Pepys who records his expectation of benefit in return for helping kin. The consensus among sociologists, however, is that kinship, even if only active on occasion, was an important force in eighteenth-century society at most levels, and not simply with regard to financial advantages. While the propertied classes had a wider knowledge of kin than the lower classes because they had the leisure to pursue relationships,[1] family connections – both consanguineal and affinal, by blood and marriage – were stressed across the social hierarchy. In general, the obligations for maintaining relationships with kin, regardless of geographic distance, were important in both pre-industrial England and France.[2]

---

1  In "The Female World of Cards and Holidays: Women, Families, and the Work of Kinship," Micaela Di Leonardo makes the point that it was women in families who wrote the letters to one another that did the work of connecting kin. Upper class women would be better situated to do this kinwork across households, since they would have the leisure and the literacy that working class women in most cases would not have (in *Rethinking the Family*, rev. ed., ed. Barrie Thorne and Marilyn Yalom [Boston: Northeastern University Press, 1992].)

2  Cressy, O'Day, Hunt, Wrightson, and Smith, among others, argue this stance; Macfarlane and Stone contend that relations with extended kin during this period declined.

Indeed, the very distance could provide opportunities for bringing kin together through hospitality given, contacts made, employment negotiated, or marriage partners found. As Cressy points out in his article "Kinship and Kin Interaction in Early Modern England," these were the "conventional expectations" of kin relations; feuds or "a defect of character" might disappoint these expectations, but most people sought to keep a sense of kinship alive through a variety of means (68). Ralph Josselin records in his late-seventeenth-century diary the many ways of maintaining connections between distant kin, including having grandchildren stay with him and his wife for extended visits (Harris 146).

Indeed, the role of grandparents in eighteenth-century family life could be an important one, though as a result of the short life expectancy, grandparents were not much in evidence (Gottlieb 176; Houlbrooke 192). Statistics indicate that three generations in one household was a relatively rare occurrence (Gillis *World* 9; Laslett *Family Life* 26); indeed, fewer than six per cent of households between 1450 and 1700 contained three generations (Houlbrooke 20). As John Gillis points out in *A World of Their Own Making,* "the two groups least likely to be living with their own kin were children in their teens and old persons" ( 9). The latter can be explained by Houlbrooke's contention in *The English Family 1450-1700* that "parental love was held to be much stronger than filial, and reluctance to help parents in old age was allegedly widespread" (21).[1] There seems to have been no clear understanding in society regarding the treatment of the elderly, the duties and responsibilities of adult children toward their parents. Conflicts between the different generations, whether living together or separate, were common and not always a result of the older generation pulling rank, since the power hierarchies were not synonymous with age hierarchies.[2]

---

1 Olivia Harris also notes that recent research challenges our assumptions regarding the affective connections with family – "We cannot assume even that solidarity between siblings or care for aging parents were generally adhered to as principles" (146).

2 Michael Mitterauer and Reinhard Sieder, *The European Family: Patriarchy to Partnership from the Middle Ages to the Present,* Trans. Karla Oosterveen and Manfred Hörzinger (Chicago: University of Chicago Press, 1982), 68.

This unease seems not to have significantly affected relationships between grandparents and grandchildren since evidence points to affectionate relationships between these two groups at all levels of society, though children of the upper classes had more of a chance of developing a relationship with their grandparents (O'Day 86; Houlbrooke 52).

As Ralph Josselin's diary makes clear, children were sometimes sent to visit grandparents who lived at a distance for extended periods of time (Davidoff and Hill 354; Harris 146). It is especially characteristic of eighteenth-century England that grandchildren resided with grandparents without their own parents present as part of the household.[1] Grandparents were viewed as more tolerant in their parenting of grandchildren than they had been as parents of their own children, and a "tempering" presence in disputes between their children and their grandchildren. Usually the relationship between grandparent and grandchild was positive for both, and this seems especially true for grandmothers and granddaughters, since women in old age looked to intergenerational relationships to sustain them, while men of the same age depended on relationships within their generation.[2] This was certainly the case for Burney and her maternal grandmother DuBois whom she depicts in her *Memoirs of Dr. Burney* as quite nurturing, especially after Burney's mother, Esther, died. Indeed, the bond between the grandmother and granddaughter was so strong that Charles Burney feared Madame DuBois' influence over his daughter and when he made plans to send his daughters to France for schooling, he did not allow Frances to go with them, fearing that her "tender veneration" for her grandmother could lead her to embrace Madame DuBois' Catholic faith (see Appendix B). The grandmother as provider of comfort and agent of harmony in the family, enjoying the play of her grandchildren, is the central image of "The Family Fire-side," a poem

---

1   Peter Laslett, "Mean Household Size in England since the Sixteenth Century." In *Household and Family in Past Time*, ed. Peter Laslett (Cambridge: Cambridge University Press, 1972), 151.

2   O'Day 86; Charles Booth, *The Aged Poor in England and Wales* (1894) (New York: Garland, 1980), 70.

in Mrs. Bonhote's *The Parental Monitor* late in the century (see Appendix B). And certainly, Sarah, Duchess of Newcastle's relationship with her granddaughter, Diana Spencer, embodied in the older woman's letters to her granddaughter written in the early 1730s, is generally an affectionate relationship, though Sarah takes a much more active and forceful role in Diana's life than the grandmother in Mrs. Bonhote's poem. Sarah is the matriarch of the family, the senior woman whose traditional role it was to guide the motherless younger woman into society. Sarah took Diana beyond this into the intimacy of her married life, until Diana's early death.[1] At points in the correspondence, however, there are indications that Sarah's attitude toward her granddaughter was not uncritical; if Sarah gave to her granddaughter – love, advice, support – she also demanded complete loyalty in return, and her efforts to guide might as easily be interpreted as attempts to dominate (see Appendix B).

Even kin farther removed from the nuclear family figured in such intangible ways in eighteenth-century families. It was generally felt that an individual's identity rested in her relationship with different family members, and that the more kin a young person related to outside the nuclear family, the more secure she would be within herself.[2] A child born of a marriage had two sets of kin to support and nurture her, and to whom she owed respect, loyalty, and affection. James Nelson, in *An Essay on the Government of Children* (1756), notes that children owe respect to *all* their relations,

> whatever be their Circumstances or Conditions. In every Family there are particular Obligations which Children must be taught to distinguish, and to reduce to Practice. Next to their Parents, Children owe to all senior Rela-

---

1 O'Day notes that older women of the upper classes often exercised significant influence over the lives of younger female family members, guiding them into society, and even arranging their marriages. This usually made for a more humane, buffered process, the matriarch's concern for the family's reputation and property being balanced by a grandmother's concern for her granddaughter's well-being (80–84).

2 O'Day 272; Davidoff and Hall, "The Family in Britain," in *The Cambridge Social History of Britain 1750-1950*, vol.2, ed. F.M.L. Thompson (Cambridge: Cambridge University Press, 1990), 321.

tions, Respect and Duty; to their Brothers and Sisters they owe not only a tender but an unalterable Affection; and all of more distant Kin have a Claim of Respect which cannot be refused them. (see Appendix B)

While in England during this period, the father's line or the patrilineal lineage was most important in determining a child's social status and in controlling property rights under the law, a child's maternal kin often proved more influential on a personal basis by providing the child with emotional support and a moral/religious education (Farber 8).

The language of kinship at this time was inexact, reflecting the vagueness of barriers between kin – the ease with which relationships could grow into something more than exact labels designated, as well as the ease with which relationships could be distanced. The term "cousin," for instance, was quite vague and could refer to relatives by marriage or blood who lived close or at a distance, to grandchildren, to nephews and nieces, to first or second cousins. It was used in its strict sense, but also as a form of address among kin of the same generation. Its use implied affection, connection, and obligation; however, while it could be used to conjure a closer bond from a more distant relationship genealogically, it could also be used to distance kin whose genealogical closeness typically implied certain expectations. As Olivia Harris cautions, while the language of kinship "is concerned with generosity and sharing, ... [it] is also a language of hierarchy and dependency, of authority and obedience" (150).[1]

*Foster Parenting and Adoption*

Household size in general was shrinking in the eighteenth century, and with it, the number of people from outside the nuclear family who lived in a household. Between 1750-1821 only 5 per cent of people in England lived with relatives other than their nuclear family; and extended kin lived in only 10 per

---

1   See also Houlbrooke 40 and Cressy 65-66.

cent of English households during the period 1650-1780. While very large households grew more and more rare, simple nuclear families were equally rare: 44 per cent of households contained at least one person from outside the nuclear family: servant, kin, visitor, lodger. Thus, while the practice of kin connecting over distance and time, and between generations, might have been less frequent, it still occurred. In many cases, kin who were distant geographically *were* less important than those kin who were closer geographically, sometimes less important even than friends. Social relations often took precedence over blood relations: biological bonds were not necessary for emotional closeness amongst those brought up in the same household. During this period, members of one's household, albeit non-kin, could be of more importance in one's life, to one's sense of family, than one's extended kin. Given this, it is not surprising that the eighteenth century saw a great deal of the fostering of the young by extended kin and non-kin alike, of which legal adoption is the ultimate manifestation.[1] Indeed, according to W. Austin Flanders in *Structures of Experience*, the number of substitute parents in fiction of the period reveals the stress the nuclear family was under in the eighteenth century; he points to the large number of adoptive relationships in many of the stories of heroes or heroines who find a sense of family outside the traditional family structure (144-46).

Legal adoption in the eighteenth century was usually undertaken by childless couples or an unmarried man in order to provide themselves with an heir – usually male – in order to ensure the continuance of the family name. Little emphasis was placed on the benefit this held for the adoptee, at least in the early part of the century; what mattered was benefit to the adopter's family and to the adopter's reputation for generosity.

---

1   Michael Anderson "The Social Implications of Demographic Change," in *The Cambridge Social History of Britain 1750-1950*, ed. F.M.L. Thompson (Cambridge University Press, 1990), 59, 65; Steven Ruggles, *Prolonged Connections: The Rise of the Extended Family in Nineteenth-Century England and America* (Madison: University of Wisconsin Press, 1987) 3; Gottlieb 193; Harris 147. Interestingly, with regard to Villars' role in the novel, Davidoff and Hall point to the evidence of non-biological parents parenting, and note that the clergy especially often took on this foster parenting role (287).

Of course, Villars seems to be motivated by less self-interested considerations in his involvement with John Evelyn's family. Villars writes that he adopted Evelina and made her his heir, but she does not bear his name, so one has to assume that the adoption was not legal, but that the stipulations of his will would be binding. Villars had been made guardian of Evelina by her mother on Caroline Evelyn's deathbed, just as he had been given the same charge with regard to the infant Caroline Evelyn by her father, John Evelyn, on his deathbed. In both cases, parents in whose care the child could have been placed remained alive but unavailable to parent: Sir John Belmont had abandoned his wife Caroline when Madame Duval disinherited her; Madame Duval, then Mrs. Evelyn, was in France but presumably living apart from John Evelyn and her daughter. John Evelyn could ask such a favor of Villars and under the law, his wife had no right to her child since a child was the property of the father, not the mother.[1]

*Illegitimacy*

Because her birth father tore up the marriage certificate that legalized his marriage to Evelina's mother, and because he has not publicly acknowledged Evelina as his daughter, Evelina would have been born, under the law, a bastard. And to all intents and purposes, despite the fact that Villars says he has adopted her, she remains a bastard in terms of her social standing throughout the novel *until* her father owns her.[2]

---

1  Pinchbeck and Hewitt further note that this was possible under a statute of Charles II that allowed a father to appoint a guardian to his children other than his wife, to take over after his death. This was such a powerful law that the courts could not reverse it in favor of the wife (362-63). In 1839 the Custody of Infants Act finally gave mothers some legal rights over their children (Alan Teague, *Social Change, Social Work, and the Adoption of Children* [Brookfield, VT: Avebury, 1989], 24).

2  See also Doody *Frances Burney* 40. The level of social ambiguity surrounding Evelina's status, the fact that the fops, including Willoughby, see her as an easy target for degradation, and that it is only the smitten and socially/economically/personally secure Lord Orville who pursues Evelina seriously as a marriage partner, make it difficult to accept Julia Epstein's view that Evelina never confronts "the unsavoury hopelessness that illegitimacy confers on women ... because from the outset she is fundamentally legitimate, a character in search not of a name but of name recognition, of public acknowledgment" ("Burney Criticism" 279).

According to William Blackstone's *Commentaries on the Laws of England* (1758), there were only two sorts of children under the law: legitimate and illegitimate. While parents owed legitimate children maintenance, protection, and an education, they owed a bastard only maintenance.[1] The bastard's rights were few because she was "kin to nobody." The *Encyclopédie*, claims a bastard has no kin except his/her children born of a legal marriage. He/she has no mother or father even: "'It is only those who are born of a legitimate marriage who are kin to their father and mother'" under the law (qtd. in Flandrin 19). Bastards then "had a personal kindred but belonged to no patrilineage" (Trumbach 161) and so would find it difficult to establish for themselves a legitimate place in society. This lack of legal connection to family caused many born in such circumstances to grow up feeling cast out from society.[2] They certainly would have experienced some degree of ostracism in "polite" society. On the other hand, such a status, while it stigmatized, could also liberate one from the pressure and control experienced by heirs to family fortunes and names. Indeed, Flanders points out, the situation of the illegitimate child and that of a middle class individual were very similar: each was faced with the freedom and the challenge to make his or her own place in the world, without an inheritance to mediate the journey (130).

The number of illegitimate births rose considerably after the mid-eighteenth century as a result of a number of different social stresses and events. These included the Hardwicke Marriage Act of 1753, which made marriage more expensive and tightened the laws governing marriage, with the result that while couples continued to court and to have sexual intercourse, they married later, if at all, and thus there was an

---

1  Blackstone 446-59. The courts would intervene in cases where a father had abandoned his child if the mother swore out an oath; the putative father could then be arrested on a justices' warrant (called a bastardy warrant) and committed to prison unless he could show he'd take responsibility to support the child. Or, if the child had been left for the parish to support it, the Poor Law would be used to secure maintenance of the child by its parents or grandparents (Pinchbeck and Hewitt 586).

2  Mary Abbott, *Family Ties: English Families 1540-1920* (London: Routledge, 1993), 34; Valerie Fildes, ed., *Women as Mothers in Pre-Industrial England* (London: Routledge, 1990), 162.

increase in pre-nuptial pregnancy (Gillis *For Better* 110); the worsening economic conditions in the country that made paying for a marriage license and setting up a household more difficult and resulted in broken engagements even when the woman was already pregnant (Spierenburg 262); and the enclosure laws that forced the struggling farmer and his family off the land and into the cities where community support and policing of morality were less in evidence (Pinchbeck and Hewitt 585; Anderson 57). Gillis points out that the incidence of bastardy in southern and eastern England was low because of the great number of "coverup" marriages made to avoid the stigma of unwedmotherhood which was particularly strong in these two regions (*For Better* 127); this may help us to understand why Evelina has not adopted her mother's surname as her own, which was typically what illegitimate children, unowned by their fathers, did; doing so would not only remind people of her mother's tragedy but mark her as a bastard. Evelina assumes a false name, neither the paternal or maternal surname, to avoid public shame. In so doing, she also manages to avoid Caroline Evelyn's family for a great while, which would not have been the usual case when the child took his mother's surname, for then her family would have adopted him. Evelina's settling (even temporarily) for the maternal line of descent in exclusion of the paternal, which is the more powerful, especially with regard to social position and inheritance, would amount to admitting her bastard status and settling, from her point of view, for a poor half, when she is entitled to the whole.

*Inheritance*

Inheritance practices structured relationships between kin.[1] Indeed, in *The Rise of the Egalitarian Family*, Randolph Trumbach goes so far as to argue that "the material tie was the

---

1   David Sabean, "Aspects of kinship behaviour and property in rural Western Europe before 1800," in *Family and Inheritance: Rural Society in Western Europe, 1200-1800*, ed. J. Goody et al. (Cambridge: Cambridge University Press, 1976), 111; Jack Goody, "Inheritance, property and women: some comparative considerations," in *Family and Inheritance: Rural Society in Western Europe 1200-1800*, ed. Jack Goody (Cam-

strongest of all ties between family members in the eighteenth century." Edmund Leach points out in his article "Complementary Filiation and Bilateral Kinship," that the basic kin structure in England is bilateral, that is, both the paternal and maternal sides of a family are important to the children born into that family; but he concedes that this is "distorted" by inheritance practices which award the bulk of a family's goods to the oldest son, as well as the use of the father's surname. These practices, he notes, result in a leaning toward a patrilineal ideology, a belief that the male is to be privileged over the female, the paternal over the maternal.[1] While the inheritance from the mother might also be significant, women's property was more often in material goods rather than land.[2] A father's

---

bridge: Cambridge University Press, 1976), 3; Brian Sutton-Smith, "The Play of Girls," in *Becoming Female*, ed. Claire Kopp (New York: Plenum Press, 1979), 1-2; Renée Hirschon, "Property, Power and Gender Relations," in *Women and Property – Women as Property*, ed. Renée Hirschon (New York: St. Martin's Press, 1984), 1.

1   56. See also Gottlieb 217-27; Elizabeth Bott, *Family and Social Networks: Roles, Norms, and External Relationships in Ordinary Urban Families* (London: Tavistock, 1957), 116-17. This patrilineal inheritance practice, or primogeniture, was in evidence among the aristocracy and gentry primarily. Indeed, according to Susan Moller Okin, among the aristocracy, daughters' property was handled by fathers very conservatively, and always with the good of the patriliny in mind ("Patriarchy and Married Women's Property in England: Questions on Some Current Views" in *Eighteenth-Century Studies* 17 (1983): 125). As Susan Staves points out, upper class women were seen as conduits for passing property between generations of men (*Married Women's Separate Property in England 1660-1833* [Cambridge, MA: Harvard University Press, 1990], 4). According to John Gillis, peasants and artisans were more prone to dividing their property among all their children evenly (*Youth* 12). Peter Earle suggests that wills of the middle classes in eighteenth-century England also evidenced the practice of equally dividing inheritance (235).

2   Women usually had more portable wealth since they were limited in their control of property because of primogeniture which allowed the bulk of an estate to the oldest son. They were also limited in the extent to which they could control their wealth, both by a lack of education in economic management as well as a lack of subject position under the law (Ann Whitehead, "Women and Men: Kinship and Property: Some General Issues" in *Women and Property – Women as Property*, ed. Renée Hirschon [New York: St. Martin's Press, 1984], 180); married women had no presence under the law, and could therefore not own property. More status was attached to property than movable goods since the former implied permanence to individuals and society (G. Mingay, *English Landed Society*, 3). There may be some significance in the fact that in marrying Lord Orville, Evelina is associated with property rather than simply the moveable goods/money Madame Duval possesses to hand down to her.

power was felt in his hold on inheritance, since he could threaten to disinherit his child if she did not act according to his wishes. William Fleetwood, in *The Relative Duties of Parents and Children* (1705), notes that children should inherit their parents' estates through "reason and natural affections." He writes that disinheriting a child is for a Christian a "case of conscience" and indicts those parents who disinherit their children for trivial reasons. Many parents during this period threatened disinheritance, but few carried it out; when they did, as in the case of Madame Duval in *Evelina*, it was usually over a child choosing a marriage partner of whom the parents did not approve (Houlbrooke 232). Certainly, control over inheritance gave parents a great deal of say in their children's behavior and the power to wreak havoc on their children's lives, as the case of Leolin, in Eliza Haywood's *The Female Spectator* illustrates. Haywood's story depicts a father disinheriting his son, whose blood tie to him he questions, in order to get back at his wife for deserting him. Disinheritance leads Leolin to abandon his wealthy fiancée out of pride and join the army in whose service he quickly dies; any potential for doing good that his life may have held is ended (see Appendix B). Conversely, many parents during this period chose to deal with their property in generous ways during their lifetimes, not waiting until death to ease the way of their children. Devolution, the transfer of property or goods from the older generation to the younger, can occur before or after death. Usually, land was passed during the lifetime of the two generations, and movables – money, personal possessions – passed after death. The settlements that occurred during the life of the older generation were usually meant to establish the younger generation's household.[1]

Ultimately, inheritance could be a unifying device in families. Without land, portable property, businesses to pass on

---

1   Lloyd Bonfield, "Normative Rules and Property Transmission: Reflections on the Link between Marriage and Inheritance in Early Modern England," in *The World We Have Gained: Histories of Population and Social Structure*, ed. Lloyd Bonfield et al. (Oxford: Basil Blackwell, 1986), 175-76.

from one generation to another, families disintegrated, having no common interest or goal. And while conflicts arising over the practice of inheritance could cause rifts in families, there seems to have been a sense that the struggle to maintain ties between family members was a necessary and worthwhile one. This was especially true for the elderly, the young, the female, the poor. "Anyone who wanted a place in society on any level had to locate herself ... in a household" (Gottlieb 252). Women especially were dependent upon family – the one they were born into, the one they married into or worked in (Rendall 4) – for their very identity since few of them held jobs outside the domestic sphere. Evelina's search for the proper family structure within which she can rest with a public as well as private identity takes her into many households and into many relationships. She is Villars' "adoptive" daughter, though she more properly fits the role of his granddaughter in terms of the difference in their ages.[1] In this role she is sheltered, protected, nurtured, but not allowed to grow until Madame Duval forces the issue by demanding her rights to her granddaughter and Lady Howard steps in to take Evelina away from Berry Hill, first to Howard Grove and then into the larger social world of London. As a member of Lady Howard's household, before the arrival of Captain Mirvan, Evelina becomes one in a household of three generations of women; it is a wholly nurturing, and very private household, one to which Evelina wishes she belonged; she calls Mrs. Mirvan her "mama" and Maria her "sister". But it is not a viable family structure, which is made clear by the father's return.[2] Captain Mirvan's return home after seven years away at sea results in a loss of comfort and stability for all the women in his household, including Evelina, whom he makes clear does not belong in his family because he has no control over her (she is Lady Howard's guest, not his);

---

1 This sense of their relationship is further enhanced by Evelina's comment in a letter to Villars that Mrs. Mirvan "could not be more kind to me, were she your daughter."

2 Gillis, writing about the structure of convents in Catholic countries, notes that they were headed by bishops in the eighteenth century because "it was simply no longer possible to imagine a family consisting entirely of women" (*World* 31).

this return also serves to foreshadow the mixed nature of Evelina's long-awaited meeting with Sir John.[1]

Evelina's discomfort with family structures is increased in her relationships with her maternal grandmother, Madame Duval, and her cousins, the Branghtons. These are connections she suffers through, feels great shame over, and finally escapes from via her marriage, at which these relatives are conspicuously absent. Evelina is Sir John Belmont's daughter, though for all the closeness the relationship naturally implies, she does not know him. His shame over his treatment of her mother is so great that it may make any future relationship between them impossible. He is, however, available for the essential public duty of a father, giving his daughter away in marriage. And finally, having turned away from those family structures that were more problematic for her (especially kin relationships), Evelina ends as Lord Orville's wife, securely situated in what Claude Levi-Strauss would call the "elemental family structure" of the nuclear family.[2]

*Female Education*

In addition to a sense of how family worked at this time, we need a general understanding of female education in order to appreciate how Evelina negotiates her way through these relationships, as well as what values inform her behavior and the attitudes she expresses in conversation and in her letters. Eighteenth-century conduct books recommend that girls obey, respect, and submit to their parents. In her *Plans of Education* (1792),[3] Clara Reeve enjoins a religious education, virtuous behavior, and an education superintended by parents and appropriate to the social level of the children, with an emphasis on practical subjects. Education for girls during this period

---

1   Doody notes that Evelina's attempts to see the Mirvan women as "a new family" succeed until Captain Mirvan joins the household and destroys the "fantasy" of domestic unity: "Quietly, Evelina desists from claiming family relationship to the Mirvans anymore; we hear no more of 'mamma Mirvan'" (*Frances Burney* 46).
2   *Structural Anthropology* (New York: Basic Books, 1963).
3   See Appendix B for excerpts of contemporary works treated in this section.

varied depending on the class to which the girl belonged. Daughters of businessmen or women, for instance – like Evelina's cousins, the Branghton girls – worked in their families' shops. Their formal education was usually not very broad or deep because they and their futures were viewed as belonging to the family business or to the business of their husbands. Daughters of this class might receive a gentlewoman's education only if their parents felt this would garner them a better marriage partner and allow the family's rise in society (Plumb 80). Sarah Pennington, in *An Unfortunate Mother's Advice to her Absent Daughters* (1766), also advises her daughters not to ignore their religious education; to find useful domestic employment; and to respect their father's decisions in all matters except where his choice of a marriage partner for them does not accord with their own desires; in such a case, if they must refuse his choice, they might not then make their own without his approval. She also admonishes her daughters to treat everyone civilly, regardless of his or her class. Several critics have noted the contradiction between the advice Sarah Pennington gives her daughters to be obedient and virtuous and her own unhappy life, the result of a lack of self-restraint in public.[1] Certainly, a part of a daughter's education was to be found in the life her mother modelled. The contradiction between their mother's role as primary educator of her daughters and her young sons, and her essential powerlessness in life (unless she were widowed), might not be something most young girls would be aware of until they themselves married and were confronted with the restrictions on individual identity, but they would eventually have to face it and accept it, as Mrs. Mirvan certainly has.

Even when daughters and mothers are separated by geographical distance, many conduct books of the period emphasize the need for a mother's supervisory role in her daughter's education. Education for children was as much a matter of

---

1   See Hemlow "FB and the Courtesy Books," 740–41; Susan Fraiman, *Unbecoming Women: British Women Writers and the Novel of Development* (New York: Columbia University Press, 1993), Chpt. 1.

what was in the world around them as it was a matter of what they read. While children's books after the 1740s stressed non-violence, innocence, sensitivity, and obedience, the cultural emphasis in the later eighteenth century on oddities of nature, the exotic, and mechanical curiosities reached out to children with their possibilities, widening their worlds (Plumb 83-87). At Cox's Museum, for instance, Evelina is impressed by these curiosities, but also somewhat repulsed by their trivial nature and the strength of their allure with the crowd of sightseers. Evelina has no biological mother to guide her, as Portia, in *The Polite Lady or a Course of Female Education* (1797), guides her daughter Sophia, through her correspondence with the girl who is, like Evelina, experiencing the world away from home for the first time. But Evelina does have mentors, chiefly Lord Orville and Villars, who support her instinctive devaluation of the gewgaws she sees, in the face of her grandmother's and cousins' enthusiastic appreciation of them. And it is Villars who instructs Evelina to "assiduously attend" to her grandmother, even in the face of Madame Duval's questionable tastes and behaviors, though he also cautions her not to rely on her grandmother's judgments in deciding how she herself should act in any given situation while Madame Duval is her sole guardian. Such instruction is certainly in keeping with the contemporary view of proper feminine behavior, a mix of passive forbearance and active defense of one's reputation.

Like Pennington, though much earlier, Halifax, in his *The Lady's New-Year's-Gift; or, Advice to a Daughter* (1688), suggests women be virtuous, calm, and reasonable; accept men's foibles; suppress any verbal criticism they might have; withhold laughter except when amongst good friends; and avoid jests. While an "*Aversion* to what is *Criminal,* a *Contempt* of what is *ridiculous,* are the *inseparable Companions* of Understanding and Vertue," it is dangerous to articulate such feelings. "You must ... take heed of *Laughing,* ... It is throwing Snow-balls against Bullets," since the victim of the laughter will generally respond violently to the insult. Instead, he urges his daughter to turn her "Eyes inwards, to see what is amiss" there. The "Triumph of *Wit* is to make your *good Nature* subdue your *Censure*; to be quick in *seeing Faults*, and slow in *exposing* them."

Instruction on a young girl's behavior vis-à-vis the comic constituted a serious portion of her social education. In her *Letters on the Improvement of the Mind* (1773), Hester Mulso Chapone notes that the young desire to laugh and for them, anything can become the object of their ridicule. Old age, personal defects, infirmities – these meet with laughter when they should meet with compassion from the young. She writes that

> It is so shocking an outrage against society to talk of, or laugh at any person in his own presence, that one would think it could only be committed by the vulgar. I am sorry however, to say, that I have too often observed it amongst young ladies, who little deserved that title whilst they indulge their overflowing spirits, in defiance of decency and good nature. The desire of laughing will make such inconsiderate young persons find a subject of ridicule, even in the most respectable characters.

Like Chapone, Reeve also notes that "the affected wisdom and garrulity of age, is a constant subject of ridicule to youth; and serves them as a touchstone to sharpen their wit upon." She quotes from the "Epilogue" to a "Dramatic Caricature" called *Taste and Feeling*, first performed in 1790, which emphasizes the distance between generations and the lack of respect given specifically to the female ancestress:

> My grand-mother told me, what her grand-mother told her,
> The times grow worser child, as they grow older.
> Oh, God-a-mercy times! – If this were true,
> What would another century dwindle to? –
> I dare maintain this time as good as any,
> In spite of whiners, grumblers, or my granny.

However, Chapone does admit that while old age is an improper object of mirth, old age masquerading as youth exemplifies vanity and affectation, which deserve ridicule because such is a deviation from nature and truth.

James Nelson, in *An Essay on the Government of Children* (1756), observes the same inclination in the young to make fun of the defects of others; he admonishes parents: "Another indispensable Duty of Parents to their Children is, that they teach them never to dare to sport with the natural Defects of others." He includes not only physical defects – "What can be more absurd than to ridicule one Man for being too tall, and another for being too short?" – but also defects of the mind: "Are we to laugh at a Man for not knowing what he has had no opportunity to learn? no surely."

Wit, in Richardson's view, is rarely coupled with wisdom and if it requires a foil to set it off, it is not wit to be proud of: "That ought not to be called Wit, in the good sense of the word, that has not justice in its sallies; nor humour, that preserves not decorum" (*Col.*). Wit in women is "always to be feared," according to John Hill in *On the Management and Education of Children* (1754). "Men have been condemned sometimes for sacrificing their Friend to their Joke; a Woman never made any Scruple of this." The Edgeworths, in *Practical Education* (1798), observe that "all vivacious young people are fond of wit," and because this is so, young people should not be given books to read in which rogues and tricksters figure since "In books we do not actually suffer by the tricks of rogues, or by the lies they tell; hence their truth is to us a quality of no value; but their wit, humour, and the ingenuity of their contrivances, are of great value to us, because they afford us entertainment."

*Pre-Nineteenth-Century Comic Works*

And indeed, eighteenth-century readers were greatly entertained by contemporary tricksters as well as those of the past. Looking back to the literature of the Renaissance, it is possible to find a number of female trickster figures – strong, assertive women who make a way for themselves in the world regardless of the obstacles: Wyddow Edyth, in *XII Mery Jests of the*

*Wyddow Edyth*, follows her mother's advice to make merry "for this world wyll not last alway;" her jests consist of deceiving others into thinking what she wishes them to, and include masquerading as a rich widow, and passing her bastard daughter off as an heiress.[1]

Widows easily filled the trickster role since they were seen as sexually and economically transgressive, "out to supplant men" (Canfield 150). The jests of Scoggin,[2] a court jester to Edward IV, were still known in the late-eighteenth century; his joke on his wife – a cruel, physically violent response to her having made him look a fool in public – is meant to re-establish the power structure in the family, with the male taking the dominant role. The lesson of the jest the reader is told is that it's "an unhappy house where the woman is master." Scoggin's practical joke is meant to redress the imbalance caused by the female trickster figures in the public world of the joke. The jests of the eighteenth-century actor, Quin, function similarly. His sexually explicit, physical, misogynistic humour offended even his eighteenth-century editor to the point that the editor assures his readers that he has suppressed the most "indelicate and indecent" of Quin's jokes and impromptus. The reader is left with jests pertaining to Quin's mother's virtue and his own illegitimacy, indicating that the bastard and his mother are both acceptable butts; jokes aimed at the French in particular, though any foreign person or custom seems fair game;[3] and stories pointing in particular to female appetites: the seemingly heartbroken widow who quickly remarries or the old woman who marries a young man.

The most popular jest book of the eighteenth century, published in 1739, *Joe Miller's Jest Book*, also uses references to the

---

1  Anon., *XII Mery Jests of the Wyddow Edyth* (1573), ed. W. Carew Hazlitt (London: Willis and Sotheran, 1866), 35.
2  Excerpts from this work, as well as many of the works discussed in this section, can be found in Appendix C.
3  Edward Bloom and Lillian Bloom note in *Satire's Persuasive Voice* (Ithaca: Cornell University Press, 1979, 269), that the anti-French bias in eighteenth-century English satire marks "a widening discontent with the collapse of native culture" which many felt was due to the infusion of French manners in England.

world of the theater, though its subject matter is wide-ranging and deals with many of the traditional topics for jesting: unequal marriages, cuckolded husbands, enterprising thieves, national stereotypes (especially of the French dandy and the penny-pinching and opportunistic Scot), women's vanity, family relations and family pride, and stereotyped relationships.[1] One of these stereotypical relationships prevalent into the eighteenth century is that of the old sea captain, that "Son of Neptune" as he is called here as well as in *Evelina*, who engages in ridiculing the affected dandy, whom he likens to a monkey; it is a joking relationship Burney revisits in her depiction of Mirvan's abuse of Lovel.

Another very popular[2] comic work of the period was Christopher Anstey's *The New Bath Guide* (1766) which Burney herself read and which Lord Orville and Evelina read. In fact, it was supposed by many contemporary readers that the anonymously published *Evelina* had been written by Anstey. Certainly the similarities in the works' satiric targets are striking. Anstey uses the letters of the unsophisticated B—R—D family, writing from Bath to friends and relations back home in the country, to reveal the shallowness and artifice of fashionable life and the lack of civility and sensitivity among the people the family meets; additionally, in the course of their commentary, members of the family reveal their own ambivalence in their feelings for their extended family. In the first of the two letters included in Appendix C of this text, for example, Miss Jenny writes of her embarrassment at her ninny cousins who mortify

---

1   This work was so popular that it "went into as many editions as *Pilgrim's Progress*" (Robert Hutchinson, ed., *Joe Miller's Jests* (London: Dover, 1963), v.). Part of the popularity of the book was in its theatrical references, including the Drury Lane comedian, Joe Miller, whose name graces the title of the book – ironically, it appears, since the book was written by John Mottley, under the pseudonym of Elijah Jenkins, without the knowledge or participation of Joe Miller who, it was said, could not read, write, or even tell a joke (vi-vii).

2   In *Eighteenth-Century Satire* (New York: Cambridge University Press, 1988), Howard Weinbrot notes that Anstey's *New Bath Guide* went through twelve editions in eighteen years, illustrating the desirability of this type of mild satire. Smollett satirized Anstey's work in his 1771 novel *Humphrey Clinker*, putting a harsher spin on Anstey's scenes. Weinbrot points out Anstey's resurrection of the misogynous Quin (197).

her by calling her "cousin" in public, reminding us of Evelina's feelings towards the Branghtons.

## Eighteenth-Century Comic Theory

Those writers theorizing on comedy during the century concern themselves with laughter, the distinctions between various types of humour, and the joking relationship. An *Essay Towards Fixing the True Standards of Wit, Humour, Raillery, Satire, and Ridicule* (1744), by Corbyn Morris, for instance, locates the distinctions between raillery, ridicule, and satire in the joking relationship: raillery is used with social equals, over minor follies. Ridicule is used to address more heinous problems and usually occurs when one wishes to degrade another, thus ensuring for oneself a position of superiority. Satire is more biting still and tends to be depersonalized.[1] Everyone, says Addison in *The Spectator* No. 47 (1711), "diverts himself with some person or other that is below him in point of understanding, and triumphs in the superiority of his genius, whilst he has such objects of derision before his eyes." In *The Spectator* No. 35 (1711), Addison notes such "False Humour" "is exceedingly given to little apish tricks and buffooneries," "ridicule[s] both friends and foes indifferently" and always in a personal manner, aiming the ridicule at the person, and not the vice.

In *Human Nature*, Hobbes writes that people laugh "at the infirmities of others".[2] Objects of derision are those who have some deformity, some weakness. This might be a weakness of character, such as vanity; but it could just as easily be a person's gender, class, physical attributes, or age that marks her as the butt of a joke, depending on the character of the jokester. For instance, in *Conceits, Clinches, Flashes, and Whimzies* (1639), it is the character of women – "crooked and perverse in their conditions"[3] – that marks them as objects of derision for the anonymous writer of this jest book. In Eliza Haywood's *Female*

---

1  Excerpts from most of the works in this section may be found in Appendix C.
2  In *The Philosophy of Laughter and Humor*, ed. John Morreall (Albany: State University of New York Press, 1987), 20.
3  Ed. W. Carew Hazlitt (London: Willis and Sotheran, 1866), 21.

*Spectator* (1744-46), it is his wife's obsession for masquerades that justifies the husband's cruel and dangerous prank on her. John Dennis, in "A Large Account of the Taste in Poetry, and the Causes of the Degeneracy of It" (1702), suggests that it is

> among People of the lower sort, that by the means of Passion and Humour, Nature appears so admirably conspicuous in all her Charming diversities: Since.... Humour is more to be found among those of the lower sort, than among those of a higher Rank, it is very plain that low Characters are more proper for Comedy than high ones....[1]

Dennis is joined in this opinion by James Beattie in his 1776 *Essays on Poetry and Music as they Affect the Mind. On Laughter and Ludicrous Composition. On the Utility of Classical Learning*: "The sphere most favourable to wit and humour is that which is occupied by the middle and lower ranks of mankind; persons in high stations being obliged to maintain a reserve unfriendly to risible emotion; and to reduce this behaviour to an artificial uniformity."[2]

William Hazlitt, writing at the beginning of the nineteenth century, in *Lectures on the English Comic Writers* (1819), and looking back on eighteenth-century writers of comedy, including Burney, chronicles the sources of laughter:

> The essence of the laughable ... is the incongruous.... The ludicrous is where there is the same contradiction between the object and our expectations, heightened by some deformity or inconvenience, that is, by its being

---

1   In Paul Lauter, ed., *Theories of Comedy* (Garden City, NY: Doubleday and Co., 1964), 221.
2   Qtd. in Shearer West, "The De-Formed Face of Democracy: Class, Comedy and Character in Eighteenth-Century British Portraiture," in *Culture and Society in Britain 1660-1800*, ed. Jeremy Black (New York: Manchester University Press, 1997), 163. In *Hogarth to Cruickshank: Social Change in Graphic Satire* (New York: Walker and Co., 1967, 73), M. Dorothy George notes that Low life was traditionally a subject for ridicule rather than compassion, its members shown to be lewd, disreputable, dirty, poor, and drunken.

contrary to what is customary or desirable.... We laugh at absurdity; we laugh at deformity.... We laugh at the dress of foreigners, and they at ours. Any one dressed in the height of fashion, or quite out of it, is equally an object of ridicule. One rich source of the ludicrous is distress with which we cannot sympathise from its absurdity or insignificance.... We laugh at mischief.... We laugh at fools, and at those who pretend to be wise – at extreme simplicity, awkwardness, hypocrisy, and affectation.

## The Joking Relationship and Family Structures in Evelina

Many modern critics of the novel have noted the violent nature of the comedy in *Evelina*;[1] interestingly enough, this seems not to have either registered with or been problematic for most eighteenth-century readers of the novel. This dearth of contemporary outcry against the violent comedy of the novel points perhaps to a greater tolerance among eighteenth-century readers for this kind of humour, despite the negative opinion of it given by conduct books of the period. Jokes in this novel *are* aggressive, violent, even hostile, as they are in the jestbooks described above and excerpted in Appendix C. Two jokes in particular stand out for modern audiences as particularly brutal. The old women's footrace, organized by the silly, irresponsible, arrogant Merton and Coverley, but viewed by the polite company which includes Evelina and Lord Orville, has received a good deal of attention by modern critics appalled at the physical abuse the two upper-class young men visit upon the two poor, old women. But little discomfort with this incident on the part of contemporary readers was voiced. Earl Anderson explains this by acknowledging "the place of this incident in the comedy of manners" (58) and pointing out that the novel's contemporary audience would "very likely have witnessed ludicrous foot-races like the [one described by

---

1   See for example Doody, *Frances Burney*; Straub, *Divided Fictions*; Zomchick, "Satire and the Bourgeois Subject in FB's *Evelina*"; Zonitch, *Familiar Violence*.

Burney], ... and would have recognized the ludicrous details [the racers' gender and age] as part of the sociological characterization of them as lower-class" (67). Audiences would have appreciated the absurdity of the race and found this aspect humorous, and the class to which the racers belonged would have insulated the audience from feeling moral outrage at the brutality experienced by the two women at the hands not only of Merton and Coverley, but also as a result of the relative passivity of the spectators. Eighteenth-century readers, then, found the footrace entertaining because it was a familiar jest; this may account as well for their general acceptance of the most spectacular example of such violent jesting in the novel, Captain Mirvan's "ditching" of Madame Duval,[1] which also received little contemporary commentary other than that indirectly represented by the *Monthly Review*'s criticism of Burney's unrealistic depiction of Captain Mirvan as a naval officer (see Appendix A).[2] The explanation for such tolerance of Captain Mirvan's brutal jest lies in the socially acceptable nature of his ridicule, aimed, as it is, at Madame Duval's vanity and affectation, and in his readily identifiable character itself, that of the stereotypical tar – rough-mannered and insensitive, but full of nationalistic fervor and staunch supporter of the status quo. Given his type, his target, and the comic tradition in which both were firmly established, Captain Mirvan was no doubt an eminently acceptable and entertaining trickster in the eyes of many eighteenth-century readers.

Newly returned from seven years at sea, Mirvan is unhappy with the addition to his household, and rather than treat Madame Duval hospitably, as part of the family, he makes her the butt of his practical joking. From Captain Mirvan's point of view, there are a number of very good reasons why Madame Duval is eminently qualified for the role as butt of his practical jokes and verbal abuse. She is foreign, in terms of both the

---

1 The frontispiece of this edition reproduces John Mortimer's 1779 depiction of Evelina helping Madame Duval out of the ditch.
2 As noted earlier in the introduction, FB herself rejected this criticism. To her mind, the boorish, quick-tempered Captain Mirvan was a realistic rendition of a sea officer.

country and class she seems to represent; she seems somehow to be affiliated with France, and she clearly does not fit into the upper-class English social scene of which she acts as if she is a part. While she was apparently born in England to a working-class family, and met John Evelyn while serving as a barmaid in an English pub, she has lived for forty years in France; her home is in Paris. Given this combination of birth, upbringing, and life experience, it makes sense that her speech is a mish-mash of French phrases and ungrammatical English, but because she is wealthy, and thereby assumes a place in polite society, her speech is a marker of her foreignness, of her not belonging in the role she has taken on. This role which her fortune allows her to assume puts her on a social level with Captain Mirvan who himself does not really fit into the upper-class social life of his wife and mother-in-law. Captain Mirvan and Madame Duval are somewhat alike, then, in that they are both out of place in London's polite society – assertive, demanding, completely unmannerly in speech and behavior; Evelina refers to them both as "gross." Captain Mirvan's behavior is less socially problematic than Madame Duval's affecting an upper-class status and French nationality since his "Franco-phobia" can be forgiven as an offshoot of his profession. According to John Hart, Mirvan's distaste for the French was shared by many naval officers whose very lives had been placed in jeopardy in violent military exchanges with members of the enemy nation. His is not a personal animosity so much as it is a public – professional and national – one (65).

In addition to her foreignness, Madame Duval's gender, age, sexuality, and marital status also operate to make her an attractive target for Captain Mirvan's jokes. The stereotype of widows prevalent in the eighteenth century goes back at least as far as the Middle Ages and Chaucer's Wife of Bath, a figure current in literature until the nineteenth century (Holderness 423). It is that of a sexually promiscuous, disorderly, non-maternal, generally shrewd and conniving woman, one intent on marrying another husband as quickly as possible, often before the year of mourning for her previous husband had been completed, though through this marriage she was often taken advantage of since she was married only for her money.[1] The stereotype can be seen in comedies performed during the late seventeenth and eighteenth centuries, from Thomas Shadwell's *A True Widow* (1678) in the character of Lady Cheatly, to William Congreve's *The Way of the World* (1700) in the character of Lady Wishfort, to contemporary dramas such as David Garrick's *The Clandestine Marriage* (1766) in the character of Mrs. Heidelberg. Eliza Haywood, writing in *The Female Spectator* (1744–46) criticizes those widows who wish to remarry in order to fulfill their sexual appetites for not living in a "regular decent manner."

Single women had rights under the law that married women did not enjoy. Unlike married women, the single woman or *feme sole*[2] could own property and material goods; she could make contracts and a will; she could sue.[3] Marriage made a woman a *feme covert*, a woman whose legal identity was subsumed by her husband, under whose "protection and influence" she was, and upon whom she was dependent (Blackstone I 442). A married woman's property in essence belonged, upon marriage, to her husband; while she might keep nominal title to property her family had settled on her, her husband had a right to all proceeds from that property. Widowhood, though it left the woman without her husband's protection, gave her back her legal identity and allowed her to control her financial resources, to run her household, and to educate her children in the manner she saw fit. Indeed, B. A. Holderness notes that "women in pre-industrial Europe

---

1 Hardwick 136; Todd 54–55, 77; Canfield 150.
2 The eighteenth-century English legal system referred to the single woman as the *feme sole*, from the French *femme seule* or "woman alone," and the married woman as the *feme covert*, from the French *femme coverte*. In his mid-century *Commentaries on the Laws of England*, Sir William Blackstone explains the latter term: "By marriage, the husband and wife are one person in law: that is, the very being or legal existence of the woman is suspended during the marriage, or at least incorporated or consolidated into that of the husband: under whose wing, protection, and *cover* she performs everything; and is therefore called in our law French a *feme covert* ... ; said to be covert-baron, or under the protection and influence of her husband" (I.442).
3 Janelle Greenberg, "The Legal Status of the English Woman in Early Eighteenth-Century Common Law and Equity," *Studies in Eighteenth-Century Culture* 4 (1974): 172.

reached the height of their social influence and enjoyed their greatest rights out of coverture, as the common law expressed it, especially in widowhood" (427).

Given the high mortality rates in early modern Europe, widowhood and remarriage were a common occurrence – in the seventeenth and eighteenth centuries, this amounted to at least one marriage in four being a remarriage.[1] Among widows and widowers in eighteenth-century England, more widowers, regardless of their age, than widows remarried, and they did so relatively soon after the death of their spouse, especially if they had young children (Holderness 431). A widow's class affiliation seems to have made a difference in whether she would remarry or not, as did her financial situation: while wealthy widows of all ages were in demand, especially those without obligations to children or kin, more women of the upper classes than of the lower remained single in England at this time (Holderness 429; Hufton 359). Indeed, in his *Letters Written to and for Particular Friends, on the Most Important Occasions* (1741), Richardson advises a rich widow not to marry a younger, poorer man; if she does so, he warns, she will be taken advantage of because the second marriage will prove detrimental to her children; reflect badly on her first marriage; and cause her to be unhappily circumstanced, having to be on her guard to protect her children's interests from her husband's desires (see Appendix B).

Rather than being concerned with meeting her own needs, as society assumed she was, a widow's life was much more likely to be consumed by the care of her children and the property left by her husband for those children – over which she acted as steward, a widow's property rights in most cases where there were children being temporary.[2] And while she had greater autonomy under the law than a married woman, this very autonomy threatened the patriarchal system under which she lived and could deprive her of privacy and personal autonomy. During the seventeenth and eighteenth centuries "Female

---

1   André Burguière and François Lebrun, "The One Hundred and One Families of Europe," in *A History of the Family*, Vol. 2, ed. Burguière et al., trans. Sarah Hanbury Tenison (Cambridge, MA: Harvard University Press, 1996), 15.
2   See Gottlieb 206; Abbott 67; Todd 55.

heads of household were anomalies in a patriarchal society, and as such all widows found themselves situated awkwardly across gender boundaries," and suspect as a result (Hardwick 134). In fact, in villages during this period in England and in France, a widow's influence in the community and her rights to inheritance of her husband's property and goods were very much dependent upon her meeting certain requirements set by the village fathers: if she did not live chastely, or if she remarried, her rights to parent her children, and to her property, could be taken from her by the men of the village exercising their "paternal responsibilities."[1] Widows at certain levels of society could make choices about their futures and could suit themselves as to the second husband they took; Hester Thrale Piozzi, friend to many prominent eighteenth-century literary figures, is a good example of a rich widow of the upper middle class who took as her second husband a man who pleased her, though he was lower in class than she, and while she lost many friends over her decision, including Frances Burney, according to her diaries she was a happy woman. But she seems to have been in the minority, since the number of impoverished widows, who of course had fewer options and were less attractive prospects in the marriage market, far surpassed the number of financially solvent widows (Holderness 428).

Burney's treatment of Madame Duval's widowhood is consistent with the stereotypical perspective common among writers of the period: her relationship with M. Du Bois, a Frenchman somewhat younger than herself, implies she is sexually active; she has given up wearing her "widow's weeds" soon after her second husband's death; it is seemingly her money and not her person that attracts potential suitors to her; she seems to be intent on attracting another, younger husband, despite her advanced age;[1] and she is "disorderly" in the

---

1 According to E.P. Thompson, a widow who had lost her rights due to incontinent behavior could petition the courts to have her rights restored, but she would have to make a fool of herself first, riding into court on the back of a black ram, backwards, its tail in her hand, reciting silly verses ("The grid of inheritance: a comment," in *Family and Inheritance; Rural Society in Western Europe, 1200-1800*, ed. J. Goody et al. [Cambridge: Cambridge University Press, 1976], 351). Widowers who lost their rights did not have to do this in order to petition to regain them.

grotesque figure she makes at all times, but especially as a consequence of Captain Mirvan's practical jokes. That she embodies the stereotype to such an extent allows Captain Mirvan's positioning her as the butt of his jokes; as a caricature she is denied the reader's sympathy, and the eighteenth-century reader, primed by the comedies of the past still being acted on stage as well as contemporary comedies, is ready to sanction Captain Mirvan's actions. Even his brutality may be acceptable to readers who see him as an agent of the status quo, a village father sent to punish an offender against the generally agreed upon standards of decency, and Madame Duval is offensive because she is an independent woman – self-centered and self-assured, unable to compromise, lacking feminine submissiveness – who thereby threatens the patriarchy (Gillis *Youth* 32). His attraction to Madame Duval as the butt of his jokes goes beyond his general misogyny to a dislike of her particular brand of femininity. As Kristina Straub asserts, "Madame Duval possesses a kind of renegade female strength, gained through ignoring the social formations that define mature female power in relationship to masculine authority" (*Divided Fictions* 28-29).

Madame Duval is, in short, Captain Mirvan's equal, a situation that allows the joking relationship between them, since according to Christopher P. Wilson, in *Jokes: Form, Content, Use, and Function*, the "norm" in joking relationships is that "equals may engage each other in hostile joking" (191), that ridicule is normally "directed downwards and sideways in a social hierarchy" (212), and that people rarely ridicule those who are older, wiser, or more powerful than they. Their equality also impels Captain Mirvan to place Madame Duval in the position of butt of the joke because he needs to degrade her from the position of equality she claims for herself and which threatens him. As in the case of the Renaissance practical joker,

---

1 Evelina takes Madame Duval to be around fifty years old, which is "elderly"; her grandmother is at least in her mid-fifties if we consider thirty-five years have elapsed since she gave birth to Caroline Evelyn. That M. Du Bois is younger than Madame Duval can be implied from Captain Mirvan's facetious question to M. Du Bois regarding what "Monseers" do with their time in Paris: "Do they game? – or drink? – or fiddle? – ... or do they spend all their time in flummering old women?"

Scoggin, Mirvan is a man normally surrounded by submissive women, content with his superior place in the hierarchy of patriarchal family relationships, and in order to maintain that position, he invokes the joking relationship in a manner typical of men, according to Judith Wilt, who contends that male joking "'is used to avoid, to impede, or to deride the possibility of free equal relationships between men and women'" (qtd. in Barreca *Last Laughs* 7).

Mirvan quickly moves beyond verbal attacks on Madame Duval and an anonymous drenching to engineering an elaborate prank designed to "play the old dowager off." The "scheme" involves Madame Duval's believing Monsieur Du Bois to have been arrested on charges of treason, and her setting out by carriage, accompanied by Evelina, to confront the country justice who is allegedly holding him. Before they can arrive at their destination, Madame Duval receives a message indicating that Monsieur Du Bois has escaped. On the return journey, they are stopped by what appear to be two highwaymen, one of whom tears Madame Duval from the carriage, drags her down the road, shaking her violently and "bumping" her about. The "robber" then ties her feet and leaves her in a ditch where Evelina finds her and releases her.

Captain Mirvan, described throughout the novel as brutish, vulgar, and violent, reacts to Madame Duval's degradation with expected rapture; his servants, Evelina notes, "were ready to die with laughter the moment they saw" Madame Duval; and though Sir Clement Willoughby asserts "the scheme was the Captain's; I even opposed it," he not only participates in the prank as the second robber and makes use of the opportunity to be alone with Evelina, but he ostensibly provides the Captain the occasion for such sportiveness, the Captain having declared upon Willoughby's arrival at Howard Grove that "I have scarce made use of [the old Frenchwoman] yet, by reason I have had nobody with me that could enjoy a joke." Regina Barreca asserts that "Male comedy is directed toward and assumes a predominantly male audience" (*Snow White* 180); Judith Wilt explains that men use joking as a "'bonding device, assisting male solidarity (and excluding women)'" (qtd. in

Barreca *Last Laughs* 7). While this is ostensibly the case between Mirvan and Willoughby, since Willoughby openly responds to the joke with laughter, Evelina's position as audience is invited by Mirvan, and both her discomfort and acquiescence is fulfilling for him. Evelina's role in the joke and her response to it offer us a way into understanding how the novel's comedy is integral to Evelina's search for a proper family structure. To fully appreciate the complexity of Evelina's involvement with this practical joke, it is helpful to consider her relationship with Madame Duval, her maternal grandmother, within the context of eighteenth-century familial relationships, as outlined above.

Madame Duval and Evelina meet for the first time when Evelina is sixteen. Evelina has grown up as an orphan under the guardianship of the Reverend Mr. Villars, with no interaction with either maternal or paternal relatives, and is presently residing in the Mirvan household where she is a beloved surrogate daughter and sister. Evelina sees Madame Duval from the beginning as a threat to her happiness with the Mirvans and with Mr. Villars since her grandmother desires to take her back to Paris to give her the social polish she feels the "rustic" Evelina lacks. Clearly, Evelina's relationship with Madame Duval, the grandmother she has never known and into whose power she is suddenly placed, is not the warm and comforting relationship enjoyed by those adolescent granddaughters lucky enough to still have had grandmothers living with whom they might share a sense of family identity, by whom they might be guided, nurtured, and loved. Their initial meeting is a shock for both of them and leaves Evelina feeling stunned and anxious. Evelina is obviously ashamed of Madame Duval's lack of feminine diffidence and decorum, her ignorance, her assertiveness. Madame Duval also provides Evelina occasion for discomfort, anxiety and embarrassment as Captain Mirvan and she are almost immediately "violent antagonists" whose continual "wrangling and ill breeding" make Evelina "blush that I belonged to them." Additionally, Madame Duval introduces Evelina to some of her relations whom Evelina describes as "so low-bred and vulgar, that I should be equally ashamed of such a connection in the country, or anywhere," and indeed, her time with her maternal relations is spent in attempting to hide that relationship from her London acquaintances and to deny the relationship to herself. (This is evident in Evelina's unwillingness to call her relations "cousin" or "grandmother"; it is only Madame Duval and the Branghtons who insist on using such terms of address.)[1]

But Evelina may also distrust Madame Duval as a maternal figure and blame her for Evelina's mother's tragedy and her neglect of Evelina herself. Evelina has been told that her mother flew into the arms of the libertine Sir John Belmont only because Madame Duval and her second husband were attempting to force Caroline to marry one of M. Duval's nephews, and that once Caroline had run off with Sir John, Madame Duval disowned her; Evelina also believes that Madame Duval was unconcerned with Caroline's fate once she'd been abandoned by Sir John, and with the fate of Caroline's child after Caroline's death in childbirth. But there is a degree of ambiguity surrounding Madame Duval's past behavior in family matters as reported in the narrative; what we and Evelina know of this subject is mediated through Mr. Villars and Lady Howard; Madame Duval's letters are not reproduced in the narrative, and neither is the difference in parenting styles and practices between England and France made clear. The reader, piecing together the events of seventeen years before, is uncertain as to the extent to which Madame Duval was simply cruel in her treatment of both her daughter and granddaughter; acting as per the accepted methods of parenting, which were much stricter in France, especially with regard to daughters, and particularly on the choice of marriage partners; controlled by Monsieur Duval's directions and concerns for his own kin – Madame Duval tells Evelina her second husband had been a difficult man; or ignorant of the very existence of her grand-

---

1  Toby Olshin sees Madame Duval and the Branghtons as providing Evelina with an "incorrect familial context" which puts Evelina in danger of being judged "incorrectly" (32). Evelina obviously feels Madame Duval and the Branghtons provide a "negative context," but it is not an "incorrect" context; they *are* her "true" family by blood if not by emotional bond.

daughter. We know that she was very ill after the events sur-rounding her failed attempts to marry Caroline within the Duval family and her disinheriting of her daughter, that she felt "agonies of grief and remorse;" we know that she was over-whelmed emotionally upon seeing Evelina, and the image of her dead daughter in Evelina, for the first time. Still, Evelina may blame her for her own orphaned state and she certainly resents the power Madame Duval's legal relationship to her gives her over Evelina, a power which her grandmother in no subtle way attempts to enforce and which Evelina strains against. While Madame Duval's voiced intention is to aid Evelina, Evelina herself sees no benefit from the relationship, though she does feel under an obligation to treat her grand-mother respectfully. Thus, while Madame Duval is the closest blood relative who has owned her, and therefore a legitimate guardian to her granddaughter; and while their individual situ-ations are somewhat similar – as William Alexander asserts in *The History of Women* (1779), the "state of the widow and the fatherless was of all others the most forlorn and miserable"[1] – Evelina's fear of Madame Duval's power and her embarrass-ment over her vulgar manners vie with her sense of duty toward kin and compassion for Madame Duval's outsider status to cause her to feel ambivalent toward her grandmother. This ambivalence sets the groundwork that allows Evelina to partic-ipate in Captain Mirvan's joke against her grandmother.

Another dimension of Evelina's ambivalent feelings toward Madame Duval can be found in the conflict she experiences within family structures. We can see that Evelina participates in quite a wide variety of household situations: in some she seeks to belong, in others she is uncomfortable with and resistant to becoming part of the family. Her feelings toward a given household might change with changes in either her situation or the situation of the other members of the household. Once

---

1   (London: W. Strahan and T. Cadell, 1779), 288. Julia Epstein notes that Madame Duval is the "most unsettling of Evelina's tormentors because the most legitimate and the most perspicacious about the younger woman's position as a statusless woman; Evelina's plight in some ways resembles that of her grandmother, who is a foreigner traveling with a man to whom she is not married" (*Iron Pen* 106).

Captain Mirvan joins the Howard/Mirvan household, for instance, Evelina ceases to wish to belong to it. While households can offer a resident non-relative such as Evelina a sense of belonging, they also harbor the potential for restrictiveness and obligation that belonging to a family implies: Mrs. Mirvan, her daughter Maria, and to a lesser extent, her mother Lady Howard, must all suffer the indignities of Captain Mirvan, since under a patriarchal system, his word is law. The "amity" she finds with the Mirvan women, "purer than that which links real kin precisely because it is not prescriptive" (Pitt-Rivers 102), is circumscribed by the Captain's insistence on an almost filial obedience from Evelina. Under such conditions, Evelina claims the freedom consequent to occupying merely an "inmate" position, as defined by Peter Laslett in *Household and Family in Past Time*: as a visitor at Lady Howard's or Mrs. Beaumont's, or even as Mr. Villars' ward, she is, like servants, borders, or lodgers, in an ambiguous position; while she inhabits the same location and shares in similar activities with the other inhabitants, she is not bound to them by blood or marriage (35). This sense of liminality, of existing on the margins, is increased by the shadow of illegitimacy that hangs about her birth, giving her an outsider status that engenders in her at once a sense of freedom from the constraint of family relations as well as a sense of being unprotected from the world's hostility (Yeazell 137; Staves "Female Difficulties" 23). Evelina's desire to belong to a family is legally restricted while she is under the shadow of illegitimacy: socially, she can become part of a family or household, but she can claim no familial or kinship relations. This may account in part for her distancing herself from her blood kin, Madame Duval and the Branghtons, since legally, until Sir John owns her and validates his marriage to her mother, she is kin to no one.

In addition, Evelina is confounded initially by the obligations and ties claimed of her by her mother's relations as they enter her life for the first time. Indeed, Evelina does not live with kin until the very end of the novel, except when her grandmother visits Lady Howard's, and when Evelina lives with her grandmother in London, since Mr. Villars, while her declared "more than father," has no legal right to that name and is limited in his guardianship of her. Evelina is related by blood to so few of the members of the households in which she stays, but those relatives who do claim her – her grandmother and the Branghtons – do so through matrilinear descent, which seems to be problematic for Evelina. Evelina's discomfort with such matrilineal owning may arise from what this signifies regarding her social status. In a society where patrilineage is emphasized, to be owned by one's mother's kin exclusively is a disadvantage. Certainly, such kin recognition highlights the lack of patrilineal owning; it marks Evelina's outsider status, and emphasizes her powerlessness within society. The value of patri-filiation *is* dominant in the novel, and not simply from an inheritance perspective. Evelina chooses to deny her mother's kin group, despite the fact that her grandmother names her heir, and that therefore, the "practical economic significance of descent through females is ... at least as significant as descent through males" (Leach 56). However, Evelina is not satisfied with being owned by members of the maternal line. If she owns family, it is through the paternal line. When she reveals to Macartney that he is her half-brother, she says: "You see, therefore, the claim we mutually have to each other's regard; we are not merely bound by the ties of friendship, but by those of blood." This statement implies that Evelina values blood ties more strongly than ties of friendship, yet this has no bearing on her relationship with her maternal kin: at the end of the novel, Madame Duval and the Branghtons are out of the picture.

While the novel may "question ... paternal authority" (Greenfield 310), it also obviously questions maternal authority. A patrilineal ideology *is* at work in the novel; kinship may theoretically be emotionally bilineal, and may, in many families, even favor the matrilineal,[1] but social power lies with the patri-

---

1    Farber 8; Leach: "once a bilateral structure is so distorted for ideological reasons that it is made to appear 'as if' it were a patrilineal structure, then it will automatically follow that the pseudo-patrilineal descent is complemented by a mystical reverence for a less pseudo principle of matrilateral filiation" (54); and Gottlieb: "At the same time that everyone was avidly pursuing good marriage alliances and making the most of them, the contributions of mothers to their children's official ancestry were systematically suppressed. This is not to say that mothers and the families they came

lineal line, not the matrilineal in the world of *Evelina*. Evelina's favoring the patrilineal line of descent and her father's inheritance over her grandmother's reflects the "growing tendency to see paternal inheritance as the only kind that mattered" (Gottlieb 226). Evelina's discomfort with her blood kin is less evident once she is owned by her birth father, recognized under the law of patrilinear descent, and once she becomes part of the simple nuclear family household her marriage to Lord Orville secures her, and which will also embrace a patrilineal ideology.[1] While Evelina's dead mother seems to be an essential presence in Evelina's search for an identity, Caroline Evelyn's line is pushed aside by Evelina as ineffective, unattractive, and demanding.

Evelina arrives at this end point by negotiating her way through this labyrinth of familial structures via the joking relationship. This relationship, according to Freud in *Jokes and Their Relation to the Unconscious*, concerns three people: the person who makes the joke (the joker); the object of the joker's hostility or sexual aggression (the butt); and the spectator of the joke, the person who receives pleasure from the joke (the audience) (118-19). The audience may also be viewed as one who is taken in by the joker. She deals with her annoyance at being captured by the joke by resolving to tell the joke later to the next person in the joking chain; thus, the joking relationship is more of a quadrilateral than a triangle (Flieger 945). In *Comedy, the Mastery of Discourse*, Susan Purdie further notes that the goal

---

from did not loom large in most people's lives. Resistance to the father's monopoly of control over the household inheritance remained strong, and the mother's family often behaved as though her children belonged to them at least as much as to the father.... The bilineal character of inheritance remained a permanent part of the European tradition. Having two sources of inheritance and two kinship groups made for complexity and, inevitably, a certain degree of ambiguity. The ambiguity was compounded by the growing preference for patrilineality, which never entirely superseded bilineality but instead made a variety of accommodations to it. A lot depended on where you were on the social ladder, or where you wanted to go" (227).

1   Julia Epstein writes that "Evelina's quest to regain her family and legitimate 'name' is paralleled by a quest to replace those original blood ties, the instant they are legalized, with ties of her own choice and determination" ("Evelina's Deceptions" 113).

of this joking relationship is a successful "exchange" between joker and audience. This exchange involves the audience allowing the transgressive element of the joke in her thoughts and marking the transgression with a laugh. The Teller of the joke receives the response back, confirming the transgressive thought as "constituting part of a meaningful discursive exchange" (13-14).

A hostile joke is often aimed at someone who claims authority and respect. The butt, Purdie points out, is often viewed by the audience and/or the joker as "other," though in reality there is much that is similar between them. Women especially end up as the butts of male jokers. According to Purdie, this is because women are viewed as "inherently disqualified from exercising power" so any powerful action on their parts invites "comic degrading" (128-48). Such a female transgressor, a woman who has assumed a central position of authority, usually reserved for the male, is viewed as grotesque, and in that grotesqueness is a potential for even further untraditionally feminine behavior which marks her as powerful; it also marks her as a target for ridicule by the patriarchy, an easy mark because she is a spectacle already. Patriarchal ridicule simply exploits the spectacular nature of such a woman.

Visual joking, which is our specific concern in Captain Mirvan's joke on Madame Duval, "is concerned with visiting unpleasant circumstances on performing targets in ways that produce an equivocally, momentarily permitted expression of hostility ..." (Purdie 44). The butt is degraded through ridicule that unmasks the butt, displays her stripped of all dignity, made commonplace. The degree to which the audience will find the joke funny depends on the distance between the audience and the butt. The greater the audience's dislike of the butt, the funnier the joke. Funniness is also evoked by the "victims['] struggle against their fate in a flurry of physical or verbal resistance which reinforces their perceived oscillation between having and not-having power – i.e., their *de*gradation" (64). The funniness of the situation "depends upon the almost simultaneous perception of the two states" (65). Degrading the butt through the joking process denies the butt's authority: "the object of laughter has been made into a joke, and a joke's effects in the world are of no consequence" (60).

The use of the joke form makes the aggression of the joker and the audience toward the butt socially acceptable (Wilson 206). Joking is a social litmus test: it allows an "assessment" of how well one fits one's social context. As Chris Powell notes: "To get the joke and to respond appropriately demonstrates one's social competence.... Not to get it threatens shared meanings and jeopardises one's social position" (99). Humor therefore teaches social hegemony: "humor operates to set apart and invalidate the behavior and ideas of those 'not like us' by creating and sustaining stereotypes" (100). As the conduct books noted two hundred and fifty years before, so Christopher Wilson observes today that it is socially acceptable to ridicule "deviants, … or members of out-groups; and there are few inhibitions against enjoyment of such derision" (149). The public nature of the ridicule the butt receives is another aspect of the socializing aspect of the joke: if the audience laughs at the butt, the butt will feel isolated and the audience will find further pleasure in the butt's discomfort. "If the butt questions the humorousness of the ridicule, when the audience seem amused, he risks further isolating himself by presenting a minority view" (204). This is most effective when the butt is already isolated because deviant in some way. As Judy Little notes, "ridiculing a deviant is … a means of societal control" (9). In order that a joke be successful, the audience must permit it, respond to it; therefore, the audience is as much implicated by the joke as the joker (Douglas 98; Palmer 12). Powell does admit that social pressure can cause some to respond to a joke even when they don't get it, or when they disagree with its direction, especially if they are subordinate and the agent is superordinate. In that case, "getting the joke" may be an indication of social cohesiveness, but cohesiveness achieved through coercion rather than through a sense of shared attitudes.

Evelina knows of Captain Mirvan's "intentions" with regard to Madame Duval when the joke is in its planning stage, since the Captain "can scarcely restrain his raptures sufficiently to conceal his design, even from [Madame Duval]" but Evelina does not "dare put Madame Duval upon her guard." Once the joke is underway, and Willoughby's report of "a poor French-man who had got into a scrape which might cost him his life" launches Madame Duval's preparations for rushing off to town, the Captain stops Evelina and "reads his commission to his ship's company," insisting on her "obedience and submission" to his rule. If she dare to "capitulate, or enter into any treaty with the enemy," the Captain assures her, "I shall look upon you as mutinying, and turn you adrift." Evelina is joined in this conspiracy of silence as the joke goes down by the Mirvan women, and by Lady Howard who suspects the Captain. How-ever, while Lady Howard is not happy with his "frolic, yet she would not hazard the consequence of discovering his designs." While the women are motivated to support Captain Mirvan in his joking by their fear of him and his not altogether facetious threat to cast them adrift, there is also something about this joke which appeals to them. Madame Duval's request that Lady Howard not tell the Captain of her plan to go to the country justice calls forth a smile from Lady Howard, and, as we shall see, Evelina's distress over the joke, her embarrassment and, eventually, her moral indignation, is not unmixed with some amusement at the joke's consequences and appreciation for its absurdity, and at Madame Duval's gullibility. Having been cor-nered by the Captain and Clement Willoughby before she joins Madame Duval in the carriage to share with them the progress of the ruse, Evelina is "quite ashamed of being engaged in so ridiculous an affair, and could only think of the absurd appearance we should make upon our arrival at" the justice's.

But when Madame Duval receives the note from the mes-senger indicating she need not go on to the justice's since Monsieur Du Bois has escaped, and Evelina also receives a note, covertly, from Willoughby telling her of the planned attack and reassuring her of her safety, Evelina does not share this information with Madame Duval, either at that instant or when the attack is underway. She explains that she remains silent out of fear of Captain Mirvan's probable resentment toward her and Madame Duval's toward him, if she were to know the truth. As Madame Duval is dragged off by the disguised Captain Mirvan, Willoughby takes the opportunity to make love to Evelina. Evelina flies to her grandmother with "unfeigned concern at her situation" once the two men leave. After Evelina has freed Madame Duval of her restraints, Madame Duval slaps her granddaughter violently on the face for having left her in her moment of need, an act which isolates her even further from both Evelina's and the reader's sympathy. However, Evelina's initial surprise and anger are replaced by compassion for Madame Duval's "real suffering," or so she writes to Villars as she records the joke for his benefit, yet it is Evelina who observes in her letter that Madame Duval "hardly looked human" and that the servants "were ready to die with laughter." While the exposing of affectation was acceptable, according to the conduct books of the period, exposure of a person's weaknesses and deficiencies was not. Madame Duval is a strange mix of vanity and vulnerability; while we understand Evelina's frustration with her grandmother's propensity for affectation, it is more difficult to sympathize with the girl's participation in a prank that reveals her grandmother's vulnerability. Even more incriminating is Evelina's confession that Madame Duval's rendition of the attack, given on their journey back to Howard Grove, "almost compelled me to laugh," though she is "irritated with the Captain, for carrying his love of tormenting – *sport*, he calls it – to such barbarous and unjustifiable extremes." Evelina resolves that she will no longer be passive to the Captain's jests: "Had I imagined he would have been so violent, I would have risked his anger in her defense much sooner."

Captain Mirvan's degradation of Madame Duval, which Evelina participates in, may be viewed simply as an opportunistic exploitation of what Ruth Yeazell terms Madame Duval's natural "propensity to make herself the object of ridicule.... It is as if Madame Duval's powder and paint were here revealed as already a kind of dirt, as if tossing her in a ditch did not so much unsettle her ordinary composure as call attention to her latent sluttishness and disarray" (132-33). Still, the ditching of Madame Duval does reduce her in the eyes of all "to a bare and unaccommodated animal, the body deconstructed to its elemental components of dirt and mud...." The scene, asserts John Zomchick, "is a perfect rendition of an attempt to purge by means of a surfeit" (357). The socially criminal excesses associated with Madame Duval – with her dress, her manners, her speech, her emotions – which embarrass Evelina so, are answered by excessive hostility on the part of Mirvan under the cover of play.[1]

Captain Mirvan's love of tormenting is captured in Jane Collier's description of the cat playing with the mouse in *The Art of Tormenting* (1753):

> She delays the gratification of her hunger, which prompted her to seek for food, and triumphs in her power over her wretched captive – She not only sticks her claws into it, making it feel the sharpness of her teeth (without touching the vitals enough to render it insensible to her tricks), but she tosses it over her head in sport, seems in the highest joy imaginable.... Yet should any thing approach her, that she fears will rob her of her play-thing (holding her prey fast in her teeth), she swears, she growls, and shews all the savage motions of her heart. As soon as her fears are over, she again resumes her sport; and is, in this one instance only, kinder to her victim, than her imitators men, that by death she at last puts a final end to the poor wretch's torments. (See Appendix C)

While Captain Mirvan's gleeful response to the ditching is to be expected because it is consistent with his brute nature, Evelina's is somewhat puzzling, given her earlier chronicling of another joke played on Madame Duval by Captain Mirvan, one which involved Madame Duval's falling into mud, spitting on the Captain, and being shaken violently by him; throughout

---

1 Are Captain Mirvan's jokes play or aggression? Elliott Oring notes that jokes "serve the emotions by allowing the expression of aggression safely 'masked' as play" (16). Aggression and play are distinct; however, "aggressive impulses may, on occasion, utilize forms of intellectual play (i.e., jokes) as weapons, but the impulse of play, mediated by the intellect, can similarly manipulate forms of aggression in the construction of jokes" (28).

her commentary on the antagonism between the two, Evelina has emphasized the violent nature of that relationship. To claim that she had no idea Captain Mirvan would be so violent in this practical joke, then, seems disingenuous. Nor does the joke simply end with the public degradation of Madame Duval. As Evelina is about to leave with Madame Duval for London, the Captain asks that she write to let him know how Madame Duval takes finding out that the Monsieur Dubois incident was "all a trick." "I answered that I would obey him, though I was very little pleased with the commission, which, to me, was highly improper: but he will either treat me as an informer, or make me a party in his frolic."

Evelina's response to the joke on Madame Duval is inappropriate if we expect that love and respect naturally exist between granddaughter and grandmother, but it can also be viewed as a not entirely unexpected response in this particular situation for a variety of reasons. Marvin Koller, in *Humor and Society*, offers us help in understanding at least one aspect of their relationship when he notes that

> among members of nuclear families ... the joking relationship is generally absent because the bonding ... cannot be jeopardized or possibly compromised without serious consequences in terms of antagonisms and alienation. On the other hand, the joking relationship is found between members of extended kin groups, ... particularly as these relatives are increasingly removed from the close, personal, and intimate relationships of nuclear families. (149)

It is primarily with those whom she has blood ties – Madame Duval and the Branghtons – but from whom she is emotionally distant, that Evelina is involved in a joking relationship. In this relationship, the discursive exchange of the joke occurs between Captain Mirvan and Evelina, and, secondarily, between Evelina and the reader of her letters, Villars; in both cases her relatives occupy the position of "butt" of the joke. This is possible not only because Evelina is emotionally distant from her extended kin, but also because she is emotionally dependent upon the community whose patriarch is Mirvan. Julian Pitt-Rivers's observation that "the initial tie of kinship can be modified or reproduced by acts of individual will," and that particular rituals or rites, such as that of blood brotherhood, can establish consubstantiality (93) aptly describes why Evelina's created relationships with Mrs. Mirvan (whom she refers to as "maman") or with Mr. Villars (her "more than father") are relatively humorless ones, involving little joking. Hobbes' observation on laughter in *Human Nature* is valid in *Evelina*: "… when a jest is broken upon ourselves, or friends of whose dishonor we participate, we never laugh thereat" (20). Bonds can be established through ritual, and they can be broken through this means. Joking becomes such a ritual in the novel, and through her participation in the joke, Evelina rejects the "accepted conventions" of kinship and remains unrepentant, as her response to Captain Mirvan's queries regarding her grandmother's presence at her wedding make clear: "I have no reason to expect her at all" and we must assume this is because Evelina has not invited her. The Captain's disappointment and frustration at having his plans spoiled are uppermost in this conversation, but the fact that even boorish Captain Mirvan obviously expects Madame Duval at her granddaughter's wedding makes us question Evelina's denial of her grandmother at such a family-oriented event.[1]

As the conduct books of the period make clear, it was not acceptable for girls to participate in jokes, and certainly not to initiate them. Regina Barreca asserts that "women who create comedy do so in order to intrude, disturb and disrupt; … com-

---

1   Much later in Letter XXI, Vol. III, Evelina reports that she has received a letter from Madame Duval in which she rejoices at Evelina's "late intelligence" and reports that "a violent cold" prevents her coming to Bristol. If Evelina's conversation with Captain Mirvan occurs before Evelina receives the letter from her grandmother (which is what the chronology within the letter itself implies), it would be reasonable to surmise that Evelina has no reason to think Madame Duval would be coming to her wedding, because Evelina has not asked her. If she has indeed had word from Madame Duval regarding her inability to attend the wedding before Evelina speaks with Captain Mirvan, Evelina's answer is unnecessarily ambiguous. In either case, this does not address the absence of Evelina's cousins, the Branghtons, at the wedding.

edy constructed by women is linked to aggression and to the need to break free of socially and culturally imposed restraints" (*Last Laughs* 6). In her relations with Captain Mirvan, Evelina is not only placed as audience to his joke, but as player in it. In her relations with the Branghtons and, to a lesser degree, Madame Duval, Evelina herself becomes the joker, sarcastically commenting on the Branghtons' *faux pas* to Mr. Villars and describing the ridiculous figure Madame Duval makes after each of Captain Mirvan's jokes; she thus implicates herself even further in the jokes.

In *Satire and the Novel in Eighteenth-Century England*, Ronald Paulson points out that joke books in the eighteenth century were generally aimed at discovering affectation and contemporary practical jokes were viewed as "symbolic acts" to expose and punish affectation. Certainly the excerpts from jestbooks of the sixteenth through eighteenth centuries included in Appendix C of this edition emphasize the didactic nature of jokes. Captain Mirvan is the traditional trickster figure, whose "rough actions" serve to scourge the community of all that threatens it – artifice, affectation, immorality.[1] His practical joke on Madame Duval functions as an invitation to its audience to transgress acknowledged social or moral bounds, to accept the butt as scapegoat in a "communal ritual ... of sacrifice,"[2] and thereby to strengthen the status quo (which, after all, his profession demands he protect). In not warning her grandmother of the joke, Evelina accepts the invitation, partakes of the exchange, permits the joke, thereby transgressing the bonds of familial relationship but supporting the status quo.[3] Evelina's comic description of the ditching, as well as of the movements leading up to and following it, are made from the vantage point of what Huang Mei terms the "alienated observer;"[4] it raises for us the specter of Evelina's bastard status and her failure to

---

1 Straub *Divided Fictions* 60; Paulson 6-7; Gillis *Youth* 25-34.
2 Michael Seidel, *Satiric Inheritance* (Princeton: Princeton University Press, 1979), 18.
3 Doody sees Evelina as an "unwilling accomplice" (*Frances Burney* 54) in Captain Mirvan's joke on her grandmother.
4 "Evelina: 'With a Consciousness of Her Sex,'" in *Transforming the Cinderella Dream* (New Brunswick: Rutgers University Press, 1990), 43.

find the "right" family structure to embrace as possible reasons for such a stance. Turning one's back on one's obligations to kin, transgressing bonds of familial relationship is easier to do if one legally is bound to no kin, and easier still if one has received no benefits from those kin. Zomchick points out that Evelina "is implicated in the satiric attacks insofar as her descriptions of [Madame Duval] ... make[s her an] appropriate target" of Mirvan's cruelty in the eyes of her audience, Mr. Villars (especially given his view of Madame Duval, established in the early letters and upheld throughout his correspondence with Lady Howard) (356). Yeazell reads in Evelina's unwillingness to interfere in and her reporting of the incident in which Mirvan ditches her grandmother "some secret satisfaction" (141).[1] Such a response would be understandable if, quoting Freud, we see the joke as making possible "'the satisfaction of an instinct – whether lustful or hostile – in the face of an obstacle which stands in its way.... By making our enemy small, inferior, despicable, or comic, we achieve in a roundabout way the enjoyment of overcoming him'" (qtd. in Flieger 943-44).

A significant issue in Evelina's participation in Captain Mirvan's joke, then, is the degree to which that participation assures her own social acceptability. Evelina may participate in Captain Mirvan's joke because she shares his attitudes toward Madame Duval or because she has adopted these attitudes in order to be a part of the community he controls, the social hegemony his joke purports. In her collusive laughter or irony or silence, Evelina betrays matrilineal bloodlines for consubstantial affiliations. Despite her reservations regarding the Mirvans' domestic bliss and her rebellion against Villars' advice in certain matters, these are the relationships that matter to Evelina, not those with strangers who happen to be related to her. Through her participation in the joke, she reveals her vulnerability to social pressure as well as the depth of her ambivalence and possibly even suppressed hostility toward the butt of

---

1   Straub also notes that "a laugh of complicity in Mirvan's pranks often hovers just
    above the surface of Evelina's discomfort with them" (*Divided Fictions* 103). ·

the joke, her anxiety as outsider at potentially being made the butt, and her wish for power over the butt. The discursive exchange that occurs through the joking relationship in *Evelina* between the joker and the audience ostensibly enables the maintenance of the status quo, as masculine humor generally does through its replication of the patriarchal ideology (Barreca *Snow White* 181). In his practical joke, Captain Mirvan exercises his patriarchally engendered power. John Hart notes that "at least within the Howard/Mirvan households, [Mirvan] comes to signify male hegemony along with other aspects of the tar" (53-54). His actions support Judith Lowder Newton's contention that the novel "presents us with a world dominated by the imposition of men upon women, a world in which male control takes the form of assault, and a world in which male assault is the most central expression of power" (59). And momentarily, as Doody says, he "seizes all the power present in the group" (*Frances Burney* 57) – but only for a moment, because once the discursive exchange occurs between joker and audience – Mirvan and Evelina – the audience is also invested with the power of the joke. Evelina's unwillingness to share the joke with her grandmother is explained by her emotional distance from her grandmother, as well as her desire to achieve power over someone who is essentially a stranger to her but who enjoys excessive power over Evelina's life by virtue of their shared bloodlines.

However, the assurance of the status quo's right to dominance in *Evelina* is questionable given the fluid nature of the joking relationship. If the audience to the joke is impelled to tell the joke to another, thus shifting her position from audience to joker, it is clear that positions within the joking triangle are somewhat fluid. It is possible that the person occupying the position of butt can take on the role of joker, as Madame Duval does when she turns the tables on Sir Clement Willoughby to prove to him that she can play him "trick for trick." While women do not usually take on such a commanding role within the joking relationship, Madame Duval is fired by feelings of revenge against Mirvan and Willoughby, and Willoughby is the safer target. Her declaration that "I'd rather be done any thing to than laughed at, for, to my mind, it's one or other the disagreeablest thing in the world," does not make her so sensitive to the position of the butt that she does not enjoy placing another person in that role.

It is equally possible that the person who occupies the position of audience, while compelled to actively take on the position of joker, may just as easily be forced into the position of butt. Negotiating the joking relationship, attempting to avoid the position of "butt," Evelina reveals her fear of not belonging and her fear of the patriarchy, both of which strengthen her desire to find a place within the nuclear, patriarchal family, either as daughter or as wife, or preferably both.[1] However, if we consider that, like Swift's Gulliver, Evelina is being used by Burney as a satiric device (Paulson 11), a young woman whose denial of one family structure for another is based primarily on what is socially and economically expedient and who is actuated by fear, it is possible to see the subversive Burney positioning her heroine as the butt of the joke. In denying her grandmother's line of descent, in acquiescing to the race of the old women as a grand "diversion,"[2] Evelina accepts as natural what is only so within "the patrilineal ideology;" the joke, finally, is on her, as well as on a society that allows such an ideology to weaken familial bonds. In this respect, it is possible to read Burney's focus in the novel on her heroine's involvement with a variety of family structures as indicating a willingness to consider that alternatives to the nuclear, patriarchal family might be viable, despite the fact that in the end, that is the type of family structure Evelina chooses.

In *Evelina*, the family romance in which the patriarchal father dominates is shown to be restrictive toward its female

---

1 Newton notes that Mirvan, as "an image of the violence potential in patriarchy ... suggests the real necessity for reconciliation to the patriarchal order" (82).
2 Yeazell contends that "the effect of careless brutality is intensified by Evelina's understated reporting of the scene" in which the group at Mrs. Beaumont's are entertained by the race between the two old women. "Like the violent practical joke that previously landed Madame Duval in the ditch, the women's footrace leads directly to an incident in which Evelina herself suffers a related form of coercion": Willoughby's corralling Evelina while Mirvan ditches Madame Duval, and Merton's grabbing Evelina after his racer wins (140).

members – as in the Mirvan household – yet the limitations of a matriarchally-dominated family romance are also clear: the Mirvan women and Madame Duval as heads of household are easily displaced and degraded by the patriarchal males through the power and allure of the patrilineal ideology within the family structure, an allure which encourages the joking relationship. Purdie concludes *Comedy, The Mastery of Discourse* by summarizing: "not only does joking often involve social 'taboos,' it operates exactly like taboo formations in establishing the bounds of what it is 'right' to do, think, say – through the *marked* transgression of rules" (170). In *Evelina*, Mirvan's joke on Madame Duval most obviously establishes that Madame Duval's deviance is not socially acceptable, but it also establishes through its violence to the concept of family the bounds of what it is right to do, think, say within a family. Evelina's response to the joke, like her feelings for family structures, is ambivalent: Evelina recognizes the limiting nature of family structures in general, but also recognizes the importance of a familial bond (as long as it is with the "right" family). Her involvement in the joking relationship is an effort to wrest what control she can from the conflicting family structures until she can situate herself, if only briefly, in an ideologically legitimate family structure – her birth father's household, where she will be the only legitimate female member[1] and where being "real kin" will allow her to be "fully part of the kinship system" in terms of inheritance and status (Pitt-Rivers 94) – until she enters the family structure of her choice, as wife to Orville, where the joking relationship is both unnecessary and impermissible.

So, while Burney's *Evelina* provides the twenty-first-century reader with an entertaining, instructive glimpse of English society in the eighteenth century, set against a vivid backdrop of pleasure gardens, palaces, picture galleries, and parades, it also confronts timeless issues of identity and relationship. Through

---

1   A shadowy paternal aunt, Mrs. Paterson, who is mentioned once in the novel (Volume III, Letter VIII) as guardian to Polly Green has no substance as a character, and Polly's marriage to Sir John Belmont's bastard son Macartney does not give her the same degree of legitimacy Evelina enjoys finally.

her depiction of Evelina and her relations with others, Burney reveals and explores the existing structures of society, both public and private. She examines the manner in which an individual's identity is formed in relation to the family which nurtures her and to the larger community which she enters. Burney is interested in the kinds of negotiations that occur between the individual, her family, and the larger community. As we've seen, Evelina uses the joking relationship as a negotiating tool because it allows her a degree of power unavailable to her through any other means, given her situation and the patriarchal ideology that informs both public and private society in eighteenth-century England. And because she is a woman and has imbibed the lessons of the conduct books, she must necessarily be the seemingly passive audience of the joke, rather than the more obviously assertive initiator of the joke.

As the research presented in the introduction makes clear, the eighteenth-century "family" could no more be pigeonholed than the twenty-first-century family can be patly defined. The nuclear family was at its core, but at its periphery other configurations existed. These alternatives to the traditional nuclear family did not require affiliation through shared bloodlines, so that non-kin might be as close as parent and child, as is the case with Evelina and Mr. Villars, or Evelina and Mrs. Mirvan. They might bring together distant kin to cobble out a more intense bond than would normally exist. They could turn from the more dominant patrilineal relations to the matrilineal, as Evelina is forced to do with Madame Duval and the Branghtons. These alternative family structures existed in the eighteenth century, and while *Evelina* makes clear their potential for providing nurturing alternatives to the nuclear family, Burney's novel also presents the reader with their limitations, limitations which impel Evelina finally to embrace the simple nuclear family as her salvation in a clearly patriarchal society.

Thus, while the concept of "family" escaped easy definition during this period, it could be prescribed. Twenty-first-century readers of this eighteenth-century novel may struggle with it for this very reason, that while we may wish to celebrate diverse family structures, we must acknowledge that our society may still harbor such prescriptive tendencies that privilege one family structure, ultimately, over another. And we must also ask what negotiations such a situation forces each of us into. Will the negotiations my daughter, the adopted child of a single parent whose race is not her own, be any less taxing to her sense of family values than the negotiations Evelina is forced to undertake in a society in which the definition of "family" could only be stretched so far?

# Frances Burney: A Brief Chronology

1752   birth of Frances Burney in King's Lynn, Norfolk
         (13 June), fourth child of Charles Burney and
         Esther Sleepe Burney

1760   move with family to Poland Street, London

1762   death of her mother, Esther Sleepe Burney (27
         September)

1767   manuscript of novel, *The History of Caroline Evelyn*,
         along with all other juvenalia, destroyed by FB;
         marriage of Charles Burney to Elizabeth Allen (2
         October); visit to Bristol Hotwells

1768   diary begun

1770   move with family to Queen's Square, London; visits
         to London entertainments, 1770–73: Marylebone
         Gardens, Ranelagh, Vauxhall, the theater and opera

1774   move with family to St. Martin's Street, Leicester
         Square; marriage proposal from Thomas Barlow
         received, rejected

1778   publication of *Evelina; or, A Young Lady's Entrance
         into the World* (29 January); visits with Hester Thrale
         and Samuel Johnson

1779   publication of four editions of *Evelina* (one pirated);
         *The Witlings, a Comedy* written, suppressed by FB at
         advice of Charles Burney and Samuel Crisp

1782   publication of *Cecilia, or Memoirs of an Heiress* (12
         June)

1783   death of Samuel "Daddy" Crisp (26 April);
         introduction to Mary Delany

1784   death of Samuel Johnson (13 December)

1786   move to court as Second Keeper of the Robes to
         Queen Charlotte, where she felt isolated, bored,
         exhausted by her duties

1790–91   verse tragedies *Hubert De Vere*, *A Pastoral Tragedy*,
         *The Siege of Pevensy*, and *Elberta* written, not pro-
         duced

| 1791 | resigned from court and Queen's service after serious illness |
|---|---|
| 1793 | marriage to Alexandre d'Arblay (28, 30 July), impoverished French emigrant refugee, in both Protestant and Catholic ceremonies; publication of pamphlet, *Brief Reflections Relative to the Emigrant French Clergy*; France at war with England and Holland; introduction to Mme. de Staël |
| 1794 | birth of son, Alexander (18 December) |
| 1795 | production of *Edwy and Elgiva* at Drury Lane (21 March) |
| 1796 | publication of *Camilla; or, a Picture of Youth* (Summer), which allowed FB and ADA to purchase Camilla Cottage; death of her stepmother (20 October) |
| 1798–99 | *Love and Fashion*, a comedy, written |
| 1800 | death of sister, Susanna (6 January) |
| 1801 | *A Busy Day; or, An Arrival from India* and *The Womanhater*, both comedies, written, not produced; cessation of war between France and England; return of d'Arblay to France over estate issues |
| 1802 | move to France to join d'Arblay who had returned to France to recover his property but had been given a military position requiring he remain in France |
| 1803 | England at war with France (18 May); return to England politically impossible |
| 1811 | mastectomy (September) |
| 1812 | return to England with Alexander while d'Arblay remains in France; reunion with her father, Charles Burney |
| 1814 | publication of *The Wanderer; or, Female Difficulties* (March); death of father (12 April); return to France, leaving Alexander at Cambridge; return of Bourbons to French throne after Napoleon is defeated at Victoria by Wellington |
| 1815 | D'Arblay a member of French royalist troops; defeat of Napoleon at Waterloo; return of FB to England with wounded d'Arblay |

1818    death of d'Arblay (3 May)
1832    publication of *Memoirs of Dr. Burney*
1837    death of son, Alexander (19 January)
1840    death of FB (6 January) in London; buried beside
        husband and son

# A Note on the Text

## Choice of Edition

Joyce Hemlow in *The History of Fanny Burney* and Edward
Bloom in his introduction to the 1968 Oxford University Press
edition of *Evelina* both comment on the nature of the substantial revisions Burney made to the several manuscript drafts of
the novel before it was published in January, 1778. Somewhere
between the first drafts of the novel and the published first edition – probably during the process of copying the manuscript
into a feigned hand – Burney revised the novel stylistically to
make distinctions between members of different classes more
apparent: Lord Orville's speech, for instance, was polished,
stripped of all vulgar colloquialisms. According to Hemlow,
Burney's improvements to the novel tended toward: "the clarifying of occasional ambiguous phrases, pruning of unimportant
or superfluous details, tightening of the sentence structure,
replacing of direct, artless, and informal effect by one of greater
finish, dignity, and elegance" (80). "Reflections or sentiments"
from popular quotations were also added to the manuscript, as
were "comments on current plays or operas;" the manuscript
was "amplified ... by character-sketches" (82). Burney was also
given the opportunity to correct the novel once its publisher,
Thomas Lowndes, had prepared a typescript. Just before he
was to bind the printed pages, Lowndes sent an incomplete and
faulty copy of the novel in sheets care of "Mr. Grafton"
at Gregg's Coffee-House for the unknown author of *Evelina*,
asking that a list of corrections might be prepared. Burney's
cousin, Edward Francesco Burney, acting in the role of Mr.
Grafton, was late in retrieving the package and as a result,
Burney had only approximately two weeks to prepare the
*Errata*, which Lowndes subsequently inserted at the beginning
of the first volume rather than correcting the text as per Burney's instructions. This list mentions thirty-three errors in the
first edition, twenty-nine of which were corrected in the second edition (Mackinnon [11]). Burney herself wrote to Lown-

des in June, 1778, continuing the pretence of anonymity, to request that "Shd the Book pass through another Edition, I shd be glad to have Timely notice, as I have many corrections & some alterations, to propose" (*Early Journals and Letters*, ed. Troide, Vol. III 33). Lowndes immediately wrote back that "I think the Impression [of five hundred copies, according to Lowndes, eight hundred according to Burney] will be sold by Christmas" and that "If, mean Time, or about that Time, you favour me with any commands, I shall be proud to observe them" (*EJL* III 55).

During the following months, Burney discussed the "corrections and alterations" to be made to the first edition with her friends and family. For instance, Samuel Crisp writes to Burney in August 1778 that "Hetty & I are agreed on one alteration you must make in the new Edition – the Captain should call the French *Monseers*, the word should be so spelt, & not (as it is printed throughout) *Monsieurs*, as that spelling may mislead some Readers …" (*EJL* III 82). Also in August 1778, while visiting the Thrales, Burney records a conversation with Samuel Johnson in which he gently admonishes her use in the first edition of the Scottish phrase "the one you had designed" where he feels she should have used the English phrase "the letter you had designed." Burney writes,

> Now was not this *extremely* good in him? Who would not have concluded the Book must have *abounded* in Errors too widely spread, & too closely weaved into the general work, to allow of his instructing me in any *one*? *EJL* (III 96)

This change was made in Willoughby's letter to Evelina in the second edition. Burney sent the page proofs for the second edition back to Lowndes in October, 1778, and late in that month (26 October 1778) he published the second edition, though the imprint date was 1779.[1]

---

1    The price for the second edition, bound, was still nine shillings. The run for the second edition was five hundred copies. Burney had written to Lowndes in Octo-

These two changes clarify the distinction between the 1778 first edition of the novel, which several modern editions reproduce, and the 1779 second edition, which R. Brimley Johnson used for his 1893 Dent & Co. edition and Frank MacKinnon reproduced in his 1930 Oxford University Press edition of *Evelina* (these latter two editions are of course out of print). The tendency in Burney studies seems to be to privilege, as Troide and Hemlow did in their editions of Burney's journals and letters, "the verve and spontaneity of Burney's original text [over] … the greater polish of Mme. D'Arblay's revisions" (*EJL* I xxxi). In the case of the journals and letters, which Burney had revised in old age, this difference in style is striking, since there is quite a gap in time from the original texts and the revisions of these. In the case of the first and second editions of *Evelina*, however, only nine months separate Burney's final revisions from the revisions that had taken her through several manuscript drafts to the first edition. The revisions she made for the second edition seem to continue the efforts to polish and sharpen the text which inform her earlier revision process as outlined by Hemlow. Given this, and the fact that it seems Burney did no substantial revisions for the third or subsequent editions of the novel published during her lifetime,[1] I look upon the second edition as a more definitive text than the first edition or subsequent editions.

*Treatment of Text*

This text is a replication of the second edition of *Evelina*. I have kept the title as it appears on the title page for the published second edition, despite the fact that Burney in a letter of October 1778 had asked that Lowndes change the title to *Evelina, or the History of a Young Lady's Entrance into the World* for the second edition. The expansion of the title did not occur until the

---

ber 1778 asking that he consider using better paper for the second edition, which he apparently did, as well as using a better binding (*EJL* III 176).

1   There is no record in her diaries, letters, or her *Memoirs of Dr. Burney* that Burney offered further revisions for the third or subsequent editions that appeared before her death.

third edition of 1779. This Broadview edition reproduces the three-volume structure of the second edition since the style, structure, and tone of each volume is distinctive. The letters within each volume are numbered independent of previous volumes. The text has been emended to correct obvious printer's errors (e.g., missing end punctuation, dropped letters, transposed letters, the use of a period to end an interrogative sentence, the use of the lower case at the beginning of a sentence, "there" for "their," etc.) and to correct the four errors noted in the *Errata* to the first edition which were not corrected in the second edition along with the other twenty nine.

This Broadview edition attempts to replicate the format and design of the original second edition as well with regard to the openings and closings of letters and the poetry included in the text. No attempt to regularize spelling within the text has been made since the use of variant spellings within a text was still an acceptable practice among printers of the period.[1] Nor have I attempted to regularize the punctuation of the text, with its overabundant use of commas, the seeming interchangeableness of colons and semicolons, along modern grammatical lines since grammatical "rules" for the English language in the eighteenth century were less rigid than modern guidelines, allowing more play, which is an interesting facet of the text; however, quotation marks, commas, and appropriate end punctuation have been added where sense would have been obscured without them. Capitalization of substantives within the text has been retained. Such features as the long "s," the display capitals used for the first word of each letter, and the running of quotations marks down the left side of the page have been silently dropped since they do not impact on Burney's text. The length of dashes has been normalized. Hyphens in compound words hyphenated at the margin in the original second edition have been retained unless the words appear unhyphenated elsewhere in the text.

---

1   Cynthia Booth Ricciardi and Susan Staves make this point in their recent edition of Elizabeth Griffith's *The Delicate Distress* (1769) for the University Press of Kentucky, though they acknowledge that the printing industry was clearly moving away from this practice toward a more regularized approach.

Burney uses italics for several reasons: to alert the reader to new terms just entering the language, to further characterize particular speakers through their idiosyncratic phrasings, to identify slang terms. This use of italics has been honored. Burney also footnotes three items in her novel; these notes have been retained and marked but incorporated into my notes on those items.

*Annotations*

Annotations for this edition of *Evelina* attempt to clarify the relationship between the novel and its cultural, historical, and literary contexts. They clarify accidental misquotation, since these are not corrected in the text, and terms, when the eighteenth-century meaning differs from present-day understanding of a word or phrase. Burney is referred to as "FB" in all annotations. I consulted a number of reference works which have been helpful, but from which I have not quoted; these include Microsoft's *Encarta Encyclopedia Deluxe 2000*, *Chambers' Biographical Dictionary*, *Bartlett's Familiar Quotations*, the *Dictionary of National Biography*, *Brewer's Dictionary of Phrase and Fable*, *The New Century Cyclopedia of Names*, and *The Concise Columbia Encyclopedia*.

# EVELINA,

## OR, A

## YOUNG LADY'S

## ENTRANCE

## INTO THE

## WORLD.

## IN A SERIES OF LETTERS.

The Second Edition.

## VOL. I.

LONDON:
Printed for T. Lowndes, N° 77, in
Fleet-Street.

M.DCC.LXXIX.

# TO ___ ___[1]

Oh author of my being!—far more dear
 To me than light, than nourishment, or rest,
Hygieia's[2] blessings, Rapture's burning tear,
 Or the life blood that mantles[3] in my breast!
If in my heart the love of Virtue glows,
 'Twas planted there by an unerring rule;
From thy example the pure flame arose,
 Thy life, my precept—thy good works, my school.
Could my weak pow'rs thy num'rous virtues trace,
 By filial love each fear should be repress'd;
The blush of Incapacity I'd chace,
 And stand, recorder of thy worth, confess'd:
But since my niggard stars that gift refuse,
 Concealment is the only boon I claim;[4]
Obscure be still the unsuccessful Muse,
 Who cannot raise, but would not sink, your fame.
Oh! of my life at once the source and joy!
 If e'er thy eyes these feeble lines survey,
Let not their folly their intent destroy;
 Accept the tribute—but forget the lay.

---

1 Charles Burney (1726–1814), FB's father.
2 The Greek goddess of health.
3 "To 'bubble' with desire" (*Oxford English Dictionary*, ed. James H. Murray et al., 2nd ed. [Oxford: Clarendon Press, 1989]). Abbreviated to "*OED*" in all subsequent references.
4 The novel was published anonymously.

# TO THE AUTHORS

## OF THE

## MONTHLY AND CRITICAL

## REVIEWS.[1]

Gentlemen,

The liberty which I take in addressing to You the trifling production of a few idle hours, will, doubtless, move your wonder,
and, probably, your contempt. I will not, however, with the
futility of apologies, intrude upon your time, but briefly
acknowledge the motives of my temerity: lest, by a premature
exercise of that patience which I hope will befriend me, I
should lessen its benevolence, and be myself accessary to my
own condemnation.

Without name, without recommendation, and unknown
alike to success and disgrace, to whom can I so properly apply
for patronage, as to those who publicly profess themselves
Inspectors of all literary performances?

The extensive plan of your critical observations, – which,
not confined to works of utility or ingenuity, is equally open to
those of frivolous amusement, – and yet worse than frivolous
dullness, – encourages me to seek for your protection, since, –
perhaps for my sins! – it entitles me to your annotations. To
resent, therefore, this offering, however insignificant, would ill
become the universality of your undertaking, though not to
despise it may, alas! be out of your power.

The language of adulation, and the incense of flattery,
though the natural inheritance, and constant resource, from
time immemorial, of the Dedicator, to me offer nothing but
the wistful regret that I dare not invoke their aid. Sinister views
would be imputed to all I could say; since, thus situated, to

---

1 The *Monthly Review* and the *Critical Review* were two of the most important journals in the second half of the eighteenth century. For their reviews of *Evelina*, see
Appendix A.

extol your judgment, would seem the effect of art, and to celebrate your impartiality, be attributed to suspecting it.

As Magistrates of the press, and Censors for the Public, – to
which you are bound by the sacred ties of integrity to exert the
most spirited impartiality, and to which your suffrages[1] should
carry the marks of pure, dauntless, irrefragable truth, – to appeal
for your MERCY, were to solicit your dishonour; and therefore,
– though 'tis sweeter than frankincense, – more grateful to the
senses than all the odorous perfumes of Arabia, – and though

> It droppeth like the gentle rain from heaven
> Upon the place beneath, —— [2]

I court it not! to your justice alone I am entitled, and by that I
must abide. Your engagements are not to the supplicating
author, but to the candid public, which will not fail to crave

> The penalty and forfeit of your bond.[3]

No hackneyed writer, inured to abuse, and callous to criticism,
here braves your severity; – neither does a half-starv'd garret-
teer,[4]

> Oblig'd by hunger, – and request of friends, – [5]

implore your lenity: your examination will be alike unbiassed
by partiality and prejudice: – no refractory murmuring will follow your censure, no private interest be gratified by your praise.

Let not the anxious solicitude with which I recommend
myself to your notice, expose me to your derision. Remember,

---

1  "A vote in support of or an opinion in favour of" (*OED*), i.e., favorable reviews.
2  Portia to Shylock in Shakespeare's *The Merchant of Venice* IV. i. 185-6. Slightly misquoted: "like" should be "as" (*The Riverside Shakespeare,* Ed. G. Blakemore Evans
   [Boston: Houghton Mifflin, 1974]).
3  Shylock to Portia, IV. i. 207. Misquoted: "your" should be "my."
4  "One who lives in a garret; especially an impecunious author or literary hack"
   (*OED*).
5  Pope, "Epistle to Dr. Arbuthnot," ln. 44 (*The Poetry and Prose of Alexander Pope,* Ed.
   A. Williams [Boston: Houghton Mifflin Co., 1969]).

Gentlemen, you were all young writers once, and the most experienced veteran of your corps, may, by recollecting his first publication, renovate his first terrors, and learn to allow for mine. For, though Courage is one of the noblest virtues of this nether sphere, and, though scarcely more requisite in the field of battle, to guard the fighting hero from disgrace, than in the private commerce of the world, to ward off that littleness of soul which leads, by steps imperceptible, to all the base train of the inferior passions, and by which the too timid mind is betrayed into a servility derogatory to the dignity of human nature; yet is it a virtue of no necessity in a situation such as mine; a situation which removes, even from cowardice itself, the sting of ignominy; – for surely that courage may easily be dispensed with, which would rather raise disgust than admiration! Indeed, it is the peculiar privilege of an author, to rob terror of contempt, and pusillanimity of reproach.

*Here let me rest,* – and snatch myself, while yet I am able, from the fascination of EGOTISM, – a monster who has more votaries than ever did homage to the most popular deity of antiquity; and whose singular quality is, that while he excites a blind and involuntary adoration in almost every individual, his influence is universally disallowed, his power universally contemned, and his worship, even by his followers, never mentioned but with abhorrence.

In addressing you jointly, I mean but to mark the generous sentiments by which liberal criticism, to the utter annihilation of envy, jealousy, and all selfish views, ought to be distinguished.

I have the honour to be,
GENTLEMEN,
Your most obedient
humble servant,
★ ★ ★ ★ ★

# PREFACE.

*In the republic of letters, there is no member of such inferior rank, or who is so much disdained by his brethren of the quill, as the humble Novelist: nor is his fate less hard in the world at large, since, among the whole class of writers, perhaps not one can be named of which the votaries are more numerous but less respectable.*

*Yet, while in the annals of those few of our predecessors, to whom this species of writing is indebted for being saved from contempt, and rescued from depravity, we can trace such names as Rousseau, Johnson★,[1] Marivaux, Fielding, Richardson, and Smollet,[2] no man need blush at starting from the same post, though many, nay, most men, may sigh at finding themselves distanced.*

*The following letters are presented to the public — for such, by novel writers, novel readers will be called, — with a very singular mixture of timidity and confidence, resulting from the peculiar situation of the editor; who, though trembling for their success from a consciousness of their imperfections, yet fears not being involved in their disgrace, while happily wrapped up in a mantle of impenetrable obscurity.*

*To draw characters from nature, though not from life, and to mark the manners of the times, is the attempted plan of the following letters. For this purpose, a young female, educated in the most secluded retirement, makes, at the age of seventeen, her first appearance upon the great and busy stage of life; with a virtuous mind, a cultivated understanding, and a feeling heart, her ignorance of the forms, and inexperience in the manners, of the world, occasion all the little incidents which*

---

1 ★FB's note: However superior the capacities in which these great writers deserve to be considered, they must pardon me that, for the dignity of my subject, I here rank the authors of Rasselas and Eloïse as Novelists.

2 Jean-Jacques Rousseau (1712-78), author of philosophical and educational works, as well as the novel *La Nouvelle Héloïse* (1761); Samuel Johnson (1709-84), poet, lexicographer, critic, and author of *The History of Rasselas, Prince of Abyssinia* (1759), an oriental tale; Pierre Carlet de Chamblain de Marivaux (1688-1763), dramatist and novelist, author of *La Vie de Marianne* (1731-41); Henry Fielding (1707-54), dramatist, essayist, and author of such popular novels as *The Adventures of Joseph Andrews and His Friend, Mr. Abraham Adams* (1742), *The History of Tom Jones, A Foundling* (1749), and *Amelia* (1751); Samuel Richardson (1689-1761), printer and novelist, author of the epistolary novels *Pamela* (1741), *Clarissa, Or the History of a Young Lady* (1748), and *Sir Charles Grandison* (1754); Tobias Smollett (1721-71), surgeon, essayist and editor, translator, historian, and novelist best known for *The Adventures of Roderick Random* (1748), *The Adventures of Peregrine Pickle* (1751), and *The Expedition of Humphry Clinker* (1771).

these volumes record, and which form the natural progression of the life of a young woman of obscure birth, but conspicuous beauty, for the first six months after her Entrance into the world.

Perhaps were it possible to effect the total extirpation of novels, our young ladies in general, and boarding-school damsels in particular, might profit from their annihilation: but since the distemper they have spread seems incurable, since their contagion bids defiance to the medicine of advice or reprehension, and since they are found to baffle all the mental art of physic, save what is prescribed by the slow regimen of Time, and bitter diet of Experience, surely all attempts to contribute to the number of those which may be read, if not with advantage, at least without injury, ought rather to be encouraged than contemned.

Let me, therefore, prepare for disappointment those who, in the perusal of these sheets, entertain the gentle expectation of being transported to the fantastic regions of Romance, where Fiction is coloured by all the gay tints of luxurious Imagination, where Reason is an outcast, and where the sublimity of the Marvellous, rejects all aid from sober Probability. The heroine of these memoirs, young, artless, and inexperienced, is

No faultless Monster, that the world ne'er saw,[1]

but the offspring of Nature, and of Nature in her simplest attire.

In all the Arts, the value of copies can only be proportioned to the scarceness of originals: among sculptors and painters, a fine statue, or a beautiful picture, of some great master, may deservedly employ the imitative talents of younger and inferior artists, that their appropriation to one spot, may not wholly prevent the more general expansion of their excellence; but, among authors, the reverse is the case, since the noblest productions of literature, are almost equally attainable with the meanest. In books, therefore, imitation cannot be shunned too sedulously; for the very perfection of a model which is frequently seen, serves but more forcibly to mark the inferiority of a copy.

To avoid what is common, without adopting what is unnatural, must limit the ambition of the vulgar herd of authors: however zealous,

---

1   John Sheffield, first Duke of Buckingham and Normanby (1648-1721), *An Essay on Poetry* (1682), line 235. Slightly misquoted: "No" should be "A" and "that" should read "which."

*therefore, my veneration of the great writers I have mentioned, however I may feel myself enlightened by the knowledge of Johnson, charmed with the eloquence of Rousseau, softened by the pathetic powers of Richardson, and exhilarated by the wit of Fielding, and humour of Smollet; I yet presume not to attempt pursuing the same ground which they have tracked; whence, though they may have cleared the weeds, they have also culled the flowers, and though they have rendered the path plain, they have left it barren.*

*The candour of my readers, I have not the impertinence to doubt, and to their indulgence, I am sensible I have no claim: I have, therefore, only to entreat, that my own words may not pronounce my condemnation, and that what I have here ventured to say in regard to imitation, may be understood, as it is meant, in a general sense, and not be imputed to an opinion of my own originality, which I have not the vanity, the folly, or the blindness, to entertain.*

*Whatever may be the fate of these letters, the editor*[1] *is satisfied they will meet with justice; and commits them to the press, though hopeless of fame, yet not regardless of censure.*

---

1  The editor is often used as a framing device to lend credibility to the epistolary form.

# EVELINA.

## IN A SERIES OF LETTERS.

---

## LETTER I.

*Lady Howard to the Rev. Mr. Villars.*

Howard Grove, Kent.[1]

CAN any thing, my good Sir, be more painful to a friendly mind, than a necessity of communicating disagreeable intelligence? Indeed, it is sometimes difficult to determine, whether the relator or the receiver of evil tidings is most to be pitied.

I have just had a letter from Madame Duval; she is totally at a loss in what manner to behave; she seems desirous to repair the wrongs she has done, yet wishes the world to believe her blameless. She would fain cast upon another the odium of those misfortunes for which she alone is answerable. Her letter is violent, sometimes abusive, and that of *you! – you,* to whom she is under obligations which are greater even than her faults, but to whose advice she wickedly imputes all the sufferings of her much-injured daughter, the late Lady Belmont. The chief purport of her writing I will acquaint you with; the letter itself is not worthy your notice.

She tells me that she has, for many years past, been in continual expectation of making a journey to England, which

---

1  Kent is a county in southeast England.

prevented her writing for information concerning this melancholy subject, by giving her hopes of making personal enquiries; but family occurrences have still detained her in France, which country she now sees no prospect of quitting. She has, therefore, lately used her utmost endeavours to obtain a faithful account of whatever related to her *ill-advised* daughter; the result of which giving her *some reason* to apprehend that, upon her death-bed, she bequeathed an infant orphan to the world, she most graciously says that if *you*, with whom *she understands* the child is placed, will procure authentic proofs of its relationship to her, you may send it to Paris, where she will properly provide for it.

This woman is, undoubtedly, at length, self-convicted of her most unnatural behaviour: it is evident, from her writing, that she is still as vulgar and illiterate as when her first husband, Mr. Evelyn, had the weakness to marry her; nor does she at all apologise for addressing herself to me, though I was only once in her company.

Her letter has excited in my daughter Mirvan, a strong desire to be informed of the motives which induced Madame Duval to abandon the unfortunate Lady Belmont, at a time when a mother's protection was peculiarly necessary for her peace and her reputation. Notwithstanding I was personally acquainted with all the parties concerned in that affair, the subject always appeared of too delicate a nature to be spoken of with the principals; I cannot, therefore, satisfy Mrs. Mirvan otherwise than by applying to you.

By saying that you *may* send the child, Madame Duval aims at *conferring*, where she most *owes* obligation. I pretend not to give you advice; you, to whose generous protection this helpless orphan is indebted for every thing, are the best and only judge of what she ought to do; but I am much concerned at the trouble and uneasiness which this unworthy woman may occasion you.

My daughter and my grandchild join with me in desiring to be most kindly remembered to the amiable girl; and they bid me remind you, that the annual visit to Howard Grove, which we were formerly promised, has been discontinued for more than four years. I am, dear Sir,

with great regard,<br>Your most obedient friend and servant,<br>M. HOWARD.

## LETTER II.

*Mr. Villars to Lady Howard.*

Berry Hill, Dorsetshire.[1]

Your Ladyship did but too well foresee the perplexity and uneasiness of which Madame Duval's letter has been productive. However, I ought rather to be thankful that I have so many years remained unmolested, than repine at my present embarrassment; since it proves, at least, that this wretched woman is at length awakened to remorse.

In regard to my answer, I must humbly request your Ladyship to write to this effect: "That I would not, upon any account, intentionally offend Madame Duval, but that I have weighty, nay unanswerable reasons for detaining her granddaughter at present in England; the principal of which is, that it was the earnest desire of one to whose Will she owes implicit duty. Madame Duval may be assured that she meets with the utmost attention and tenderness; that her education, however short of my wishes, almost exceeds my abilities; and I flatter myself, when the time arrives that she shall pay her duty to her grandmother, Madame Duval will find no reason to be dissatisfied with what has been done for her."

Your Ladyship will not, I am sure, be surprised at this answer. Madame Duval is by no means a proper companion or guardian for a young woman: she is at once uneducated and unprincipled; ungentle in her temper, and unamiable in her manners. I have long known that she has persuaded herself to

---

1 Dorset is a county on the south coast of England.

harbour an aversion for me – Unhappy woman! I can only regard her as an object of pity!

I dare not hesitate at a request from Mrs. Mirvan, yet, in complying with it, I shall, for her own sake, be as concise as I possibly can; since the cruel transactions which preceded the birth of my ward, can afford no entertainment to a mind so humane as her's.

Your Ladyship may probably have heard, that I had the honour to accompany Mr. Evelyn, the grandfather of my young charge, when upon his travels, in the capacity of a tutor.[1] His unhappy marriage, immediately upon his return to England, with Madame Duval, then a waiting-girl at a tavern, contrary to the advice and entreaties of all his friends, among whom I was myself the most urgent, induced him to abandon his native land, and fix his abode in France. Thither he was followed by shame and repentance; feelings which his heart was not framed to support: for, notwithstanding he had been too weak to resist the allurements of beauty, which nature, though a niggard to her of every other boon, had with a lavish hand bestowed on his wife; yet he was a young man of excellent character, and, till thus unaccountably infatuated, of unblemished conduct. He survived this ill-judged marriage but two years. Upon his death-bed, with an unsteady hand, he wrote me the following note:

"My friend! forget your resentment, in favour of your humanity; – a father, trembling for the welfare of his child, bequeaths her to your care. – O Villars! hear! pity! and relieve me!"

Had my circumstances permitted me, I should have answered these words by an immediate journey to Paris; but I was obliged to act by the agency of a friend, who was upon the spot, and present at the opening of the will.

Mr. Evelyn left to me a legacy of a thousand pounds, and the sole guardianship of his daughter's person till her eighteenth

---

1  Mr. Evelyn, like many other well-to-do young Englishmen of the period, completed his education with a "grand tour" of the continent of Europe; he was accompanied by Mr. Villars, who served as guide and companion.

year, conjuring me, in the most affecting terms, to take the charge of her education till she was able to act with propriety for herself; but in regard to fortune, he left her wholly dependent on her mother, to whose tenderness he earnestly recommended her.

Thus, though he would not, to a woman low-bred and illiberal as Mrs. Evelyn, trust the conduct and morals of his daughter, he nevertheless thought proper to secure to her the respect and duty which, from her own child, were certainly her due; but, unhappily, it never occurred to him that the mother, on her part, could fail in affection or justice.

Miss Evelyn, Madam, from the second to the eighteenth year of her life, was brought up under my care, and, except when at school, under my roof. I need not speak to your Ladyship of the virtues of that excellent young creature. She loved me as her father; nor was Mrs. Villars less valued by her; while to me she became so dear, that her loss was little less afflicting than that which I have since sustained of Mrs. Villars herself.

At that period of her life we parted; her mother, then married to Monsieur Duval, sent for her to Paris. How often have I since regretted that I did not accompany her thither! protected and supported by me, the misery and disgrace which awaited her, might, perhaps, have been avoided. But – to be brief, Madame Duval, at the instigation of her husband, earnestly, or rather tyrannically, endeavoured to effect a union between Miss Evelyn and one of his nephews. And, when she found her power inadequate to her attempt, enraged at her non-compliance, she treated her with the grossest unkindness, and threatened her with poverty and ruin.

Miss Evelyn, to whom wrath and violence had hitherto been strangers, soon grew weary of such usage; and rashly, and without a witness, consented to a private marriage[1] with Sir

---

1    Sir John Belmont and Caroline Evelyn were married in France in what would at that time – a few years after Lord Hardwicke's Marriage Act of 1753 – have been an irregular ceremony, one in which the banns had not been published, nor a license procured, and for which no witnesses were present. In addition, in his notes to the 1930 Oxford University Press edition of *Evelina*, Frank D. MacKinnon questions the likelihood of there even being "a certificate of a marriage between two British subjects in Paris about 1758 ..." (510).

John Belmont, a very profligate young man, who had but too successfully found means to insinuate himself into her favour. He promised to conduct her to England – he did. – O, Madam, you know the rest! – Disappointed of the fortune he expected, by the inexorable rancour of the Duvals, he infamously burnt the certificate of their marriage, and denied that they had ever been united!

She flew to me for protection. With what mixed transports of joy and anguish did I again see her! By my advice she endeavoured to procure proofs of her marriage; – but in vain: her credulity had been no match for his art.

Every body believed her innocent, from the guiltless tenor of her unspotted youth, and from the known libertinism[1] of her barbarous betrayer. Yet her sufferings were too acute for her tender frame, and the same moment that gave birth to her infant, put an end at once to the sorrows and the life of its mother.

The rage of Madame Duval at her elopement, abated not while this injured victim of cruelty yet drew breath. She probably intended, in time, to have pardoned her, but time was not allowed. When she was informed of her death, I have been told, that the agonies of grief and remorse, with which she was seized, occasioned her a severe fit of illness. But, from the time of her recovery to the date of her letter to your Ladyship, I had never heard that she manifested any desire to be made acquainted with the circumstances which attended the death of Lady Belmont, and the birth of her helpless child.

That child, Madam, shall never, while life is lent me, know the loss she has sustained. I have cherished, succoured, and supported her, from her earliest infancy to her sixteenth year; and so amply has she repaid my care and affection, that my fondest wish is now circumscribed by the desire of bestowing her on one who may be sensible of her worth, and then sinking to eternal rest in her arms.

Thus it has happened that the education of the father, daughter, and grand-daughter, has devolved on me. What

---

1    The licentiousness practiced by some young men belonging to the upper classes in seventeenth- and eighteenth-century England.

infinite misery have the two first caused me! Should the fate of the dear survivor be equally adverse, how wretched will be the end of my cares – the end of my days!

Even had Madame Duval merited the charge she claims, I fear my fortitude would have been unequal to such a parting; but, being such as she is, not only my affection, but my humanity recoils, at the barbarous idea of deserting the sacred trust reposed in me. Indeed, I could but ill support her former yearly visits to the respectable mansion at Howard Grove; pardon me, dear Madam, and do not think me insensible of the honour which your Ladyship's condescension confers upon us both; but so deep is the impression which the misfortunes of her mother have made on my heart, that she does not, even for a moment, quit my sight, without exciting apprehensions and terrors which almost overpower me. Such, Madam, is my tenderness, and such my weakness! – But she is the only tie I have upon earth, and I trust to your Ladyship's goodness not to judge of my feelings with severity.

I beg leave to present my humble respects to Mrs. and Miss Mirvan; and have the honour to be,

Madam,
Your Ladyship's most obedient
and most humble servant,
ARTHUR VILLARS.

## LETTER III.

[Written some months after the last.]

*Lady Howard to the Rev. Mr. Villars.*

Howard Grove, March 8.

Dear and Rev. Sir,
Your last letter gave me infinite pleasure: after so long and tedious an illness, how grateful to yourself and to your friends must be your returning health! You have the hearty wishes

of every individual of this place for its continuance and increase.

Will you not think I take advantage of your acknowledged recovery, if I once more venture to mention your pupil and Howard Grove together? Yet you must remember the patience with which we submitted to your desire of not parting with her during the bad state of your health, though it was with much reluctance we forbore to solicit her company. My grand-daughter, in particular, has scarce been able to repress her eagerness to again meet the friend of her infancy; and for my own part, it is very strongly my wish to manifest the regard I had for the unfortunate Lady Belmont, by proving serviceable to her child; which seems to me the best respect that can be paid to her memory. Permit me, therefore, to lay before you a plan which Mrs. Mirvan and I have formed, in consequence of your restoration to health.

I would not frighten you; – but do you think you could bear to part with your young companion for two or three months? Mrs. Mirvan proposes to spend the ensuing spring in London, whither, for the first time, my grandchild will accompany her: Now, my good friend, it is very earnestly their wish to enlarge and enliven their party by the addition of your amiable ward, who would share, equally with her own daughter, the care and attention of Mrs. Mirvan. Do not start at this proposal; it is time that she should see something of the world. When young people are too rigidly sequestered from it, their lively and romantic imaginations paint it to them as a paradise of which they have been beguiled; but when they are shown it properly, and in due time, they see it such as it really is, equally shared by pain and pleasure, hope and disappointment.

You have nothing to apprehend from her meeting with Sir John Belmont, as that abandoned man is now abroad, and not expected home this year.

Well, my good Sir, what say you to our scheme? I hope it will meet with your approbation; but if it should not, be assured I can never object to any decision of one who is so much respected and esteemed as Mr. Villars, by

His most faithful humble servant,
M. HOWARD.

## LETTER IV.

### Mr. Villars to Lady Howard

Berry Hill, March 12.

I am grieved, Madam, to appear obstinate, and I blush to incur the imputation of selfishness. In detaining my young charge thus long with myself in the country, I consulted not solely my own inclination. Destined, in all probability, to possess a very moderate fortune, I wished to contract her views to something within it. The mind is but too naturally prone to pleasure, but too easily yielded to dissipation: it has been my study to guard her against their delusions, by preparing her to expect, – and to despise them. But the time draws on for experience and observation to take place of instruction: if I have, in some measure, rendered her capable of using one with discretion, and making the other with improvement, I shall rejoice myself with the assurance of having largely contributed to her welfare. She is now of an age that happiness is eager to attend, – let her then enjoy it! I commit her to the protection of your Ladyship, and only hope she may be found worthy half the goodness I am satisfied she will meet with at your hospitable mansion.

Thus far, Madam, I chearfully submit to your desire. In confiding my ward to the care of Lady Howard, I can feel no uneasiness from her absence, but what will arise from the loss of her company, since I shall be as well convinced of her safety as if she were under my own roof; – but, can your Ladyship be serious in proposing to introduce her to the gaieties of a London life? Permit me to ask, for what end, or what purpose? A youthful mind is seldom totally free from ambition; to curb that, is the first step to contentment, since to diminish expectation, is to increase enjoyment. I apprehend nothing more than too much raising her hopes and her views, which the natural vivacity of her disposition would render but too easy to effect. The town-acquaintance of Mrs. Mirvan are all in the circle of high life; this artless young creature, with too much beauty to escape notice, has too much sensibility[1] to be indifferent to it; but she has too little wealth to be sought with propriety by men of the fashionable world.

Consider, Madam, the peculiar cruelty of her situation; only child of a wealthy Baronet,[2] whose person she has never seen, whose character she has reason to abhor, and whose name she is forbidden to claim; entitled as she is to lawfully inherit his fortune and estate, is there any probability that he will *properly* own her? And while he continues to persevere in disavowing his marriage with Miss Evelyn, she shall never, at the expence of her mother's honour, receive a part of her right, as the donation of his bounty.

And as to Mr. Evelyn's estate, I have no doubt but that Madame Duval and her relations will dispose of it among themselves.

It seems, therefore, as if this deserted child, though legally heiress of two large fortunes, must owe all her rational expectations to adoption and friendship. Yet her income will be such as may make her happy, if she is disposed to be so in private life; though it will by no means allow her to enjoy the luxury of a London fine lady.

Let Miss Mirvan, then, Madam, shine in all the splendor of high life;[3] but suffer my child still to enjoy the pleasures of humble retirement, with a mind to which greater views are unknown.

I hope this reasoning will be honoured with your approbation; and I have yet another motive which has some weight with me; I would not willingly give offence to any human being, and surely Madame Duval might accuse me of injustice, if, while I refuse to let her grand-daughter wait upon her, I consent that she should join a party of pleasure to London.

In sending her to Howard Grove, not one of these scruples arise; and therefore Mrs. Clinton, a most worthy woman,

---

1 Sensitivity.
2 "A titled order, the lowest that is hereditary, ranking next below a baron.... A baronet is a commoner" (*OED*).
3 Fashionable life.

formerly her nurse, and now my housekeeper, shall attend her thither next week.

Though I have always called her by the name of Anville, and reported in this neighbourhood that her father, my intimate friend, left her to my guardianship, yet I have thought it necessary she should herself be acquainted with the melancholy circumstances attending her birth; for, though I am very desirous of guarding her from curiosity and impertinence, by concealing her name, family, and story, yet I would not leave it in the power of chance, to shock her gentle nature with a tale of so much sorrow.

You must not, Madam, expect too much from my pupil. She is quite a little rustic, and knows nothing of the world; and though her education has been the best I could bestow in this retired place, to which Dorchester,[1] the nearest town, is seven miles distant, yet I shall not be surprised if you should discover in her a thousand deficiencies of which I have never dreamt. She must be very much altered since she was last at Howard Grove, – but I will say nothing of her; I leave her to your Ladyship's own observations, of which I beg a faithful relation; and am,

Dear Madam, with great respect,
Your obedient and most humble servant,
ARTHUR VILLARS.

## LETTER V.

*Mr. Villars to Lady Howard.*

March 18.

Dear Madam,

This letter will be delivered to you by my child, – the child of my adoption,[2] – my affection! Unblest with one natural

---

1   Dorchester, on the Frome River, is the capital of Dorset in Southern England.
2   Villars writes to Lady Howard later in Volume I, Letter XXVIII, that it was his plan to "adopt [Evelina] … the heiress of my small fortune."

friend,[1] she merits a thousand. I send her to you, innocent as an angel, and artless as purity itself: and I send you with her the heart of your friend, the only hope he has on earth, the subject of his tenderest thoughts, and the object of his latest cares. She is one, Madam, for whom alone I have lately wished to live; and she is one whom to serve I would with transport die! Restore her but to me all innocence as you receive her, and the fondest hope of my heart will be amply gratified!

A. VILLARS.

## LETTER VI.

*Lady Howard to the Rev. Mr. Villars.*

Howard Grove.

Dear and Rev. Sir,

The solemn manner in which you have committed your child to my care, has in some measure dampt the pleasure which I receive from the trust, as it makes me fear that you suffer from your compliance, in which case I shall very sincerely blame myself for the earnestness with which I have requested this favour; but remember, my good Sir, she is within a few days summons, and be assured I will not detain her a moment longer than you wish.

You desire my opinion of her.

She is a little angel! I cannot wonder that you sought to monopolize her. Neither ought you, at finding it impossible.

Her face and person answer my most refined ideas of complete beauty: and this, though a subject of praise less important to you, or to me, than any other, is yet so striking, it is not possible to pass it unnoticed. Had I not known from whom she received her education, I should, at first sight of so perfect a face, have been in pain for her understanding; since it has been long and justly remarked, that folly has ever sought alliance with beauty.

---

1   Relative by blood or marriage.

She has the same gentleness in her manners, the same natural grace in her motions, that I formerly so much admired in her mother. Her character seems truly ingenuous and simple; and, at the same time that nature has blessed her with an excellent understanding, and great quickness of parts, she has a certain air of inexperience and innocency that is extremely interesting.

You have no reason to regret the retirement in which she has lived; since that politeness which is acquired by an acquaintance with high life, is in her so well supplied by a natural desire of obliging, joined to a deportment infinitely engaging.

I observe with great satisfaction a growing affection between this amiable girl and my grand-daughter, whose heart is as free from selfishness or conceit, as that of her young friend is from all guile. Their regard may be mutually useful, since much is to be expected from emulation, where nothing is to be feared from envy. I would have them love each other as sisters, and reciprocally supply the place of that tender and happy relationship, to which neither of them have a natural claim.

Be satisfied, my good Sir, that your child shall meet with the same attention as our own.

We all join in most hearty wishes for your health and happiness, and in returning our sincere thanks for the favour you have conferred on us.

I am, Dear Sir,
Your most faithful servant,
M. HOWARD.

## LETTER VII.

*Lady Howard to the Rev. Mr. Villars.*

Howard Grove, March 26.

Be not alarmed, my worthy friend, at my so speedily troubling you again; I seldom use the ceremony of waiting for answers, or writing with any regularity, and I have at present immediate occasion for begging your patience.

Mrs. Mirvan has just received a letter from her long-absent husband, containing the welcome news of his hoping to reach London by the beginning of next week. My daughter and the Captain have been separated almost seven years, and it would therefore be needless to say what joy, surprise, and consequently confusion, his, at present, unexpected return has caused at Howard Grove. Mrs. Mirvan, you cannot doubt, will go instantly to town to meet him; her daughter is under a thousand obligations to attend her; I grieve that her mother cannot.

And now, my good Sir, I almost blush to proceed; – but, tell me, may I ask – will you permit – that your child may accompany them? Do not think us unreasonable, but consider the many inducements which conspire to make London the happiest place at present she can be in. The joyful occasion of the journey; the gaiety of the whole party; opposed to the dull life she must lead if left here, with a solitary old woman for her sole companion, while she so well knows the chearfulness and felicity enjoyed by the rest of the family, – are circumstances that seem to merit your consideration. Mrs. Mirvan desires me to assure you, that one week is all she asks, as she is certain that the Captain, who hates London, will be eager to revisit Howard Grove: and Maria is so very earnest in wishing to have the company of her friend, that, if you are inexorable, she will be deprived of half the pleasure she otherwise hopes to receive.

However, I will not, my good Sir, deceive you into an opinion that they intend to live in a retired manner, as that cannot be fairly expected. But you have no reason to be uneasy concerning Madame Duval; she has not any correspondent in England, and obtains no intelligence[1] but by common report. She must be a stranger to the name your child bears; and, even should she hear of this excursion, so short a time as a week, or less, spent in town upon so particular an occasion, though previous to their meeting, cannot be construed into disrespect to herself.

Mrs. Mirvan desires me to assure you, that if you will oblige her, her *two* children shall equally share her time and her atten-

---

1 News.

tion. She has sent a commission to a friend in town to take a house for her, and while she waits for an answer concerning it, I shall for one from you to our petition. However, your child is writing herself, and that, I doubt not, will more avail than all we can possibly urge.

My daughter desires her best compliments to you, *if*, she says, you will grant her request, but *not else*.

Adieu, my dear Sir, – we all hope every thing from your goodness.

M. HOWARD.

## LETTER VIII.

*Evelina to the Rev. Mr. Villars.*

Howard Grove, March 26.

This house seems to be the house of joy; every face wears a smile, and a laugh is at every body's service. It is quite amusing to walk about, and see the general confusion; a room leading to the garden is fitting up for Captain Mirvan's study. Lady Howard does not sit a moment in a place; Miss Mirvan is making caps; every body so busy! – such flying from room to room! – so many orders given, and retracted, and given again! – nothing but hurry and perturbation.

Well but, my dear Sir, I am desired to make a request to you. I hope you will not think me an incroacher; Lady Howard insists upon my writing! – yet I hardly know how to go on; a petition implies a want, – and have you left me one? No, indeed.

I am half ashamed of myself for beginning this letter. But these dear ladies are so pressing – I cannot, for my life, resist wishing for the pleasures they offer me, – provided you do not disapprove them.

They are to make a very short stay in town. The Captain will meet them in a day or two. Mrs. Mirvan and her sweet daughter both go; – what a happy party! Yet I am not *very* eager to accompany them: at least, I shall be contented to remain where I am, if you desire that I should.

Assured, my dearest Sir, of your goodness, your bounty, and your indulgent kindness, ought I to form a wish that has not your sanction? Decide for me, therefore, without the least apprehension that I shall be uneasy, or discontented. While I am yet in suspense, perhaps I may *hope*, but I am most certain, that when you have once determined, I shall not repine.

They tell me that London is now in full splendour. Two Play-houses are open,[1] – the Opera-House,[2] – Ranelagh,[3] – and the Pantheon.[4] – You see I have learned all their names. However, pray don't suppose that I make any point of going, for I shall hardly sigh to see them depart without me; though I shall probably never meet with such another opportunity. And, indeed, their domestic happiness will be so great, – it is natural to wish to partake of it.

I believe I am bewitched! I made a resolution when I began, that I would not be urgent; but my pen – or rather my thoughts, will not suffer me to keep it – for I acknowledge, I must acknowledge, I cannot help wishing for your permission.

I almost repent already that I have made this confession; pray forget that you have read it, if this journey is displeasing to you. But I will not write any longer; for the more I think of this affair, the less indifferent to it I find myself.

Adieu, my most honoured, most reverenced, most beloved father! for by what other name can I call you? I have no happiness or sorrow, no hope or fear, but what your kindness bestows, or your displeasure may cause. You will not, I am sure, send a refusal, without reasons unanswerable, and therefore I

---

1  Drury Lane Theatre and Covent Garden Theatre were open from late September until late June.

2  The Opera House, managed by Mary Ann Yates and Frances Brooke from 1773–78, was open from October until June on Tuesdays and Saturdays, and produced Italian opera.

3  Ranelagh was a pleasure garden in Chelsea where people might walk, view the ornamental lake or Chinese pavilion, listen to concerts, attend masquerades or dances, play cards, watch fireworks, or take tea in the rotunda.

4  The Pantheon, in Oxford Street, was an elegant indoor pleasure garden opened in 1772 to house masquerades, concerts, and dances.

shall chearfully acquiesce. Yet I hope – I hope you will be able to permit me to go!

I am,
With the utmost affection,
gratitude, and duty,
Your
EVELINA — .

I cannot to *you* sign *Anville*, and what other name may I claim?

## LETTER IX.

*Mr. Villars to Evelina.*

Berry-Hill, March 28.

To resist the urgency of entreaty, is a power which I have not yet acquired: I aim not at an authority which deprives you of liberty, yet I would fain guide myself by a prudence which should save me the pangs of repentance. Your impatience to fly to a place which your imagination has painted to you in colours so attractive, surprises me not; I have only to hope that the liveliness of your fancy may not deceive you: to refuse, would be raising it still higher. To see my Evelina happy, is to see myself without a wish: go then, my child, and may that Heaven which alone can, direct, preserve, and strengthen you! To That, my love, will I daily offer prayers for your felicity; O may it guard, watch over you! defend you from danger, save you from distress, and keep vice as distant from your person as from your heart! And to Me, may it grant the ultimate blessing of closing these aged eyes in the arms of one so dear – so deservedly beloved!

ARTHUR VILLARS.

## LETTER X.

*Evelina to the Rev. Mr. Villars.*

Queen-Ann-Street,[1] London, Saturday, April 2.

This moment arrived. Just going to Drury-Lane theatre. The celebrated Mr. Garrick performs Ranger.[2] I am quite in extacy. So is Miss Mirvan. How fortunate, that he should happen to play! We would not let Mrs. Mirvan rest till she consented to go; her chief objection was to our dress, for we have had no time to *Londonize*[3] ourselves; but we teized her into compliance, and so we are to sit in some obscure place, that she may not be seen. As to me, I should be alike unknown in the most conspicuous or most private part of the house.

I can write no more now. I have hardly time to breathe – only just this, the houses and streets are not quite so superb as I expected. However, I have seen nothing yet, so I ought not to judge.

Well, adieu, my dearest Sir, for the present; I could not forbear writing a few words instantly on my arrival; though I suppose my letter of thanks for your consent is still on the road.

Saturday Night.

O my dear Sir, in what raptures am I returned! Well may Mr. Garrick be so celebrated, so universally admired – I had not any idea of so great a performer.

Such ease! such vivacity in his manner! such grace in his motions! such fire and meaning in his eyes! – I could hardly believe he had studied a written part, for every word seemed to be uttered from the impulse of the moment.

---

1   Queen-Ann-Street is in the West End of London on the Portland Estate.
2   David Garrick (1717-79), dramatist, manager of Drury Lane Theatre from 1747-76, and popular actor, played Ranger, the hero of Benjamin Hoadly's *The Suspicious Husband* (1747), numerous times in 1776, the year he retired as actor and manager.
3   "To make like London or its inhabitants" (*OED*, which credits *Evelina* with being the first publication in which the word appeared).

His action – at once so graceful and so free! – his voice – so clear, so melodious, yet so wonderfully various in its tones – such animation! – every look *speaks!*

I would have given the world to have had the whole play acted over again. And when he danced – O how I envied Clarinda![1] I almost wished to have jumped on the stage and joined them.

I am afraid you will think me mad, so I won't say any more; yet I really believe Mr. Garrick would make you mad too, if you could see him. I intend to ask Mrs. Mirvan to go to the play every night while we stay in town. She is extremely kind to me, and Maria, her charming daughter, is the sweetest girl in the world.

I shall write to you every evening all that passes in the day, and that in the same manner as, if I could see, I should tell you.

Sunday.

This morning we went to Portland chapel,[2] and afterwards we walked in the Mall of St. James's Park,[3] which by no means answered my expectations: it is a long straight walk, of dirty gravel, very uneasy to the feet; and at each end, instead of an open prospect, nothing is to be seen but houses built of brick. When Mrs. Mirvan pointed out the *Palace*[4] to me – I think I was never much more surprised.

However, the walk was very agreeable to us; every body looked gay, and seemed pleased, and the ladies were so much

---

1  Clarinda is the heroine of *The Suspicious Husband*, but she dances with her fiancé, Frankly, at the end of the play, and not with Ranger (who dances with Mrs. Strickland).

2  Designed by S. Leadbetter, and built 1765-66, Portland Chapel was a "chapel of ease to the parish of St. Marylebone" (Henry Wheatley, *London Past and Present* [London: Murray, 1891], 62).

3  St. James Park is "the oldest of the royal parks; it extends to about 90 acres with the Mall as the northern boundary and Birdcage Walk as the southern" (*The London Encyclopedia*, Ed. Ben Weinreb and Christopher Hibbert [London: Macmillan, 1983] 716). Pall Mall was the most fashionable street in London during the eighteenth century, lined with expensive shops and fine houses.

4  St. James Palace was the "principal royal residence in London" during the eighteenth century (Weinreb 716).

dressed, that Miss Mirvan and I could do nothing but look at them. Mrs. Mirvan met several of her friends. No wonder, for I never saw so many people assembled together before. I looked about for some of *my* acquaintance, but in vain, for I saw not one person that I knew, which is very odd, for all the world seemed there.

Mrs. Mirvan says we are not to walk in the Park again next Sunday, even if we should be in town, because there is better company in Kensington Gardens.[1] But really if you had seen how much every body was dressed, you would not think that possible.

Monday.

We are to go this evening to a private ball, given by Mrs. Stanley, a very fashionable lady of Mrs. Mirvan's acquaintance.

We have been *a shopping*, as Mrs. Mirvan calls it, all this morning, to buy silks, caps, gauzes, and so forth.

The shops are really very entertaining, especially the mercers;[2] there seem to be six or seven men belonging to each shop, and every one took care, by bowing and smirking, to be noticed; we were conducted from one to another, and carried from room to room, with so much ceremony, that at first I was almost afraid to go on.

I thought I should never have chosen a silk, for they produced so many I knew not which to fix upon, and they recommended them all so strongly, that I fancy they thought I only wanted persuasion to buy every thing they shewed me. And, indeed, they took so much trouble, that I was almost ashamed I could not.

At the milliners,[3] the ladies we met were so much dressed, that I should rather have imagined they were making visits than purchases. But what most diverted me was, that we were more

---

1   The Broad Walk in Kensington Gardens was a fashionable meeting place.
2   A mercer "deals in textile fabrics, esp. ... in silks, velvets, and other costly materials" (*OED*).
3   A milliner is "a vendor of 'fancy' wares and articles of apparel, ... esp. bonnets and other headgear" (*OED*).

frequently served by men than by women; and such men! so finical, so affected! they seemed to understand every part of a woman's dress better than we do ourselves; and they recommended caps and ribbands with an air of so much importance, that I wished to ask them how long they had left off wearing them!

The dispatch with which they work in these great shops is amazing, for they have promised me a compleat suit of linen[1] against the evening.

I have just had my hair dressed.[2] You can't think how oddly my head feels; full of powder and black pins, and a great *cushion* on the top of it. I believe you would hardly know me, for my face looks quite different to what it did before my hair was dressed. When I shall be able to make use of a comb for myself I cannot tell, for my hair is so much entangled, *frizled* they call it, that I fear it will be very difficult.

I am half afraid of this ball to-night, for, you know, I have never danced but at school;[3] however, Miss Mirvan says there is nothing in it. Yet I wish it was over.

Adieu, my dear Sir; pray excuse the wretched stuff I write, perhaps I may improve by being in this town, and then my letters will be less unworthy your reading. Mean time I am,

Your dutiful and affectionate,

though unpolished,

EVELINA.

Poor Miss Mirvan cannot wear one of the caps she made, because they dress her hair too large for them.

---

1 "In earlier use, an entire set of garments for wear at one time; in recent use, a costume (i.e., coat and skirt)" (*OED*).

2 Fashionable women's hair was teased up high over padding, kept in place by grease and pins, powdered, and ornamented with jewels, ribbons, and even miniature scenes.

3 Evelina probably attended a boarding school and would have danced with other girls.

# LETTER XI.

*Evelina in continuation.*

Queen-Ann-Street, April 5, Tuesday morning.

I have a vast deal to say, and shall give all this morning to my pen. As to my plan of writing every evening the adventures of the day, I find it impracticable; for the diversions here are so very late, that if I begin my letters after them, I could not go to bed at all.

We past a most extraordinary evening. A *private* ball[1] this was called, so I expected to have seen about four or five couple; but Lord! my dear Sir, I believe I saw half the world! Two very large rooms were full of company; in one, were cards for the elderly ladies, and in the other, were the dancers. My mamma Mirvan, for she always calls me her child, said she would sit with Maria and me till we were provided with partners, and then join the card-players.

The gentlemen, as they passed and repassed, looked as if they thought we were quite at their disposal, and only waiting for the honour of their commands; and they sauntered about, in a careless indolent manner, as if with a view to keep us in suspense. I don't speak of this in regard to Miss Mirvan and myself only, but to the ladies in general; and I thought it so provoking, that I determined, in my own mind, that, far from humouring such airs, I would rather not dance at all, than with any one who should seem to think me ready to accept the first partner who would condescend to take me.

Not long after, a young man, who had for some time looked at us with a kind of negligent impertinence, advanced, on tiptoe, towards me; he had a set smile on his face, and his dress was so foppish,[2] that I really believe he even wished to be stared at; and yet he was very ugly.

Bowing almost to the ground, with a sort of swing, and

---

1 A ball given by a family in their home to specified guests.
2 "Resembling or befitting a fop or dandy ... (one who is foolishly attentive to and vain of his appearance, dress, or manners)" (*OED*).

waving his hand with the greatest conceit, after a short and silly pause, he said, "Madam – may I presume?" – and stopt, offering to take my hand. I drew it back, but could scarce forbear laughing. "Allow me, Madam," (continued he, affectedly breaking off every half moment) "the honour and happiness – if I am not so unhappy as to address you too late – to have the happiness and honour – "

Again he would have taken my hand, but, bowing my head, I begged to be excused, and turned to Miss Mirvan to conceal my laughter. He then desired to know if I had already engaged myself to some more fortunate man? I said No, and that I believed I should not dance at all. He would keep himself, he told me, disengaged, in hopes I should relent; and then, uttering some ridiculous speeches of sorrow and disappointment, though his face still wore the same invariable smile, he retreated.

It so happened, as we have since recollected, that during this little dialogue, Mrs. Mirvan was conversing with the lady of the house. And very soon after another gentleman, who seemed about six-and-twenty years old, gayly, but not foppishly, dressed, and indeed extremely handsome, with an air of mixed politeness and gallantry, desired to know if I was engaged, or would honour him with my hand. So he was pleased to say, though I am sure I know not what honour he could receive from me; but these sort of expressions, I find, are used as words of course, without any distinction of persons, or study of propriety.

Well, I bowed, and I am sure I coloured; for indeed I was frightened at the thoughts of dancing before so many people, all strangers, and, which was worse, *with* a stranger; however, that was unavoidable, for though I looked round the room several times, I could not see one person that I knew. And so, he took my hand, and led me to join in the dance.

The minuets were over before we arrived,[1] for we were kept late by the milliner's making us wait for our things.

---

1   "A slow, stately dance ... for two dancers; derived from France in the latter part of the seventeenth century, and fashionable throughout the eighteenth" (*OED*).

He seemed very desirous of entering into conversation with me; but I was seized with such a panic, that I could hardly speak a word, and nothing but the shame of so soon changing my mind, prevented my returning to my seat, and declining to dance at all.

He appeared to be surprised at my terror, which I believe was but too apparent: however, he asked no questions, though I fear he must think it very strange; for I did not choose to tell him it was owing to my never before dancing but with a school-girl.

His conversation was sensible and spirited; his air and address were open and noble; his manners gentle, attentive, and infinitely engaging; his person is all elegance, and his countenance, the most animated and expressive I have ever seen.

In a short time we were joined by Miss Mirvan, who stood next couple to us. But how was I startled, when she whispered me that my partner was a nobleman! This gave me a new alarm; how will he be provoked, thought I, when he finds what a simple rustic he has honoured with his choice! one whose ignorance of the world makes her perpetually fear doing something wrong!

That he should be so much my superior every way, quite disconcerted me; and you will suppose my spirits were not much raised, when I heard a lady, in passing us, say, "This is the most difficult dance I ever saw."

"O dear, then," cried Maria to her partner, "with your leave, I'll sit down till the next."

"So will I too, then," cried I, "for I am sure I can hardly stand."

"But you must speak to your partner first," answered she; for he had turned aside to talk with some gentlemen. However, I had not sufficient courage to address him, and so away we all three tript, and seated ourselves at another end of the room.

But, unfortunately for me, Miss Mirvan soon after suffered herself to be prevailed upon to attempt the dance; and just as she rose to go, she cried, "My dear, yonder is your partner, Lord Orville, walking about the room in search of you."

"Don't leave me, then, dear girl!" cried I; but she was obliged to go. And now I was more uneasy than ever; I would have given the world to have seen Mrs. Mirvan, and begged of her to make my apologies; for what, thought I, can I possibly say to him in excuse for running away? he must either conclude me a fool, or half mad; for any one brought up in the great world, and accustomed to its ways, can have no idea of such sort of fears as mine.

My confusion encreased when I observed that he was every where seeking me, with apparent perplexity and surprise; but when, at last, I saw him move towards the place where I sat, I was ready to sink with shame and distress. I found it absolutely impossible to keep my seat, because I could not think of a word to say for myself, and so I rose, and walked hastily towards the card-room, resolving to stay with Mrs. Mirvan the rest of the evening, and not to dance at all. But before I could find her, Lord Orville saw and approached me.

He begged to know if I was not well? You may easily imagine how much I was embarrassed. I made no answer, but hung my head, like a fool, and looked on my fan.

He then, with an air the most respectfully serious, asked if he had been so unhappy as to offend me?

"No, indeed!" cried I: and, in hopes of changing the discourse, and preventing his further inquiries, I desired to know if he had seen the young lady who had been conversing with me?

No; – but would I honour him with any commands to her?

"O by no means!"

Was there any other person with whom I wished to speak?

I said *no*, before I knew I had answered at all.

Should he have the pleasure of bringing me any refreshment?

I bowed, almost involuntarily. And away he flew.

I was quite ashamed of being so troublesome, and so much *above* myself as these seeming airs made me appear; but indeed I was too much confused to think or act with any consistency.

If he had not been swift as lightning, I don't know whether I should not have stolen away again; but he returned in a moment. When I had drunk a glass of lemonade, he hoped, he said, that I would again honour him with my hand, as a new dance was just begun. I had not the presence of mind to say a single word, and so I let him once more lead me to the place I had left.

Shocked to find how silly, how childish a part I had acted, my former fears of dancing before such a company, and with such a partner, returned more forcibly than ever. I suppose he perceived my uneasiness, for he intreated me to sit down again, if dancing was disagreeable to me. But I was quite satisfied with the folly I had already shewn, and therefore declined his offer, tho' I was really scarce able to stand.

Under such conscious disadvantages, you may easily imagine, my dear Sir, how ill I acquitted myself. But, though I both expected and deserved to find him very much mortified and displeased at his ill fortune in the choice he had made, yet, to my very great relief, he appeared to be even contented, and very much assisted and encouraged me. These people in high life have too much presence of mind, I believe, to *seem* disconcerted, or out of humour, however they may feel: for had I been the person of the most consequence in the room, I could not have met with more attention and respect.

When the dance was over, seeing me still very much flurried, he led me to a seat, saying that he would not suffer me to fatigue myself from politeness.

And then, if my capacity, or even if my spirits had been better, in how animated a conversation might I have been engaged! It was then I saw that the rank of Lord Orville was his least recommendation, his understanding and his manners being far more distinguished. His remarks upon the company in general were so apt, so just, so lively, I am almost surprised myself that they did not re-animate me; but indeed I was too well convinced of the ridiculous part I had myself played before so nice an observer, to be able to enjoy his pleasantry: so self-compassion gave me feeling for others. Yet I had not the courage to attempt either to defend them, or to rally in my turn,[1] but listened to him in silent embarrassment.

---

1    "To treat or assail with banter, pleasantry, or good-humoured ridicule; to make fun or game of" (*OED*).

When he found this, he changed the subject, and talked of public places, and public performers; but he soon discovered that I was totally ignorant of them.

He then, very ingeniously, turned the discourse to the amusements and occupations of the country.

It now struck me, that he was resolved to try whether or not I was capable of talking upon *any* subject. This put so great a constraint upon my thoughts, that I was unable to go further than a monosyllable, and not even so far, when I could possibly avoid it.

We were sitting in this manner, he conversing with all gaiety, I looking down with all foolishness, when that fop who had first asked me to dance, with a most ridiculous solemnity, approached, and after a profound bow or two, said, "I humbly beg pardon, Madam, – and of you too, my Lord, – for breaking in upon such agreeable conversation – which must, doubtless, be much more delectable – than what I have the honour to offer – but – "

I interrupted him – I blush for my folly, – with laughing; yet I could not help it, for, added to the man's stately foppishness, (and he actually took snuff[1] between every three words) when I looked round at Lord Orville, I saw such extreme surprise in his face, – the cause of which appeared so absurd, that I could not for my life preserve my gravity.

I had not laughed before from the time I had left Miss Mirvan, and I had much better have cried then; Lord Orville actually stared at me; the beau,[2] I know not his name, looked quite enraged. "Refrain – Madam," (said he, with an important air,) "a few moments refrain! – I have but a sentence to trouble you with. – May I know to what accident I must attribute not having the honour of your hand?"

"Accident, Sir!" repeated I, much astonished.

"Yes, accident, Madam – for surely, – I must take the liberty to observe – pardon me, Madam, – it ought to be no common

---

1   "A preparation of powdered tobacco for inhaling through the nostrils. The practice of taking snuff appears to have become fashionable about 1680 ..." (*OED*).

2   "A man who gives particular, or excessive, attention to dress, mien, and social etiquette" (*OED*).

one – that should tempt a lady – so young a one too, – to be guilty of ill manners."

A confused idea now for the first time entered my head, of something I had heard of the rules of an assembly;[1] but I was never at one before, – I have only danced at school, – and so giddy and heedless I was, that I had not once considered the impropriety of refusing one partner, and afterwards accepting another. I was thunderstruck at the recollection: but, while these thoughts were rushing into my head, Lord Orville, with some warmth, said, "This lady, Sir, is incapable of meriting such an accusation!"

The creature – for I am very angry with him, – made a low bow, and with a grin the most malicious I ever saw, "My Lord," said he, "far be it from me to *accuse* the lady, for having the discernment to distinguish and prefer – the superior attractions of your Lordship."

Again he bowed, and walked off.

Was ever any thing so provoking? I was ready to die with shame. "What a coxcomb!"[2] exclaimed Lord Orville; while I, without knowing what I did, rose hastily, and moving off, "I can't imagine," cried I, "where Mrs. Mirvan has hid herself!"

"Give me leave to see," answered he. I bowed and sat down again, not daring to meet his eyes; for what must he think of me, between my blunder, and the supposed preference?

He returned in a moment, and told me that Mrs. Mirvan was at cards, but would be glad to see me; and I went immediately. There was but one chair vacant, so, to my great relief, Lord Orville presently left us. I then told Mrs. Mirvan my disasters, and she good-naturedly blamed herself for not having better instructed me, but said she had taken it for granted that I must know such common customs. However, the man may,

---

1   A woman who refused to dance with a man, but was not engaged to another, would not dance for two further dances. It was also understood that agreeing to dance one dance really meant agreeing to dance two dances with the same partner (Timothy Dow Adams, "To Know the Dancer from the Dance," *Studies in the Novel* 14 [1982]: 55).

2   "A foolish, conceited, showy person, vain of his accomplishments, appearance, or dress" (*OED*).

I think, be satisfied with his pretty speech, and carry his resentment no farther.

In a short time, Lord Orville returned. I consented, with the best grace I could, to go down another dance, for I had had time to recollect myself, and therefore resolved to use some exertion, and, if possible, appear less a fool than I had hitherto done; for it occurred to me that, insignificant as I was, compared to a man of his rank and figure, yet, since he had been so unfortunate as to make choice of me for a partner, why I should endeavour to make the best of it.

The dance, however, was short, and he spoke very little; so I had no opportunity of putting my resolution in practice. He was satisfied, I suppose, with his former successless efforts to draw me out: or, rather, I fancied, he had been inquiring *who I was*. This again disconcerted me, and the spirits I had determined to exert, again failed me. Tired, ashamed, and mortified, I begged to sit down till we returned home, which we did soon after. Lord Orville did me the honour to hand me to the coach, talking all the way of the honour *I* had done *him!* O these fashionable people!

Well, my dear Sir, was it not a strange evening? I could not help being thus particular, because, to me, every thing is so new. But it is now time to conclude. I am, with all love and duty,

Your<br>EVELINA.

## LETTER XII.

*Evelina in continuation.*

Tuesday, April 5.

There is to be no end to the troubles of last night. I have this moment, between persuasion and laughter, gathered from Maria the most curious dialogue that ever I heard. You will, at first, be startled at my vanity; but, my dear Sir, have patience!

It must have passed while I was sitting with Mrs. Mirvan in the card-room. Maria was taking some refreshment, and saw Lord Orville advancing for the same purpose himself; but he did not know her, though she immediately recollected him. Presently after, a very gay-looking man, stepping hastily up to him, cried, "Why, my Lord, what have you done with your lovely partner?"

"*Nothing!*" answered Lord Orville, with a smile and a shrug.

"By Jove," cried the man, "she is the most beautiful creature I ever saw in my life!"

Lord Orville, as he well might, laughed, but answered, "Yes, a pretty modest-looking girl."

"O my Lord!" cried the madman, "she is an angel!"

"A *silent* one," returned he.

"Why ay, my Lord, how stands she as to that? She looks all intelligence and expression."

"A poor weak girl!" answered Lord Orville, shaking his head.

"By Jove," cried the other, "I am glad to hear it!"

At that moment, the same odious creature who had been my former tormentor, joined them. Addressing Lord Orville with great respect, he said, "I beg pardon, my Lord, – if I was – as I fear might be the case – rather too severe in my censure of the lady who is honoured with your protection – but, my Lord, ill-breeding is apt to provoke a man."

"Ill-breeding!" cried my unknown champion, "impossible! that elegant face can never be so vile a mask!"

"O Sir, as to that," answered he, "you must allow *me* to judge; for though I pay all deference to your opinion – in other things, – yet I hope you will grant – and I appeal to your Lordship also – that I am not totally despicable as a judge of good or ill manners."

"I was so wholly ignorant," said Lord Orville gravely, "of the provocation you might have had, that I could not but be surprised at your singular resentment."

"It was far from my intention," answered he, "to offend your Lordship; but really, for a person who is nobody, to give herself such airs, – I own I could not command my passions. For, my

Lord, though I have made diligent enquiry – I cannot learn who she is."

"By what I can make out," cried my defender, "she must be a country parson's daughter."

"He! he! he! very good, 'pon honour!" cried the fop, – "well, so I could have sworn by her manners."

And then, delighted at his own wit, he laughed, and went away, as I suppose, to repeat it.

"But what the deuce is all this?" demanded the other.

"Why a very foolish affair," answered Lord Orville; "your Helen[1] first refused this coxcomb, and then – danced with me. This is all I can gather of it."

"O Orville," returned he, "you are a happy man! – But, *ill-bred*? – I can never believe it! And she looks too sensible to be *ignorant*."

"Whether ignorant or mischievous, I will not pretend to determine, but certain it is, she attended to all *I* could say to her, though I have really fatigued myself with fruitless endeavours to entertain her, with the most immoveable gravity; but no sooner did Lovel begin his complaint, than she was seized with a fit of laughing, first affronting the poor beau, and then enjoying his mortification."

"Ha! ha! ha! why there's some *genius* in that, my Lord, though perhaps rather – *rustick*."

Here Maria was called to dance, and so heard no more.

Now tell me, my dear Sir, did you ever know any thing more provoking? "*A poor weak girl!*" "*ignorant or mischievous!*" What mortifying words! I am resolved, however, that I will never again be tempted to go to an assembly. I wish I had been in Dorsetshire.

Well, after this, you will not be surprised that Lord Orville contented himself with an enquiry after our healths this morning, by his servant, without troubling himself to call; as Miss Mirvan had told me he would: but perhaps it may be only a country custom.[2]

---

1   Helen of Troy's beauty was legendary.

2   It was customary for a man who had danced with a woman to call on her the next day to ask after her health. That Lord Orville sends his servant rather than visiting himself indicates his lack of commitment to the relationship.

I would not live here for the world. I care not how soon we leave town. London soon grows tiresome. I wish the Captain would come. Mrs. Mirvan talks of the opera for this evening; however, I am very indifferent about it.

Wednesday morning.

Well, my dear Sir, I have been pleased against my will, I could almost say, for I must own I went out in very ill-humour, which I think you cannot wonder at: but the music and the singing were charming; they soothed me into a pleasure the most grateful, the best suited to my present disposition in the world. I hope to persuade Mrs. Mirvan to go again on Saturday. I wish the opera was every night. It is, of all entertainments, the sweetest, and most delightful. Some of the songs seemed to melt my very soul. It was what they call a *serious* opera, as the *comic* first singer was ill.

To-night we go to Ranelagh. If any of those three gentlemen who conversed so freely about me should be there — but I won't think of it.

Thursday morning.

Well, my dear Sir, we went to Ranelagh. It is a charming place, and the brilliancy of the lights, on my first entrance, made me almost think I was in some inchanted castle, or fairy palace, for all looked like magic to me.

The very first person I saw was Lord Orville. I felt so confused! – but he did not see me. After tea, Mrs. Mirvan being tired, Maria and I walked round the room alone. Then again we saw him, standing by the orchestra. We, too, stopt to hear a singer. He bowed to me; I courtsied, and I am sure I coloured. We soon walked on, not liking our situation: however, he did not follow us, and when we passed by the orchestra again, he was gone. Afterwards, in the course of the evening, we met him several times, but he was always with some party, and never spoke to us, tho' whenever he chanced to meet my eyes, he condescended to bow.

I cannot but be hurt at the opinion he entertains of me. It is true, my own behaviour incurred it – yet he is himself the most agreeable and, seemingly, the most amiable man in the world, and therefore it is, that I am grieved to be thought ill of by him: for of whose esteem ought we to be ambitious, if not of those who most merit our own? – But it is too late to reflect upon this now. Well, I can't help it; – However, I think I have done with assemblies!

This morning was destined for *seeing sights*, auctions,[1] curious shops,[2] and so forth; but my head ached, and I was not in a humour to be amused, and so I made them go without me, though very unwillingly. They are all kindness.

And now I am sorry I did not accompany them, for I know not what to do with myself. I had resolved not to go to the play to-night; but I believe I shall. In short, I hardly care whether I do or not.

★    ★    ★    ★    ★

I thought I had done wrong! Mrs. Mirvan and Maria have been half the town over, and so entertained! – while I, like a fool, stayed at home to do nothing. And, at an auction in Pall-mall, who should they meet but Lord Orville! He sat next to Mrs. Mirvan, and they talked a great deal together: but she gave me no account of the conversation.

I may never have such another opportunity of seeing London; I am quite sorry that I was not of the party; but I deserve this mortification, for having indulged my ill-humour.

Thursday night.

We are just returned from the play, which was King Lear,[3] and has made me very sad. We did not see any body we knew. Well, adieu, it is too late to write more.

---

1  Christie's auction house in Pall Mall was opened in 1766.
2  Curious shops catered to shoppers interested in the exotic, the ornamental.
3  Evelina would have seen Garrick's version of *King Lear*, which did not depart from Shakespeare's original to the extent of other adaptations of the play performed during the eighteenth century. In Nahum Tate's version, for instance, Lear is restored to his throne and Cordelia marries Edgar.

Captain Mirvan is arrived. I have not spirits to give an account of his introduction, for he has really shocked me. I do not like him. He seems to be surly, vulgar, and disagreeable.

Almost the same moment that Maria was presented to him, he began some rude jests upon the bad shape of her nose, and called her a tall, ill-formed thing. She bore it with the utmost good-humour; but that kind and sweet-tempered woman, Mrs. Mirvan, deserved a better lot. I am amazed she would marry him.

For my own part, I have been so shy, that I have hardly spoken to him, or he to me. I cannot imagine why the family was so rejoiced at his return. If he had spent his whole life abroad, I should have supposed they might rather have been thankful than sorrowful. However, I hope they do not think so ill of him as I do. At least, I am sure they have too much prudence to make it known.

Saturday night.

We have been to the opera, and I am still more pleased than I was on Tuesday. I could have thought myself in paradise, but for the continual talking of the company around me. We sat in the pit, where every body was dressed in so high a style, that, if I had been less delighted with the performance, my eyes would have found me sufficient entertainment from looking at the ladies.[1]

I was very glad I did not sit next the Captain, for he could not bear the music, or singers, and was extremely gross in his observations on both. When the opera was over, he went into a place called the coffee-room, where ladies as well as gentlemen assemble. There are all sorts of refreshments, and the company walk about, and *chat* with the same ease and freedom as in a private room.

---

1   Fashionable people attending the opera sat in the pit (comparable to today's orchestra), and while admittance was expensive and people were expected to dress well, the pit was noisy and the seating uncomfortable (benches without backs or arms).

On Monday we go to a ridotto,[1] and on Wednesday we return to Howard Grove. The Captain says he won't stay here to be *smoked with filth* any longer; but, having been seven years *smoked with a burning sun*, he will retire to the country, and sink into a *fair-weather chap*.[2]

Adieu, my dear Sir.

## LETTER XIII.

*Evelina in continuation.*

Tuesday, April 12.

My dear Sir,

We came home from the ridotto so late, or rather, so early, that it was not possible for me to write. Indeed we did not *go*, you will be frightened to hear it, — till past eleven o'clock: but nobody does. A terrible reverse of the order of nature! We sleep with the sun, and wake with the moon.

The room was very magnificent, the lights and decorations were brilliant, and the company gay and splendid. But I should have told you, that I made many objections to being of the party, according to the resolution I had formed. However, Maria laughed me out of my scruples, and so, once again — I went to an assembly.

Miss Mirvan danced a minuet, but I had not the courage to follow her example. In our walks I saw Lord Orville. He was quite alone, but did not observe us. Yet, as he seemed of no party, I thought it was not impossible that he might join us; and tho' I did not much wish to dance at all, — yet, as I was more acquainted with him than with any other person in the room, I must own I could not help thinking it would be infinitely more desirable to dance again with him, than with an entire

---

1 "An entertainment or social assembly consisting of music and dancing. Introduced into England 'in the year 1722, at the Opera House in the Haymarket' ... and a marked feature of London social life during the eighteenth century" (*OED*).

2 A landlubber who cannot stomach bad weather at sea; a derogatory term.

stranger. To be sure, after all that had passed, it was very ridiculous to suppose it even probable, that Lord Orville would again honour me with his choice; yet I am compelled to confess my absurdity, by way of explaining what follows.

Miss Mirvan was soon engaged; and, presently after, a very fashionable, gay-looking man, who seemed about 30 years of age, addressed himself to me, and begged to have the honour of dancing with me. Now Maria's partner was a gentleman of Mrs. Mirvan's acquaintance; for she had told us it was highly improper for young women to dance with strangers, at any public assembly. Indeed it was by no means my wish so to do; yet I did not like to confine myself from dancing at all; neither did I dare refuse this gentleman, as I had done Mr. Lovel, and then, if any acquaintance should offer, accept him: and so, all these reasons combining, induced me to tell him – yet I blush to write it to you! – that I was *already engaged*; by which I meant to keep myself at liberty to dance or not, as matters should fall out.

I suppose my consciousness betrayed my artifice, for he looked at me as if incredulous; and, instead of being satisfied with my answer, and leaving me, according to my expectation, he walked at my side, and, with the greatest ease imaginable, began a conversation, in the free style which only belongs to old and intimate acquaintance. But, what was most provoking, he asked me a thousand questions concerning *the partner to whom I was engaged*. And, at last, he said, "Is it really possible that a man whom you have honoured with your acceptance, can fail to be at hand to profit from your goodness?"

I felt extremely foolish, and begged Mrs. Mirvan to lead to a seat, which she very obligingly did. The Captain sat next her, and, to my great surprise, this gentleman thought proper to follow, and seat himself next to me.

"What an insensible!" continued he, "why, Madam, you are missing the most delightful dance in the world! The man must be either mad, or a fool. – Which do you incline to think him yourself?"

"Neither, Sir," answered I in some confusion.

He begged my pardon for the freedom of his supposition,

saying, "I really was off my guard, from astonishment that any man can be so much and so unaccountably his own enemy. But where, Madam, can he possibly be? – has he left the room? – or has not he been in it?"

"Indeed, Sir," said I peevishly, "I know nothing of him."

"I don't wonder that you are disconcerted, Madam, it is really very provoking. The best part of the evening will be absolutely lost. He deserves not that you should wait for him."

"I do not, Sir," said I, "and I beg you not to – "

"Mortifying, indeed, Madam," interrupted he, "a lady to wait for a gentleman: – O fie! – careless fellow! – what can detain him? – Will you give me leave to seek him?"

"If you please, Sir," answered I, quite terrified lest Mrs. Mirvan should attend to him, for she looked very much surprised at seeing me enter into conversation with a stranger.

"With all my heart," cried he; "pray what coat has he on?"

"Indeed I never looked at it."

"Out upon him!" cried he; "What! did he address you in a coat not worth looking at? – What a shabby wretch!"

How ridiculous! I really could not help laughing, which, I fear, encouraged him, for he went on.

"Charming creature! – and can you really bear ill usage with so much sweetness? – Can you, *like patience on a monument,*[1] smile in the midst of disappointment? – For my part, though I am not the offended person, my indignation is so great, that I long to kick the fellow round the room! – unless, indeed, – (hesitating and looking earnestly at me,) unless, indeed – it is a partner of your own *creating*?"

I was dreadfully abashed, and could not make any answer.

"But no!" cried he, (again, and with warmth,) "it cannot be that you are so cruel! Softness itself is painted in your eyes: – You could not, surely, have the barbarity so wantonly to trifle with my misery."

I turned away from this nonsense, with real disgust. Mrs. Mirvan saw my confusion, but was perplexed what to think of it, and I could not explain to her the cause, lest the Captain

---

1 Viola speaking to the Duke in Shakespeare's *Twelfth Night, or What You Will* II. iv. 114, of the sad end of the woman who never told her love.

should hear me. I therefore proposed to walk, she consented, and we all rose; but, would you believe it? this man had the assurance to rise too, and walk close by my side, as if of my party!

"Now," cried he, "I hope we shall see this ingrate. – Is that he?" – pointing to an old man, who was lame, "or that?" And in this manner he asked me of whoever was old or ugly in the room. I made no sort of answer; and when he found that I was resolutely silent, and walked on, as much as I could, without observing him, he suddenly stamped his foot, and cried out, in a passion, "Fool! idiot! booby!"

I turned hastily toward him: "O Madam," continued he, "forgive my vehemence, but I am distracted to think there should exist a wretch who can slight a blessing for which I would forfeit my life! – O! that I could but meet him! – I would soon —— But I grow angry: pardon me, Madam, my passions are violent, and your injuries affect me!"

I began to apprehend he was a madman, and stared at him with the utmost astonishment. "I see you are moved, Madam," said he, "generous creature! – but don't be alarmed, I am cool again, I am indeed, – upon my soul I am, – I entreat you, most lovely of mortals! I entreat you to be easy."

"Indeed, Sir," said I very seriously, "I must insist upon your leaving me; you are quite a stranger to me, and I am both unused, and averse to your language and your manners."

This seemed to have some effect on him. He made me a low bow, begged my pardon, and vowed he would not for the world offend me.

"Then, Sir, you must leave me," cried I.

"I am gone, Madam, I am gone!" with a most tragical air; and he marched away, a quick pace, out of sight in a moment; but before I had time to congratulate myself, he was again at my elbow.

"And could you really let me go, and not be sorry? – Can you see me suffer torments inexpressible, and yet retain all your favour for that miscreant who flies you? – Ungrateful puppy! – I could bastinado him!"[1]

---

1   "To beat with a stick" especially on the soles of the feet (*OED*).

"For Heaven's sake, my dear," cried Mrs. Mirvan, "who is he talking of?"

"Indeed – I do not know, Madam," said I, "but I wish he would leave me."

"What's all that there?" cried the Captain.

The man made a low bow, and said, "Only, Sir, a slight objection which this young lady makes to dancing with me, and which I am endeavouring to obviate. I shall think myself greatly honoured, if you will intercede for me."

"That lady, Sir," said the Captain coldly, "is her own mistress." And he walked sullenly on.

"You, Madam," said the man, (who looked delighted, to Mrs. Mirvan,) "you, I hope, will have the goodness to speak for me."

"Sir," answered she gravely, "I have not the pleasure of being acquainted with you."

"I hope when you have, Ma'am," cried he, (undaunted,) "you will honour me with your approbation; but, while I am yet unknown to you, it would be truly generous in you to countenance me; and, I flatter myself, Madam, that you will not have cause to repent it."

Mrs. Mirvan, with an embarrassed air, replied, "I do not at all mean, Sir, to doubt your being a gentleman, – but, – "

"But *what*, Madam? – that doubt removed, why a *but?*"

"Well, Sir," said Mrs. Mirvan, (with a good-humoured smile,) "I will even treat you with your own plainness, and try what effect that will have on you: I must therefore tell you, once for all – "

"O pardon me, Madam!" interrupted he eagerly, "you must not proceed with those words, *once for all*; no, if *I* have been too *plain*, and though a *man*, deserve a rebuke, remember, dear ladies, that if you *copy*, you ought, in justice, to *excuse* me."

We both stared at the man's strange behaviour.

"Be nobler than your sex," continued he, turning to me, "honour me with one dance, and give up the ingrate who has merited so ill your patience."

Mrs. Mirvan looked with astonishment at us both. "Who does he speak of, my dear? – you never mentioned — "

"O Madam!" exclaimed he, "he was not worth mentioning – it is pity he was ever thought of; but let us forget his existence. One dance is all I solicit; permit me, Madam, the honour of this young lady's hand; it will be a favour I shall ever most gratefully acknowledge."

"Sir," answered she, "favours and strangers have with me no connection."

"If you have hitherto," said he, "confined your benevolence to your intimate friends, suffer me to be the first for whom your charity is enlarged."

"Well, Sir, I know not what to say to you, – but – "

He stopt her *but* with so many urgent entreaties, that she at last told me, I must either go down one dance, or avoid his importunities by returning home. I hesitated which alternative to chuse; but this impetuous man at length prevailed, and I was obliged to consent to dance with him.

And thus was my deviation from truth punished; and thus did this man's determined boldness conquer.

During the dance, before we were too much engaged in it for conversation, he was extremely provoking about *my partner*, and tried every means in his power to make me own that I had deceived him; which, though I would not so far humble myself as to acknowledge, was, indeed, but too obvious.

Lord Orville, I fancy, did not dance at all; he seemed to have a large acquaintance, and joined several different parties: but you will easily suppose I was not much pleased to see him, in a few minutes after I was gone, walk towards the place I had just left, and bow to, and join Mrs. Mirvan!

How unlucky I thought myself, that I had not longer withstood this stranger's importunities! The moment we had gone down the dance, I was hastening away from him, but he stopt me, and said that I could by no means return to my party, without giving offence, before we had *done our duty of walking up the dance.*[1] As I know nothing at all of these rules and customs, I

---

[1] In a country dance, the couple first dances down the aisle of couples facing one another, but in order to complete their role in the dance, they must then return "up the dance" to take their places so that the next couple may pass down the aisle (Mackinnon 516).

was obliged to submit to his directions; but I fancy I looked rather uneasy, for he took notice of my inattention, saying, in his free way, "Whence that anxiety? – Why are those lovely eyes perpetually averted?"

"I wish you would say no more to me, Sir," (cried I peevishly) "you have already destroyed all my happiness for this evening."

"Good Heaven! what is it I have done? – How have I merited this scorn?"

"You have tormented me to death; you have forced me from my friends, and intruded yourself upon me, against my will, for a partner."

"Surely, my dear Madam, we ought to be better friends, since there seems to be something of sympathy in the frankness of our dispositions. – And yet, were you not an angel – how do you think I could brook such contempt?"

"If I have offended you," cried I, "you have but to leave me – and O how I wish you would!"

"My dear creature," (said he, half laughing) "why where could you be educated?"

"Where I most sincerely wish I now was!"

"How conscious you must be, all beautiful that you are, that those charming airs serve only to heighten the bloom of your complexion!"

"Your freedom, Sir, where you are more acquainted, may perhaps be less disagreeable; but to *me* – "

"You do me justice," (cried he, interrupting me) "yes, I do indeed improve upon acquaintance; you will hereafter be quite charmed with me."

"Hereafter, Sir, I hope I shall never – "

"O hush! – hush! – have you forgot the situation in which I found you? – Have you forgot, that when deserted, I pursued you, – when betrayed, I adored you? – but for me – "

"But for you, Sir, I might, perhaps, have been happy."

"What then, am I to conclude that, *but for me*, your *partner* would have appeared? – poor fellow! – and did my presence awe him?"

"I wish *his* presence, Sir, could awe *you*!"

"His presence! – perhaps then you see him?"

"Perhaps, Sir, I do;" cried I, quite wearied of his raillery.

"Where? – where? – for Heaven's sake shew me the wretch!"

"Wretch, Sir?"

"O, a very savage! – a sneaking, shamefaced, despicable puppy!"

I know not what bewitched me – but my pride was hurt, and my spirits were tired, and – in short – I had the folly, looking at Lord Orville, to repeat, "*Despicable*, you think?"

His eyes instantly followed mine; "Why, is *that* the gentleman?"

I made no answer; I could not affirm, and I could not deny; for I hoped to be relieved from his teizing, by his mistake.

The very moment we had done what he called our duty, I eagerly desired to return to Mrs. Mirvan.

"To your *partner*, I presume, Madam?" said he, very gravely.

This quite confounded me; I dreaded lest this mischievous man, ignorant of his rank, should address himself to Lord Orville, and say something which might expose my artifice. Fool! to involve myself in such difficulties! I now feared what I had before wished, and, therefore, to *avoid* Lord Orville, I was obliged myself to *propose* going down another dance, though I was ready to sink with shame while I spoke.

"But your *partner*, Ma'am?" (said he, affecting a very solemn air) "perhaps he may resent my detaining you: if you will give me leave to ask his consent – "

"Not for the universe."

"Who is he, Madam?"

I wished myself a hundred miles off. He repeated his question, "What is his name?"

"Nothing – nobody – I don't know. – "

He assumed a most important solemnity; "How! – not know? – Give me leave, my dear Madam, to recommend this caution to you; Never dance in public with a stranger, – with one whose name you are unacquainted with, – who may be a mere adventurer, – a man of no character, – consider to what impertinence you may expose yourself."

Was ever any thing so ridiculous? I could not help laughing, in spite of my vexation.

At this instant, Mrs. Mirvan, followed by Lord Orville, walked up to us. You will easily believe it was not difficult for me to recover my gravity; but what was my consternation, when this strange man, destined to be the scourge of my artifice, exclaimed, "Ha! my Lord Orville! – I protest I did not know your Lordship. What can I say for my usurpation? – Yet, faith, my Lord, such a prize was not to be neglected."

My shame and confusion were unspeakable. Who could have supposed or foreseen that this man knew Lord Orville! But falsehood is not more unjustifiable than unsafe.

Lord Orville – well he might, – looked all amazement.

"The philosophic coldness of your Lordship," continued this odious creature, "every man is not endowed with. I have used my utmost endeavours to entertain this lady, though I fear without success; and your Lordship would not be a little flattered, if acquainted with the difficulty which attended my procuring the honour of only one dance." Then, turning to me, who was sinking with shame, while Lord Orville stood motionless, and Mrs. Mirvan astonished, – he suddenly seized my hand, saying, "Think, my Lord, what must be my reluctance to resign this fair hand to your Lordship!"

In the same instant, Lord Orville took it of him; I coloured violently, and made an effort to recover it. "You do me too much honour, Sir," cried he, (with an air of gallantry, pressing it to his lips before he let it go) "however, I shall be happy to profit by it, if this lady," (turning to Mrs. Mirvan) "will permit me to seek for her party."

To compel him thus to dance, I could not endure, and eagerly called out, "By no means, – not for the world! – I must beg – "

"Will you honour *me*, Madam, with your commands," cried my tormentor; "may *I* seek the lady's party?"

"No, Sir," answered I, turning from him.

"What *shall* be done, my dear," said Mrs. Mirvan.

"Nothing, Ma'am; – any thing, I mean – "

"But do you dance, or not? you see his Lordship waits."

"I hope not, – I beg that – I would not for the world – I am sure I ought to – to – "

I could not speak; but that confident man, determined to discover whether or not I had deceived him, said to Lord Orville, who stood suspended, "My Lord, this affair, which, at present, seems perplexed, I will briefly explain; – this lady proposed to me another dance, – nothing could have made me more happy – I only wished for your Lordship's permission, which, if now granted, will, I am persuaded, set every thing right."

I glowed with indignation. "No, Sir – It is your absence, and that alone, can set every thing right."

"For Heaven's sake, my dear," (cried Mrs. Mirvan, who could no longer contain her surprise,) "what does all this mean? – were you pre-engaged? – had Lord Orville – "

"No, Madam," cried I, " – only – only I did not know that gentleman, – and so, – and so I thought – I intended – I – "

Overpowered by all that had passed, I had not strength to make my mortifying explanation; – my spirits quite failed me, and I burst into tears.

They all seemed shocked and amazed.

"What is the matter, my dearest love?" cried Mrs. Mirvan, with the kindest concern.

"What have I done?" exclaimed my evil genius, and ran officiously for a glass of water.

However, a hint was sufficient for Lord Orville, who comprehended all I would have explained. He immediately led me to a seat, and said, in a low voice, "Be not distressed, I beseech you; I shall ever think my name honoured by your making use of it."

This politeness relieved me. A general murmur had alarmed Miss Mirvan, who flew instantly to me; while Lord Orville, the moment Mrs. Mirvan had taken the water, led my tormentor away.

"For Heaven's sake, dear Madam," cried I, "let me go home, – indeed I cannot stay here any longer."

"Let us all go," cried my kind Maria.

"But the Captain – what will he say? – I had better go home in a chair."[1]

Mrs. Mirvan consented, and I rose to depart. Lord Orville and that man both came to me. The first, with an attention I had but ill merited from him, led me to a chair, while the other followed, pestering me with apologies. I wished to have made mine to Lord Orville, but was too much ashamed.

It was about one o'clock. Mrs. Mirvan's servants saw me home.

And now, – what again shall ever tempt me to an assembly? I dread to hear what you will think of me, my most dear and honoured Sir: you will need your utmost partiality, to receive me without displeasure.

This morning Lord Orville has sent to enquire after our healths: and Sir Clement Willoughby, for that, I find, is the name of my persecutor, has called: but I would not go down stairs till he was gone.

And now, my dear Sir, I can somewhat account for the strange, provoking, and ridiculous conduct of this Sir Clement last night; for Miss Mirvan says, he is the very man with whom she heard Lord Orville conversing at Mrs. Stanley's, when I was spoken of in so mortifying a manner. He was pleased to say he was glad to hear I was a fool, and therefore, I suppose, he concluded he might talk as much nonsense as he pleased to me: however, I am very indifferent as to his opinion; – but for Lord Orville, – if then he thought me an idiot, now, I am sure, he must suppose me both bold and presuming. Make use of his name! – what impertinence! – he can never know how it happened, – he can only imagine it was from an excess of vanity: – well, however, I shall leave this bad city to-morrow, and never again will I enter it!

The Captain intends to take us to-night to the Fantocini.[2] I cannot bear that Captain; I can give you no idea how gross he is. I heartily rejoice that he was not present at the disagreeable

---

1  An enclosed chair on poles carried by two men, licensed, for hire at one shilling per mile.
2  An Italian puppet show.

conclusion of yesterday's adventure, for I am sure he would have contributed to my confusion; which might perhaps have diverted him, as he seldom or never smiles but at some other person's expence.

And here I conclude my London letters, – and without any regret, for I am too inexperienced and ignorant to conduct myself with propriety in this town, where every thing is new to me, and many things are unaccountable and perplexing.

Adieu, my dear Sir; Heaven restore me safely to you! I wish I was to go immediately to Berry Hill; yet the wish is ungrateful to Mrs. Mirvan, and therefore I will repress it. I shall write an account of the Fantocini from Howard Grove. We have not been to half the public places that are now open, though I dare say you will think we have been to all. But they are almost as innumerable as the persons who fill them.


## LETTER XIV.

*Evelina in continuation.*

Queen-Ann-street, April 13.

How much will you be surprised, my dearest Sir, at receiving another letter from London of your Evelina's writing! But, believe me, it was not my fault, neither is it my happiness, that I am still here: our journey has been postponed by an accident equally unexpected and disagreeable.

We went last night to see the Fantocini, where we had infinite entertainment from the performance of a little comedy, in French and Italian, by puppets, so admirably managed, that they both astonished and diverted us all, except the Captain, who has a fixed and most prejudiced hatred of whatever is not English.

When it was over, while we waited for the coach, a tall elderly woman brushed quickly past us, calling out, "My God! what shall I do?"

"Why what *would* you do," cried the Captain.

"*Ma foi, Monsieur*,"[1] answered she, "I have lost my company, and in this place I don't know nobody."

There was something foreign in her accent, though it was difficult to discover whether she was an English or a French woman. She was very well dressed, and seemed so entirely at a loss what to do, that Mrs. Mirvan proposed to the Captain to assist her.

"Assist her!" cried he, "ay, with all my heart; – let a link-boy[2] call her a coach."

There was not one to be had, and it rained very fast.

"*Mon Dieu*," exclaimed the stranger, "what shall become of me? *Je suis au désespoir*."[3]

"Dear Sir," cried Miss Mirvan, "pray let us take the poor lady into our coach. She is quite alone, and a foreigner. – "

"She's never the better for that," answered he: "she may be a woman of the town,[4] for any thing you know."

"She does not appear such," said Mrs. Mirvan, "and indeed she seems so much distressed, that we shall but follow the golden rule,[5] if we carry her to her lodgings."

"You are mighty fond of new acquaintance," returned he, "but first let us know if she be going our way."

Upon enquiry, we found that she lived in Oxford Road, and, after some disputing, the Captain, surlily, and with a very bad grace, consented to admit her into his coach; though he soon convinced us, that he was determined she should not be too much obliged to him, for he seemed absolutely bent upon quarrelling with her: for which strange inhospitality, I can assign no other reason, than that she appeared to be a foreigner.

The conversation began, by her telling us, that she had been in England only two days; that the gentlemen belonging to her were Parisians, and had left her, to see for a hackney-coach,[6] as her own carriage was abroad; and that she had waited for them

---

1   "Faith, Sir."
2   Boys who carried torches to show passengers the way to their carriages.
3   "My God, ... I am in despair!"
4   Prostitute.
5   To treat others as you would have them treat you.
6   A coach pulled by two horses, licensed, for hire.

till she was quite frightened, and concluded that they had lost themselves.

"And pray," said the Captain, "why did you go to a public place without an Englishman?"

"*Ma foi*, Sir," answered she, "because none of my acquaintance is in town."

"Why then," said he, "I'll tell you what; your best way is to go out of it yourself."

"*Pardi,*[1] *Monsieur,*" returned she, "and so I shall; for, I promise you, I think the English a parcel of brutes; and I'll go back to France as fast as I can, for I would not live among none of you."

"Who wants you?" cried the Captain; "do you suppose, Madam French, we have not enough of other nations to pick our pockets already? I'll warrant you, there's no need for you for to put in your oar."

"Pick your pockets, Sir! I wish nobody wanted to pick your pockets no more than I do; and I'll promise you, you'd be safe enough. But there's no nation under the sun can beat the English for ill-politeness: for my part, I hate the very sight of them, and so I shall only just visit a person of quality[2] or two, of my particular acquaintance, and then I shall go back again to France."

"Ay, do," cried he, "and then go to the devil together, for that's the fittest voyage for the French and the quality."

"We'll take care, however," cried the stranger, with great vehemence, "not to admit none of your vulgar, unmannered English among us."

"O never fear," (returned he coolly) "we shan't dispute the point with you; you and the quality may have the devil all to yourselves."

Desirous of changing the subject of a conversation which now became very alarming, Miss Mirvan called out, "Lord, how slow the man drives!"

"Never mind, Moll," said her father, "I'll warrant you he'll drive fast enough to-morrow, when you're going to Howard Grove."

---

1 Derived from "par dieu" meaning "by God."
2 An aristocrat or member of the gentry.

"To Howard Grove!" exclaimed the stranger; "why, *mon Dieu*, do you know Lady Howard?"

"Why, what if we do?" answered he, "that's nothing to you; she's none of *your* quality, I'll promise you."

"Who told you that?" cried she, "you don't know nothing about the matter; besides, you're the ill-bredest person ever I see; and as to your knowing Lady Howard, I don't believe no such a thing; unless, indeed, you are her steward."

The Captain, swearing terribly, said, with great fury, "*you* would much sooner be taken for her wash-woman."

"Her wash-woman, indeed! – Ha, ha, ha! – why you han't no eyes; did you ever see a wash-woman in such a gown as this? – besides, I'm no such mean person, for I'm as good as Lady Howard, and as rich too; and besides, I'm now come to England to visit her."

"You may spare yourself that there trouble," said the Captain, "she has paupers enough about her already."

"Paupers, Mr.! – no more a pauper than yourself, nor so much neither; – but you are a low, dirty fellow, and I shan't stoop to take no more notice of you."

"Dirty fellow!" (exclaimed the Captain, seizing both her wrists) "hark you, Mrs. Frog,[1] you'd best hold your tongue, for I must make bold to tell you, if you don't, that I shall make no ceremony of tripping you out of the window; and there you may lie in the mud till some of your *Monseers* come to help you out of it."

Their encreasing passion quite terrified us; and Mrs. Mirvan was beginning to remonstrate with the Captain, when we were all silenced by what follows.

"Let me go, villain that you are, let me go, or I'll promise you I'll get you put to prison for this usage; I'm no common person, I assure you, and, *ma foi*, I'll go to Justice Fielding[2] about you; for I'm a person of fashion, and I'll make you know it, or my name i'n't Duval."

---

1   The Captain's term derives from the practice common among impoverished people in France of eating frogs.

2   A magistrate in the City of London from mid- to late-eighteenth century, Sir John Fielding tried cases of assault, such as the one Madame Duval threatens to claim against Captain Mirvan, in his office in Bow Street.

I heard no more: amazed, frightened, and unspeakably shocked, an involuntary exclamation of *Gracious Heaven!* escaped me, and, more dead than alive, I sunk into Mrs. Mirvan's arms. But let me draw a veil over a scene too cruel for a heart so compassionately tender as yours; it is sufficient that you know this supposed foreigner proved to be Madame Duval, – the grandmother of your Evelina!

O, Sir, to discover so near a relation in a woman who had thus introduced herself! – what would become of me, were it not for you, my protector, my friend, and my refuge?

My extreme concern, and Mrs. Mirvan's surprise, immediately betrayed me. But I will not shock you with the manner of her acknowledging me, or the bitterness, the *grossness* – I cannot otherwise express myself, – with which she spoke of those unhappy past transactions you have so pathetically related to me. All the misery of a much-injured parent, dear, though never seen, regretted, though never known, crowded so forcibly upon my memory, that they rendered this interview – one only excepted – the most afflicting I can ever know.

When we stopt at her lodgings, she desired me to accompany her into the house, and said she could easily procure a room for me to sleep in. Alarmed and trembling, I turned to Mrs. Mirvan. "My daughter, Madam," said that sweet woman, "cannot so abruptly part with her young friend; you must allow a little time to wean them from each other."

"Pardon me, Ma'am," answered Madame Duval, (who, from the time of her being known, somewhat softened her manners) "Miss can't possibly be so nearly connected to this child as I am."

"No matter for that," cried the Captain, (who espoused my cause to satisfy his own pique, though an awkward apology had passed between them) "she was sent to us, and so, d'ye see, we don't chuse for to part with her."

I promised to wait upon her at what time she pleased the next day, and, after a short debate, she desired me to breakfast with her, and we proceeded to Queen-Ann-street.

What an unfortunate adventure! I could not close my eyes the whole night. A thousand times I wished I had never left

Berry Hill; however, my return thither shall be accelerated to the utmost of my power; and, once more in that abode of tranquil happiness, I will suffer no temptation to allure me elsewhere.

Mrs. Mirvan was so kind as to accompany me to Madame Duval's house this morning. The Captain, too, offered his service, which I declined, from a fear she should suppose I meant to insult her.

She frowned most terribly upon Mrs. Mirvan, but she received me with as much tenderness as I believe she is capable of feeling. Indeed, our meeting seems really to have affected her; for when, overcome by the variety of emotions which the sight of her occasioned, I almost fainted in her arms, she burst into tears, and said, "Let me not lose my poor daughter a second time!" This unexpected humanity softened me extremely; but she very soon excited my warmest indignation, by the ungrateful mention she made of the best of men, my dear, and most generous benefactor. However, grief and anger mutually gave way to terror, upon her avowing the intention of her visiting England was to make me return with her to France. This, she said, was a plan she had formed from the instant she had heard of my birth, which, she protested, did not reach her ears till I must have been twelve years of age; but Monsieur Duval, who, she declared, was the worst husband in the world, would not permit her to do any thing she wished: he had been dead but three months, which had been employed in arranging certain affairs, that were no sooner settled, than she set off for England. She was already out of mourning,[1] for she said nobody here could tell how long she had been a widow.

She must have been married very early in life; what her age is, I do not know, but she really looks to be less than fifty. She dresses very gaily, paints very high,[2] and the traces of former beauty are still very visible in her face.

---

1  Members of the upper classes wore mourning clothes in various shades of black or grey, depending on the nearness of relation of the deceased to the wearer, and the amount of time that had passed since his/her death (the darker the color, the closer the relation, the more recent the death, the greater the depth of grief).

2  Wears a great deal of make-up, a negative judgment of an older woman's desperate attempts to attract a man.

I know not when, or how, this visit would have ended, had not the Captain called for Mrs. Mirvan, and absolutely insisted upon my attending her. He is become, very suddenly, so warmly my friend, that I quite dread his officiousness. Mrs. Mirvan, however, whose principal study seems to be healing those wounds which her husband inflicts, appeased Madame Duval's wrath, by a very polite invitation to drink tea and spend the evening here. Not without great difficulty was the Captain prevailed upon to defer his journey some time longer; but what could be done? it would have been indecent for me to have quitted town the very instant I discovered that Madame Duval was in it; and to have stayed here solely under her protection – Mrs. Mirvan, thank Heaven, was too kind for such a thought. That she should follow us to Howard Grove, I almost equally dreaded; it is, therefore, determined that we remain in London for some days, or a week: though the Captain has declared that the *old French hag*, as he is pleased to call her, shall fare never the better for it.

My only hope, is to get safe to Berry Hill; where, counselled and sheltered by you, I shall have nothing more to fear. Adieu, my ever dear and most honoured Sir! I shall have no happiness till I am again with you!

### LETTER XV.

*Mr. Villars to Evelina.*

Berry Hill, April 16.

In the belief and hope that my Evelina would ere now have bid adieu to London, I had intended to have deferred writing, till I heard of her return to Howard Grove; but the letter I have this moment received, with intelligence of Madame Duval's arrival in England, demands an immediate answer.

Her journey hither equally grieves and alarms me: how much did I pity my child, when I read of a discovery at once so unexpected and unwished! I have long dreaded this meeting and its consequence; to claim you, seems naturally to follow acknowledging you: I am well acquainted with her disposition, and have for many years foreseen the contest which now threatens us.

Cruel as are the circumstances of this affair, you must not, my love, suffer it to depress your spirits; remember, that while life is lent me, I will devote it to your service; and, for future time, I will make such provision as shall seem to me most conducive to your future happiness. Secure of my protection, and relying on my tenderness, let no apprehensions of Madame Duval disturb your peace; conduct yourself towards her with all the respect and deference due to so near a relation, remembering always, that the failure of duty on her part, can by no means justify any neglect on yours: indeed, the more forcibly you are struck with improprieties and misconduct in another, the greater should be your observance and diligence to avoid even the shadow of similar errors. Be careful, therefore, that no remissness of attention, no indifference of obliging, make known to her the independence I assure you of; but when she fixes the time for her leaving England, trust to me the task of refusing your attending her: disagreeable to myself I own it will be, yet to you, it would be improper, if not impossible.

In regard to her opinion of me, I am more sorry than surprised at her determined blindness; the palliation which she feels the want of, for her own conduct, leads her to seek for failings in all who were concerned in those unhappy transactions which she has so much reason to lament. And this, as it is the cause, so we must, in some measure, consider it as the excuse of her inveteracy.

How grateful to me are your wishes to return to Berry Hill! your lengthened stay in London, and the dissipation in which I find you are involved, fill me with uneasiness: I mean not however that I would have you sequester yourself from the party to which you belong, since Mrs. Mirvan might thence infer a reproof which your youth and her kindness would render inexcusable. I will not, therefore, enlarge upon this subject, but content myself with telling you, that I shall heartily rejoice when I hear of your safe arrival at Howard Grove, for which place I hope you will be preparing at the time you receive this letter.

I cannot too much thank you, my best Evelina, for the minuteness of your communications; continue to me this indulgence, for I should be miserable if in ignorance of your proceedings.

How new to you is the scene of life in which you are now engaged, – balls – plays – operas – ridottos – Ah, my child! at your return hither, how will you bear the change? My heart trembles for your future tranquillity. – Yet I will hope every thing from the unsullied whiteness of your soul, and the native liveliness of your disposition.

I am sure I need not say, how much more I was pleased with the mistakes of your inexperience at the private ball, than with the attempted adoption of more fashionable manners at the ridotto. But your confusion and mortifications were such as to entirely silence all reproofs on my part.

I hope you will see no more of Sir Clement Willoughby, whose conversation and boldness are extremely disgustful to me. I was gratified by the good-nature of Lord Orville, upon your making use of his name, but I hope you will never again put it to such a trial.

Heaven bless thee, my dear child, and grant that neither misfortune nor vice may ever rob thee of that gaiety of heart which, resulting from innocence, while it constitutes your own, contributes also to the felicity of all who know you!

ARTHUR VILLARS.

## LETTER XVI.

*Evelina to the Rev. Mr. Villars.*

Queen-Ann-street, Thursday morning, April 14.

Before our dinner was over yesterday, Madame Duval came to tea: though it will lessen your surprise, to hear that it was near five o'clock, for we never dine till the day is almost over. She was asked into another room, while the table was cleared, and then was invited to partake of the desert.

She was attended by a French gentleman, whom she introduced by the name of Monsieur Du Bois: Mrs. Mirvan received them both with her usual politeness; but the Captain looked very much displeased, and, after a short silence, very sternly said to Madame Duval, "Pray who asked you to bring that there spark[1] with you?"

"O," cried she, "I never go no-where without him."

Another short silence ensued, which was terminated by the Captain's turning roughly to the foreigner, and saying, "Do you know, *Monseer*, that you're the first Frenchman I ever let come into my house?"

Monsieur Du Bois made a profound bow. He speaks no English, and understands it so imperfectly, that he might, possibly, imagine he had received a compliment.

Mrs. Mirvan endeavoured to divert the Captain's ill-humour, by starting new subjects; but he left to her all the trouble of supporting them, and leant back in his chair in gloomy silence, except when any opportunity offered of uttering some sarcasm upon the French. Finding her efforts to render the evening agreeable were fruitless, Mrs. Mirvan proposed a party to Ranelagh. Madame Duval joyfully consented to it, and the Captain, though he railed against the dissipation of the women, did not oppose it, and therefore Maria and I ran up stairs to dress ourselves.

Before we were ready, word was brought us, that Sir Clement Willoughby was in the drawing-room. He introduced himself under the pretence of enquiring after all our healths, and entered the room with the easy air of an old acquaintance; though Mrs. Mirvan confesses that he seemed embarrassed, when he found how coldly he was received, not only by the Captain, but by herself.

I was extremely disconcerted at the thoughts of seeing this man again, and did not go down stairs till I was called to tea. He was then deeply engaged in a discourse upon French man-

---

1  "A beau, lover, or suitor" (*OED*).

ners with Madame Duval and the Captain, and the subject seemed so entirely to engross him, that he did not, at first, observe my entrance into the room. Their conversation was supported with great vehemence; the Captain roughly maintaining the superiority of the English in every particular, and Madame Duval warmly refusing to allow of it in any; while Sir Clement exerted all his powers of argument and of ridicule to second and strengthen whatever was advanced by the Captain: for he had the sagacity to discover, that he could take no method so effectual for making the master of the house his friend, as to make Madame Duval his enemy: and indeed, in a very short time, he had reason to congratulate himself upon his successful discernment.

As soon as he saw me, he made a most respectful bow, and hoped I had not suffered from the fatigue of the ridotto: I made no other answer than a slight inclination of the head, for I was very much ashamed of that whole affair. He then returned to the disputants, where he managed the argument so skillfully, at once provoking Madame Duval, and delighting the Captain, that I could not forbear admiring his address, though I condemned his subtlety. Mrs. Mirvan, dreading such violent antagonists, attempted frequently to change the subject; and she might have succeeded, but for the interposition of Sir Clement, who would not suffer it to be given up, and supported it with such humour and satire, that he seems to have won the Captain's heart; though their united forces so enraged and overpowered Madame Duval, that she really trembled with passion.

I was very glad when Mrs. Mirvan said it was time to be gone. Sir Clement arose to take leave; but the Captain very cordially invited him to join our party: he *had* an engagement, he said, but would give it up to have that pleasure.

Some little confusion ensued in regard to our manner of setting off: Mrs. Mirvan offered Madame Duval a place in her coach, and proposed that we four females should go all together: however, this she rejected, declaring she would by no means go so far without a gentleman, and wondering so polite a lady could make *so English* a proposal. Sir Clement Willoughby said his chariot was waiting at the door, and begged to know if it could be of any use. It was, at last, decided, that a hackney-coach should be called for Monsieur Du Bois and Madame Duval, in which the Captain, and, at his request, Sir Clement, went also; Mrs. and Miss Mirvan and I had a peaceful and comfortable ride by ourselves.

I doubt not but they quarreled all the way; for when we met at Ranelagh, every one seemed out of humour: and, though we joined parties, poor Madame Duval was avoided as much as possible by all but me.

The room was so very much crowded, that, but for the uncommon assiduity of Sir Clement Willoughby, we should not have been able to procure a box (which is the name given to the arched recesses that are appropriated for tea-parties) till half the company had retired. As we were taking possession of our places, some ladies of Mrs. Mirvan's acquaintance stopped to speak to her, and persuaded her to *take a round*[1] with them. When she returned to us, what was my surprise, to see that Lord Orville had joined her party! The ladies walked on; Mrs. Mirvan seated herself, and made a slight, though respectful, invitation to Lord Orville to drink his tea with us, which, to my no small consternation, he accepted.

I felt a confusion unspeakable at again seeing him, from the recollection of the ridotto adventure: nor did my situation lessen it, for I was seated between Madame Duval and Sir Clement, who seemed as little as myself to desire Lord Orville's presence. Indeed, the continual wrangling and ill-breeding of Captain Mirvan and Madame Duval, made me blush that I belonged to them. And poor Mrs. Mirvan and her amiable daughter had still less reason to be satisfied.

A general silence ensued after he was seated: his appearance, from different motives, gave a universal restraint to every body. What his own reasons were for honouring us with his company, I cannot imagine, unless, indeed, he had a curiosity to know whether I should invent any new impertinence concerning him.

The first speech was made by Madame Duval, who said, "It's

---

1 Walk once around the room.

quite a shocking thing to see ladies come to so genteel a place as Ranelagh with hats on; it has a monstrous vulgar look: I can't think what they wear them for. There's no such a thing to be seen in Paris."

"Indeed," cried Sir Clement, "I must own myself no advocate for hats; I am sorry the ladies ever invented or adopted so tantalizing a fashion; for, where there is beauty, they only serve to shade it, and where there is none, to excite a most unavailing curiosity. I fancy they were originally worn by some young and whimsical coquet."

"More likely," answered the Captain, "they were invented by some wrinkled old hag, who'd a mind for to keep the young fellows in chace, let them be never so weary."

"I don't know what you may do in England," cried Madame Duval, "but I know in Paris no woman need n't be at such a trouble as that, to be taken very genteel notice of."

"Why, will you pretend for to say," returned the Captain, "that they don't distinguish the old from the young there as well as here?"

"They don't make no distinguishments at all," said she; "they're vastly too polite."

"More fools they!" cried the Captain, sneeringly.

"Would to Heaven," cried Sir Clement, "that, for our own sakes, we Englishmen too were blest with so accommodating a blindness!"

"Why the devil do you make such a prayer as that?" demanded the Captain: "them are the first foolish words I've heard you speak; but I suppose you're not much used to that sort of work. Did you ever make a prayer before, since you were a sniveler?"

"Ay, now," cried Madame Duval, "that's another of the unpolitenesses of you English, to go to talking of such things as that: now in Paris, nobody never says nothing about religion, no more than about politics."

"Why then," answered he, "it's a sign they take no more care of their souls, than of their country, and so both one and t'other go to old Nick."[1]

---

1  The devil.

"Well, if they do," said she, "who's the worse, so long as they don't say nothing about it? it's the tiresomest thing in the world to be always talking of them sort of things, and nobody that's ever been abroad troubles their heads about them."

"Pray then," cried the Captain, "since you know so much of the matter, be so good as to tell us what they *do* trouble their heads about? – hay, Sir Clement! ha'n't we a right to know that much?"

"A very comprehensive question," said Sir Clement, "and I expect much instruction from the lady's answer."

"Come, Madam," continued the Captain, "never flinch; speak at once; don't stop for thinking."

"I assure you I am not going," answered she; "for as to what they *do* do, why they've enough to do, I promise you, what with one thing or another."

"But *what, what* do they do, these famous *Monseers*?" demanded the Captain; "can't you tell us? do they game? – or drink? – or fiddle? – or are they jockies? – or do they spend all their time in flummering¹ old women?"

"As to that, Sir, – but indeed I shan't trouble myself to answer such a parcel of low questions, so don't ask me no more about it." And then, to my great vexation, turning to Lord Orville, she said, "Pray, Sir, was you ever in Paris?"

He only bowed.

"And pray, Sir, how did you like it?"

This *comprehensive* question, as Sir Clement would have called it, though it made him smile, also made him hesitate; however, his answer was expressive of his approbation.

"I thought you would like it, Sir, because you look so like a gentleman. As to the Captain, and as to that other gentleman, why they may very well not like what they don't know: for I suppose, Sir, you was never abroad?"

"Only three years, Ma'am," answered Sir Clement, drily.

"Well, that's very surprising! I should never have thought it: however, I dare say you only kept company with the English."

"Why pray, who *should* he keep company with?" cried the

---

1  "To deceive by flattery, to humbug" (*OED*).

Captain: "what, I suppose you'd have him ashamed of his own nation, like some other people, not a thousand miles off, on purpose to make his own nation ashamed of him?"

"I'm sure it wou'd be a very good thing if you'd go abroad yourself."

"How will you make out that, hay, Madam? come, please to tell me, where wou'd be the good of that?"

"Where! why a great deal. They'd make quite another person of you."

"What, I suppose you'd have me learn to cut capers? – and dress like a monkey? – and palaver[1] in French gibberish? – hay, would you? – And powder, and daub, and make myself up, like some other folks?"

"I would have you learn to be more politer, Sir, and not to talk to ladies in such a rude, old-fashion way as this. You, Sir, as have been in Paris" (again addressing herself to Lord Orville) "can tell this English gentleman how he'd be despised, if he was to talk in such an ungenteel manner as this, before any foreigners. Why there is n't a hair-dresser, nor a shoe-maker, nor nobody, that would n't blush to be in your company."

"Why look ye, Madam," answered the Captain, "as to your hair-pinchers and shoe-blacks, you may puff off[2] their manners, and welcome; and I am heartily glad you like 'em so well; but as to me, since you must needs make so free of your advice, I must e'en tell you, I never kept company with any such gentry."

"Come, ladies and gentlemen," said Mrs. Mirvan, "as many of you as have done tea, I invite to walk with me." Maria and I started up instantly; Lord Orville followed; and I question whether we were not half round the room ere the angry disputants knew that we had left the box.

As the husband of Mrs. Mirvan had borne so large a share in this disagreeable altercation, Lord Orville forbore to make any

---

1 "To talk profusely or unnecessarily; to 'jaw,' 'jabber'; to talk plausibly or flatteringly" (*OED*). Originally nautical slang, it passed into colloquial use in the latter half of the eighteenth century in England.

2 "To praise, extol, or commend in inflated or extravagant terms, usually from interested motives" (*OED*).

comments upon it; so that the subject was immediately dropt, and the conversation became calmly sociable, and politely chearful, and, to every body but me, must have been highly agreeable: – but, as to myself, I was so eagerly desirous of making some apology to Lord Orville for the impertinence of which he must have thought me guilty at the ridotto, and yet so utterly unable to assume sufficient courage to speak to him concerning an affair in which I had so terribly exposed myself, that I hardly ventured to say a word all the time we were walking. Besides, the knowledge of his contemptuous opinion, haunted and dispirited me, and made me fear he might possibly misconstrue whatever I should say. So that, far from enjoying a conversation which might, at any other time, have delighted me, I continued silent, uncomfortable, and ashamed. O Sir, shall I ever again involve myself in so foolish an embarrassment? I am sure that if I do, I shall deserve yet greater mortification.

We were not joined by the rest of the party till we had taken three or four turns round the room, and then, they were so quarrelsome, that Mrs. Mirvan complained of being fatigued, and proposed going home. No one dissented. Lord Orville joined another party, having first made an offer of his services, which the gentlemen declined, and we proceeded to an outward room, where we waited for the carriages. It was settled that we should return to town in the same manner we came to Ranelagh, and, accordingly, Monsieur Du Bois handed Madame Duval into a hackney-coach, and was just preparing to follow her, when she screamed, and jumpt hastily out, declaring she was wet through all her clothes. Indeed, upon examination, the coach was found to be in a dismal condition; for the weather proved very bad, and the rain had, though I know not how, made its way into the carriage.

Mrs. and Miss Mirvan, and myself, were already disposed of as before; but no sooner did the Captain hear this account, than, without any ceremony, he was so civil as to immediately take possession of the vacant seat in his own coach, leaving Madame Duval and Monsieur Du Bois to take care of themselves. As to Sir Clement Willoughby, his own chariot was in waiting.

I instantly begged permission to offer Madame Duval my own place, and made a motion to get out; but Mrs. Mirvan stopped me, saying that I should then be obliged to return to town with only the foreigner, or Sir Clement.

"O never mind the old Beldame,"[1] cried the Captain, "she's weather-proof, I'll answer for her; and besides, as we are all, I hope, *English*, why she'll meet with no worse than she expects from us."

"I do not mean to defend her," said Mrs. Mirvan; "but indeed, as she belongs to our party, we cannot, with any decency, leave the place, till she is, by some means, accommodated."

"Lord, my dear," cried the Captain, whom the distress of Madame Duval had put into very good humour, "why she'll break her heart, if she meets with any civility from a filthy Englishman."

Mrs. Mirvan, however, prevailed, and we all got out of the coach, to wait till Madame Duval could meet with some better carriage. We found her, attended by Monsieur Du Bois, standing amongst the servants, and very busy in wiping her negligee, and endeavouring to save it from being stained by the wet, as she said it was a new Lyons silk.[2] Sir Clement Willoughby offered her the use of his chariot,[3] but she had been too much piqued by his raillery to accept it. We waited some time, but in vain, for no hackney-coach could be procured. The Captain, at last, was persuaded to accompany Sir Clement himself, and we four females were handed into Mrs. Mirvan's carriage, though not before Madame Duval had insisted upon our making room for Monsieur Du Bois, to which the Captain only consented in preference to being incommoded by him in Sir Clement's chariot.

Our party drove off first. We were silent and unsociable; for

---

1   Captain Mirvan uses "Beldame" in a depreciative sense to mean "a loathsome old woman, a hag; a witch; a furious raging woman ... , a virago," but interestingly, the term also refers to "an aged woman, a matron of advanced years, ... a grandmother or great-grandmother" in the sense of an ancestress, particularly of female descendants (*OED*).

2   A negligee was "a kind of loose gown worn by women in the eighteenth century" (*OED*). Madame Duval's dress was made in Lyons, France, which was known for its manufacture of high quality, expensive silk.

3   A light, closed carriage seating two and drawn by two horses.

the difficulties attending this arrangement had made every one languid and fatigued. Unsociable, I must own, we continued; but very short was the duration of our silence, as we had not proceeded thirty yards, before every voice was heard at once, – for the coach broke down! I suppose we concluded of course, that we were all half killed, by the violent shrieks that seemed to come from every mouth. The chariot was stopped, the servants came to our assistance, and we were taken out of the carriage, without having been at all hurt. The night was dark and wet; but I had scarce touched the ground, when I was lifted suddenly from it, by Sir Clement Willoughby, who begged permission to assist me, though he did not wait to have it granted, but carried me in his arms back to Ranelagh.

He enquired very earnestly if I was not hurt by the accident? I assured him I was perfectly safe, and free from injury, and desired he would leave me, and return to the rest of the party, for I was very uneasy to know whether they had been equally fortunate. He told me he was happy in being honoured with my commands, and would joyfully execute them; but insisted upon first conducting me to a warm room, as I had not wholly escaped being wet. He did not regard my objections, but made me follow him to an apartment, where we found an excellent fire, and some company waiting for carriages. I readily accepted a seat, and then begged he would go.

And go, indeed, he did; but he returned in a moment, telling me that the rain was more violent than ever, and that he had sent his servants to offer their assistance, and acquaint *the Mirvans* of my situation. I was very mad that he would not go himself; but as my acquaintance with him was so very slight, I did not think proper to urge him contrary to his inclination.

Well, he drew a chair close to mine, and, after again enquiring how I did, said, in a low voice, "You will pardon me, Miss Anville, if the eagerness I feel to vindicate myself, induces me to snatch this opportunity of making sincere acknowledgments for the impertinence with which I tormented you at the last ridotto. I can assure you, Madam, I have been a true and sorrowful penitent ever since; but – shall I tell you honestly what encouraged me to – "

He stopt; but I said nothing, for I thought instantly of the conversation Miss Mirvan had overheard, and supposed he was going to tell me himself what part Lord Orville had borne in it; and really I did not wish to hear it repeated. Indeed, the rest of his speech convinces me that such was his intention; with what view, I know not, except to make a merit of his defending me.

"And yet," he continued, "my excuse may only expose my own credulity, and want of judgment and penetration. I will, therefore, merely beseech your pardon, and hope that some future time – "

Just then, the door was opened by Sir Clement's servant, and I had the pleasure of seeing the Captain, Mrs. and Miss Mirvan, enter the room.

"O ho," cried the former, "you have got a good warm birth here; but we shall beat up your quarters.[1] Here, Lucy, Moll, come to the fire, and dry your trumpery.[2] But, hey-day, – why where's old Madam French?"

"Good God," cried I, "is not Madame Duval then with you?"

"With me! No, – thank God."

I was very uneasy to know what might have become of her, and, if they would have suffered me, I should have gone out in search of her myself; but all the servants were dispatched to find her, and the Captain said we might be very sure her *French beau* would take care of her.

We waited some time without any tidings, and were soon the only party in the room. My uneasiness encreased so much, that Sir Clement now made a voluntary offer of seeking her. However, the same moment that he opened the door with this design, she presented herself at it, attended by Monsieur Du Bois.

"I was this instant, Madam," said he, "coming to see for you."

"You are mighty good, truly," cried she, "to come when all the mischief's over."

She then entered, – in such a condition! – entirely covered with mud, and in so great a rage, it was with difficulty she could

---

1    "To arouse, disturb, ... visit unceremoniously" (*OED*).
2    "Showy but unsubstantial apparel; worthless finery" (*OED*).

speak. We all expressed our concern, and offered our assistance, – except the Captain; who no sooner beheld her, than he burst into a loud laugh.

We endeavoured, by our enquiries and condolements, to prevent her attending to him; and she was, for some time, so wholly engrossed by her anger and her distress, that we succeeded without much trouble. We begged her to inform us how this accident had happened. "How!" repeated she, – "why it was all along of your all going away, – and there poor Monsieur Du Bois – but it was n't his fault, – for he's as bad off as me."

All eyes were then turned to Monsieur Du Bois, whose clothes were in the same miserable plight with those of Madame Duval, and who, wet, shivering, and disconsolate, had crept to the fire.

The Captain laughed yet more heartily; while Mrs. Mirvan, ashamed of his rudeness, repeated her enquiries to Madame Duval; who answered, "Why, as we were a-coming along, all in the rain, Monsieur Du Bois was so obliging, though I'm sure it was an unlucky obligingness for me, as to lift me up in his arms, to carry me over a place that was ancle-deep in mud; but instead of my being ever the better for it, just as we were in the worst part, – I'm sure I wish we had been fifty miles off, – for, somehow or other, his foot slipt, – at least, I suppose so, – though I can't think how it happened, for I'm no such great weight, – but, however that was, down we both came together, all in the mud; and the more we tried to get up, the more deeper we got covered with the nastiness – and my new Lyons negligee, too, quite spoilt! – however, it's well we got up at all, for we might have laid there till now, for aught you all cared; for nobody never came near us."

This recital put the Captain into an extacy; he went from the lady to the gentleman, and from the gentleman to the lady, to enjoy alternately the sight of their distress. He really shouted with pleasure; and, shaking Monsieur Du Bois strenuously by the hand, wished him joy of having *touched English ground*;[1] and

---

1 England offered sanctuary to the oppressed; foreigners seeking freedom rejoiced at "touching English ground." Captain Mirvan uses the phrase facetiously.

then he held a candle to Madame Duval, that he might have a more complete view of her disaster, declaring repeatedly, that he had never been better pleased in his life.

The rage of poor Madame Duval was unspeakable; she dashed the candle out of his hand, stamped upon the floor, and, at last, spat in his face.

This action seemed immediately to calm them both, as the joy of the Captain was converted into resentment, and the wrath of Madame Duval into fear; for he put his hands upon her shoulders, and gave her so violent a shake, that she screamed out for help; assuring her, at the same time, that if she had been one ounce less old, or less ugly, she should have had it all returned on her own face.

Monsieur Du Bois, who had seated himself very quietly at the fire, approached them, and expostulated very warmly with the Captain; but he was neither understood nor regarded, and Madame Duval was not released, till she quite sobbed with passion.

When they were parted, I entreated her to permit the woman who has the charge of the ladies cloaks to assist in drying her clothes; she consented, and we did what was possible to save her from catching cold. We were obliged to wait in this disagreeable situation near an hour, before a hackney-coach could be found; and then we were disposed in the same manner as before our accident.

I am going this morning to see poor Madame Duval, and to enquire after her health, which I think must have suffered by her last night's misfortunes; though, indeed, she seems to be naturally strong and hearty.

Adieu, my dear Sir, till to-morrow.

# LETTER XVII.

*Evelina in continuation.*

Friday morning, April 15.

Sir Clement Willoughby called here yesterday at noon, and Captain Mirvan invited him to dinner. For my part, I spent the day in a manner the most uncomfortable imaginable.

I found Madame Duval at breakfast in bed, though Monsieur Du Bois was in the chamber; which so much astonished me, that I was, involuntarily, retiring, without considering how odd an appearance my retreat would have, when Madame Duval called me back, and laughed very heartily at my ignorance of foreign customs.[1]

The conversation, however, very soon took a more serious turn; for she began, with great bitterness, to inveigh against the *barbarous brutality of that fellow the Captain,* and the horrible ill-breeding of the English in general, declaring she should make her escape with all expedition from so *beastly a nation.* But nothing can be more strangely absurd, than to hear politeness recommended in language so repugnant to it as that of Madame Duval.

She lamented, very mournfully, the fate of her Lyons silk, and protested she had rather have parted with all the rest of her wardrobe, because it was the first gown she had bought to wear upon leaving off her weeds.[2] She has a very bad cold, and Monsieur Du Bois is so hoarse, he can hardly speak.

She insisted upon my staying with her all day, as she intended, she said, to introduce me to some of my own relations. I would very fain have excused myself, but she did not allow me any choice.

Till the arrival of these relations, one continued series of questions on her side, and of answers on mine, filled up all the

---

1 It was customary for French gentlewomen to receive men and women in their bedrooms.
2 Widow's weeds, "the deep mourning worn by a widow, including a crape veil, 'weepers,' etc." (*OED*).

time we passed together. Her curiosity was insatiable; she enquired into every action of my life, and every particular that had fallen under my observation, in the lives of all I knew. Again, she was so cruel as to avow the most inveterate rancour against the sole benefactor her deserted child and grandchild have met with; and such was the indignation her ingratitude raised, that I would actually have quitted her presence and house, had she not, in a manner the most peremptory, absolutely forbid me. But what, good Heaven! can induce her to such shocking injustice? O my friend and father! I have no command of myself when this subject is started.

She talked very much of taking me to Paris, and said I greatly wanted the polish of a French education. She lamented that I had been brought up in the country, which, she observed, had given me a very *bumpkinish air.* However, she bid me not despair, for she had known many girls, much worse than me, who had become very fine ladies after a few years residence abroad; and she particularly instanced a Miss Polly Moore, daughter of a chandler's-shop woman,[1] who, by an accident not worth relating, happened to be sent to Paris, where, from an awkward, ill-bred girl, she so much improved, that she has since been taken for a woman of quality.

The relations to whom she was pleased to introduce me, consisted of a Mr. Branghton, who is her nephew, and three of his children, the eldest of which is a son, and the two younger are daughters.

Mr. Branghton appears about forty years of age. He does not seem to want a common understanding, though he is very contracted and prejudiced: he has spent his whole time in the city,[2] and I believe feels a great contempt for all who reside elsewhere.

His son seems weaker in his understanding, and more gay in his temper; but his gaiety is that of a foolish, over-grown

---

1 A woman working in a shop that makes and sells candles.

2 The City of London covers one square mile, reaching to Temple Bar and Holborn Bars on the west, to Smithfield and Moorfields on the north, to Aldgate and Tower Hill on the east, and to the Thames River on the south. A center of trade and finance, the City was not the home of the fashionable (Weinreb 172-73).

school-boy, whose mirth consists in noise and disturbance. He disdains his father for his close attention to business, and love of money, though he seems himself to have no talents, spirit, or generosity, to make him superior to either. His chief delight appears to be tormenting and ridiculing his sisters, who, in return, most heartily despise him.

Miss Branghton, the eldest daughter, is by no means ugly, but looks proud, ill-tempered, and conceited. She hates the city, though without knowing why; for it is easy to discover she has lived no where else.

Miss Polly Branghton is rather pretty, very foolish, very ignorant, very giddy, and, I believe, very good-natured.

The first half hour was allotted to *making themselves comfortable,* for they complained of having had a very dirty walk, as they came on foot from Snow Hill,[1] where Mr. Branghton keeps a silver-smith's shop; and the young ladies had not only their coats to brush, and shoes to dry, but to adjust their head-dress, which their bonnets had totally discomposed.

The manner in which Madame Duval was pleased to introduce me to this family, extremely shocked me. "Here, my dears," said she, "here's a relation you little thought of; but you must know my poor daughter Caroline had this child after she run away from me, – though I never knew nothing of it, not I, for a long while after; for they took care to keep it a secret from me, though the poor child has never a friend in the world besides."

"Miss seems very tender-hearted, aunt," said Miss Polly, "and to be sure she's not to blame for her mama's undutifulness, for she could n't help it."

"Lord no," answered she, "and I never took no notice of it to her; for indeed, as to that, my own poor daughter was n't so much to blame as you may think, for she'd never have gone astray, if it had not been for that meddling old parson I told you of."

---

1  Snow Hill was a "steep winding hill extending from Central Markets to Holborn Viaduct. Before the viaduct was built wild young men used to capture elderly women at the top and roll them down to the bottom in barrels, a practice much enjoyed by the eighteenth-century gangs known as Mohocks" (Weinreb 791).

"If aunt pleases," said young Mr. Branghton, "we'll talk o' somewhat else, for Miss looks very uneasy-like."

The next subject that was chosen, was the age of the three young Branghtons and myself. The son is twenty; the daughters, upon hearing that I was seventeen, said that was just the age of Miss Polly; but their brother, after a long dispute, proved that she was two years older, to the great anger of both sisters, who agreed that he was very ill-natured and spiteful.

When this point was settled, the question was put, Which was tallest? – We were desired to measure, as the Branghtons were all of different opinions. None of them, however, disputed my being the tallest in the company, but, in regard to one another, they were extremely quarrelsome: the brother insisted upon their measuring *fair*, and not with *heads* and *heels*; but they would by no means consent to lose those privileges of our sex, and therefore the young man was *cast*,[1] as shortest; though he appealed to all present upon the injustice of the decree.

This ceremony over, the young ladies began, very freely, to examine my dress, and to interrogate me concerning it. "This apron's your own work, I suppose, Miss? but these sprigs a'n't in fashion now. Pray, if it is not impertinent, what might you give a yard for this lutestring? – Do you make your own caps, Miss? – " and many other questions equally interesting and well-bred.

They then asked me *how I liked London*? and whether I should not think the country a very *dull place*, when I returned thither? "Miss must try if she can't get a good husband," said Mr. Branghton, "and then she may stay and live here."

The next topic was public places, or rather the theatres, for they knew of no other; and the merits and defects of all the actors and actresses were discussed: the young man here took the lead, and seemed to be very conversant on the subject. But during this time, what was my concern, and, suffer me to add, my indignation, when I found, by some words I occasionally heard, that Madame Duval was entertaining Mr. Branghton with all the most secret and cruel particulars of my situation!

---

1   Three meanings of the word might apply: "to reckon, calculate, estimate;" "a contrivance, device, artifice, trick;" and "the assignment of the parts in a play to the several actors" (*OED*).

The eldest daughter was soon drawn to them by the recital; the youngest and the son still kept their places, intending, I believe, to divert me, though the conversation was all their own.

In a few minutes, Miss Branghton, coming suddenly up to her sister, exclaimed, "Lord, Polly, only think! Miss never saw her papa!"

"Lord, how odd!" cried the other; "why then, Miss, I suppose you would n't know him?"

This was quite too much for me; I rose hastily, and ran out of the room: but I soon regretted I had so little command of myself, for the two sisters both followed, and insisted upon comforting me, notwithstanding my earnest entreaties to be left alone.

As soon as I returned to the company, Madame Duval said, "Why, my dear, what was the matter with you? why did you run away so?"

This question almost made me run again, for I knew not how to answer it. But is it not very extraordinary, that she can put me in situations so shocking, and then wonder to find me sensible of any concern?

Mr. Branghton junior now enquired of me, whether I had seen the Tower, or St. Paul's church?[1] and, upon my answering in the negative, they proposed making a party to shew them to me. Among other questions, they also asked if I had ever seen *such a thing as an Opera*? I told them I had. "Well," said Mr. Branghton, " I never saw one in my life, so long as I've lived in London, and I never desire to see one, if I live here as much longer."

"Lord, Papa," cried Miss Polly, "why not? you might as well for once, for the curiosity of the thing: besides, Miss Pomfret saw one, and she says it was very pretty."

"Miss will think us very vulgar," said Miss Branghton, "to

---

1   The Tower of London, originally a medieval fortress, was a popular tourist attraction during the eighteenth century, chiefly for the royal menagerie and the crown jewels housed there, though it was still a working prison. St. Paul's Church or Cathedral was the fifth cathedral to stand in the place where once a Roman temple stood. The cathedral had been rebuilt after the Great Fire in 1666 over a period of thirty-five years under the direction of architect Christopher Wren, its most remarkable feature being the dome (Weinreb 871-77).

live in London, and never have been to an Opera; but it's no fault of mine, I assure you, Miss, only Papa don't like to go."

The result was, that a party was proposed, and agreed to, for some early opportunity. I did not dare contradict them; but I said that my time, while I remained in town, was at the disposal of Mrs. Mirvan. However, I am sure I will not attend them, if I can possibly avoid so doing.

When we parted, Madame Duval desired to see me the next day; and the Branghtons told me, that the first time I went towards Snow Hill, they should be very glad if I would call upon them.

I wish we may not meet again till that time arrives.

I am sure I shall not be very ambitious of being known to any more of my relations, if they have any resemblance to those whose acquaintance I have been introduced to already.


## LETTER XVIII.

*Evelina in continuation.*

I had just finished my letter to you this morning, when a violent rapping at the door made me run down stairs; and who should I see in the drawing-room, but – Lord Orville!

He was quite alone, for the family had not assembled to breakfast. He enquired, first of mine, then of the health of Mrs. and Miss Mirvan, with a degree of concern that rather surprised me, till he said that he had just been informed of the accident we had met with at Ranelagh. He expressed his sorrow upon the occasion with the utmost politeness, and lamented that he had not been so fortunate as to hear of it in time to offer his services. "But, I think," he added, "Sir Clement Willoughby had the honour of assisting you?"

"He was with Captain Mirvan, my Lord."

"I had heard of his being of your party."

I hope that flighty man has not been telling Lord Orville he only assisted *me*! however, he did not pursue the subject, but said, "This accident, though extremely unfortunate, will not, I hope, be the means of frightening you from gracing Ranelagh with your presence in future?"

"Our time, my Lord, for London, is almost expired already."

"Indeed! do you leave town so very soon?"

"O yes, my Lord, our stay has already exceeded our intentions."

"Are you, then, so particularly partial to the country?"

"We merely came to town, my Lord, to meet Captain Mirvan."

"And does Miss Anville feel no concern at the idea of the many mourners her absence will occasion?"

"O, my Lord, – I'm sure you don't think – " I stopt there, for, indeed, I hardly knew what I was going to say. My foolish embarrassment, I suppose, was the cause of what followed; – for he came to me, and took my hand, saying, "I *do* think, that whoever has once seen Miss Anville, must receive an impression never to be forgotten."

This compliment, – from Lord Orville, – so surprised me, that I could not speak; but felt myself change colour, and stood, for some moments, silent and looking down: however, the instant I recollected my situation, I withdrew my hand, and told him that I would see if Mrs. Mirvan was not dressed. He did not oppose me, so away I went.

I met them all on the stairs, and returned with them to breakfast.

I have since been extremely angry with myself for neglecting so excellent an opportunity of apologizing for my behaviour at the ridotto: but, to own the truth, that affair never once occurred to me during the short *tête-à-tête* which we had together. But, if ever we should happen to be so situated again, I will certainly mention it; for I am inexpressibly concerned at the thought of his harbouring an opinion that I am bold or impertinent, and I could almost kill myself for having given him the shadow of a reason for so shocking an idea.

But was it not very odd that he should make me such a compliment? I expected it not from him; – but gallantry, I believe, is common to all men, whatever other qualities they may have in particular.

Our breakfast was the most agreeable meal, if it may be called a *meal*, that we have had since we came to town. Indeed, but for Madame Duval I should like London extremely.

The conversation of Lord Orville is really delightful. His manners are so elegant, so gentle, so unassuming, that they at once engage esteem, and diffuse complacence. Far from being indolently satisfied with his own accomplishments, as I have already observed many men here are, though without any pretensions to his merit, he is most assiduously attentive to please and to serve all who are in his company; and, though his success is invariable, he never manifests the smallest degree of consciousness.

I could wish that *you*, my dearest Sir, knew Lord Orville, because I am sure you would love him; and I have felt that wish for no other person I have seen since I came to London. I sometimes imagine, that, when his youth is flown, his vivacity abated, and his life is devoted to retirement, he will, perhaps, resemble him whom I most love and honour. His present sweetness, politeness, and diffidence, seem to promise in future the same benevolence, dignity, and goodness. But I must not expatiate upon this subject.

When Lord Orville was gone, – and he made but a very short visit, – I was preparing, most reluctantly, to wait upon Madame Duval; but Mrs. Mirvan proposed to the Captain, that she should be invited to dinner in Queen-Ann-Street, and he readily consented, for he said he wished to ask after her Lyons negligee.

The invitation is accepted, and we expect her every moment. But to me, it is very strange, that a woman, who is the uncontrolled mistress of her time, fortune, and actions, should chuse to expose herself voluntarily to the rudeness of a man who is openly determined to make her his sport. But she has very few acquaintance, and, I fancy, scarce knows how to employ herself.

How great is my obligation to Mrs. Mirvan, for bestowing her time in a manner so disagreeable to herself, merely to promote my happiness! every dispute in which her undeserving husband engages, is productive of pain, and uneasiness to herself; of this I am so sensible, that I even besought her not to send to Madame Duval, but she declared she could not bear to have me pass all my time, while in town, with her only. Indeed she could not be more kind to me, were she your daughter.

## LETTER XIX.

*Evelina in continuation.*

Saturday morning, April 16.

Madame Duval was accompanied by Monsieur Du Bois. I am surprised that she should chuse to introduce him where he is so unwelcome; and, indeed, it is strange that they should be so constantly together: though I believe I should not have taken notice of it, but that Captain Mirvan is perpetually rallying me upon my *grandmama's beau.*

They were both received by Mrs. Mirvan with her usual good-breeding; but the Captain, most provokingly, attacked her immediately, saying, "Now, Madam, you that have lived abroad, please to tell me this here; Which did you like best, the *warm room* at Ranelagh, or the *cold bath* you went into afterwards? though, I assure you, you look so well that I should advise you to take another dip."

"*Ma foi*, Sir," cried she, "nobody asked for your advice, so you may as well keep it to yourself: besides, it's no such great joke to be splashed, and to catch cold, and spoil all one's things, whatever you may think of it."

"*Splashed*, quoth-a! – why I thought you were soused all over. – Come, come, don't mince the matter, never spoil a good story; you know you had n't a dry thread about you – 'Fore George, I shall never think on't without hallowing![1] such a poor, forlorn, draggle-tailed[2] – *gentlewoman*! and poor *Monseer* French, here, like a drowned rat, by your side! – "

---

1  "To shout ... aloud" (*OED*).
2  "A woman whose skirts are wet and draggled, or whose dress hangs about her untidily and dirty; a slut" (*OED*).

"Well, the worse pickle we was in, so much the worser in you not to help us, for you knowed where we was fast enough, because, while I laid in the mud, I'm pretty sure I heard you snigger; so it's like enough you jostled us down yourself, for Monsieur Du Bois says, that he is sure he had a great jolt given him, or he should n't have fell."

The Captain laughed so immoderately, that he really gave me also a suspicion that he was not entirely innocent of the charge: however, he disclaimed it very peremptorily.

"Why then," continued she, "if you did n't do that, why did n't you come to help us?"

"Who, I? – what, do you suppose I had forgot I was an *Englishman*, a filthy, beastly *Englishman?*"

"Very well, Sir, very well; but I was a fool to expect any better, for it's all of a piece with the rest; you know you wanted to fling me out of the coach-window, the very first time ever I see you: but I'll never go to Ranelagh with you no more, that I'm resolved; for I dare say, if the horses had runn'd over me, as I laid in that nastiness, you'd never have stirred a step to save me."

"Lord, no, to be sure, Ma'am, not for the world! I know your opinion of our nation too well, to affront you by supposing a *Frenchman* would want *my* assistance to protect you. Did you think that *Monseer* here, and I, had changed characters, and that he should pop you into the mud, and I help you out of it? Ha, ha, ha!"

"O, very well, Sir, laugh on, it's like your manners; however, if poor Monsieur Du Bois had n't met with that unlucky accident himself, I should n't have wanted nobody's help."

"O, I promise you, Madam, you'd never have had mine; I knew my distance better; and as to your being a little ducked, or so, why, to be sure, *Monseer* and you settled that between yourselves; so it was no business of mine."

"What, then, I suppose, you want to make me believe as Monsieur Du Bois served me that trick o' purpose?"

"O' purpose! ay, certainly, who ever doubted that? Do you think a *Frenchman* ever made a blunder? If he had been some clumsy-footed *English* fellow, indeed, it might have been accidental: but what the devil signifies all your hopping and

capering with your dancing-masters, if you can't balance yourselves upright?"

In the midst of this dialogue, Sir Clement Willoughby made
his appearance. He affects to enter the house with the freedom
of an old acquaintance, and this very *easiness*, which, to me, is
astonishing, is what most particularly recommends him to the
Captain. Indeed, he seems very successfully to study all the
humours of that gentleman.

After having heartily welcomed him, "You are just come in
time, my boy," said he, "to settle a little matter of a dispute
between this here gentlewoman and I; do you know, she has
been trying to persuade me, that she did not above half like the
ducking *Monseer* gave her t'other night?"

"I should have hoped," (said Sir Clement, with the utmost
gravity) "that the friendship subsisting between that lady and
gentleman, would have guarded them against any actions professedly disagreeable to each other; but, probably, they might
not have discussed the matter previously; in which case, the
gentleman, I must own, seems to have been guilty of inattention, since, in my humble opinion, it was his business first to
have enquired whether the lady preferred soft, or hard ground,
before he dropt her."

"O very fine, Gentlemen, very fine," cried Madame Duval,
"you may try to set us together by the ears as much as you will;
but I'm not such an ignorant person as to be made a fool of so
easily; so you need n't talk no more about it, for I sees into your
designs."

Monsieur Du Bois, who was just able to discover the subject
upon which the conversation turned, made his defence, in
French, with great solemnity: he hoped, he said, that the company would at least acknowledge, he did not come from a
nation of brutes, and consequently, that to wilfully offend any
lady, was, to him, utterly impossible; but that, on the contrary, in
endeavouring, as was his duty, to save and guard her, he had
himself suffered, in a manner which he would forbear to relate,
but which, he greatly apprehended, he should feel the ill effects
of for many months; and then, with a countenance exceedingly
lengthened, he added, that he hoped it would not be attributed

to him as national prejudice, when he owned that he must, to the best of his memory, aver, that his unfortunate fall was owing to a sudden, but violent push, which, he was shocked to say, some malevolent person, with a design to his injury, must certainly have given him; but whether with a view to mortify him, by making him let the lady fall, or whether merely to spoil his clothes, he could not pretend to determine.

This disputation was, at last, concluded by Mrs. Mirvan's proposing that we should all go to Cox's Museum.[1] Nobody objected, and carriages were immediately ordered.

In our way down stairs, Madame Duval, in a very passionate manner, said, "*Ma foi*, if I would n't give fifty guineas only to know who gave us that shove!"

This Museum is very astonishing, and very superb; yet, it afforded me but little pleasure, for it is a mere show, though a wonderful one.

Sir Clement Willoughby, in our walk round the room, asked me what my opinion was of this brilliant *spectacle*?

"It is very fine, and very ingenious," answered I, "and yet – I don't know how it is, – but I seem to *miss something*."

"Excellently answered!" cried he, "you have exactly defined my own feelings, though in a manner I should never have arrived at. But I was certain your taste was too well formed, to be pleased at the expence of your understanding."

"*Pardi*," cried Madame Duval, "I hope you two is difficult enough! I'm sure if you don't like this, you like nothing; for it's the grandest, prettiest, finest sight that ever I see, in England."

"What," (cried the Captain, with a sneer) "I suppose this may be in your French taste? it's like enough, for it's all *kickshaw* work.[2] But, pr'ythee, friend," (turning to the person who explained the devices) "will you tell me the *use* of all this? for I'm not enough of a conjurer to find it out."

---

1   Located in Spring Gardens, the museum opened in 1772 to display 56 jewel-studded mechanisms designed by Nollekens and Zoffany, assembled by James Cox, a jeweller and silversmith, and said to be worth £197,000 when they were sold in 1775 (Weinreb 206).

2   "Something dainty or elegant, but unsubstantial or comparatively valueless; a toy, trifle, gew-gaw" (*OED*). Also applied to French cooking.

"Use, indeed!" (repeated Madame Duval disdainfully) "Lord, if every thing's to be useful! – "

"Why, Sir, as to that, Sir," said our conductor, "the ingenuity of the mechanism, – the beauty of the workmanship, – the – undoubtedly, Sir, any person of taste may easily discern the utility of such extraordinary performances."

"Why then, Sir," answered the Captain, "your person of taste must be either a coxcomb, or a Frenchman; though, for the matter of that, 'tis the same thing."

Just then, our attention was attracted by a pine-apple, which, suddenly opening, discovered a nest of birds, who immediately began to sing. "Well," cried Madame Duval, "this is prettier than all the rest! I declare, in all my travels, I never see nothing eleganter."

"Hark ye, friend," said the Captain, "hast never another pine-apple?"

"Sir? – "

"Because, if thou hast, pr'ythee give it us without the birds; for, d'ye see, I'm no Frenchman, and should relish something more substantial."

This entertainment concluded with a concert of mechanical music: I cannot explain how it was produced, but the effect was pleasing. Madame Duval was in extacies; and the Captain flung himself into so many ridiculous distortions, by way of mimicking her, that he engaged the attention of all the company; and, in the midst of the performance of the Coronation Anthem,[1] while Madame Duval was affecting to beat time, and uttering many expressions of delight, he called suddenly for salts,[2] which a lady, apprehending some distress, politely handed to him, and which, instantly applying to the nostrils of poor Madame Duval, she involuntarily snuffed up such a quantity, that the pain and surprise made her scream aloud. When she recovered, she reproached him, with her usual vehemence; but

---

1  George Frederick Handel (1685-1759) composed four anthems for George II's coronation in 1727. The anthem known as the "Coronation Anthem" was the first of the four, entitled "Zadock the Priest." The anthem was used for George III's coronation as well.

2  "Smelling salts, consisting usually of ammonium carbonate" (*OED*).

he protested he had taken that measure out of pure friendship, as he concluded, from her raptures, that she was going into hysterics. This excuse by no means appeased her, and they had a violent quarrel; but the only effect her anger had on the Captain, was to encrease his diversion. Indeed, he laughs and talks so terribly loud in public, that he frequently makes us ashamed of belonging to him.

Madame Duval, notwithstanding her wrath, made no scruple of returning to dine in Queen-Ann-street. Mrs. Mirvan had secured places for the play at Drury Lane Theatre, and, though ever uneasy in her company, she very politely invited Madame Duval to be of our party; however, she had a bad cold, and chose to nurse it. I was sorry for her indisposition, but I knew not how to be sorry she did not accompany us, for she is – I must not say what, but very unlike other people.

## LETTER XX.

*Evelina in continuation.*

Our places were in the front row of a side-box. Sir Clement Willoughby, who knew our intention, was at the door of the Theatre, and handed us from the carriage.

We had not been seated five minutes, before Lord Orville, who we saw in the stage-box,[1] came to us; and he honoured us with his company all the evening. Miss Mirvan and I both rejoiced that Madame Duval was absent, as we hoped for the enjoyment of some conversation, uninterrupted by her quarrels with the Captain: but I soon found that her presence would have made very little alteration, for so far was I from daring to speak, that I knew not where even to look.

The play was Love for Love,[2] and though it is fraught with

---

1   "A side-box was at the side of the theatre beyond the front of the stage. The two stage-boxes were over the part of the stage which was in front of the curtain." Mackinnon also notes that while these seats were the most expensive in the theater, the boxes were not private (519).

2   *Love for Love*, a comedy by William Congreve (1670-1729), was first performed in 1695 at Lincoln's Inn Fields Theatre and every season until 1766-67, and, according

wit and entertainment, I hope I shall never see it represented again; for it is so extremely indelicate, – to use the softest word I can, – that Miss Mirvan and I were perpetually out of countenance, and could neither make any observations ourselves, nor venture to listen to those of others. This was the more provoking, as Lord Orville was in excellent spirits, and exceedingly entertaining.

When the Play was over, I flattered myself I should be able to look about me with less restraint, as we intended to stay the Farce;[1] but the curtain had hardly dropped, when the box-door opened, and in came Mr. Lovel, the man by whose foppery and impertinence I was so much teazed at the ball where I first saw Lord Orville.

I turned away my head, and began talking to Miss Mirvan, for I was desirous to avoid speaking to him; – but in vain, for as soon as he had made his compliments to Lord Orville and Sir Clement Willoughby, who returned them very coldly, he bent his head forward, and said to me, "I hope, Ma'am, you have enjoyed your health since I had the honour – I beg ten thousand pardons, but I protest I was going to say the honour of *dancing* with you – however, I mean the honour of *seeing* you dance?"

He spoke with a self-complacency that convinced me he had studied this address, by way of making reprisals for my conduct at the ball: I therefore bowed slightly, but made no answer.

---

to Edward Bloom, in his notes to the 1968 Oxford University Press edition of *Evelina*, at least ten times in the nine years before Burney published *Evelina* (411). As is reflected in this exchange between Burney's characters, late-eighteenth-century genteel audiences found it entertaining (if male) or embarrassing (if female) for the explicitly sexual nature of its witty humor. Such examples of the older Restoration plays were in competition with the newer, more sentimental plays. *Love for Love*'s characters include Mr. Tattle, whom Congreve describes as "a half-witted beau, vain of his amours, yet valuing himself for secrecy;" Ben, who is Sir Sampson's younger son, "half home-bred, and half sea-bred;" Miss Prue, who is "a silly, awkward, country girl;" Angelica, who is the self-possessed heroine of the piece, controlling her fortune and her future; and Valentine, who is an extravagant hero who yet manages to win Angelica. (*Love for Love* [1695]. Ed M.M. Kelsall [London: Ernest Benn Ltd, 1969].)

1  Plays were often followed by a short entertainment or *petite-piece*. The farce presented is *The Deuce Is in Him*, by George Colman the Elder (1732-94), first produced at Drury Lane Theatre in 1763 and "performed [there] at least forty times between 1767 and 1776" (Bloom 411).

After a short silence, he again called my attention, by saying, in an easy, negligent way, "I think, Ma'am, you was never in town before?"

"No, Sir."

"So I did presume. Doubtless, Ma'am, every thing must be infinitely novel to you. Our customs, our manners, and *les etiquettes de nous autres*,[1] can have very little resemblance to those you have been used to. I imagine, Ma'am, your retirement is at no very small distance from the capital?"

I was so much disconcerted at this sneering speech, that I said not a word; though I have since thought my vexation both stimulated and delighted him.

"The air we breathe here, however, Ma'am," (continued he, very conceitedly) "though foreign to that you have been accustomed to, has not, I hope, been at variance with your health?"

"Mr. Lovel," said Lord Orville, "could not your *eye* have spared that question?"

"O, my Lord," answered he, "if *health* were the only cause of a lady's bloom, my eye, I grant, had been infallible from the first glance; but – "

"Come, come," cried Mrs. Mirvan, "I must beg no insinuations of that sort; Miss Anville's colour, as you have successfully tried, may, you see, be heightened; – but I assure you, it would be past your skill to lessen it."

"'Pon honour, Madam," returned he, "you wrong me; I presumed not to infer that *rouge* was the only succedaneum[2] for health; but, really, I have known so many different causes for a lady's colour, such as flushing, – anger, – *mauvaise honte*,[3] – and so forth, that I never dare decide to which it may be owing."

"As to such causes as them there," cried the Captain, "they must belong to those that they keep company with."

"Very true, Captain," said Sir Clement; "the natural complexion has nothing to do with occasional sallies of the passions, or any accidental causes."

"No, truly," returned the Captain, "for now here's me, why I

---

1   Our etiquette.
2   Substitute.
3   Shame.

look like any other man just now; and yet, if you were to put me in a passion, 'fore George, you'd soon see me have as fine a high colour as any painted Jezabel[1] in all this place, be she never so bedaubed."

"But," said Lord Orville, "the difference of natural and of artificial colour, seems to me very easily discerned; that of Nature, is mottled, and varying; that of art, *set*, and *too* smooth; it wants that animation, that glow, that *indescribable something* which, even now that I see it, wholly surpasses all my powers of expression."

"Your Lordship," said Sir Clement; "is universally acknowledged to be a *connoisseur* in beauty."

"And you, Sir Clement," returned he, "an *enthusiast*."[2]

"I am proud to own it," cried Sir Clement; "in such a cause, and before such objects, enthusiasm is simply the consequence of not being blind."

"Pr'ythee a truce with all this palavering," cried the Captain, "the women are vain enough already; no need for to puff 'em up more."

"We must all submit to the commanding officer," said Sir Clement, "therefore let us call another subject. Pray, Ladies, how have you been entertained with the play?"

"Want of entertainment," said Mrs. Mirvan, "is its least fault; but I own there are objections to it, which I should be glad to see removed."

"I could have ventured to answer for the Ladies," said Lord Orville, "since I am sure this is not a play that can be honoured with their approbation."

"What, I suppose it is not sentimental enough!" cried the Captain, "or else it's too good for them; for I'll maintain it's one

---

1   Jezebel was the wife of Ahab, King of Israel, and viewed by many in her time as a witch. When she heard that Jehu was coming to see her, "she put paint on her eyes and adorned her head"; he killed her and dogs ate her (*Women's Study Bible*, ed. D. Patterson [Nashville: Thomas Nelson Publishers, 1995], 2 Kings 9).

2   As opposed to the *connoisseur*, whose ability to judge the worth of something is based on her/his knowledge, the *enthusiast* exhibits "rapturous intensity of feeling in favour of a person, principle, cause, etc.; passionate eagerness in any pursuit, proceeding from an intense conviction of the worthiness of the object" (*OED*), but not necessarily from grounded knowledge of it.

of the best comedies in the language, and has more wit in one scene, than there is in all the new plays put together."

"For my part," said Mr. Lovel, "I confess I seldom listen to the players: one has so much to do, in looking about, and finding out one's acquaintance, that, really, one has no time to mind the stage. Pray, – (most affectedly fixing his eyes upon a diamond-ring on his little finger) pray – what was the play to-night?"

"Why, what the D——l," cried the Captain, "do you come to the play, without knowing what it is?"

"O yes, Sir, yes, very frequently; I have no time to read play-bills; one merely comes to meet one's friends, and shew that one's alive."

"Ha, ha, ha! – and so," cried the Captain, "it costs you five shillings a night, just to shew that you're alive! Well, faith, my friends should all think me dead and under ground, before I'd be at that expence for 'em. Howsomever, this here you may take from me; – they'll find you out fast enough, if you've any thing to give 'em. – And so you've been here all this time, and don't know what the play was?"

"Why, really, Sir, a play requires so much attention, – it is scarce possible to keep awake, if one listens; – for, indeed, by the time it is evening, one has been so fatigued, with dining, – or wine, – or the house,[1] – or studying, – that it is – it is perfectly an impossibility. But, now I think of it, I believe I have a bill[2] in my pocket; O, ay, here it is – Love for Love, ay, – true, – ha, ha, – how could I be so stupid!"

"O, easily enough as to that, I warrant you," said the Captain; "but, by my soul, this is one of the best jokes I ever heard! Come to a play, and not know what it is! – Why, I suppose you would n't have found it out, if they had *fob'd* you off with a scraping of fidlers, or an opera? – Ha! ha! ha! – why now, I should have thought you might have taken some notice of one Mr. *Tattle* that is in this play!"

This sarcasm, which caused a general smile, made him

---

1  Lovel is a member of the House of Commons.
2  Playbill: "a bill or placard announcing a play and giving the names of the actors to whom the various parts are assigned" (*OED*).

colour: but, turning to the Captain with a look of conceit, which implied that he had a retort ready, he said, "Pray, Sir, give me leave to ask, – what do *you* think of *one Mr. Ben*, who is also in this play?"

The Captain, regarding him with the utmost contempt, answered in a loud voice, "Think of him! – why I think he's a *man*!" And then, staring full in his face, he struck his cane on the ground, with a violence that made him start. He did not, however, chuse to take any notice of this; but, having bit his nails some time, in manifest confusion, he turned very quick to me, and, in a sneering tone of voice, said, "For my part, I was most struck with the *country* young lady, Miss Prue; pray what do *you* think of her, Ma'am?"

"Indeed, Sir," cried I, very much provoked, "I think – that is, I do not think any thing about her."

"Well, really, Ma'am, you prodigiously surprise me! – *mais apparemment ce n'est qu'un façon de parler?*[1] – though I should beg your pardon, for probably you do not understand French?"

I made no answer, for I thought his rudeness intolerable; but Sir Clement, with great warmth, said, "I am surprised that you can suppose such an object as Miss Prue would engage the attention of Miss Anville even for a moment."

"O Sir," returned this fop, "'tis the first character in the piece! – so well drawn, – so much the thing! – such true country-breeding, – such rural ignorance! – ha! ha! ha! – 'tis most admirably hit off, 'pon honour!"

I could almost have cried, that such impertinence should be levelled at me; and yet, chagrined as I was, I could never behold Lord Orville and this man at the same time, and feel any regret for the cause I had given of displeasure.

"The only female in the play," said Lord Orville, "worthy of being mentioned to these ladies, is Angelica."

"Angelica," cried Sir Clement, "is a noble girl; she tries her lover severely, but she rewards him generously."

"Yet, in a trial so long," said Mrs. Mirvan, "there seems rather too much consciousness of her power."

---

1   But, apparently it is only a manner of speaking.

"Since my opinion has the sanction of Mrs. Mirvan's," added Lord Orville, "I will venture to say, that Angelica bestows her hand rather with the air of a benefactress, than with the tenderness of a mistress. Generosity without delicacy, like wit without judgment, generally give as much pain as pleasure. The uncertainty in which she keeps Valentine, and her manner of trifling with his temper, give no very favourable idea of her own."

"Well, my Lord," said Mr. Lovel, "it must, however, be owned, that uncertainty is not the *ton*[1] among our ladies at present; nay, indeed, I think they say, though, faith," taking a pinch of snuff, "I hope it is not true — but they say, that *we* now are most shy and backward."

The curtain then drew up, and our conversation ceased. Mr. Lovel, finding we chose to attend to the players, left the box. How strange it is, Sir, that this man, not contented with the large share of foppery and nonsense which he has from nature, should think proper to affect yet more! for what he said of Tattle and of Miss Prue, convinced me that he really had listened to the play, though he was so ridiculous and foolish as to pretend ignorance.

But how malicious and impertinent in this creature to talk to me in such a manner! I am sure I hope I shall never see him again. I should have despised him heartily as a fop, had he never spoken to me at all; but now, that he thinks proper to resent his supposed ill-usage, I am really quite afraid of him.

The entertainment was, The Deuce is in him, which Lord Orville observed to be the most finished and elegant *petite piece* that was ever written in English.

In our way home, Mrs. Mirvan put me into some consternation, by saying it was evident, from the resentment which this Mr. Lovel harbours of my conduct, that he would think it a provocation sufficiently important for a duel, if his courage equalled his wrath.

I am terrified at the very idea. Good Heaven! that a man so weak and frivolous should be so revengeful! However, if bravery would have excited him to affront Lord Orville, how much

---

1   "The fashion, the vogue, the mode" (*OED*).

reason have I to rejoice, that cowardice makes him contented with venting his spleen upon me! But we shall leave town soon, and, I hope, see him no more.

It was some consolation to me, to hear, from Miss Mirvan, that, while he was speaking to me so cavalierly, Lord Orville regarded him with great indignation.

But, really, I think there ought to be a book, of the laws and customs *à-la-mode*, presented to all young people, upon their first introduction into public company.[1]

To-night we go to the opera, where I expect very great pleasure. We shall have the same party as at the play; for Lord Orville said he should be there, and would look for us.

## LETTER XXI.

*Evelina in continuation.*

I have a volume to write, of the adventures of yesterday. In the afternoon, – at Berry Hill, I should have said the *evening*, for it was almost six o'clock, – while Miss Mirvan and I were dressing for the opera, and in high spirits, from the expectation of great entertainment and pleasure, we heard a carriage stop at the door, and concluded that Sir Clement Willoughby, with his usual assiduity, was come to attend us to the Haymarket;[2] but, in a few moments, what was our surprise, to see our chamber-door flung open, and the two Miss Branghtons enter the room! They advanced to me with great familiarity, saying, "How do you do, cousin? – so we've caught you at the glass! – well, I'm determined I'll tell my brother of that!"

Miss Mirvan, who had never before seen them, and could not, at first, imagine who they were, looked so much astonished, that I was ready to laugh myself, till the eldest said,

---

1 The popular conduct books of the day provided moral instruction with some emphasis on proper behavior, but did not specifically address how one should behave in fashionable society where the "customs *à-la-mode*" changed from season to season.

2 The King's Opera House.

"We're come to take you to the opera, Miss; papa and my brother are below, and we are to call for your grandmama as we go along."

"I am very sorry," answered I, "that you should have taken so much trouble, as I am engaged already."

"Engaged! Lord, Miss, never mind that," cried the youngest, "this young lady will make your excuses, I dare say; it's only doing as one would be done by, you know."

"Indeed, Ma'am," said Miss Mirvan, "I shall myself be very sorry to be deprived of Miss Anville's company this evening."

"Well, Miss, that is not so very good-natured in you," said Miss Branghton, "considering we only come to give our cousin pleasure; it's no good to us; it's all upon her account; for we came, I don't know how much round about to take her up."

"I am extremely obliged to you," said I, "and very sorry you have lost so much time; but I cannot possibly help it, for I engaged myself without knowing you would call."

"Lord, what signifies that?" said Miss Polly, "you're no old maid, and so you need n't be so very formal: besides, I dare say those you are engaged to, a'n't half so near related to you as we are."

"I must beg you not to press me any further, for I assure you it is not in my power to attend you."

"Why we came all out of the city on purpose: besides, your grand-mama expects you; – and, pray, what are we to say to her?"

"Tell her, if you please, that I am much concerned, – but that I am pre-engaged."

"And who to?" demanded the abrupt Miss Branghton.

"To Mrs. Mirvan, – and a large party."

"And, pray, what are you all going to do, that it would be such a mighty matter for you to come along with us?"

"We are going to – to the opera."

"O dear, if that be all, why can't we go all together?"

I was extremely disconcerted at this forward and ignorant behaviour, and yet their rudeness very much lessened my concern at refusing them. Indeed, their dress was such as would have rendered their scheme of accompanying our party impracticable, even if I had desired it; and this, as they did not themselves find out, I was obliged, in terms the least mortifying I could think of, to tell them.

They were very much chagrined, and asked where I should sit?

"In the pit," answered I.

"In the pit!" repeated Miss Branghton, "well, really, I must own I should never have supposed that my gown was not good enough for the pit: but come, Polly, let's go; if Miss does not think us fine enough for her, why to be sure she may chuse."

Surprised at this ignorance, I would have explained to them that the pit at the opera required the same dress as the boxes; but they were so much affronted, they would not hear me, and, in great displeasure, left the room, saying they would not have troubled me, only they thought I should not be so proud with my own relations, and that they had at least as good a right to my company as strangers.

I endeavoured to apologize, and would have sent a long message to Madame Duval; but they hastened away without listening to me; and I could not follow them down stairs, because I was not dressed. The last words I heard them say, were, "Well, her grand-mama will be in a fine passion, that's one good thing."

Though I was extremely mad at this visit, yet I so heartily rejoiced at their going, that I would not suffer myself to think gravely about it.

Soon after, Sir Clement actually came, and we all went down stairs. Mrs. Mirvan ordered tea; and we were engaged in a very lively conversation, when the servant announced Madame Duval, who instantly followed him into the room.

Her face was the colour of scarlet, and her eyes sparkled with fury. She came up to me with a hasty step, saying, "So, Miss, you refuses to come to me, do you? And pray who are you, to dare to disobey me?"

I was quite frightened; – I made no answer; – I even attempted to rise, and could not, but sat still, mute and motionless.

Every body, but Miss Mirvan, seemed in the utmost astonishment; and the Captain, rising and approaching Madame Duval, with a voice of authority, said, "Why how now, Mrs. Turkey Cock, what's put you into this here fluster?"

"It's nothing to you," answered she, "so you may as well hold your tongue, for I sha'n't be called to no account by you, I assure you."

"There you're out, Madam Fury," returned he, "for you must know I never suffer any body to be in a passion in my house, but myself."

"But you *shall*," cried she, in a great rage, "for I'll be in as great a passion as ever I please, without asking your leave, so don't give yourself no more airs about it. And as for you, Miss," again advancing to me, "I order you to follow me this moment, or else I'll make you repent it all your life." And, with these words, she flung out of the room.

I was in such extreme terror, at being addressed and threatened in a manner to which I am so wholly unused, that I almost thought I should have fainted.

"Don't be alarmed, my love," cried Mrs. Mirvan, "but stay where you are, and I will follow Madame Duval, and try to bring her to reason."

Miss Mirvan took my hand, and most kindly endeavoured to raise my spirits: Sir Clement, too, approached me, with an air so interested in my distress, that I could not but feel myself oblig-ed to him; and, taking my other hand, said, "For Heaven's sake, my dear Madam, compose yourself; surely the violence of such a wretch ought merely to move your contempt: she can have no right, I imagine, to lay her commands upon you, and I only wish that you would allow *me* to speak to her."

"O no! not for the world! – indeed, I believe, – I am afraid – I had better follow her."

"Follow her! Good God, my dear Miss Anville, would you trust yourself with a mad woman? for what else can you call a creature whose passions are so insolent? No, no; send her word at once to leave the house, and tell her you desire that she will never see you again."

"O Sir! you don't know who you talk of! – it would ill become me to send Madame Duval such a message."

"But *why*," cried he, (looking very inquisitive,) "*why* should you scruple to treat her as she deserves?"

I then found that his aim was to discover the nature of her connection with me; but I felt so much ashamed of my near relationship to her, that I could not persuade myself to answer him, and only entreated that he would leave her to Mrs. Mirvan, who just then entered the room.

Before she could speak to me, the Captain called out, "Well, Goody,[1] what have you done with Madame French? is she cooled a little? 'cause if she be n't, I've just thought of a most excellent device to bring her to."

"My dear Evelina," said Mrs. Mirvan, "I have been vainly endeavouring to appease her; I pleaded your engagement, and promised your future attendance: but I am sorry to say, my love, that I fear her rage will end in a total breach (which I think you had better avoid) if she is any further opposed."

"Then I will go to her, Madam," cried I, "and, indeed, it is now no matter, for I should not be able to recover my spirits sufficiently to enjoy much pleasure *any* where this evening."

Sir Clement began a very warm expostulation, and entreaty, that I would not go; but I begged him to desist, and told him, very honestly, that, if my compliance were not indispensably necessary, I should require no persuasion to stay. He then took my hand, to lead me down stairs; but the Captain desired him to be quiet, saying he would 'squire me himself, "because," he added, (exultingly rubbing his hands) "I have a wipe ready for the old lady, which may serve her to *chew* as she goes along."[2]

We found her in the parlour. "O, you're come at last, Miss, are you? – fine airs you give yourself, indeed! – *ma foi*, if you

---

1 "A term of civility formerly applied to a woman, usually a married woman, in humble life" (*OED*). Since Mrs. Mirvan's status as the daughter of Lady Howard would not seem to merit such a form of address, one can only assume Captain Mirvan is using the term in a denigrating manner, somewhat comparable to the names he has just called Madame Duval (Mrs. Turkey Cock, Madam Fury), perhaps because Mrs. Mirvan has taken the role of peacemaker in attempting to calm Madame Duval after Captain Mirvan's incendiary applications.

2 The Captain might be ready to make "a cutting remark; a sarcastic reproof or rebuff; a jeer, jibe" (*OED*) or to give Madame Duval a handkerchief to chew on to vent her frustration over his baiting her.

had n't come, you might have stayed, I assure you, and have been a beggar for your pains."

"Heyday, Madam," cried the Captain, (prancing forward, with a look of great glee,) "what, a'n't you got out of that there passion yet? why then, I'll tell you what to do to cool yourself; call upon your old friend, *Monseer* Slippery, who was with you at Ranelagh, and give my service to him, and tell him, if he sets any store by your health, that I desire he'll give you such another souse as he did before: he'll know what I mean, and I'll warrant you he'll do't for my sake."

"Let him, if he dares!" cried Madame Duval; "but I sha'n't stay to answer you no more; you are a vulgar fellow, – and so, child, let us leave him to himself."

"Hark ye, Madam," cried the Captain, "you'd best not call names, because, d'ye see, if you do, I shall make bold to show you the door."

She changed colour, and saying, "*Pardi*, I can shew it myself," hurried out of the room, and I followed her into a hackney-coach. But, before we drove off, the Captain, looking out of the parlour window, called out, "D'ye hear, Madam, – don't forget my message to *Monseer*."

You will believe our ride was not the most agreeable in the world; indeed, it would be difficult to say which was least pleased, Madame Duval or me, though the reasons of our discontent were so different: however, Madame Duval soon got the start of me; for we had hardly turned out of Queen-Ann-street, when a man, running full speed, stopt the coach. He came up to the window, and I saw he was the Captain's servant. He had a broad grin on his face, and panted for breath. Madame Duval demanded his business; "Madam," answered he, "my master desires his compliments to you, and – and – and he says he wishes it well over with you. He! he! he! – "

Madame Duval instantly darted forward, and gave him a violent blow on the face; "Take that back for your answer, sirrah," cried she, "and learn to grin at your betters another time. Coachman, drive on!"

The servant was in a violent passion, and swore terribly; but we were soon out of hearing.

The rage of Madame Duval was greater than ever, and she inveighed against the Captain with such fury, that I was even apprehensive she would have returned to his house, purposely to reproach him, which she repeatedly threatened to do; nor would she, I believe, have hesitated a moment, but that, notwithstanding her violence, he has really made her afraid of him.

When we came to her lodgings, we found all the Branghtons in the passage, impatiently waiting for us, with the door open.

"Only see, here's Miss!" cried the brother.

"Well, I declare I thought as much!" said the younger sister.

"Why, Miss," said Mr. Branghton, "I think you might as well have come with your cousins at once; it's throwing money in the dirt, to pay two coaches for one fare."

"Lord, father," cried the son, "make no words about that; for I'll pay for the coach that Miss had."

"O, I know very well," answered Mr. Branghton, "that you're always more ready to spend than to earn."

I then interfered, and begged that I might myself be allowed to pay the fare, as the expence was incurred upon my account; they all said *no*, and proposed that the same coach should carry us on to the opera.

While this passed, the Miss Branghtons were examining my dress, which, indeed, was very improper for my company; and, as I was extremely unwilling to be so conspicuous amongst them, I requested Madame Duval to borrow a hat or bonnet for me of the people of the house. But she never wears either herself, and thinks them very *English* and barbarous; therefore she insisted that I should go full dressed, as I had prepared myself for the pit, though I made many objections.

We were then all crowded into the same carriage; but when we arrived at the opera-house, I contrived to pay the coach-man. They made a great many speeches; but Mr. Branghton's reflection had determined me not to be indebted to him.

If I had not been too much chagrined to laugh, I should have been extremely diverted at their ignorance of whatever belongs to an opera. In the first place, they could not tell at what door we ought to enter, and we wandered about for some time, without knowing which way to turn: they did not chuse to apply to me, though I was the only person of the party who had ever before been at an opera; because they were unwilling to suppose that their *country cousin*, as they were pleased to call me, should be better acquainted with any London public place than themselves. I was very indifferent and careless upon this subject, but not a little uneasy at finding that my dress, so different from that of the company to which I belonged, attracted general notice and observation.

In a short time, however, we arrived at one of the door-keeper's *bars*.[1] Mr. Branghton demanded for what part of the house they took money? They answered the pit, and regarded us all with great earnestness. The son then advancing, said, "Sir, if you please, I beg that I may treat Miss."

"We'll settle that another time," answered Mr. Branghton, and put down a guinea.

Two tickets of admission were given to him.

Mr. Branghton, in his turn, now stared at the door-keeper, and demanded what he meant by giving him only two tickets for a guinea?

"Only two, Sir!" said the man, "why don't you know that the tickets are half a guinea each?"

"Half a guinea each!" repeated Mr. Branghton, "why I never heard of such a thing in my life! And pray, Sir, how many will they admit?"

"Just as usual, Sir, one person each."

"But one person for half a guinea! – why I only want to sit in the pit, friend."

"Had not the Ladies better sit in the gallery, Sir; for they'll hardly chuse to go into the pit with their hats on?"

"O, as to that," cried Miss Branghton, "if out hats are too high, we'll take them off when we get in. I sha'n't mind it, for I did my hair on purpose."

---

1   A ticket counter or barrier between the entrance to the opera house and the seating area. According to Margaret Anne Doody in her notes to the 1994 Penguin edition of *Evelina*, there were "different entrances and different posts of ticket-selling for various parts of the auditorium" (467 n. 161).

Another party then approaching, the door-keeper could no longer attend to Mr. Branghton, who, taking up the guinea, told him it should be long enough before he'd see it again, and walked away.

The young ladies, in some confusion, expressed their surprise, that their *papa* should not know the Opera prices, which, for their parts, they had read in the papers a thousand times.

"The price of stocks," said he, "is enough for me to see after; and I took it for granted it was the same thing here as at the play-house."[1]

"I knew well enough what the price was," said the son, "but I would not speak, because I thought perhaps they'd take less, as we're such a large party."

The sisters both laughed very contemptuously at this idea, and asked him if he ever heard of *people's abating*[2] any thing at a public place?

"I don't know whether I have or no," answered he, "but I'm sure if they would, you'd like it so much the worse."

"Very true, Tom," cried Mr. Branghton; "tell a woman that any thing is reasonable, and she'll be sure to hate it."

"Well," said Miss Polly, "I hope that Aunt and Miss will be of our side, for Papa always takes part with Tom."

"Come, come," cried Madame Duval, "if you stand talking here, we sha'n't get no place at all."

Mr. Branghton then enquired the way to the gallery, and, when we came to the door-keeper, demanded what was to pay.

"The usual price, Sir," said the man.

"Then give me change," cried Mr. Branghton, again putting down his guinea.

"For how many, Sir?"

"Why – let's see, – for six."

"For six, Sir? why you've given me but a guinea."

"*But* a guinea! why how much would you have? I suppose it i'n't half a guinea apiece here too?"

"No, Sir, only five shillings."

---

1  The price of seats at the opera house was much higher than at the theater.
2  Lowering the price.

Mr. Branghton again took up his unfortunate guinea, and protested he would submit to no such imposition. I then proposed that we should return home, but Madame Duval would not consent, and we were conducted, by a woman who sells books of the Opera, to another gallery-door, where, after some disputing, Mr. Branghton at last paid, and we all went up stairs.

Madame Duval complained very much of the trouble of going so high, but Mr. Branghton desired her not to hold the place too cheap, "for, whatever you may think," cried he, "I assure you I paid pit price; so don't suppose I come here to save my money."

"Well, to be sure," said Miss Branghton, "there's no judging of a place by the outside, else, I must needs say, there's nothing very extraordinary in the stair-case."

But, when we entered the gallery, their amazement and disappointment became general. For a few instants, they looked at one another without speaking, and then they all broke silence at once.

"Lord, Papa," exclaimed Miss Polly, "why you have brought us to the one-shilling gallery!"[1]

"I'll be glad to give you two shillings, though," answered he, "to pay. I was never so fooled out of my money before, since the hour of my birth. Either the door-keeper's a knave, or this is the greatest imposition that ever was put upon the public."

"*Ma foi*," cried Madame Duval, "I never sat in such a mean place in all my life; – why it's as high! – we sha'n't see nothing."

"I thought at the time," said Mr. Branghton, "that three shillings was an exorbitant price for a place in the gallery, but as we'd been asked so much more at the other doors, why I paid it without many words; but then, to be sure, thinks I, it can never be like any other gallery, – we shall see some *crinkum-crankum*[2] or other for our money; – but I find it's as arrant a take-in as ever I met with."

"Why it's as like the twelvepenny gallery at Drury-lane,"

---

1 Also known as "the Gods," the one-shilling gallery contained the cheapest seats because it was at the top of the house, furthest from the stage.
2 "A word applied playfully to anything full of twists and turns, or intricately or fancifully elaborated" (*OED*).

cried the son, "as two peas are one to another. I never knew father so bit before."[1]

"Lord," said Miss Branghton, "I thought it would have been quite a fine place, – all over I don't know what, – and done quite in taste."

In this manner they continued to express their dissatisfaction till the curtain drew up; after which, their observations were very curious. They made no allowance for the customs, or even for the language of another country, but formed all their remarks upon comparisons with the English theatre.

Notwithstanding my vexation at having been forced into a party so very disagreeable, and that, too, from one so much – so very much the contrary – yet, would they have suffered me to listen, I should have forgotten every thing unpleasant, and felt nothing but delight, in hearing the sweet voice of Signor Millico,[2] the first singer; but they tormented me with continual talking.

"What a jabbering they make!" cried Mr. Branghton; "there's no knowing a word they say. Pray what's the reason they can't as well sing in English? – but I suppose the fine folks would not like it, if they could understand it."

"How unnatural their action is!" said the son; "why now who ever saw an Englishman put himself in such out-of-the-way postures?"

"For my part," said Miss Polly, "I think it's very pretty, only I don't know what it means."

"Lord, what does that signify?" cried her sister; "mayn't one like a thing without being so very particular? – You may see that Miss likes it, and I don't suppose she knows more of the matter than we do."

A gentleman, soon after, was so obliging as to make room in the front row for Miss Branghton and me. We had no sooner seated ourselves, than Miss Branghton exclaimed, "Good gracious! only see! – why, Polly, all the people in the pit are without hats, dressed like any thing!"

---

1   Taken advantage of.
2   Giuseppe Millico (1737–1802), a castrato soprano, composer, teacher; a very popular entertainer during the 1770s in London.

"Lord, so they are," cried Miss Polly, "well, I never saw the like! – it's worth coming to the Opera if one saw nothing else."

I was then able to distinguish the happy party I had left; and I saw that Lord Orville had seated himself next to Mrs. Mirvan. Sir Clement had his eyes perpetually cast towards the five-shilling gallery, where I suppose he concluded that we were seated; however, before the Opera was over, I have reason to believe that he had discovered me, high and distant as I was from him. Probably he distinguished me by my head-dress.

At the end of the first act, as the green curtain dropped, to prepare for the dance, they imagined that the Opera was done, and Mr. Branghton expressed great indignation that he had been *tricked* out of his money with so little trouble. "Now if any Englishman was to do such an impudent thing as this," said he, "why he'd be pelted; – but here, one of these outlandish gentry may do just what he pleases, and come on, and squeak out a song or two, and then pocket your money without further ceremony."

However, so determined he was to be dissatisfied, that, before the conclusion of the third act, he found still more fault with the Opera for being too long, and wondered whether they thought their singing good enough to serve us for supper.

During the symphony of a song of Signor Millico's, in the second act, young Mr. Branghton said, "It's my belief that that fellow's going to sing another song! – why there's nothing but singing! – I wonder when they'll speak."

This song, which was slow and pathetic, caught all my attention, and I lean'd my head forward to avoid hearing their observations, that I might listen without interruption; but, upon turning round, when the song was over, I found that I was the object of general diversion to the whole party; for the Miss Branghtons were tittering, and the two gentlemen making signs and faces at me, implying their contempt of my affectation.

This discovery determined me to appear as inattentive as themselves; but I was very much provoked at being thus prevented enjoying the only pleasure, which, in such a party, was within my power.

"So, Miss," said Mr. Branghton, "you're quite in the fashion, I see; – so you like Operas? Well, I'm not so polite; I can't like nonsense, let it be never so much the taste."

"But pray, Miss," said the son, "what makes that fellow look so doleful while he's singing?"

"Probably because the character he performs is in distress."

"Why then I think he might as well let alone singing 'till he's in better cue: it's out of all nature for a man to be piping when he's in distress. For my part, I never sing but when I'm merry; yet I love a song as well as most people."

When the curtain dropt, they all rejoiced.

"How do *you* like it? – and how do *you* like it?" passed from one to another with looks of the utmost contempt.

"As for me," said Mr. Branghton, "they've caught me once, but if ever they do again, I'll give 'em leave to sing me to Bedlam[1] for my pains: for such a heap of stuff never did I hear; there is n't one ounce of sense in the whole Opera, nothing but one continued squeaking and squalling from beginning to end."

"If I had been in the pit," said Madame Duval, "I should have liked it vastly, for music is my passion; but sitting in such a place as this, is quite unbearable."

Miss Branghton, looking at me, declared, that she was not *genteel* enough to admire it.

Miss Polly confessed, that, if they would but sing *English*, she should like it *very well*.

The brother wished he could raise a riot in the house, because then he might get his money again.

And, finally, they all agreed, that it was *monstrous dear*.

During the last dance, I perceived, standing near the gallery-door, Sir Clement Willoughby. I was extremely vexed, and would have given the world to have avoided being seen by him: my chief objection was, from the apprehension that he

---

1  Bethlehem Royal Hospital was founded in 1247 as a priory hospital; in 1377 it began to treat "distracted patients." At the beginning of the seventeenth century, paying visitors were allowed in to look at the patients and by the eighteenth century, Bedlam was a tourist attraction.

wou'd hear Miss Branghton call me *cousin*. – I fear you will think this London journey has made me grow very proud, but indeed this family is so low-bred and vulgar, that I should be equally ashamed of such a connexion in the country, or any where. And really I had already been so much chagrined that Sir Clement had been a witness of Madame Duval's power over me, that I could not bear to be exposed to any further mortification.

As the seats cleared, by parties going away, Sir Clement approached nearer to us; the Miss Branghtons observed with surprise, what a fine gentleman was come into the gallery, and they gave me great reason to expect, that they would endeavour to attract his notice, by familiarity with me, whenever he should join us; and so, I formed a sort of plan, to prevent any conversation. I am afraid you will think it wrong; and so I do myself now, – but, at the time, I only considered how I might avoid immediate humiliation.

As soon as he was within two seats of us, he spoke to me, "I am very happy, Miss Anville, to have found you, for the Ladies below have each an humble attendant, and therefore I am come to offer my services here."

"Why then," cried I, (not without hesitating) "if you please, – I will join them."

"Will you allow me the honour of conducting you?" cried he eagerly; and, instantly taking my hand, he would have marched away with me: but I turned to Madame Duval, and said, "As our party is so large, Madam, if you will give me leave, I will go down to Mrs. Mirvan, that I may not crowd you in the coach."

And then, without waiting for an answer, I suffered Sir Clement to hand me out of the gallery.

Madame Duval, I doubt not, will be very angry, and so I am with myself, now, and therefore I cannot be surprised: but Mr. Branghton, I am sure, will easily comfort himself, in having escaped the additional coach expence of carrying me to Queen-Ann-street: as to his daughters, they had no time to speak, but I saw they were in utter amazement.

My intention was to join Mrs. Mirvan, and accompany her

home. Sir Clement was in high spirits and good-humour; and, all the way we went, I was fool enough to rejoice in secret at the success of my plan; nor was it till I got down stairs, and amidst the servants, that any difficulty occurred to me of meeting with my friends.

I then asked Sir Clement how I should contrive to acquaint Mrs. Mirvan that I had left Madame Duval?

"I fear it will be almost impossible to find her," answered he; "but you can have no objection to permitting me to see you safe home."

He then desired his servant, who was waiting, to order his chariot to draw up.

This quite startled me; I turned to him hastily, and said that I could not think of going away without Mrs. Mirvan.

"But how can we meet with her?" cried he; "you will not chuse to go into the pit yourself; I cannot send a servant there; and it is impossible for *me* to go and leave you alone."[1]

The truth of this was indisputable, and totally silenced me. Yet, as soon as I could recollect myself, I determined not to go in his chariot, and told him I believed I had best return to my party up stairs.

He would not hear of this; and earnestly entreated me not to withdraw the trust I had reposed in him.

While he was speaking, I saw Lord Orville, with several ladies and gentlemen, coming from the pit passage: unfortunately, he saw me too, and, leaving his company, advanced instantly towards me, and, with an air and voice of surprise, said, "Good God, do I see Miss Anville!"

I now most severely felt the folly of my plan, and the awkwardness of my situation; however, I hastened to tell him, though in a hesitating manner, that I was waiting for Mrs. Mirvan: but what was my disappointment, when he acquainted me that she was already gone home!

I was inexpressibly distressed; to suffer Lord Orville to think me satisfied with the single protection of Sir Clement Willoughby, I could not bear; yet I was more than ever averse

---

1  It is improper for Evelina to move about the theater without a chaperon or escort. The only women to be found alone in the theater were prostitutes.

to returning to a party which I dreaded his seeing: I stood some moments in suspense, and could not help exclaiming, "Good Heaven, what can I do!"

"Why, my dear Madam," cried Sir Clement, "should you be thus uneasy? – you will reach Queen-Ann-street almost as soon as Mrs. Mirvan, and I am sure you cannot doubt being as safe."

I made no answer, and Lord Orville then said, "My coach is here; and my servants are ready to take any commands Miss Anville will honour me with for them. I shall myself go home in a chair, and therefore – "

How grateful did I feel for a proposal so considerate, and made with so much delicacy! I should gladly have accepted it, had I been permitted, but Sir Clement would not let him even finish his speech; he interrupted him with evident displeasure, and said, "My Lord, my own chariot is now at the door."

And just then the servant came, and told him the carriage was ready. He begged to have the honour of conducting me to it, and would have taken my hand, but I drew it back, saying, "I can't – I can't indeed! pray go by yourself – and as to me, let me have a chair."

"Impossible!" (cried he with vehemence) "I cannot think of trusting you with strange chairmen, – I cannot answer it to Mrs. Mirvan, – come, dear Madam, we shall be home in five minutes."

Again I stood suspended. With what joy would I then have compromised with my pride, to have been once more with Madame Duval and the Branghtons, provided I had not met with Lord Orville! However, I flatter myself that he not only saw, but pitied my embarrassment, for he said, in a tone of voice unusually softened, "To offer my services in the presence of Sir Clement Willoughby would be superfluous; but I hope I need not assure Miss Anville, how happy it would make me to be of the least use to her."

I courtsied my thanks. Sir Clement with great earnestness pressed me to go; and while I was thus uneasily deliberating what to do, the dance, I suppose, finished, for the people crowded down stairs. Had Lord Orville then repeated his offer, I would have accepted it, notwithstanding Sir Clement's repugnance; but I fancy he thought it would be impertinent. In a very few minutes I heard Madame Duval's voice, as she descended from the gallery; "Well," cried I, hastily, "if I must go –" I stopt, but Sir Clement immediately handed me into his chariot, called out "Queen-Ann-street," and then jumped in himself. Lord Orville, with a bow and a half smile, wished me good night.

My concern was so great, at being seen and left by Lord Orville in so strange a situation, that I should have been best pleased to have remained wholly silent during our ride home: but Sir Clement took care to prevent that.

He began by making many complaints of my unwillingness to trust myself with him, and begged to know what could be the reason? This question so much embarrassed me, that I could not tell what to answer, but only said, that I was sorry to have taken up so much of his time.

"O Miss Anville," (cried he, taking my hand) "if you knew with what transport I would dedicate to you not only the present but all the future time allotted to me, you would not injure me by making such an apology."

I could not think of a word to say to this, nor to a great many other equally fine speeches with which he ran on, though I would fain have withdrawn my hand, and made almost continual attempts; but in vain, for he actually grasped it between both his, without any regard to my resistance.

Soon after, he said that he believed the coachman was going the wrong way, and he called to his servant, and gave him directions. Then again addressing himself to me, "How often, how assiduously have I sought an opportunity of speaking to you, without the presence of that brute Captain Mirvan! Fortune has now kindly favoured me with one, and permit me," (again seizing my hand) "permit me to use it, in telling you that I adore you."

I was quite thunderstuck at this abrupt and unexpected declaration. For some moments I was silent, but, when I recovered from my surprise, I said, "Indeed, Sir, if you were determined to make me repent leaving my own party so foolishly, you have very well succeeded."

"My dearest life," cried he, "is it possible you can be so cruel? Can your nature and your countenance be so totally opposite? Can the sweet bloom upon those charming cheeks, which appears as much the result of good-humour as of beauty – "

"O, Sir," cried I, interrupting him, "this is very fine; but I had hoped we had had enough of this sort of conversation at the Ridotto, and I did not expect you would so soon resume it."

"What I then said, my sweet reproacher, was the effect of a mistaken, a prophane idea, that your understanding held no competition with your beauty; but now, now that I find you equally incomparable in both, all words, all powers of speech, are too feeble to express the admiration I feel of your excellencies."

"Indeed," cried I, "if your thoughts had any connexion with your language, you would never suppose that I could give credit to praise so very much above my desert."

This speech, which I made very gravely, occasioned still stronger protestations, which he continued to pour forth, and I continued to disclaim, till I began to wonder that we were not in Queen-Ann-street, and begged he would desire the coachman to drive faster.

"And does this little moment," cried he, "which is the first of happiness I have ever known, does it already appear so very long to you?"

"I am afraid the man has mistaken the way," answered I, "or else we should ere now have been at our journey's end. I must beg you will speak to him."

"And can you think me so much my own enemy? – if my good genius has inspired the man with a desire of prolonging my happiness, can you expect that I should counter-act its indulgence?"

I now began to apprehend that he had himself ordered the man to go a wrong way, and I was so much alarmed at the idea, that, the very instant it occurred to me, I let down the glass, and made a sudden effort to open the chariot-door myself, with a view of jumping into the street; but he caught hold of me, exclaiming, "For Heaven's sake, what is the matter?"

"I – I don't know," cried I, (quite out of breath) "but I am sure the man goes wrong, and, if you will not speak to him, I am determined I will get out myself."

"You amaze me," answered he, (still holding me) "I cannot imagine what you apprehend. Surely you can have no doubts of my honour?"

He drew me towards him as he spoke. I was frightened dreadfully, and could hardly say, "No, Sir, no, – none at all, – only Mrs. Mirvan, – I think she will be uneasy."

"Whence this alarm, my dearest angel? – What can you fear? – my life is at your devotion, and can you, then, doubt my protection?"

And so saying, he passionately kissed my hand.

Never, in my whole life, have I been so terrified. I broke forcibly from him, and, putting my head out of the window, called aloud to the man to stop. Where we then were I know not, but I saw not a human being, or I should have called for help.

Sir Clement, with great earnestness, endeavoured to appease and compose me; "If you do not intend to murder me," cried I, "for mercy's, for pity's sake, let me get out!"

"Compose your spirits, my dearest life," cried he, "and I will do every thing you would have me." And then he called to the man himself, and bid him make haste to Queen-Ann-street. "This stupid fellow," continued he, "has certainly mistaken my orders; but I hope you are now fully satisfied."

I made no answer, but kept my head at the window, watching which way he drove, but without any comfort to myself, as I was quite unacquainted with either the right or the wrong.

Sir Clement now poured forth abundant protestations of honour, and assurances of respect, entreating my pardon for having offended me, and beseeching my good opinion: but I was quite silent, having too much apprehension to make reproaches, and too much anger to speak without.

In this manner we went through several streets, till at last, to my great terror, he suddenly ordered the man to stop, and said, "Miss Anville, we are now within twenty yards of your house;

but I cannot bear to part with you, till you generously forgive me for the offence you have taken, and promise not to make it known to the Mirvans."

I hesitated between fear and indignation.

"Your reluctance to speak, redoubles my contrition for having displeased you, since it shews the reliance I might have on a promise which you will not give without consideration."

"I am very, very much distressed," cried I, "you ask a promise which you must be sensible I ought not to grant, and yet dare not refuse."

"Drive on!" cried he to the coachman; – "Miss Anville, I will not compel you; I will exact no promise, but trust wholly to your generosity."

This rather softened me; which advantage he no sooner perceived, than he determined to avail himself of, for he flung himself on his knees, and pleaded with so much submission, that I was really obliged to forgive him, because his humiliation made me quite ashamed: and, after that, he would not let me rest till I gave him my word that I would not complain of him to Mrs. Mirvan.

My own folly and pride, which had put me in his power, were pleas which I could not but attend to in his favour. However, I shall take very particular care never to be again alone with him.

When, at last, we arrived at our house, I was so overjoyed, that I should certainly have pardoned him then, if I had not before. As he handed me up stairs, he scolded his servant aloud, and very angrily, for having gone so much out of the way. Miss Mirvan ran out to meet me, – and who should I see behind her, but – Lord Orville!

All my joy now vanished, and gave place to shame and confusion; for I could not endure that he should know how long a time Sir Clement and I had been together, since I was not at liberty to assign any reason for it.

They all expressed great satisfaction at seeing me, and said they had been extremely uneasy and surprised that I was so long coming home, as they had heard from Lord Orville that I was not with Madame Duval. Sir Clement, in an affected passion, said that his booby of a servant had misunderstood his orders, and was driving us to the upper end of Piccadilly.[1] For my part, I only coloured, for though I would not forfeit my word, I yet disdained to confirm a tale in which I had myself no belief.

Lord Orville, with great politeness, congratulated me, that the troubles of the evening had so happily ended, and said, that he had found it impossible to return home, before he enquired after my safety.

In a very short time he took leave, and Sir Clement followed him. As soon as they were gone, Mrs. Mirvan, though with great softness, blamed me for having quitted Madame Duval. I assured her, and with truth, that for the future I would be more prudent.

The adventures of the evening so much disconcerted me, that I could not sleep all night. I am under the most cruel apprehensions, lest Lord Orville should suppose my being on the gallery-stairs with Sir Clement was a concerted scheme, and even that our continuing so long together in his chariot, was with my approbation, since I did not say a word on the subject, nor express any dissatisfaction at the coachman's pretended blunder.

Yet his coming hither to wait our arrival, though it seems to imply some doubt, shews also some anxiety. Indeed Miss Mirvan says, that he appeared *extremely* anxious, nay uneasy and impatient for my return. If I did not fear to flatter myself, I should think it not impossible but that he had a suspicion of Sir Clement's design, and was therefore concerned for my safety.

What a long letter is this! however, I shall not write many more from London, for the Captain said this morning, that he would leave town on Tuesday next. Madame Duval will dine here to-day, and then she is to be told his intention.

I am very much amazed that she accepted Mrs. Mirvan's invitation, as she was in such wrath yesterday. I fear that to-day

1   The driver was taking them east rather than west, from Haymarket to Piccadilly, not Haymarket to Queen-Ann-street in the West End of London where Evelina is staying with the Mirvans.

I shall myself be the principal object of her displeasure; but I must submit patiently, for I cannot defend myself.

Adieu, my dearest Sir. Should this letter be productive of any uneasiness to you, more than ever shall I repent the heedless imprudence which it recites.

## LETTER XXII.

*Evelina in continuation.*

Monday morning, April 18.

Mrs. Mirvan has just communicated to me an anecdote concerning Lord Orville, which has much surprised, half pleased, and half pained me.

While they were sitting together during the opera, he told her that he had been greatly concerned at the impertinence which the young lady under her protection had suffered from Mr. Lovel; but that he had the pleasure of assuring her, she had no future disturbance to apprehend from him.

Mrs. Mirvan, with great eagerness, begged he would explain himself, and said she hoped he had not thought so insignificant an affair worthy his serious attention.

"There is nothing," answered he, "which requires more immediate notice than impertinence, for it ever encroaches when it is tolerated." He then added, that he believed he ought to apologize for the liberty he had taken of interfering, but that, as he regarded himself in the light of a *party concerned*, from having had the honour of dancing with Miss Anville, he could not possibly reconcile to himself a patient neutrality.

He then proceeded to tell her, that he had waited upon Mr. Lovel[1] the morning after the play; that the visit had proved an amicable one, but the particulars were neither entertaining nor necessary; he only assured her, Miss Anville might be perfectly easy, since Mr. Lovel had engaged his honour never more to

---

1   It is implied that Lord Orville had "waited upon Mr. Lovel" in order to challenge him to a duel if he did not discontinue harassing Evelina.

mention, or even to hint at what had passed at Mrs. Stanley's assembly.

Mrs. Mirvan expressed her satisfaction at this conclusion, and thanked him for his polite attention to her young friend.

"It would be needless," said he, "to request that this affair may never transpire, since Mrs. Mirvan cannot but see the necessity of keeping it inviolably secret; but I thought it incumbent upon me, as the young lady is under your protection, to assure both you and her of Mr. Lovel's future respect."

Had I known of this visit previous to Lord Orville's making it, what dreadful uneasiness would it have cost me! Yet that he should so much interest himself in securing me from offence, gives me, I must own, an internal pleasure greater than I can express; for I feared he had too contemptuous an opinion of me, to take any trouble upon my account. Though, after all, this interference might rather be to satisfy his own delicacy, than from thinking well of me.

But how cool, how quiet is true courage! Who, from seeing Lord Orville at the play, would have imagined his resentment would have hazarded his life? yet his displeasure was evident, though his real bravery and his politeness equally guarded him from entering into any discussion in our presence.

Madame Duval, as I expected, was most terribly angry yesterday; she scolded me for I believe two hours, on account of having left her, and protested she had been so much surprised at my going, without giving her time to answer, that she hardly knew whether she was awake or asleep. But she assured me, that if ever I did so again, she would never more take me into public. And she expressed an equal degree of displeasure against Sir Clement, because he had not even spoken to her, and because he was always of the Captain's side in an argument. The Captain, as bound in honour, warmly defended him, and then followed a dispute in the usual style.

After dinner, Mrs. Mirvan introduced the subject of our leaving London. Madame Duval said she should stay a month or two longer. The Captain told her she was welcome, but that he and his family should go into the country on Tuesday morning.

A most disagreeable scene followed; Madame Duval insisted upon keeping me with her; but Mrs. Mirvan said, that as I was actually engaged on a visit to Lady Howard, who had only consented to my leaving her for a few days, she could not think of returning without me.

Perhaps if the Captain had not interfered, the good-breeding and mildness of Mrs. Mirvan might have had some effect upon Madame Duval; but he passes no opportunity of provoking her, and therefore made so many gross and rude speeches, all of which she retorted, that, in conclusion, she vowed she would sooner go to law, in right of her relationship, than that I should be taken away from her.[1]

I heard this account from Mrs. Mirvan, who was so kindly considerate as to give me a pretence for quitting the room, as soon as this dispute began, lest Madame Duval should refer to me, and insist on my obedience.

The final result of the conversation was, that, to soften matters for the present, Madame Duval should make one in the party for Howard Grove, whither we are positively to go next Wednesday. And though we are none of us satisfied with this plan, we know not how to form a better.

Mrs. Mirvan is now writing to Lady Howard, to excuse bringing this unexpected guest, and to prevent the disagreeable surprise, which must, otherwise, attend her reception. This dear lady seems eternally studying my happiness and advantage.

To-night we go to the Pantheon, which is the last diversion we shall partake of in London, for to-morrow –

\*       \*       \*       \*       \*

This moment, my dearest Sir, I have received your kind letter.

If you thought us too dissipated the first week, I almost fear

---

1   As her grandmother, Madame Duval's claim to Evelina under the law would be stronger than that of Villars', since he is not related to Evelina by blood. However, Sir John Belmont's claim would supersede even Madame Duval's, if he chose to claim Evelina, and a will in Lady Belmont's hand naming Villars as guardian would also make Madame Duval's claim less certain. Any such lawsuit would make public the shaky nature of Evelina's legitimacy and would therefore be something to be avoided from Evelina's perspective.

to know what you will think of us this second; – however, the Pantheon this evening will probably be the last public place which I shall ever see.

The assurance of your support and protection in regard to Madame Duval, though what I never doubted, excites my utmost gratitude: how, indeed, cherished under your roof, the happy object of your constant indulgence, how could I have borne to become the slave of her tyrannical humours? – pardon me that I speak so hardly of her, but, whenever the idea of passing my days with her occurs to me, the comparison which naturally follows, takes from me all that forbearance, which, I believe, I owe her.

You are already displeased with Sir Clement: to be sure, then, his behaviour after the Opera will not make peace with you. Indeed, the more I reflect upon it, the more angry I am. I was entirely in his power, and it was cruel in him to cause me so much terror.

O my dearest Sir, were I but worthy the prayers and the wishes you offer for me, the utmost ambition of my heart would be fully satisfied! but I greatly fear you will find me, now that I am out of the reach of your assisting prudence, more weak and imperfect than you could have expected.

I have not now time to write another word, for I must immediately hasten to dress for the evening.

## LETTER XXIII.

*Evelina in continuation.*

Queen-Ann-street, Tuesday, April 19.

There is something to me half melancholy in writing an account of our last adventures in London; however, as this day is merely appropriated to packing, and preparations for our journey, and as I shall shortly have no more adventures to write, I think I may as well complete my town journal at once. And, when you have it all together, I hope, my dear Sir, you will send me your observations and thoughts upon it to Howard Grove.

About eight o'clock we went to the Pantheon. I was extremely struck with the beauty of the building, which greatly surpassed whatever I could have expected or imagined. Yet, it has more the appearance of a chapel, than of a place of diversion; and, though I was quite charmed with the magnificence of the room, I felt that I could not be as gay and thoughtless there as at Ranelagh, for there is something in it which rather inspires awe and solemnity, than mirth and pleasure. However, perhaps it may only have this effect upon such a novice as myself.

I should have said, that our party consisted only of Captain, Mrs. and Miss Mirvan, as Madame Duval spent the day in the city: – which I own I could not lament.

There was a great deal of company; but the first person we saw was Sir Clement Willoughby. He addressed us with his usual ease, and joined us for the whole evening. I felt myself very uneasy in his presence; for I could not look at him, nor hear him speak, without recollecting the chariot adventure; but to my great amazement, I observed that he looked at *me* without the least apparent discomposure, though certainly he ought not to think of his behaviour without blushing. I really wish I had not forgiven him, and then he could not have ventured to speak to me any more.

There was an exceeding good concert, but too much talking to hear it well. Indeed I am quite astonished to find how little music is attended to in silence; for though every body seems to admire, hardly any body listens.

We did not see Lord Orville, till we went into the tea-room, which is large, low, and under ground, and serves merely as a foil to the apartments above; he then sat next to us; he seemed to belong to a large party, chiefly of ladies; but, among the gentlemen attending them, I perceived Mr. Lovel.

I was extremely irresolute whether or not I ought to make any acknowledgments to Lord Orville for his generous conduct in securing me from the future impertinence of that man; and I thought, that as he had seemed to allow Mrs. Mirvan to acquaint me, though no one else, of the measures which he had taken, he might perhaps suppose me ungrateful if silent:

however, I might have spared myself the trouble of deliberating, as I never once had the shadow of an opportunity of speaking unheard by Sir Clement. On the contrary, he was so exceedingly officious and forward, that I could not say a word to any body, but instantly he bent his head forward, with an air of profound attention, as if I had addressed myself wholly to him: and yet, I never once looked at him, and would not have spoken to him on any account.

Indeed, Mrs. Mirvan herself, though unacquainted with the behaviour of Sir Clement after the opera, says it is not right for a young woman to be seen so frequently in public with the same gentleman; and, if our stay in town was to be lengthened, she would endeavour to represent to the Captain the impropriety of allowing his constant attendance; for Sir Clement, with all his *easiness*, could not be so eternally of our parties, if the Captain was less fond of his company.

At the same table with Lord Orville, sat a gentleman, – I call him so only because he *was* at the same table, – who, almost from the moment I was seated, fixed his eyes stedfastly on my face, and never once removed them to any other object during tea-time, notwithstanding my dislike of his staring must, I am sure, have been very evident. I was quite surprised, that a man whose boldness was so offensive, could have gained admission into a party of which Lord Orville made one; for I naturally concluded him to be some low-bred, and uneducated man; and I thought my idea was indubitably confirmed, when I heard him say to Sir Clement Willoughby, in an *audible whisper*, – which is a mode of speech very distressing and disagreeable to by-standers, – "For Heaven's sake, Willoughby, who is that lovely creature?"

But what was my amazement, when, listening attentively for the answer, though my head was turned another way, I heard Sir Clement say, "I am sorry I cannot inform your Lordship, but I am ignorant myself."

*Lordship!* – how extraordinary! that a *nobleman*, accustomed, in all probability, to the first rank of company in the kingdom, from his earliest infancy, can possibly be deficient in *good manners*, however faulty in morals and principles! Even Sir Clement

Willoughby appeared modest in comparison with this person.

During tea, a conversation was commenced upon the times, fashions, and public places, in which the company of both tables joined. It began by Sir Clement's enquiring of Miss Mirvan and of me if the Pantheon had answered our expectations.

We both readily agreed that it had greatly exceeded them.

"Ay, to be sure," said the Captain, "why you don't suppose they'd confess they did n't like it, do you? Whatever's the fashion, they must like of course; – or else I'd be bound for it they'd own, that there never was such a dull place as this here invented."

"And has, then, this building," said Lord Orville, "no merit that may serve to lessen your censure? Will not your eye, Sir, speak something in its favour?"

"Eye!" cried the Lord, (I don't know his name,) "and is there any eye here, that can find pleasure in looking at dead walls or statues, when such heavenly living objects as I now see demand all their admiration?"

"O, certainly," said Lord Orville, "the lifeless symmetry of architecture, however beautiful the design and proportion, no man would be so mad as to put in competition with the animated charms of nature: but when, as to-night, the eye may be regaled at the same time, and in one view, with all the excellence of art, and all the perfection of nature, I cannot think that either suffer by being seen together."

"I grant, my Lord," said Sir Clement, "that the cool eye of unimpassioned philosophy may view both with equal attention, and equal safety; but, where the heart is not so well guarded, it is apt to interfere, and render, even to the eye, all objects but one insipid and uninteresting."

"Aye, aye," cried the Captain, "you may talk what you will of your eye here, and your eye there, and, for the matter of that, to be sure you have two, – but we all know they both squint one way."

"Far be it from me," said Lord Orville, "to dispute the *magnetic* power of beauty, which irresistibly draws and attracts whatever has soul and sympathy: and I am happy to acknowledge, that though we have now no *gods* to occupy a mansion professedly built for them, yet we have secured their *better halves*, for we have *goddesses* to whom we all most willingly bow down." And then, with a very droll air, he made a profound reverence to the ladies.

"They'd need be goddesses with a vengeance," said the Captain, "for they're mortal dear to look at. Howsomever, I should be glad to know what you can see in e'er a face among them that's worth half a guinea for a sight."

"Half a guinea!" exclaimed that same Lord, "I would give half I am worth, for a sight of only *one*, provided I make my own choice. And, prithee, how can money be better employed than in the service of fine women?"

"If the ladies of his own party can pardon the Captain's speech," said Sir Clement, "I think he has a fair claim to the forgiveness of all."

"Then you depend very much, as I doubt not but you may," said Lord Orville, "upon the general sweetness of the sex; – but, as to the ladies of the Captain's party, they may easily pardon, for they cannot be hurt."

"But they must have a devilish good conceit of themselves, though," said the Captain, "to believe all that. Howsomever, whether or no, I should be glad to be told, by some of you, who seem to be knowing in them things, what kind of diversion can be found in such a place as this here, for one who has had, long ago, his full of face-hunting?"

Every body laughed, but nobody spoke.

"Why look you there, now," continued the Captain, "you're all at a dead stand! – not a man among you can answer that there question. Why, then, I must make bold to conclude, that you all come here for no manner of purpose but to stare at one another's pretty faces; – though, for the matter of that, half of 'em are plaguy ugly, – and, as to t'other half, – I believe it's none of God's manufactory."

"What the ladies may come hither for, Sir," said Mr. Lovel, (stroking his ruffles, and looking down,) "it would ill become *us* to determine; but as to we men, doubtless we can have no other view, than to admire them."

"If I be n't mistaken," cried the Captain, (looking earnestly

in his face,) "you are that same person we saw at Love for Love
t'other night; be n't you?"

Mr. Lovel bowed.

"Why then, Gentlemen," continued he, with a loud laugh, "I
must tell you a most excellent good joke; – when all was over,
as sure as you're alive, he asked what the play was! Ha, ha, ha!"

"Sir," said Mr. Lovel, colouring, "if you were as much used
to a town life as I am, – which, I presume, is not precisely the
case, – I fancy you would not find so much diversion from a
circumstance so common."

"Common! what, is it common?" repeated the Captain;
"why then, 'fore George, such chaps are more fit to be sent to
school, and well disciplined with a cat o' nine tails,[1] than to
poke their heads into a play-house. Why, a play is the only
thing left, now-a-days, that has a grain of sense in it; for as to all
the rest of your public places, d'ye see, if they were all put
together, I would n't give *that* for 'em!" snapping his fingers.
"And now we're talking of them sort of things, there's your
operas, – I should like to know, now, what any of you can find
to say for them."

Lord Orville, who was most able to have answered, seemed
by no means to think the Captain worthy an argument, upon a
subject concerning which he had neither knowledge nor feeling: but, turning to us, he said, "The ladies are silent, and we
seem to have engrossed the conversation to ourselves, in which
we are much more our own enemies than theirs. But," addressing himself to Miss Mirvan and me, "I am most desirous to hear
the opinions of these young ladies, to whom all public places
must, as yet, be new."

We both, and with eagerness, declared that we had received
as much, if not more pleasure, at the opera than any where: but
we had better have been silent; for the Captain, quite displeased, said, "What signifies asking them girls? Do you think
they know their own minds yet? Ask 'em after any thing that's
called diversion, and you're sure they'll say it's vastly fine; – they
are a set of parrots, and speak by rote, for they all say the same

---

1  "A whip with nine knotted lashes; till 1881 an authorized instrument of punishment in the British navy and army" (*OED*).

thing: but ask 'em how they like making puddings and pies, and I'll warrant you'll pose 'em. As to them operas, I desire I may hear no more of their liking such nonsense; and for you, Moll," to his daughter, "I charge you, as you value my favour, that you'll never again be so impertinent as to have a taste of your own before my face. There are fools enough in the world, without your adding to their number. I'll have no daughter of mine affect them sort of megrims.[1] It is a shame they a'n't put down; and if I'd my will, there's not a magistrate in this town, but should be knocked of the head for suffering them. If you've a mind to praise any thing, why you may praise a play, and welcome, for I like it myself."

This reproof effectually silenced us both for the rest of the evening. Nay, indeed, for some minutes it seemed to silence every body else; till Mr. Lovel, not willing to lose an opportunity of returning the Captain's sarcasm, said, "Why, really, Sir, it is but natural to be most pleased with what is most familiar, and, I think, of all our diversions, there is not one so much in common between us and the country, as a play. Not a village but has its barns and comedians;[2] and as for the stage business, why it may be pretty equally done any where; and even in regard to *us*, and the *canaille*,[3] confined as we all are within the semi-circle of a theatre, there is no place where the distinction is less obvious."

While the Captain seemed considering for Mr. Lovel's meaning, Lord Orville, probably with a view to prevent his finding it, changed the subject to Cox's Museum, and asked what he thought of it?

"Think! – " said he, "why I think as how it i'n't worth thinking about. I like no such *jemcracks*.[4] It is only fit, in my mind, for monkeys, – though, for aught I know, they too might turn up their noses at it."

---

1   "A whim, fancy, fad" (*OED*).
2   "A player in general, a stage-player" (*OED*).
3   "A contemptuous name given to the populace; the "vile" herd, vile populace; the rabble, the mob" (*OED*). Originally French for "pack of dogs."
4   Obsolete form of gimcracks, "a showy, insubstantial thing; esp. ... a useless ornament, a trumpery article, a knick-knack" (*OED*).

"May we ask your Lordship's own opinion?" said Mrs. Mirvan.

"The mechanism," answered he, "is wonderfully ingenious: I am sorry it is turned to no better account; but its purport is so frivolous, so very remote from all aim at instruction or utility, that the sight of so fine a shew, only leaves a regret on the mind, that so much work, and so much ingenuity, should not be better bestowed."

"The truth is," said the Captain, "that in all this huge town, so full as it is of folks of all sorts, there i'n't so much as one public place, besides the play-house, where a man, that's to say a man who *is* a man, ought not to be ashamed to shew his face. T'other day they got me to a ridotto; but I believe it will be long enough before they get me to another. I knew no more what to do with myself, than if my ship's company had been metamorphosed into Frenchmen. Then, again, there's your famous Ranelagh, that you make such a fuss about, – why what a dull place is that! – it's the worst of all."

"Ranelagh dull!" – "Ranelagh dull!" was echoed from mouth to mouth, and all the ladies, as if of one accord, regarded the Captain with looks of the most ironical contempt.

"As to Ranelagh," said Mr. Lovel, "most indubitably, though the price is plebeian, it is by no means adapted to the plebeian taste. It requires a certain acquaintance with high life, and – and – and something of – of – something *d'un vrai goût*, to be really sensible of its merit. Those whose – whose connections, and so forth, are not among *les gens comme il faut*, can feel nothing but *ennui*[1] at such a place as Ranelagh."

"Ranelagh!" cried Lord ——, "O, 'tis the divinest place under heaven, – or, indeed, – for aught I know ——"

"O you creature!" cried a pretty, but affected young lady, patting him with her fan, "you sha'n't talk so; I know what you are going to say; but, positively, I won't sit by you, if you're so wicked."

"And how can one sit by you, and be good?" said he, "when only to look at you is enough to make one wicked – or wish to be so?"

---

1   A true taste. The right people. Boredom.

"Fie, my Lord!" returned she, "you are really insufferable. I don't think I shall speak to you again these seven years."

"What a metamorphosis," cried Lord Orville, "should you make a patriarch of his Lordship!"[1]

"Seven years!" said he, "dear Madam, be contented with telling me you will not speak to me *after* seven years, and I will endeavour to submit."

"O, very well, my Lord," answered she, "pray date the end of our speaking to each other as early as you please, I'll promise to agree to your time."

"You know, dear Madam," said he, sipping his tea, "you know I only live in your sight."

"O yes, my Lord, I have long known that. But I begin to fear we shall be too late for Ranelagh this evening."

"O no, Madam," said Mr. Lovel, looking at his watch, "it is but just past ten."

"No more!" cried she, "O then we shall do very well."

All the ladies now started up, and declared they had no time to lose.

"Why what the D——l," cried the Captain, leaning forward with both his arms on the table, "are you going to Ranelagh at this time of night?"

The ladies looked at one another, and smiled.

"To Ranelagh?" cried Lord ——, "Yes, and I hope you are going too; for we cannot possibly excuse these ladies."

"I go to Ranelagh? – if I do, I'll be – ."

Every body now stood up, and the stranger Lord, coming round to me, said, "*You* go, I hope?"

"No, my Lord, I believe not."

"O you cannot, must not be so barbarous." And he took my hand, and ran on saying such fine speeches and compliments, that I might almost have supposed myself a goddess, and him a pagan, paying me adoration. As soon as I possibly could, I drew back my hand; but he frequently, in the course of conversation, contrived to take it again, though it was extremely disagreeable to me; and the more so, as I saw that Lord Orville

---

1   Allusion to the seven years Jacob served Laban so that he might marry his daughter, Rachel (Genesis 29).

had his eyes fixed upon us, with a gravity of attention that made me uneasy.

And, surely, my dear Sir, it was a great liberty in this Lord, notwithstanding his rank, to treat me so freely. As to Sir Clement, he seemed in misery.

They all endeavoured to prevail with the Captain to join the Ranelagh party; and this Lord told me, in a low voice, that *it was tearing his heart out* to go without me.

During this conversation, Mr. Lovel came forward, and assuming a look of surprise, made me a bow, and enquired how I did, protesting, upon his honour, that he had not seen me before, or would sooner have paid his respects to me.

Though his politeness was evidently constrained, yet I was very glad to be thus assured of having nothing more to fear from him.

The Captain, far from listening to their persuasions of accompanying them to Ranelagh, was quite in a passion at the proposal, and vowed he would sooner go to the *Black-hole in Calcutta*.[1]

"But," said Lord ——, "if the *ladies* will take their tea at Ranelagh, you may depend upon our seeing them safe home, for we shall all be proud of the honour of attending them."

"May be so," said the Captain; "but I'll tell you what, if one of these places be n't enough for them to-night, why to-morrow they shall go to ne'er a one."

We instantly declared ourselves very ready to go home.

"It is not for yourselves that we petition," said Lord ——, "but for *us*; if you have any charity, you will not be so cruel as to deny us; we only beg you to prolong our happiness for a few minutes, – the favour is but a small one for you to grant, though so great a one for us to receive."

"To tell you a piece of my mind," said the Captain, surlily, "I think you might as well not give the girls so much of this palaver: they'll take it all for gospel. As to Moll, why she's well enough, but nothing extraordinary, though, perhaps, you may

---

1 In 1756, 146 European residents of Calcutta, most of them British, were taken hostage by Indian insurgents under the Nawab of Bengal and placed in a small cell at Fort William where all but 23 died.

persuade her that her pug-nose is all the fashion: and as to the other, why she's good white and red,[1] to be sure; but what of that? – I'll warrant she'll moulder away as fast as her neighbours."

"Is there," cried Lord ——, "another man in this place, who, seeing such objects, could make such a speech?"

"As to that there," returned the Captain, "I don't know whether there be or no, and, to make free, I don't care; for I sha'n't go for to model myself by any of these fair-weather chaps, who dare not so much as say their souls are their own, – and, for aught I know, no more they ben't. I'm almost as much ashamed of my countrymen, as if I was a Frenchman, and I believe in my heart there i'n't a pin to chuse between them; and, before long, we shall hear the very sailors talking that lingo, and see never a swabber without a bag and a sword."[2]

"He, he, he! – well, 'pon honour," cried Mr. Lovel, "you gentlemen of the ocean have a most severe way of judging."

"Severe! 'fore George, that is impossible; for, to cut the matter short, the men, as they call themselves, are no better than monkeys; and as to the women, why they are mere dolls. So, now you've got my opinion of this subject; and so I wish you good night."

The ladies, who were very impatient to be gone, made their courtsies, and tripped away, followed by all the gentlemen of their party, except the Lord I have before mentioned, and Lord Orville, who stayed to make enquiries of Mrs. Mirvan concerning our leaving town; and then saying, with his usual politeness, something civil to each of us, with a very grave air, he quitted us.

Lord —— remained some minutes longer, which he spent in making a profusion of compliments to me, by which he prevented my hearing distinctly what Lord Orville said, to my

---

1 Slight misquote of Shakespeare's *Twelfth Night, or What You Will* I. v. 239-40. Viola (disguised as Cesario) describes Lady Olivia's unpainted face to her: "'Tis beauty truly blent, whose red and white Nature's own sweet and cunning hand laid on."

2 Gentlemen wore bags (wigs) and swords. A swabber is "one of a ship's crew whose business it was to swab the decks" or "one who behaves like a sailor of low rank; a low or unmannerly fellow; a term of contempt" (*OED*).

great vexation, especially as he looked – I thought so, at least, – as if displeased at his particularity of behaviour to me.

In going to an outward room, to wait for the carriage, I walked, and could not possibly avoid it, between this nobleman and Sir Clement Willoughby; and, when the servant said the coach stopped the way, though the latter offered me his hand, which I should much have preferred, this same Lord, without any ceremony, took mine himself; and Sir Clement, with a look extremely provoked, conducted Mrs. Mirvan.

In all ranks and all stations of life, how strangely do characters and manners differ! Lord Orville, with a politeness which knows no intermission, and makes no distinction, is as unassuming and modest, as if he had never mixed with the great, and was totally ignorant of every qualification he possesses; this other Lord, though lavish of compliments and fine speeches, seems to me an entire stranger to real good-breeding; whoever strikes his fancy, engrosses his whole attention. He is forward and bold, has an air of haughtiness towards men, and a look of libertinism towards women, and his conscious quality seems to have given him a freedom in his way of speaking to either sex, that is very little short of rudeness.

When we returned home, we were all low-spirited; the evening's entertainment had displeased the Captain, and his displeasure, I believe, disconcerted us all.

And here I thought to have concluded my letter; but, to my great surprise, just now we had a visit from Lord Orville. He called, he said, to pay his respects to us before we left town, and made many enquiries concerning our return; and, when Mrs. Mirvan told him we were going into the country without any view of again quitting it, he expressed his concern in such terms – so polite, so flattering, so serious – that I could hardly forbear being sorry myself. Were I to go immediately to Berry Hill, I am sure I should feel nothing but joy; – but, now we are joined by this Captain, and by Madame Duval, I must own I expect very little pleasure at Howard Grove.

Before Lord Orville went, Sir Clement Willoughby called. He was more grave than I had ever seen him, and made several attempts to speak to me in a low voice, and to assure me that his regret upon the occasion of our journey, was entirely upon my account. But I was not in spirits, and could not bear to be teazed by him. However, he has so well paid his court to Captain Mirvan, that he gave him a very hearty invitation to the Grove. At this, he brightened, – and, just then, Lord Orville took leave!

No doubt but he was disgusted at this ill-timed, ill-bred partiality; for surely it was very wrong to make an invitation before Lord Orville, in which he was not included! I was so much chagrined, that, as soon as he went, I left the room; and I shall not go down stairs till Sir Clement is gone.

Lord Orville cannot but observe his assiduous endeavours to ingratiate himself into my favour; and does not this extravagant civility of Captain Mirvan, give him reason to suppose, that it meets with our general approbation? I cannot think upon this subject, without inexpressible uneasiness; – and yet, I can think of nothing else.

Adieu, my dearest Sir. Pray write to me immediately. How many long letters has this one short fortnight[1] produced! More than I may, probably, ever write again: I fear I shall have tired you with reading them; but you will now have time to rest, for I shall find but little to say in future.

And now, most honoured Sir, with all the follies and imperfections which I have thus faithfully recounted, can you, and with unabated kindness, suffer me to sign myself

Your dutiful,
and most affectionate
EVELINA?

---

1  Mackinnon notes that Evelina arrives in town on Saturday April 2 and leaves April 20, which makes a stay of eighteen days, not fourteen, as the phrase "one short fortnight" would imply (520-21).

# LETTER XXIV.

*Mr. Villars to Evelina.*

Berry Hill, April 22.

How much do I rejoice that I can again address my letters to Howard Grove! My Evelina would have grieved, had she known the anxiety of my mind, during her residence in the great world. My apprehensions have been inexpressibly alarming; and your journal, at once exciting and relieving my fears, has almost wholly occupied me, since the time of your dating it from London.

Sir Clement Willoughby must be an artful, designing man; I am extremely irritated at his conduct. The passion he pretends for you has neither sincerity nor honour; the manner and the opportunities he has chosen to declare it, are bordering upon insult.

His unworthy behaviour after the opera, convinces me, that, had not your vehemence frightened him, Queen-Ann-street would have been the last place whither he would have ordered his chariot. O my child, how thankful am I for your escape! I need not now, I am sure, enlarge upon your indiscretion and want of thought, in so hastily trusting yourself with a man so little known to you, and whose gaiety and flightiness should have put you on your guard.

The nobleman you met at the Pantheon, bold and forward as you describe him to be, gives me no apprehension; a man who appears so openly licentious, and who makes his attack with so little regard to decorum, is one who, to a mind such as my Evelina's, can never be seen but with the disgust which his manners ought to excite.

But Sir Clement, though he seeks occasion to give real offence, contrives to avoid all appearance of intentional evil. He is far more dangerous, because more artful; but I am happy to observe, that he seems to have made no impression upon your heart, and therefore a very little care and prudence may secure you from those designs which I fear he has formed.

Lord Orville appears to be of a better order of beings. His spirited conduct to the meanly impertinent Lovel, and his anxiety for you after the opera, prove him to be a man of sense and of feeling. Doubtless he thought there was much reason to tremble for your safety, while exposed to the power of Sir Clement; and he acted with a regard to real honour, that will always incline me to think well of him, in so immediately acquainting the Mirvan family with your situation. Many men of this age, from a false and pretended delicacy to a friend, would have quietly pursued their own affairs, and thought it more honourable to leave an unsuspecting young creature to the mercy of a libertine, than to risk his displeasure by taking measures for her security.

Your evident concern at leaving London, is very natural; and yet it afflicts me. I ever dreaded your being too much pleased with a life of dissipation, which youth and vivacity render but too alluring; and I almost regret the consent for your journey, which I had not the resolution to withhold.

Alas, my child, the artlessness of your nature, and the simplicity of your education, alike unfit you for the thorny paths of the great and busy world. The supposed obscurity of your birth and situation, makes you liable to a thousand disagreeable adventures. Not only my views, but my hopes for your future life, have ever centered in the country. Shall I own to you, that, however I may differ from Captain Mirvan in other respects, yet my opinion of the town, its manners, inhabitants, and diversions, is much upon a level with his own? Indeed it is the general harbour of fraud and of folly, of duplicity and of impertinence; and I wish few things more fervently, than that you may have taken a lasting leave of it.

Remember, however, that I only speak in regard to a public and dissipated life; in private families, we may doubtless find as much goodness, honesty, and virtue, in London as in the country.

If contented with a retired station, I still hope I shall live to see my Evelina the ornament of her neighbourhood, and the pride and delight of her family: giving and receiving joy from such society as may best deserve her affection, and employing herself in such useful and innocent occupations as may secure and merit the tenderest love of her friends, and the worthiest satisfaction of her own heart.

Such are my hopes, and such have been my expectations. Disappoint them not, my beloved child, but chear me with a few lines, that may assure me, this one short fortnight spent in town, has not undone the work of seventeen years spent in the country.

. ARTHUR VILLARS.

## LETTER XXV.

*Evelina to the Rev. Mr. Villars.*

Howard Grove, April 25.

No, my dear Sir, no; *the work of seventeen years* remains such as it was, ever unworthy your time and your labour, but not more so now, – at least I hope not, – than before that fortnight which has so much alarmed you.

And yet, I must confess, that I am not half so happy here at present, as I was ere I went to town: but the change is in the place, not in me. Captain Mirvan and Madame Duval have ruined Howard Grove. The harmony that reigned here, is disturbed, our schemes are broken, our way of life is altered, and our comfort is destroyed. But do not suppose *London* to be the source of these evils; for, had our excursion been any where else, so disagreeable an addition to our houshold, must have caused the same change at our return.

I was sure you would be displeased with Sir Clement Willoughby, and therefore I am by no means surprised at what you say of him: but for Lord Orville – I must own I had greatly feared, that my weak and imperfect account would not have procured him the good opinion which he so well deserves, and which I am delighted to find you seem to have of him. O Sir, could I have done justice to the merit of which I believe him possessed, – could I have painted him to *you* such as he appeared to *me*, – then, indeed, you would have had some idea of the claim which he has to your approbation!

After the last letter which I wrote in town, nothing more passed previous to our journey hither, except a very violent quarrel between Captain Mirvan and Madame Duval. As the Captain intended to travel on horseback, he had settled that we four females should make use of his coach. Madame Duval did not come to Queen-Ann-street, till the carriage had waited some time at the door, and then, attended by Monsieur Du Bois, she made her appearance.

The Captain, impatient to be gone, would not suffer them to enter the house, but insisted that we should immediately get into the coach. We obeyed; but were no sooner seated, than Madame Duval said, "Come, Monsieur Du Bois, these girls can make very good room for you; sit closer, children."

Mrs. Mirvan looked quite confounded, and M. Du Bois, after making some apologies about crowding us, actually got into the coach, on the side with Miss Mirvan and me. But no sooner was he seated, than the Captain, who had observed this transaction very quietly, walked up to the coach-door, saying, "What, neither with your leave, nor by your leave?"

M. Du Bois seemed rather shocked, and began to make abundance of excuses; but the Captain neither understood nor regarded him, and, very roughly, said, "Look'ee, *Monseer*, this here may be a French fashion, for aught I know; – but Give and Take is fair in all nations; and so now, d'ye see, I'll make bold to shew you an English one."

And then, seizing his wrist, he made him jump out of the coach.

M. Du Bois instantly put his hand upon his sword, and threatened to resent this indignity. The Captain, holding up his stick, bid him draw at his peril. Mrs. Mirvan, greatly alarmed, got out of the coach, and, standing between them, entreated her husband to re-enter the house.

"None of your clack!" cried he, angrily, "what the D—l, do you suppose I can't manage a Frenchman?"

Mean time, Madame Duval called out to M. Du Bois, "*Eh, laissez-le, mon ami, ne le corrigez pas; c'est un vilain bête qui n'en vaut pas la peine.*"

"*Monsieur le Capitaine,*" cried M. Du Bois, "*voulez-vous bien me demander pardon?*"[1]

"O ho, you demand pardon; do you?" said the Captain, "I thought as much; I thought you'd come to; – so you have lost your relish for an English salutation, have you?" strutting up to him with looks of defiance.

A crowd was now gathering, and Mrs. Mirvan again besought her husband to go into the house.

"Why what a plague is the woman afraid of? – did you ever know a Frenchman that could not take an affront? – I warrant, *Monseer* knows what he is about; – don't you, *Monseer?*"

M. Du Bois, not understanding him, only said, "*plait-il, Monsieur?*"

"No, nor *dish* me, neither,"[2] answered the Captain; "but be that as it may, what signifies our parleying here? If you've any thing to propose, speak at once; if not, why let us go on our journey without more ado."

"*Parbleu, je n'entends rien, moi!*"[3] cried M. Du Bois, shrugging his shoulders, and looking very dismal.

Mrs. Mirvan then advanced to him, and said, in French, that she was sure the Captain had not any intention to affront him, and begged he would desist from a dispute which could only be productive of mutual misunderstanding, as neither of them knew the language of the other.

This sensible remonstrance had the desired effect, and M. Du Bois, making a bow to every one, except the Captain, very wisely gave up the point, and took leave.

We then hoped to proceed quietly on our journey; but the turbulent Captain would not yet permit us: he approached

---

1   "Leave him, my friend, don't correct him; he is an ignorant man who is not worth the trouble."
    "Captain, do you wish to ask my pardon?"
2   Captain Mirvan's pun on M. Du Bois's "plait-il" for "please, Sir" (as in, "What did you say?"). The slang term, to "dish," means "to 'do for,' defeat completely, ruin; to cheat, circumvent [from the notion of food being *done*, and *dished*]" (*OED*).
3   "Indeed, I understand nothing!"

Madame Duval with an exulting air, and said, "Why how's this, Madam? what, has your champion deserted you? why I thought you told me, that you old gentlewomen had it all your own way, among them French sparks?"

"As to that, Sir," answered she, "it's not of no consequence what you thought; for a person who can behave in such a low way, may think what he pleases for me, for I sha'n't mind."

"Why, then, Mistress, since you must needs make so free," cried he, "please to tell me the reason why you took the liberty for to ask any of your followers into my coach, without my leave? Answer me to that."

"Why then, pray, Sir," returned she, "tell me the reason why you took the liberty to treat the gentleman in such a unpolite way, as to take and pull him neck and heels out? I'm sure he had n't done nothing to affront you, nor nobody else; and I don't know what great hurt he would have done you, by just sitting still in the coach; he would not have eat it."

"What, do you think, then, that my horses have nothing to do, but to carry about your sniveling Frenchmen? If you do, Madam, I must make bold to tell you, you are out, for I'll see 'em hanged first."

"More brute you, then! for they've never carried nobody half so good."

"Why, look'ee, Madam, if you must needs provoke me, I'll tell you a piece of my mind; you must know, I can see as far into a mill-stone as another man;[1] and so, if you thought for to fob me off with one of your smirking French puppies for a son-in-law, why you'll find yourself in a hobble,[2] – that's all."

"Sir, you're a —— but I won't say what; – but, I protest, I had n't no such a thought, no more had n't Monsieur Du Bois."

"My dear," said Mrs. Mirvan, "we shall be very late."

"Well, well," answered he, "get away then; off with you, as fast as you can, it's high time. As to Molly, she's fine lady

---

1   "Used chiefly in ironical commendation of pretended extraordinary acuteness" (*OED*).
2   "An awkward or perplexing situation from which extrication is difficult" (*OED*). Bloom notes that "the expression conveys a legal threat for it was slang for 'seized, apprehended, taken up by a constable'" (412).

enough in all conscience; I want none of your French chaps to make her worse."

And so saying, he mounted his horse, and we drove off. And I could not but think with regret of the different feelings we experienced upon leaving London, to what had belonged to our entering it!

During the journey, Madame Duval was so very violent against the Captain, that she obliged Mrs. Mirvan to tell her, that, when in her presence, she must beg her to chuse some other subject of discourse.

We had a most affectionate reception from Lady Howard, whose kindness and hospitality cannot fail of making every body happy, who is disposed so to be.

Adieu, my dearest Sir. I hope, though I have hitherto neglected to mention it, that you have always remembered me to whoever has made any enquiry concerning me.


# LETTER XXVI.

*Evelina to the Rev. Mr. Villars.*

Howard Grove, April 27.

O my dear Sir, I now write in the greatest uneasiness! Madame Duval has made a proposal which terrifies me to death, and which was as unexpected, as it is shocking.

She had been employed for some hours this afternoon in reading letters from London, and, just about tea-time, she sent for me into her room, and said, with a look of great satisfaction, "Come here, child, I've got some very good news to tell you: something that will surprise you, I'll give you my word, for you ha'n't no notion of it."

I begged her to explain herself; and then, in terms which I cannot repeat, she said she had been considering what a shame it was, to see me such a poor country, shame-faced thing, when I ought to be a fine lady; and that she had long, and upon several occasions, blushed for me, though she must own the fault was none of mine: for nothing better could be expected from a girl who had been so immured. However, she assured me she had, at length, hit upon a plan, which would make quite another creature of me.

I waited, without much impatience, to hear what this preface led to; but I was soon awakened to more lively sensations, when she acquainted me, that her intention was to prove my birthright, and to claim, by law, the inheritance of my real family!

It would be impossible for me to express my extreme consternation, when she thus unfolded her scheme. My surprise and terror were equally great. I could say nothing; I heard her with a silence which I had not the power to break.

She then expatiated very warmly upon the advantages I should reap from her plan; talked in a high style of my future grandeur; assured me how heartily I should despise almost every body and every thing I had hitherto seen; predicted my marrying into some family of the first rank in the kingdom; and, finally, said I should spend a few months in Paris, where my education and manners might receive their last polish.

She enlarged also upon the delight she should have, in common with myself, from mortifying the pride of certain people, and shewing them, that she was not to be slighted with impunity.

In the midst of this discourse, I was relieved by a summons to tea. Madame Duval was in great spirits; but my emotion was too painful for concealment, and every body enquired into the cause. I would fain have waved the subject, but Madame Duval was determined to make it public. She told them, that she had it in her head to *make something* of me, and that they should soon call me by another name than that of Anville, and yet that she was not going to have the child married, neither.

I could not endure to hear her proceed, and was going to leave the room; which, when Lady Howard perceived, she begged Madame Duval would defer her intelligence to some other opportunity; but she was so eager to communicate her scheme, that she could bear no delay, and therefore they suffered me to go, without opposition. Indeed, whenever my situation or affairs are mentioned by Madame Duval, she speaks of them with such bluntness and severity, that I cannot be enjoined a task more cruel than to hear her.

I was afterwards acquainted with some particulars of the conversation by Miss Mirvan, who told me that Madame Duval informed them of her plan with the utmost complacency, and seemed to think herself very fortunate in having suggested it; but soon after, she accidentally betrayed, that she had been instigated to the scheme by her relations the Branghtons, whose letters, which she received to-day, first mentioned the proposal. She declared that she would have nothing to do with any *round-about ways*, but go openly and instantly to law, in order to prove my birth, real name, and title to the estate of my ancestors.

How impertinent and officious, in these Branghtons, to interfere thus in my concerns! You can hardly imagine what a disturbance this plan has made in the family. The Captain, without enquiring into any particulars of the affair, has peremptorily declared himself against it, merely because it has been proposed by Madame Duval, and they have battled the point together with great violence. Mrs. Mirvan says she will not even *think*, till she hears your opinion. But Lady Howard, to my great surprise, openly avows her approbation of Madame Duval's intention: however, she will write her reasons and sentiments upon the subject to you herself.

As to Miss Mirvan, she is my second self, and neither hopes nor fears but as I do. And as to *me*, – I know not what to say, nor even what to wish; I have often thought my fate peculiarly cruel, to have but one parent, and from that one to be banished for ever; – while, on the other side, I have but too well known and felt the propriety of the separation. And yet, you may much better imagine than I can express, the internal anguish which sometimes oppresses my heart, when I reflect upon the strange indifferency, that must occasion a father never to make the least enquiry after the health, the welfare, or even the life of his child!

O Sir, to *me*, the loss is nothing! – greatly, sweetly, and most benevolently have you guarded me from feeling it; – but for *him*, I grieve indeed! – I must be divested, not merely of all filial piety, but of all humanity, could I ever think upon this subject, and not be wounded to the soul.

Again I must repeat, I know not what to *wish*: think for me, therefore, my dearest Sir, and suffer my doubting mind, that knows not which way to direct its hopes, to be guided by your wisdom and unerring counsel.

EVELINA.

## LETTER XXVII.

*Lady Howard to the Rev. Mr. Villars.*

Howard Grove.

Dear Sir,

I cannot give a greater proof of the high opinion I have of your candour, than by the liberty I am now going to take, of presuming to offer you advice, upon a subject concerning which you have so just a claim to act for yourself: but I know you have too unaffected a love of justice, to be partially tenacious of your own judgment.

Madame Duval has been proposing a scheme which has put us all in commotion, and against which, at first, in common with the rest of my family, I exclaimed; but upon more mature consideration, I own my objections have almost wholly vanished.

This scheme is no other than to commence a law-suit with Sir John Belmont, to prove the validity of his marriage with Miss Evelyn; the necessary consequence of which proof, will be securing his fortune and estate to his daughter.

And why, my dear Sir, should not this be? I know that, upon first hearing, such a plan conveys ideas that must shock you; but I know, too, that your mind is superior to being governed by prejudices, or to opposing any important cause on account of a few disagreeable attendant circumstances.

Your lovely charge, now first entering into life, has merit

which ought not to be buried in obscurity. She seems born for an ornament to the world. Nature has been bountiful to her of whatever she had to bestow; and the peculiar attention you have given to her education, has formed her mind to a degree of excellence, that, in one so young, I have scarce ever seen equalled. Fortune, alone, has hitherto been sparing of her gifts; and she, too, now opens the way which leads to all that is left to wish for her.

What your reasons may have been, my good Sir, for so carefully concealing the birth, name, and pretensions of this amiable girl, and forbearing to make any claim upon Sir John Belmont, I am totally a stranger to; but, without knowing, I respect them, from the high opinion I have of your character and judgment: but I hope they are not insuperable; for I cannot but think, that it was never designed, for one who seems meant to grace the world, to have her life devoted to retirement.

Surely Sir John Belmont, wretch as he has shewn himself, could never see his accomplished daughter, and not be proud to own her, and eager to secure her the inheritance of his fortune. The admiration she met with in town, though merely the effect of her external attractions, was such, that Mrs. Mirvan assures me, she would have had the most splendid offers, had there not seemed to be some mystery in regard to her birth, which, she was well informed, was assiduously, though vainly, endeavoured to be discovered.

Can it be right, my dear Sir, that this promising young creature should be deprived of the fortune, and rank of life, to which she is lawfully entitled, and which you have prepared her to support and to use so nobly? To despise riches, may, indeed, be philosophic, but to dispense them worthily, must surely be more beneficial to mankind.

Perhaps a few years, or, indeed, a much shorter time, may make this scheme impracticable: Sir John, though yet young, leads a life too dissipated for long duration; and, when too late, we may regret that something was not sooner done; for it will be next to impossible, after he is gone, to settle or prove any thing with his heirs and executors.

Pardon the earnestness with which I write my sense of this affair; but your charming ward has made me so warmly her friend, that I cannot be indifferent upon a subject of such importance to her future life.

Adieu, my dear Sir; – send me speedily an answer to this remonstrance, and believe me to be, &c.

M. HOWARD.

## LETTER XXVIII.

*Mr. Villars to Lady Howard.*

Berry Hill, May 2.

Your letter, Madam, has opened a source of anxiety to which I look forward with dread, and which to see closed, I scarcely dare expect. I am unwilling to oppose my opinion to that of your Ladyship, nor, indeed, can I, but by arguments which, I believe, will rather rank me as a hermit, ignorant of the world, and fit only for my cell, than as a proper guardian, in an age such as this, for an accomplished young woman. Yet, thus called upon, it behoves me to explain, and endeavour to vindicate, the reasons by which I have been hitherto guided.

The mother of this dear child, – who was led to destruction by her own imprudence, the hardness of heart of Madame Duval, and the villainy of Sir John Belmont, – was once, what her daughter is now, the best beloved of my heart; and her memory, so long as my own holds, I shall love, mourn, and honour! On the fatal day that her gentle soul left its mansion, and not many hours ere she ceased to breathe, I solemnly plighted my faith, *That her child, if it lived, should know no father, but myself, or her acknowledged husband.*

You cannot, Madam, suppose that I found much difficulty in adhering to this promise, and forbearing to make any *claim* upon Sir John Belmont. Could I feel an affection the most paternal for this poor sufferer, and not abominate her destroyer?

Could I wish to deliver to *him*, who had so basely betrayed the mother, the helpless and innocent offspring, who, born in so much sorrow, seemed entitled to all the compassionate tenderness of pity?

For many years, the *name* alone of that man, accidentally spoken in my hearing, almost divested me of my christianity, and scarce could I forbear to execrate him. Yet I sought not, neither did I desire, to deprive him of his child, had he, with any appearance of contrition, or, indeed, of humanity, endeavoured to become less unworthy such a blessing; – but he is a stranger to all parental feelings, and has, with a savage insensibility, forborne to enquire even into the existence of this sweet orphan, though the situation of his injured wife was but too well known to him.

You wish to be acquainted with my intentions. – I must acknowledge, they were such as I now perceive would not be honoured with your Ladyship's approbation: for though I have sometimes thought of presenting Evelina to her father, and demanding the justice which is her due, yet, at other times, I have both disdained and feared the application; disdained, lest it should be refused, and feared, lest it should be accepted!

Lady Belmont, who was firmly persuaded of her approaching dissolution, frequently and earnestly besought me, that if her infant was a female, I would not abandon her to the direction of a man so wholly unfit to take the charge of her education; but, should she be importunately demanded, that I would retire with her abroad, and carefully conceal her from Sir John, till some apparent change in his sentiments and conduct should announce him less improper for such a trust. And often would she say, "Should the poor babe have any feelings correspondent with its mother's, it will have no want, while under your protection." Alas! she had no sooner quitted it herself, than she was plunged into a gulph of misery, that swallowed up her peace, reputation, and life.

During the childhood of Evelina, I suggested a thousand plans for the security of her birth-right; – but I as oftentimes rejected them. I was in a perpetual conflict, between the desire that she should have justice done her, and the apprehension that, while I improved her fortune, I should endanger her mind. However, as her character began to be formed, and her disposition to be displayed, my perplexity abated; the road before me seemed less thorny and intricate, and I thought I could perceive the right path from the wrong: for, when I observed the artless openness, the ingenuous simplicity of her nature; when I saw that her guileless and innocent soul fancied all the world to be pure and disinterested as herself, and that her heart was open to every impression with which love, pity, or art might assail it; – then did I flatter myself, that to follow my own inclination, and to secure her welfare, was the same thing; since, to expose her to the snares and dangers inevitably encircling a house of which the master is dissipated and unprincipled, without the guidance of a mother, or any prudent and sensible female, seemed to me no less than suffering her to stumble into some dreadful pit, when the sun was in its meridian. My plan, therefore, was not merely to educate and to cherish her as my own, but to adopt her the heiress of my small fortune, and to bestow her upon some worthy man, with whom she might spend her days in tranquillity, chearfulness, and good-humour, untainted by vice, folly, or ambition.

So much for the time past. Such have been the motives by which I have been governed; and I hope they will be allowed not merely to account for, but also to justify, the conduct which has resulted from them. It now remains to speak of the time to come.

And here, indeed, I am sensible of difficulties which I almost despair of surmounting according to my wishes. I pay the highest deference to your Ladyship's opinion, which it is extremely painful to me not to concur with; yet, I am so well acquainted with your goodness, that I presume to hope it would not be absolutely impossible for me to offer such arguments as might lead you to think with me, that this young creature's chance of happiness seems less doubtful in retirement, than it would be in the gay and dissipated world: but why should I perplex your Ladyship with reasoning that can turn to so little account? for, alas! what arguments, what persuasions can I make use of, with any prospect of success, to such a woman as Madame Duval? Her character, and the violence of her disposition, intimidate me from making the attempt: she is too ignorant for instruction, too obstinate for entreaty, and too weak for reason.

I will not, therefore, enter into a contest from which I have nothing to expect but altercation and impertinence. As soon would I discuss the effect of sound with the deaf, or the nature of colours with the blind, as aim at illuminating with conviction a mind so warped by prejudice, so much the slave of unruly and illiberal passions. Unused as she is to controul, persuasion would but harden, and opposition incense her. I yield, therefore, to the necessity which compels my reluctant acquiescence, and shall now turn all my thoughts upon considering of such methods for conducting this enterprize, as may be most conducive to the happiness of my child, and least liable to wound her sensibility.

The law-suit, therefore, I wholly and absolutely disapprove.

Will you, my dear Madam, forgive the freedom of an old man, if I own myself greatly surprised, that you could, even for a moment, listen to a plan so violent, so public, so totally repugnant to all female delicacy? I am satisfied your Ladyship has not weighed this project. There was a time, indeed, when, to assert the innocence of Lady Belmont, and to blazon[1] to the world the *wrongs*, not *guilt*, by which she suffered, I proposed, nay attempted, a similar plan: but then, all assistance and encouragement was denied. How cruel to the remembrance I bear of her woes, is this tardy resentment of Madame Duval! She was deaf to the voice of Nature, though she has hearkened to that of Ambition.

Never can I consent to have this dear and timid girl brought forward to the notice of the world by such a method; a method, which will subject her to all the impertinence of curiosity, the sneers of conjecture, and the stings of ridicule. And for what? – the attainment of wealth, which she does not want, and the gratification of vanity, which she does not feel. – A child to appear against a father! – no, Madam, old and infirm

---

1  "To describe fitly, set forth honourably in words, ... to proclaim, make public" (*OED*).

as I am, I would even yet sooner convey her myself to some remote part of the world, though I were sure of dying in the expedition.

Far different had been the motives which would have stimulated her unhappy mother to such a proceeding; all her felicity in this world was irretrievably lost; her life was become a burthen to her, and her fair fame, which she had early been taught to prize above all other things, had received a mortal wound: therefore, to clear her own honour, and to secure from blemish the birth of her child, was all the good which Fortune had reserved herself the *power* of bestowing. But even this last consolation was with-held from her!

Let milder measures be adopted; and – since it must be so, – let application be made to Sir John Belmont; but as to a lawsuit, I hope, upon this subject, never more to hear it mentioned.

With Madame Duval, all pleas of delicacy would be ineffectual; her scheme must be opposed by arguments better suited to her understanding. I will not, therefore, talk of its impropriety, but endeavour to prove its inutility. Have the goodness, then, to tell her, that her own intentions would be frustrated by her plan, since, should the law-suit be commenced, and even should the cause be gained, Sir John Belmont would still have it in his power, and, if irritated, no doubt in his inclination, to cut off her grand-daughter with a shilling.[1]

She cannot do better, herself, than to remain quiet and inactive in the affair: the long and mutual animosity between her and Sir John, will make her interference merely productive of debates and ill-will. Neither would I have Evelina appear till summoned. And as to myself, I must wholly decline *acting*, though I will, with unwearied zeal, devote all my thoughts to giving counsel: but, in truth, I have neither inclination nor spirits adequate to engaging personally with this man.

My opinion is, that he would pay more respect to a letter

---

1   Doody notes that "it was legally safer to disinherit someone specifically by mentioning that person by name in the will and bequeathing the lowest sum legally convenient, a token shilling; an individual not named in a will could claim that a natural or inevitable claim had been overlooked" (472 n. 209).

from your Ladyship upon this subject, than from any other person. I therefore advise and hope, that you will yourself take the trouble of writing to him, in order to open the affair. When he shall be inclined to see Evelina, I have for him a posthumous letter, which his much-injured lady left to be presented to him, if ever such a meeting should take place.

The views of the Branghtons, in suggesting this scheme, are obviously interested; they hope, by securing to Evelina the fortune of her father, to induce Madame Duval to settle her own upon themselves. In this, however, they would probably be mistaken, for little minds have ever a propensity to bestow their wealth upon those who are already in affluence, and, therefore, the less her grand-child requires her assistance, the more gladly she will give it.

I have but one thing more to add, from which, however, I can by no means recede: my word so solemnly given to Lady Belmont, that her child should never be owned[1] but with herself, must be inviolably adhered to.

> I am, dear Madam, with great respect,
> Your Ladyship's most obedient servant,
> ARTHUR VILLARS.

## LETTER XXIX.

*Mr. Villars to Evelina.*

Berry Hill, May 2.

How sincerely do I sympathise in the uneasiness and concern which my beloved Evelina has so much reason to feel! The cruel scheme in agitation is equally repugnant to my judgment and my inclination, – yet to oppose it, seems impracticable. To follow the dictates of my own heart, I should instantly recall you to myself, and never more consent to your being separated from me; but the manners and opinion of the world demand a

---

1  Acknowledged.

different conduct. Hope, however, for the best, and be satisfied you shall meet with no indignity; if you are not received into your own family as you ought to be, and with the distinction that is your due, you shall leave it for ever; and, once again restored to my protection, secure your own tranquillity, and make, as you have hitherto done, all the happiness of my life!

## LETTER XXX.

*Evelina to the Rev. Mr. Villars.*

Howard Grove, May 6.

The die is thrown, and I attend the event in trembling! Lady Howard has written to Paris, and sent her letter to town, to be forwarded in the ambassador's packet, and in less than a fortnight, therefore, she expects an answer. O Sir, with what anxious impatience shall I wait its arrival! upon it seems to depend the fate of my future life. My solicitude is so great, and my suspence so painful, that I cannot rest a moment in peace, or turn my thoughts into any other channel.

Deeply interested as I now am in the event, most sincerely do I regret that the plan was ever proposed: methinks it *cannot* end to my satisfaction; for either I must be torn from the arms of my *more* than father, – or I must have the misery of being finally convinced, that I am cruelly rejected by him who has the natural claim to that dear title; a title, which to write, mention, or think of, fills my whole soul with filial tenderness.

The subject is discussed here eternally. Captain Mirvan and Madame Duval, as usual, quarrel whenever it is started: but I am so wholly engrossed by my own reflections, that I cannot even listen to them. My imagination changes the scene perpetually: one moment, I am embraced by a kind and relenting parent, who takes me to that heart from which I have hitherto been banished, and supplicates, through me, peace and forgiveness from the ashes of my mother! – at another, he regards me with detestation, considers me as the living image of an injured saint, and repulses me with horror! – But I will not afflict you with the melancholy phantasms of my brain. I will endeavour to compose my mind to a more tranquil state, and forbear to write again, till I have, in some measure, succeeded.

May heaven bless you, my dearest Sir! and long, long may it continue you on earth, to bless

Your grateful
EVELINA!

## LETTER XXXI.

*Lady Howard to Sir John Belmont, Bart.*

Howard Grove, May 5.

Sir,

You will, doubtless, be surprised at receiving a letter from one who had for so short a period the honour of your acquaintance, and that at so great a distance of time; but the motive which has induced me to take this liberty, is of so delicate a nature, that were I to commence making apologies for my officiousness, I fear my letter would be too long for your patience.

You have, probably, already conjectured the subject upon which I mean to treat. My regard for Mr. Evelyn and his amiable daughter was well known to you: nor can I ever cease to be interested in whatever belongs to their memory or family.

I must own myself somewhat distressed in what manner to introduce the purport of my writing; yet, as I think that, in affairs of this kind, frankness is the first requisite to a good understanding between the parties concerned, I will neither torment you nor myself with punctilious ceremonies, but proceed instantly and openly to the business which occasions my giving you this trouble.

I presume, Sir, it would be superfluous to tell you, that your child resides still in Dorsetshire, and is still under the protection of the Reverend Mr. Villars, in whose house she was born: for, though no enquiries concerning her have reached his ears, or mine, I can never suppose it possible you have forborne to make them. It only remains, therefore, to tell you, that your daughter is now grown up; that she has been educated with the utmost care, and the utmost success; and that she is now a most deserving, accomplished, and amiable young woman.

Whatever may be your view for her future destination in life, it seems time to declare it. She is greatly admired, and, I doubt not, will be very much sought after: it is proper, therefore, that her future expectations, and your pleasure concerning her, should be made known.

Believe me, Sir, she merits your utmost attention and regard. You could not see and know her, and remain unmoved by those sensations of affection which belong to so near and tender a relationship. She is the lovely resemblance of her lovely mother; − pardon, Sir, the liberty I take in mentioning that unfortunate lady, but I think it behoves me, upon this occasion, to shew the esteem I felt for her; allow me, therefore, to say, and be not offended at my freedom, that the memory of that excellent lady has but too long remained under the aspersions of calumny; surely it is time to vindicate her fame! − and how can that be done in a manner more eligible, more grateful to her friends, or more honourable to yourself, than by openly receiving as your child, *the daughter of the late Lady Belmont*?

The venerable man who has had the care of her education, deserves your warmest acknowledgments, for the unremitting pains he has taken, and attention he has shewn, in the discharge of his trust. Indeed she has been peculiarly fortunate in meeting with such a friend and guardian: a more worthy man, or one whose character seems nearer to perfection, does not exist.

Permit me to assure you, Sir, she will amply repay whatever regard and favour you may hereafter shew her, by the comfort and happiness you cannot fail to find in her affection and duty. To be owned *properly* by you, is the first wish of her heart; and I am sure, that to merit your approbation will be the first study of her life.

I fear that you will think this address impertinent; but I must rest upon the goodness of my intention to plead my excuse. I am, Sir,

Your most obedient humble servant,
M. HOWARD.

## END OF THE FIRST VOLUME.

EVELINA,

OR, A

YOUNG LADY'S

ENTRANCE

INTO THE

WORLD.

IN A SERIES OF LETTERS.

The Second Edition.

VOL. II.

LONDON:
Printed for T. Lowndes, N° 77, in
Fleet-Street.

M.DCC.LXXIX.

# EVELINA

## IN A SERIES OF LETTERS.

## LETTER I.

*Evelina to the Rev. Mr. Villars.*

Howard Grove, Kent, May 10.

OUR house has been enlivened to-day, by the arrival of a London visitor; and the necessity I have been under of concealing the uneasiness of my mind, has made me exert myself so effectually, that I even think it is really diminished; or, at least, my thoughts are not so totally, so very anxiously occupied by one only subject, as they lately were.

I was strolling this morning with Miss Mirvan, down a lane about a mile from the grove, when we heard the trampling of horses; and, fearing the narrowness of the passage, we were turning hastily back, but stopped upon hearing a voice call out "Pray, Ladies, don't be frightened, for I will walk my horse." We turned again, and then saw Sir Clement Willoughby. He dismounted, and approaching us, with the reins in his hand, presently recollected us. "Good Heaven," cried he, with his usual quickness, "do I see Miss Anville? – and you, too, Miss Mirvan?"

He immediately ordered his servant to take charge of his horse, and then, advancing to us, took a hand of each, which he pressed to his lips, and said a thousand fine things concerning his good fortune, our improved looks, and the charms of the country, when inhabited by such rural deities. "The town, Ladies, has languished since your absence, – or, at least, I have so much languished myself, as to be absolutely insensible to all it had to offer. One refreshing breeze, such as I now enjoy, awakens me to new vigour, life, and spirit. But I never before had the good luck to see the country in such perfection."

"Has not almost every body left town, Sir?" said Miss Mirvan.

"I am ashamed to answer you, Madam – but indeed it is as full as ever, and will continue so, till after the birth-day.[1] However, you Ladies were so little seen, that there are but few who know what it has lost. For my own part, I felt it too sensibly, to be able to endure the place any longer."

"Is there any body remaining there, that we were acquainted with!" cried I.

"O yes, Ma'am." And then he named two or three persons we had seen when with him; but he did not mention Lord Orville, and I would not ask him, lest he should think me curious. Perhaps, if he stays here some time, he may speak of him by accident.

He was proceeding in this complimentary style, when we were met by the Captain; who no sooner perceived Sir Clement, than he hastened up to him, gave him a hearty shake of the hand, a cordial slap on the back, and some other equally gentle tokens of satisfaction, assuring him of his great joy at his visit, and declaring he was as glad to see him as if he had been a messenger who brought news that a French ship was sunk.[2] Sir Clement, on the other side, expressed himself with equal warmth, and protested he had been so eager to pay his respects to Captain Mirvan, that he had left London in its full lustre, and a thousand engagements unanswered, merely to give himself that pleasure.

"We shall have rare sport," said the Captain, "for do you know the old French-woman is among us? 'Fore George, I have scarce made any use of her yet, by reason I have had nobody with me that could enjoy a joke: howsomever, it shall go hard but we'll have some diversion now."

---

1 King George III's birthday, June 4, the final major event of the London season, after which many people returned to their country homes.

2 A reference to Captain Mirvan's professional involvement as a member of the English navy with the French at sea in recent engagements.

Sir Clement very much approved of the proposal; and we then went into the house, where he had a very grave reception from Mrs. Mirvan, who is by no means pleased with his visit, and a look of much discontent from Madame Duval, who said to me, in a low voice, "I'd as soon have seen Old Nick as that man, for he's the most impertinentest person in the world, and is n't never of my side."

The Captain is now actually occupied in contriving some scheme which, he says, is *to play the old Dowager off;*[1] and so eager and delighted is he at the idea, that he can scarcely constrain his raptures sufficiently to conceal his design, even from herself. I wish, however, since I do not dare put Madame Duval upon her guard, that he had the delicacy not to acquaint me with his intention.

## LETTER II.

*Evelina in continuation.*

May 13th.

The Captain's operations are begun, – and, I hope, ended; for indeed, poor Madame Duval has already but too much reason to regret Sir Clement's visit to Howard Grove.

Yesterday morning, during breakfast, as the Captain was reading the news-paper, Sir Clement suddenly begged to look at it, saying he wanted to know if there was any account of a transaction, at which he had been present the evening before his journey hither, concerning a poor Frenchman, who had got into a scrape which might cost him his life.

The Captain demanded particulars; and then Sir Clement told a long story, of being with a party of country friends, at the Tower, and hearing a man call out for mercy in French; and

---

1 To play off is "To set in opposition, oppose, pit (one person, thing, or party against another), esp. for one's own advantage" (*OED*). Captain Mirvan's reference to Madame Duval as "an old dowager," while disrespectful in the use of the adjective "old," does recognize her standing as a titled, or in this case, propertied widow, and possibly therefore a worthy opponent.

that, when he enquired into the occasion of his distress, he was informed, that he had been taken up upon suspicion of treasonable practices against the government.[1] "The poor fellow," continued he, "no sooner found that I spoke French, than he besought me to hear him, protesting that he had no evil designs; that he had been but a short time in England, and only waited the return of a Lady from the country, to quit it for ever."

Madame Duval changed colour, and listened with the utmost attention.

"Now, though I by no means approve of so many foreigners continually flocking into our country," added he, addressing himself to the Captain, "yet I could not help pitying the poor wretch, because he did not know enough of English to make his defence: however, I found it impossible to assist him, for the mob would not suffer me to interfere. In truth, I am afraid he was but roughly handled."

"Why, did they duck him?"[2] said the Captain.

"Something of that sort," answered he.

"So much the better! so much the better!" cried the Captain, "an impudent French puppy! – I'll bet you what you will he was a rascal. I only wish all his countrymen were served the same."

"I wish you had been in his place, with all my soul!" cried Madame Duval, warmly; – "but pray, Sir, did n't nobody know who this poor gentleman was?"

"Why, I did hear his name," answered Sir Clement, "but I cannot recollect it."

"It was n't, – it was n't – Du Bois?" stammered out Madame Duval.

"The very name!" answered he, "yes, Du Bois, I remember it now."

Madame Duval's cup fell from her hand, as she repeated "Du Bois! Monsieur Du Bois, did you say?"

---

1  At the time of the novel's publication, England was at war with the American colonies; France signed a treaty with the American colonies in 1778, and was thereby at war with England. Given this alliance, England was suspicious of the French who came to England during this time.

2  "To plunge (a person or thing) in, into, or under water" (*OED*).

"Du Bois! why that's *my* friend," cried the Captain, that's *Monseer Slippery,* i'n't it? – Why he's plaguy fond of sousing[1] work; howsomever, I'll be sworn they gave him his fill of it."

"And I'll be sworn," cried Madame Duval, "that you're a – but I don't believe nothing about it, so you need n't be so over-joyed, for I dare say it was no more Monsieur Du Bois than I am."

"I thought at the time," said Sir Clement, very gravely, "that I had seen the gentleman before, and now I recollect, I think it was in company with you, Madam."

"With *me*, Sir!" cried Madame Duval.

"Say you so!" said the Captain, "why then, it must be he, as sure as you're alive! – Well but, my good friend, what will they do with poor *Monseer*?"

"It is difficult to say," answered Sir Clement, very thought-fully, "but I should suppose, that if he has not good friends to appear for him, he will be in a very unpleasant situation; for these are serious sort of affairs."

"Why, do you think they'll hang him?" demanded the Captain.

Sir Clement shook his head, but made no answer.

Madame Duval could no longer contain her agitation; she started from her chair, repeating, with a voice half choaked, "Hang him! – they can't, – they sha'n't, – let them at their peril! – however, it's all false, and I won't believe a word of it; – but I'll go to town this very moment, and see M. Du Bois myself; – I won't wait for nothing."

Mrs. Mirvan begged her not to be alarmed; but she flew out of the room, and up stairs into her own apartment. Lady Howard blamed both the gentlemen for having been so abrupt, and followed her. I would have accompanied her, but the Captain stopped me; and, having first laughed very heartily, said he was going to read his commission to his ship's company.[2]

"Now, do you see," said he, "as to Lady Howard, I sha'n't pretend for to enlist her into my service, and so I shall e'en

---

1  "Drenching, soaking" (*OED*).

2  "To order (a ship) for active service, put in commission; to assume the charge of (a ship) as the commanding officer" (*OED*).

leave her to make it out as well as she can; but as to all you, I expect obedience and submission to orders; I am now upon a hazardous expedition, having undertaken to convoy a crazy vessel[1] to the shore of Mortification; so, d'ye see, if any of you have any thing to propose, that will forward the enterprize, – why speak and welcome; but if any of you, that are of my chosen crew, capitulate, or enter into any treaty with the enemy, – I shall look upon you as mutinying, and turn you adrift."[2]

Having finished this harangue, which was interlarded with many expressions, and sea-phrases, that I cannot recollect, he gave Sir Clement a wink of intelligence, and left us to ourselves.

Indeed, notwithstanding the attempts I so frequently make of writing some of the Captain's conversation, I can only give you a faint idea of his language; for almost every other word he utters, is accompanied by an oath, which, I am sure, would be as unpleasant for you to read, as for me to write. And, besides, he makes use of a thousand sea-terms, which are to me quite unintelligible.

Poor Madame Duval sent to enquire at all probable places, whether she could be conveyed to town in any stage-coach; but the Captain's servant brought her for answer, that no London stage would pass near Howard Grove till to-day. She then sent to order a chaise; but was soon assured, that no horses could be procured. She was so much inflamed by these disappointments, that she threatened to set out for town on foot, and it was with difficulty that Lady Howard dissuaded her from this mad scheme.

The whole morning was filled up with these enquiries. But, when we were all assembled to dinner, she endeavoured to appear perfectly unconcerned, and repeatedly protested that she gave not any credit to the report, as far as it regarded M. Du Bois, being very certain that he was not the person in question.

---

1  "Full of cracks or flaws; damaged, impaired, unsound; liable to break or fall to pieces; frail, 'shaky.' (Now usually used of ships …)" (*OED*).

2  Crew members who unsuccessfully rebelled against their commander could be hung, but instead were often put off the ship with few provisions and little prospect for survival.

The Captain used the most provoking efforts to convince her that she deceived herself; while Sir Clement, with more art, though not less malice, affected to be of her opinion; but, at the same time that he pretended to relieve her uneasiness, by saying that he doubted not having mistaken the name, he took care to enlarge upon the danger to which the *unknown gentleman* was exposed, and expressed great concern at his perilous situation.

Dinner was hardly removed, when a letter was delivered to Madame Duval. The moment she had read it, she hastily demanded from whom it came? "A country boy brought it," answered the servant, "but he would not wait."

"Run after him this instant!" cried she, "and be sure you bring him back. *Mon Dieu! quel avanture! que ferai-je?*"[1]

"What's the matter? what's the matter?" said the Captain.

"Why nothing, – nothing's the matter. *O mon Dieu!*"

And she rose, and walked about the room.

"Why, what – has *Monseer* sent to you?" continued the Captain: "is that there letter from him?"

"No, – it i'n't; – besides, if it is, it's nothing to you."

"O then, I'm sure it is! Pray now, Madame, don't be so close; come, tell us all about it, – what does he say? how did he relish the horse-pond? – which did he find best, sousing *single* or *double*? – 'Fore George, 'twas plaguy unlucky you was not with him!"

"It's no such a thing, Sir," cried she, very angrily, "and if you're so very fond of a horse-pond, I wish you'd put yourself into one, and not be always a thinking about other people's being served so."

The man then came in, to acquaint her they could not overtake the boy. She scolded violently, and was in such perturbation, that Lady Howard interfered, and begged to know the cause of her uneasiness, and whether she could assist her?

Madame Duval cast her eyes upon the Captain and Sir Clement, and said she should be glad to speak to her Ladyship, without so many witnesses.

---

1   "My God! what a thing! what shall I do?"

"Well, then, Miss Anville," said the Captain, turning to me, "do you and Molly go into another room, and stay there till Mrs. Duval has opened her mind to us."

"So you may think, Sir," cried she, "but who's fool then? no, no, you need n't trouble yourself to make a ninny of me, neither, for I'm not so easily taken in, I'll assure you."

Lady Howard then invited her into the dressing-room, and I was desired to attend her.

As soon as we had shut the door, "O my Lady," exclaimed Madame Duval, "here's the most cruellest thing in the world has happened! – But that Captain is such a beast, I can't say nothing before him, – but it's all true! poor M. Du Bois is tooked up!"

Lady Howard begged her to be comforted, saying that, as M. Du Bois was certainly innocent, there could be no doubt of his ability to clear himself.

"To be sure, my Lady," answered she, "I know he is innocent; and to be sure they'll never be so wicked as to hang him for nothing?"

"Certainly not;" replied Lady Howard, "you have no reason to be uneasy. This is not a country where punishment is inflicted without proof."[1]

"Very true, my Lady; but the worst thing is this; I cannot bear that that fellow, the Captain, should know about it; for if he does, I sha'n't never hear the last of it; – no more won't poor M. Du Bois."

"Well, well," said Lady Howard, "shew me the letter, and I will endeavour to advise you."

The letter was then produced. It was signed by the clerk of a country justice; who acquainted her, that a prisoner, then upon trial for suspicion of treasonable practices against the government, was just upon the point of being committed to jail, but

---

1 Opposing Britain's due process of law with France's *lettres de cachet* or secret letters which were issued by the king's ministers in order to cut through bureaucratic red tape; sometimes used constructively to right a wrong, they could just as easily be used despotically. Ariel Durant and Will Durant note that "any offense to a noble by a commoner, any major criticism of the government, might bring a 'lettre de cachet' and imprisonment without trial or stated cause" (*The Story of Civilization*, Vol. 9 [New York: Simon and Schuster, 1954-75], 267).

having declared that he was known to her, this clerk had been prevailed upon to write, in order to enquire if she really could speak to the character and family of a Frenchman who called himself Pierre Du Bois.

When I heard the letter, I was quite amazed at its success. So improbable did it seem, that a foreigner should be taken before a *country* justice of peace, for a crime of so dangerous a nature,[1] that I cannot imagine how Madame Duval could be alarmed, even for a moment. But, with all her violence of temper, I see that she is easily frightened, and, in fact, more cowardly than many who have not half her spirit; and so little does she reflect upon circumstances, or probability, that she is continually the dupe of her own – I ought not to say *ignorance*, but yet, I can think of no other word.

I believe that Lady Howard, from the beginning of the transaction, suspected some contrivance of the Captain, and this letter, I am sure, must confirm her suspicion: however, though she is not at all pleased with his frolick, yet she would not hazard the consequence of discovering his designs: her looks, her manner, and her character, made me draw this conclusion from her apparent perplexity; for not a word did she say, that implied any doubt of the authenticity of the letter. Indeed there seems to be a sort of tacit agreement between her and the Captain, that she should not appear to be acquainted with his schemes; by which means she at once avoids quarrels, and supports her dignity.

While she was considering what to propose, Madame Duval begged to have the use of her Ladyship's chariot, that she might go immediately to the assistance of her friend. Lady Howard politely assured her, that it would be extremely at her service; and then Madame Duval besought her not to own to the Captain what had happened, protesting that she could not endure he should know poor M. Du Bois had met with so unfortunate an accident. Lady Howard could not help smiling, though she readily promised not to *inform* the Captain of the affair. As to

---

1    If Du Bois had been arrested for such a serious crime as treason in London, he would have been brought before a magistrate there, not transferred to a country magistrate.

me, she desired my attendance; which I was by no means rejoiced at, as I was certain she was going upon a fruitless errand.

I was then commissioned to order the chariot.

At the foot of the stairs I met the Captain, who was most impatiently waiting the result of the conference. In an instant we were joined by Sir Clement. A thousand enquiries were then made concerning Madame Duval's opinion of the letter, and her intentions upon it: and when I would have left them, Sir Clement, pretending equal eagerness with the Captain, caught my hand, and repeatedly detained me, to ask some frivolous question, to the answer of which he must be totally indifferent. At length, however, I broke from them; they retired into the parlour, and I executed my commission.

The carriage was soon ready, and Madame Duval having begged Lady Howard to say she was not well, stole softly down stairs, desiring me to follow her. The chariot was ordered at the garden-door; and when we were seated, she told the man, according to the clerk's directions, to drive to Mr. Justice Tyrell's, asking, at the same time, how many miles off he lived?

I expected he would have answered that he knew of no such person; but, to my great surprise, he said, "Why 'Squire Tyrell lives about nine miles beyond the park."

"Drive fast, then," cried she, "and you sha'n't be no worse for it."

During our ride, which was extremely tedious, she tormented herself with a thousand fears for M. Du Bois' safety; and piqued herself very much upon having escaped unseen by the Captain, not only that she avoided his triumph, but because she knew him to be so much M. Du Bois' enemy, that she was sure he would prejudice the Justice against him, and endeavour to take away his life. For my part, I was quite ashamed of being engaged in so ridiculous an affair, and could only think of the absurd appearance we should make upon our arrival at Mr. Tyrell's.

When we had been out near two hours, and expected every moment to stop at the place of our destination, I observed that Lady Howard's servant, who attended us on horseback, rode on forward till he was out of sight, and soon after returning, came up to the chariot-window, and delivering a note to Madame Duval, said he had met a boy, who was just coming with it to Howard Grove, from the Clerk of Mr. Tyrell.

While she was reading it, he rode round to the other window, and, making a sign for secrecy, put into my hand a slip of paper, on which was written, "Whatever happens, be not alarmed, – for *you* are safe, – though you endanger all mankind!"

I readily imagined that Sir Clement must be the author of this note, which prepared me to expect some disagreeable adventure: but I had no time to ponder upon it, for Madame Duval had no sooner read her own letter, than, in an angry tone of voice, she exclaimed, "Why now what a thing is this! here we're come all this way for nothing!"

She then gave me the note, which informed her, that she need not trouble herself to go to Mr. Tyrell's, as the prisoner had had the address[1] to escape. I congratulated her upon this fortunate incident; but she was so much concerned at having rode so far in vain, that she seemed less pleased than provoked. However, she ordered the man to make what haste he could home, as she hoped, at least, to return before the Captain should suspect what had passed.

The carriage turned about, and we journeyed so quietly for near an hour, that I began to flatter myself we should be suffered to proceed to Howard Grove without further molestation, when, suddenly, the footman called out, "John, are we going right?"

"Why, I a'n't sure," said the coachman, "but I'm afraid we turned wrong."

"What do you mean by that, Sirrah?" said Madame Duval, "why if you lose your way, we shall be all in the dark."

"I think we should turn to the left," said the footman.

"To the left!" answered the other, "No, no, I'm partly sure we should turn to the right."

"You had better make some enquiry," said I.

---

1  "Skill, dexterity, adroitness" (*OED*).

"*Ma foi*," cried Madame Duval, "we're in a fine hole, here! – they neither of them know no more than the post. However, I'll tell my Lady, as sure as you're born, so you'd better find the way."

"Let's try this lane" said the footman.

"No," said the coachman, "that's the road to Canterbury; we had best go straight on."

"Why that's the direct London road," returned the footman, "and will lead us twenty miles about."

"*Pardi*," cried Madame Duval, "why they won't go one way nor t'other! and, now we're come all this jaunt for nothing, I suppose we sha'n't get home to-night!"

"Let's go back to the public-house," said the footman, "and ask for a guide."

"No, no," said the other, "if we stay here a few minutes, somebody or other will pass by: and the horses are almost knocked up already."

"Well, I protest," cried Madame Duval, "I'd give a guinea to see them sots both horse-whipped! As sure as I'm alive, they're drunk! Ten to one but they'll overturn us next!"

After much debating, they, at length, agreed to go on, till we came to some inn, or met with a passenger who could direct us. We soon arrived at a small farm-house, and the footman alighted, and went into it.

In a few minutes he returned, and told us we might proceed, for that he had procured a direction; "But," added he, "it seems there are some thieves hereabouts; and so the best way will be for you to leave your watches and purses with the farmer, who I know very well, and who is an honest man, and a tenant of my Lady's."

"Thieves!" cried Madame Duval, looking aghast, "the Lord help us! – I've no doubt but we shall be all murdered!"

The farmer came up to us, and we gave him all we were worth, and the servants followed our example. We then proceeded, and Madame Duval's anger so entirely subsided, that, in the mildest manner imaginable, she intreated them to make haste, and promised to tell their Lady how diligent and obliging they had been. She perpetually stopped them, to ask if they apprehended any danger; and was, at length, so much overpowered by her fears, that she made the footman fasten his horse to the back of the carriage, and then come and seat himself within it. My endeavours to encourage her were fruitless; she sat in the middle, held the man by the arm, and protested that if he did but save her life, she would make his fortune. Her uneasiness gave me much concern, and it was with the utmost difficulty I forbore to acquaint her that she was imposed upon; but the mutual fear of the Captain's resentment to me, and of her own to him, neither of which would have any moderation, deterred me. As to the footman, he was evidently in torture from restraining his laughter, and I observed that he was frequently obliged to make most horrid grimaces, from pretended fear, in order to conceal his risibility.

Very soon after, "The robbers are coming!" cried the coachman.

The footman opened the door, and jumped out of the chariot.

Madame Duval gave a loud scream.

I could no longer preserve my silence. "For Heaven's sake, my dear Madam," said I, "don't be alarmed, – you are in no danger – you are quite safe, – there is nothing but – "

Here the chariot was stopped, by two men in masks, who, at each side, put in their hands, as if for our purses. Madame Duval sunk to the bottom of the chariot, and implored their mercy. I shrieked involuntarily, although prepared for the attack: one of them held me fast, while the other tore poor Madame Duval out of the carriage, in spite of her cries, threats, and resistance.

I was really frightened, and trembled exceedingly. "My angel!" cried the man who held me, "you cannot surely be alarmed, – do you not know me? – I shall hold myself in eternal abhorrence, if I have really terrified you."

"Indeed, Sir Clement, you have," cried I, – "but, for Heaven's sake, where is Madame Duval? – why is she forced away?"

"She is perfectly safe; the Captain has her in charge: but suffer me now, my adored Miss Anville, to take the only opportunity that is allowed me, to speak upon another, a much dearer, much sweeter subject."

And then he hastily came into the chariot, and seated himself next to me. I would fain have disengaged myself from him, but he would not let me; "Deny me not, most charming of women," cried he, "deny me not this only moment that is lent me, to pour forth my soul into your gentle ears, – to tell you how much I suffer from your absence, – how much I dread your displeasure, – and how cruelly I am affected by your coldness!"

"O Sir, this is no time for such language, – pray leave me, pray go to the relief of Madame Duval, – I cannot bear that she should be treated with such indignity."

"And will you, – can you command my absence? – When may I speak to you, if not now? – does the Captain suffer me to breathe a moment out of his sight? – and are not a thousand *impertinent*[1] *people* for ever at your elbow?"

"Indeed, Sir Clement, you must change your style, or I will not hear you. The impertinent people you mean, are among my best friends, and you would not, if you really wished me well, speak of them so disrespectfully."

"Wish you well! – O Miss Anville, point but out to me how, in what manner I may convince you of the fervour of my passion, – tell me but what services you will accept from me, – and you shall find my life, my fortune, my whole soul at your devotion."

"I want *nothing*, Sir, that you can offer; – I beg you not to talk to me so – so strangely. Pray leave me, and pray assure yourself, you cannot take any method so successless to shew any regard for me, as entering into schemes so frightful to Madame Duval, and so disagreeable to myself."

"The scheme was the Captain's; I even opposed it: though, I own, I could not refuse myself the so-long-wished-for happiness, of speaking to you once more, without so many of – your *friends* to watch me. And I had flattered myself, that the note I charged the footman to give you would have prevented the alarm you have received."

"Well, Sir, you have now, I hope, said enough; and, if you will

---

1   "Unsuitable" (*OED*).

not go yourself to see for Madame Duval, at least suffer *me* to enquire what is become of her."

"And when may I speak to you again?"

"No matter when, – I don't know, – perhaps – "

"Perhaps what, my angel?"

"Perhaps *never*, Sir, – if you torment me thus."

"Never! O Miss Anville, how cruel, how piercing to my soul is that icy word! – Indeed, I cannot endure such displeasure."

"Then, Sir, you must not provoke it. Pray leave me directly."

I will, Madam: but let me, at least, make a merit of my obedience, – allow me to hope that you will, in future, be less averse to trusting yourself for a few moments alone with me."

I was surprised at the freedom of this request; but, while I hesitated how to answer it, the other mask came up to the chariot-door, and, in a voice almost stifled with laughter, said, "I've done for her! – the old buck is safe; – but we must sheer off directly, or we shall be all aground."[1]

Sir Clement instantly left me, mounted his horse, and rode off. The Captain, having given some directions to the servants, followed him.

I was both uneasy and impatient to know the fate of Madame Duval, and immediately got out of the chariot to seek her. I desired the footman to shew me which way she was gone; he pointed with his finger, by way of answer, and I saw that he dared not trust his voice to make any other. I walked on, a very quick pace, and soon, to my great consternation, perceived the poor lady, seated upright in a ditch. I flew to her, with unfeigned concern at her situation. She was sobbing, nay, almost roaring, and in the utmost agony of rage and terror. As soon as she saw me, she redoubled her cries, but her voice was so broken, I could not understand a word she said. I was so much shocked, that it was with difficulty I forbore exclaiming against the cruelty of the Captain, for thus wantonly ill-treating

---

1   "Old buck" in this instance probably means "old washtub," likening Madame Duval to a vessel of sorts; to "sheer off directly" is, with reference to a ship, to "turn aside, alter its direction, swerve to either side of its course" immediately or the ship will "run aground" (*OED*).

her; and I could not forgive myself for having passively suffered the deception. I used my utmost endeavours to comfort her, assuring her of our present safety, and begging her to rise, and return to the chariot.

Almost bursting with passion, she pointed to her feet, and with frightful violence, she actually beat the ground with her hands.

I then saw, that her feet were tied together with a strong rope, which was fastened to the upper branch of a tree, even with an hedge which ran along the ditch where she sat. I endeavoured to untie the knot, but soon found it was infinitely beyond my strength. I was, therefore, obliged to apply to the footman; but being very unwilling to add to his mirth, by the sight of Madame Duval's situation, I desired him to lend me a knife; I returned with it, and cut the rope. Her feet were soon disentangled, and then, though with great difficulty, I assisted her to rise. But what was my astonishment, when, the moment she was up, she hit me a violent slap on the face! I retreated from her with precipitation and dread, and she then loaded me with reproaches, which, though almost unintelligible, convinced me that she imagined I had voluntarily deserted her; but she seemed not to have the slightest suspicion that she had not been attacked by real robbers.

I was so much surprised and confounded at the blow, that, for some time, I suffered her to rave without making any answer; but her extreme agitation, and real suffering, soon dispelled my anger, which all turned into compassion. I then told her, that I had been forcibly detained from following her, and assured her of my real sorrow at her ill usage.

She began to be somewhat appeased; and I again entreated her to return to the carriage, or give me leave to order that it should draw up to the place where we stood. She made no answer, till I told her, that the longer we remained still, the greater would be the danger of our ride home. Struck with this hint, she suddenly, and with hasty steps, moved forward.

Her dress was in such disorder, that I was quite sorry to have her figure exposed to the servants, who all of them, in imitation of their master, hold her in derision: however, the disgrace was unavoidable.

The ditch, happily, was almost quite dry, or she must have suffered still more seriously; yet, so forlorn, so miserable a figure, I never before saw. Her head-dress had fallen off; her linen was torn; her negligee had not a pin left in it; her petti-coats she was obliged to hold on; and her shoes were perpetu-ally slipping off. She was covered with dirt, weeds, and filth, and her face was really horrible, for the pomatum[1] and powder from her head, and the dust from the road, were quite *pasted* on her skin by her tears, which, with her *rouge*, made so frightful a mixture, that she hardly looked human.

The servants were ready to die with laughter, the moment they saw her; but not all my remonstrances could prevail upon her to get into the carriage, till she had most vehemently reproached them both, for not rescuing her. The footman, fixing his eyes on the ground, as if fearful of again trusting him-self to look at her, protested that the robbers had vowed they would shoot him, if he moved an inch, and that one of them had stayed to watch the chariot, while the other carried her off; adding, that the reason of their behaving so barbarously, was to revenge our having secured our purses. Notwithstanding her anger, she gave immediate credit to what he said, and really imagined that her want of money had irritated the pretended robbers to treat her with such cruelty. I determined, therefore, to be carefully upon my guard, not to betray the imposition, which could now answer no other purpose, than occasioning an irreparable breach between her and the Captain.

Just as we were seated in the chariot, she discovered the loss which her head had sustained, and called out, "My God! what is becomed of my hair? – why the villain has stole all my curls!"[2]

She then ordered the man to run and see if he could find any of them in the ditch. He went, and presently returning, produced a great quantity of hair, in such a nasty condition, that I was amazed she would take it; and the man, as he deliv-

---

1 Pomade or pomatum is a "scented ointment (in which apples are said to have been originally an ingredient) for application to the skin; now used esp. for the skin of the head and for dressing the hair" (*OED*).
2 Her wig.

ered it to her, found it impossible to keep his countenance; which she no sooner observed, than all her stormy passions were again raised. She flung the battered curls in his face, saying, "Sirrah, what do you grin for? I wish you'd been served so yourself, and you would n't have found it no such joke: you are the impudentest fellow ever I see, and if I find you dare grin at me any more, I shall make no ceremony of boxing your ears."

Satisfied with the threat, the man hastily retired, and we drove on.

Her anger now subsiding into grief, she began most sorrowfully to lament her case. "I believe," she cried, "never nobody was so unlucky as I am! and so here, because I ha'n't had misfortunes enough already, that puppy has made me lose my curls! – Why, I can't see nobody without them: – only look at me, – I was never so bad off in my life before. *Pardi*, if I'd know'd as much, I'd have brought two or three sets with me: but I'd never a thought of such a thing as this."

Finding her now somewhat pacified, I ventured to ask an account of her adventure, which I will endeavour to write in her own words.

"Why, child, all this misfortune comes of that puppy's making us leave our money behind us; for as soon as the robber see I did not put nothing in his hands, he lugged me out of the chariot by main force, and I verily thought he'd have murdered me. He was as strong as a lion; I was no more in his hands than a child. But I believe never nobody was so abused before, for he dragged me down the road, pulling and hawling me all the way, as if I'd no more feeling than a horse. I'm sure I wish I could see that man cut up and quartered alive! however, he'll come to the gallows, that's one good thing. So, as soon as we'd got out of sight of the chariot, – though he need n't have been afraid, for if he'd beat me to a mummy,[1] those cowardly fellows would n't have said nothing to it. – So, when I was got there, what does he do, but, all of a sudden, he takes me by both the shoulders, and he gives me such a shake! – *Mon Dieu*! I shall never forget it, if I live to be an hundred. I'm sure I dare say I'm out of joint

---

1 Beat to a "pulpy substance or mass" (*OED*).

all over.[1] And, though I made as much noise as ever I could, he took no more notice of it than nothing at all, but there he stood, shaking me in that manner, as if he was doing it for a wager. I'm determined, if it costs me all my fortune, I'll see that villain hanged. He shall be found out, if there's e'er a justice in England. So when he had shooked me till he was tired, and I felt all over like a jelly, without saying never a word, he takes and pops me into the ditch! I'm sure I thought he'd have murdered me, as much as I ever thought any thing in my life, for he kept bumping me about, as if he thought nothing too bad for me. However, I'm resolved I'll never leave my purse behind me again, the longest day I have to live. So when he could n't stand over me no longer, he holds out his hands again for my money; but he was as cunning as could be, for he would n't speak a word, because I should n't swear to his voice; however, that sha'n't save him, for I'll swear to him any day in the year, if I can but catch him. So, when I told him I had no money, he fell to jerking me again, just as if he had but that moment begun! And, after that, he got me close by a tree, and out of his pocket he pulls a great cord! – It's a wonder I did not swoon away, for as sure as you're alive, he was going to hang me to that tree. I screamed like any thing mad, and told him if he would but spare my life, I'd never prosecute him, nor tell nobody what he'd done to me: so he stood some time, quite in a brown study, a thinking what he should do. And so, after that, he forced me to sit down in the ditch, and he tied my feet together, just as you see them, and then, as if he had not done enough, he twitched off my cap, and, without saying nothing, got on his horse, and left me in that condition, thinking, I suppose, that I might lie there and perish."

Though this narrative almost compelled me to laugh, yet I was really irritated with the Captain, for carrying his love of tormenting, – *sport*, he calls it, – to such barbarous and unjustifiable extremes. I consoled and soothed her as well as I was able, and told her that, since M. Du Bois had escaped, I hoped, when she recovered from her fright, all would end well.

---

1    In a figurative sense, "disordered" (*OED*).

"Fright, child!" repeated she, "why, that's not half; – I promise you, I wish it was; but here I'm bruised from top to toe, and it's well if ever I have the right use of my limbs again. However, I'm glad the villain got nothing but his trouble for his pains. But here the worst is to come, for I can't go out, because I've got no curls, and so he'll be escaped, before I can get to the Justice to stop him. I'm resolved I'll tell Lady Howard how her man served me, for if he had n't made me fling 'em away, I dare say I could have pinned them up well enough for the country."

"Perhaps Lady Howard may be able to lend you a cap that will wear without them."

"Lady Howard, indeed! why, do you think I'd wear one of her dowdies?[1] No, I'll promise you, I sha'n't put on no such disguisement. It's the unluckiest thing in the world that I did not make the man pick up the curls again; but he put me in such a passion, I could not think of nothing. I know I can't get none at Howard Grove for love nor money, for of all the stupid places ever I see, that Howard Grove is the worst! there's never no getting nothing one wants."

This sort of conversation lasted till we arrived at our journey's end; and then, a new distress occurred; Madame Duval was eager to speak to Lady Howard and Mrs. Mirvan, and to relate her misfortunes, but she could not endure that Sir Clement or the Captain should see her in such disorder, for she said they were so ill-natured, that instead of pitying her, they would only make a jest of her disasters. She therefore sent me first into the house, to wait for an opportunity of their being out of the way, that she might steal up stairs unobserved. In this I succeeded, as the gentlemen thought it most prudent not to seem watching for her; though they both contrived to divert themselves with peeping at her as she passed.

She went immediately to bed, where she had her supper. Lady Howard and Mrs. Mirvan both of them very kindly sat with her, and listened to her tale with compassionate attention; while Miss Mirvan and I retired to our own room, where I was

---

1 A "dowd" is "a woman's cap or night-cap;" a "dowdy" is "a woman or girl shabbily or unattractively dressed" (*OED*). Unattractive caps.

very glad to end the troubles of the day in a comfortable conversation.

The Captain's raptures, during supper, at the success of his plan, were boundless. I spoke, afterwards, to Mrs. Mirvan, with the openness which her kindness encourages, and begged her to remonstrate with him upon the cruelty of tormenting Madame Duval so causelessly. She promised to take the first opportunity of starting the subject, but said he was, at present, so much elated that he would not listen to her with any patience. However, should he make any new efforts to molest her, I can by no means consent to be passive. Had I imagined he would have been so violent, I would have risked his anger in her defence much sooner.

She has kept her bed all day, and declares she is almost bruised to death.

Adieu, dear Sir. What a long letter have I written! I could almost fancy I sent it you from London!

## LETTER III.

*Evelina in continuation.*

Howard Grove, May 15th.

This insatiable Captain, if left to himself, would not, I believe, rest, till he had tormented Madame Duval into a fever. He seems to have no delight but in terrifying or provoking her and all his thoughts apparently turn upon inventing such methods as may do it most effectually.

She had her breakfast again in bed yesterday morning; but during ours, the Captain, with a very significant look at Sir Clement, gave us to understand, that he thought she had now rested long enough to bear the hardships of a fresh campaign.[1]

His meaning was obvious, and, therefore, I resolved to endeavour immediately to put a stop to his intended exploits.

---

1   Military personnel were allowed rest leaves between bouts of fighting.

When breakfast was over, I followed Mrs. Mirvan out of the parlour, and begged her to lose no time in pleading the cause of Madame Duval with the Captain. "My love," answered she, "I have already expostulated with him; but all I can say is fruitless, while his favourite Sir Clement contrives to urge him on."

"Then I will go and speak to Sir Clement," said I, "for I know he will desist, if I request him."

"Have a care, my dear!" said she, smiling, "it is sometimes dangerous to make requests to men, who are too desirous of receiving them."

"Well then, my dear Madam, will you give me leave to speak myself to the Captain?"

"Willingly; nay, I will accompany you to him."

I thanked her, and we went to seek him. He was walking in the garden with Sir Clement. Mrs. Mirvan most obligingly made an opening for my purpose, by saying, "Mr. Mirvan, I have brought a petitioner with me."

"Why what's the matter now?" cried he.

I was fearful of making him angry, and stammered very much, when I told him, I hoped he had no new plan for alarming Madame Duval.

"*New* plan!" cried he, "why, you don't suppose the *old* one would do again, do you? Not but what it was a very good one, only I doubt she would n't bite."

"Indeed, Sir," said I, "she has already suffered too much, and I hope you will pardon me, if I take the liberty of telling you, that I think it my duty to do all in my power to prevent her being again so much terrified."

A sullen gloominess instantly clouded his face, and, turning short from me, he said, I might do as I pleased, but that I should much sooner repent than repair my officiousness.

I was too much disconcerted at this rebuff, to attempt making any answer, and, finding that Sir Clement warmly espoused my cause, I walked away, and left them to discuss the point together.

Mrs. Mirvan, who never speaks to the Captain when he is out of humour, was glad to follow me, and, with her usual sweetness, made a thousand apologies for her husband's ill-manners.

When I left her, I went to Madame Duval, who was just risen, and employed in examining the cloaths she had on the day of her ill usage.

"Here's a sight!" cried she. "Come here, child, – only look – *Pardi*, so long as I've lived, I never see so much before! Why, all my things are spoilt, and, what's worse, my sacque[1] was as good as new. Here's the second negligee I've had used in this manner! – I am sure I was a fool to put it on, in such a lone-some place as this; however, if I stay here these ten years, I'll never put on another good gown, that I'm resolved."

"Will you let the maid try if she can iron it out, or clean it, Ma'am?"

"No, she'll only make bad worse. – But look here, now, here's a cloak! *Mon Dieu!* why, it looks like a dish-clout![2] Of all the unluckinesses that ever I met, this is the worst! for, do you know, I bought it but the day before I left Paris? – Besides, into the bargain, my cap's quite gone;where the villain twitched it, I don't know, but I never see no more of it, from that time to this. Now you must know this was the becomingest cap I had in the world, for I've never another with pink ribbon in it; and, to tell you the truth, if I had n't thought to have seen M. Du Bois, I'd no more have put it on than I'd have flown; for as to what one wears in such a stupid place as this, it signifies no more than nothing at all."

She then told me, that she had been thinking all night of a contrivance to hinder the Captain from finding out her loss of curls; which was, having a large gauze handkerchief pinned on her head as a hood, and saying she had the tooth-ach.

"To tell you the truth," added she, "I believe that Captain is one of the worst men in the world; he's always making a joke of me; and as to his being a gentleman, he has no more man-ners than a bear, for he's always upon the grin when one's in distress; and, I declare, I'd rather be done any thing to than laugh'd at, for, to my mind, it's one or other the disagreeablest thing in the world."

---

1   "A French fashion of [loose] gown ... worn by ladies" in the eighteenth century (*OED*).
2   Dish cloth.

Mrs. Mirvan, I found, had been endeavouring to dissuade her from the design she had formed, of having recourse to the law, in order to find out the supposed robbers; for she dreads a discovery of the Captain, during Madame Duval's stay at Howard Grove, as it could not fail being productive of infinite commotion. She has, therefore, taken great pains to shew the inutility of applying to justice, unless she were more able to describe the offenders against whom she would appear, and has assured her, that as she neither heard their voices, nor saw their faces, she cannot possibly swear to their persons, or obtain any redress.

Madame Duval, in telling me this, extremely lamented her hard fate, that she was thus prevented from revenging her injuries; which, however, she vowed she would not be persuaded to *pocket tamely*,[1] "because," added she, "if such villains as these are let to have their own way, and nobody takes no notice of their impudence, they'll make no more ado than nothing at all of tying people in ditches, and such things as that: however, I shall consult with M. Du Bois, as soon as I can ferret out where he's hid himself. I'm sure I've a right to his advice, for it's all along of his gaping about at the Tower that I've met with these misfortunes."

"M. Du Bois, said I, will, I am sure, be very sorry when he hears what has happened."

"And what good will that do now? – that won't unspoil all my cloaths; I can tell him, I a'n't much obliged to him, though it's no fault of his; – yet it i'n't the less provokinger for that. I'm sure, if he had been there, to have seen me served in that manner, and put neck and heels into a ditch, he'd no more have thought it was me, than the Pope of Rome. I'll promise you, whatever you may think of it, I sha'n't have no rest, night nor day, till I find out that rogue."

"I have no doubt, Madam, but you will soon discover him."

"*Pardi*, if I do, I'll hang him, as sure as fate! – but what's the oddest, is that he should take such a 'special spite against *me*, above all the rest! it was as much for nothing, as could be, for I

---

1  "To take or accept (an affront, etc.) without showing resentment; to submit to, endure meekly" (*OED*).

don't know what I had done, so particular bad, to be used in that manner: I'm sure, I had n't given him no offence, as I know of, for I never see his face all the time; and as to screaming a little, I think it's very hard if one must n't do such a thing as that, when one's put in fear of one's life."

During this conversation, she endeavoured to adjust her head dress, but could not at all please herself. Indeed, had I not been present, I should have thought it impossible for a woman at her time of life to be so very difficult in regard to dress. What she may have in view, I cannot imagine, but the labour of the toilette[1] seems the chief business of her life.

When I left her, in my way down stairs, I met Sir Clement, who, with great earnestness, said he must not be denied the honour of a moment's conversation with me; and then, without waiting for an answer, he led me to the garden, at the door of which, however, I absolutely insisted upon stopping.

He seemed very serious, and said, in a grave tone of voice, "At length, Miss Anville, I flatter myself I have hit upon an expedient that will oblige you, and therefore, though it is death to myself, I will put it in practice."

I begged him to explain himself.

"I saw your desire of saving Madame Duval, and scarce could I refrain giving the brutal Captain my real opinion of his savage conduct; but I am unwilling to quarrel with him, lest I should be denied entrance into a house which you inhabit: I have been endeavouring to prevail with him to give up his absurd new scheme, but I find him impenetrable; – I have therefore determined to make a pretence for suddenly leaving this place, dear as it is to me, and containing all I most admire and adore; – and I will stay in town till the violence of this boobyish humour is abated."

He stopped; but I was silent, for I knew not what I ought to say. He took my hand, which he pressed to his lips, saying, "And must I, then, Miss Anville, must I quit you – sacrifice voluntarily my greatest felicity, – and yet not be honoured with one word, one look of approbation?"

---

1  "The action or process of dressing, or, more recently, of washing and grooming" (*OED*).

I withdrew my hand, and said, with a half laugh, "You know so well, Sir Clement, the value of the favours you confer, that it would be superfluous for me to point it out."

"Charming, charming girl! how does your wit, your understanding rise upon me daily! and must I, can I part with you? – will no other method – "

"O Sir, do you so soon repent the good office you had planned for Madame Duval?"

"For Madame Duval! – cruel creature, and will you not even suffer me to place to your account the sacrifice I am about to make?"

"You must place it, Sir, to what account you please; but I am too much in haste now to stay here any longer."

And then I would have left him, but he held me, and, rather impatiently, said, "If, then, I cannot be so happy as to oblige *you*, Miss Anville, you must not be surprised, should I seek to oblige myself. If my scheme is not honoured with your approbation, for which alone it was formed, why should I, to my own infinite dissatisfaction, pursue it?"

We were then, for a few minutes, both silent; I was really unwilling he should give up a plan which would so effectually break into the Captain's designs, and, at the same time, save me the pain of disobliging him; and I should instantly and thankfully have accepted his offered civility, had not Mrs. Mirvan's caution made me fearful. However, when he pressed me to speak, I said, in an ironical voice, "I had thought, Sir, that the very strong sense you have yourself of the favour you propose to me, would sufficiently have repaid you, but, as I was mistaken, I must thank you myself. And now," making a low court'sy, "I hope, Sir, you are satisfied."

"Loveliest of thy sex – " he began, but I forced myself from him, and ran up stairs.

Soon after, Miss Mirvan told me that Sir Clement had just received a letter, which obliged him instantly to leave the Grove, and that he had actually ordered a chaise. I then acquainted her with the real state of the affair. Indeed, I conceal nothing from her, she is so gentle and sweet-tempered, that it gives me great pleasure to place an entire confidence in her.

At dinner, I must own, we all missed him; for though the flightiness of his behaviour to me, when we are by ourselves, is very distressing, yet, in large companies, and general conversation, he is extremely entertaining and agreeable. As to the Captain, he has been so much chagrined at his departure, that he has scarce spoken a word since he went: but Madame Duval, who made her first public appearance since her accident, was quite in raptures that she escaped seeing him.

The money which we left at the farm-house, has been returned to us. What pains the Captain must have taken to arrange and manage the adventures which he chose we should meet with! Yet he must certainly be discovered, for Madame Duval is already very much perplexed, at having received a letter this morning from M. Du Bois, in which he makes no mention of his imprisonment. However, she has so little suspicion, that she imputes his silence upon the subject, to his fears that the letter might be intercepted.

Not one opportunity could I meet with, while Sir Clement was here, to enquire after his friend Lord Orville: but I think it was strange he should never mention him unasked. Indeed, I rather wonder that Mrs. Mirvan herself did not introduce the subject, for she always seemed particularly attentive to him.

And now, once more, all my thoughts involuntarily turn upon the letter I so soon expect from Paris. This visit of Sir Clement has, however, somewhat diverted my fears, and therefore I am very glad he made it at this time. Adieu, my dear Sir.

## LETTER IV.

*Sir John Belmont to Lady Howard.*

Paris, May 11.

Madam,

I have this moment the honour of your Ladyship's letter, and I will not wait another, before I return an answer.

It seldoms happens that a man, though extolled as a saint, is really without blemish; or that another, though reviled as a devil, is really without humanity. Perhaps the time is not very distant, when I may have the honour to convince your Ladyship of this truth, in regard to Mr. Villars and myself.

As to the young lady, whom Mr. Villars so obligingly proposes presenting to me, I wish her all the happiness to which, by your Ladyship's account, she seems entitled; and, if she has a third part of the merit of *her* to whom you compare her, I doubt not but Mr. Villars will be more successful in every other application he may make for her advantage, than he can ever be in any with which he may be pleased to favour me.

I have the honour to be,

Madam,

your Ladyship's most humble

and most

obedient servant

JOHN BELMONT.

## LETTER V.

*Evelina to the Rev. Mr. Villars.*

Howard Grove, May 18.

Well, my dear Sir, all is now over! the letter so anxiously expected, is at length arrived, and my doom is fixed. The various feelings which oppress me, I have not language to describe; nor need I, – you know my heart, you have yourself formed it, – and its sensations upon this occasion, you may but too readily imagine.

Outcast as I am,[1] and rejected for ever by him to whom I of right belong, – shall I now implore *your* continued protection? – no, no, – I will not offend your generous heart, which, open to distress, has no wish but to relieve it, with an application that

---

1    In failing to own Evelina properly as his daughter and to admit to the legality of his marriage to her mother, Sir John Belmont not only leaves her feeling rejected emotionally but legally a bastard, an outcast in society.

would seem to imply a doubt. I am more secure than ever of your kindness, since you now know upon that is my sole dependance.

I endeavour to bear this stroke with composure, and in such a manner as if I had already received your counsel and consolation. Yet, at times, my emotions are almost too much for me. O Sir, what a letter for a parent to write! must I not myself be deaf to the voice of Nature, if I could endure to be thus absolutely abandoned, without regret? I dare not even to you, nor would I, could I help it, to myself, acknowledge all that I think; for, indeed, I have, sometimes, sentiments upon this rejection, which my strongest sense of duty can scarcely correct. Yet, suffer me to ask, – might not this answer have been softened? – was is not enough to disclaim me for ever, without treating me with contempt, and wounding me with derision?

But, while I am thus thinking of myself, I forget how much more he is the object of sorrow, than I am! Alas, what amends can he make himself, for the anguish he is hoarding up for time to come! My heart bleeds for him, whenever this reflection occurs to me.

What is said of *you*, my protector, my friend, my benefactor! – I dare not trust myself to comment upon. Gracious Heaven! what a return for goodness so unparalleled!

I would fain endeavour to divert my thoughts from this subject, but even that is not in my power; for, afflicting as this letter is to me, I find that it will not be allowed to conclude the affair, though it does all my expectations: for Madame Duval has determined not to let it rest here. She heard the letter in great wrath, and protested she would not be so easily answered; she regretted her facility in having been prevailed upon to yield the direction of this affair to those who knew not how to manage it, and vowed she would herself undertake and conduct it in future.

It is in vain that I have pleaded against her resolution, and besought her to forbear an attack, where she has nothing to expect but resentment; especially as there seems to be a hint, that Lady Howard will one day be more openly dealt with: she will not hear me; she is furiously bent upon a project which is terrible to think of, – for she means to go herself to Paris, take me with her, and there, *face to face*, demand justice!

How to appease or to persuade her, I know not; but for the universe would I not be dragged, in such a manner, to an interview so awful, with a parent I have never yet beheld!

Lady Howard and Mrs. Mirvan are both of them infinitely shocked at the present situation of affairs, and they seem to be even more kind to me than ever; and my dear Maria, who is the friend of my heart, uses her utmost efforts to console me, and, when she fails in her design, with still greater kindness, she sympathises in my sorrow.

I very much rejoice, however, that Sir Clement Willoughby had left us before this letter arrived. I am sure the general confusion of the house would, otherwise, have betrayed to him the whole of a tale which I now, more than ever, wish to have buried in oblivion.

Lady Howard thinks I ought not to disoblige Madame Duval, yet she acknowledges the impropriety of my accompanying her abroad upon such an enterprize. Indeed I would rather die, than force myself into his presence. But so vehement is Madame Duval, that she would instantly have compelled me to attend her to town, in her way to Paris, had not Lady Howard so far exerted herself, as to declare she could by no means consent to my quitting her house, till she gave me up to you, by whose permission I had entered it.

She was extremely angry at this denial; and the Captain, by his sneers and raillery, so much encreased her rage, that she has positively declared, should your next letter dispute her authority to guide me by her own pleasure, she will, without hesitation, make a journey to Berry Hill, and *teach you to know who she is*.

Should she put this threat in execution, nothing could give me greater uneasiness, for her violence and volubility would almost distract you.

Unable as I am to act for myself, or to judge what conduct I ought to pursue, how grateful do I feel myself, that I have such a guide and director to counsel and instruct me as yourself!

Adieu, my dearest Sir! Heaven, I trust, will never let me live to be repulsed and derided by *you*, to whom I may now sign myself

Wholly your<br>EVELINA.

## LETTER VI.

*Mr. Villars to Evelina.*

Berry Hill, May 21.

Let not my Evelina be depressed by a stroke of fortune for which she is not responsible. No breach of duty on your part, has incurred the unkindness which has been shewn you; nor have you, by any act of imprudence, provoked either censure or reproach. Let me entreat you, therefore, my dearest child, to support yourself with that courage which your innocency ought to inspire; and let all the affliction you allow yourself, be for him only, who, not having that support, must one day be but too severely sensible how much he wants it.

The hint thrown out concerning myself, is wholly unintelligible to me: my heart, I dare own, fully acquits me of vice, but *without blemish*, I have never ventured to pronounce myself. However, it seems his intention to be hereafter more explicit, and *then*, – should any thing appear, that has on *my* part, contributed to those misfortunes we lament, let me, at least, say, that the most partial of my friends cannot be so much astonished as I shall myself be, at such a discovery.

The mention, also, of any *future applications* I may make, is equally beyond my comprehension. But I will not dwell upon a subject which almost compels from me reflections that cannot but be wounding to a heart so formed for filial tenderness as my Evelina's. There is an air of mystery throughout the letter, the explanation of which I will await in silence.

The scheme of Madame Duval is such as might be reasonably expected from a woman so little inured to disappointment, and so totally incapable of considering the delicacy of your situation. Your averseness to her plan gives me pleasure, for it exactly corresponds with my own. Why will she not make the journey she projects by herself? She would not have even the wish of an opposition to encounter. And then, once more, might my child and myself be left to the quiet enjoyment of that peaceful happiness, which she alone has interrupted. As to her coming hither, I could, indeed, dispense with such a visit; but, if she will not be satisfied with my refusal by letter, I must submit to the task of giving it her in person.

My impatience for your return is encreased by your account of Sir Clement Willoughby's visit to Howard Grove. I am but little surprised at the perseverance of his assiduities to interest you in his favour; but I am very much hurt that you should be exposed to addresses, which, by their privacy, have an air that shocks me. You cannot, my love, be too circumspect; the slightest carelessness on your part, will be taken advantage of, by a man of his disposition. It is not sufficient for you to be reserved; his conduct even calls for your resentment: and should he again, as will doubtless be his endeavour, contrive to solicit your favour in private, let your disdain and displeasure be so marked, as to constrain a change in his behaviour. Though, indeed, should his visit be repeated while you remain at the Grove, Lady Howard must pardon me if I shorten your's.

Adieu, my child. You will always make my respects to the hospitable family to which we are so much obliged.


## LETTER VII.

*Mr. Villars to Lady Howard.*

Berry Hill, May 27.

Dear Madam,
I believe your Ladyship will not be surprised at hearing I have had a visit from Madame Duval, as I doubt not her having

made known her intention before she left Howard Grove. I would gladly have excused myself this meeting, could I have avoided it decently; but, after so long a journey, it was not possible to refuse her admittance.

She told me, that she came to Berry Hill, in consequence of a letter I had sent to her grand-daughter, in which I had forbid her going to Paris. Very roughly, she then called me to account for the authority which I assumed; and, had I been disposed to have argued with her, she would very angrily have disputed the right by which I used it. But I declined all debating. I therefore listened very quietly, till she had so much fatigued herself with talking, that she was glad, in her turn, to be silent. And then, I begged to know the purport of her visit.

She answered, that she came to make me relinquish the power I had usurped over her grand-daughter, and assured me she would not quit the place till she succeeded.

But I will not trouble your Ladyship with the particulars of this disagreeable conversation; nor should I, but on account of the result, have chosen so unpleasant a subject for your perusal. However, I will be as concise as I possibly can, that the better occupations of your Ladyship's time may be the less impeded.

When she found me inexorable in refusing Evelina's attending her to Paris, she peremptorily insisted, that she should, at least, live with her in London, till Sir John Belmont's return. I remonstrated against this scheme with all the energy in my power; but the contest was vain; she lost her patience, and I my time. She declared that if I was resolute in opposing her, she would instantly make a will, in which she would leave all her fortune to strangers, though, otherwise, she intended her grand-daughter for her sole heiress.

To me, I own, this threat seemed of little consequence; I have long accustomed myself to think, that, with a competency,[1] of which she is sure, my child might be as happy as in the possession of millions: but the incertitude of her future fate, deters me from following implicitly the dictates of my present judgment. The connections she may hereafter form, the style

---

1 "A sufficiency, without superfluity, of the means of life; a competent . . . income" (*OED*).

of life for which she may be destined, and the future family to which she may belong, are considerations which give but too much weight to the menaces of Madame Duval. In short, Madam, after a discourse infinitely tedious, I was obliged, though very reluctantly, to compromise with this ungovernable woman, by consenting that Evelina should pass one month with her.

I never made a concession with so bad a grace, or so much regret. The violence and vulgarity of this woman, her total ignorance of propriety, the family to which she is related, and the company she is likely to keep, are objections so forcible to her having the charge of this dear child, that nothing less than my diffidence of the right I have of depriving her of so large a fortune, would have induced me to listen to her proposal. Indeed we parted, at last, equally discontented, she, at what I had refused, I, at what I had granted.

It now only remains for me to return your Ladyship my humble acknowledgements for the kindness which you have so liberally shewn to my ward; and to beg you would have the goodness to part with her, when Madame Duval thinks proper to claim the promise which she has extorted from me. I am,

Dear Madam, &c.

ARTHUR VILLARS.

## LETTER VIII.

*Mr. Villars to Evelina.*

Berry Hill, May 28.

With a reluctance which occasions me inexpressible uneasiness, I have been almost compelled to consent that my Evelina should quit the protection of the hospitable and respectable Lady Howard, and accompany Madame Duval to a city which I had hoped she would never again have entered. But alas, my dear child, we are the slaves of custom, the dupes of prejudice, and dare not stem the torrent of an opposing world, even though our judgments condemn our compliance! however, since the die is cast, we must endeavour to make the best of it.

You will have occasion, in the course of the month you are to pass with Madame Duval, for all the circumspection and prudence you can call to your aid: she will not, I know, propose any thing to you which she thinks wrong herself; but you must learn not only to *judge* but to *act* for yourself: If any schemes are started, any engagements made, which your understanding represents to you as improper, exert yourself resolutely in avoiding them, and do not, by a too passive facility, risk the censure of the world, or your own future regret.

You cannot too assiduously attend to Madame Duval herself; but I would wish you to mix as little as possible with her associates, who are not likely to be among those whose acquaintance would reflect credit upon you. Remember, my dear Evelina, nothing is so delicate as the reputation of a woman: it is, at once, the most beautiful and most brittle of all human things.

Adieu, my beloved child; I shall be but ill at ease till this month is elapsed.

A. V.

## LETTER IX.

*Evelina to the Rev. Mr. Villars.*

London, June 6.

Once more, my dearest Sir, I write to you from this great city. Yesterday morning, with the truest concern, I quitted the dear inhabitants of Howard Grove, and most impatiently shall I count the days till I see them again. Lady Howard and Mrs. Mirvan took leave of me with the most flattering kindness; but indeed I knew not how to part with Maria, whose own apparent sorrow redoubled mine. She made me promise to send her a letter every post. And I shall write to her with the same freedom, and almost the same confidence, you allow me to make use of to yourself.

The Captain was very civil to me, but he wrangled with poor Madame Duval to the last moment; and, taking me aside, just before we got into the chaise, he said, "Hark'ee, Miss Anville, I've a favour for to ask of you, which is this; that you will write us word how the old gentlewoman finds herself, when she sees it was all a trick: and what the French lubber[1] says to it, and all about it."

I answered that I would obey him, though I was very little pleased with the commission, which, to me, was highly improper: but he will either treat me as an *informer*, or make me a party in his frolic.

As soon as we drove away, Madame Duval, with much satisfaction, exclaimed "*Dieu Merci*, we've got off at last! I'm sure I never desire to see that place again. It's a wonder I've got away alive; for I believe I've had the worst luck ever was known, from the time I set my foot upon the threshold. I know I wish I'd never a gone. Besides, into the bargain, it's the most dullest place in all Christendom: there's never no diversions, nor nothing at all."

Then she bewailed M. Du Bois, concerning whose adventures she continued to make various conjectures during the rest of our journey.

When I asked her what part of London she should reside in, she told me that Mr. Branghton was to meet us at an inn, and would conduct us to a lodging. Accordingly, we proceeded to a house in Bishopsgate-street,[2] and were led by a waiter into a room where we found Mr. Branghton.

He received us very civilly, but seemed rather surprized at seeing me, saying "Why I did n't think of your bringing Miss; however she's very welcome."

"I'll tell you how it was," said Madame Duval; "you must know I've a mind to take the girl to Paris, that she may see something of the world, and improve herself a little; besides,

---

1   "A seaman's term for: A clumsy sailor; an unseamanlike fellow" (*OED*).

2   Bishopsgate-street runs through the City of London. During Elizabeth I's reign, this area was home to many well-to-do merchants (Weinreb 67).

I've another reason, that you and I will talk more about; but do you know, that meddling old parson as I told you of, would not let her go: however, I'm resolved I'll be even with him, for I shall take her on with me, without saying never a word more to nobody."

I started at this intimation, which very much surprised me. But I am very glad she has discovered her intention, as I shall be carefully upon my guard not to venture from town with her.

Mr. Branghton then hoped we had passed our time agreeably in the country.

"O Lord, Cousin," cried she, "I've been the miserablest creature in the world! I'm sure all the horses in London sha'n't drag me into the country again of one while: why how do you think I've been served? – only guess."

"Indeed Cousin, I can't pretend to do that."

"Why then I'll tell you. Do you know, I've been robbed! – that is, the villain would have robbed me if he could, only I'd secured all my money."

"Why then, Cousin, I think your loss can't have been very great."

"O Lord, you don't know what you're a saying; you're talking in the unthinkingest manner in the world: why it was all along of not having no money, that I met with that misfortune."

"How's that, Cousin? I don't see what great misfortune you can have met with, if you'd secured all your money."

"That's because you don't know nothing of the matter; for there the villain came to the chaise, and because we had n't got nothing to give him, though he'd no more right to our money than the man in the moon, yet, do you know, he fell into the greatest passion ever you see, and abused me in such a manner, and put me in a ditch, and got a rope, o' purpose to hang me, – and I'm sure, if that was n't misfortune enough, why I don't know what is."

"This is a hard case indeed, Cousin. But why don't you go to Justice Fielding?"

"O, as to that, I'm a going to him directly; but only I want first to see poor M. Du Bois, for the oddest thing of all is, that he has wrote to me, and never said nothing of where he is, nor what's become of him, nor nothing else."

"M. Du Bois! why he's at my house at this very time."

"M. Du Bois at your house! well, I declare this is the surprisingest part of all! however, I assure you, I think he might have comed for me, as well as you, considering what I have gone through on his account; for, to tell you the truth, it was all along of him that I met with that accident; so I don't take it very kind of him, I promise you."

"Well but, Cousin, tell me some of the particulars of this affair."

"As to the particulars, I'm sure they'd make your hair stand an end to hear them; however, the beginning of it all was through the fault of M. Du Bois: but I'll assure you, he may take care of himself in future, since he don't so much as come to see if I'm dead or alive; – but there I went for him to a justice of peace, and rode all out of the way, and did every thing in the world, and was used worser than a dog, and all for the sake of serving of him, and now, you see, he don't so much – well, I was a fool for my pains, – however, he may get somebody else to be treated so another time, for if he's taken up every day in the week, I'll never go after him no more."

This occasioned an explanation, in the course of which, Madame Duval, to her utter amazement, heard that M. Du Bois had never left London during her absence! nor did Mr. Branghton believe that he had ever been to the Tower, or met with any kind of accident.

Almost instantly, the whole truth of the transaction seemed to *rush upon her mind*, and her wrath was inconceivably violent. She asked me a thousand questions in a breath, but, fortunately, was too vehement to attend to my embarrassment, which must, otherwise, have betrayed my knowledge of the deceit. Revenge was her first wish, and she vowed she would go the next morning to Justice Fielding, and enquire what punishment she might lawfully inflict upon the Captain for his assault.

I believe we were an hour in Bishopsgate-street, before poor Madame Duval could allow any thing to be mentioned but her own story; at length, however, Mr. Branghton told her, that M. Du Bois, and all his own family, were waiting for her at his house. A hackney-coach was then called, and we proceeded to Snow-hill.

Mr. Branghton's house is small and inconvenient, though his shop, which takes in all the ground floor, is large and commodious. I believe I told you before that he is a silver-smith.

We were conducted up two pair of stairs; for the dining-room, Mr. Branghton told us, was *let*. His two daughters, their brother, M. Du Bois, and a young man, were at tea. They had waited some time for Madame Duval, but I found they had not any expectation that I should accompany her; and the young ladies, I believe, were rather more surprised than pleased when I made my appearance; for they seemed hurt that I should see their apartment. Indeed I would willingly have saved them that pain, had it been in my power.

The first person who saw me was M. Du Bois: "*Ah, mon Dieu!*" exclaimed he, "*voilà Mademoiselle!*"[1]

"Goodness," cried young Branghton, "if there is n't Miss!"

"Lord, so there is," said Miss Polly; "well, I'm sure I should never have dreamed of Miss's coming."

"Nor I neither, I'm sure," cried Miss Branghton, "or else I would not have been in this room to see her; I'm quite ashamed about it, – only not thinking of seeing any body but my aunt – however, Tom, it's all your fault, for you know very well I wanted to borrow Mr. Smith's room, only you were so *grumpy* you would not let me."

"Lord, what signifies?" said the brother, "I dare be sworn Miss has been up two pair of stairs before now; – Ha'n't you, Miss?"

I begged that I might not give them the least disturbance, and assured them that I had not any choice in regard to what room we sat in.

"Well," said Miss Polly, "when you come next, Miss, we'll have Mr. Smith's room; and it's a very pretty one, and only up one pair of stairs, and nicely furnished, and every thing."

---

1 "Oh, my God! Here's Miss!"

"To say the truth," said Miss Branghton, "I thought that my cousin would not, upon any account, have come to town in the summer-time; for it's not at all the *fashion*, – so, to be sure, thinks I, she'll stay till September, when the play-houses open."

This was my reception, which I believe you will not call a very *cordial* one. Madame Duval, who, after having severely reprimanded M. Du Bois for his negligence, was just entering upon the story of her misfortunes, now wholly engaged the company.

M. Du Bois listened to her with a look of the utmost horror, repeatedly lifting up his eyes and hands, and exclaiming, "*O ciel! quel barbare!*"[1] The young ladies gave her the most earnest attention; but their brother, and the young man, kept a broad grin upon their faces during the whole recital. She was, however, too much engaged to observe them: but, when she mentioned having been tied in a ditch, young Branghton, no longer able to constrain himself, burst into a loud laugh, declaring that he had never heard any thing so *funny* in his life! His laugh was heartily re-echoed by his friend; the Miss Branghtons could not resist the example; and poor Madame Duval, to her extreme amazement, was absolutely overpowered and stopped by the violence of their mirth.

For some minutes the room seemed quite in an uproar; the rage of Madam Duval, the astonishment of M. Du Bois, and the angry interrogatories of Mr. Branghton, on one side; the convulsive tittering of the sisters, and the loud laughs of the young men, on the other, occasioned such noise, passion, and confusion, that had any one stopped an instant on the stairs, he must have concluded himself in Bedlam. At length, however, the father brought them to order; and, half laughing, half frightened, they made Madame Duval some very awkward apologies. But she would not be prevailed upon to continue her narrative, till they had protested they were laughing at the Captain, and not at her. Appeased by this, she resumed her story; which, by the help of stuffing handkerchiefs into their mouths, the young people heard with tolerable decency.

---

1   "Oh, heavens! What barbarity!"

Every body agreed, that the ill usage the Captain had given her was *actionable*,[1] and Mr. Branghton said he was sure she might recover what damages she pleased, since she had been put in fear of her life.

She then, with great delight, declared, that she would lose no time in satisfying her revenge, and vowed she would not be contented with less than half his fortune: "For though," said she, "I don't put no value upon the money, because, *Dieu merci*,[2] I ha'n't no want of it, yet I don't wish for nothing so much as to punish that fellow; for, I'm sure, whatever's the cause of it, he owes me a great *grudge*,[3] and I know no more what it's for than you do, but he's always been doing me one spite or other, ever since I knew him."

Soon after tea, Miss Branghton took an opportunity to tell me, in a whisper, that the young man I saw was a lover of her sister's, that his name was Brown, and that he was a haber-dasher,[4] with many other particulars of his circumstances and family; and then she declared her utter aversion to the thoughts of such a match; but added, that her sister had no manner of spirit or ambition, though, for her part, she would ten times rather die an old maid, than marry any person but a gentleman. "And, for that matter," added she, "I believe Polly herself don't care much for him, only she's in such a hurry, because, I suppose, she's a mind to be married before me; however, she's very welcome, for, I'm sure, I don't care a pin's point whether I ever marry at all; – it's all one to me."

Some time after this, Miss Polly contrived to tell *her* story. She assured me, with much tittering, that her sister was in a great fright, lest she should be married first, "So I make her believe that I will," continued she, "for I love dearly to plague

---

1    "Subject or liable to an action at law" (the "taking of legal steps to establish a claim or obtain judicial remedy; legal process") (*OED*).

2    "Thank God!"

3    "He has a great grudge against me."

4    "Formerly, a dealer in a variety of articles now dealt with by other trades, including caps, and probably hats…. In the course of the sixteenth century the trade seems to have been split into two, those of a. A dealer in, or maker of, hats and caps, a hatter … ; b. A dealer in small articles appertaining to dress, as thread, tape, ribbons, etc." (*OED*).

her a little; though, I declare, I don't intend to have Mr. Brown in reality; I'm sure I don't like him half well enough, – do you, Miss?"

"It is not possible for me to judge of his merits," said I, "as I am entirely a stranger to him."

"But, what do you think of him, Miss?"

"Why, really, I – I don't know – "

"But do you think him handsome? Some people reckon him to have a good pretty person, – but, I'm sure, for my part, I think he's monstrous ugly: – don't *you*, Miss?"

"I am no judge, – but I think his person is very – very well."

"*Very well!* – Why, pray, Miss," in a tone of vexation, "what fault can you find with it?"

"O, none at all!"

"I'm sure you must be very ill-natured if you could. Now there's Biddy says she thinks nothing of him, – but I know its all out of spite. You must know, Miss, it makes her as mad as can be, that I should have a lover before her, but she's so proud, that nobody will court her, and I often tell her she'll die an old maid. But, the thing is, she has taken it into her head, to have a liking for Mr. Smith, as lodges on the first floor; but, Lord, he'll never have her, for he's quite a fine gentleman; and besides, Mr. Brown heard him say, one day, that he'd never marry as long as he lived, for he'd no opinion of matrimony."

"And did you tell your sister this?"

"O, to be sure, I told her directly; but she did not mind me; however, if she will be a fool, she must."

This extreme want of affection, and good-nature, increased the distaste I already felt for these unamiable sisters; and a confidence so entirely unsolicited and unnecessary, manifested equally their folly and their want of decency.

I was very glad when the time for our departing arrived. Mr. Branghton said our lodgings were in Holborn,[1] that we might

---

1   Holborn, which runs from High Holborn to Holborn Circus in East Central London and dates back to 1249, was principally a business center. Burney interchanges High Holborn for Holborn later in the novel. High Holborn continues Holborn but is distant from Snow Hill, which makes it more likely that the lodgings of Evelina and Madame Duval are in Holborn.

be near his house, and neighbourly. He accompanied us to them himself.

Our rooms are large, and not inconvenient; our landlord is an hosier.[1] I am sure I have a thousand reasons to rejoice that I am so little known; for my present situation is, in every respect, very unenviable; and I would not, for the world, be seen by any acquaintance of Mrs. Mirvan.

This morning Madame Duval, attended by all the Branghtons, actually went to a Justice in the neighbourhood, to report the Captain's ill usage of her. I had great difficulty in excusing myself from being of the party, which would have given me very serious concern. Indeed, I was extremely anxious, though at home, till I heard the result of the application; for I dread to think of the uneasiness which such an affair would occasion the amiable Mrs. Mirvan. But, fortunately, Madame Duval has received very little encouragement to proceed in her design, for she has been informed that, as she neither heard the voice, nor saw the face of the person suspected, she will find it difficult to cast him upon *conjecture*,[2] and will have but little probability of gaining her cause, unless she can procure witnesses of the transaction. Mr. Branghton, therefore, who has considered all the circumstances of the affair, is of opinion, that the lawsuit will not only be expensive, but tedious and hazardous, and has advised against it. Madame Duval, though very unwillingly, has acquiesced in his decision; but vows that if ever she is so affronted again, she will be revenged, even if she ruins herself. I am extremely glad that this ridiculous adventure seems now likely to end without more serious consequences.

Adieu, my dearest Sir. My direction[3] is at Mr. Dawkins's, a hosier in High Holborn.

---

1   "One who makes or deals in hose (stockings and socks) and frame-knitted or woven underclothing generally. Also used more generally for a men's outfitter or haberdasher" (*OED*).
2   To turn him over to the authorities based on suspicion of wrong doing.
3   Address.

# LETTER X.

*Evelina to Miss Mirvan.*

June 7th.

I have no words, my sweet friend, to express the thankfulness I feel for the unbounded kindness which you, your dear mother, and the much-honoured Lady Howard, have shewn me; and still less can I find language to tell you with what reluctance I parted from such dear and generous friends, whose goodness reflects, at once, so much honour on their own hearts, and on her to whom it has been so liberally bestowed. But I will not repeat what I have already written to the kind Mrs. Mirvan; I will remember your admonitions, and confine to my own breast that gratitude with which you have filled it, and teach my pen to dwell upon subjects less painful to my generous correspondent.

O Maria, London now seems no longer the same place where I lately enjoyed so much happiness; every thing is new and strange to me; even the town itself has not the same aspect: – my situation so altered! my home so different! – my companions so changed! – But you well know my averseness to this journey.

Indeed, to me, London now seems a desart;[1] that gay and busy appearance it so lately wore, is now succeeded by a look of gloom, fatigue, and lassitude; the air seems stagnant, the heat is intense, the dust intolerable, and the inhabitants illiterate and under-bred. At least, such is the face of things in the part of the town where I at present reside.

Tell me, my dear Maria, do you never re-trace in your memory the time we past here when together? to mine, it recurs for ever! And yet, I think I rather recollect a dream, or some visionary fancy, than a reality. – That I should ever have been known to Lord Orville, – that I should have spoken to – have danced with him, – seems now a romantic illusion: and that

---

1  Desert.

elegant politeness, that flattering attention, that high-bred delicacy, which so much distinguished him above all other men,
and which struck us with such admiration, I now re-trace the
remembrance of, rather as belonging to an object of ideal perfection, formed by my own imagination, than to a being of the
same race and nature as those with whom I at present converse.

I have no news for you, my dear Miss Mirvan; for all that I
could venture to say of Madame Duval, I have already written
to your sweet mother; and as to adventures, I have none to
record. Situated as I now am, I heartily hope I shall not meet
with any; my wish is to remain quiet and unnoticed.

Adieu! excuse the gravity of this letter, and believe me,

Your most sincerely
affectionate and obliged
EVELINA ANVILLE.

## LETTER XI.

*Evelina to the Rev. Mr. Villars.*

Holborn, June 9.

Yesterday morning, we received an invitation to dine and spend
the day at Mr. Branghton's; and M. Du Bois, who was also
invited, called to conduct us to Snow-hill.

Young Branghton received us at the door, and the first
words he spoke were, "Do you know, sisters a'n't dressed yet?"

Then, hurrying us into the house, he said to me, "Come,
Miss, you shall go up stairs and catch 'em, – I dare say they're at
the glass."

He would have taken my hand, but I declined this civility,
and begged to follow Madame Duval. Mr. Branghton then
appeared, and led the way himself. We went, as before, up two
pair of stairs; but the moment the father opened the door, the
daughters both gave a loud scream. We all stopped, and then
Miss Branghton called out, "Lord, Papa, what do you bring the
company up here for? why, Polly and I a'n't half dressed."

"More shame for you," answered he, "here's your aunt, and cousin, and M. Du Bois, all waiting, and ne'er a room to take them to."

"Who'd have thought of their coming so soon?" cried she: "I'm sure for my part I thought Miss was used to nothing but quality hours."[1]

"Why, I shan't be ready this half-hour yet," said Miss Polly; "can't they stay in the shop, till we're dressed?"

Mr. Branghton was very angry, and scolded them violently; however, we were obliged to descend, and stools were procured for us in the shop, where we found the brother, who was highly delighted, he said, that his sisters had been *catched*; and he thought proper to entertain me with a long account of their tediousness, and the many quarrels they all had together.

When, at length, these ladies were equipped to their satisfaction, they made their appearance; but before any conversation was suffered to pass between them and us, they had a long and most disagreeable dialogue with their father, to whose reprimands, though so justly incurred, they replied with the utmost pertness and rudeness, while their brother, all the time, laughed aloud.

The moment they perceived this, they were so much provoked, that, instead of making any apologies to Madame Duval, they next began a quarrel with him. "Tom, what do you laugh for? I wonder what business you have to be always a laughing when Papa scolds us."

"Then what business have you to be such a while getting on your cloaths? You're never ready, you know well enough."

"Lord, Sir, I wonder what that's to you! I wish you'd mind your own affairs, and not trouble yourself about ours. How should a boy like you know any thing?"

"A boy, indeed! not such a boy, neither; I'll warrant you'll be glad to be as young, when you come to be old maids."

This sort of dialogue we were amused with till dinner was ready, when we again mounted up two pair of stairs.

In our way, Miss Polly told me that her sister had asked Mr.

---

1   Fashionable hours consisted of late nights, late risings, late mealtimes.

Smith for his room to dine in, but he had refused to lend it; "because," she said, "one day it happened to be a little greased: however, we shall have it to drink tea in, and then, perhaps, you may see him, and I assure you he's quite like one of the quality, and dresses as fine, and goes to balls and dances, and every thing quite in taste; – and besides, Miss, he keeps a foot-boy of his own, too."

The dinner was ill-served, ill-cooked, and ill-managed. The maid who waited had so often to go down stairs for something that was forgotten, that the Branghtons were perpetually oblig-ed to rise from table themselves, to get plates, knives and forks, bread or beer. Had they been without *pretensions*, all this would have seemed of no consequence; but they aimed at appearing to advantage, and even fancied they succeeded. However, the most disagreeable part of our fare was, that the whole family continually disputed whose turn it was to rise, and whose to be allowed to sit still.

When this meal was over, Madame Duval, ever eager to dis-course upon *her travels*, entered into an argument with Mr. Branghton, and in broken English, M. Du Bois, concerning the French nation: and Miss Polly, then addressing herself to me, said, "Don't you think, Miss, it's very dull sitting up stairs here? we'd better go down *to shop*, and then we shall see the people go by."

"Lord, Poll," said the brother, "you're always wanting to be staring and gaping; and I'm sure you need n't be so fond of shewing yourself, for you're ugly enough to frighten a horse."

"Ugly, indeed! I wonder which is best, you or me. But, I tell you what, Tom, you've no need to give yourself such airs, for if you do, I'll tell Miss of you know what – ."

"Who cares if you do? you may tell what you will; I don't mind – "

"Indeed," cried I, "I do not desire to hear any secrets."

"O, but I'm resolved I'll tell you, because Tom's so very spiteful. You must know, Miss, t'other night – "

"Poll," cried the brother, "if you tell of that, Miss shall know all about your meeting young Brown, – you know when! – So I'll be quits with you, one way or another."

Miss Polly coloured, and again proposed our going down stairs till Mr. Smith's room was ready for our reception.

"Aye, so we will," said Miss Branghton; "I'll assure you, Cousin, we have some very genteel people pass by our shop sometimes. Polly and I always go and sit there, when we've cleaned ourselves."

"Yes, Miss," cried the brother, "they do nothing else all day long, when father don't scold them. But the best fun is, when they've got all their dirty things on, and all their hair about their ears, sometimes I send young Brown up stairs to them; and then, there's such a fuss! – there they hide themselves, and run away, and squeel and squall like any thing mad: and so then I puts the two cats into the room, and I gives 'em a good whipping, and so that sets them a squalling too; so there's such a noise, and such an uproar! – Lord, you can't think, Miss, what fun it is!"

This occasioned a fresh quarrel with the sisters; at the end of which, it was, at length, decided that we should go to the shop.

In our way down stairs, Miss Branghton said aloud, "I wonder when Mr. Smith's room will be ready."

"So do I," answered Polly; "I'm sure we should not do any harm to it now."

This hint had not the desired effect; for we were suffered to proceed very quietly.

As we entered the shop, I observed a young man, in deep mourning,[1] leaning against the wall, with his arms folded, and his eyes fixed on the ground, apparently in profound and melancholy meditation: but the moment he perceived us, he started, and, making a passing bow, very abruptly retired. As I found he was permitted to go quite unnoticed, I could not forbear enquiring who he was.

"Lord!" answered Miss Branghton, "he's nothing but a poor Scotch poet."[2]

"For my part," said Miss Polly, "I believe he's just starved, for

---

1  Indicates that the person McCartney is mourning was someone to whom he was closely attached and that the bereavement was recent.

2  Miss Branghton expresses her negative opinion of McCartney's profession and nationality through this phrase; it was an opinion shared by many English. Many

I don't find he has any thing to live upon."

"Live upon!" cried the brother, "why he's a poet, you know, so he may live upon learning."

"Aye, and good enough for him too," said Miss Branghton, "for he's as proud as he's poor."

"Like enough," replied the brother, "but, for all that, you won't find he will live without meat and drink: no, no, catch a Scotchman at that if you can! why, they only come here for what they can get."

"I'm sure," said Miss Branghton, "I wonder Papa 'll be such a fool as to let him stay in the house, for I dare say he'll never pay for his lodging."

"Why, no more he would if he could get another Lodger: you know the bill's been put up this fortnight. Miss, if you should hear of a person that wants a room, I assure you it is a very good one, for all it's up three pair of stairs."

I answered that as I had no acquaintance in London, I had not any chance of assisting them: but both my compassion and my curiosity were excited for this poor young man; and I asked them some further particulars concerning him.

They then acquainted me, that they had only known him three months. When he first lodged with them, he agreed to board also; but had lately told them, he would eat by himself, though they all believed he had hardly ever tasted a morsel of meat since he left their table. They said, that he had always appeared very low-spirited, but, for the last month, he had been *duller* than ever, and, all of a sudden, had put himself into mourning, though they knew not for whom, nor for what, but they supposed it was only for convenience, as no person had ever been to see or enquire for him since his residence amongst them: and they were sure he was very poor, as he had not paid for his lodgings the last three weeks: and finally, they concluded he was a poet, or else half-crazy, because they had, at different times, found scraps of poetry in his room.

---

Scots had come to London since the Union between the two countries in 1707, hoping to find their fortunes there. The English resented the competition for jobs this created, ridiculed the Scots for their speech and dress, and, after the Jacobite Rebellions of 1715 and 1745, remained suspicious of their loyalty to the Union and their potential for provoking political upheaval.

They then produced some unfinished verses, written on small pieces of paper, unconnected, and of a most melancholy cast. Among them was the fragment of an ode,[1] which, at my request, they lent me to copy; and, as you may perhaps like to see it, I will write it now.

> O LIFE! thou lingering dream of grief, of pain,
> And every ill that Nature can sustain,
> Strange, mutable, and wild!
> Now flattering with Hope most fair,
> Depressing now with fell Despair,
> The nurse of Guilt, the slave of Pride,
> That, like a wayward child,
> Who, to himself a foe,
> Sees joy alone in what's denied,
> In what is granted, woe!
>
> ───────────
>
> O thou poor, feeble, fleeting pow'r,
> By Vice seduc'd, by Folly woo'd,
> By Mis'ry, Shame, Remorse, pursu'd;
> And as thy toilsome steps proceed,
> Seeming to Youth the fairest flow'r,
> Proving to Age the rankest weed,
> A gilded, but a bitter pill,
> Of varied, great, and complicated ill!

These lines are harsh, but they indicate an internal wretchedness which, I own, affects me. Surely this young man must be involved in misfortunes of no common nature: but I cannot imagine what can induce him to remain with this unfeeling family, where he is, most unworthily, despised for being poor, and, most illiberally, detested for being a Scotchman. He may, indeed, have motives which he cannot surmount, for submitting to such a situation. Whatever they are, I most heartily pity him, and cannot but wish it were in my power to afford him some relief.

---

1  An ode in ancient literature referred to a poem meant to be sung (e.g., the odes of Horace). "In modern use: a rimed (rarely unrimed) lyric, often in the form of an address; generally dignified or exalted in subject, feeling, and style …" (*OED*).

During this conversation, Mr. Smith's foot-boy came to Miss Branghton, and informed her, that his master said she might have the room now when she liked it, for that he was presently going out.

This very genteel message, though it perfectly satisfied the Miss Branghtons, by no means added to my desire of being introduced to this gentleman: and upon their rising, with intention to accept his offer, I begged they would excuse my attending them, and said I would sit with Madame Duval till the tea was ready.

I therefore once more went up two pair of stairs, with young Branghton, who insisted upon accompanying me; and there we remained, till Mr. Smith's foot-boy summoned us to tea, when I followed Madame Duval into the dining-room.

The Miss Branghtons were seated at one window, and Mr. Smith was lolling indolently out of the other. They all approached us at our entrance, and Mr. Smith, probably to shew he was master of the apartment, most officiously handed me to a great chair, at the upper end of the room, without taking any notice of Madame Duval, till I rose, and offered her my own seat.

Leaving the rest of the company to entertain themselves, he, very abruptly, began to address himself to me, in a style of gallantry equally new and disagreeable to me. It is true, no man can possibly pay me greater compliments, or make more fine speeches, than Sir Clement Willoughby, yet his language, though too flowery, is always that of a gentleman, and his address and manners are so very superior to those of the inhabitants of this house, that to make any comparison between him and Mr. Smith would be extremely unjust. This latter seems very desirous of appearing a man of gaiety and spirit; but his vivacity is so low-bred, and his whole behaviour so forward and disagreeable, that I should prefer the company of *dullness* itself, even as that goddess is described by Pope,[1] to that of this *sprightly* young man.

---

1  In his *Dunciad* (1728; 1743), Pope describes Dulness (sic) as "Laborious, heavy, busy, bold, and blind, / She rul'd in native Anarchy, the mind" (I. 15-16). His satire attacks the literary and social establishments of London during the early to mid-eighteenth century.

He made many apologies that he had not lent his room for our dinner, which, he said, he should certainly have done, had he seen me first; and he assured me, that when I came again, he should be very glad to oblige me.

I told him, and with sincerity, that every part of the house was equally indifferent to me.

"Why, Ma'am, the truth is, Miss Biddy and Polly take no care of any thing, else, I'm sure, they should be always welcome to my room; for I'm never so happy as in obliging the ladies, – that's my character, Ma'am; – but, really, the last time they had it, every thing was made so greasy and so nasty, that, upon my word, to a man who wishes to have things a little genteel, it was quite cruel. Now, as to you, Ma'am, it's quite another thing; for I should not mind if every thing I had was spoilt, for the sake of having the pleasure to oblige you; and, I assure you, Ma'am, it makes me quite happy, that I have a room good enough to receive you."

This elegant speech was followed by many others, so much in the same style, that to write them would be superfluous; and, as he did not allow me a moment to speak to any other person, the rest of the evening was consumed in a painful attention to this irksome young man, who seemed to intend appearing before me to the utmost advantage.

Adieu, my dear Sir. I fear you will be sick of reading about this family; yet I must write of them, or not of any, since I mix with no other. Happy shall I be, when I quit them all, and again return to Berry Hill!

# LETTER XII.

*Evelina in continuation.*

June 10<sup>th</sup>.

This morning, Mr. Smith called, *on purpose*, he said, to offer me a ticket for the next Hampstead assembly.[1] I thanked him, but desired to be excused accepting it; he would not, however, be denied, nor answered, and, in a manner both vehement and free, pressed and urged his offer till I was wearied to death: but, when he found me resolute, he seemed thunderstruck with amazement, and thought proper to desire I would tell him my reasons.[2]

Obvious as they must, surely, have been to any other person, they were such as I knew not how to repeat to him; and, when he found I hesitated, he said, "Indeed, Ma'am, you are too modest; I assure you the ticket is quite at your service, and I shall be very happy to dance with you; so pray don't be so coy."

"Indeed, Sir," returned I, "you are mistaken; I never supposed you would offer a ticket, without wishing it should be accepted; but it would answer no purpose to mention the reasons which make me decline it, since they cannot possibly be removed."

This speech seemed very much to mortify him, which I could not be concerned at, as I did not chuse to be treated by him with so much freedom. When he was, at last, convinced that his application to me was ineffectual, he addressed himself to Madame Duval, and begged she would interfere in his favour, offering, at the same time, to procure another ticket for herself.

"*Ma foi,* Sir," answered she, angrily, "you might as well have had the complaisance[3] to ask me before, for, I assure you, I

---

1 A public dance at Hampstead, in northwest London, a fashionable spa in the eighteenth century.
2 Evelina declines Mr. Smith's offer of a ticket to the assembly because it would not be proper for her, as an unchaperoned young woman unacquainted with him, to accept it.
3 Courtesy.

don't approve of no such rudeness: however, you may keep your tickets to yourself, for we don't want none of 'em."

This rebuke almost overset him; he made many apologies, and said that he should certainly have first applied to her, but that he had no notion the *young* lady would have refused him, and, on the contrary, had concluded that she would have assisted him to persuade Madame Duval herself.

This excuse appeased her; and he pleaded his cause so successfully, that, to my great chagrin, he gained it: and Madame Duval promised that she would go herself, and take me to the Hampstead assembly whenever he pleased.

Mr. Smith then, approaching me with an air of triumph, said, "Well, Ma'am, now, I think, you can't possibly keep to your denial."

I made no answer, and he soon took leave, though not till he had so wonderfully gained the favour of Madame Duval, that she declared, when he was gone, he was the prettiest young man she had seen since she came to England.

As soon as I could find an opportunity, I ventured, in the most humble manner, to entreat Madame Duval would not insist upon my attending her to this ball; and represented to her, as well as I was able, the impropriety of my accepting any present from a young man so entirely unknown to me: but she laughed at my scruples, called me a foolish, ignorant country girl, and said she should make it her business to teach me something of the world.

This ball is to be next week. I am sure it is not more improper for, than unpleasant to me, and I will use every possible endeavour to avoid it. Perhaps I may apply to Miss Branghton for advice, as I believe she will be willing to assist me, from disliking, equally with myself, that I should dance with Mr. Smith.

June 11<sup>th</sup>.

O, my dear Sir! I have been shocked to death, – and yet, at the same time, delighted beyond expression, in the hope that I have happily been the instrument of saving a human creature from destruction!

This morning, Madame Duval said she would invite the Branghton family to return our visit to-morrow; and, not chusing to rise herself, – for she generally spends the morning in bed, – she desired me to wait upon them with her message. M. Du Bois, who just then called, insisted upon attending me.

Mr. Branghton was in the shop, and told us that his son and daughters were out; but desired me to step up stairs, as he very soon expected them home. This I did, leaving M. Du Bois below. I went into the room where we had dined the day before, and, by a wonderful chance, I happened so to seat myself, that I had a view of the stairs, and yet could not be seen from them.

In about ten minutes time, I saw, passing by the door, with a look perturbed and affrighted, the same young man I mentioned in my last letter. Not heeding, as I suppose, how he went, in turning the corner of the stairs, which are narrow and winding, his foot slipped, and he fell, but, almost instantly rising, I plainly perceived the end of a pistol, which started from his pocket, by hitting against the stairs.

I was inexpressibly shocked. All that I had heard of his misery occurring to my memory, made me conclude, that he was, at that very moment, meditating suicide! Struck with the dreadful idea, all my strength seemed to fail me. He moved on slowly, yet I soon lost sight of him; I sat motionless with terror; all power of action forsook me; and I grew almost stiff with horror: till, recollecting that it was yet possible to prevent the fatal deed, all my faculties seemed to return, with the hope of saving him.

My first thought was to fly to Mr. Branghton, but I feared that an instant of time lost, might for ever be rued; and therefore, guided by the impulse of my apprehensions, as well as I was able, I followed him up stairs, stepping very softly, and obliged to support myself by the banisters.

When I came within a few stairs of the landing-place, I stopped, for I could then see into his room, as he had not yet shut the door.

He had put the pistol upon a table, and had his hand in his pocket, whence, in a few moments, he took out another: He then emptied something on the table from a small leather bag;[1] after which, taking up both the pistols, one in each hand, he dropt hastily upon his knees, and called out "O God! – forgive me!"

In a moment, strength and courage seemed lent me as by inspiration: I started, and rushing precipitately into the room, just caught his arm, and then, overcome by my own fears, I fell down at his side, breathless and senseless. My recovery, however, was, I believe, almost instantaneous; and then the sight of this unhappy man, regarding me with a look of unutterable astonishment, mixed with concern, presently restored to me my recollection. I arose, though with difficulty; he did the same; the pistols, as I soon saw, were both on the floor.

Unwilling to leave them, and, indeed, too weak to move, I leant one hand on the table, and then stood perfectly still: while he, his eyes cast wildly towards me, seemed too infinitely amazed to be capable of either speech or action.

I believe we were some minutes in this extraordinary situation; but, as my strength returned, I felt myself both ashamed and awkward, and moved towards the door. Pale, and motionless, he suffered me to pass, without changing his posture, or uttering a syllable; and, indeed,

He looked a bloodless image of despair![2*]

When I reached the door, I turned round; I looked fearfully at the pistols, and, impelled by an emotion I could not repress, I hastily stepped back, with an intention of carrying them away: but their wretched owner, perceiving my design, and recovering from his astonishment, darting suddenly down, seized them both himself.

Wild with fright, and scarce knowing what I did, I caught, almost involuntarily, hold of both his arms, and exclaimed, "O Sir! have mercy on yourself!"

The guilty pistols fell from his hands, which, disengaging

---

1   The bag probably contains gun powder and shot, as Macartney purchases these items with the guns (see Letter XX).
2   *FB's note: Pope's Iliad. Pope's translation of Homer's *Iliad* (1715-20), Book XIII, line 365: "And looks a bloodless image of despair."

from me, he fervently clasped, and cried, "Sweet Heaven! is this thy angel?"

Encouraged by such gentleness, I again attempted to take the pistols, but, with a look half frantic, he again prevented me, saying, "What would you do?"

"Awaken you," I cried, with a courage I now wonder at, "to worthier thoughts, and rescue you from perdition."

I then seized the pistols; he said not a word, – he made no effort to stop me; – I glided quick by him, and tottered down stairs, ere he had recovered from the extremest amazement.

The moment I reached again the room I had so fearfully left, I threw away the pistols, and flinging myself on the first chair, gave free vent to the feelings I had most painfully stifled, in a violent burst of tears, which, indeed, proved a happy relief to me.

In this situation I remained some time; but when, at length, I lifted up my head, the first object I saw, was the poor man who had occasioned my terror, standing, as if petrified, at the door, and gazing at me with eyes of wild wonder.

I started from the chair, but trembled so excessively, that I almost instantly sunk again into it. He then, though without advancing, and in a faltering voice, said, "Whoever or whatever you are, relieve me, I pray you, from the suspence under which my soul labours – and tell me if indeed I do not dream!"

To this address, so singular and so solemn, I had not then the presence of mind to frame any answer: but, as I presently perceived that his eyes turned from me to the pistols, and that he seemed to intend regaining them, I exerted all my strength, and saying "O for Heaven's sake forbear!" I rose and took them myself.

"Do my senses deceive me!" cried he, "do *I* live – ? and do *you*?"

As he spoke, he advanced towards me, and I, still guarding the pistols, retreated, saying "No, no – you must not – must not have them!" –

"Why – for what purpose, tell me! – do you withhold them?" –

"To give you time to *think*, – to save you from eternal misery, – and, I hope, to reserve you for mercy and forgiveness."

"Wonderful!" cried he, with uplifted hands and eyes, "most wonderful!"

For some time, he seemed wrapped in deep thought, till a sudden noise of tongues below, announcing the approach of the Branghtons, made him start from his reverie: he sprung hastily forward, – dropt on one knee, – caught hold of my gown, which he pressed to his lips, and then, quick as lightening, he rose, and flew up stairs to his own room.

There was something in the whole of this extraordinary and shocking adventure, really too affecting to be borne; and so entirely had I spent my spirits and exhausted my courage, that, before the Branghtons reached me, I had sunk on the ground, without sense or motion.

I believe I must have been a very horrid sight to them, on their entrance into the room; for, to all appearance, I seemed to have suffered a violent death, either by my own rashness, or the cruelty of some murderer; as the pistols had fallen close by my side.

How soon I recovered, I know not, but, probably, I was more indebted to the loudness of their cries, than to their assistance; for they all concluded that I was dead, and, for some time, did not make any effort to revive me.

Scarcely could I recollect *where*, or, indeed, *what* I was, ere they poured upon me such a torrent of questions and enquiries, that I was almost stunned with their vociferation. However, as soon and as well as I was able, I endeavoured to satisfy their curiosity, by recounting what had happened as clearly as was in my power. They all looked aghast at the recital, but, not being well enough to enter into any discussions, I begged to have a chair called, and to return instantly home.

Before I left them, I recommended, with great earnestness, a vigilant observance of their unhappy lodger, and that they would take care to keep from him, if possible, all means of self-destruction.

M. Du Bois, who seemed extremely concerned at my disposition, walked by the side of the chair, and saw me safe to my own apartment.

The rashness and the misery of this ill-fated young man, engross all my thoughts. If, indeed, he is bent upon destroying himself, all efforts to save him will be fruitless. How much do I wish it were in my power to discover the nature of the malady which thus maddens him, and to offer or to procure alleviation to his sufferings! I am sure, my dearest Sir, you will be much concerned for this poor man; and, were you here, I doubt not but you would find some method of awakening him from the error which blinds him, and of pouring the balm of peace and comfort into his afflicted soul!

## LETTER XIII.

*Evelina in continuation.*

Holborn, June 13th.

Yesterday all the Branghtons dined here.

Our conversation was almost wholly concerning the adventure of the day before. Mr. Branghton said, that his first thought was instantly to turn his lodger out of doors, "Lest," continued he, "his killing himself in my house, should bring me into any trouble; but then, I was afraid I should never get the money he owes me, whereas, if he dies in my house, I have a right to all he leaves behind him, if he goes off in my debt. Indeed, I would put him in prison,[1] – but what should I get by that? he could not earn any thing there to pay me. So I considered about it some time, and then I determined to ask him, point-blank, for my money out of hand. And so I did, but he told me he'd pay me next week: however, I gave him to understand, that, though I was no Scotchman, yet I did not like to be over-reached[2] any more than he; so then, he gave me a ring, which, to my certain knowledge, must be worth ten guineas, and told me he would not part with it for his life, and a good deal more such sort of stuff, but that I might keep it till he could pay me."

"It is ten to one, Father," said young Branghton, "if he came fairly by it."

---

1  Many were incarcerated for debt in inhumane conditions from which it was difficult to escape unless one's friends paid off one's debt.
2  "The gaining of an advantage by deception" (*OED*).

"Very likely not," answered he, "but that will make no great difference; for I shall be able to prove my right to it all one."[1]

What principles! I could hardly stay in the room.

"I'm determined," said the son, "I'll take some opportunity to affront him soon, now I know how poor he is, because of the airs he gave himself to me when he first came."

"And pray how was that, child?" said Madame Duval.

"Why you never knew such a fuss in your life as he made, because, one day at dinner, I only happened to say, that I supposed he had never got such a good meal in his life, before he came to England: there he fell in such a passion as you can't think; but, for my part, I took no notice of it, for to be sure, thinks I, he must needs be a gentleman, or he'd never go to be so angry about it. However, he won't put his tricks upon me again, in a hurry."

"Well," said Miss Polly, "he's grown quite another creature to what he was, and he does n't run away from us, nor hide himself, nor any thing; and he's as civil as can be, and he's always in the shop, and he saunters about the stairs, and he looks at every body as comes in."

"Why you may see what he's after plain enough," said Mr. Branghton; "he wants to see Miss again."

"Ha, ha, ha! Lord, how I should laugh," said the son, "if he should have fell in love with Miss!"

"I'm sure," said Miss Branghton, "Miss is welcome; but, for my part, I should be quite ashamed of such a beggarly conquest."

Such was the conversation till tea-time, when the appearance of Mr. Smith gave a new turn to the discourse.

Miss Branghton desired me to remark with what a *smart air* he entered the room, and asked me if he had not very much a *quality look*?

"Come," cried he, advancing to us, "you ladies must not sit together; wherever I go, I always make it a rule to part the ladies."

---

1   Mr. Branghton is sure he will be able to legally obtain all of Macartney's goods in lieu of the rent the young man owes him.

And then, handing Miss Branghton to the next chair, he seated himself between us.

"Well, now, ladies, I think we sit very well. What say you? for my part, I think it was a very good motion."

"If my Cousin likes it," said Miss Branghton, "I'm sure I've no objection."

"O," cried he, "I always study what the ladies like, – that's my first thought. And, indeed, it is but natural that you should like best to sit by the gentlemen, for what can you find to say to one another?"

"Say?" cried young Branghton, "O, never you think of that, they'll find enough to say, I'll be sworn. You know the women are never tired of talking."

"Come, come, Tom," said Mr. Smith, "don't be severe upon the ladies; when I'm by, you know I always take their part."

Soon after, when Miss Branghton offered me some cake, this man of gallantry said, "Well, if I was that lady, I'd never take any thing from a woman."

"Why not, Sir?"

"Because I should be afraid of being poisoned for being so handsome."

"Who is severe upon the ladies *now?*" said I.

"Why, really, Ma'am, it was a slip of the tongue; I did not intend to say such a thing; but one can't always be on one's guard."

Soon after, the conversation turning upon public places, young Branghton asked if I had ever been to *George's* at Hampstead?[1]

"Indeed I never heard the place mentioned."

"Did n't you, Miss?" cried he, eagerly, "why then you've a deal of fun to come, I'll promise you; and, I tell you what, I'll treat you there some Sunday soon. So now, Bid and Poll, be sure you don't tell Miss about the chairs, and all that, for I've a mind to surprise her; and if I pay, I think I've a right to have it my own way."

---

1  Possibly New Georgia, a tea house and garden in Hampstead, full of curiosities, or simply a tavern in the growing town (Bloom 414; Doody 478 n. 57).

"George's at Hampstead!" repeated Mr. Smith, contemptuously, "how came you to think the young Lady would like to go to such a low place as that! But, pray Ma'am, have you ever been to Don Saltero's at Chelsea?"[1]

"No, Sir."

"No! – nay, then, I must insist on having the pleasure of conducting you there before long. I assure you, Ma'am, many genteel people go, or else, I give you my word, *I* should not recommend it."

"Pray, Cousin," said Mr. Branghton, "have you been at Sadler's Wells,[2] yet?"

"No, Sir."

"No! why then you've seen nothing!"

"Pray, Miss," said the Son, "how do you like the Tower of London?"

"I have never been to it, Sir."

"Goodness!" exclaimed he, "not seen the Tower! – why may be you ha' n't been o' top of the Monument,[3] neither?"

"No, indeed, I have not."

"Why then you might as well not have come to London, for aught I see, for you've been no where."

"Pray, Miss," said Polly, "have you been all over Paul's Church, yet?"

"No, Ma'am."

"Well, but, Ma'am," said Mr. Smith, "how do you like Vauxhall and Marybone?"[4]

---

1  A coffee house and museum of curiosities on Cheyne Walk in Chelsea run by a barber named Salter until 1768, and then by his daughter until 1799 when the collection was sold. One of the sights attractive to foreign tourists visiting London during the eighteenth century (Wheatley 511-12; Weinreb 152).

2  Originally a music hall, then a theater, Sadler's Wells in Islington (East London) was founded in 1683 by a surveyor named Sadler who discovered the mineral spring there. It was popular at the beginning of the eighteenth century with fashionable society, but by 1770 was on the decline as a resort (Wheatley 199-200).

3  The Monument, in East-Central London, was a stone pillar in the doric mode designed by Christopher Wren and Robert Hooke and erected in 1671-77 to commemorate the Great Fire of London. At 202 feet, it is the "tallest isolated stone column in the world" (Weinreb 525-6). Eighteenth-century visitors could climb to the gallery at the top of the monument where they had a view of London.

4  Vauxhall, called The New Spring Garden until 1785, opened in 1660 and was initially free to the public (from 1732-92 a shilling was charged for admission). In

"I never saw either, Sir."

"No! – God bless me! – you really surprise me, – why Vaux-hall is the first pleasure in life! – I know nothing like it. – Well, Ma'am, you must have been with strange people, indeed, not to have taken you to Vauxhall. Why you have seen nothing of London yet. – However, we must try if *we* can't make you amends."

In the course of this *catechism*, many other places were mentioned, of which I have forgotten the names; but the looks of surprise and contempt that my repeated negatives incurred, were very diverting.

"Come," said Mr. Smith, after tea, "as this Lady has been with such a queer set of people, let's shew her the difference; suppose we go somewhere to-night! – I love to do things with spirit! – Come, Ladies, where shall we go? For my part, I should like Foote's,[1] – but the Ladies must chuse; I never speak myself."

"Well, Mr. Smith is always in such spirits!" said Miss Branghton.

"Why yes, Ma'am, yes, thank God, pretty good spirits; – I have not yet the cares of the world upon me, – I am not *married*, – ha, ha, ha, – you'll excuse me, Ladies, – but I can't help laughing! – "

---

1778 there were two ways to get to the fashionable gardens: by boat on the Thames River, or by foot or carriage using Westminster Bridge. The main avenues of the gardens were well lit, unlike the "dark walks" which were often used for clandestine rendezvous (attempts to bar people from entering these walks were made in 1764 but proved ineffective). One might enjoy instrumental or vocal concerts; walking in the landscaped gardens, complete with a man-made waterfall or cascade which was activated at 9:00 p.m. each evening; eating and drinking in the boxes; visiting the Picture Room. The last night of the season at Vauxhall could become riotous, as it had during the 1770s. Marylebone Gardens was opened in 1650 as fields where such entertainments as cock-fighting and bear-baiting could occur; in 1739 rooms were built to house concerts, balls, and allow for covered walking. In the 1770s until their closure in 1778, the gardens were known for their musical entertainments, mineral spring, refreshments, and spectacular fireworks displays.

1 Samuel Foote's little theater in the Haymarket. Foote (1720–77), actor and satiric playwright, as well as theater manager, built the theater in 1760 and redecorated it in 1767. This establishment provided entertainment to those who remained in London after the season was over in June and before it began again in September (a period during which the larger theaters such as Drury Lane and Covent Garden were closed).

No objection being made, to my great relief, we all proceeded to the little theatre in the Haymarket, where I was extremely entertained by the performance of the Minor and the
Commissary.[1]

They all returned hither to supper.


## LETTER XIV.

*Evelina in continuation.*

June 15th.

Yesterday morning, Madame Duval again sent me to Mr.
Branghton's attended by M. Du Bois, to make some party for
the evening; because she had had the vapours the preceding
day, from staying at home.

As I entered the shop, I perceived the unfortunate North
Briton,[2] seated in a corner, with a book in his hand. He cast his
melancholy eyes up, as we came in, and, I believe, immediately
recollected my face, for he started and changed colour. I delivered Madame Duval's message to Mr. Branghton; who told me
I should find Polly up stairs, but that the others were gone out.

Up stairs, therefore, I went; and seated on a window, with
Mr. Brown at her side, sat Miss Polly. I felt a little awkward at
disturbing them, and much more so, at their behaviour afterwards: for, as soon as the common enquiries were over, Mr.
Brown grew so fond,[3] and so foolish, that I was extremely disgusted. Polly, all the time, only rebuked him with "La, now, Mr.
Brown, do be quiet, can't you? – you should not behave so
before company. – Why now what will Miss think of me?" –
while her looks plainly shewed not merely the pleasure, but the
pride which she took in his caresses.

I did not, by any means, think it necessary to punish myself
by witnessing their tenderness, and, therefore, telling them I

---

1  *The Minor* (1760) and *The Commissary* (1765) were two farces by Foote.
2  Macartney, the Scot.
3  "Infatuated, foolish, silly" (*OED*).

would see if Miss Branghton were returned home, I soon left them, and again descended into the shop.

"So, Miss, you've come again," said Mr. Branghton, "what, I suppose, you've a mind to sit a little in the shop, and see how the world goes, hay, Miss?"

I made no answer; and M. Du Bois instantly brought me a chair.

The unhappy stranger, who had risen at my entrance, again seated himself; and, though his head leant towards his book, I could not help observing, that his eyes were most intently and earnestly turned towards me.

M. Du Bois, as well as his broken English would allow him, endeavoured to entertain us, till the return of Miss Branghton and her brother.

"Lord, how tired I am!" cried the former, "I have not a foot to stand upon." And then, without any ceremony, she flung herself into the chair from which I had risen to receive her.

"You tired!" said the brother, "why then what must I be, that have walked twice as far?" And with equal politeness, he paid the same compliment to M. Du Bois which his sister had done to me.

Two chairs and three stools compleated the furniture of the shop, and Mr. Branghton, who chose to keep his own seat himself, desired M. Du Bois to take another; and then, seeing that I was without any, called out to the stranger, "Come, Mr. Macartney, lend us your stool."

Shocked at their rudeness, I declined the offer, and approaching Miss Branghton, said, "If you will be so good as to make room for me on your chair, there will be no occasion to disturb that gentleman."

"Lord, what signifies that?" cried the brother, "he has had his share of sitting, I'll be sworn."

"And if he has not," said the sister, "he has a chair up stairs; and the shop is our own, I hope."

This grossness so much disgusted me, that I took the stool, and carrying it back to Mr. Macartney myself, I returned him thanks, as civilly as I could, for this politeness, but said that I had rather stand.

He looked at me as if unaccustomed to such attention, bowed very respectfully, but neither spoke, nor yet made use of it.

I soon found that I was an object of derision to all present, except M. Du Bois, and, therefore, I begged Mr. Branghton would give me an answer for Madame Duval, as I was in haste to return.

"Well, then, Tom, – Biddy, – where have you a mind to go to-night? your Aunt and Miss want to be abroad and amongst them."

"Why then, Papa," said Miss Branghton, "we'll go to Don Saltero's. Mr. Smith likes that place, so may be he'll go along with us."

"No, no," said the son, "I'm for White-Conduit House;[1] so let's go there."

"White-Conduit House, indeed?" cried his sister, "no, Tom, that I won't."

"Why then let it alone; nobody wants your company; – we shall do as well without you, I'll be sworn, and better too."

"I'll tell you what, Tom, if you don't hold your tongue, I'll make you repent it, – that I assure you."

Just then, Mr. Smith came into the shop, which he seemed to intend passing through; but when he saw me, he stopped and began a most courteous enquiry after my health, protesting that, had he known I was there, he should have come down sooner. "But, bless me, Ma'am," added he, "what is the reason you stand?" and then he flew to bring me the seat from which I had just parted.

"Mr. Smith, you are come in very good time," said Mr. Branghton, "to end a dispute between my son and daughter, about where they shall all go to-night."

"O fie, Tom, – dispute with a lady!" cried Mr. Smith, "Now, as for me, I'm for where you will, provided this young Lady is of the party, – one place is the same as another to me, so that it

---

1 The White Conduit House was a tavern in Islington near the White Conduit; opened in the 1640s, it was a refuge for eighteenth-century families from the city, offering fresh bread and milk. Diversions included cricket, a shrubbery maze, gardens and a fishpond (Weinreb 953).

be but agreeable to the ladies, – I would go any where with you, Ma'am," (to me) "unless, indeed, it were to *church*; – ha, ha, ha, – you'll excuse me, Ma'am, but, really, I never could conquer my fear of a parson; – ha, ha, ha, – really, ladies, I beg your pardon, for being so rude, but I can't help laughing for my life!"

"I was just saying, Mr. Smith," said Miss Branghton, "that I should like to go to Don Saltero's; – now pray where should *you* like to go?"

"Why really, Miss Biddy, you know I always let the ladies decide; I never fix any thing myself; but I should suppose it would be rather hot at the coffee-house, – however, pray, Ladies, settle it among yourselves, – I'm agreeable to whatever you chuse."

It was easy for me to discover, that this man, with all his parade of *conformity*, objects to every thing that is not proposed by himself: but he is so much admired, by this family, for his *gentility*, that he thinks himself a complete fine gentleman!

"Come," said Mr. Branghton, "the best way will be to put it to the vote, and then every body will speak their minds. Biddy, call Poll down stairs. We'll start fair."

"Lord, Papa," said Miss Branghton, "why can't you as well send Tom? – you're always sending me of the errands."

A dispute then ensued, but Miss Branghton was obliged to yield.

When Mr. Brown and Miss Polly made their appearance, the latter uttered many complaints of having been called, saying she did not want to come, and was very well where she was.

"Now, Ladies, your votes;" cried Mr. Smith, "and so, Ma'am," (to me) "we'll begin with you. What place shall you like best?" and then, in a whisper, he added, "I assure you, I shall say the same as you do, whether I like it or not."

I said, that as I was ignorant what choice was in my power, I must beg to hear their decisions first. This was reluctantly assented to; and then Miss Branghton voted for Saltero's Coffee-house; her sister, for a party to *Mother Red Cap's*;[1] the

---

1   Mother Red Cap's was a popular tavern in Kentish Town. Mackinnon notes that the sign outside the public house had a woman in a tall red hat holding cakes in

brother, for White-Conduit House; Mr. Brown, for Bagnigge Wells;[1] Mr. Branghton for Sadler's Wells; and Mr. Smith for Vauxhall.

"Well now, Ma'am," said Mr. Smith, "we have all spoken, and so you must give the casting vote. Come, what will you fix upon?"

"Sir," answered I, "I was to speak *last*."

"Well, so you will," said Miss Branghton, "for we've all spoke first."

"Pardon me," returned I, "the voting has not yet been quite general."

And I looked towards Mr. Macartney, to whom I wished extremely to shew that I was not of the same brutal nature with those by whom he was treated so grossly.

"Why pray," said Mr. Branghton, "who have we left out? would you have the cats and dogs vote?"

"No, Sir," cried I, with some spirit, "I would have *that gentleman* vote, – if, indeed, he is not superior to joining our party."

They all looked at me, as if they doubted whether or not they had heard me right: but, in a few moments, their surprise gave way to a rude burst of laughter.

Very much displeased, I told M. Du Bois that if he was not ready to go, I would have a coach called for myself.

O yes, he said, he was always ready to attend me.

Mr. Smith then advancing, attempted to take my hand, and begged me not to leave them till I had settled the evening's plan.

"I have nothing, Sir," said I, "to do with it, as it is my intention to stay at home; and therefore Mr. Branghton will be so good as to send Madame Duval word what place is fixed upon, when it is convenient to him."

---

one hand and a pot of ale in the other. He suggests that the name of the tavern was derived from "a remarkable shrew of Kentish Town who was also called Mother Damnable" (529).

1 Bagnigge Wells at King's Cross Road was a popular and fashionable spa during the mid- to late-eighteenth century. "In the grounds were honeysuckle-covered tea arbours, a bun house, skittle alley, bowling green, grotto, flower garden, fish pond, fountain and formal walks edged with holly and box…. Concerts and other entertainments were frequently held in the pump-room" (Weinreb 32).

And then, making a slight courtesie, I left them.

How much does my disgust for these people encrease my pity for poor Mr. Macartney! I will not see them when I can avoid so doing; but I am determined to take every opportunity in my power, to shew civility to this unhappy man, whose misfortunes, with this family, only render him an object of scorn. I was, however, very well pleased with M. Du Bois, who, far from joining in their mirth, expressed himself extremely shocked at their ill-breeding.

We had not walked ten yards before we were followed by Mr. Smith, who came to make excuses, and to assure me they were *only joking*, and hoped I took nothing ill, for, if I did, he would make a quarrel of it himself with the Branghtons, rather than I should receive any offence.

I begged him not to take any trouble about so immaterial an affair, and assured him I should not myself. He was so officious, that he would not be prevailed upon to return home, till he had walked with us to Mr. Dawkins's.

Madame Duval was very much displeased that I brought her so little satisfaction. White-Conduit House was, at last, fixed upon; and, notwithstanding my great dislike of such parties and such places, I was obliged to accompany them.

Very disagreeable, and much according to my expectations, the evening proved. There were many people all smart and gaudy, and so pert and low-bred, that I could hardly endure being amongst them; but the party to which, unfortunately, I belonged, seemed all *at home*.


## LETTER XV.

*Evelina in continuation.*

Holborn, June 17<sup>th</sup>.

Yesterday Mr. Smith carried his point, of making a party for Vauxhall, consisting of Madame Duval, M. Du Bois, all the Branghtons, Mr. Brown, himself, – and me! – for I find all endeavours vain to escape any thing which these people desire I should not.

There were twenty disputes previous to our setting out; first, as to the *time* of our going: Mr. Branghton, his son, and young Brown, were for six o'clock; and all the ladies and Mr. Smith were for eight; – the latter, however, conquered.

Then, as to the *way* we should go; some were for a boat, others for a coach, and Mr. Branghton himself was for walking: but the boat, at length, was decided upon. Indeed this was the only part of the expedition that was agreeable to me, for the Thames was delightfully pleasant.

The Garden is very pretty, but too formal; I should have been better pleased, had it consisted less of strait walks, where

Grove nods at grove, each alley has its brother.[1]

The trees, the numerous lights, and the company in the circle round the orchestra make a most brilliant and gay appearance; and, had I been with a party less disagreeable to me, I should have thought it a place formed for animation and pleasure. There was a concert, in the course of which, a hautbois[2] concerto was so charmingly played, that I could have thought myself upon enchanted ground, had I had spirits more gentle to associate with. The hautboy in the open air is heavenly.

Mr. Smith endeavoured to attach himself to me, with such officious assiduity, and impertinent freedom, that he quite sickened me. Indeed, M. Du Bois was the only man of the party to whom, voluntarily, I ever addressed myself. He is civil and respectful, and I have found nobody else so since I left Howard Grove. His English is very bad, but I prefer it to speaking French myself, which I dare not venture to do. I converse with him frequently, both to disengage myself from others, and to oblige Madame Duval, who is always pleased when he is attended to.

As we were walking about the orchestra, I heard a bell ring, and, in a moment, Mr. Smith, flying up to me, caught my hand,

---

1  Pope's *Moral Essays*, "Epistle IV: To Burlington," line 117; slightly misquoted: "its" should read "a."
2  An oboe.

and, with a motion too quick to be resisted, ran away with me many yards before I had breath to ask his meaning, though I struggled as well as I could to get from him. At last, however, I insisted upon stopping; "Stopping, Ma'am!" cried he, "why, we must run on, or we shall lose the cascade!"

And then again, he hurried me away, mixing with a crowd of people, all running with so much velocity, that I could not imagine what had raised such an alarm. We were soon followed by the rest of the party; and my surprise and ignorance proved a source of diversion to them all, which was not exhausted the whole evening. Young Branghton, in particular, laughed till he could hardly stand.

The scene of the cascade I thought extremely pretty, and the general effect striking and lively.

But this was not the only surprise which was to divert them at my expence; for they led me about the garden, purposely to enjoy my first sight of various other deceptions.[1]

About ten o'clock, Mr. Smith having chosen a *box* in a very conspicuous place, we all went to supper. Much fault was found with every thing that was ordered, though not a morsel of any thing was left; and the dearness of the provisions, with conjectures upon what profit was made by them, supplied discourse during the whole meal.

When wine and cyder were brought, Mr. Smith said, "Now let's enjoy ourselves; now is the time, or never. Well, Ma'am, and how do you like Vauxhall?"

"Like it!" cried young Branghton, "why, how can she help liking it? she has never seen such a place before, that I'll answer for."

"For my part," said Miss Branghton, "I like it because it is not vulgar."

"This must have been a fine treat for you, Miss," said Mr. Branghton; "why, I suppose you was never so happy in all your life before?"

I endeavoured to express my satisfaction with some pleasure, yet I believe they were much amazed at my coldness.

---

1　Doody notes that "the ornaments of Vauxhall Gardens, especially those put in when Tyers became the owner, included many decorative effects of artificial ruins and fake classical arches, as well as statues" (481, n. 81).

"Miss ought to stay in town till the last night," said young Branghton, "and then, it's my belief, she'd say something to it! Why, Lord, it's the best night of any; there's always a riot, – and there the folks run about, – and then there's such squealing and squalling! – and there all the lamps are broke, – and the women run skimper scamper; – I declare I would not take five guineas to miss the last night!"

I was very glad when they all grew tired of sitting, and called for the waiter to pay the bill. The Miss Branghtons said they would walk on, while the gentlemen settled the account, and asked me to accompany them; which, however, I declined.

"You girls may do as you please," said Madame Duval, "but as to me, I promise you, I sha'n't go no where without the gentlemen."

"No more, I suppose, will my *Cousin*," said Miss Branghton, looking reproachfully towards Mr. Smith.

This reflection, which I feared would flatter his vanity, made me, most unfortunately, request Madame Duval's permission to attend them. She granted it, and away we went, having promised to meet in the room.[1]

To the room therefore, I would immediately have gone: but the sisters agreed that they would first have a *little pleasure*, and they tittered, and talked so loud, that they attracted universal notice.

"Lord, Polly," said the eldest, "suppose we were to take a turn in the dark walks!"

"Ay, do," answered she, "and then we'll hide ourselves, and then Mr. Brown will think we are lost."

I remonstrated very warmly against this plan, telling them that it would endanger our missing the rest of the party all the evening.

"O dear," cried Miss Branghton, "I thought how uneasy Miss would be, without a beau!"

This impertinence I did not think worth answering; and, quite by compulsion, I followed them down a long alley, in which there was hardly any light.

---

1    The Picture Room.

By the time we came near the end, a large party of gentlemen, apparently very riotous, and who were hallowing, leaning on one another, and laughing immoderately, seemed to rush suddenly from behind some trees, and, meeting us face to face, put their arms at their sides, and formed a kind of circle, which first stopped our proceeding, and then our retreating, for we were presently entirely inclosed. The Miss Branghtons screamed aloud, and I was frightened exceedingly: our screams were answered with bursts of laughter, and, for some minutes, we were kept prisoners, till, at last, one of them, rudely, seizing hold of me, said I was a pretty little creature.

Terrified to death, I struggled with such vehemence to disengage myself from him, that I succeeded, in spite of his efforts to detain me; and immediately, and with a swiftness which fear only could have given me, I flew rather than ran up the walk, hoping to secure my safety by returning to the lights and company we had so foolishly left: but, before I could possibly accomplish my purpose, I was met by another party of men, one of whom placed himself so directly in my way, calling out, "Whither so fast, my love?" – that I could only have proceeded, by running into his arms.

In a moment, both my hands, by different persons, were caught hold of; and one of them, in a most familiar manner, desired, when I ran next, to accompany me in a race; while the rest of the party stood still and laughed.

I was almost distracted with terror, and so breathless with running, that I could not speak, till another advancing, said, I was as handsome as an angel, and desired to be of the party. I then just articulated, "For Heaven's sake, Gentlemen, let me pass!"

Another, then, rushing suddenly forward, exclaimed, "Heaven and earth! what voice is that? – "

"The voice of the prettiest little actress[1] I have seen this age," answered one of my persecutors.

---

1   Evelina is mistaken for an actress/prostitute since she is in the disreputable "dark walks" of Vauxhall. Actresses were assumed to be open to prostitution as a means to increasing their incomes.

"No, – no, – no, – " I *panted* out, "I am no actress, – pray let me go, – pray let me pass – ."

"By all that's sacred," cried the same voice, which I then knew for Sir Clement Willoughby's, "'tis herself!"

"Sir Clement Willloughby!" cried I. "O Sir, assist – assist me – or I shall die with terror! – "

"Gentlemen," cried he, disengaging them all from me in an instant, "pray leave this lady to me."

Loud laughs proceeded from every mouth, and two or three said, "*Willoughby has all the luck!*" But one of them, in a passionate manner, vowed he would not give me up, for that he had the first right to me, and would support it.

"You are mistaken," said Sir Clement, "this lady is – I will explain myself to you another time; but, I assure you, you are all mistaken."

And then, taking my willing hand, he led me off, amidst the loud acclamations, laughter, and gross merriment of his impertinent companions.

As soon as we had escaped from them, Sir Clement, with a voice of surprise, exclaimed, "My dearest creature, what wonder, what strange revolution, has brought you to such a spot as this?"

Ashamed of my situation, and extremely mortified to be thus recognized by him, I was for some time silent, and when he repeated his question, only stammered out, "I have, – I hardly know how, – lost myself from my party. – "

He caught my hand, and eagerly pressing it, in a passionate voice, said, "O that I had sooner met with thee!"

Surprised at a freedom so unexpected, I angrily broke from him, saying, "Is this the protection you give me, Sir Clement?"

And then I saw, what the perturbation of my mind had prevented my sooner noticing, that he had led me, though I know not how, into another of the dark alleys, instead of the place whither I meant to go.

"Good God!" I cried, "where am I? – What way are you going? – "

"Where," answered he, "we shall be least observed."

Astonished at this speech, I stopped short, and declared I would go no further.

"And why not, my angel?" again endeavouring to take my hand.

My heart beat with resentment; I pushed him away from me with all my strength, and demanded how he dared treat me with such insolence?

"Insolence!" repeated he.

"Yes, Sir Clement, *insolence*; from you, who know me, I had a claim for protection, – not to such treatment as this."

"By Heaven," cried he with warmth, "you distract me, – why, tell me, – why do I see you here? – Is this a place for Miss Anville? – these dark walks! – no party! – no companion! – by all that's good, I can scarce believe my senses!"

Extremely offended at this speech, I turned angrily from him, and, not deigning to make any answer, walked on towards that part of the garden whence I perceived the lights and company.

He followed me; but we were both some time silent.

"So you will not explain to me your situation?" said he, at length.

"No, Sir," answered I, disdainfully.

"Nor yet – suffer me to make my own interpretation? – "

I could not bear this strange manner of speaking; it made my very soul shudder, – and I burst into tears.

He flew to me, and actually flung himself at my feet, as if regardless who might see him, saying, "O Miss Anville – loveliest of women – forgive my – my – I beseech you forgive me; – if I have offended, – if I have hurt you – I could kill myself at the thought! – "

"No matter, Sir, no matter," cried I, "if I can but find my friends, – I will never speak to – never see you again!"

"Good God! – good Heaven! – my dearest life, what is it I have done? – what is it I have said? – "

"You best know, Sir, *what* and *why*; – but don't hold me here, – let *me* be gone, and do *you*!"

"Not till you forgive me! – I cannot part with you in anger."

"For shame, for shame, Sir!" cried I indignantly, "do you suppose I am to be thus compelled? – do you take advantage of the absence of my friends, to affront me?"

"No, Madam," cried he, rising, "I would sooner forfeit my

life than act so mean a part. But you have flung me into amazement unspeakable, and you will not condescend to listen to my request of giving me some explanation."

"The manner, Sir," said I, "in which you spoke that request, made, and will make me scorn to answer it."

"Scorn! – I will own to you, I expected not such displeasure from Miss Anville."

"Perhaps, Sir, if you had, you would less voluntarily have merited it."

"My dearest life, surely it must be known to you, that the man does not breathe, who adores you so passionately, so fervently, so tenderly as I do! – why then will you delight in perplexing me? – in keeping me in suspence – in torturing me with doubt? – "

"I, Sir, delight in perplexing you! – You are much mistaken. – Your suspence, your doubts, your perplexities, – are of your own creating; and, believe me, Sir, they may *offend*, but they can never *delight* me: – but, as you have yourself raised, you must yourself satisfy them."

"Good God! – that such haughtiness and such sweetness can inhabit the same mansion!"

I made no answer, but quickening my pace, I walked on silently and sullenly; till this most impetuous of men, snatching my hand, which he grasped with violence, besought me to forgive him, with such earnestness of supplication, that, merely to escape his importunities, I was forced to speak, and, in some measure, to grant the pardon he requested: though it was accorded with a very ill grace; but, indeed, I knew not how to resist the humility of his entreaties: yet never shall I recollect the occasion he gave me of displeasure, without feeling it renewed.

We now soon arrived in the midst of the general crowd, and my own safety being then insured, I grew extremely uneasy for the Miss Branghtons, whose danger, however imprudently incurred by their own folly, I too well knew how to tremble for. To this consideration all my pride of heart yielded, and I determined to seek my party with the utmost speed; though not without a sigh did I recollect the fruitless attempt I had made, after the opera, of concealing from this man my unfortunate connections, which I was now obliged to make known.

I hastened, therefore, to the room, with a view of sending young Branghton to the aid of his sisters. In a very short time, I perceived Madame Duval, and the rest, looking at one of the paintings. I must own to you, honestly, my dear Sir, that an involuntary repugnance seized me, at presenting such a set to Sir Clement, – he, who had been used to see me in parties so different! – My pace slackened as I approached them, – but they presently perceived me.

"*Ah, Mademoiselle!*" cried M. Du Bois, "*Que je suis charmé de vous voir!*"[1]

"Pray, Miss," cried Mr. Brown, "where's Miss Polly?"

"Why, Miss, you've been a long while gone," said Mr. Branghton; "we thought you'd been lost. But what have you done with your cousins?"

I hesitated, – for Sir Clement regarded me with a look of wonder.

"*Pardi*," cried Madame Duval, "I sha'n't let you leave me again in a hurry. Why, here we've been in such a fright! – and, all the while, I suppose you've been thinking nothing about the matter."

"Well," said young Branghton, "as long as Miss is come back, I don't mind, for as to Bid and Poll, they can take care of themselves. But the best joke is, Mr. Smith is gone all about a-looking for you."

These speeches were made almost all in a breath: but when, at last, they waited for an answer, I told them, that in walking up one of the long alleys, we had been frightened and separated.

"The long alleys!" repeated Mr. Branghton, "and, pray, what had you to do in the long alleys? why, to be sure, you must all of you have had a mind to be affronted!"

This speech was not more impertinent to me, than surpris-

---

1  "Ah, Miss! How happy I am to see you!"

ing to Sir Clement, who regarded all the party with evident astonishment. However, I told young Branghton that no time ought to be lost, for that his sisters might require his immediate protection.

"But how will they get it?" cried this brutal brother; "if they've a mind to behave in such a manner as that, they ought to protect themselves; and so they may for me."

"Well," said the simple Mr. Brown, "whether you go or no, I think I may as well see after Miss Polly."

The father, then, interfering, insisted that his son should accompany him; and away they went.

It was now that Madame Duval first perceived Sir Clement; to whom turning with a look of great displeasure, she angrily said, "*Ma foi*, so you are comed here, of all the people in the world! – I wonder, child, you would let such a – such a *person* as that keep company with you."

"I am very sorry, Madam," said Sir Clement, in a tone of surprise, "if I have been so unfortunate as to offend you; but I believe you will not regret the honour I now have of attending Miss Anville, when you hear that I have been so happy as to do her some service."

Just as Madame Duval, with her usual *Ma foi*, was beginning to reply, the attention of Sir Clement was wholly drawn from her, by the appearance of Mr. Smith, who coming suddenly behind me, and freely putting his hands on my shoulders, cried, "O ho, my little runaway, have I found you at last? I have been scampering all over the gardens for you, for I was determined to find you, if you were above ground. – But how could you be so cruel as to leave us?"

I turned round to him, and looked with a degree of contempt that I hoped would have quieted him; but he had not the sense to understand me; and, attempting to take my hand, he added, "Such a demure looking lady as you are, who'd have thought of your leading one such a dance? – Come, now, don't be so coy, – only think what a trouble I have had in running after you!"

"The trouble, Sir," said I, "was of your own choice, – not mine." And I walked round to the other side of Madame Duval.

Perhaps I was too proud, – but I could not endure that Sir Clement, whose eyes followed him with looks of the most surprised curiosity, should witness his unwelcome familiarity.

Upon my removal, he came up to me, and, in a low voice, said, "You are not, then, with the Mirvans?"

"No, Sir."

"And pray – may I ask, – have you left them long?"

"No, Sir."

"How unfortunate I am! – but yesterday I sent to acquaint the Captain I should reach the Grove by tomorrow noon! However, I shall get away as fast as possible. Shall you be long in town?"

"I believe not, Sir."

"And then, when you leave it, – which way – will you allow me to ask, which way you shall travel?"

"Indeed, – I don't know."

"Not know! – But do you return to the Mirvans any more?"

"I – I can't tell, Sir."

And then, I addressed myself to Madame Duval, with such a pretended earnestness, that he was obliged to be silent.

As he cannot but observe the great change in my situation, which he knows not how to account for, there is something in all these questions, and this unrestrained curiosity, that I did not expect from a man, who when he pleases can be so well-bred, as Sir Clement Willoughby. He seems disposed to think that the alteration in my companions authorises an alteration in his manners. It is true, he has always treated me with uncommon freedom, but never before with so disrespectful an abruptness. This observation, which he has given me cause to make, of his *changing with the tide*, has sunk him more in my opinion, than any other part of his conduct.

Yet I could almost have laughed, when I looked at Mr. Smith, who no sooner saw me addressed by Sir Clement, than, retreating aloof from the company, he seemed to lose at once all his happy self-sufficiency and conceit; looking now at the baronet, now at himself, surveying, with sorrowful eyes, his dress, struck with his air, his gestures, his easy gaiety; he gazed at him with envious admiration, and seemed himself, with conscious inferiority, to shrink into nothing.

Soon after, Mr. Brown, running up to us, called out, "La, what, i'n't Miss Polly come yet?"

"Come!" said Mr. Branghton, "why, I thought you went to fetch her yourself, did n't you?"

"Yes, but I could n't find her; – yet I dare say I've been over half the garden."

"Half! but why did not you go over it all?"

"Why, so I will: but only I thought I'd just come and see if she was here first?"

"But where's Tom?"

"Why, I don't know; for he would not stay with me, all as ever I could say; for we met some young gentlemen of his acquaintance, and so he bid me go and look by myself, for he said, says he, I can divert myself better another way, says he."

This account being given, away again went this silly young man; and Mr. Branghton, extremely incensed, said he would go and see after them himself.

"So now," cried Madame Duval, "he's gone too! why, at this rate we shall have to wait for one or other of them all night!"

Observing that Sir Clement seemed disposed to renew his enquiries, I turned towards one of the paintings, and, pretending to be very much occupied in looking at it, asked M. Du Bois some questions concerning the figures.

"O, *Mon Dieu!*" cried Madame Duval, "don't ask him; your best way is to ask Mr. Smith, for he's been here the oftenest. Come, Mr. Smith, I dare say you can tell us all about them."

"Why, yes, Ma'am, yes," said Mr. Smith, who, brightening up at this application, advanced towards us, with an air of assumed importance, which, however, sat very uneasily upon him, and begged to know what he should explain first; "For I have attended," said he, "to all these paintings, and know every thing in them perfectly well; for I am rather fond of pictures, Ma'am;

and, really, I must say, I think a pretty picture is a – a very – is really a very – is something very pretty. – "

"So do I too," said Madame Duval, "but pray now, Sir, tell us who that is meant for," pointing to a figure of Neptune.[1]

"That! – why that, Ma'am, is, – Lord bless me, I can't think how I come to be so stupid, but really I have forgot his name, – and yet, I know it as well as my own, too, – however, he's a *General*, Ma'am, they are all Generals."

I saw Sir Clement bite his lips; and, indeed, so did I mine.

"Well," said Madame Duval, "it's the oddest dress for a General ever I see!"

"He seems so capital a figure," said Sir Clement to Mr. Smith, "that I imagine he must be *Generalissimo* of the whole army."

"Yes, Sir, yes," answered Mr. Smith, respectfully bowing, and highly delighted at being thus referred to, "you are perfectly right, – but I cannot for my life think of his name; – perhaps, Sir, you may remember it?"

"No, really," replied Sir Clement, "my acquaintance among the Generals is not so extensive."

The ironical tone of voice in which Sir Clement spoke, entirely disconcerted Mr. Smith; who, again retiring to an humble distance, seemed sensibly mortified at the failure of his attempt to recover his consequence.

Soon after, Mr. Branghton returned, with his youngest daughter, whom he had rescued from a party of insolent young men; but he had not yet been able to find the eldest. Miss Polly was really frightened, and declared she would never go into the dark walks again. Her father, leaving her with us, went in quest of her sister.

While she was relating her adventures, to which nobody listened more attentively than Sir Clement, we saw Mr. Brown enter the room. "O la!" cried Miss Polly "let me hide myself, and don't tell him I'm come."

---

1  In his introduction to the 1903 Macmillan edition of *Evelina,* Austin Dobson identifies this painting in the Picture Room at Vauxhall as "Hayman's allegorical representation of Admiral Hawke's defeat [of the French navy] at Quiberon Bay" in 1759 (xvii). Gordon Fulton notes that while "The Triumph of Britannia" has not survived, an engraving is reproduced in Brian Allen's *Francis Hayman* (Yale UP, 1987), 65.

She then placed herself behind Madame Duval, in such a manner that she could not be seen.

"So Miss Polly is not come yet!" said the simple swain;[1] "well, I can't think where she can be! I've been a looking, and looking, and looking all about, and I can't find her, all I can do."

"Well but, Mr. Brown," said Mr. Smith, "sha'n't you go and look for the lady again?"

"Yes, Sir," said he, sitting down, "but I must rest me a little bit first. You can't think how tired I am."

"O fie, Mr. Brown, fie," cried Mr. Smith, winking at us, "tired of looking for a lady! Go, go, for shame!"

"So I will, Sir, presently; but you'd be tired too, if you'd walked so far: besides, I think she's gone out of the garden, or else I must have seen something or other of her."

A *he, he, he!* of the tittering Polly, now betrayed her, and so ended this ingenious little artifice.

At last appeared Mr. Branghton and Miss Biddy, who, with a face of mixed anger and confusion, addressing herself to me, said, "So Miss, so you ran away from me! Well, see if I don't do as much by you, some day or other! But I thought how it would be, you'd no mind to leave the *gentlemen*, though you'd run away from *me*."

I was so much surprised at this attack, that I could not answer her for very amazement; and she proceeded to tell us how ill she had been used, and that two young men had been making her walk up and down the dark walks by absolute force, and as fast as ever they could tear her along; and many other particulars, which I will not tire you with relating. In conclusion, looking at Mr. Smith, she said, "But, to be sure, thought I, at least all the company will be looking for me; so I little expected to find you all here, talking as comfortably as ever you can. However, I know I may thank my cousin for it!"

"If you mean *me*, Madam," said I, very much shocked, "I am

---

1  A "swain" is "a country gallant or lover; hence generally a lover, wooer, sweetheart, especially in pastoral poetry" (*OED*). Evelina's description of Mr. Brown as a "simple swain" captures her condescending attitude toward his lack of intelligence, his low class, and his obvious disinterest in his supposed loved one.

quite ignorant in what manner I can have been accessary to your distress."

"Why, by running away so. If you'd stayed with us, I'll answer for it, Mr. Smith and M. Du Bois would have come to look for us; but I suppose they could not leave your ladyship."

The folly and unreasonableness of this speech would admit of no answer. But what a scene was this for Sir Clement! his surprise was evident; and, I must acknowledge, my confusion was equally great.

We had now to wait for young Branghton, who did not appear for some time; and, during this interval, it was with difficulty that I avoided Sir Clement, who was on the rack of curiosity, and dying to speak to me.

When, at last, the hopeful youth returned, a long and fright-ful quarrel ensued between him and his father, in which his sisters occasionally joined, concerning his neglect; and he defended himself only by a brutal mirth, which he indulged at their expence.

Every one, now, seemed inclined to depart, – when, as usual, a dispute arose, upon the *way* of our going, whether in a coach or a boat. After much debating, it was determined that we should make two parties, one by the water and the other by land; for Madame Duval declared she would not, upon any account, go into a boat at night.

Sir Clement then said, that if she had no carriage in waiting, he should be happy to see her and me safe home, as his was in readiness.

Fury started into her eyes, and passion inflamed every fea-ture, as she answered, "*Pardi*, no, – you may take care of your-self, if you please; but as to me, I promise you I sha'n't trust myself with no such person."

He pretended not to comprehend her meaning, yet, to wave a discussion, acquiesced in her refusal. The coach-party fixed upon consisted of Madame Duval, M. Du Bois, Miss Branghton, and myself.

I now began to rejoice, in private, that, at least, our lodgings would be neither seen nor known by Sir Clement. We soon met with an hackney-coach, into which he handed me, and then took leave.

Madame Duval, having already given the coachman her direction, he mounted the box, and we were just driving off, when Sir Clement exclaimed, "By Heaven, this is the very coach I had in waiting for myself!"

"This coach, your honour!" said the man, "no, that it i'n't."

Sir Clement, however, swore that it was, and, presently, the man, begging his pardon, said he had really forgotten that he was engaged.

I have no doubt but that this scheme occurred to him at the moment, and that he made some sign to the coachman, which induced him to support it: for there is not the least probability that the accident really happened, as it is most likely his own chariot was in waiting.

The man then opened the coach-door, and Sir Clement advancing to it, said, "I don't believe there is another carriage to be had, or I would not incommode you; but, as it may be dis-agreeable to you to wait here any longer, I beg you will not get out, for you shall be set down before I am carried home, if you will be so good as to make a little room."

And so saying, in he jumpt, and seated himself between M. Du Bois and me, while our astonishment at the whole transaction was too great for speech. He then ordered the coachman to drive on, according to the directions he had already received.

For the first ten minutes, no one uttered a word; and then, Madame Duval, no longer able to contain herself, exclaimed, "*Ma foi*, if this is n't one of the impudentest things ever I see!"

Sir Clement, regardless of this rebuke, attended only to me; however, I answered nothing he said, when I could possibly avoid so doing. Miss Branghton made several attempts to attract his notice, but in vain, for he would not take the trouble of paying her any regard.

Madame Duval, during the rest of the ride, addressed herself to M. Du Bois in French, and in that language exclaimed with great vehemence against boldness and assurance.

I was extremely glad when I thought our journey must be nearly at an end, for my situation was very uneasy to me, as Sir

Clement perpetually endeavoured to take my hand. I looked out of the coach-window, to see if we were near home; Sir Clement, stooping over me did the same, and then, in a voice of infinite wonder, called out, "Where the d − l is the man driving to? − why we are in Broad St. Giles's!"[1]

"O, he's very right," cried Madame Duval, "so never trouble your head about that, for I sha'n't go by no directions of yours, I promise you."

When, at last, we stopped, at *an Hosier's* in *High Holborn*, − Sir Clement said nothing, but his *eyes*, I saw, were very busily employed in viewing the place, and the situation of the house. The coach, he said, belonged to him, and therefore he insisted upon paying for it; and then he took leave. M. Du Bois walked home with Miss Branghton, and Madame Duval and I retired to our apartments.

How disagreeable an evening's adventure! not one of the party seemed satisfied, except Sir Clement, who was in high spirits: but Madame Duval, was enraged at meeting with him; Mr. Branghton, angry with his children; the frolic of the Miss Branghtons had exceeded their plan, and ended in their own distress; their brother was provoked that there had been no riot; Mr. Brown was tired; and Mr. Smith mortified. As to myself, I must acknowledge, nothing could be more disagreeable to me, than being seen by Sir Clement Willoughby with a party at once so vulgar in themselves, and so familiar to me.

And you, too, my dear Sir, will, I know, be sorry that I have met him; however, there is no apprehension of his visiting here, as Madame Duval is far too angry to admit him.

---

1  Mackinnon identifies this as a reference to Broad Street, from the top of Drury Lane towards St. Giles-in-the-Fields (530), whereas Stewart Cooke, in his notes to the 1998 Norton edition of *Evelina*, interprets Sir Clement to mean that they are "well into the parish of St. Giles," quite far from where he expects them to be, given Evelina's previous address and the rough, working class nature of her present address (171).

# LETTER XVI.

*Evelina in continuation.*

Holborn, June 18th.

Madame Duval rose very late this morning, and, at one o'clock, we had but just breakfasted, when Miss Branghton, her brother, Mr. Smith, and Monsieur Du Bois, called to enquire after our healths.

This civility in young Branghton, I much suspect, was merely the result of his father's commands; but his sister and Mr. Smith, I soon found, had motives of their own. Scarce had they spoken to Madame Duval, when, advancing eagerly to me, "Pray, Ma'am," said Mr. Smith, "who was that gentleman?"

"Pray, Cousin," cried Miss Branghton, "was not he the same gentleman you ran away with that night at the opera?"

"Goodness! that he was," said young Branghton; "and, I declare, as soon as ever I saw him, I thought I knew his face."

"I'm sure I'll defy you to forget him," answered his sister, "if once you had seen him: he is the finest gentleman I ever saw in my life; don't you think so, Mr. Smith?"

"Why, you won't give the Lady time to speak," said Mr. Smith. – "Pray, Ma'am, what is the gentleman's name?"

"Willoughby, Sir."

"Willoughby! I think I have heard the name. Pray, Ma'am, is he married?"

"Lord, no, that he is not," cried Miss Branghton; "he looks too smart, by a great deal, for a married man. Pray, Cousin, how did you get acquainted with him?"

"Pray, Miss," said young Branghton, in the same breath, "what's his business?"

"Indeed I don't know," answered I.

"Something very genteel, I dare say," added Miss Branghton, "because he dresses so fine."

"It ought to be something that brings in a good income," said Mr. Smith, "for I'm sure he did not get that suit of cloaths he had on, under thirty or forty pounds; for I know the price of cloaths pretty well; – pray, Ma'am, can you tell me what he has a year?"

"Don't talk no more about him," cried Madame Duval, "for I don't like to hear his name; I believe he's one of the worst persons in the world; for, though I never did him no manner of harm, nor so much as hurt a hair of his head, I know he was an accomplice with that fellow, Captain Mirvan, to take away my life."

Every body but myself, now crowding around her for an explanation, a violent rapping at the street-door was unheard; and, without any previous notice, in the midst of her narration, Sir Clement Willoughby entered the room. They all started, and, with looks of guilty confusion, as if they feared his resentment for having listened to Madame Duval, they scrambled for chairs, and, in a moment were all formally seated.

Sir Clement, after a general bow, singling out Madame Duval, said, with his usual easiness, "I have done myself the honour of waiting on you, Madam, to enquire if you have any commands to Howard Grove, whither I am going to-morrow morning."

Then, seeing the storm that gathered in her eyes, before he allowed her time to answer, he addressed himself to me; – "And if you, Madam, have any with which you will honour me, I shall be happy to execute them."

"None at all, Sir."

"None! – not to Miss Mirvan! – no message! no letter! – "

"I wrote to Miss Mirvan yesterday by the post."

"My application should have been earlier, had I sooner known your address."

"*Ma foi*," cried Madame Duval, recovering from her surprise, "I believe never nobody saw the like of this!"

"Of what! Madam!" cried the undaunted Sir Clement, turning quick towards her, "I hope no one has offended you!"

"You don't hope no such a thing!" cried she, half choked with passion, and rising from her chair. This motion was followed by the rest, and, in a moment, every body stood up.

Still Sir Clement was not abashed; affecting to make a bow of *acknowledgement* to the company in general, he said, "Pray –

I beg – Ladies, – Gentlemen, – pray don't let me disturb you, pray keep your seats."

"Pray, Sir," said Miss Branghton, moving a chair towards him, "won't you sit down yourself?"

"You are extremely good, Ma'am: – rather than make any disturbance – "

And so saying, this strange man seated himself, as did, in an instant, every body else, even Madame Duval herself, who, overpowered by his boldness, seemed too full for utterance.

He then, and with as much composure as if he had been an expected guest, began to discourse on the weather, – its uncertainty, – the heat of the public places in summer, – the emptiness of the town, – and other such common topics.

Nobody, however, answered him; Mr. Smith seemed afraid, young Branghton ashamed, M. Du Bois amazed, Madame Duval enraged, and myself determined not to interfere. All that he could obtain, was the notice of Miss Branghton, whose nods, smiles, and attention, had some appearance of entering into conversation with him.

At length, growing tired, I suppose, of engaging every body's eyes, and nobody's tongue, addressing himself to Madame Duval and to me, he said, "I regard myself as peculiarly unfortunate, Ladies, in having fixed upon a time for my visit to Howard Grove, when you are absent from it."

"So I suppose, Sir, so I suppose," cried Madame Duval, hastily rising, and the next moment as hastily seating herself, "you'll be a wanting of somebody to make your game of, and so you may think to get *me* there again; – but, I promise you, Sir, you won't find it so easy a matter to make me a fool: and besides that," raising her voice, "I've found you out, I assure you; so if ever you go to play your tricks upon me again, I'll make no more ado, but go directly to a justice of peace; so, Sir, if you can't think of nothing but making people ride about the country, at all hours of the night, just for your diversion, why you'll find I know some justices, as well as Justice Tyrrel."

Sir Clement was evidently embarrassed at this attack; yet he affected a look of surprise, and protested he did not understand her meaning.

"Well," cried she, "if I don't wonder where people can get such impudence! if you'll say that, you'll say any thing; however, if you swear till you're black in the face, I sha'n't believe you; for nobody sha'n't persuade me out of my senses, that I'm resolved."

"Doubtless not, Madam," answered he with some hesitation, "and I hope you do not suspect I ever had such an intention; my respect for you – "

"O Sir, you're vastly polite, all of a sudden! but I know what it's all for; – it's only for what you can get! – you could treat me like nobody at Howard Grove – but now you see I've a house of my own, you've a mind to wheedle yourself into it; but I sees your design, so you need n't trouble yourself to take no more trouble about that, for you shall never get nothing at my house, – not so much as a dish of tea: – so now, Sir, you see I can play you trick for trick."

There was something so extremely gross in this speech, that it even disconcerted Sir Clement, who was too much confounded to make any answer.

It was curious to observe the effect which his embarrassment, added to the freedom with which Madame Duval addressed him, had upon the rest of the company: every one, who, before, seemed at a loss how, or if at all, to occupy a chair, now filled it with the most easy composure: and Mr. Smith, whose countenance had exhibited the most striking picture of mortified envy, now began to recover his usual expression of satisfied conceit. Young Branghton, too, who had been apparently awed by the presence of so fine a gentleman, was again himself, rude and familiar; while his mouth was wide distended into a broad grin, at hearing *his aunt give the beau such a trimming.*[1]

Madame Duval, encouraged by this success, looked around her with an air of triumph, and continued her harangue: "And so, Sir, I suppose you thought to have had it all your own way, and to have comed here as often as you pleased, and to have got me to Howard Grove again, on purpose to have served me as

---

1  "A beating, a drubbing; a sharp censure" (*OED*).

you did before; but you shall see I'm as cunning as you, so you may go and find somebody else to use in that manner, and to put your mask on, and to make a fool of; for as to me, if you go to tell me your stories about the Tower again, for a month together, I'll never believe 'em no more; and I'll promise you, Sir, if you think I like such jokes, you'll find I'm no such person."

"I assure you, Ma'am, – upon my honour – I really don't comprehend – I fancy there is some misunderstanding – "

"What, I suppose you'll tell me next you don't know nothing of the matter?"

"Not a word, upon my honour."

O Sir Clement! thought I, is it thus you prize your honour!

"*Pardi*," cried Madame Duval "this is the most provokingest part of all! why you might as well tell me I don't know my own name."

"Here is certainly some mistake; for I assure you, Ma'am – "

"Don't assure me nothing," cried Madame Duval, raising her voice, "I know what I'm saying, and so do you too; for did not you tell me all that about the Tower, and about M. Du Bois? – why M. Du Bois was n't never there, nor nigh it, and so it was all your own invention."

"May there not be two persons of the same name? the mistake was but natural, – "

"Don't tell me of no mistake, for it was all on purpose; besides, did not you come, all in a mask, to the chariot-door, and help to get me put in that ditch? – I'll promise you, I've had the greatest mind in the world to take the law of you ever since, and if ever you do as much again, so I will, I assure you!"

Here Miss Branghton tittered; Mr. Smith smiled contemptuously, and young Branghton thrust his handkerchief into his mouth to stop his laughter.

The situation of Sir Clement, who saw all that passed, became now very awkward, even to himself, and he stammered very much in saying, "Surely, Madam – surely you – you cannot do me the – the injustice to think – that I had any share in the – the – the misfortune which – "

"*Ma foi*, Sir," cried Madame Duval, with encreasing passion, "you'd best not stand talking to me at that rate; I know it *was* you, – and if you stay there, a provoking me in such a manner, I'll send for a constable[1] this minute."

Young Branghton, at these words, in spite of all his efforts, burst into a loud laugh; nor could either his sister, or Mr. Smith, though with more moderation, forbear joining in his mirth.

Sir Clement darted his eyes towards them, with looks of the most angry contempt, and then told Madame Duval, that he would not now detain her to make his vindication, but would wait on her some time when she was alone.

"O *pardi*, Sir," cried she, "I don't desire none of your company; and if you was n't the most boldest person in the world, you would not dare look me in the face."

The ha, ha, ha's, and he, he, he's, grew more and more uncontroulable, as if the restraint from which they had burst, had added to their violence. Sir Clement could no longer endure being the object who excited them, and, having no answer ready for Madame Duval, he hastily stalked towards Mr. Smith and young Branghton, and sternly demanded what they laughed at?

Struck by the air of importance which he assumed, and alarmed at the angry tone of his voice, their merriment ceased, as instantaneously as if it had been directed by clock work, and they stared foolishly, now at him, now at each other, without making any answer but a simple "*Nothing*, Sir!"

"O *pour le coup*,"[2] cried Madame Duval, "this is too much! pray, Sir, what business have you to come here, a ordering people that comes to see me? I suppose next, nobody must laugh but yourself!"

"With me, Madam," said Sir Clement, bowing, "a *lady* may do any thing, and, consequently, there is no liberty in which I shall not be happy to indulge *you*: – but it has never been my custom to give the same licence to *gentlemen*."

Then, advancing to me, who had sat very quietly, on a window, during this scene, he said, "Miss Anville, I may at least acquaint our friends at Howard Grove, that I had the honour of

---

1  "An officer of the peace" (*OED*).
2  "This time this is too much."

leaving you in good health." And then, lowering his voice, he added, "For Heaven's sake, my dearest creature, who are these people? and how came you so strangely situated?"

"I beg my respects to all the family, Sir," answered I, aloud, "and I hope you will find them well."

He looked at me reproachfully, but kissed my hand; and then, bowing to Madame Duval and Miss Branghton, passed hastily by the men, and made his exit.

I fancy he will not be very eager to repeat his visits, for I should imagine he has rarely, if ever, been before in a situation so awkward and disagreeable.

Madame Duval has been all spirits and exultation ever since he went, and only wishes Captain Mirvan would call, that she might *do the same by him*. Mr. Smith, upon hearing that he was a Baronet, and seeing him drive off in a very beautiful chariot, declared that he would not have laughed upon any account, had he known his rank, and regretted extremely having missed such an opportunity of making so *genteel* an *acquaintance*. Young Branghton vowed, that, if he had known as much, he would have *asked for his custom*:[1] and his sister has sung his praises ever since, protesting she thought, *all along*, he was a man of *quality* by his *look*.

### LETTER XVII.

*Evelina in continuation.*

June 21.

The last three evenings have passed tolerably quiet, for the Vauxhall adventures had given Madame Duval a surfeit of public places: home, however, soon growing tiresome, she determined to night, she said, to relieve her *ennui*, by some amusement; and it was therefore settled that we should call

---

1    "Business patronage or support" (*OED*).

upon the Branghtons, at their house, and thence proceed to Marybone Gardens.

But, before we reached Snow-Hill, we were caught in a shower of rain: we hurried into the shop, where the first object I saw was Mr. Macartney, with a book in his hand, seated in the same corner where I saw him last; but his looks were still more wretched than before, his face yet thinner, and his eyes sunk almost hollow into his head. He lifted them up as we entered, and I even thought that they emitted a gleam of joy: involuntarily, I made to him my first courtesie; he rose and bowed, with a precipitation that manifested surprise and confusion.

In a few minutes, we were joined by all the family, except Mr. Smith, who fortunately was engaged.

Had all the future prosperity of our lives depended upon the good or bad weather of this evening, it could not have been treated as a subject of greater importance. "Sure never any thing was so unlucky! – " "Lord, how provoking! – " "It might rain for ever, if it would hold up now! – " These, and such expressions, with many anxious observations upon the kennels,[1] filled up all the conversation till the shower was over.

And then a very warm debate arose, whether we should pursue our plan, or defer it to some finer evening; Miss Branghtons were for the former; their father was sure it would rain again; Madame Duval, though she detested returning home, yet dreaded the dampness of the gardens.

M. Du Bois then proposed going to the top of the house, to examine whether the clouds looked threatening or peaceable; Miss Branghton, starting at this proposal, said they might go to Mr. Macartney's room, if they would, but not to her's.

This was enough for the brother; who, with a loud laugh, declared he would have some *fun*, and immediately led the way, calling to us all to follow. His sisters both ran after him, but no one else moved.

In a few minutes, young Branghton, coming half way down

---

1   "The surface drain of a street; the gutter" (*OED*).

stairs, called out, "Lord, why don't you all come? why here's Poll's things all about the room!"

Mr. Branghton then went, and Madame Duval, who cannot bear to be excluded from whatever is going forward, was handed up stairs by M. Du Bois.

I hesitated a few moments, whether or not to join them; but, soon perceiving that Mr. Macartney had dropped his book, and that I engrossed his whole attention, I prepared, from mere embarrassment, to follow them.

As I went, I heard him move from his chair, and walk slowly after me. Believing that he wished to speak to me, and earnestly desiring myself to know if, by your means, I could possibly be of any service to him, I first slackened my pace, and then turned back. But, though I thus met him half-way, he seemed to want courage or resolution to address me; for when he saw me returning, with a look extremely disordered, he retreated hastily from me.

Not knowing what I ought to do, I went to the street-door, where I stood some time, hoping he would be able to recover himself: but, on the contrary, his agitation encreased every moment; he walked up and down the room, in a quick, but unsteady pace, seeming equally distressed and irresolute: and, at length, with a deep sigh, he flung himself into a chair.

I was so much affected by the appearance of such extreme anguish, that I could remain no longer in the room; I therefore glided by him, and went up stairs; but, ere I had gone five steps, he precipitately followed me, and, in a broken voice, called out, "Madam! – for Heaven's sake – "

He stopped, but I instantly descended, restraining, as well as I was able, the fullness of my own concern. I waited some time, in painful expectation, for his speaking: all that I had heard of his poverty, occurring to me, I was upon the point of presenting him my purse, but the fear of mistaking or offending him, deterred me. Finding, however, that he continued silent, I ventured to say, "Did you – Sir, wish to speak to me?"

"I did!" cried he, with quickness, "but now – I cannot!" –

"Perhaps, Sir, another time, – perhaps if you recollect yourself – "

"Another time!" repeated he mournfully, "alas! I look not forward but to misery and despair!"

"O Sir," cried I, extremely shocked, "you must not talk thus! – if you forsake *yourself*, how can you expect – "

I stopped. "Tell me, tell me," cried he, with eagerness, "who you are? – whence you come? – and by what strange means you seem to be arbitress and ruler of the destiny of such a wretch as I am?"

"Would to Heaven," cried I, "I could serve you!"

"You can!"

"And how? pray tell me how?"

"To tell you – is death to me! yet I *will* tell you, – I have a *right* to your assistance, – you have deprived me of the only resource to which I could apply, – and therefore – "

"Pray, pray, speak;" cried I, putting my hand into my pocket, "they will be down stairs in a moment!"

"I will, Madam. – Can you – will you – I think you will! – may I then – " he stopped and paused, "say, will you —— " then suddenly turning from me, "Great Heaven! I cannot speak!" and he went back to the shop.

I now put my purse in my hand, and following him, said, "If indeed, Sir, I can assist you, why should you deny me so great a satisfaction? Will you permit me to – "

I dared not go on; but with a countenance very much softened, he approached me, and said, "Your voice, Madam, is the voice of compassion! – such a voice as these ears have long been strangers to!"

Just then, young Branghton called out vehemently to me, to come up stairs; I seized the opportunity of hastening away: and therefore saying, "Heaven, Sir, protect and comfort you! – " I let fall my purse upon the ground, not daring to present it to him, and ran up stairs with the utmost swiftness.

Too well do I know you, my ever honoured Sir, to fear your displeasure for this action: I must, however, assure you I shall need no fresh supply during my stay in town, as I am at little expence, and hope soon to return to Howard Grove.

Soon, did I say! when not a fortnight is yet expired, of the long and tedious month I must linger out here!

I had many witticisms to endure from the Branghtons, upon account of my staying so long with the *Scotch mope*,[1] as they call him; but I attended to them very little, for my whole heart was filled with pity and concern. I was very glad to find the Mary-bone scheme was deferred, another shower of rain having put a stop to the dissention upon this subject; the rest of the evening was employed in most violent quarrelling between Miss Polly and her brother, on account of the discovery made by the latter, of the state of her apartment.

We came home early; and I have stolen from Madame Duval and M. Du Bois, who is here for ever, to write to my best friend.

I am most sincerely rejoiced that this opportunity has offered for my contributing what little relief was in my power, to this unhappy man; and I hope it will be sufficient to enable him to pay his debts to this pitiless family.

## LETTER XVIII.

*Mr. Villars to Evelina.*

Berry Hill.

Displeasure? my Evelina! – you have but done your duty; you have but shewn that humanity without which I should blush to own my child. It is mine, however, to see that your generosity be not repressed by your suffering from indulging it; I remit to you, therefore, not merely a token of my approbation, but an acknowledgement of my desire to participate in your charity.

O my child, were my fortune equal to my confidence in thy benevolence, with what transport should I, through thy means, devote it to the relief of indigent virtue! yet let us not repine at the limitation of our power, for, while our bounty is propor-tioned to our ability, the difference of the greater or less dona-tion, can weigh but little in the scale of justice.

---

1  The Branghtons may view Macartney as either "a fool" or "a gloomy, listless per-son" (*OED*), both of which define "mope."

In reading your account of the misguided man, whose misery has so largely excited your compassion, I am led to apprehend, that his unhappy situation is less the effect of misfortune, than of misconduct. If he is reduced to that state of poverty represented by the Branghtons, he should endeavour by activity and industry to retrieve his affairs; and not pass his time in idle reading in the very shop of his creditor.

The pistol scene made me shudder: the courage with which you pursued this desperate man, at once delighted and terrified me. Be ever thus, my dearest Evelina, dauntless in the cause of distress! let no weak fears, no timid doubts, deter you from the exertion of your duty, according to the fullest sense of it that Nature has implanted in your mind. Though gentleness and modesty are the peculiar attributes of your sex, yet fortitude and firmness, when occasion demands them, are virtues as noble and as becoming in women as in men: the right line of conduct is the same for both sexes, though the manner in which it is pursued, may somewhat vary, and be accommodated to the strength or weakness of the different travellers.

There is, however, something so mysterious in all you have yet seen or heard of this wretched man, that I am unwilling to stamp a bad impression of his character, upon so slight and partial a knowledge of it. Where any thing is doubtful, the ties of society, and the laws of humanity, claim a favourable interpretation; but remember, my dear child, that those of discretion have an equal claim to your regard.

As to Sir Clement Willoughby, I know not how to express my indignation at his conduct. Insolence so insufferable, and the implication of suspicions so shocking, irritate me to a degree of wrath, which I hardly thought my almost worn-out passions were capable of again experiencing. You must converse with him no more; he imagines, from the pliability of your temper, that he may offend you with impunity; but his behaviour justifies, nay, calls for, your avowed resentment: do not, therefore, hesitate in forbidding him your sight.

The Branghtons, Mr. Smith, and young Brown, however ill-bred and disagreeable, are objects too contemptible for serious displeasure: yet I grieve much that my Evelina should be exposed to their rudeness and impertinence.

The very day that this tedious month expires, I shall send Mrs. Clinton to town, who will accompany you to Howard Grove. Your stay there will, I hope, be short, for I feel daily an encreasing impatience to fold my beloved child to my bosom!

ARTHUR VILLARS.

## LETTER XIX.

*Evelina to the Rev. Mr. Villars.*

Holborn, June 27<sup>th</sup>.

I have just received, my dearest Sir, your kind present, and still kinder letter. Surely never had orphan so little to regret as your grateful Evelina! Though motherless, though worse than fatherless, bereft from infancy of the two first and greatest blessings of life, never has she had cause to deplore their loss; never has she felt the omission of a parent's tenderness, care, or indulgence; never, but from sorrow for *them*, had reason to grieve at the separation! Most thankfully do I receive the token of your approbation, and most studiously will I endeavour so to dispose of it, as may merit your generous confidence in my conduct.

Your doubts concerning Mr. Macartney give me some uneasiness. Indeed, Sir, he has not the appearance of a man whose sorrows are the effect of guilt. But I hope, before I leave town, to be better acquainted with his situation, and enabled, with more certainty of his worth, to recommend him to your favour.

I am very willing to relinquish all acquaintance with Sir Clement Willoughby, as far as it may depend upon myself so to do; but indeed, I know not how I should be able to absolutely *forbid him my sight.*

Miss Mirvan, in her last letter, informs me that he is now at Howard Grove, where he continues in high favour with the Captain, and is the life and spirit of the house. My time, since I wrote last, has passed very quietly; Madame Duval having been kept at home by a bad cold, and the Branghtons by bad weather. The young man, indeed, has called two or three times, and his behaviour, though equally absurd, is more unaccountable than ever: he speaks very little, takes hardly any notice of Madame Duval, and never looks at me, without a broad grin. Sometimes he approaches me, as if with intention to communicate intelligence of importance, and then, suddenly stopping short, laughs rudely in my face.

O how happy shall I be, when the worthy Mrs. Clinton arrives!

June 29<sup>th</sup>.

Yesterday morning, Mr. Smith called, to acquaint us that the Hampstead assembly was to be held that evening; and then he presented Madame Duval with one ticket, and brought another to me. I thanked him for his intended civility, but told him I was surprised he had so soon forgotten my having already declined going to the ball.

"Lord, Ma'am," cried he, "how should I suppose you was in earnest? come, come, don't be cross; here's your Grandmama ready to take care of you, so you can have no fair objection, for she'll see that I don't run away with you. Besides, Ma'am, I got the tickets on purpose."

"If you were determined, Sir," said I, "in making me this offer, to allow me no choice of refusal or acceptance, I must think myself less obliged to your intention, than I was willing to do."

"Dear Ma'am," cried he, "you're so smart, there is no speaking to you; – indeed, you are monstrous smart, Ma'am! but come, your Grandmama shall ask you, and then I know you'll not be so cruel."

Madame Duval was very ready to interfere; she desired me to make no further opposition, said she should go herself, and insisted upon my accompanying her. It was in vain that I remonstrated; I only incurred her anger, and Mr. Smith, having given both the tickets to Madame Duval, with an air of triumph, said he should call early in the evening, and took leave.

I was much chagrined at being thus compelled to owe even the shadow of an obligation to so forward a young man; but I determined that nothing should prevail upon me to dance with him, however my refusal might give offence.

In the afternoon, when he returned, it was evident that he purposed to both charm and astonish me by his appearance; he was dressed in a very showy manner, but without any taste, and the inelegant smartness of his air and deportment, his visible struggle, against education, to put on the fine gentleman, added to his frequent conscious glances at a dress to which he was but little accustomed, very effectually destroyed his aim of *figuring*,[1] and rendered all his efforts useless.

During tea, entered Miss Branghton and her brother. I was sorry to observe the consternation of the former, when she perceived Mr. Smith. I had intended applying to her for advice upon this occasion, but been always deterred by her disagreeable abruptness. Having cast her eyes several times from Mr. Smith to me, with manifest displeasure, she seated herself sullenly in the window, scarce answering Madame Duval's enquiries, and when I spoke to her, turning absolutely away from me.

Mr. Smith delighted at this mark of his importance, sat indolently quiet on his chair, endeavouring by his looks rather to display, than to conceal, his inward satisfaction.

"Good gracious!" cried young Branghton, "why, you're all as fine as five-pence![2] Why, where are you going?"

"To the Hampstead ball," answered Mr. Smith.

"To a ball!" cried he, "Why, what, is Aunt going to a ball? Ha, ha, ha!"

"Yes, to be sure," cried Madame Duval; "I don't know nothing need hinder me."

"And pray, Aunt, will you dance too?"

"Perhaps I may; but I suppose, Sir, that's none of your business, whether I do or not."

---

1  Making "a distinguished appearance" (*OED*).

2  As attractive as five pennies.

"Lord! well, I should like to go! I should like to see Aunt dance, of all things! But the joke is, I don't believe she'll get ever a partner."

"You're the most rudest boy ever I see," cried Madame Duval, angrily: "but, I promise you, I'll tell your father what you say, for I've no notion of such vulgarness."

"Why, Lord, Aunt, what are you so angry for? there's no speaking a word, but you fly into a passion: you're as bad as Biddy or Poll for that, for you're always a scolding."

"I desire, Tom," cried Miss Branghton, "you'd speak for yourself, and not make so free with my name."

"There, now, she's up! there's nothing but quarreling with the women: it's my belief they like it better than victuals and drink."

"Fie, Tom," cried Mr. Smith, "you never remember your manners before the ladies: I'm sure you never heard *me* speak so rude to them."

"Why, Lord, *you* are a beau; but that's nothing to me. So, if you've a mind, you may be so polite as to dance with Aunt yourself." Then, with a loud laugh, he declared it would be *good fun* to see them.

"Let it be never so good, or never so bad," cried Madame Duval, "you won't see nothing of it, I promise you; so pray don't let me hear no more of such vulgar pieces of fun; for, I assure you, I don't like it. And as to my dancing with Mr. Smith, you may see wonderfuller things than that any day in the week."

"Why, as to that, Ma'am," said Mr. Smith, looking much surprised, "I always thought you intended to play at cards, and so I thought to dance with the young lady."

I gladly seized this opportunity to make my declaration, that I should not dance at all.

"Not dance at all!" repeated Miss Branghton; "yes, that's a likely matter truly, when people go to balls."

"I wish she may'n't," said the brother; "'cause then Mr. Smith will have nobody but Aunt for a partner. Lord, how mad he'll be!"

"O, as to that," said Mr. Smith, "I don't at all fear prevailing with the young lady, if once I get her to the room."

"Indeed, Sir," cried I, much offended by his conceit, "you are mistaken; and therefore I beg leave to undeceive you, as you may be assured my resolution will not alter."

"Then pray, Miss, if it is not impertinent," cried Miss Branghton, sneeringly, "what do you go for?"

"Merely and solely," answered I, "to comply with the request of Madame Duval."

"Miss," cried young Branghton, "Bid only wishes it was she, for she has cast a sheep's-eye[1] at Mr. Smith this long while."

"Tom," cried the sister, rising, "I've the greatest mind in the world to box your ears! How dare you say such a thing of me?"

"No, hang it, Tom, no, that's wrong," said Mr. Smith, simpering, "it is indeed, to tell the lady's secrets. – But never mind him, Miss Biddy, for I won't believe him."

"Why, I know Bid would give her ears to go," returned the brother; "but only Mr. Smith likes Miss best, – so does every body else."

While the sister gave him a very angry answer, Mr. Smith said to me, in a low voice, "Why now, Ma'am, how can you be so cruel as to be so much handsomer than your cousins? Nobody can look at them when you are by."

"Miss," cried young Branghton, "whatever he says to you, don't mind him, for he means no good; I'll give you my word for it, he'll never marry you, for he has told me again and again, he'll never marry as long as he lives; besides, if he'd any mind to be married, there's Bid would have had him long ago, and thanked him too."

"Come, come, Tom, don't tell secrets; you'll make the ladies afraid of me: but, I assure you," lowering his voice, "if I *did* marry, it should be your cousin."

*Should* be! – did you ever, my dear Sir, hear such unauthorised freedom? I looked at him with a contempt I did not wish to repress, and walked to the other end of the room.

Very soon after, Mr. Smith sent for a hackney-coach. When I would have taken leave of Miss Branghton, she turned angrily from me, without making any answer. She supposes, perhaps,

---

1   "To look lovingly, amorously, or longingly at" (*OED*).

that I have rather sought, than endeavoured to avoid, the notice and civilities of this conceited young man.

The ball was at the *long room*[1] at Hampstead.

This room seems very well named, for I believe it would be difficult to find any other epithet which might, with propriety, distinguish it, as it is without ornament, elegance, or any sort of singularity, and merely to be marked by its length.

I was saved from the importunities of Mr. Smith, the beginning of the evening, by Madame Duval's declaring her intention to dance the two first dances with him herself. Mr. Smith's chagrin was very evident, but as she paid no regard to it, he was necessitated to lead her out.

I was, however, by no means pleased, when she said she was determined to dance a minuet. Indeed, I was quite astonished, not having had the least idea she would have consented to, much less proposed, such an exhibition of her person. She had some trouble to make her intentions known, as Mr. Smith was rather averse to speaking to the Master of the ceremonies.[2]

During this minuet, how much did I rejoice in being surrounded only with strangers! She danced in a style so uncommon; her age, her showy dress, and an unusual quantity of *rouge*, drew upon her the eyes, and, I fear, the derision of the whole company. Who she danced with, I know not; but Mr. Smith was so ill-bred as to laugh at her very openly, and to speak of her with as much ridicule as was in his power. But I would neither look at, nor listen to him; nor would I suffer him to proceed with a speech which he began, expressive of his vexation at being forced to dance with her. I told him, very gravely, that complaints upon such a subject might, with less impropriety, be made to every person in the room, than to me.

When she returned to us, she distressed me very much, by asking what I thought of her minuet. I spoke as civilly as I could, but the coldness of my compliment evidently disappointed her. She then called upon Mr. Smith to secure a good

---

1 The dance room at Hampstead spa.
2 The Master of Ceremonies is responsible for overseeing the socializing during an assembly; new parties are introduced to him; he then introduces members of new parties to others in the room as dancing partners.

place among the country-dancers; and away they went, though not before he had taken the liberty to say to me in a low voice, "I protest to you, Ma'am, I shall be quite out of countenance, if any of my acquaintance should see me dancing with the old lady!"

For a few moments I very much rejoiced at being relieved from this troublesome man; but scarce had I time to congratulate myself, before I was accosted by another, who *begged the favour of hopping a dance* with me.

I told him that I should not dance at all; but he thought proper to importune me, very freely, not to be so cruel; and I was obliged to assume no little haughtiness before I could satisfy him I was serious.

After this, I was addressed, much in the same manner, by several other young men, of whom the appearance and language were equally inelegant and low-bred: so that I soon found my situation was both disagreeable and improper; since, as I was quite alone, I fear I must seem rather to invite, than to forbid, the offers and notice I received. And yet, so great was my apprehension at this interpretation, that I am sure, my dear Sir, you would have laughed had you seen how proudly grave I appeared.

I knew not whether to be glad or sorry, when Madame Duval and Mr. Smith returned. The latter instantly renewed his tiresome entreaties, and Madame Duval said she would go to the card-table: and as soon as she was accommodated, she desired us to join the dancers.

I will not trouble you with the arguments which followed. Mr. Smith teazed me till I was weary of resistance; and I should at last have been obliged to submit, had I not fortunately recollected the affair of Mr. Lovel, and told my persecutor, that it was impossible I should dance with him, even if I wished it, as I had refused several persons in his absence.

He was not contented with being extremely chagrined, but took the liberty, openly and warmly, to expostulate with me upon not having said I was engaged.

The total disregard with which, involuntarily, I heard him, made him soon change the subject. In truth, I had no power to attend to him, for all my thoughts were occupied in re-tracing the transactions of the two former balls at which I had been present. The party – the conversation – the company – O how great the contrast!

In a short time, however, he contrived to draw my attention to himself, by his extreme impertinence; for he chose to express what he called his *admiration* of me, in terms so open and familiar, that he forced me to express my displeasure with equal plainness.

But how was I surprised, when I found he had the temerity – what else can I call it? – to impute my resentment to doubts of his honour; for he said, "My dear Ma'am, you must be a little patient; I assure you I have no bad designs, I have not upon my word; but, really, there is no resolving upon such a thing as matrimony all at once; what with the loss of one's liberty, and what with the ridicule of all one's acquaintance, – I assure you, Ma'am, you are the first lady who ever made me even demur upon this subject; for, after all, my dear Ma'am, marriage is the devil!"

"Your opinion, Sir," answered I, "of either the married or the single life, can be of no manner of consequence to me, and therefore I would by no means trouble you to discuss their different merits."

"Why, really, Ma'am, as to your being a little out of sorts, I must own I can't wonder at it, for, to be sure, marriage is all in all with the ladies; but with us gentlemen it's quite another thing! Now only put yourself in my place, – suppose you had such a large acquaintance of gentlemen as I have, – and that you had always been used to appear a little – a little smart among them, – why now, how should you like to let yourself down all at once into a married man?"

I could not tell what to answer; so much conceit, and so much ignorance, both astonished and silenced me.

"I assure you, Ma'am," added he, "there is not only Miss Biddy, – though I should have scorned to mention her, if her brother had not blab'd, for I'm quite particular in keeping ladies' secrets, – but there are a great many other ladies that have been proposed to me, – but I never thought twice of any of them, – that is, not in a *serious* way, – so you may very well be proud," offering to take my hand, "for I assure you, there is nobody so likely to catch me at last as yourself."

"Sir," cried I, drawing myself back as haughtily as I could, "you are totally mistaken, if you imagine you have given me any pride I felt not before, by this conversation; on the contrary, you must allow me to tell you, I find it too humiliating to bear with it any longer."

I then placed myself behind the chair of Madame Duval; who, when she heard of the partners I had refused, pitied my ignorance of the world, but no longer insisted upon my dancing.

Indeed, the extreme vanity of this man makes me exert a spirit which I did not, till now, know that I possessed: but I cannot endure that he should think me at his disposal.

The rest of the evening passed very quietly, as Mr. Smith did not again attempt speaking to me; except, indeed, after we had left the room, and while Madame Duval was seating herself in the coach, he said, in a voice of *pique*, "Next time I take the trouble to get any tickets for a young lady, I'll make a bargain beforehand that she sha'n't turn me over to her grandmother."

We came home very safe; and thus ended this so long projected, and most disagreeable affair.


## LETTER XX.

*Evelina in continuation.*

I have just received a most affecting letter from Mr. Macartney. I will inclose it, my dear Sir, for your perusal. More than ever have I cause to rejoice that I was able to assist him.

*Mr. Macartney to Miss Anville.*

Madam,
Impressed with the deepest, the most heart-felt sense of the exalted humanity with which you have rescued from destruc-

tion an unhappy stranger, allow me, with the humblest gratitude, to offer you my fervent acknowledgements, and to
implore your pardon for the terror I have caused you.

You bid me, Madam, live: I have now, indeed, a motive for
life, since I should not willingly quit the world, while I withhold from the needy and distressed any share of that charity
which a disposition so noble would, otherwise, bestow upon
them.

The benevolence with which you have interested yourself in
my affairs, induces me to suppose you would wish to be
acquainted with the cause of that desperation from which you
snatched me, and the particulars of that misery of which you
have so wonderfully, been a witness. Yet, as this explanation
will require that I should divulge secrets of a nature the most
delicate, I must entreat you to regard them as sacred, even
though I forbear to mention the names of the parties concerned.

I was brought up in Scotland, though my mother, who had
the sole care of me, was an Englishwoman, and had not one
relation in that country. She devoted to me her whole time.
The retirement in which we lived, and the distance from our
natural friends, she often told me, were the effect of an uncon-
querable melancholy with which she was seized, upon the sudden loss of my father, some time before I was born.

At Aberdeen where I finished my education, I formed a
friendship with a young man of fortune, which I considered as
the chief happiness of my life; — but, when he quitted his studies, I considered it as my chief misfortune, for he immediately
prepared, by direction of his friends, to make the tour of
Europe. As I was designed for the church, and had no prospect
even of maintenance but from my own industry, I scarce dared
permit even a wish of accompanying him. It is true, he would
joyfully have borne my expences; but my affection was as free
from meanness as his own, and I made a determination the
most solemn, never to lessen its dignity, by submitting to pecuniary obligations.

We corresponded with great regularity, and the most
unbounded confidence, for the space of two years, when he

arrived at Lyons in his way home. He wrote me, thence, the most pressing invitation to meet him at Paris, where he intended to remain some time. My desire to comply with his request, and shorten our absence, was so earnest, that my mother, too indulgent to controul me, lent me what assistance was in her power, and, in an ill-fated moment, I set out for that capital.

My meeting with this dear friend was the happiest event of my life: he introduced me to all his acquaintance; and so quickly did time seem to pass at that delightful period, that the six weeks I had allotted for my stay were gone, ere I was sensible I had missed so many days. But I must now own, that the company of my friend was not the sole subject of my felicity: I became acquainted with a young lady, daughter of an Englishman of distinction, with whom I formed an attachment which I have a thousand times vowed, a thousand times sincerely thought would be lasting as my life. She had but just quitted a convent,[1] in which she had been placed when a child, and though English by birth, she could scarcely speak her native language. Her person and disposition were equally engaging; but chiefly I adored her for the greatness of the expectations which, for my sake she was willing to resign.

When the time for my residence in Paris expired, I was almost distracted at the idea of quitting her; yet I had not the courage to make our attachment known to her father, who might reasonably form for her such views as would make him reject, with a contempt which I could not bear to think of, such an offer as mine. Yet I had free access to the house, where she seemed to be left almost wholly to the guidance of an old servant, who was my fast friend.

But, to be brief, the sudden and unexpected return of her father, one fatal afternoon, proved the beginning of the misery which has ever since devoured me. I doubt not but he had listened to our conversation, for he darted into the room with the rage of a madman. Heavens! what a scene followed! – what abusive language did the shame of a clandestine affair, and the consciousness of acting ill, induce me to brook! At length,

---

1   Many English girls were still educated in French convents during the eighteenth century.

however, his fury exceeded my patience, – he called me a beggarly, cowardly Scotchman. Fired at the words, I drew my sword; he, with equal alertness, drew his; for he was not an old man, but, on the contrary, strong and able as myself. In vain his daughter pleaded; – in vain did I, repentant of my anger, retreat – his reproaches continued; myself, my country, were loaded with infamy, till, no longer constraining my rage, – we fought, – and he fell!

At that moment I could almost have destroyed myself! The young lady fainted with terror; the old servant, drawn to us by the noise of the scuffle, entreated me to escape, and promised to bring intelligence of what should pass to my apartment. The disturbance which I heard raised in the house obliged me to comply, and, in a state of mind inconceivably wretched, I tore myself away.

My friend, who I found at home, soon discovered the whole affair. It was near midnight before the woman came. She told me that her master was living, and her young mistress restored to her senses. The absolute necessity for my leaving Paris, while any danger remained, was forcibly urged by my friend: the servant promised to acquaint him of whatever passed, and he to transmit to me her information. Thus circumstanced, with the assistance of this dear friend, I effected my departure from Paris, and, not long after, I returned to Scotland. I would fain have stopped by the way, that I might have been nearer the scene of all my concerns, but the low state of my finances denied me that satisfaction.

The miserable situation of my mind was soon discovered by my mother; nor would she rest till I communicated the cause. She heard my whole story with an agitation which astonished me; – the *name* of the parties concerned, seemed to strike her with horror; – but when I said, *We fought, and he fell*; – "My son," cried she, "you have then murdered your father!" and she sunk breathless at my feet. Comments, Madam, upon such a scene as this, would to you be superfluous, and to me agonizing: I cannot, for both our sakes, be too concise. When she recovered, she confessed all the particulars of a tale which she had hoped never to have revealed. – Alas! the loss she had sustained of my father was not by death! – bound to her by no ties but those of honour, he had voluntarily deserted her! – Her settling in Scotland was not the effect of choice, – she was banished thither by a family but too justly incensed; – pardon, Madam, that I cannot be more explicit!

My senses, in the greatness of my misery, actually forsook me, and for more than a week I was wholly delirious. My unfortunate mother was yet more to be pitied, for she pined with unmitigated sorrow, eternally reproaching herself for the danger to which her too strict silence had exposed me. When I recovered my reason, my impatience to hear from Paris almost deprived me of it again; and though the length of time I waited for letters might justly be attributed to contrary winds, I could not bear the delay, and was twenty times upon the point of returning thither at all hazards. At length, however, several letters arrived at once, and from the most insupportable of my afflictions I was then relieved, for they acquainted me that the horrors of parricide were not in reserve for me. They informed me also, that as soon as the wound was healed, a journey would be made to England, where my unhappy *sister* was to be received by an aunt with whom she was to live.

This intelligence somewhat quieted the violence of my sorrows. I instantly formed a plan of meeting them in London, and, by revealing the whole dreadful story, convincing this irritated parent that he had nothing more to apprehend from his daughter's unfortunate choice. My mother consented, and gave me a letter to prove the truth of my assertions. As I could but ill afford to make this journey, I travelled in the cheapest way that was possible. I took an obscure lodging, I need not, Madam, tell you where, – and boarded with the people of the house.

Here I languished, week after week, vainly hoping for the arrival of my *family*; but my impetuosity had blinded me to the imprudence of which I was guilty in quitting Scotland so hastily. My wounded father, after his recovery, relapsed; and when I had waited in the most comfortless situation, for six weeks, my friend wrote me word, that the journey was yet deferred for some time longer.

My finances were then nearly exhausted, and I was obliged,

though most unwillingly, to beg further assistance from my mother, that I might return to Scotland. Oh! Madam! – my answer was not from herself, – it was written by a lady who had long been her companion, and acquainted me that she had been taken suddenly ill of a fever, – and was no more!

The compassionate nature of which you have given such noble proofs, assures me I need not, if I could, paint to you the anguish of a mind overwhelmed with such accumulated sorrows.

Inclosed was a letter to a near relation, which she had, during her illness, with much difficulty, written, and in which, with the strongest maternal tenderness, she described my deplorable situation, and entreated his interest to procure me some preferment. Yet so sunk was I by misfortune, that a fortnight elapsed before I had the courage or spirit to attempt delivering this letter. I was then compelled to it by want. To make my appearance with some decency, I was necessitated, myself, to the melancholy task of changing my coloured cloaths for a suit of mourning; – and then I proceeded to seek my relation.

I was informed that he was not in town.

In this desperate situation, the pride of my heart, which hitherto had not bowed to adversity, gave way, and I determined to entreat the assistance of my friend, whose offered services I had a thousand times rejected. Yet, Madam, so hard is it to root from the mind its favourite principles, or prejudices, call them which you please, that I lingered another week ere I had the resolution to send away a letter which I regarded as the death of my independence.

At length, reduced to my last shilling, dunned insolently by the people of the house, and almost famished, I sealed this fatal letter, and, with a heavy heart, determined to take it to the post-office. But Mr. Branghton and his son suffered me not to pass through their shop with impunity; they insulted me grossly, and threatened me with imprisonment, if I did not immediately satisfy their demands. Stung to the soul, I bid them have but a day's patience, and flung from them, in a state of mind too terrible for description.

My letter, which I now found would be received too late to

save me from disgrace, I tore into a thousand pieces, and scarce could I refrain from putting an instantaneous, an unlicensed period to my existence.

In this disorder of my senses, I formed the horrible plan of turning foot-pad;[1] for which purpose I returned to my lodging, and collected whatever of my apparel I could part with, which I immediately sold, and with the profits purchased a brace of pistols, powder and shot. I hope, however, you will believe me, when I most solemnly assure you, my sole intention was to *frighten* the passengers[2] I should assault, with these dangerous weapons, which I had not loaded, but from a resolution, – a dreadful one, I own, – to save *myself* from an ignominious death if seized. And, indeed, I thought that if I could but procure money sufficient to pay Mr. Branghton, and make a journey to Scotland, I should soon be able, by the public papers, to discover whom I had injured, and to make private retribution.

But, Madam, new to every species of villainy, my perturbation was so great that I could with difficulty support myself: yet the Branghtons observed it not as I passed through the shop.

Here I stop: what followed is better known to yourself. But no time can ever efface from my memory that moment, when in the very action of preparing for my own destruction, or the lawless seizure of the property of others, you rushed into the room, and arrested my arm! – It was, indeed, an awful moment! – the hand of Providence seemed to intervene between me and eternity; I beheld you as an angel! – I thought you dropt from the clouds; – the earth, indeed, had never before presented to my view a form so celestial! – What wonder, then, that a spectacle so astonishing should, to a man disordered as I was, appear too beautiful to be human?

And now, Madam, that I have performed this painful task, the more grateful one remains of rewarding, as far as is in my power, your generous goodness, by assuring you it shall not be thrown away. You have awakened me to a sense of the false pride by which I have been actuated, – a pride which, while it scorned assistance from a friend, scrupled not to compel it from

---

1  "A highwayman who robs on foot" (*OED*).
2  Referring to people passing in the street on foot rather than in a vehicle.

a stranger, though at the hazard of reducing that stranger to a situation as destitute as my own. Yet, Oh! how violent was the struggle which tore my conflicting soul, ere I could persuade myself to profit by the benevolence which you were so evidently disposed to exert in my favour!

By means of a ring, the gift of my much-regretted mother, I have for the present satisfied Mr. Branghton; and by means of your compassion, I hope to support myself, either till I hear from my friend, to whom, at length, I have written, or till the relation of my mother returns to town.

To talk to you, Madam, of paying my debt, would be vain; I never can! the service you have done me exceeds all power of return; you have restored me to my senses, you have taught me to curb those passions which bereft me of them, and, since I cannot avoid calamity, to bear it as a man! An interposition so wonderfully circumstanced can never be recollected without benefit. Yet allow me to say, the pecuniary part of my obligation must be settled by my first ability.

I am, Madam, with the most profound respect, and heart-felt gratitude,

Your obedient,
and devoted humble servant,
J. MACARTNEY.

## LETTER XXI.

*Evelina in continuation.*

Holborn, July 1, 5 o'clock in the morn.

O Sir, what an adventure have I to write! – all night it has occupied my thoughts, and I am now risen thus early, to write it to you.

Yesterday it was settled that we should spend the evening in Marybone-gardens, where M. Torre,[1] a celebrated foreigner,

---

1  Giovanni Battista Torré (d. 1780) of Italy became director of fireworks at Marylebone Gardens in 1772.

was to exhibit some fireworks. The party consisted of Madame Duval, all the Branghtons, M. Du Bois, Mr. Smith, and Mr. Brown.

We were almost the first persons who entered the Gardens, Mr. Branghton having declared he would have *all he could get for his money*, which, at best, was only fooled away, at such silly and idle places.

We walked in parties, and very much detached from one another; Mr. Brown and Miss Polly led the way by themselves; Miss Branghton and Mr. Smith followed, and the latter seemed determined to be revenged for my behaviour at the ball, by transferring all his former attention for me, to Miss Branghton, who received it with an air of exultation: and very frequently they each of them, though from different motives, looked back, to discover whether I observed their good intelligence. Madame Duval walked with M. Du Bois; and Mr. Branghton by himself; but his son would willingly have attached himself wholly to me, saying frequently, "Come, Miss, let's you and I have a little fun together; you see they have all left us, so now let us leave them." But I begged to be excused, and went to the other side of Madame Duval.

This Garden, as it is called, is neither striking for magnificence nor for beauty; and we were all so dull and languid, that I was extremely glad when we were summoned to the orchestra, upon the opening of a concert; in the course of which, I had the pleasure of hearing a concerto on the violin by Mr. Barthelemon,[1] who, to me, seems a player of exquisite fancy, feeling, and variety.

When notice was given us, that the fireworks were preparing, we hurried along to secure good places for the sight: but, very soon, we were so encircled and incommoded by the crowd, that Mr. Smith proposed the *ladies* should make interest for a form to stand upon;[2] this was soon effected, and the men then left us, to accommodate themselves better, saying they would return the moment the exhibition was over.

---

1  François-Hippolite Barthélemon (1741-1808), composer, violinist, conductor, who came to work in London in the mid-1760s from France.
2  "A long seat without a back, a bench" (*OED*).

The firework was really beautiful, and told, with wonderful ingenuity, the story of Orpheus and Eurydice;[1] but, at the moment of the fatal look, which separated them for ever, there was such an explosion of fire, and so horrible a noise, that we all as of one accord, jumpt hastily from the form, and ran away some paces, fearing that we were in danger of mischief, from the innumerable sparks of fire which glittered in the air.

For a moment or two, I neither knew nor considered whither I had run; but my recollection was soon awakened by a stranger's addressing me with, "Come along with me, my dear, and I'll take care of you."

I started, and then, to my great terror, perceived that I had out-run all my companions, and saw not one human being I knew! with all the speed in my power, and forgetful of my first fright, I hastened back to the place I had left; – but found the form occupied by a new set of people.

In vain, from side to side, I looked for some face I knew; I found myself in the midst of a crowd, yet without party, friend, or acquaintance. I walked, in disordered haste, from place to place, without knowing which way to turn, or whither I went. Every other moment, I was spoken to, by some bold and unfeeling man, to whom my distress, which, I think, must be very apparent, only furnished a pretence for impertinent witticisms, or free gallantry.

At last, a young officer, marching fiercely up to me, said, "You are a sweet pretty creature, and I enlist you in my service;" and then, with great violence, he seized my hand. I screamed aloud with fear, and, forcibly snatching it away, I ran hastily up to two ladies, and cried, "For Heaven's sake, dear ladies, afford me some protection!"

They heard me with a loud laugh, but very readily said, "Ay,

---

1  Happily married to Orpheus, who could charm all nature with his lyre, Eurydice was pursued by Aristaeus and bitten by a poisonous snake as she fled his advances. She died and descended to the underworld where Orpheus sought her. Pluto and Persephone agreed that Orpheus might take Eurydice back with him to the world on condition that he did not look back at Eurydice as she followed him to the surface. Orpheus failed to keep his end of the bargain, and as a consequence, lost Eurydice to the underworld forever.

let her walk between us;" and each of them took hold of an arm.

Then, in a drawling, ironical tone of voice, they asked *what had frightened my little Ladyship*? I told them my adventure very simply, and intreated they would have the goodness to assist me in finding my friends.

O yes, to be sure, they said, I should not want for friends, whilst I was with them.[1] Mine, I said, would be very grateful for any civilities with which they might favour me. But imagine, my dear Sir, how I must be confounded, when I observed, that every other word I spoke produced a loud laugh! However, I will not dwell upon a conversation, which soon, to my inexpressible horror, convinced me I had sought protection from insult, of those who were themselves most likely to offer it! You, my dearest Sir, I well know, will both feel for, and pitty my terror, which I have no words to describe.

Had I been at liberty, I should have instantly run away from them, when I made the shocking discovery; but, as they held me fast, that was utterly impossible: and such was my dread of their resentment or abuse, that I did not dare make any open attempt to escape.

They asked me a thousand questions, accompanied by as many hallows, of who I was, what I was, and whence I came. My answers were very incoherent, – but what, good Heaven, were my emotions, when, a few moments afterwards, I perceived advancing our way, – Lord Orville!

Never shall I forget what I felt at that instant: had I, indeed, been sunk to the guilty state, which such companions might lead him to suspect, I could scarce have had feelings more cruelly depressing.

However, to my infinite joy, he passed us without distinguishing me; though I saw that, in a careless manner, his eyes surveyed the party.

As soon as he was gone, one of these unhappy women said, "Do you know that young fellow?"

---

1 . "Friends" as in men seeking her services as a prostitute.

Not thinking it possible she should mean Lord Orville by such a term, I readily answered, "No, Madam."

"Why then," answered she, "you have a monstrous good stare, for a little country Miss."

I now found I had mistaken her, but was glad to avoid an explanation.

A few minutes after, what was my delight, to hear the voice of Mr. Brown, who called out, "Lord, i'n't that Miss what's her name?"

"Thank God," cried I, suddenly springing from them both, "thank God, I have found my party."

Mr. Brown was, however, alone, and, without knowing what I did, I took hold of his arm.

"Lord, Miss," cried he, "we've had such a hunt you can't think! some of them thought you was gone home; but I says, says I, I don't think, says I, that she's like to go home all alone, says I."

"So that gentleman belongs to you, Miss, does he?" said one of the women.

"Yes, Madam," answered I, "and I now thank you for your civility; but, as I am safe, will not give you any further trouble."

I courtsied slightly, and would have walked away; but, most unfortunately, Madame Duval and the two Miss Branghtons just then joined us.

They all began to make a thousand enquiries, to which I briefly answered, that I had been obliged to these two ladies for walking with me, and would tell them more another time: for, though I felt great *comparative* courage, I was yet too much intimidated by their presence, to dare be explicit.

Nevertheless, I ventured, once more, to wish them good night, and proposed seeking Mr. Branghton. These unhappy women listened to all that was said with a kind of callous curiosity, and seemed determined not to take any hint. But my vexation was terribly augmented, when, after having whispered something to each other, they very cavalierly declared, that they intended joining our party! and then, one of them, very boldly took hold of my arm, while the other, going round, seized that of Mr. Brown; and thus, almost forcibly, we were moved on between them, and followed by Madame Duval and the Miss Branghtons.

It would be very difficult to say which was greatest, my fright, or Mr. Brown's consternation; who ventured not to make the least resistance, though his uneasiness made him tremble almost as much as myself. I would instantly have withdrawn my arm; but it was held so tight, I could not move it; and poor Mr. Brown was circumstanced in the same manner on the other side; for I heard him say, "Lord, Ma'am, there's no need to squeeze one's arm so!"

And this was our situation, – for we had not taken three steps, when, – O Sir, – we again met Lord Orville! – but not again did he pass quietly by us, – unhappily I caught his eye; – both mine, immediately, were bent to the ground; but he approached me, and we all stopped.

I then looked up. He bowed. Good God, with what expressive eyes did he regard me! Never were surprise and concern so strongly marked, – yes, my dear Sir, he looked *greatly* concerned; and that, the remembrance of that, is the only consolation I feel, for an evening the most painful of my life.

What he first said I know not; for, indeed, I seemed to have neither ears nor understanding; but I recollect that I only courtsied in silence. He paused for an instant, as if – I believe so, – as if unwilling to pass on; but then, finding the whole party detained, he again bowed, and took leave.

Indeed, my dear Sir, I thought I should have fainted, so great was my emotion from shame, vexation, and a thousand other feelings, for which I have no expressions. I absolutely tore myself from the woman's arm, and then, disengaging myself from that of Mr. Brown, I went to Madame Duval, and besought that she would not suffer me to be again parted from her.

I fancy – that Lord Orville saw what passed; for scarcely was I at liberty, ere he returned. Methought, my dear Sir, the pleasure, the surprise of that moment, recompensed me for all the chagrin I had before felt: for do you not think, that this return manifests, from a character so quiet, so reserved as Lord Orville's, something like solicitude in my concerns? – such, at least, was the interpretation I involuntarily made upon again seeing him.

With a politeness to which I have been some time very little used, he apologised for returning, and then enquired after the health of Mrs. Mirvan, and the rest of the Howard Grove family. The flattering conjecture which I have just acknowledged, had so wonderfully restored my spirits, that I believe I never answered him so readily, and with so little constraint. Very short, however, was the duration of this conversation: for we were soon most disagreeably interrupted.

The Miss Branghtons, though they saw almost immediately the characters of the women to whom I had so unfortunately applied, were, nevertheless, so weak and foolish, as merely to *titter* at their behaviour. As to Madame Duval, she was for some time so strangely imposed upon, that she thought they were two real fine ladies. Indeed it is wonderful to see how easily and how frequently she is deceived: our disturbance, however, arose from young Brown, who was now between the two women, by whom his arms were absolutely pinioned to his sides: for a few minutes, his complaints had been only murmured; but he now called out aloud, "Goodness, Ladies, you hurt me like any thing! why I can't walk at all, if you keep pinching my arms so!"

This speech raised a loud laugh in the women, and redoubled the tittering of the Miss Branghtons. For my own part, I was most cruelly confused; while the countenance of Lord Orville manifested a sort of indignant astonishment; and, from that moment, he spoke to me no more, till he took leave.

Madame Duval, who now began to suspect her company, proposed our taking the first box we saw empty, bespeaking a supper, and waiting till Mr. Branghton should find us.

Miss Polly mentioned one she had remarked, to which we all turned; Madame Duval instantly seated herself; and the two bold women, forcing the frightened Mr. Brown to go between them, followed her example.

Lord Orville, with an air of gravity that wounded my very soul, then wished me good night. I said not a word; but my face, if it had any connection with my heart, must have looked melancholy indeed: and so, I have some reason to believe, it did; for he added, with much more softness, though not less dignity, "Will Miss Anville allow me to ask her address, and to pay my respects to her before I leave town?"

O how I changed colour at this unexpected request! – yet what was the mortification I suffered, in answering, "My Lord, I am – in Holborn!"

He then bowed and left us.

What, what can he think of this adventure! how strangely, how cruelly have all appearances turned against me! Had I been blessed with any presence of mind, I should instantly have explained to him the accident which occasioned my being in such terrible company; – but I have none!

As to the rest of the evening, I cannot relate the particulars of what passed; for, to you, I only write of what I think, and I can think of nothing but this unfortunate, this disgraceful meeting. These two wretched women continued to torment us all, but especially poor Mr. Brown, who seemed to afford them uncommon diversion, till we were discovered by Mr. Branghton, who very soon found means to release us from their persecutions, by frightening them away. We stayed but a short time after they left us, which was all employed in explanations.

Whatever may be the construction which Lord Orville may put upon this affair, to me it cannot fail of being unfavourable; to be seen – gracious Heaven! – to be seen in company with two women of such character! – How vainly, how proudly have I wished to avoid meeting him when only with the Branghtons and Madame Duval, – but now, how joyful should I be had he seen me to no greater disadvantage! – Holborn, too! what a direction! – he who had always – but I will not torment you, my dearest Sir, with any more of my mortifying conjectures and apprehensions: perhaps he may call, – and then I shall have an opportunity of explaining to him all the most shocking part of the adventure. And yet, as I did not tell him at whose house I lived, he may not be able to discover me; I merely said *in Holborn*, and he, who I suppose saw my embarrassment, forbore to ask any other direction.

Well, I must take my chance!

Yet let me, in justice to Lord Orville, and in justice to the high opinion I have always entertained of his honour and delicacy, – let me observe the difference of his behaviour, when nearly in the same situation to that of Sir Clement Willoughby. He had at least equal cause to depreciate me in his opinion, and to mortify and sink me in my own: but far different was his conduct; – perplexed, indeed, he looked, and much surprised, – but it was benevolently, not with insolence. I am even inclined to think, that he could not see a young creature whom he had so lately known in a higher sphere, appear so suddenly, so strangely, so disgracefully altered in her situation, without some pity and concern. But, whatever might be his doubts and suspicions, far from suffering them to influence his behaviour, he spoke, he looked, with the same politeness and attention with which he had always honoured me when countenanced by Mrs. Mirvan.

Once again, let me drop this subject.

In every mortification, every disturbance, how grateful to my heart, how sweet to my recollection, is the certainty of your never-failing tenderness, sympathy, and protection! Oh Sir, could I, upon this subject, could I write as I feel, – how animated would be the language of

Your devoted
EVELINA!

## LETTER XXII.

*Evelina to the Rev. Mr. Villars.*

Holborn, July 1.

Listless, uneasy, and without either spirit or courage to employ myself, from the time I had finished my last letter, I indolently seated myself at the window, where, while I waited Madame Duval's summons to breakfast, I perceived, among the carriages which passed by, a coronet coach,[1] and, in a few minutes, from the window of it, Lord Orville! I instantly retreated but not, I believe, unseen; for the coach immediately drove up to our door.

Indeed, my dear Sir, I must own I was greatly agitated; the idea of receiving Lord Orville by myself, – the knowledge that his visit was entirely to *me*, – the wish of explaining the unfortunate adventure of yesterday, – and the mortification of my present circumstances, – all these thoughts, occurring to me nearly at the same time, occasioned me more anxiety, confusion, and perplexity, than I can possibly express.

I believe he meant to send up his name; but the maid, unused to such a ceremony, forgot it by the way, and only told me, that a great Lord was below, and desired to see me: and, the next moment, he appeared himself.

If formerly, when in the circle of high life, and accustomed to its manners, I so much admired and distinguished the grace, the elegance of Lord Orville, think, Sir, how they must strike me now, – now, when, far removed from that splendid circle, I live with those to whom even civility is unknown, and decorum a stranger!

I am sure I received him very awkwardly; depressed by a situation so disagreeable, could I do otherwise? When his first enquiries were made, "I think myself very fortunate," he said, "in meeting with Miss Anville at home, and still more so, in finding her disengaged."

I only courtsied. He then talked of Mrs. Mirvan; asked how long I had been in town, and other such general questions, which, happily, gave me time to recover from my embarrassment. After which, he said, "If Miss Anville will allow me the honour of sitting by her a few minutes (for we were both standing) I will venture to tell her the motive which, next to enquiring after her health, has prompted me to wait on her thus early."

We were then both seated, and, after a short pause, he said, "How to apologize for so great a liberty as I am upon the point

---

1   A coach with a small crown on its side door which indicated that its owner was a member of the peerage.

of taking, I know not; – shall I, therefore, rely wholly upon your goodness, and not apologize at all?"

I only bowed.

"I should be extremely sorry to appear impertinent, – yet hardly know how to avoid it."

"Impertinent! O my Lord," cried I, eagerly, "that, I am sure, is impossible!"

"You are very good," answered he, "and encourage me to be ingenuous – "

Again he stopped: but my expectation was too great for speech: at last, without looking at me, in a low voice and hesitating manner, he said, "Were those ladies with whom I saw you last night, ever in your company before?"

"No, my Lord," cried I, rising, and colouring violently, "nor will they ever be again."

He rose too, and, with an air of the most condescending concern, said, "Pardon, Madam, the abruptness of a question which I knew not how to introduce as I ought, and for which I have no excuse to offer, but my respect for Mrs. Mirvan, joined to the sincerest wishes for your happiness: yet I fear I have gone too far!"

"I am very sensible of the honour of your Lordship's attention," said I, "but – ."

"Permit me to assure you," cried he, finding I hesitated, "that officiousness is not my characteristic, and that I would by no means have risked your displeasure, had I not been fully satisfied you were too generous to be offended, without a real cause of offence."

"Offended!" cried I, "no, my Lord, I am only grieved, – grieved, indeed! to find myself in a situation so unfortunate, as to be obliged to make explanations which cannot but mortify and shock me."

"It is I alone," cried he, with some eagerness, "who am shocked, as it is I who deserve to be mortified; I seek no explanation, for I have no doubt; but, in mistaking me, Miss Anville injures herself: allow me, therefore, frankly and openly to tell you the intention of my visit."

I bowed, and we both returned to our seats.

"I will own myself to have been greatly surprised," continued he, "when I met you yesterday evening, in company with two persons who I was sensible merited not the honour of your notice; nor was it easy for me to conjecture the cause of your being so situated; yet, believe me, my incertitude did not for a moment do you injury; I was satisfied that their characters must be unknown to you, and I thought with concern of the shock you would sustain, when you discovered their unworthiness. I should not, however, upon so short an acquaintance, have usurped the privilege of intimacy, in giving my unasked sentiments upon so delicate a subject, had I not known that credulity is the sister of innocence, and therefore feared you might be deceived. A something, which I could not resist, urged me to the freedom I have taken to caution you; but I shall not easily forgive myself, if I have been so unfortunate as to give you pain."

The pride which his first question had excited, now subsided into delight and gratitude, and I instantly related to him, as well as I could, the accident which had occasioned my joining the unhappy women with whom he had met me. He listened with an attention so flattering, seemed so much interested during the recital, and, when I had done, thanked me, in terms so polite, for what he was pleased to call my condescension, that I was almost ashamed either to look at, or hear him.

Soon after, the maid came to tell me, that Madame Duval desired to have breakfast made in her own room.

"I fear," cried Lord Orville, instantly rising, "that I have intruded upon your time, – yet who, so situated, could do otherwise?" Then, taking my hand, "Will Miss Anville allow me thus to seal my peace?" He pressed it to his lips, and took leave.

Generous, noble Lord Orville! how disinterested his conduct! how delicate his whole behaviour! willing to advise, yet afraid to wound me! – Can I ever, in future, regret the adventure I met with at Marybone, since it has been productive of a visit so flattering? Had my mortifications been still more humiliating, my terrors still more alarming, such a mark of esteem – may I not call it so? – from Lord Orville, would have made me ample amends.

And indeed, my dear Sir, I require some consolation in my present very disagreeable situation; for, since he went, two incidents have happened, that, had not my spirits been particularly elated, would greatly have disconcerted me.

During breakfast, Madame Duval, very abruptly, asked if I should like to be married? and added, that Mr. Branghton had been proposing a match for me with his son. Surprised, and, I must own, provoked, I assured her that, in thinking of me, Mr. Branghton would very vainly lose his time.

"Why," cried she, "I have had grander views for you, myself, if once I could get you to Paris, and make you be owned; but, if I can't do that, and you can do no better, why, as you are both my relations, I think to leave my fortune between you, and then, if you marry, you never need want for nothing."

I begged her not to pursue the subject, as, I assured her, Mr. Branghton was totally disagreeable to me: but she continued her admonitions and reflections, with her usual disregard of whatever I could answer. She charged me, very peremptorily, neither wholly to discourage, nor yet to accept Mr. Branghton's offer, till she saw what could be done for me: the young man, she added, had often intended to speak to me himself, but, not well knowing how to introduce the subject, he had desired her to pave the way for him.

I scrupled not, warmly and freely to declare my aversion to this proposal; but it was to no effect; she concluded, just as she had begun, by saying, that I should not *have him, if I could do better.*

Nothing, however, shall persuade me to listen to any other person concerning this odious affair.

My second cause of uneasiness arises, very unexpectedly, from M. Du Bois, who, to my infinite surprise, upon Madame Duval's quitting the room after dinner, put into my hand a note, and immediately left the house.

This note contains an open declaration of an attachment to me, which, he says, he should never have presumed to have acknowledged, had he not been informed that Madame Duval destined my hand to young Branghton, – a match which he cannot endure to think of. He beseeches me, earnestly to pardon his temerity, professes the most inviolable respect, and commits his fate to time, patience, and pity.

This conduct in M. Du Bois gives me real concern, as I was disposed to think very well of him. It will not, however, be difficult to discourage him, and therefore I shall not acquaint Madame Duval of his letter, as I have reason to believe it would greatly displease her.

## LETTER XXIII.

*Evelina in continuation.*

July 3.

O Sir, how much uneasiness must I suffer, to counterbalance one short morning of happiness!

Yesterday, the Branghtons proposed a party to Kensington-gardens,[1] and, as usual, Madame Duval insisted upon my attendance.

We went in a hackney-coach to Piccadilly, and then had a walk through Hyde Park,[2] which, in any other company, would have been delightful. I was much pleased with Kensington-gardens, and think them infinitely preferable to those of Vauxhall.

---

1  The grounds of Nottingham House in West London became Kensington Gardens when William III bought the house in 1689, renovated it, and renamed it Kensington Palace. Throughout the eighteenth century the gardens were landscaped, walks laid (the Broad Walk became a fashionable place to walk and meet others), ponds dug and filled with water, summer houses and temples built (Weinreb 424).

2  Hyde Park is one of the oldest and "the largest of the London parks, extending over 340 acres … [until] it merges with Kensington Gardens" (Weinreb 400). Originally belonging to the manor of Eia, then given to the monks of Westminster, the park became a royal hunting ground when Henry VIII dissolved the monasteries. The park was opened to the public in the seventeenth century, cut up and sold in 1652, and then taken by Charles II in 1660 and enclosed; its reputation as a fashionable meeting place was only enhanced during this period, though it was also frequented by highwaymen and duellists.

Young Branghton was extremely troublesome; he insisted upon walking by my side, and talked with me almost by compulsion: however, my reserve and coldness prevented his entering upon the hateful subject which Madame Duval had prepared me to apprehend. Once, indeed, when I was, accidentally, a few yards before the rest, he said, "I suppose, Miss, aunt has told you about you know what? – ha'n't she, Miss?" – But I turned from him without making any answer. Neither Mr. Smith nor Mr. Brown were of the party; and poor M. Du Bois, when he found that I avoided him, looked so melancholy, that I was really sorry for him.

While we were strolling round the garden, I perceived, walking with a party of ladies at some distance, Lord Orville! I instantly retreated behind Miss Branghton, and kept out of sight till we had passed him:[1] for I dreaded being seen by him again, in a public walk, with a party of which I was ashamed.

Happily I succeeded in my design, and saw no more of him; for a sudden and violent shower of rain made us all hasten out of the gardens. We ran till we came to a small green-shop,[2] where we begged shelter. Here we found ourselves in company with two footmen, whom the rain had driven into the shop. Their livery,[3] I thought, I had before seen; and upon looking from the window, I perceived the same upon a coachman belonging to a carriage, which I immediately recollected to be Lord Orville's.

Fearing to be known, I whispered Miss Branghton not to speak my name. Had I considered but a moment, I should have been sensible of the inutility of such a caution, since not one of the party call me by any other appellation than that of *Cousin*, or of *Miss*; but I am perpetually involved in some distress or dilemma from my own heedlessness.

This request excited very strongly her curiosity; and she attacked me with such eagerness and bluntness of enquiry, that I could not avoid telling her the reason of my making it, and,

---

1   The *Errata* to the first edition indicates "them" should be changed to "him." This change was not made in the second edition, but was made in the third.
2   A green-grocer's shop which sells vegetables.
3   "The distinctive uniform style of dress worn by a person's servants" (*OED*).

consequently, that I was known to Lord Orville: an acknowledgment which proved the most unfortunate in the world; for she would not rest till she had drawn from me the circumstances attending my first making the acquaintance. Then, calling to her sister, she said, "Lord, Polly, only think! Miss has danced with a Lord!"

"Well," cried Polly, "that's a thing I should never have thought of! And pray Miss, what did he say to you?"

This question was much sooner asked than answered; and they both became so very inquisitive and earnest, that they soon drew the attention of Madame Duval and the rest of the party, to whom, in a very short time, they repeated all they had gathered from me.

"Goodness, then," cried young Branghton, "if I was Miss, if I would not make free with his Lordship's coach to take me to town."

"Why ay," said the father, "there would be some sense in that; that would be making some use of a Lord's acquaintance, for it would save us coach-hire."

"Lord, Miss," cried Polly, "I wish you would, for I should like of all things to ride in a coronet coach!"

"I promise you," said Madame Duval, "I'm glad you've thought of it, for I don't see no objection; – so let's have the coachman called."

"Not for the world," cried I, very much alarmed, "indeed it is utterly impossible."

"Why so?" demanded Mr. Branghton; "pray where's the good of your knowing a Lord, if you're never the better for him?"

"*Ma foi*, child," said Madame Duval, "you don't know no more of the world than if you was a baby. Pray, Sir, (to one of the footmen,) tell that coachman to draw up, for I wants to speak to him."

The man stared, but did not move. "Pray, pray, Madam," said I, "pray, Mr. Branghton, have the goodness to give up this plan; I know but very little of his Lordship, and cannot, upon any account, take so great a liberty."

"Don't say nothing about it," said Madame Duval, "for I shall have it my own way: so if *you* won't call the coachman, Sir, I'll promise you I'll call him myself."

The footman, very impertinently, laughed and turned upon his heel. Madame Duval, extremely irritated, ran out in the rain, and beckoned the coachman, who instantly obeyed her summons. Shocked beyond all expression, I flew after her, and entreated her with the utmost earnestness, to let us return in a hackney-coach: – but oh! – she is impenetrable to persuasion! She told the man she wanted him to carry her directly to town, and that she would answer for him to Lord Orville. The man, with a sneer, thanked her, but said he should answer for himself; and was driving off, when another footman came up to him, with information that his Lord was gone into Kensington Palace,[1] and would not want him for an hour or two.

"Why then, friend," said Mr. Branghton, (for we were followed by all the party) "where will be the great harm of your taking us to town?"

"Besides," said the son, "I'll promise you a pot of beer[2] for my own share."

These speeches had no other answer from the coachman than a loud laugh, which was echoed by the insolent footmen. I rejoiced at their resistance, though I was certain, that if their Lord had witnessed their impertinence, they would have been instantly dismissed his service.

"*Pardi*," cried Madame Duval, "if I don't think all the footmen are the most impudentest fellows in the kingdom! But I'll promise you I'll have your master told of your airs, so you'll get no good by 'em."

"Why pray," said the coachman, rather alarmed, "did my Lord give you leave to use the coach?"

---

1 Kensington Palace was the royal residence from 1689 when William III and his family took up residence there, until 1760 when George II died and his son, George III, moved to Buckingham House. In 1798 George III's son, the Duke of Kent, refurbished the Palace, and while he never really took up residence there, other members of the royal family lived there from time to time, including Princess Victoria (Weinreb 425-27).

2 At this time in ale houses beer was served in pots by pot-boys who also hawked pots of beer in the neighborhood of the ale house. Lord Orville's servants are not appreciative of Branghton's offer of a simple pot of beer as a tip.

"It's no matter for that," answered she; "I'm sure if he's a gentleman, he'd let us have it sooner than we should be wet to the skin: but I'll promise you he shall know how saucy you've been, for this young lady knows him very well."

"Ay, that she does," said Miss Polly; "and she's danced with him too."

Oh how I repented my foolish mismanagement! The men bit their lips, and looked at one another in some confusion. This was perceived by our party, who, taking advantage of it, protested they would write Lord Orville word of their ill behaviour without delay. This quite startled them, and one of the footmen offered to run to the palace and ask his Lord's permission for our having the carriage.

This proposal really made me tremble; and the Branghtons all hung back upon it: but Madame Duval is never to be dissuaded from a scheme she has once formed. "Do so," cried she, and give this child's compliments to your master, and tell him, as we ha'n't no coach here, we should be glad to go just as far as Holborn in his."

"No, no, no!" cried I; "don't go, – I know nothing of his Lordship, – I send no message, – I have nothing to say to him!"

The men, very much perplexed, could with difficulty restrain themselves from resuming their impertinent mirth. Madame Duval scolded me very angrily, and then desired them to go directly. "Pray, then," said the coachman, "what name is to be given to my Lord?"

"Anville," answered Madame Duval, "tell him Miss Anville wants the coach; the young lady he danced with once."

I was really in an agony; but the winds could not have been more deaf to me, than those to whom I pleaded! and therefore the footman, urged by the repeated threats of Madame Duval, and perhaps recollecting the name himself, actually went to the palace with this strange message!

He returned in a few minutes, and bowing to me with the greatest respect, said, "My Lord desires his compliments, and his carriage will be always at Miss Anville's service."

I was so much affected by this politeness, and chagrined at the whole affair, that I could scarce refrain from tears. Madame

Duval and the Miss Branghtons eagerly jumped into the coach, and desired me to follow. I would rather have submitted to the severest punishment; – but all resistance was vain.

During the whole ride, I said not a word; however, the rest of the party were so talkative, that my silence was very immaterial. We stopped at our lodgings; but when Madame Duval and I alighted, the Branghtons asked if they could not be carried on to Snow Hill? The servants, now all civility, made no objection. Remonstrances from me, would, I too well knew, be fruitless; and therefore, with a heavy heart, I retired to my room, and left them to their own direction.

Seldom have I passed a night in greater uneasiness: – so lately to have cleared myself in the good opinion of Lord Orville, – so soon to forfeit it! – to give him reason to suppose I presumed to boast of his acquaintance, – to publish his having danced with me! – to take with him a liberty I should have blushed to have taken with the most intimate of my friends! – to treat with such impertinent freedom one who has honoured *me* with such distinguished respect! – indeed, Sir, I could have met with no accident that would so cruelly have tormented me!

If such were, then, my feelings, imagine, – for I cannot describe, what I suffered during the scene I am now going to write.

This morning, while I was alone in the dining-room, young Branghton called. He entered with a most important air, and strutting up to me, said, "Miss, *Lord Orville* sends his compliments to you."

"Lord Orville!" – repeated I, much amazed.

"Yes, Miss, Lord Orville; – for *I* know his Lordship now, as well as you. – And a very civil gentleman he is, for all he's a Lord."

"For Heaven's sake," cried I, "explain yourself."

"Why you must know, Miss, after we left you, we met with a little misfortune; but I don't mind it now, for it's all turned out for the best: but, just as we were a going up Snow Hill, plump we comes against a cart, with such a jogg it almost pulled the coach-wheel off; however, that i'n't the worst, for as I went to open the door in a hurry, a thinking the coach would be broke down, as ill-luck would have it, I never minded that the glass was up, and so I poked my head fairly through it. Only see, Miss, how I've cut my forehead!"

A much worse accident to himself, would not, I believe, at that moment, have given me any concern for him: however, he proceeded with his account, for I was too much confounded to interrupt him.

"Goodness, Miss, we were in such a stew, us, and the servants, and all, as you can't think; for, besides the glass being broke, the coachman said how the coach would n't be safe to go back to Kensington. So we did n't know what to do; however, the footmen said they'd go and tell his Lordship what had happened. So then father grew quite uneasy, like, for fear of his Lordship's taking offence, and prejudicing us in our business: so he said I should go this morning and ask his pardon, 'cause of having broke the glass. So then I asked the footman the direction, and they told me he lived in Berkeley-square;[1] so this morning I went, – and I soon found out the house."

"You did!" cried I, quite out of breath with apprehension.

"Yes, Miss, and a very fine house it is. Did you ever see it?"

"No."

"No! – why then, Miss, I know more of his Lordship than you do, for all you knew him first. So, when I came to the door, I was in a peck of troubles, a thinking what I should say to him; however, the servants had no mind I should see him, for they told me he was busy, but I might leave my message. So I was just a coming away, when I bethought myself to say I come from you."

"From *me*! –"

"Yes, Miss, – for you know why should I have such a long walk as that for nothing? So I says to the porter, says I, tell his Lordship, says I, one wants to speak to him as comes from one Miss Anville, says I."

---

1   North of Piccadilly, Berkeley Square was designed in the 1730s by Cock and Hill-yard with large houses on the east and west sides, and gardens on the north and in the center of the square.

"Good God," cried I, "and by what authority did you take such a liberty?"

"Goodness, Miss, don't be in such a hurry, for you'll be as glad as me when you hear how well it all turned out. So then they made way for me, and said his Lordship would see me directly; and there I was led through such a heap of servants, and so many rooms, that my heart quite misgave me; for I thought, thinks I, he'll be so proud he'll hardly let me speak; but he's no more proud than I am, and he was as civil as if I'd been a lord myself. So then I said, I hoped he would n't take it amiss about the glass, for it was quite an accident; but he bid me not mention it, for it did n't signify. And then he said he hoped you got safe home, and was n't frightened; and so I said yes, and I gave your duty to him."

"My duty to him!" exclaimed I, – "and who gave you leave? – who desired you?"

"O, I did it of my own head, just to make him think I came from you. But I should have told you before how the footman said he was going out of town to-morrow evening, and that his sister was soon to be married, and that he was a ordering a heap of things for that; so it come into my head, as he was so affable, that I'd ask him for his custom. So I says, says I, my Lord, says I, if your Lordship i'n't engaged particularly, my father is a silver-smith, and he'd be very proud to serve you, says I; and Miss Anville, as danced with you, is his cousin, and she's my cousin too, and she'd be very much obliged to you, I'm sure."

"You'll drive me wild," (cried I, starting from my seat) "you have done me an irreparable injury; – but I will hear no more!" – and then I ran into my own room.

I was half frantic, I really raved; the good opinion of Lord Orville seemed now irretrievably lost: a faint hope, which in the morning I had vainly encouraged, that I might see him again, and explain the transaction, wholly vanished, now I found he was so soon to leave town: and I could not but conclude that, for the rest of my life, he would regard me as an object of utter contempt.

The very idea was a dagger to my heart! – I could not support it, and – but I blush to proceed – I fear your disapprobation, yet I should not be conscious of having merited it, but that the repugnance I feel to relate to you what I have done, makes me suspect I must have erred. Will you forgive me, if I own that I *first* wrote an account of this transaction to Miss Mirvan? – and that I even thought of *concealing* it from you? – Short-lived, however, was the ungrateful idea, and sooner will I risk the justice of your displeasure, than unworthily betray your generous confidence.

You are now probably prepared for what follows – which is a letter, – a hasty letter, that, in the height of my agitation, I wrote to Lord Orville.

"My Lord,

I am so infinitely ashamed of the application made yesterday for your Lordship's carriage in my name, and so greatly shocked at hearing how much it was injured, that I cannot forbear writing a few lines, to clear myself from the imputation of an impertinence which I blush to be suspected of, and to acquaint you, that the request for your carriage was made against my consent, and the visit with which you were importuned this morning, without my knowledge.

I am inexpressibly concerned at having been the instrument, however innocently, of so much trouble to your Lordship; but I beg you to believe, that reading these lines is the only part of it which I have given voluntarily.

I am, my Lord,
Your Lordship's most humble servant,
EVELINA ANVILLE."

I applied to the maid of the house to get this note conveyed to Berkeley-square; but scarce had I parted with it, before I regretted having written at all, and I was flying down stairs to recover it, when the voice of Sir Clement Willoughby stopped me. As Madame Duval had ordered we should be denied to him, I was obliged to return up stairs; and after he was gone, my application was too late, as the maid had given it to a porter.[1]

---

1    A person who carries messages throughout the town.

My time did not pass very serenely while he was gone; however, he brought me no answer, but that Lord Orville was not at home. Whether or not he will take the trouble to send any; – or whether he will condescend to call; – or whether the affair will rest as it is, I know not; – but, in being ignorant, am most cruelly anxious.

## LETTER XXIV.

*Evelina in continuation.*

July 4.

You may now, my dear Sir, send Mrs. Clinton for your Evelina with as much speed as she can conveniently make the journey, for no further opposition will be made to her leaving this town: happy had it perhaps been for her had she never entered it!

This morning Madame Duval desired me to go to Snow-hill, with an invitation to the Branghtons and Mr. Smith, to spend the evening with her: and she desired M. Du Bois, who breakfasted with us, to accompany me. I was very unwilling to obey her, as I neither wished to walk with M. Du Bois, nor yet to meet young Branghton. And, indeed, another, a yet more powerful reason, added to my reluctance, – for I thought it possible that Lord Orville might send some answer, or perhaps might call, during my absence; however, I did not dare dispute her commands.

Poor M. Du Bois spoke not a word during our walk, which was, I believe, equally unpleasant to us both. We found all the family assembled in the shop. Mr. Smith, the moment he perceived me, addressed himself to Miss Branghton, whom he entertained with all the gallantry in his power. I rejoice to find that my conduct at the Hampstead ball has had so good an effect. But young Branghton was extremely troublesome, he repeatedly laughed in my face, and looked so impertinently significant, that I was obliged to give up my reserve to

M. Du Bois, and enter into conversation with him, merely to avoid such boldness.

"Miss," said Mr. Branghton, "I'm sorry to hear from my son that you was n't pleased with what we did about that Lord Orville; but I should like to know what it was you found fault with, for we did all for the best."

"Goodness!" cried the son, "why if you'd seen Miss, you'd have been surprised – she went out of the room quite in a huff, like."

"It is too late, now," said I, "to reason upon this subject; but, for the future, I must take the liberty to request, that my name may never be made use of without my knowledge. May I tell Madame Duval that you will do her the favour to accept her invitation?"

"As to me, Ma'am," said Mr. Smith, "I am much obliged to the old lady, but I've no mind to be taken in by her again; you'll excuse me, Ma'am."

All the rest promised to come, and I then took leave: but as I left the shop, I heard Mr. Branghton say, "Take courage, Tom, she's only coy." And, before I had walked ten yards, the youth followed.

I was so much offended that I would not look at him, but began to converse with M. Du Bois, who was now more lively than I had ever before seen him; for, most unfortunately, he misinterpreted the reason of my attention to him.

The first intelligence I received when I came home, was that two gentlemen had called, and left cards. I eagerly enquired for them, and read the names of Lord Orville and Sir Clement Willoughby. I by no means regretted that I missed seeing the latter, but perhaps I may all my life regret that I missed the former, for probably he has now left town, – and I may see him no more!

"My goodness!" cried young Branghton, rudely looking over me, "only think of that Lord's coming all this way! It's my belief he'd got some order ready for father, and so he'd a mind to call and ask you if I'd told him the truth."

"Pray, Betty," cried I, "how long has he been gone?"

"Not two minutes, Ma'am."

"Why then I'll lay you any wager," said young Branghton, "he saw you and I a-walking up Holborn Hill!"

"God forbid!" cried I, impatiently; and too much chagrined to bear with any more of his remarks, I ran up stairs: but I heard him say to M. Du Bois, "Miss is so *uppish* this morning, that I think I had better not speak to her again."

I wish M. Du Bois had taken the same resolution; but he chose to follow me into the dining-room, which we found empty.

"*Vous ne l'aimez donc pas, ce garçon, Mademoiselle!*" cried he.

"Me!" cried I, "no, I detest him!" for I was quite sick at heart.

"*Ah, tu me rends la vie!*"[1] cried he, and flinging himself at my feet, he had just caught my hand, as the door was opened by Madame Duval.

Hastily, and with marks of guilty confusion in his face, he arose; but the rage of that lady quite amazed me! advancing to the retreating M. Du Bois, she began, in French, an attack which her extreme wrath and wonderful volubility almost rendered unintelligible; yet I understood but too much, since her reproaches convinced me she had herself proposed being the object of his affection.

He defended himself in a weak and evasive manner, and upon her commanding him from her sight, very readily withdrew: and then, with yet greater violence, she upbraided me with having *seduced* his heart, called me an ungrateful, designing girl, and protested she would neither take me to Paris, nor any more interest herself in my affairs, unless I would instantly agree to marry young Branghton.

Frightened as I had been at her vehemence, this proposal restored all my courage; and I frankly told her that in this point I never could obey her. More irritated than ever, she ordered me to quit the room.

Such is the present situation of affairs. I shall excuse myself from seeing the Branghtons this afternoon: indeed, I never wish

---

1    M. Du Bois exclaims to Evelina: "So you don't love that man, Miss!" and when she agrees that this is so, he is so relieved that he drops the formal "vous" and uses the more intimate "tu" in addressing her: "Ah, you give me life!"

to see them again. I am sorry, however innocently, that I have displeased Madame Duval, yet I shall be very glad to quit this town, for I believe it does not, now, contain one person I ever wish to again meet. Had I but seen Lord Orville, I should regret nothing: I could then have more fully explained what I so hastily wrote; yet it will always be a pleasure to me to recollect that he called, since I flatter myself it was in consequence of his being satisfied with my letter.

Adieu, my dear Sir; the time now approaches when I hope once more to receive your blessing, and to owe all my joy, all my happiness to your kindness.

## LETTER XXV.

*Mr. Villars to Evelina.*

Berry Hill, July 7.

Welcome, thrice welcome, my darling Evelina, to the arms of the truest, the fondest of your friends! Mrs. Clinton, who shall hasten to you with these lines, will conduct you directly hither, for I can consent no longer to be parted from the child of my bosom! – the comfort of my age! – the sweet solace of all my infirmities! Your worthy friends at Howard Grove must pardon me that I rob them of the visit you proposed to make them before your return to Berry Hill, for I find my fortitude unequal to a longer separation.

I have much to say to you, many comments to make upon your late letters, some parts of which give me no little uneasiness; but I will reserve my remarks for our future conversations. Hasten, then, to the spot of thy nativity, the abode of thy youth, where never yet care or sorrow had power to annoy thee; – O that they might ever be banished this peaceful dwelling!

Adieu, my dearest Evelina! I pray but that thy satisfaction at our approaching meeting, may bear any comparison with mine!

ARTHUR VILLARS.

# LETTER XXVI.

*Evelina to Miss Mirvan.*

Berry Hill, July 14.

My sweet Maria will be much surprised, and, I am willing to flatter myself, concerned, when, instead of her friend, she receives this letter; – this cold, this inanimate letter, which will but ill express the feelings of the heart which indites it.

When I wrote to you last Friday, I was in hourly expectation of seeing Mrs. Clinton, with whom I intended to have set out for Howard Grove; Mrs. Clinton came, but my plan was necessarily altered, for she brought me a letter, – the sweetest that ever was penned, from the best and kindest friend that ever orphan was blest with, requiring my immediate attendance at Berry Hill.

I obeyed, – and pardon me if I own I obeyed without reluctance; after so long a separation, should I not else have been the most ungrateful of mortals? – And yet, – oh Maria? though I *wished* to leave London, the gratification of my wish afforded me no happiness! and though I felt an impatience inexpressible to return hither, no words, no language can explain the heaviness of heart with which I made the journey. I believe you would hardly have known me; – indeed, I hardly know myself. Perhaps had I first seen *you*, in your kind and sympathizing bosom I might have ventured to have reposed every secret of my soul; and then – but let me pursue my journal.

Mrs. Clinton delivered Madame Duval a letter from Mr. Villars, which requested her leave for my return, and, indeed, it was very readily accorded: yet, when she found, by my willingness to quit town, that M. Du Bois was really indifferent to me, she somewhat softened in my favour, and declared that, but for punishing his folly in thinking of such a child, she would not have consented to my being again buried in the country.

All the Branghtons called to take leave of me: but I will not write a word more about them; indeed I cannot with any patience think of that family, to whose forwardness and impertinence is owing all the uneasiness I at this moment suffer!

So great was the depression of my spirits upon the road, that it was with difficulty I could persuade the worthy Mrs. Clinton I was not ill: but alas, the situation of my mind was such as would have rendered any mere bodily pain, by comparison, even enviable!

And yet, when we arrived at Berry Hill, – when the chaise[1] stopped at this place, – how did my heart throb with joy! And when, through the window, I beheld the dearest, the most venerable of men, with uplifted hands, returning, as I doubt not, thanks for my safe arrival, – good God! I thought it would have burst my bosom! – I opened the chaise-door myself, I flew, – for my feet did not seem to touch the ground, – into the parlour; he had risen to meet me, but the moment I appeared, he sunk into his chair, uttering with a deep sigh, though his face *beamed* with delight, "My God, I thank thee!"

I sprung forward, and with a pleasure that bordered upon agony, I embraced his knees, I kissed his hands, I wept over them, but could not speak: while he, now raising his eyes in thankfulness towards heaven, now bowing down his reverend head, and folding me in his arms, could scarce articulate the blessings with which his kind and benevolent heart overflowed.

O Miss Mirvan, to be so beloved by the best of men, – should I not be happy? – Should I have one wish save that of meriting his goodness? – Yet think me not ungrateful; indeed I am not, although the internal sadness of my mind unfits me, at present, for enjoying as I ought the bounties of Providence.

I cannot journalise;[2] cannot arrange my ideas into order.

How little has situation to do with happiness! I had flattered myself that, when restored to Berry Hill, I should be restored to tranquillity: far otherwise have I found it, for never yet had tranquillity and Evelina so little intercourse.

I blush for what I have written. Can you, Maria, forgive my gravity? but I restrain it so much and so painfully in the pres-

---

1   "A light open carriage for one or two persons, often having a top or calash; those with four wheels resembling a phaeton, those with two the curricle" (*OED*).
2   "To enter, record, or describe in or as in a private journal" (*OED*).

ence of Mr. Villars, that I know not how to deny myself the consolation of indulging it to you.

Adieu, my dear Miss Mirvan.

Yet one thing I must add; do not let the seriousness of this letter deceive you; do not impute to a wrong cause the melancholy I confess, by supposing that the heart of your friend mourns a too great susceptibility; no, indeed! believe me it never was, never can be, more assuredly her own than at this moment. So witness in all truth,

Your affectionate
EVELINA.

You will make my excuses to the honoured Lady Howard, and to your dear mother.

## LETTER XXVII.

*Evelina in continuation.*

Berry Hill, July 21.

You accuse me of mystery, and charge me with reserve: I cannot doubt but I must have merited the accusation; – yet, to clear myself, – you know not how painful will be the task. But I cannot resist your kind entreaties, – indeed, I do not wish to resist them, for your friendship and affection will soothe my chagrin. Had it arisen from any other cause, not a moment would I have deferred the communication you ask; – but, as it is, I would, were it possible, not only conceal it from all the world, but endeavour to disbelieve it myself. Yet, since I *must* tell you, why trifle with your impatience?

I know not how to come to the point; twenty times have I attempted it in vain; – but I will *force* myself to proceed.

Oh, Miss Mirvan, could you ever have believed, that one who seemed formed as a pattern for his fellow-creatures, as a model of perfection, – one whose elegance surpassed all description, – whose sweetness of manners disgraced all comparison, – Oh, Miss Mirvan, could you ever have believed that *Lord Orville* would have treated me with indignity?

Never, never again will I trust to appearances, – never confide in my own weak judgment, – never believe that person to be good, who seems to be amiable! What cruel maxims are we taught by a knowledge of the world! – But while my own reflections absorb me, I forget you are still in suspence.

I had just finished the last letter which I wrote to you from London, when the maid of the house brought me a note. It was given to her, she said, by a footman, who told her he would call the next day for an answer.

This note, – but let it speak for itself.

### To Miss Anville.

"With transport, most charming of thy sex, did I read the letter with which you yesterday morning favoured me. I am sorry the affair of the carriage should have given you any concern, but I am highly flattered by the anxiety you express so kindly. Believe me, my lovely girl, I am truly sensible of the honour of your good opinion, and feel myself deeply penetrated with love and gratitude. The correspondence you have so sweetly commenced I shall be proud of continuing, and I hope the strong sense I have of the favour you do me, will prevent your withdrawing it. Assure yourself that I desire nothing more ardently, than to pour forth my thanks at your feet, and to offer those vows which are so justly the tribute of your charms and accomplishments. In your next, I entreat you to acquaint me how long you shall remain in town. The servant whom I shall commission to call for an answer, has orders to ride post with it to me.[1] My impatience for his arrival will be very great, though inferior to that with which I burn, to tell you, in person, how much I am, my sweet girl,

> Your grateful admirer,
> ORVILLE."

---

1   To ride "with speed or haste" (*OED*). Rather than relying on the post to deliver the letter, the sender will have his servant bring Evelina's answer to him.

What a letter! how has my proud heart swelled every line I have copied! What I wrote to him you know; tell me then, my dear friend, do you think it merited such an answer? – and that I have deservedly incurred the liberty he has taken? I meant nothing but a simple apology, which I thought as much due to my own character, as to his; yet, by the construction he seems to have put upon it, should you not have imagined it contained the avowal of sentiments which might, indeed, have provoked his contempt?

The moment the letter was delivered to me, I retired to my own room to read it, and so eager was my first perusal, that, – I am ashamed to own it gave me no sensation but of delight. Unsuspicious of any impropriety from Lord Orville, I perceived not immediately the impertinence it implied, – I only marked the expressions of his own regard; and I was so much surprised, that I was unable, for some time, to compose myself, or read it again, – I could only walk up and down the room, repeating to myself, "Good God, is it possible? – am I, then, loved by Lord Orville?"

But this dream was soon over, and I awoke to far different feelings; upon a second reading, I thought every word changed, – it did not seem the same letter, – I could not find one sentence that I could look at without blushing: my astonishment was extreme, and it was succeeded by the utmost indignation.

If, as I am very ready to acknowledge, I erred in writing to Lord Orville, was it for *him* to punish the error? If he was offended, could he not have been silent? If he thought my letter ill-judged, should he not have pitied my ignorance? have considered my youth, and allowed for my inexperience.

Oh Maria, how have I been deceived in this man! Words have no power to tell the high opinion I had of him; to that was owing the unfortunate solicitude which prompted my writing, – a solicitude I must for ever repent!

Yet perhaps I have rather reason to rejoice than to grieve, since this affair has shewn me his real disposition, and removed that partiality, which, covering his every imperfection, left only his virtues and good qualities exposed to view. Had the deception continued much longer, had my mind received any additional prejudice in his favour, who knows whither my mistaken ideas might have led me? Indeed I fear I was in greater danger than I apprehended, or can now think of without trembling, – for oh, if this weak heart of mine had been penetrated with too deep an impression of his merit, – my peace and happiness had been lost for ever!

I would fain encourage more chearful thoughts, fain drive from my mind the melancholy that has taken possession of it, – but I cannot succeed; for, added to the humiliating feelings which so powerfully oppress me, I have yet another cause of concern; – alas, my dear Maria, I have broken the tranquillity of the best of men!

I have never had the courage to shew him this cruel letter: I could not bear so greatly to depreciate in his opinion, one whom I had, with infinite anxiety, raised in it myself. Indeed, my first determination was to confine my chagrin totally to my own bosom; but your friendly enquiries have drawn it from me; and now I wish I had made no concealment from the beginning, since I know not how to account for a gravity which not all my endeavours can entirely hide or repress.

My greatest apprehension is, lest he should imagine that my residence in London has given me a distaste to the country. Every body I see takes notice of my being altered, and looking pale and ill. I should be very indifferent to all such observations, did I not perceive that they draw upon me the eyes of Mr. Villars, which glisten with affectionate concern.

This morning, in speaking of my London expedition, he mentioned Lord Orville. I felt so much disturbed, that I would instantly have changed the subject; but he would not allow me, and, very unexpectedly, he began his panegyric, extolling, in strong terms, his manly and honourable behaviour in regard to the Marybone adventure. My cheeks glowed with indignation every word he spoke; – so lately as I had myself fancied him the noblest of his sex, now that I was so well convinced of my mistake, I could not bear to hear his undeserved praises uttered by one so really good, so unsuspecting, so pure of heart!

What he thought of my silence and uneasiness I fear to know, but I hope he will mention the subject no more. I will not, however, with ungrateful indolence, give way to a sadness which I find infectious to him who merits the most chearful exertion of my spirits. I am thankful that he has forborne to probe my wound, and I will endeavour to heal it by the consciousness that I have not deserved the indignity I have received. Yet I cannot but lament to find myself in a world so deceitful, where we must suspect what we see, distrust what we hear, and doubt even what we feel!

## LETTER XXVIII.

*Evelina in continuation.*

Berry Hill, July 29.

I must own myself somewhat distressed how to answer your raillery: yet believe me, my dear Maria, your suggestions are those of *fancy*, not of *truth*. I am unconscious of the weakness you suspect; yet, to dispel your doubts, I will animate myself more than ever to conquer my chagrin, and to recover my spirits.

You wonder, you say, since my *heart* takes no part in this affair, why it should make me so unhappy? And can you, acquainted as you are with the high opinion I entertained of Lord Orville, can you wonder that so great a disappointment in his character should affect me? indeed, had so strange a letter been sent to me from *any* body, it could not have failed shocking me; how much more sensibly, then, must I feel such an affront, when received from the man in the world I had imagined least capable of giving it?

You are glad I made no reply; assure yourself, my dear friend, had this letter been the most respectful that could be written, the clandestine air given to it, by his proposal of sending his servant for my answer, instead of having it directed to his house, would effectually have prevented my writing. Indeed, I have an aversion the most sincere to all mysteries, all private actions; however foolishly and blameably, in regard to this letter, I have deviated from the open path which, from my earliest infancy, I was taught to tread.

He talks of my having *commenced a correspondence*[1] with him; and could Lord Orville indeed believe I had such a design? believe me so forward, so bold, so strangely ridiculous? I know not if his man called or not, but I rejoice that I quitted London before he came, and without leaving any message for him. What, indeed, could I have said? it would have been a condescension very unmerited to have taken any, the least notice of such a letter.

Never shall I cease to wonder how he could write it. Oh, Maria, what, what could induce him so causelessly to wound and affront one who would sooner have died than wilfully offended *him*? – How mortifying a freedom of style! how cruel an implication conveyed by his *thanks*, and expressions of gratitude! Is it not astonishing, that any man can *appear* so modest, who is so vain?

Every hour I regret the secrecy I have observed with my beloved Mr. Villars; I know not what bewitched me, but I felt, at first, a repugnance to publishing this affair that I could not surmount, – and now, I am ashamed of confessing that I have any thing to confess! Yet I deserve to be punished for the false delicacy which occasioned my silence; since, if Lord Orville himself was contented to forfeit his character, was it for me, almost at the expence of my own, to support it?

Yet I believe I should be very easy, now the first shock is over, and now that I see the whole affair, with the resentment it merits, did not all my good friends in this neighbourhood, who think me extremely altered, teaze me about my gravity, and torment Mr. Villars with observations upon my dejection, and falling away.[2] The subject is no sooner started, than a deep gloom overspreads his venerable countenance, and he looks at me with a tenderness so melancholy, that I know not how to endure the consciousness of exciting it.

Mrs. Selwyn, a lady of large fortune, who lives about three

---

1 Proper young ladies did not "commence a correspondence" with a man unrelated to them.
2 Decline in health, loss of weight.

miles from Berry Hill, and who has always honoured me with very distinguishing marks of regard, is going, in a short time, to Bristol,[1] and has proposed to Mr. Villars to take me with her, for the recovery of my health. He seemed very much distressed whether to consent or refuse; but I, without any hesitation, warmly opposed the scheme, protesting my health could no where be better than in this pure air. He had the goodness to thank me for this readiness to stay with him: but he is all goodness! Oh that it were in my power to be, indeed, what in the kindness of his heart he has called me, the comfort of his age, and solace of his infirmities!

Never do I wish to be again separated from him. If here I am grave, elsewhere I should be unhappy. In his presence, with a very little exertion, all the chearfulness of my disposition seems ready to return; the benevolence of his countenance reanimates, the harmony of his temper composes, the purity of his character edifies me! I owe to him every thing; and, far from finding my debt of gratitude a weight, the first pride, first pleasure of my life is the recollection of the obligations conferred upon me by a goodness so unequalled.

Once, indeed, I thought there existed another, – who, when *time had wintered o'er his locks*, would have shone forth among his fellow-creatures, with the same brightness of worth which dignifies my honoured Mr. Villars; a brightness, how superior in value to that which results from mere quickness of parts, wit, or imagination! a brightness, which, not contented with merely diffusing smiles, and gaining admiration from the sallies of the spirits, reflects a real and a glorious lustre upon all mankind! Oh how great was my error! how ill did I judge! how cruelly have I been deceived!

I will not go to Bristol, though Mrs. Selwyn is very urgent with me; – but I desire not to see any more of the world; the few months I have already passed in it, have sufficed to give me a disgust even to its name.

I hope, too, I shall see Lord Orville no more; accustomed,

---

1   Bristol Hotwells was a spa town, like Bath, and just to the northwest of that city, located close to the southwest coast of England. It was a fashionable summer resort in the eighteenth century.

from my first knowledge of him, to regard him as a *being superior to his race*, his presence, perhaps, might banish my resentment, and I might forget his ill conduct, – for oh, Maria! – I should not know how to see *Lord Orville* – and to think of displeasure!

As a sister I loved him, – I could have entrusted him with every thought of my heart, had he deigned to wish my confidence; so steady did I think his honour, so *feminine* his delicacy, and so amiable his nature! I have a thousand times imagined that the whole study of his life, and whole purport of his reflections, tended solely to the good and happiness of others: – but I will talk, – write, – think of him no more!

Adieu, my dear friend!


## LETTER XXIX.

*Evelina in continuation.*

Berry Hill, August 10.

You complain of my silence, my dear Miss Mirvan, – but what have I to write? Narrative does not offer, nor does a lively imagination supply the deficiency. I have, however, at present, sufficient matter for a letter, in relating a conversation I had yesterday with Mr. Villars.

Our breakfast had been the most chearful we have had since my return hither; and, when it was over, he did not, as usual, retire to his study, but continued to converse with me while I worked. We might, probably, have passed all the morning thus sociably, but for the entrance of a farmer, who came to solicit advice concerning some domestic affairs. They withdrew together into the study.

The moment I was alone, my spirits failed me; the exertion with which I had supported them, had fatigued my mind: I flung away my work, and, leaning my arms on the table, gave way to a train of disagreeable reflections, which, bursting from the restraint that had smothered them, filled me with unusual sadness.

This was my situation, when, looking towards the door, which was open, I perceived Mr. Villars, who was earnestly regarding me. "Is Farmer Smith gone, Sir?" cried I, hastily rising, and snatching up my work.[1]

"Don't let me disturb you," said he, gravely; "I will go again to my study."

"Will you, Sir? – I was in hopes you were coming to sit here."

"In hopes! – and why, Evelina, should you hope it?"

This question was so unexpected, that I knew not how to answer it; but, as I saw he was moving away, I followed, and begged him to return. "No, my dear, no," said he, with a forced smile, "I only interrupt your meditations."

Again I knew not what to say; and while I hesitated, he retired. My heart was with him, but I had not the courage to follow. The idea of an explanation, brought on in so serious a manner, frightened me. I recollected the inference *you* had drawn from my uneasiness, and I feared that he might make a similar interpretation.

Solitary and thoughtful, I passed the rest of the morning in my own room. At dinner I again attempted to be chearful; but Mr. Villars himself was grave, and I had not sufficient spirits to support a conversation merely by my own efforts. As soon as dinner was over, he took a book, and I walked to the window. I believe I remained near an hour in this situation. All my thoughts were directed to considering how I might dispel the doubts which I apprehended Mr. Villars had formed, without acknowledging a circumstance which I had suffered so much pain merely to conceal. But, while I was thus planning for the future, I forgot the present; and so intent was I upon the subject which occupied me, that the strange appearance of my unusual inactivity and extreme thoughtfulness, never occurred to me. But when, at last, I recollected myself, and turned round, I saw that Mr. Villars, who had parted with his book, was wholly engrossed in attending to me. I started from my reverie, and, hardly knowing what I said, asked if he had been reading?

1 Her needle work.

He paused a moment, and then replied, "Yes, my child; – a book that both afflicts and perplexes me!"

He means *me*, thought I; and therefore I made no answer.

"What if we read it together?" continued he, "will you assist me to clear its obscurity?"

I knew not what to say, but I sighed, involuntarily, from the bottom of my heart. He rose, and, approaching me, said, with emotion, "My child, I can no longer be a silent witness of thy sorrow, – is not *thy* sorrow *my* sorrow? – and ought I to be a stranger to the cause, when I so deeply sympathise in the effect?"

"Cause, Sir!" cried I, greatly alarmed, "what cause? – I don't know, – I can't tell – I – "

"Fear not," said he, kindly, "to unbosom thyself to me, my dearest Evelina; open to me thy whole heart, – it can have no feelings for which I will not make allowance. Tell me, therefore, what it is that thus afflicts us both, and who knows but I may suggest some means of relief?"

"You are too, too good," cried I, greatly embarrassed; "but indeed I know not what you mean."

"I see," said he, "it is painful to you to speak: suppose then, I endeavour to save you by guessing?"

"Impossible! impossible!" cried I, eagerly, "no one living could ever guess, ever suppose – " I stopped abruptly; for I then recollected I was acknowledging something *was* to be guessed: however, he noticed not my mistake.

"At least let me try," answered he, mildly; "perhaps I may be a better diviner than you imagine: if I guess every thing that is probable, surely I must approach near the real reason. Be honest, then, my love, and speak without reserve, – does not the country, after so much gaiety, so much variety, does it not appear insipid and tiresome?"

"No, indeed! I love it more than ever, and more than ever do I wish I had never, never quitted it!"

"Oh my child! that I had not permitted the journey! My judgment always opposed it, but my resolution was not proof against persuasion."

"I blush, indeed," cried I, "to recollect my earnestness; – but I have been my own punisher!"

"It is too late, now," answered he, "to reflect upon this subject; let us endeavour to avoid repentance for the time to come, and we shall not have erred without reaping some instruction." Then seating himself, and making me sit by him, he continued: "I must now guess again; perhaps you regret the loss of those friends you knew in town, – perhaps you miss their society, and fear you may see them no more? – perhaps Lord Orville — "

I could not keep my seat, but rising hastily, said, "Dear Sir, ask me nothing more! – for I have nothing to own, – nothing to say; – my gravity has been merely accidental, and I can give no reason for it at all. Shall I fetch you another book? – or will you have this again?"

For some minutes he was totally silent, and I pretended to employ myself in looking for a book: at last, with a deep sigh, "I see," said he, "I see but too plainly, that though Evelina is returned, – I have lost my child!"

"No, Sir, no," cried I, inexpressibly shocked, "she is more yours than ever! Without you, the world would be a desart to her, and life a burthen; – forgive her, then, and, – if you can, – condescend to be, once more, the confident of all her thoughts."

"How highly I value, how greatly I wish for her confidence," returned he, "she cannot but know; – yet to extort, to tear it from her, – my justice, my affection, both revolt at the idea. I am sorry that I was so earnest with you; – leave me, my dear, leave me and compose yourself; – we will meet again at tea."

"Do you then refuse to hear me?"

"No, but I abhor to compel you. I have long seen that your mind has been ill at ease, and mine has largely partaken of your concern: I forbore to question you, for I hoped that time, and absence from whatever excited your uneasiness, might best operate in silence: but alas; your affliction seems only to augment, – your health declines, – your look alters, – Oh Evelina, my aged heart bleeds to see the change! – bleeds to behold the darling it had cherished, the prop it had reared for its support, when bowed down by years and infirmities, sinking itself under the pressure of internal grief! – struggling to hide, what it should seek to participate! – But go, my dear, go to your own room, – we both want composure, and we will talk of this matter some other time."

"Oh Sir," cried I, penetrated to the soul, "bid me not leave you! – think me not so lost to feeling, to gratitude – "

"Not a word of that," interrupted he; "it pains me you should think upon that subject; pains me you should ever remember that you have not a natural, an hereditary right to every thing within my power. I meant not to affect you thus, – I hoped to have soothed you! – but my anxiety betrayed me to an urgency that has distressed you. Comfort yourself, my love, and doubt not but that time will stand your friend, and all will end well."

I burst into tears: with difficulty had I so long restrained them; for my heart, while it glowed with tenderness and gratitude, was oppressed with a sense of its own unworthiness. "You are all, all goodness!" cried I, in a voice scarce audible, "little as I deserve, – unable as I am to repay, such kindness, – yet my whole soul feels, – thanks you for it!"

"My dearest child," cried he, "I cannot bear to see thy tears; – for *my* sake dry them, – such a sight is too much for me: think of that, Evelina, and take comfort, I charge thee!"

"Say then," cried I, kneeling at his feet, "say then that you forgive me! that you pardon my reserve, – that you will again suffer me to tell you my most secret thoughts, and rely upon my promise never more to forfeit your confidence! – my father! my protector! – my ever-honoured – ever-loved – my best and only friend! – say you forgive your Evelina, and she will study better to deserve your goodness!"

He raised, he embraced me; he called me his sole joy, his only earthly hope, and the child of his bosom! He folded me to his heart, and, while I wept from the fullness of mine, with words of sweetest kindness and consolation, he soothed and tranquilised me.

Dear to my remembrance will ever be that moment, when, banishing the reserve I had so foolishly planned and so painfully supported, I was restored to the confidence of the best of men!

When, at length, we were again quietly and composedly seated by each other, and Mr. Villars waited for the explanation I had begged him to hear, I found myself extremely embarrassed how to introduce the subject which must lead to it. He saw my distress, and, with a kind of benevolent pleasantry, asked me if I would let him *guess* any more? I assented in silence.

"Shall I, then, go back to where I left off!"

"If – if you please; – I believe so, – " said I, stammering.

"Well then, my love, I think I was speaking of the regret it was natural you should feel upon quitting those from whom you had received civility and kindness, with so little certainty of ever seeing them again, or being able to return their good offices? These are circumstances that afford but melancholy reflections to young minds; and the affectionate disposition of my Evelina, open to all social feelings, must be hurt more than usual by such considerations. – You are silent, my dear? – Shall I name those whom I think most worthy the regret I speak of? We shall then see if our opinions coincide."

Still I said nothing, and he continued.

"In your London journal, nobody appears in a more amiable, a more respectable light, than Lord Orville, and perhaps——"

"I knew what you would say," cried I, hastily, "and I have long feared where your suspicions would fall; but indeed, Sir, you are mistaken: I hate Lord Orville, – he is the last man in the world in whose favour I should be prejudiced."

I stopped; for Mr. Villars looked at me with such infinite surprise, that my own warmth made me blush.

"You *hate* Lord Orville!" repeated he.

I could make no answer, but took from my pocket book the letter, and giving it to him, "See, Sir," said I, "how differently the same man can *talk* and *write*!"

He read it three times before he spoke; and then said, "I am so much astonished, that I know not what I read. When had you this letter?"

I told him. Again he read it; and, after considering its contents some time, said, "I can form but one conjecture concerning this most extraordinary performance: he must certainly have been intoxicated when he wrote it."

"Lord Orville intoxicated!" repeated I; "once I thought him a stranger to all intemperance, – but it is very possible, for I can believe any thing now."

"That a man who had behaved with so strict a regard to delicacy," continued Mr. Villars, "and who, as far as occasion had allowed, manifested sentiments the most honourable, should thus insolently, thus wantonly insult a modest young woman, in his perfect senses, I cannot think possible. But, my dear, you should have inclosed this letter in an empty cover,[1] and have returned it to him again: such a resentment would at once have become *your* character, and have given him an opportunity, in some measure, of clearing his own. He could not well have read this letter the next morning, without being sensible of the impropriety of having written it."

Oh Maria! why had not I this thought? I might then have received some apology; the mortification would then have been *his*, not *mine*. It is true, he could not have reinstated himself so highly in my opinion as I had once ignorantly placed him, since the conviction of such intemperance would have levelled him with the rest of his imperfect race; yet, my humbled pride might have been consoled by his acknowledgments.

But why should I allow myself to be humbled by a man who can suffer his reason to be thus abjectly debased, when I am exalted by one who knows no vice, and scarcely a failing, – but by hearsay? To think of his kindness, and reflect upon his praises, might animate and comfort me even in the midst of affliction. "Your indignation," said he, "is the result of virtue; you fancied Lord Orville was without fault – he had the appearance of infinite worthiness, and you supposed his character accorded with his appearance: guileless yourself, how could you prepare against the duplicity of another? Your disappointment has but been proportioned to your expectations, and you have chiefly owed its severity to the innocence which hid its approach."

I will bid these words dwell ever in my memory, and they

---

1   A blank piece of paper in which a letter could be enclosed.

shall cheer, comfort, and enliven me! This conversation, though extremely affecting to me at the time it passed, has relieved my mind from much anxiety. Concealment, my dear Maria, is the foe of tranquillity: however I may err in future, I will never be disingenuous in acknowledging my errors. To you, and to Mr. Villars, I vow an unremitting confidence.

And yet, though I am more at ease, I am far from well: I have been some time writing this letter; but I hope I shall send you, soon, a more chearful one.

Adieu, my sweet friend. I entreat you not to acquaint even your dear mother with this affair; Lord Orville is a favourite with her, and why should I publish that he deserves not that honour?

## LETTER XXX.

*Evelina in continuation.*

Bristol Hotwell, August 28.

You will be again surprised, my dear Maria, at seeing whence I date my letter: but I have been very ill, and Mr. Villars was so much alarmed, that he not only insisted upon my accompanying Mrs. Selwyn hither, but earnestly desired she would hasten her intended journey.

We travelled very slowly, and I did not find myself so much fatigued as I expected. We are situated upon a most delightful spot; the prospect is beautiful, the air pure, and the weather very favourable to invalids. I am already better, and I doubt not but I shall soon be well; as well, in regard to mere health, as I wish to be.

I cannot express the reluctance with which I parted from my revered Mr. Villars: it was not like that parting which, last April, preceded my journey to Howard Grove, when, all expectation and hope, though I wept, I rejoiced, and though I sincerely grieved to leave him, I yet wished to be gone: the sorrow I now felt was unmixed with any livelier sensation; expectation was vanished, and hope I had none! All that I held most dear upon earth, I quitted, and that upon an errand to the success of which I was totally indifferent, the re-establishment of my health. Had it been to have seen my sweet Maria, or her dear mother, I should not have repined.

Mrs. Selwyn is very kind and attentive to me. She is extremely clever; her understanding, indeed, may be called *masculine;* but, unfortunately, her manners deserve the same epithet; for, in studying to acquire the knowledge of the other sex, she has lost all the softness of her own. In regard to myself, however, as I have neither courage nor inclination to argue with her, I have never been personally hurt at her want of gentleness; a virtue which, nevertheless, seems so essential a part of the female character, that I find myself more awkward, and less at ease, with a woman who wants it, than I do with a man. She is not a favourite with Mr. Villars, who has often been disgusted at her unmerciful propensity to satire: but his anxiety that I should try the effect of the Bristol waters, overcame his dislike of committing me[1] to her care. Mrs. Clinton is also here; so that I shall be as well attended as his utmost partiality could desire.

I will continue to write to you, my dear Miss Mirvan, with as much constancy as if I had no other correspondent; though during my absence from Berry Hill, my letters may, perhaps, be shortened on account of the minuteness of the journal which I must write to my beloved Mr. Villars: but you, who know his expectations, and how many ties bind me to fulfil them, will, I am sure, rather excuse any omission to yourself, than any negligence to him.

## END OF THE SECOND VOLUME.

---

1   The *Errata* to the first edition indicates "dislike to committing me" should read instead "dislike of committing me." This change was not made in the second edition, but was made in the third.

EVELINA,

OR, A

YOUNG LADY'S

ENTRANCE

INTO THE

WORLD.

IN A SERIES OF LETTERS.

The Second Edition.

VOL. III.

LONDON:
Printed for T. Lowndes, N° 77, in
Fleet-Street.

M.DCC.LXXIX.

# EVELINA

# IN A SERIES OF LETTERS.

## LETTER I.

*Evelina to the Rev. Mr. Villars.*

Bristol Hotwells, Sept. 12.

THE first fortnight that I passed here, was so quiet, so serene, that it gave me reason to expect a settled calm during my stay; but if I may now judge of the time to come, by the present state of my mind, the calm will be succeeded by a storm, of which I dread the violence!

This morning, in my way to the pump-room,[1] with Mrs. Selwyn, we were both very much incommoded by three gentlemen, who were sauntering by the side of the Avon,[2] laughing and talking very loud, and lounging so disagreeably, that we knew not how to pass them. They all three fixed their eyes very boldly upon me, alternately looking under my hat, and whispering one another. Mrs Selwyn assumed an air of uncommon sternness, and said, "You will please, Gentlemen, either to proceed yourselves, or to suffer us."

---

1 "A place at a spa where the medicinal water is dispensed for drinking" (*OED*).
2 A river that "flows past Bristol to enter the Bristol Channel at Avonmouth" (*Collier's Encyclopedia* [New York: Crowell-Collier Pub., 1965], 401).

"Oh! Ma'am," cried one of them, "we will suffer *you*, with the greatest pleasure in life."

"You will suffer us *both*," answered she, "or I am much mistaken; you had better, therefore, make way quietly, for I should be sorry to give my servant the trouble of teaching you better manners."

Her commanding air struck them, yet they all chose to laugh, and one of them wished the fellow would begin his lesson, that he might have the pleasure of rolling him into the Avon; while another, advancing to me with a freedom which made me start, said, "By my soul I did not know you! – but I am sure I cannot be mistaken; – had not I the honour of seeing you, once, at the Pantheon?"

I then recollected the nobleman who, at that place, had so much embarrassed me. I courtsied without speaking. They all bowed, and making, though in a very easy manner, an apology to Mrs. Selwyn, they suffered us to pass on, but chose to accompany us.

"And where," continued this Lord, "can you so long have hid yourself? do you know I have been in search of you this age? I could neither find you out, nor hear of you: not a creature could inform me what was become of you. I cannot imagine where you could be immured. I was at two or three public places every night, in hopes of meeting you. Pray did you leave town?"

"Yes, my Lord."

"So early in the season! – what could possibly induce you to go before the birth-day?"

"I had nothing, my Lord, to do with the birth-day."

"By my soul, all the women who *had*, may rejoice you were away. Have you been here any time?"

"Not above a fortnight, my Lord."

"A fortnight! – how unlucky that I did not meet you sooner! but I have had a run of ill luck ever since I came. How long shall you stay?"

"Indeed, my Lord, I don't know."

"Six weeks, I hope; for I shall wish the place at the devil when you go."

"Do you, then, flatter yourself, my Lord," said Mrs. Selwyn, who had hitherto listened in silent contempt, "that you shall see such a beautiful spot as this, when you visit the dominions of the devil?"

"Ha, ha, ha! Faith, my Lord," said one of his companions, who still walked with us, though the other had taken leave; "the Lady is rather hard upon you."

"Not at all," answered Mrs. Selwyn; "for as I cannot doubt but his Lordship's rank and interest will secure him a place there, it would be reflecting on his understanding, to suppose he should not wish to enlarge and beautify his dwelling."

Much as I was disgusted with this Lord, I must own Mrs. Selwyn's severity rather surprised me: but you, who have so often observed it, will not wonder she took so fair an opportunity of indulging her humour.

"As to *places*," returned he, totally unmoved, "I am so indifferent to them, that the devil take me if I care which way I go! *objects*, indeed, I am not so easy about; and therefore I expect that those angels with whose beauty I am so much enraptured in this world, will have the goodness to afford me some little consolation in the other."

"What, my Lord!" cried Mrs. Selwyn, "would you wish to degrade the habitation of your friend, by admitting into it the insipid company of the upper regions?"

"What do you do with yourself this evening?" said his Lordship, turning to me.

"I shall be at home, my Lord."

"O, à-propos – where are you?"

"Young ladies, my Lord," said Mrs. Selwyn, "are *no where*."

"Prithee," whispered his Lordship, "is that queer woman your mother?"

Good Heavens, Sir, what words for such a question!

"No, my Lord."

"Your maiden aunt, then?"

"No."

"Whoever she is, I wish she would mind her own affairs: I don't know what the devil a woman lives for after thirty: she is only in other folks way. Shall you be at the assembly?"

"I believe not, my Lord."

"No! – why then how in the world can you contrive to pass your time?"

"In a manner which your Lordship will think very extraordinary," cried Mrs. Selwyn; "for the young Lady *reads.*"

"Ha, ha, ha! Egad, my Lord," cried the facetious companion, "you are got into bad hands."

"You had better, Madam," answered he, "attack Jack Coverley, here, for you will make nothing of me."

"Of *you*, my lord!" cried she; "Heaven forbid I should ever entertain so idle an expectation! I only talk, like a silly woman, for the sake of talking; but I have by no means so low an opinion of your Lordship, as to suppose you vulnerable to censure."

"Do, pray, Ma'am," cried he, "turn to Jack Coverley; he's the very man for you; – he'd be a wit himself if he was not too modest."

"Prithee, my Lord, be quiet," returned the other; "if the Lady is contented to bestow all her favours upon *you*, why should you make such a point of my going snacks?"[1]

"Don't be apprehensive, Gentlemen," said Mrs. Selwyn, drily, "I am not romantic,[2] – I have not the least design of doing good to either of you."

"Have not you been ill since I saw you?" said his Lordship again, addressing himself to me.

"Yes, my Lord."

"I thought so; you are paler than you was, and I suppose that's the reason I did not recollect you sooner."

"Has not your Lordship too much gallantry," cried Mrs. Selwyn, "to discover a young lady's illness by her looks?"

"The devil a word can I speak for that woman," said he, in a low voice; "do, prithee, Jack, take her in hand."

"Excuse me, my Lord!" answered Mr. Coverley.

"When shall I see you again?" continued his Lordship; "do you go to the pump-room every morning?"

"No, my Lord."

---

1   "To share, divide" (*OED*).

2   "Fantastic, extravagant, quixotic; going beyond what is customary or practical" (*OED*).

"Do you ride out?"

"No, my Lord."

Just then we arrived at the pump-room, and an end was put to our conversation, if it is not an abuse of words to give such a term to a string of rude questions and free compliments.

He had not opportunity to say much more to me, as Mrs. Selwyn joined a large party, and I walked home between two ladies. He had, however, the curiosity to see us to the door.

Mrs. Selwyn was very eager to know how I had made acquaintance with this nobleman, whose manners so evidently announced the character of a confirmed libertine: I could give her very little satisfaction, as I was ignorant even of his name. But, in the afternoon, Mr. Ridgeway, the apothecary,[1] gave us very ample information.

As his person was easily described, for he is remarkably tall, Mr. Ridgeway told us he was Lord Merton, a nobleman who is but lately come to his title, though he has already dissipated more than half his fortune: a professed admirer of beauty, but a man of most licentious character: that among men, his companions consisted chiefly of gamblers and jockies, and among women, he was rarely admitted.

"Well, Miss Anville," said Mrs. Selwyn, "I am glad I was not more civil to him. You may depend upon *me* for keeping him at a distance."

"O, Madam," said Mr. Ridgeway, "he may now be admitted any where, for he is going to *reform*."

"Has he, under that notion, persuaded any fool to marry him?"

"Not yet, Madam, but a marriage is expected to take place shortly: it has been some time in agitation, but the friends of the Lady have obliged her to wait till she is of age: however, her brother, who has chiefly opposed the match, now that she is near being at her own disposal, is tolerably quiet. She is very pretty, and will have a large fortune. We expect her at the Wells every day."

---

1   "One who prepared and sold drugs for medicinal purposes.... From about 1700 apothecaries gradually took a place as general medical practitioners ..." (*OED*).

"What is her name?" said Mrs. Selwyn.

"Larpent," answered he, "Lady Louisa Larpent, sister of Lord Orville."

"Lord Orville!" repeated I, all amazement.

"Yes, Ma'am; his Lordship is coming with her. I have had certain information. They are to be at the honourable[1] Mrs. Beaumont's. She is a relation of my Lord's, and has a very fine house upon Clifton Hill."[2]

*His Lordship is coming with her!* − Good God, what an emotion did those words give me! How strange, my dear Sir, that, just at this time, he should visit Bristol! It will be impossible for me to avoid seeing him, as Mrs. Selwyn is very well acquainted with Mrs. Beaumont. Indeed, I have had an escape in not being under the same roof with him, for Mrs. Beaumont invited us to her house immediately upon our arrival; but the inconveniency of being so distant from the pump-room made Mrs. Selwyn decline her civility.

Oh that the first meeting was over! − or that I could quit Bristol without seeing him! − inexpressibly do I dread an interview: should the same impertinent freedom be expressed by his looks, which dictated his cruel letter, I shall not know how to endure either him or myself. Had I but returned it, I should be easier, because my sentiments of it would then be known to him; but now, he can only gather them from my behaviour, and I tremble lest he should mistake my indignation for confusion! − lest he should misconstrue my reserve into embarrassment! − for how, my dearest Sir, how shall I be able totally to divest myself of the respect with which I have been used to think of him? − the pleasure with which I have been used to see him?

Surely he, as well as I, must recollect the letter at the moment of our meeting, and he will, probably, mean to gather my thoughts of it from my looks; − oh that they could but convey to him my real detestation of impertinence and vanity!

---

1    "A courtesy title of honour or distinction, … the prefix 'Honourable' (Hon.) is given to sons of peers below the rank of Marquess and to daughters of peers below the rank of Earl" (*OED*).

2    Clifton Hill, standing on cliffs above the Avon River just west of Bristol, was lined with the expensive homes of the wealthy.

then would he see how much he had mistaken my disposition when he imagined them my due.

There was a time when the very idea that such a man as Lord Merton should ever be connected with Lord Orville, would have both surprised and shocked me, and even yet I am pleased to hear of his repugnance to the marriage.

But how strange, that a man of so abandoned a character should be the choice of a sister of Lord Orville! and how strange that, almost at the moment of the union, he should be so importunate in gallantry to another woman! What a world is this we live in! how corrupt! how degenerate! well might I be contented to see no more of it! If I find that the *eyes* of Lord Orville agree with his *pen*, – I shall then think, that of all mankind, the only virtuous individual resides at Berry Hill.

## LETTER II.

*Evelina in continuation.*

Bristol Hotwells, Sept. 16.

Oh Sir, Lord Orville is still himself! still, what from the moment I beheld, I believed him to be – all that is amiable in man! and your happy Evelina, restored at once to spirits and tranquillity, is no longer sunk in her own opinion, nor discontented with the world; – no longer, with dejected eyes, sees the prospect of passing her future days in sadness, doubt, and suspicion! – with revived courage she now looks forward, and expects to meet with goodness, even among mankind; – though still she feels, as strongly as ever, the folly of hoping, in any *second* instance, to meet with *perfection*.

Your conjecture was certainly right; Lord Orville, when he wrote that letter, could not be in his senses. Oh that intemperance should have power to degrade so low, a man so noble!

This morning I accompanied Mrs. Selwyn to Clifton Hill, where, beautifully situated, is the house of Mrs. Beaumont. Most uncomfortable were my feelings during our walk, which was very slow, for the agitation of my mind made me more than usually sensible how weak I still continue. As we entered the house, I summoned all my resolution to my aid, determined rather to die than give Lord Orville reason to attribute my weakness to a wrong cause. I was happily relieved from my perturbation, when I saw Mrs. Beaumont was alone. We sat with her for, I believe, an hour without interruption, and then we saw a phaeton[1] drive up to the gate, and a lady and gentleman alight from it.

They entered the parlour with the ease of people who were at home. The gentleman, I soon saw, was Lord Merton; he came shuffling into the room with his boots on, and his whip in his hand; and, having made something like a bow to Mrs. Beaumont, he turned towards me. His surprise was very evident, but he took no manner of notice of me. He waited, I believe, to discover, first, what chance had brought me to that house, where he did not look much rejoiced at meeting me. He seated himself very quietly at the window, without speaking to any body.

Mean time, the lady, who seemed very young, hobbling rather than walking into the room, made a passing courtsie to Mrs. Beaumont, saying, "How are you, Ma'am?" and then, without noticing any body else, with an air of languor, she flung herself upon a sofa, protesting, in a most affected voice, and speaking so softly she could hardly be heard, that she was fatigued to death. "Really, Ma'am, the roads are so monstrous dusty, – you can't imagine how troublesome the dust is to one's eyes! – and the sun, too, is monstrous disagreeable! – I dare say I shall be so tanned I sha'n't be fit to be seen this age.[2] Indeed, my Lord, I won't go out with you any more, for you don't care where you take one."

"Upon my honour," said Lord Merton, "I took you the pleasantest ride in England; the fault was in the sun, not me."

"Your Lordship is in the right," said Mrs. Selwyn, "to transfer the fault to the *sun*, because it has so many excellencies to

---

1   "A four-wheeled open carriage, of light construction; usually drawn by a pair of horses and with one or ... two seats facing forward" (*OED*).
2   Fashionable women during this period sought to maintain a pale complexion.

counterbalance partial inconveniences, that a *little* blame will not injure *that* in our estimation."

Lord Merton looked by no means delighted at this attack; which I believe she would not so readily have made, but to revenge his neglect of us.

"Did you meet your brother, Lady Louisa?" said Mrs. Beaumont.

"No Ma'am. Is he rode out this morning?"

I then found, what I had before suspected, that this Lady was Lord Orville's sister: how strange, that such near relations should be so different to each other! There is, indeed, some resemblance in their features, but in their manners, not the least.

"Yes," answered Mrs. Beaumont, "and I believe he wished to see you."

"My Lord drove so monstrous fast," said Lady Louisa, "that perhaps we passed him. He frighted me out of my senses; I declare my head is quite giddy. Do you know, Ma'am, we have done nothing but quarrel all the morning? – You can't think how I've scolded; – have not I, my Lord?" and she smiled expressively at Lord Merton.

"You have been, as you always are," said he, twisting his whip with his fingers, "all sweetness."

"O fie, my Lord," cried she, "I know you don't think so; I know you think me very ill-natured; – don't you, my Lord?"

"No, upon my honour; – how can your Ladyship ask such a question? Pray how goes time? my watch stands."[1]

"It is almost three," answered Mrs. Beaumont.

"Lord, Ma'am, you frighten me!" cried Lady Louisa; and then turning to Lord Merton, "why now, you wicked creature, you, did not you tell me it was but one?"

Mrs. Selwyn then rose to take leave; but Mrs. Beaumont asked if she would look at the shrubbery. "I should like it much," answered she, "but that I fear to fatigue Miss Anville."

Lady Louisa then, raising her head from her hand, on which it had leant, turned round to look at me, and, having fully

---

1  "My watch has stopped."

satisfied her curiosity, without any regard to the confusion it gave me, turned about, and, again leaning on her hand, took no further notice of me.

I declared myself very able to walk, and begged that I might accompany them. "What say *you*, Lady Louisa," cried Mrs. Beaumont, "to a strole in the garden?"

"Me, Ma'am! – I declare I can't stir a step; the heat is so excessive, it would kill me. I'm half dead with it already; besides, I shall have no time to dress. Will any body be here to-day, Ma'am?"

"I believe not, unless Lord Merton will favour us with his company."

"With great pleasure, Madam."

"Well, I declare you don't deserve to be asked," cried Lady Louisa, "you wicked creature, you! – I *must* tell you one thing, Ma'am, – you can't think how abominable he was! do you know we met Mr. Lovel in his new phaeton, and my Lord was so cruel as to drive against it? – we really flew. I declare I could not breathe. Upon my word, my Lord, I'll never trust myself with you again, – I won't indeed!"

We then went into the garden, leaving them to discuss the point at their leisure.

Do you remember a *pretty but affected young lady* I mentioned to have seen, in Lord Orville's party, at the Pantheon? How little did I then imagine her to be his sister! yet Lady Louisa Larpent is the very person. I can now account for the piqued manner of her speaking to Lord Merton that evening, and I can now account for the air of displeasure with which Lord Orville marked the undue attention of his future brother-in-law to me.

We had not walked long, ere, at a distance, I perceived Lord Orville, who seemed just dismounted from his horse, enter the garden. All my perturbation returned at the sight of him! – yet I endeavoured to repress every feeling but resentment. As he approached us, he bowed to the whole party; but I turned away my head, to avoid taking any share in his civility. Addressing himself immediately to Mrs. Beaumont, he was beginning to enquire after his sister, but upon seeing my face, he suddenly exclaimed "Miss Anville! – " and then he advanced, and made

his compliments to me, – not with an air of vanity or impertinence, nor yet with a look of consciousness or shame, – but
with a countenance open, manly, and charming! – with a smile
that indicated pleasure, and eyes that sparkled with delight! on
*my* side was all the consciousness, for by him, I really believe,
the letter was, at that moment, entirely forgotten.

With what politeness did he address me! with what sweetness did he look at me! the very tone of his voice seemed
flattering! he congratulated himself upon his good fortune in
meeting with me, – hoped I should spend some time at Bristol,
and enquired, even with anxiety enquired, if my health was the
cause of my journey, in which case his satisfaction would be
converted into apprehension.

Yet, struck as I was with his manner, and charmed to find
him such as he was wont to be, imagine not, my dear Sir, that I
forgot the resentment I owe him, or the cause he has given me
of displeasure; no, my behaviour was such as, I hope, had you
seen, you would not have disapproved: I was grave and distant, I
scarce looked at him when he spoke, or answered him when he
was silent.

As he must certainly observe this alteration in my conduct, I
think it could not fail making him both recollect and repent
the provocation he had so causelessly given me: for surely he
was not so wholly lost to reason, as to be now ignorant he had
ever offended me.

The moment that, without absolute rudeness, I was able, I
turned entirely from him, and asked Mrs. Selwyn if we should
not be late home? How Lord Orville looked I know not, for I
avoided meeting his eyes, but he did not speak another word as
we proceeded to the garden-gate. Indeed I believe my abruptness surprised him, for he did not seem to expect I had so
much spirit. And, to own the truth, convinced as I was of the
propriety, nay, necessity of shewing my displeasure, I yet almost
hated myself for receiving his politeness so ungraciously.

When we were taking leave, my eyes accidentally meeting
his, I could not but observe that his gravity equalled my own,
for it had entirely taken place of the smiles and good-humour
with which he had met me.

"I am afraid this young Lady," said Mrs. Beaumont, "is too weak for another long walk till she is again rested."

"If the Ladies will trust to my driving," said Lord Orville, "and are not afraid of a phaeton, mine shall be ready in a moment."

"You are very good, my Lord," said Mrs. Selwyn, "but my will is yet unsigned, and I don't chuse to venture in a phaeton with a young man while that is the case."

"O," cried Mrs. Beaumont, "you need not be afraid of my Lord Orville, for he is remarkably careful."

"Well, Miss Anville," answered she, "what say you?"

"Indeed," cried I, "I had much rather walk. – " But then, looking at Lord Orville, I perceived in his face a surprise so serious at my abrupt refusal, that I could not forbear adding, "for I should be sorry to occasion so much trouble."

Lord Orville brightening at these words, came forward, and pressed his offer in a manner not to be denied; – so the phaeton was ordered! And indeed, my dear Sir, – I know not how it was, – but, from that moment, my coldness and reserve insensibly wore away! You must not be angry, – it was my intention, nay, my endeavour, to support them with firmness; but when I formed the plan, I thought only of the letter, – not of Lord Orville! – and how is it possible for resentment to subsist without provocation? yet, believe me, my dearest Sir, had he sustained the part he began to act when he wrote the ever-to-be-regretted letter, your Evelina would not have forfeited her title to your esteem, by contentedly submitting to be treated with indignity.

We continued in the garden till the phaeton was ready. When we parted from Mrs. Beaumont, she repeated her invitation to Mrs. Selwyn to accept an apartment in her house, but the reason I have already mentioned made it be again declined.

Lord Orville drove very slow, and so cautiously, that, notwithstanding the height of the phaeton, fear would have been ridiculous. I supported no part in the conversation, but Mrs. Selwyn extremely well supplied the place of two. Lord Orville himself did not speak much, but the excellent sense and refined good-breeding which accompany every word he utters, give value and weight to whatever he says.

"I suppose, my Lord," said Mrs. Selwyn, when we stopped at our lodgings, "you would have been extremely confused had we met any gentlemen who have the honour of knowing you."

"If I had," answered he, gallantly, "it would have been from mere compassion at their envy."

"No, my Lord," answered she, "it would have been from mere shame, that, in an age so daring, you alone should be such a coward as to forbear to frighten women."

"O," cried he laughing, "when a man is in a fright for himself, the ladies cannot but be in security; for you have not had half the apprehension for the safety of your persons, that I have for that of my heart." He then alighted, handed us out, took leave, and again mounting the phaeton, was out of sight in a minute.

"Certainly," said Mrs. Selwyn, when he was gone, "there must have been some mistake in the birth of that young man; he was, undoubtedly, designed for the last age; for he is really polite!"

And now, my dear Sir, do not you think, according to the present situation of affairs, I may give up my resentment, without imprudence or impropriety? I hope you will not blame me. Indeed, had you, like me, seen his respectful behaviour, you would have been convinced of the impracticability of supporting any further indignation.


## LETTER III.

*Evelina in continuation.*

Bristol Hotwells, Sept. 19<sup>th</sup>.

Yesterday morning, Mrs. Selwyn received a card from Mrs. Beaumont, to ask her to dine with her to-day; and another, to the same purpose, came to me. The invitation was accepted, and we are but just arrived from Clifton-Hill.

We found Mrs. Beaumont alone in the parlour. I will write you the character of that lady, in the words of our satirical friend Mrs. Selwyn. "She is an absolute *Court Calendar bigot*;[1] for, chancing herself to be born of a noble and ancient family, she thinks proper to be of opinion, that *birth* and *virtue* are one and the same thing. She has some good qualities, but they rather originate from pride than principle, as she piques herself upon being too high born to be capable of an unworthy action, and thinks it incumbent upon her to support the dignity of her ancestry. Fortunately for the world in general, she has taken it into her head, that condescension is the most distinguishing virtue of high life; so that the same pride of family which renders others imperious, is with her the motive of affability. But her civility is too formal to be comfortable, and too mechanical to be flattering. That she does *me* the honour of so much notice, is merely owing to an accident which, I am sure, is very painful to her remembrance; for it so happened that I once did her some service, in regard to an apartment, at Southampton; and I have since been informed, that, at the time she accepted my assistance, she thought I was a woman of quality: and I make no doubt but she was miserable when she discovered me to be a mere country gentlewoman: however, her nice notions of decorum have made her load me with favours ever since. But I am not much flattered by her civilities, as I am convinced I owe them neither to attachment nor gratitude, but solely to a desire of cancelling an obligation which she cannot brook being under, to one whose name is no where to be found in the Court Calendar."

You well know, my dear Sir, the delight this lady takes in giving way to her satirical humour.

Mrs. Beaumont received us very graciously, though she somewhat distressed me by the questions she asked concerning my family, – such as, Whether I was related to the Anvilles in the North? – Whether some of my name did not live in Lincolnshire? and many other enquiries, which much embarrassed me.

---

1   A *Court Calendar* is "an annual handbook of royal families and their courts" (*OED*).

The conversation, next, turned upon the intended marriage in her family. She treated the subject with reserve, but it was evident she disapproved Lady Louisa's choice. She spoke in terms of the highest esteem of Lord Orville, calling him, in Marmontel's words, *Un jeune homme comme il y en a peu.*[1]

I did not think this conversation very agreeably interrupted by the entrance of Mr. Lovel. Indeed I am heartily sorry he is now at the Hot-wells. He made his compliments with the most obsequious respect to Mrs. Beaumont, but took no sort of notice of any other person.

In a few minutes Lady Louisa Larpent made her appearance. The same manners prevailed; for courtsying, with, "I hope you are well, Ma'am," to Mrs. Beaumont, she passed straight forward to her seat on the sofa, where, leaning her head on her hand, she cast her languishing eyes round the room, with a vacant stare, as if determined, though she looked, not to see who was in it.

Mr. Lovel, presently approaching her, with reverence the most profound, hoped her Ladyship was not indisposed.

"Mr. Lovel!" cried she, raising her head, "I declare I did not see you: Have you been here long?"

"By my *watch*, Madam," said he, "only five minutes, – but by your Ladyship's absence, as many hours."

"O! now I think of it," cried she, "I am very angry with you, – so go along, do, for I sha'n't speak to you all day."

"Heaven forbid your La'ship's displeasure should last so long! in such cruel circumstances, a day would seem an age. But in what have I been so unfortunate as to offend?"

"O, you half killed me, the other morning, with terror! I have not yet recovered from my fright. How could you be so cruel as to drive your phaeton against my Lord Merton's?"

"'Pon honour, Ma'am, your La'ship does me wrong; it was all owing to the horses, – there was no curbing them. I protest I suffered more than your Ladyship from the terror of alarming you."

---

1 Allusion to "La femme comme il y en a peu," a story in *Contes moraux* (1761) by Jean François Marmontel (1723-99); its title can be translated as "a woman like no other."

Just then entered Lord Merton; stalking up to Mrs. Beaumont, to whom alone he bowed, he hoped he had not made her wait; and then advancing to Lady Louisa, said, in a careless manner, "How is your Ladyship this morning?"

"Not well at all," answered she; "I have been dying with the head-ach ever since I got up."

"Indeed!" cried he, with a countenance wholly unmoved, "I am very unhappy to hear it. But should not your Ladyship have some advice?"[1]

"I am quite sick of advice," answered she; "Mr. Ridgeway has but just left me, – but he has done me no good. Nobody here knows what is the matter with me, yet they all see how indifferent I am."[2]

"Your Ladyship's constitution," said Mr. Lovel, "is infinitely delicate."

"Indeed it is," cried she, in a low voice, "I am *nerve* all over!"[3]

"I am glad, however," said Lord Merton, "that you did not take the air this morning, for Coverley has been driving against me as if he was mad: he has got two of the finest spirited horses I ever saw."

"Pray, my Lord," cried she, "why did not you bring Mr. Coverley with you? he's a droll creature; I like him monstrously."

"Why, he promised to be here as soon as me. I suppose he'll come before dinner's over."

In the midst of this trifling conversation, Lord Orville made his appearance. O how different was his address![4] how superior did he look and move, to all about him! Having paid his respects to Mrs. Beaumont, and then to Mrs. Selwyn, he came up to me, and said, "I hope Miss Anville has not suffered from the fatigue of Monday morning!" Then, turning to Lady Louisa, who seemed rather surprised at his speaking to me, he added, "Give me leave, Sister, to introduce Miss Anville to you."

Lady Louisa, half-rising, said, very coldly, that she should be

---

1    Medical advice.
2    Poorly.
3    "Nervous fibre" (*OED*). A bundle of nerves.
4    "Manner of speaking to another, bearing in conversation" (*OED*).

glad of the honour of knowing me; and then, abruptly turning to Lord Merton and Mr. Lovel, continued, in a half-whisper, her conversation.

For my part, I had risen and courtsied, and now, feeling very foolish, I seated myself again; first I blushed at the unexpected politeness of Lord Orville, and immediately afterwards, at the contemptuous failure of it in his sister. How can that young lady see her brother so universally admired for his manners and deportment, and yet be so unamiably opposite to him in her's! But while *his* mind, enlarged and noble, rises superior to the little prejudices of rank, *her's*, feeble and unsteady, sinks beneath their influence.

Lord Orville, I am sure, was hurt and displeased: he bit his lips, and turning from her, addressed himself wholly to me, till we were summoned to dinner. Do you think I was not grateful for his attention? yes, indeed, and every angry idea I had entertained, was totally obliterated.

As we were seating ourselves at the table, Mr. Coverley came into the room: he made a thousand apologies in a breath for being so late, but said he had been retarded by a little accident, for that he had overturned his phaeton, and broke it all to pieces. Lady Louisa screamed at this intelligence, and looking at Lord Merton, declared she would never go into a phaeton again.

"O," cried he, "never mind Jack Coverley, for he does not know how to drive."

"My Lord," cried Mr. Coverley, "I'll drive against *you* for a thousand pounds."

"Done!" returned the other; "Name your day, and we'll each chuse a judge."

"The sooner the better," cried Mr. Coverley; "to-morrow, if the carriage can be repaired."

"These enterprises," said Mrs. Selwyn, "are very proper for men of rank, since 'tis a million to one but both parties will be incapacitated for any better employment."

"For Heaven's sake," cried Lady Louisa, changing colour, "don't talk so shockingly! Pray, my Lord, pray Mr. Coverley, don't alarm me in this manner."

"Compose yourself, Lady Louisa," said Mrs. Beaumont, "the gentlemen will think better of the scheme; they are neither of them in earnest."

"The very mention of such a scheme," said Lady Louisa, taking out her salts, "makes me tremble all over! Indeed, my Lord, you have frightened me to death! I sha'n't eat a morsel of dinner."

"Permit me," said Lord Orville, "to propose some other subject for the present, and we will discuss this matter another time."

"Pray, Brother, excuse me; my Lord must give me his word to drop this project, – for, I declare, it has made me sick as death."

"To compromise the matter," said Lord Orville, "suppose, if both parties are unwilling to give up the bet, that, to make the ladies easy, we change its object to something less dangerous?"

This proposal was so strongly seconded by all the party, that both Lord Merton and Mr. Coverley were obliged to comply with it: and it was then agreed that the affair should be finally settled in the afternoon.

"I shall now be entirely out of conceit[1] with phaetons again," said Mrs. Selwyn, "though Lord Orville had almost reconciled me to them."

"My Lord Orville!" cried the witty Mr. Coverley, "why, my Lord Orville is as careful, – egad, as careful as an old woman! Why, I'd drive a one-horse cart against my Lord's phaeton for a hundred guineas!"

This sally occasioned much laughter; for Mr. Coverley, I find, is regarded as a man of infinite humour.

"Perhaps, Sir," said Mrs. Selwyn, "you have not discovered the *reason* my Lord Orville is so careful?"

"Why, no, Ma'am; I must own, I never heard any particular reason for it."

"Why then, Sir, I'll tell it you; and I believe you will confess it to be *very* particular; his Lordship's friends are not yet tired of him."

---

1  "Dissatisfied with, no longer pleased with" (*OED*).

Lord Orville laughed and bowed. Mr. Coverley, a little confused, turned to Lord Merton, and said, "No foul play, my Lord! I remember your Lordship recommended me to the notice of this lady the other morning, and, egad, I believe you have been doing me the same office to-day."

"Give you joy, Jack!" cried Lord Merton, with a loud laugh.

After this, the conversation turned wholly upon eating, a subject which was discussed with the utmost delight; and, had I not known they were men of rank and fashion, I should have imagined that Lord Merton, Mr. Lovel, and Mr. Coverley, had all been professed cooks; for they displayed so much knowledge of sauces and made dishes, and of the various methods of dressing the same things, that I am persuaded they must have given much time, and much study, to make themselves such adepts in this *art*. It would be very difficult to determine, whether they were most to be distinguished as *gluttons*, or *epicures*; for they were, at once, dainty and voracious, understood the right and the wrong of every dish, and alike emptied the one and the other. I should have been quite sick of their remarks, had I not been entertained by seeing that Lord Orville, who, I am sure, was equally disgusted, not only read my sentiments, but, by his countenance, communicated to me his own.

When dinner was over, Mrs. Beaumont recommended the gentlemen to the care of Lord Orville, and then attended the ladies to the drawing-room.

The conversation, till tea-time, was extremely insipid; Mrs. Selwyn reserved herself for the gentlemen, Mrs. Beaumont was grave, and Lady Louisa languid.

But, at tea, every body revived; we were joined by the gentlemen, and gaiety took place of dullness.

Since I, as Mr. Lovel says, am *Nobody*,[1]* I seated myself quietly on a window, and not very near to any body: Lord Merton, Mr. Coveley, and Mr. Lovel, severally passed me without notice, and surrounded the chair of Lady Louisa Larpent. I must own, I was rather piqued at the behaviour of Mr. Lovel, as he had formerly known me. It is true, I most sincerely despise

---

1   *FB's note: Vol. I., Letter XII.

his foppery, yet I should be grieved to meet with *contempt* from any body. But I was by no means sorry to find that Lord Merton was determined not to know me before Lady Louisa, as his neglect relieved me from much embarrassment. As to Mr. Coverley, his attention or disregard were equally indifferent to me. Yet, altogether, I felt extremely uncomfortable in finding myself considered in a light very inferior to the rest of the company.

But, when Lord Orville appeared, the scene changed: he came up stairs last, and seeing me sit alone, not only spoke to me directly, but drew a chair next mine, and honoured me with his entire attention.

He enquired very particularly after my health, and hoped I had already found benefit from the Bristol air.

"How little did I imagine," added he, "when I had last the pleasure of seeing you in town, that ill health would, in so short a time, have brought you hither! I am ashamed of myself for the satisfaction I feel at seeing you, – yet how can I help it!"

He then enquired after the Mirvan family, and spoke of Mrs. Mirvan in terms of most just praise. "She is gentle and amiable," said he, "a true feminine character."

"Yes, indeed," answered I, "and her sweet daughter, to say every thing of her at once, is just the daughter such a mother deserves."

"I am glad of it," said he, "for both their sakes, as such near relations must always reflect credit or disgrace on each other."

After this, he began to speak of the beauties of Clifton; but, in a few moments, he was interrupted by a call from the company, to discuss the affair of the wager. Lord Merton and Mr. Coverley, though they had been discoursing upon the subject some time, could not fix upon any thing that satisfied them both.

When they asked the assistance of Lord Orville, he proposed that every body present should vote something, and that the two gentlemen should draw lots which, from the several votes, should decide the bet.

"We must then begin with the ladies," said Lord Orville; and applied to Mrs. Selwyn.

"With all my heart," answered she, with her usual readiness; "and, since the gentlemen are not allowed to risk their *necks*, suppose we decide the bet by their *heads*?"

"By our heads?" cried Mr. Coverley; "Egad, I don't understand you."

"I will then explain myself more fully. As I doubt not but you are both excellent classics, suppose, for the good of your own memories, and the entertainment and surprise of the company, the thousand pounds should fall to the share of him who can repeat by heart the longest ode of Horace?"[1]

Nobody could help laughing, the two gentlemen applied to excepted; who seemed, each of them, rather at a loss in what manner to receive this unexpected proposal. At length Mr. Coverley, bowing low, said, "Will your Lordship please to begin?"

"Devil take me if I do!" answered he, turning on his heel, and stalking to the window.

"Come, Gentlemen," said Mrs. Selwyn, "why do you hesitate? I am sure you cannot be afraid of a weak *woman*? Besides, if you should chance to be out, Mr. Lovel, I dare say, will have the goodness to assist you."

The laugh, now, turned against Mr. Lovel, whose change of countenance manifested no great pleasure at the transition.

"Me, Madam!" said he, colouring, "no, really I must beg to be excused."

"Why so, Sir?"

"Why so, Ma'am? – Why, really, – as to that, – 'pon honour, Ma'am, you are rather – a little severe; – for how is it possible for a man who is in the House, to study the classics?[2] I assure you, Ma'am," (with an affected shrug) "I find quite business enough for *my* poor head, in studying politics."

"But, did you study politics at school, and at the university?"

"At the university!" repeated he with an embarrassed look;

---

1 Doody notes that the longest ode of Roman poet Quintus Horatius Flaccus (65-8 B.C.) is "Carmen Saeculare" (493 n. 21).

2 A gentleman's education included learning Greek and Latin and the Roman and Greek literatures of the classical period. Women, generally, did not study the classics.

"why, as to that, Ma'am, – no, I can't say I did; but then, what with riding, – and – and – and so forth, – really, one has not much time, even at the university, for mere reading."

"But, to be sure, Sir, you *have* read the classics?"

"O dear, yes, Ma'am! – very often, – but not very – not very lately."

"Which of the odes do you recommend to these gentlemen to begin with?"

"Which of the odes! – Really, Ma'am, as to that, I have no very particular choice, – for, to own the truth, that Horace was never a very great favourite with me."

"In truth I believe you!" said Mrs. Selwyn, very drily.

Lord Merton, again advancing into the circle, with a nod and a laugh, said, "Give you joy, Lovel!"

Lord Orville next applied to Mrs. Beaumont for her vote.

"It would very agreeably remind me of past times," said she, "when *bowing* was in fashion, if the bet was to depend upon the best-made bow."

"Egad, my Lord!" cried Mr. Coverley, "there I should beat you hollow, for your Lordship never bows at all."

"And, pray Sir, do *you*?" said Mrs. Selwyn.

"Do *I*, Ma'am?" cried he, "Why, only see!"

"I protest," cried she, "I should have taken *that* for a *shrug*, if you had not told me 'twas a bow."

"My Lord," cried Mr. Coverley, "let's practise;" and then, most ridiculously, they pranced about the room, making bows.

"We must now," said Lord Orville, turning to me, "call upon Miss Anville."

"O no, my Lord," cried I, "indeed I have nothing to propose." He would not, however, be refused, but urged me so much to say *something*, that at last, not to make him wait any longer, I ventured to propose an extempore couplet upon some given subject.

Mr. Coverley instantly made me a bow, or, according to Mrs. Selwyn, a *shrug*, crying, "Thank you, Ma'am; egad, that's my *fort*!¹ – Why, my Lord, the Fates² seem against you."

---

1  Strength.

2  The three Fates in classical mythology are Atropos, Clotho and Lachesis, daughters

Lady Louisa was then applied to; and every body seemed eager to hear her opinion. "I don't know what to say, I declare," cried she, affectedly; "can't you pass me?"

"By no means!" said Lord Merton.

"Is it possible your Ladyship can make so cruel a request?" said Mr. Lovel.

"Egad," cried Mr. Coverley, "if your Ladyship does not help us in this dilemma, we shall be forced to return to our phaetons."

"Oh," cried Lady Louisa, screaming, "you frightful creature, you, how can you be so abominable!"

I believe this trifling lasted near half an hour; when, at length, every body being tired, it was given up, and she said she would consider against another time.

Lord Orville now called upon Mr. Lovell, who, after about ten minutes deliberation, proposed, with a most important face, to determine the wager by who should draw the longest straw!

I had much difficulty to forbear laughing at this unmeaning scheme; but saw, to my great surprise, not the least change of countenance in any other person: and, since we came home, Mrs. Selwyn has informed me, that to *draw straws* is a fashion of betting by no means uncommon! Good God! my dear Sir, does it not seem as if money were of no value or service, since those who possess, squander it away in a manner so infinitely absurd!

It now only remained for Lord Orville to speak; and the attention of the company shewed the expectations he had raised; yet, I believe, they by no means prevented his proposal from being heard with amazement; for it was no other, than that the money should be his due, who, according to the opinion of two judges, should bring the worthiest object with whom to share it!

They all stared, without speaking. Indeed, I believe every one, for a moment at least, experienced something like shame, from having either proposed or countenanced an extravagance

---

of Erebus and Nyx. "Atropos carries the shears and cuts the thread of life; Clotho carries the spindle and spins the thread of life; Lachesis carries the globe or scroll and determines the length of the thread of life" (J. E. Zimmerman, *Dictionary of Classical Mythology* [New York: Bantam, 1978], 37).

so useless and frivolous. For my part, I was so much struck and affected by a rebuke so noble to these spendthrifts, that I felt my eyes filled with tears.

The short silence, and momentary reflection into which the company was surprised, Mr. Coverley was the first to dispel, by saying, "Egad, my Lord, your Lordship has a most remarkable odd way of taking things."

"Faith," said the incorrigible Lord Merton, "if this scheme takes, I shall fix upon my Swiss[1] to share with me; for I don't know a worthier fellow breathing."

After a few more of these attempts at wit, the two gentlemen agreed that they would settle the affair the next morning.

The conversation then took a different turn, but I did not give it sufficient attention to write any account of it. Not long after, Lord Orville resuming his seat next mine, said, "Why is Miss Anville so thoughtful?"

"I am sorry, my Lord," said I, "to consider myself among those who have so justly incurred your censure."

"My censure! – you amaze me!"

"Indeed, my Lord, you have made me quite ashamed of myself, for having given my vote so foolishly, when an opportunity offered, if, like your Lordship, I had had the sense to use it, of shewing some humanity."

"You treat this too seriously," said he, smiling; "and I hardly know if you do not now mean a rebuke to *me*."

"To you, my Lord!"

"Nay, who are most deserving of it, those who adapt the conversation to the company, or, those who affect to be superior to it?"

"O, my Lord, who else would do you so little justice?"

"I flatter myself," answered he, "that, in fact, your opinion and mine, in this point, are the same, though you condescended to comply with the humour of the company. It is for me, therefore, to apologize for so unseasonable a gravity, which, but for the particular interest that I now take in the affairs of Lord Merton, I should not have been so officious to display."

---

1   Manservant from Switzerland.

Such a compliment as this could not fail to reconcile me to myself; and with revived spirits, I entered into a conversation, which he supported with me till Mrs. Selwyn's carriage was announced, and we returned home.

During our ride, Mrs. Selwyn very much surprised me, by asking if I thought my health would now permit me to give up my morning walks to the pump-room, for the purpose of spending a week at Clifton? "for this poor Mrs. Beaumont," added she, "is so eager to have a discharge in full of her debt to me, that, out of mere compassion, I am induced to listen to her. Besides, she has always a house full of people, and though they are chiefly fools and coxcombs, yet there is some pleasure in cutting them up."

I begged I might not, by any means, prevent her following her inclination, as my health was now very well established. And so, my dear Sir, to-morrow we are to be, actually, the guests of Mrs. Beaumont.

I am not much delighted at this scheme; for, greatly as I am flattered by the attention of Lord Orville, it is not very comfortable to be neglected by every body else. Besides, as I am sure I owe the particularity of his civility to a generous feeling for my situation, I cannot expect him to support it so long as a week.

How often do I wish, since I am absent from you, that I was under the protection of Mrs. Mirvan! It is true, Mrs. Selwyn is very obliging, and, in every respect, treats me as an equal; but she is contented with behaving well herself, and does not, with a distinguishing politeness, raise and support me with others. Yet I mean not to blame her, for I know she is sincerely my friend; but the fact is, she is herself so much occupied in conversation, when in company, that she has neither leisure nor thought to attend to the silent.

Well, I must take my chance! But I knew not, till now, how requisite are birth and fortune to the attainment of respect and civility.

# LETTER IV.

*Evelina in continuation.*

Clifton, Sept. 20th.

Here I am, my dear Sir, under the same roof, and inmate of the same house, as Lord Orville! Indeed, if this were not the case, my situation would be very disagreeable, as you will easily believe, when I tell you the light in which I am generally considered.

"My dear," said Mrs. Selwyn, "did you ever before meet with that egregious fop, Lovel?"

I very readily satisfied her as to my acquaintance with him.

"O then," said she, I am the less surprised at his ill-nature, since he has already injured you."

I begged her to explain herself; and then she told me, that while Lord Orville was speaking to me, Lady Louisa said to Mr. Lovel, "Do you know who that is?"

"Why, Ma'am, no, 'pon honour," answered he, "I can't absolutely say I do; I only know she is a kind of a toad-eater.[1] She made her first appearance in that capacity last Spring, when she attended Miss Mirvan, a young lady of Kent."

How cruel is it, my dear Sir, to be thus exposed to the impertinent suggestions of a man who is determined to do me ill offices! Lady Louisa may well despise a *toad-eater*; but, thank Heaven, her brother has not heard, or does not credit, the mortifying appellation. Mrs. Selwyn said, she would advise me to *pay my court* to this Mr. Lovel; "for," said she, "though he is malicious, he is fashionable, and may do you some harm in the great world." But I should disdain myself as much as I do him, were I capable of such duplicity, as to flatter a man who I scorn and despise.

We were received by Mrs. Beaumont with great civility, and by Lord Orville with something more. As to Lady Louisa, she scarcely perceived that we were in the room.

---

1   "A humble friend or dependent; specifically a female companion or attendant" (*OED*).

There has been company here all day; part of which I have spent most happily; for after tea, when the ladies played at cards, Lord Orville, who does not, and I who cannot, play, were consequently at our own disposal; and then his Lordship entered into a conversation with me, which lasted till supper-time.

Almost insensibly, I find the constraint, the reserve, I have been wont to feel in his presence, wear away; the politeness, the sweetness, with which he speaks to me, restore all my natural chearfulness, and make me almost as easy as he is himself; and the more so, as, if I may judge by his looks, I am rather raised, than sunk, of late in his opinion.

I asked him, how the bet was, at last, to be decided? He told me, that, to his great satisfaction, the parties had been prevailed upon to lower the sum from one thousand to one hundred pounds; and that they had agreed it should be determined, by a race between two old women, one of which was to be chosen by each side, and both were to be proved more than eighty years of age, though, in other respects, strong and healthy as possible.[1]

When I expressed my surprise at this extraordinary method of spending so much money, "I am charmed," said he, "at the novelty of meeting with one so unhackneyed in the world, as not to be yet influenced by custom to forget the use of reason: for certain it is, that the prevalence of fashion makes the greatest absurdities pass uncensured, and the mind naturally accommodates itself, even to the most ridiculous improprieties, if they occur frequently."

"I should have hoped," said I, "that the humane proposal made yesterday by your Lordship, would have had more effect."

"O," cried he, laughing, "I was so far from expecting any success, that I shall think myself very fortunate if I escape the wit of Mr. Coverley in a lampoon! yet I spoke openly, because I do not wish to conceal that I am no friend to gaming."

---

1 Pedestrian races between unequal or equally challenged contestants were a specta-tor sport on a small scale in eighteenth-century England. See Earl R. Anderson, "Footnotes More Pedestrian than Sublime: A Historical Background for the Foot-Races in *Evelina* and *Humphry Clinker*," *Eighteenth-Century Studies* 14 (1980): 56-68.

After this, he took up the New Bath Guide,[1] and read it with me till supper-time. In our way down stairs, Lady Louisa said, "I thought, Brother, you were engaged this evening?"

"Yes, Sister," answered he, "and I *have* been engaged." And he bowed to me with an air of gallantry that rather confused me.

September 23d.

Almost insensibly have three days glided on since I wrote last, and so serenely, that, but for your absence, I could not have formed a wish. My residence here is much happier than I had dared expect. The attention with which Lord Orville honours me is as uniform as it is flattering, and seems to result from a benevolence of heart that proves him as much a stranger to caprice as to pride; for, as his particular civilities arose from a generous resentment at seeing me neglected, so will they, I trust, continue, as long as I shall, in any degree, deserve them. I am now not merely easy, but even gay in his presence: such is the effect of true politeness, that it banishes all restraint and embarrassment. When we walk out, he condescends to be my companion, and keeps by my side all the way we go. When we read, he marks the passages most worthy to be noticed, draws out my sentiments, and favours me with his own. At table, where he always sits next to me, he obliges me by a thousand nameless attentions, while the distinguishing good-breeding with which he treats me, prevents my repining at the visibly-felt superiority of the rest of the company. A thousand occasional meetings could not have brought us to that degree of social freedom, which four days spent under the same roof have, insensibly, been productive of: and, as my only friend in this house, Mrs. Selwyn, is too much engrossed in perpetual conversation to attend much to me, Lord Orville seems to regard me as a helpless stranger, and, as such, to think me entitled to his good offices and pro-

---

1    Christopher Anstey (1724-1805) wrote his immensely popular long comic poem, *The New Bath Guide: or, Memoirs of the B-r-d Family. In A Series of Poetical Epistles,* a satire on social customs in the fashionable resort, in 1766. See Appendix C for an excerpt from this work.

tection. Indeed, my dear Sir, I have reason to hope, that the depreciating opinion he formerly entertained of me is succeeded by one infinitely more partial. – It may be that I flatter myself, but yet his looks, his attentions, his desire of drawing me into conversation, and his solicitude to oblige me, all conspire to make me hope I do not. In short, my dearest Sir, these last four happy days would repay me for months of sorrow and pain!

## LETTER V.

*Evelina in continuation.*

Clifton, Sept. 24$^{th}$.

This morning I came down stairs very early, and, supposing that the family would not assemble for some time, I strolled out, purposing to take a long walk, in the manner I was wont to do at Berry Hill, before breakfast. But I had scarce shut the garden-gate, before I was met by a gentleman, who, immediately bowing to me, I recollected to be the unhappy Mr. Macartney. Very much surprised, I courtsied, and stopped till he came up to me. He was still in mourning, but looked better than when I saw him last, though he had the same air of melancholy which so much struck me at first sight of him.

Addressing me with the utmost respect, "I am happy, Madam," said he, "to have met with you so soon. I came to Bristol but yesterday, and have had no small difficulty in tracing you to Clifton."

"Did you know, then, of my being here?"

"I did, Madam; the sole motive of my journey was to see you. I have been to Berry Hill, and there I had my intelligence, and, at the same time, the unwelcome information of your ill health."

"Good God! Sir, – and can you possibly have taken so much trouble?"

"Trouble! Oh, Madam, could there be any, to return you, the

moment I had the power, my personal acknowledgments for your goodness?"

I then enquired after Madame Duval, and the Snow-Hill family. He told me, they were all well, and that Madame Duval proposed soon returning to Paris. When I congratulated him upon looking better, "It is *yourself*, Madam," said he, "you should congratulate, for to your humanity alone it may now be owing that I exist at all." He then told me, that his affairs were now in a less desperate situation, and that he hoped, by the assistance of time and reason, to accommodate his mind to a more chearful submission to his fate. "The interest you so generously took in my affliction," added he, "assures me you will not be displeased to hear of my better fortune: I was therefore eager to acquaint you with it." He then told me, that his friend, the moment he had received his letter, quitted Paris, and flew to give him his personal assistance and consolation. With a heavy heart, he acknowledged, he accepted it; "but yet," he added, "I *have* accepted it, and therefore, as bound equally by duty and honour, my first step was to hasten to the benefactress of my distress, and to return" (presenting me something in a paper) "the only part of my obligations that *can* be returned; for the rest, I have nothing but my gratitude to offer, and must always be contented to consider myself her debtor."

I congratulated him most sincerely upon his dawning prosperity, but begged he would not deprive me of the pleasure of being his friend, and declined receiving the money, till his affairs were more settled.

While this point was in agitation, I heard Lord Orville's voice, enquiring of the gardener if he had seen me? I immediately opened the garden-gate, and his Lordship, advancing to me with quickness, said, "Good God, Miss Anville, have you been out alone? Breakfast has been ready some time, and I have been round the garden in search of you."

"Your Lordship has been very good," said I; "but I hope you have not waited."

"Not waited!" repeated he, smiling, "do you think we could sit down quietly to breakfast, with the idea that you had run away from us? But come," (offering to hand me) "if we do not return, they will suppose *I* am run away too; and they very naturally may, as they know the attraction of the magnet that draws me."

"I will come, my Lord," said I, rather embarrassed, "in two minutes." Then, turning to Mr. Macartney, with yet more embarrassment, I wished him good morning.

He advanced towards the garden, with the paper still in his hand.

"No, no," cried I, "some other time."

"May I then, Madam, have the honour of seeing you again?"

I did not dare take the liberty of inviting any body to the house of Mrs. Beaumont, nor yet had I the presence of mind to make an excuse; and therefore, not knowing how to refuse him, I said, "Perhaps you may be this way again to-morrow morning, – and I believe I shall walk out before breakfast."

He bowed, and went away; while I, turning again to Lord Orville, saw his countenance so much altered, that I was frightened at what I had so hastily said. He did not again offer me his hand, but walked, silent and slow, by my side. Good Heaven! thought I, what may he not suppose from this adventure? May he not, by my desire of meeting Mr. Macartney to-morrow, imagine it was by design I walked out to meet him to-day? Tormented by this apprehension, I determined to avail myself of the freedom which his behaviour since I came hither has encouraged; and, since he would not ask any questions, begin an explanation myself. I therefore slackened my pace, to gain time, and then said, "Was not your Lordship surprised to see me speaking with a stranger?"

"A stranger!" repeated he; "is it possible that gentleman can be a stranger to you?"

"No, my Lord," – said I, stammering, "not to *me*, – but only it might look – he might seem – "

"No, believe me," said he, with a forced smile, "I could never suppose Miss Anville would make an appointment with a stranger."

"An appointment, my Lord!" repeated I, colouring violently.

"Pardon me, Madam," answered he, "but I thought I had heard one."

I was so much confounded, that I could not speak; yet, find-ing he walked quietly on, I could not endure he should make his own interpretation of my silence; and therefore, as soon as I recovered from my surprise, I said, "Indeed, my Lord, you are much mistaken, – Mr. Macartney had particular business with me, – and I could not, – I knew not how to refuse seeing him, – but indeed, my Lord, – I had not, – he had not, – " I stam-mered so terribly that I could not go on.

"I am very sorry," said he, gravely, "that I have been so unfor-tunate as to distress you; but I should not have followed you, had I not imagined you were merely walked out for the air."

"And so I was!" cried I, eagerly, "indeed, my Lord, I was! My meeting with Mr. Macartney was quite accidental; and if your Lordship thinks there is any impropriety in my seeing him to-morrow, I am ready to give up that intention."

"If *I* think!" said he, in a tone of surprise; "surely Miss Anville must best judge for herself! surely she cannot leave the arbitration of a point so delicate, to one who is ignorant of all the circumstances which attend it?"

"If," said I, "it was worth your Lordship's time to hear them, – you should *not* be ignorant of the circumstances which attend it."

"The sweetness of Miss Anville's disposition," said he, in a softened voice, "I have long admired, and the offer of a com-munication which does me so much honour, is too grateful to me not to be eagerly caught at."

Just then, Mrs. Selwyn opened the parlour-window, and our conversation ended. I was rallied upon my passion for solitary walking, but no questions were asked me.

When breakfast was over, I hoped to have had some oppor-tunity of speaking with Lord Orville; but Lord Merton and Mr. Coverley came in, and insisted upon his opinion of the spot they had fixed upon for the old women's race. The ladies declared they would be of the party, and, accordingly, we all went.

The race is to be run in Mrs. Beaumont's garden; the two gentlemen are as anxious as if their joint lives depended upon it. They have, at length, fixed upon objects, but have found great difficulty in persuading them to practise running, in order to try their strength. This grand affair is to be decided next Thursday.

When we returned to the house, the entrance of more company still prevented my having any conversation with Lord Orville. I was very much chagrined, as I knew he was engaged at the Hotwells in the afternoon. Seeing, therefore, no probability of speaking to him before the time of my meeting Mr. Macartney arrived, I determined that, rather than risk his ill opinion, I would leave Mr. Macartney to his own suggestions.

Yet, when I reflected upon his peculiar situation, his poverty, his sadness, and, more than all the rest, the idea I knew he entertained of what he calls his obligations to me, I could not resolve upon a breach of promise, which might be attributed to causes of all others the most offensive to one whom misfortune has made extremely suspicious of slights and contempt.

After the most uneasy consideration, I at length determined upon writing an excuse, which would, at once, save me from either meeting or affronting him. I therefore begged Mrs. Selwyn's leave to send her man to the Hotwells, which she instantly granted; and then I wrote the following note.

*To Mr. Macartney.*

Sir,
As it will not be in my power to walk out to-morrow morning, I would by no means give you the trouble of coming to Clifton. I hope, however, to have the pleasure of seeing you before you quit Bristol. I am,

Sir,
Your obedient servant,
EVELINA ANVILLE.

I desired the servant to enquire at the pump-room where Mr. Macartney lived, and returned to the parlour.

As soon as the company dispersed, the ladies retired to dress. I then, unexpectedly, found myself alone with Lord Orville; who, the moment I rose to follow Mrs. Selwyn, advanced to me, and said, "Will Miss Anville pardon my impatience, if I remind her of the promise she was so good as to make me this morning?"

I stopped, and would have returned to my seat, but, before I had time, the servants came to lay the cloth. He retreated, and went towards the window; and while I was considering in what manner to begin, I could not help asking myself what *right* I had to communicate the affairs of Mr. Macartney; and I doubted whether, to clear myself from one act of imprudence, I had not committed another.

Distressed by this reflection, I thought it best to quit the room, and give myself some time for consideration before I spoke; and therefore, only saying I must hasten to dress, I ran up stairs: rather abruptly, I own, and so, I fear, Lord Orville must think; yet what could I do? unused to the situations in which I find myself, and embarrassed by the slightest difficulties, I seldom, till too late, discover how I ought to act.

Just as we were all assembled to dinner, Mrs. Selwyn's man, coming into the parlour, presented to me a letter, and said, "I can't find out Mr. Macartney, Madam; but the post-office people[1] will let you know if they hear of him."

I was extremely ashamed of this public message; and meeting the eyes of Lord Orville, which were earnestly fixed on me, my confusion redoubled, and I knew not which way to look. All dinner-time, he was as silent as myself, and, the moment it was in my power, I left the table, and went to my own room. Mrs. Selwyn presently followed me, and her questions obliged me to own almost all the particulars of my acquaintance with Mr. Macartney, in order to excuse my writing to him. She said it was a most romantic affair, and spoke her sentiments with great severity, declaring that she had no doubt but he was an adventurer and an impostor.

And now, my dear Sir, I am totally at a loss what I ought to do: the more I reflect, the more sensible I am of the utter impropriety, nay, treachery, of revealing the story, and publishing the misfortunes and poverty of Mr. Macartney; who has an

---

1  According to Doody, the post office where "the penny post was handled [for Clifton] was at the Clifton Hotel" (494 n. 32).

undoubted right to my secrecy and discretion, and whose letter charges me to regard his communication as sacred. – And yet, the appearance of mystery, – perhaps something worse, which this affair must have to Lord Orville, – his seriousness, – and the promise I have made him, are inducements scarce to be resisted for trusting him, with the openness he has reason to expect from me.

I am equally distressed, too, whether or not I should see Mr. Macartney to-morrow morning.

Oh Sir, could I now be enlightened by your counsel, from what anxiety and perplexity should I be relieved!

But no, – I ought not to betray Mr. Macartney, and I will not forfeit a confidence which would never have been reposed in me, but from a reliance upon my honour which I should blush to find myself unworthy of. Desirous as I am of the good opinion of Lord Orville, I will endeavour to act as if I was guided by your advice, and, making it my sole aim to *deserve* it, leave to time and to fate my success or disappointment.

Since I have formed this resolution, my mind is more at ease; but I will not finish my letter till the affair is decided.

Sept. 25th.

I rose very early this morning, and, after a thousand different plans, not being able to resolve upon giving poor Mr. Macartney leave to suppose I neglected him, I thought it incumbent upon me to keep my word, since he had not received my letter; I therefore determined to make my own apologies, not to stay with him two minutes, and to excuse myself from meeting him any more.

Yet, uncertain whether I was wrong or right, it was with fear and trembling that I opened the garden-gate, – judge, then, of my feelings, when the first object I saw was Lord Orville! – he, too, looked extremely disconcerted, and said, in a hesitating manner, "Pardon me, Madam, – I did not intend, – I did not imagine you would have been here so soon – or, – or I would not have come." – And then, with a hasty bow, he passed me, and proceeded to the garden.

I was scarce able to stand, so greatly did I feel myself shocked; but, upon my saying, almost involuntarily, "Oh my Lord!" – he turned back, and, after a short pause, said, "Did you speak to *me*, Madam?"

I could not immediately answer; I seemed *choaked*, and was even forced to support myself by the garden-gate.

Lord Orville, soon recovering his dignity, said, "I know not how to apologise for being, just now, at this place; – and I cannot immediately, – if *ever*, – clear myself from the imputation of impertinent curiosity, to which I fear you will attribute it: however, at present, I will only entreat your pardon, without detaining you any longer." Again he bowed, and left me.

For some moments, I remained fixed to the same spot, and in the same position, immoveably as if I had been transformed to stone. My first impulse was to call him back, and instantly tell him the whole affair; but I checked this desire, though I would have given the world to have indulged it; something like pride aided what I thought due to Mr. Macartney, and I determined not only to keep his secret, but to delay any sort of explanation, till Lord Orville should condescend to request it.

Slowly he walked, and before he entered the house, he looked back, but hastily withdrew his eyes, upon finding I observed him.

Indeed, my dear Sir, you cannot easily imagine a situation more uncomfortable than mine was at that time; to be suspected by Lord Orville of any clandestine actions, wounded my soul; I was too much discomposed to wait for Mr. Macartney, nor, in truth, could I endure to have the design of my staying so well known. Yet I was so extremely agitated, that I could hardly move, and, I have reason to believe, Lord Orville, from the parlour-window, saw me tottering along, for, before I had taken five steps, he came out, and hastening to meet me, said, "I fear you are not well; pray allow me, (offering his arm) to assist you."

"No, my Lord," said I, with all the resolution I could assume; yet I was affected by an attention, at that time so little expected, and forced to turn away my head to conceal my emotion.

"You *must*," said he, with earnestness, "indeed you must, – I am sure you are not well; – refuse me not the honour of assisting you;" and, almost forcibly, he took my hand, and drawing it under his arm, obliged me to lean upon him. That I submitted, was partly the effect of surprise at an earnestness so uncommon in Lord Orville, and partly, that I did not, just then, dare trust my voice to make any objection.

When we came to the house, he led me into the parlour, and to a chair, and begged to know if I would not have a glass of water.

"No, my Lord, I thank you," said I, "I am perfectly recovered;" and, rising, I walked to the window, where, for some time, I pretended to be occupied in looking at the garden.

Determined as I was to act honourably by Mr. Macartney, I yet most anxiously wished to be restored to the good opinion of Lord Orville; but his silence, and the thoughtfulness of his air, discouraged me from speaking.

My situation soon grew disagreeable and embarrassing, and I resolved to return to my chamber till breakfast was ready. To remain longer, I feared, might seem *asking* for his enquiries; and I was sure it would ill become me to be more eager to speak, than he was to hear.

Just as I reached the door, turning to me hastily, he said, "Are you going, Miss Anville?"

"I am, my Lord," answered I, yet I stopped.

"Perhaps to return to – but I beg your pardon!" he spoke with a degree of agitation that made me readily comprehend he meant to *the garden*, and I instantly said, "To my own room, my Lord." And again I would have gone; but, convinced by my answer that I understood him, I believe he was sorry for the insinuation; he approached me with a very serious air, though, at the same time, he forced a smile, and said, "I know not what evil genius pursues me this morning, but I seem destined to do or to say something I ought not: I am so much ashamed of myself, that I can scarce solicit your forgiveness."

"My forgiveness! my Lord?" cried I, abashed, rather than elated by his condescension, "surely you cannot – you are not serious?"

"Indeed never more so; yet, if I may be my own interpreter, Miss Anville's countenance pronounces my pardon."

"I know not, my Lord, how any one can *pardon*, who has never been offended."

"You are very good; yet I could expect no less from a sweetness of disposition which baffles all comparison: will you not think I am an encroacher, and that I take advantage of your goodness, should I once more remind you of the promise you vouchsafed me yesterday?"

"No, indeed; on the contrary, I shall be very happy to acquit myself in your Lordship's opinion."

"Acquittal you need not," said he, leading me again to the window, "yet I own my curiosity is strongly excited."

When I was seated, I found myself much at a loss what to say; yet, after a short silence, assuming all the courage in my power, "Will you not, my Lord," said I, "think me trifling and capricious, should I own I have repented the promise I made, and should I entreat your Lordship not to insist upon my strict performance of it? – I spoke so hastily, that I did not, at the time, consider the impropriety of what I said."

As he was entirely silent, and profoundly attentive, I continued to speak without interruption.

"If your Lordship, by any other means, knew the circumstances attending my acquaintance with Mr. Macartney, I am most sure you would yourself disapprove my relating them. He is a gentleman, and has been very unfortunate, – but I am not, – I think, – at liberty to say more: yet I am sure, if he knew your Lordship wished to hear any particulars of his affairs, he would readily consent to my acknowledging them; – shall I, my Lord, ask his permission?"

"*His* affairs!" repeated Lord Orville; "by no means, I have not the least curiosity about them."

"I beg your Lordship's pardon, – but indeed I had understood the contrary."

"Is it possible, Madam, you could suppose the affairs of an utter stranger can excite my curiosity?"

The gravity and coldness with which he asked this question, very much abashed me; but Lord Orville is the most delicate of men, and, presently recollecting himself, he added, "I mean not to speak with indifference of any friend of yours, – far from it;

any such will always command my good wishes: yet I own I am rather disappointed; and though I doubt not the justice of your reasons, to which I implicitly submit, you must not wonder, that, when upon the point of being honoured with your confidence, I should feel the greatest regret at finding it withdrawn."

Do you think, my dear Sir, I did not, at that moment, require all my resolution to guard me from frankly telling him whatever he wished to hear? yet I rejoice that I did not; for, added to the actual wrong I should have done, Lord Orville himself, when he had heard, would, I am sure, have blamed me. Fortunately, this thought occurred to me, and I said, "Your Lordship shall yourself be my judge; the promise I made, though voluntary, was rash and inconsiderate; yet, had it concerned myself, I would not have hesitated in fulfilling it; but the gentleman whose affairs I should be obliged to relate – "

"Pardon me," cried he, "for interrupting you; yet allow me to assure you, I have not the slightest desire to be acquainted with his affairs, further than what belongs to the motives which induced you yesterday morning – " He stopped; but there was no occasion to say more.

"That, my Lord," cried I, "I will tell you honestly. Mr. Macartney had some particular business with me, – and I could not take the liberty to ask him hither."

"And why not? – Mrs. Beaumont, I am sure, – "

"I could not, my Lord, think of intruding upon Mrs. Beaumont's complaisance; and so, with the same hasty folly I promised your Lordship, I much *more* rashly, promised to meet him."

"And did you?"

"No, my Lord," said I, colouring, "I returned before he came."

Again, for some time, we were both silent; yet, unwilling to leave him to reflections which could not but be to my disadvantage, I summoned sufficient courage to say, "There is no young creature, my Lord, who so greatly wants, or so earnestly wishes for, the advice and assistance of her friends, as I do; I am new to the world, and unused to acting for myself, – my intentions are never wilfully blameable, yet I err perpetually! – I have, hitherto, been blest with the most affectionate of friends, and, indeed, the ablest of men, to guide and instruct me upon every occasion; – but he is too distant, now, to be applied to at the moment I want his aid; – and *here*, – there is not a human being whose counsel I can ask!"

"Would to Heaven," cried he, with a countenance from which all coldness and gravity were banished, and succeeded by the mildest benevolence, "that *I* were worthy, – and capable, – of supplying the place of such a friend to Miss Anville!"

"You do me but too much honour," said I; "yet I hope your Lordship's candour, – perhaps I ought to say indulgence, – will make some allowance, on account of my inexperience, for behaviour, so inconsiderate: – May I, my Lord, hope that you will?"

"May *I*," cried he, "hope that you will pardon the ill-grace with which I have submitted to my disappointment? and that you will permit me," (kissing my hand) "thus to seal my peace?"

"*Our* peace, my Lord," said I, with revived spirits.

"This, then," said he, again pressing it to his lips, "for *our* peace: and now, – are we not friends?"

Just then, the door opened, and I had only time to withdraw my hand, before the ladies came in to breakfast.

I have been, all day, the happiest of human beings! – to be thus reconciled to Lord Orville, and yet to adhere to my resolution, – what could I wish for more? – he, too, has been very chearful, and more attentive, more obliging to me than ever. Yet Heaven forbid I should again be in a similar situation, for I cannot express how much uneasiness I have suffered from the fear of incurring his ill opinion.

But what will poor Mr. Macartney think of me? happy as I am, I much regret the necessity I have been under of disappointing him.

Adieu, my dearest Sir.

# LETTER VI.

*Mr. Villars to Evelina.*

Berry Hill, Sept. 28.

Dead to the world, and equally insensible to its pleasures or its pains, I long since bid adieu to all joy, and defiance to all sorrow, but what should spring from my Evelina, – sole source, to me, of all earthly felicity. How strange, then, is it, that the letter in which she tells me she is the *happiest of human beings*, should give me the most mortal inquietude!

Alas, my child! – that innocence, the first, best gift of Heaven, should, of all others, be the blindest to its own danger, – the most exposed to treachery, – and the least able to defend itself, in a world where it is little known, less valued, and perpetually deceived!

Would to Heaven you were here! – then, by degrees, and with gentleness, I might enter upon a subject too delicate for distant discussion. Yet is it too interesting, and the situation too critical, to allow of delay. – Oh my Evelina, your situation is critical indeed! – your peace of mind is at stake, and every chance for your future happiness may depend upon the conduct of the present moment.

Hitherto I have forborne to speak with you upon the most important of all concerns, the state of your heart: – alas, I needed no information! I have been silent, indeed, but I have not been blind.

Long, and with the deepest regret, have I perceived the ascendancy which Lord Orville has gained upon your mind. – You will start at the mention of his name, – you will tremble every word you read; – I grieve to give pain to my gentle Evelina, but I dare not any longer spare her.

Your first meeting with Lord Orville was decisive. Lively, fearless, free from all other impressions, such a man as you describe him could not fail exciting your admiration, and the more dangerously, because he seemed as unconscious of his power as you of your weakness; and therefore you had no alarm, either from *his* vanity or *your own* prudence.

Young, animated, entirely off your guard, and thoughtless of consequences, *Imagination* took the reins, and *Reason*, slow-paced, though sure-footed, was unequal to a race with so eccentric and flighty a companion. How rapid was then my Evelina's progress through those regions of fancy and passion whither her new guide conducted her! – She saw Lord Orville at a ball, – and he was *the most amiable of men!* – She met him again at another, – and *he had every virtue under heaven!*

I mean not to depreciate the merit of Lord Orville, who, one mysterious instance alone excepted, seems to have deserved the idea you formed of his character; but it was not time, it was not the knowledge of his worth, obtained your regard; your new comrade had not patience to wait any trial; her glowing pencil,[1] dipt in the vivid colours of her creative ideas, painted to you, at the moment of your first acquaintance, all the excellencies, all the good and rare qualities, which a great length of time, and intimacy, could alone have really discovered.

You flattered yourself, that your partiality was the effect of esteem, founded upon a general love of merit, and a principle of justice: and your heart, which fell the sacrifice of your error, was totally gone ere you suspected it was in danger.

A thousand times have I been upon the point of shewing you the perils of your situation; but the same inexperience which occasioned your mistake, I hoped, with the assistance of time and absence, would effect a cure: I was, indeed, most unwilling to destroy your illusion, while I dared hope it might itself contribute to the restoration of your tranquillity; since your ignorance of the danger and force of your attachment, might possibly prevent that despondency with which young people, in similar circumstances, are apt to persuade themselves that what is only difficult, is absolutely impossible.

But now, since you have again met, and are become more intimate than ever, all my hope from silence and seeming ignorance is at an end.

---

1   "An artist's paint-brush" (*OED*).

Awake, then, my dear, my deluded child, awake to the sense of your danger, and exert yourself to avoid the evils with which it threatens you, – evils which, to a mind like yours, are most to be dreaded, secret repining, and concealed, yet consuming regret! Make a noble effort for the recovery of your peace, which now, with sorrow I see it, depends wholly upon the presence of Lord Orville. This effort, may, indeed, be painful, but trust to my experience, when I assure you it is requisite.

You must quit him! – his sight is baneful to your repose, his society is death to your future tranquility! Believe me, my beloved child, my heart aches for your suffering, while it dictates its necessity.

Could I flatter myself that Lord Orville would, indeed, be sensible of your worth, and act with a nobleness of mind which should prove it congenial to his own, then would I leave my Evelina to the unmolested enjoyment of the chearful society and encreasing regard of a man she so greatly admires: but this is not an age in which we may trust to appearances, and imprudence is much sooner regretted than repaired. Your health, you tell me, is much mended, – can you then consent to leave Bristol? – not abruptly, that I do not desire, but in a few days from the time you receive this? I will write to Mrs. Selwyn, and tell her how much I wish your return; and Mrs. Clinton can take sufficient care of you.

I have meditated upon every possible expedient that might tend to your happiness, ere I fixed upon exacting from you a compliance which I am convinced will be most painful to you; but I can satisfy myself in none. This will at least be safe, and as to success, – we must leave it to time.

I am very glad to hear of Mr. Macartney's welfare.

Adieu, my dearest child; Heaven preserve and strengthen you!

A.V.

# LETTER VII.

*Evelina to the Rev. Mr. Villars.*

Clifton, Sept. 28.

Sweetly, most sweetly, have two days more passed since I wrote; but I have been too much engaged to be exact in my journal.

To-day has been less tranquil. It was destined for the decision of the important bet, and has been productive of general confusion throughout the house. It was settled that the race should be run at five o'clock in the afternoon. Lord Merton breakfasted here, and stayed till noon. He wanted to engage the Ladies to *bet on his side*, in the true spirit of gaming, without seeing the racers. But he could only prevail on Lady Louisa, as Mrs. Selwyn said she never laid a wager against her own wishes, and Mrs. Beaumont would not *take sides*. As for *me*, I was not applied to. It is impossible for negligence to be more pointed, than that of Lord Merton to me, in the presence of Lady Louisa.

But, just before dinner, I happened to be alone in the drawing-room, when his Lordship suddenly returned, and coming in with his usual familiarity, he was beginning, "You see, Lady Louisa, –" but, stopping short, "Pray where's every body gone?"

"Indeed I don't know, my Lord."

He then shut the door, and, with a great alteration in his face and manner, advanced eagerly towards me, and said, "How glad I am, my sweet girl, to meet you, at last, alone! By my soul, I began to think there was a plot against me, for I've never been able to have you a minute to myself." And, very freely, he seized my hand.

I was so much surprised at this address, after having been so long totally neglected, that I could make no other answer than staring at him with unfeigned astonishment.

"Why now," continued he, "if you was not the cruellest little angel in the world, you would have helped me to some expedient: for you see how I am watched here; Lady Louisa's eyes are never off me. She gives me a charming foretaste of the pleasures of a wife! however, it won't last long."

Disgusted to the greatest degree, I attempted to draw away my hand, but I believe I should not have succeeded, if Mrs. Beaumont had not made her appearance. He turned from me with the greatest assurance, and said, "How are you, Ma'am? – how is Lady Louisa? – you see I can't live a moment out of the house."

Could you, my dearest Sir, have believed it possible for such effrontery to be in man?

Before dinner, came Mr. Coverley, and before five o'clock, Mr. Lovel and some other company. The place marked out for the race, was a gravel-walk in Mrs. Beaumont's garden, and the length of the ground twenty yards. When we were summoned to the *course*, the two poor old women made their appearance. Though they seemed very healthy for their time of life, they yet looked so weak, so infirm, so feeble, that I could feel no sensation but that of pity at the sight. However, this was not the general sense of the company, for they no sooner came forward, than they were greeted with a laugh from every beholder, Lord Orville excepted, who looked very grave during the whole transaction. Doubtless he must be greatly discontented at the dissipated conduct and extravagance, of a man with whom he is, soon, to be so nearly connected.

For some time, the scene was truly ridiculous; the agitation of the parties concerned, and the bets that were laid upon the old women, were absurd beyond measure. *Who are you for?* and *whose side are you of?* was echoed from mouth to mouth by the whole company. Lord Merton and Mr. Coverley were both so excessively gay and noisy, that I soon found they had been too free in drinking to their success. They handed, with loud shouts, the old women to the race-ground, and encouraged them, by liberal promises, to exert themselves.

When the signal was given for them to set off, the poor creatures, feeble and frightened, ran against each other, and, neither of them able to support the shock, they both fell on the ground.

Lord Merton and Mr. Coverley flew to their assistance. Seats were brought for them, and they each drank a glass of wine. They complained of being much bruised; for, heavy and helpless, they had not been able to save themselves, but fell, with their whole weight upon the gravel. However, as they seemed equal sufferers, both parties were too eager to have the affair deferred.

Again, therefore, they set off, and hobbled along, nearly even with each other, for some time, yet frequently, and to the inexpressible diversion of the company, they stumbled and tottered; and the confused hallowing of *"Now Coverley!" "Now Merton!"* rung from side to side during the whole affair.

Not long after, a foot of one of the poor women slipt, and, with great force, she came again to the ground. Involuntarily, I sprung forward to assist her, but Lord Merton, to whom she did not belong, stopped me, calling out "No foul play! no foul play!"

Mr. Coverley, then, repeating the same words, went himself to help her, and insisted that the other should stop. A debate ensued; but the poor creature was too much hurt to move, and declared her utter inability to make another attempt. Mr. Coverley was quite brutal; he swore at her with unmanly rage, and seemed scarce able to refrain even from striking her.

Lord Merton then, in great rapture, said it was a *hallow thing;*[1] but Mr. Coverley contended that the fall was accidental, and time should be allowed for the woman to recover. However, all the company being against him, he was pronounced the loser.

We then went to the drawing-room, to tea. After which, the evening being remarkably warm we all walked in the garden. Lord Merton was quite riotous, and Lady Louisa in high spirits; but Mr. Coverley endeavoured in vain to conceal his chagrin.

As Lord Orville was thoughtful, and walked by himself, I expected that, as usual, *I* should pass unnoticed, and be left to my own meditations; but this was not the case, for Lord Merton, entirely off his guard, giddy equally from wine and success, was very troublesome to me; and, regardless of the presence of Lady Louisa, which, hitherto, has restrained him even from

---

1    "Hallow" or "hollow" is "complete, thorough, out-and-out" (*OED*).

common civility, he attached himself to me, during the walk, with a freedom of gallantry that put me extremely out of countenance. He paid me the most high-flown compliments, and frequently and forcibly seized my hand, though I repeatedly, and with undissembled anger, drew it back. Lord Orville, I saw, watched us with earnestness, and Lady Louisa's smiles were converted into looks of disdain.

I could not bear to be thus situated, and complaining I was tired, I quickened my pace, with intention to return to the house; but Lord Merton, hastily following, caught my hand, and saying the *day was his own*, vowed he would not let me go.

"You *must*, my Lord," cried I, extremely flurried.

"You are the most charming girl in the world," said he, "and never looked better than at this moment."

"My Lord," cried Mrs. Selwyn, advancing to us, "you don't consider, that the better Miss Anville looks, the more striking is the contrast with your Lordship; therefore, for your own sake, I would advise you not to hold her."

"Egad, my Lord," cried Mr. Coverley, "I don't see what right you have to the best *old*, and the best *young* woman too, in the same day."

"*Best young woman!*" repeated Mr. Lovel; "'pon honour, Jack, you have made a most unfortunate speech; however, if Lady Louisa can pardon you, – and her Ladyship is all goodness, – I am sure nobody else can, for you have committed an outrageous solecism in good manners."

"And pray, Sir," said Mrs. Selwyn, "under what denomination may your own speech pass?"

Mr. Lovel, turning another way, affected not to hear her: and Mr. Coverley, bowing to Lady Louisa, said, "Her Ladyship is well acquainted with my devotion, – but egad, I don't know how it is, – I had always an unlucky turn at an epigram,[1] and never could resist a smart play upon words in my life."

"Pray, my Lord," cried I, "let go my hand! pray, Mrs. Selwyn, speak for me."

"My Lord," said Mrs. Selwyn, "in detaining Miss Anville any

---

1   An unlucky ability to speak pointedly.

longer, you only lose time, for we are already as well convinced of your valour and your strength as if you were to hold her an age."

"My Lord," said Mrs. Beaumont, "I must beg leave to interfere; I know not if Lady Louisa can pardon you, but, as this young Lady is at my house, I do not chuse to have her made uneasy."

"*I* pardon him!" cried Lady Louisa, "I declare I am monstrous glad to get rid of him."

"Egad, my Lord," cried Mr. Coverley, "while you are grasping at a shadow, you'll lose a substance; you'd best make your peace while you can."

"Pray, Mr. Coverley, be quiet," said Lady Louisa, peevishly, "for I declare I won't speak to him. Brother," (taking hold of Lord Orville's arm) "will you walk in with me?"

"Would to Heaven," cried I, frightened to see how much Lord Merton was in liquor, "that I, too, had a brother! – and then I should not be exposed to such treatment!"

Lord Orville, instantly quitting Lady Louisa, said, "Will Miss Anville allow *me* the honour of taking that title?" and then, without waiting for any answer, he disengaged me from Lord Merton, and, handing me to Lady Louisa, "Let me," added he, "take equal care of *both* my sisters;" and then, desiring her to take hold of one arm, and begging me to make use of the other, we reached the house in a moment. Lord Merton, disordered as he was, attempted not to stop us.

As soon as we entered the house I withdrew my arm, and courtsied my thanks, for my heart was too full for speech. Lady Louisa, evidently hurt at her brother's condescension, and piqued extremely by Lord Merton's behaviour, silently drew away her's, and biting her lips, with a look of infinite vexation, walked sullenly up the hall.

Lord Orville asked her if she would not go into the parlour?

"No," answered she, haughtily; "I leave you and your new sister together;" and then she walked up stairs.

I was quite confounded at the pride and rudeness of this speech. Lord Orville himself seemed thunderstruck; I turned from him, and went into the parlour; he followed me, saying,

"Must I, now, apologise to Miss Anville for the liberty of my interference? — or ought I to apologise that I did not, as I wished, interfere sooner?"

"O my Lord," cried I, with an emotion I could not repress, "it is from you alone I meet with any respect, — all others treat me with impertinence or contempt!"

I am sorry I had not more command of myself, as he had reason, just then, to suppose I particularly meant his sister; which, I am sure, must very much hurt him.

"Good Heaven," cried he, "that so much sweetness and merit can fail to excite the love and admiration so justly their due! I cannot, — I dare not express to you half the indignation I feel at this moment!"

"I am sorry, my Lord," said I, more calmly, "to have raised it; but yet, — in a situation that calls for protection, to meet only with mortifications, — indeed, I am but ill formed to bear them!"

"My *dear* Miss Anville," cried he, warmly, "allow *me* to be your friend; think of me as if I were indeed your brother, and let me entreat you to accept my best services, if there is any thing in which I can be so happy as to shew my regard, — my respect for you!"

Before I had time to speak, the rest of the party entered the parlour, and, as I did not wish to see any thing more of Lord Merton, at least before he had slept, I determined to leave it. Lord Orville, seeing my design, said, as I passed him, "Will you go?" "Had not I best, my Lord?" said I. "I am afraid," said he, smiling, "since I must now speak as your *brother*, I am afraid you *had*; — you see you may trust me, since I can advise against my own interest."

I then left the room, and have been writing ever since. And methinks I can never lament the rudeness of Lord Merton, as it has more than ever confirmed to me the esteem of Lord Orville.

# LETTER VIII.

*Evelina in continuation.*

Sept. 30.

Oh Sir, what a strange incident have I to recite! what a field of conjecture to open!

Yesterday evening, we all went to an assembly. Lord Orville presented tickets to the whole family, and did me the honour, to the no small surprise of all here, I believe, to dance with me. But every day abounds in fresh instances of his condescending politeness, and he now takes every opportunity of calling me his *friend*, and his *sister*.

Lord Merton offered a ticket to Lady Louisa; but she was so much incensed against him, that she refused it with the utmost disdain; neither could he prevail upon her to dance with him; she sat still the whole evening, and deigned not to look at, or speak to him. To me, her behaviour is almost the same, for she is cold, distant, and haughty, and her eyes express the greatest contempt. But for Lord Orville, how miserable would my residence here make me!

We were joined, in the ball-room, by Mr. Coverley, Mr. Lovel, and Lord Merton, who looked as if he was doing penance, and sat all the evening next to Lady Louisa, vainly endeavouring to appease her anger.

Lord Orville began the minuets; he danced with a young Lady who seemed to engage the general attention, as she had not been seen here before. She is pretty, and looks mild and good-humoured.

"Pray, Mr. Lovel," said Lady Louisa, "who is that?"

"Miss Belmont," answered he, "the young heiress; she came to the Wells yesterday."

Struck with the name, I involuntarily repeated it, but nobody heard me.

"What is her family?" said Mrs. Beaumont.

"Have you not heard of her, Ma'am?" cried he, "she is only daughter and heiress of Sir John Belmont."

Good Heaven, how did I start! the name struck my ear like a thunder-bolt. Mrs. Selwyn, who immediately looked at me, said, "Be calm, my dear, and we will learn the truth of all this."

Till then, I had never imagined her to be acquainted with my story; but she has since told me, that she knew my unhappy mother, and was well informed of the whole affair.

She asked Mr. Lovel a multitude of questions, and I gathered from his answers, that this young Lady was just come from abroad, with Sir John Belmont, who was now in London; that she was under the care of his sister, Mrs. Paterson; and that she would inherit a considerable estate.

I cannot express the strange feelings with which I was agitated during this recital. What, my dearest Sir, can it possibly mean? Did you ever hear of any after-marriage?[1] – or must I suppose, that, while the lawful child is rejected, another is adopted? – I know not what to think! I am bewildered with a contrariety of ideas!

When we came home, Mrs. Selwyn passed more than an hour in my room, conversing upon this subject. She says that I ought instantly to go to town, find out my father, and have the affair cleared up. She assures me I have too strong a resemblance to my dear, though unknown mother, to allow of the least hesitation in my being owned, when once I am seen. For my part, I have no wish but to act by your direction.

I cannot give any account of the evening; so disturbed, so occupied am I by this subject, that I can think of no other. I have entreated Mrs. Selwyn to observe the strictest secrecy, and she has promised that she will. Indeed, she has too much sense to be idly communicative.

Lord Orville took notice of my being absent and silent, but I ventured not to entrust him with the cause. Fortunately, he was not of the party at the time Mr. Lovel made the discovery.

Mrs. Selwyn says that if you approve my going to town, she will herself accompany me. I had a thousand times rather ask the protection of Mrs. Mirvan, but, after this offer, that will not be possible.

---

1 A second marriage.

Adieu, my dearest Sir. I am sure you will write immediately, and I shall be all impatience till your letter arrives.

## LETTER IX.

*Evelina in continuation.*

Oct. 1$^{st}$.

Good God, my dear Sir, what a wonderful tale have I again to relate! even yet, I am not recovered from my extreme surprise.

Yesterday morning, as soon as I had finished my hasty letter, I was summoned to attend a walking party to the Hotwells. It consisted only of Mrs. Selwyn and Lord Orville. The latter walked by my side all the way, and his conversation dissipated my uneasiness, and insensibly restored my serenity.

At the pump-room, I saw Mr. Macartney; I courtsied to him twice ere he would speak to me. When he did, I began to apologise for having disappointed him; but I did not find it very easy to excuse myself, as Lord Orville's eyes, with an expression of anxiety that distressed me, turned from him to me, and me to him, every word I spoke. Convinced, however, that I had really trifled with Mr. Macartney, I scrupled not to beg his pardon. He was then, not merely appeased, but even grateful.

He requested me to see him to-morrow: but I had not the folly to be again guilty of an indiscretion which had, already, caused me so much uneasiness; and therefore, I told him, frankly, that it was not in my power, at present, to see him, but by accident; and, to prevent his being offended, I hinted to him the reason I could not receive him as I wished to do.

When I had satisfied both him and myself upon this subject, I turned to Lord Orville, and saw, with concern, the gravity of his countenance. I would have spoken to him, but knew not how; I believe, however, he read my thoughts, for, in a little time, with a sort of serious smile, he said, "Does not Mr. Macartney complain of his disappointment?"

"Not much, my Lord."

"And how have you appeased him?" Finding I hesitated what to answer, "Am I not your brother," continued he, "and must I not enquire into your affairs?"

"Certainly, my Lord," said I, laughing, "I only wish it were better worth your Lordship's while."

"Let me, then, make immediate use of my privilege. When shall you see Mr. Macartney again?"

"Indeed, my Lord, I can't tell."

"But, – do you know that I shall not suffer *my sister* to make a private appointment?"

"Pray, my Lord," cried I, earnestly, "use that word no more! Indeed you shock me extremely."

"That would I not do for the world," cried he; "yet you know not how warmly, how deeply I am interested, not only in all your concerns, but in all your actions."

This speech, – the most particular one Lord Orville had ever made to me, ended our conversation at that time; for I was too much struck by it to make any answer.

Soon after, Mr. Macartney, in a low voice, entreated me not to deny him the gratification of returning the money. While he was speaking, the young Lady I saw yesterday at the assembly, with a large party, entered the pump-room. Mr. Macartney turned as pale as death, his voice faltered, and he seemed not to know what he said. I was myself almost equally disturbed, by the croud of confused ideas that occurred to me. Good Heaven, thought I, why should he be thus agitated? – is it possible this can be the young Lady he loved? –

In a few minutes, we quitted the pump-room, and though I twice wished Mr. Macartney good morning, he was so absent he did not hear me.

We did not immediately return to Clifton, as Mrs. Selwyn had business at a pamphlet-shop.[1] While she was looking at some new poems, Lord Orville again asked me when I should see Mr. Macartney?

"Indeed, my Lord," cried I, "I know not, but I would give the universe for a few moments conversation with him!" I

---

1  Pamphlet-shops sold pamphlets dealing with contemporary political and social
   issues, as well as newspapers.

spoke this with a simple sincerity, and was not aware of the force of my own words.

"The universe!" repeated he, "Good God, Miss Anville, do you say this to *me*?"

"I would say it," returned I, "to any body, my Lord."

"I beg your pardon," said he, in a voice that shewed him ill pleased, "I am answered!"

"My Lord," cried I, "you must not judge hardly of me. I spoke inadvertently; but if you knew the painful suspense I suffer at this moment, you would not be surprised at what I have said."

"And would a meeting with Mr. Macartney relieve you from that suspense?"

"Yes, my Lord, two words might be sufficient."

"Would to Heaven," cried he, after a short pause, "that I were worthy to know their import!"

"Worthy, my Lord! – O, if that were all, your Lordship could ask nothing I should not be ready to answer! If I were but at liberty to speak, I should be *proud* of your Lordship's enquiries; but indeed I am not, I have not any right to communicate the affairs of Mr. Macartney, – your Lordship cannot suppose I have."

"I will own to you," answered he, "I know not *what* to suppose; yet there seems a frankness even in your mystery, – and such an air of openness in your countenance, that I am willing to hope – " He stopped a moment, and then added, "This meeting, you say, is essential to your repose?"

"I did not say *that*, my Lord; but yet I have the most important reasons for wishing to speak to him."

He paused a few minutes, and then said, with warmth, "Yes, you *shall* speak to him! – I will myself assist you! – Miss Anville, I am sure, cannot form a wish against propriety, I will ask no questions, I will rely upon her own purity, and uninformed, blindfold as I am, I will serve her with all my power!" And then he went into the shop, leaving me so strangely affected by his generous behaviour, that I almost wished to follow him with my thanks.

When Mrs. Selwyn had transacted her affairs, we returned home.

The moment dinner was over, Lord Orville went out, and did not come back till just as we were summoned to supper. This is the longest time he has spent from the house since I have been at Clifton, and you cannot imagine, my dear Sir, how much I missed him. I scarce knew before how infinitely I am indebted to him alone for the happiness I have enjoyed since I have been at Mrs. Beaumont's.

As I generally go down stairs last, he came to me the moment the ladies had passed by, and said, "Shall you be at home to-morrow morning?"

"I believe so, my Lord."

"And will you, then, receive a visitor for me?"

"For you, my Lord!"

"Yes; — I have made acquaintance with Mr. Macartney, and he has promised to call upon me to-morrow about three o'clock."

And then, taking my hand, he led me down stairs.

O Sir! — was there ever such another man as Lord Orville? — Yes, *one* other now resides at Berry Hill!

This morning there has been a great deal of company here, but at the time appointed by Lord Orville, doubtless with that consideration, the parlour is almost always empty, as every body is dressing.

Mrs. Beaumont, however, was not gone up stairs, when Mr. Macartney sent in his name.

Lord Orville immediately said, "Beg the favour of him to walk in. You see, Madam, that I consider myself as at home."

"I hope so," answered Mrs. Beaumont, "or I should be very uneasy."

Mr. Macartney then entered. I believe we both felt very conscious to whom the visit was paid: but Lord Orville received him as his own guest, and not merely entertained him as such while Mrs. Beaumont remained in the room, but for some time after she had left it; a delicacy that saved me from the embarrassment I should have felt, had he immediately quitted us.

In a few minutes, however, he gave Mr. Macartney a book, — for I, too, by way of pretence for continuing in the room, pretended to be reading, — and begged he would be so good as to look it over, while he answered a note, which he would dispatch in a few minutes, and return to him.

When he was gone, we both parted with our books, and Mr. Macartney, again producing the paper with the money, besought me to accept it.

"Pray," said I, still declining it, "did you know the young lady who came into the pump-room yesterday morning?"

"Know her!" repeated he, changing colour, "Oh, but too well!"

"Indeed!"

"Why, Madam, do you ask?"

"I must beseech you to satisfy me further upon this subject; pray tell me who she is."

"Inviolably as I meant to keep my secret, I can refuse you, Madam, nothing; – that lady – is the daughter of Sir John Belmont! – of my father!"

"Gracious Heaven!" cried I, involuntarily laying my hand on his arm, "you are then –," *my brother*, I would have said, but my voice failed me, and I burst into tears.

"Oh, Madam," cried he, "what does this mean? – What can thus distress you?"

I could not answer, but held out my hand to him. He seemed greatly surprised, and talked in high terms of my condescension.

"Spare yourself," cried I, wiping my eyes, "spare yourself this mistake, – you have a *right* to all I can do for you; the similarity of our circumstances – "

We were then interrupted by the entrance of Mrs. Selwyn; and Mr. Macartney, finding no probability of our being left alone, was obliged to take leave, though I believe, very reluctantly, while in such suspence.

Mrs. Selwyn then, by dint of interrogatories, drew from me the state of this affair. She is so penetrating, that there is no possibility of evading to give her satisfaction.

Is not this a strange event? Good Heaven, how little did I think that the visits I so unwillingly paid at Mr. Branghton's would have introduced me to so near a relation! I will never again regret the time I spent in town this summer: a circumstance so fortunate will always make me think of it with pleasure.

$$\star \qquad \star \qquad \star \qquad \star \qquad \star$$

I have just received your letter, – and it has almost broken my heart! – Oh, Sir! the illusion is over indeed! – How vainly have I flattered, how miserably deceived myself! Long since, doubtful of the situation of my heart, I dreaded a scrutiny, – but now, now that I have so long escaped, I began, indeed, to think my safety insured, to hope that my fears were causeless, and to believe that my good opinion and esteem of Lord Orville might be owned without suspicion, and felt without danger: – miserably deceived, indeed!

*His sight is baneful to my repose, – his society is death to my future tranquility!* – Oh, Lord Orville! could I have believed that a friendship so grateful to my heart, so soothing to my distresses, – a friendship which, in every respect, did me so much honour, would only serve to embitter all my future moments! – What a strange, what an unhappy circumstance, that my gratitude, though so justly excited, should be so fatal to my peace!

Yes, Sir, I *will* quit him; – would to Heaven I could at this moment! without seeing him again, – without trusting to my now conscious emotion! – Oh, Lord Orville, how little do you know the evils I owe to you! how little suppose that, when most dignified by your attention, I was most to be pitied, – and when most exalted by your notice, you were most my enemy!

You, Sir, relied upon my ignorance; – I, alas, upon your experience; and, whenever I doubted the weakness of my heart, the idea that *you* did not suspect it, reassured me, – restored my courage, and confirmed my error! – Yet am I most sensible of the kindness of your silence.

Oh, Sir! why have I ever quitted you! why been exposed to dangers to which I am so unequal?

But I will leave this place, – leave Lord Orville, – leave him, perhaps, for ever! – no matter; your counsel, your goodness, may teach me how to recover the peace and the serenity of which my unguarded folly has beguiled me. To you alone do I trust, – in you alone confide for every future hope I may form.

The more I consider of parting with Lord Orville, the less fortitude do I feel to bear the separation; – the friendship he has shewn me, – his politeness, – his sweetness of manners, – his concern in my affairs, – his solicitude to oblige me, – all, all to be given up! –

No, I cannot tell him I am going, – I dare not trust myself to take leave of him, – I will run away without seeing him: – implicitly will I follow your advice, avoid his sight, and shun his society!

To-morrow morning I will set off for Berry Hill. Mrs. Selwyn and Mrs. Beaumont shall alone know my intention. And to-day, – I will spend in my own room. The readiness of my obedience is the only atonement I can offer, for the weakness which calls for its exertion.

Can you, will you, most honoured, most dear Sir! sole prop by which the poor Evelina is supported, – can you, without reproach, without displeasure, receive the child you have so carefully reared, – from whose education better fruit might have been expected, and who, blushing for her unworthiness, fears to meet the eye by which she has been cherished? – Oh yes, I am sure you will! Your Evelina's errors are those of the judgment, – and you, I well know, pardon all but those of the heart!


## LETTER X.

*Evelina in continuation.*

Clifton, October 1<sup>st</sup>.

I have only time, my dearest Sir, for three words, to overtake my last letter, and prevent your expecting me immediately; for, when I communicated my intention to Mrs. Selwyn, she would not hear of it, and declared it would be highly ridiculous for me to go before I received an answer to my intelligence concerning the journey from Paris. She has, therefore, insisted upon my waiting till your next letter arrives. I hope you will not be displeased at my compliance, though it is rather against my own judgment; but Mrs. Selwyn quite overpowered me with the force of her arguments. I will, however, see very little of Lord Orville; I will never come down stairs before breakfast; give up all my walks in the garden, – seat myself next to Mrs. Selwyn, and not merely avoid his conversation, but shun his presence. I will exert all the prudence and all the resolution in my power, to prevent this short delay from giving you any further uneasiness.

Adieu, my dearest Sir. I shall not now leave Clifton till I have your directions.

## LETTER XI.

*Evelina in continuation.*

October 2d.

Yesterday, from the time I received your kind, though heart-piercing letter, I kept my room, – for I was equally unable and unwilling to see Lord Orville: but this morning, finding I seemed destined to pass a few days longer here, I endeavoured to calm my spirits, and to appear as usual; though I determined to avoid him to the utmost of my power. Indeed, as I entered the parlour, when called to breakfast, my thoughts were so much occupied with your letter, that I felt as much confusion at his sight, as if he had himself been informed of its contents.

Mrs. Beaumont made me a slight compliment upon my recovery, for I had pleaded illness to excuse keeping my room: Lady Louisa spoke not a word: but Lord Orville, little imagining himself the cause of my indisposition, enquired concerning my health with the most distinguishing politeness. I hardly made any answer, and, for the first time since I have been here, contrived to sit at some distance from him.

I could not help observing that my reserve surprised him; yet he persisted in his civilities, and seemed to wish to remove it. But I paid him very little attention; and the moment breakfast was over, instead of taking a book, or walking in the garden, I retired to my own room.

Soon after, Mrs. Selwyn came to tell me that Lord Orville had been proposing I should take an airing, and persuading her to let him drive us both in his phaeton. She delivered the message with an archness that made me blush; and added, that an airing, in *my Lord Orville's carriage*, could not fail to revive my spirits. There is no possibility of escaping her discernment; she has frequently rallied me upon his Lordship's attention, – and, alas! – upon the pleasure with which I have received it! However, I absolutely refused the offer.

"Well," said she, laughing, "I cannot just now indulge you with any solicitation; for, to tell you the truth, I have business to transact at the Wells, and am glad to be excused myself. I would ask you to walk with *me*, – but, since *Lord Orville* is refused, *I* have not the presumption to hope for success."

"Indeed," cried I, "you are mistaken; I will attend *you* with pleasure."

"O rare coquetry!" cried she, "surely it must be inherent in our sex, or it could not have been imbibed at Berry Hill."

I had not spirits to answer her, and therefore put on my hat and cloak in silence.

"I presume," continued she, drily, "his Lordship may walk with us?"

"If so, Madam," said I, "you will have a companion, and I will stay at home."

"My dear child," cried she, "did you bring the certificate of your birth with you?"

"Dear Madam, no!"

"Why then, we shall never be known again at Berry Hill."

I felt too conscious to enjoy her pleasantry; but I believe she was determined to torment me; for she asked if she should inform Lord Orville that I desired him not to be of the party?

"By no means, Madam; – but, indeed, I had rather not walk myself."

"My dear," cried she, "I really do not know you this morning, – you have certainly been taking a lesson of Lady Louisa."

She then went down stairs; but presently returning, told me she had acquainted Lord Orville that I did not choose to go out in the phaeton, but preferred a walk, *tête-à-tête* with her, by way of *variety*.

I said nothing, but was really vexed. She bid me go down stairs, and said she would follow immediately.

Lord Orville met me in the hall. "I fear," said he, "Miss Anville is not yet quite well?" and he would have taken my hand, but I turned from him, and courtsying slightly, went into the parlour.

Mrs. Beaumont and Lady Louisa were at work: Lord Merton was talking with the latter; for he has now made his peace, and is again received into favour.

I seated myself, as usual, by the window. Lord Orville, in a few minutes, came to me, and said, "Why is Miss Anville so grave?"

"Not grave, my Lord," said I, "only stupid;"[1] and I took up a book.

"You will go," said he, after a short pause, "to the assembly to-night?"

"No, my Lord, certainly not."

"Neither, then, will I; for I should be sorry to sully the remembrance I have of the happiness I enjoyed at the last."

Mrs. Selwyn then coming in, general enquiries were made, to all but me, of who would go to the assembly. Lord Orville instantly declared he had letters to write at home; but every one else settled to go.

I then hastened Mrs. Selwyn away, though not before she had said to Lord Orville, "Pray, has your Lordship obtained Miss Anville's leave to favour us with your company?"

"I have not, Madam," answered he, "had the vanity to ask it."

During our walk, Mrs. Selwyn tormented me unmercifully. She told me, that since I declined any addition to our party, I must, doubtless, be conscious of my own powers of entertainment; and begged me, therefore, to exert them freely. I repented a thousand times having consented to walk alone with her; for though I made the most painful efforts to appear in spirits, her raillery quite overpowered me.

We went first to the pump-room. It was full of company! and the moment we entered, I heard a murmuring of, "*That's she!*" and, to my great confusion, I saw every eye turned

---

1  "Dull" (*OED*).

towards me. I pulled my hat over my face, and, by the assistance of Mrs. Selwyn, endeavoured to screen myself from observation: nevertheless, I found I was so much the object of general attention, that I entreated her to hasten away. But unfortunately, she had entered into conversation, very earnestly, with a gentleman of her acquaintance, and would not listen to me, but said, that if I was tired of waiting, I might walk on to the milliner's with the Miss Watkins, two young ladies I had seen at Mrs. Beaumont's, who were going thither.

I accepted the offer very readily, and away we went. But we had not gone three yards, before we were followed by a party of young men, who took every possible opportunity of looking at us, and, as they walked behind, talked aloud, in a manner at once unintelligible and absurd. "Yes," cried one, "'tis certainly she! – mark but her *blushing cheek!*"

"And then her *eye*, – her *downcast eye!*" cried another.

"True, oh most true," said a third, "*every beauty is her own!*"

"But then," said the first, "her *mind*, – now the difficulty is, to find out the truth of *that*, for she will not say a word."

"She is *timid*," answered another; "mark but her *timid air.*"

During this conversation, we walked on silent and quick; as we knew not to whom it was particularly addressed, we were all equally ashamed, and equally desirous to avoid such unaccountable observations.

Soon after, we were caught in a shower of rain. We hurried on, and these gentlemen, following us, offered their services in the most pressing manner, begging us to make use of their arms; and while I almost ran, in order to avoid their impertinence, I was suddenly met by Sir Clement Willoughby!

We both started; "Good God," he exclaimed, "Miss Anville!" and then, regarding my tormentors with an air of displeasure, he earnestly enquired, if any thing had alarmed me?

"No, no;" cried I, for I found no difficulty, now, to disengage myself from these youths, who, probably, concluding from the commanding air of Sir Clement, that he had a right to protect me, quietly gave way to him, and entirely quitted us.

With his usual impetuosity, he then began a thousand enquiries, accompanied with as many compliments; and he told me, that he arrived at Bristol but this morning, which he had entirely devoted to endeavours to discover where I lodged.

"Did you know, then," said I, "that I was at Bristol?"

"Would to Heaven," cried he, "that I *could* remain in ignorance of your proceedings with the same contentment you do of mine! then should I not for ever journey upon the wings of hope, to meet my own despair! *You* cannot even judge of the cruelty of my fate, for the ease and serenity of your mind, incapacitates you from feeling for the agitation of mine."

The ease and serenity of *my* mind! alas, how little do I merit those words!

"But," added he, "had *accident* brought me hither, had I not known of your journey, the voice of fame would have proclaimed it to me instantly upon my arrival."

"The voice of fame!" repeated I.

"Yes, for your's was the first name I heard at the pump-room. But, had I *not* heard your name, such a description could have painted no one else."

"Indeed," said I, "I do not understand you." But, just then arriving at the milliner's, our conversation ended; for Miss Watkins called me to look at caps and ribbons.

Sir Clement, however, has the art of being always *at home*; he was very soon engaged, as busily as ourselves, in looking at lace ruffles. Yet he took an opportunity of saying to me in a low voice, "How charmed I am to see you look so well! I was told you were ill, – but I never saw you in better health, – never more infinitely lovely!"

I turned away, to examine the ribbons, and soon after Mrs. Selwyn made her appearance. I found that she was acquainted with Sir Clement, and her manner of speaking to him, convinced me that he was a favourite with her.

When their mutual compliments were over, she turned to me, and said, "Pray, Miss Anville, how long can you live without nourishment?"

"Indeed, Ma'am," said I, laughing, "I have never tried."

"Because so long, and no longer," answered she, "you may remain at Bristol."

"Why, what is the matter, Ma'am?"

"The matter! – why, all the ladies are at open war with you, – the whole pump-room is in confusion; and you, innocent as you pretend to look, are the cause. However, if you take my advice, you will be very careful how you eat and drink during your stay."

I begged her to explain herself: and she then told me, that a copy of verses had been dropt in the pump-room, and read there aloud: "The Beauties of the Wells," said she, "are all mentioned, but *you* are the Venus[1] to whom the prize is given."

"Is it then possible," cried Sir Clement, "that you have not seen these verses?"

"I hardly know," answered I, "whether *any* body has."

"I assure you," said Mrs. Selwyn, "if you give *me* the invention of them, you do me an honour I by no means deserve."

"I wrote down in my tablets," said Sir Clement, "the stanzas which concern Miss Anville, this morning at the pump-room; and I will do myself the honour of copying them for her this evening."

"But why the part that concerns *Miss Anville*?" said Mrs. Selwyn; "Did you ever see her before this morning?"

"Oh yes," answered he, "I have had that happiness frequently at Captain Mirvan's. Too, too frequently!" added he, in a low voice, as Mrs. Selwyn turned to the milliner: and, as soon as she was occupied in examining some trimmings, he came to me, and, almost whether I would or not, entered into conversation with me.

"I have a thousand things," cried he, "to say to you. Pray where are you?"

"With Mrs. Selwyn, Sir."

"Indeed! – then, for once, Chance is my friend. And how long have you been here?"

"About three weeks."

"Good Heaven! what an anxious search have I had, to discover your abode, since you so suddenly left town! The termagant Madame Duval refused me all intelligence. Oh, Miss Anville, did you know what I have endured! the sleepless, rest-

---

1   Goddess of beauty; the Trojan warrior Paris judged her to be the fairest, over Hera and Athena, and awarded her the golden apple.

less state of suspense I have been tortured with, you could not, all cruel as you are, you could not have received me with such frigid indifference!"

"*Received* you, Sir!"

"Why, is not my visit to *you*? Do you think I should have made this journey, but for the happiness of again seeing you?"

"Indeed it is possible I might, – since so many others do."

"Cruel, cruel girl! you *know* that I adore you! you *know* you are the mistress of my soul, and arbitress of my fate!"

Mrs. Selwyn then advancing to us, he assumed a more disengaged air, and asked if he should not have the pleasure of seeing her, in the evening, at the assembly?

"Oh yes," cried she, "we shall certainly be there; so you may bring the verses with you, if Miss Anville can wait for them so long."

"I hope, then," returned he, "that you will do me the honour to dance with me?"

I thanked him, but said I should not be at the assembly.

"Not be at the assembly!" cried Mrs. Selwyn, "Why, have *you*, too, letters to write?"

She looked at me with a significant archness that made me colour; and I hastily answered, "No, indeed, Ma'am!"

"You have not!" cried she, yet more drily, "then pray, my dear, do you stay at home to *help*, – or to *hinder* others?"

"To do neither, Ma'am," answered I, in much confusion; "so, if you please, I will *not* stay at home."

"You allow me, then," said Sir Clement, "to hope for the honour of your hand?"

I only bowed, – for the dread of Mrs. Selwyn's raillery made me not dare refuse him.

Soon after this we walked home; Sir Clement accompanied us, and the conversation that passed between Mrs. Selwyn and him was supported in so lively a manner, that I should have been much entertained, had my mind been more at ease: but alas! I could think of nothing but the capricious, the unmeaning appearance which the alteration in my conduct must make in the eyes of Lord Orville! And, much as I wish to avoid him, greatly as I desire to save myself from having my weakness known to him, – yet I cannot endure to incur his ill opinion, – and, unacquainted as he is with the reasons by which I am actuated, how can he fail contemning a change, to him so unaccountable?

As we entered the garden, he was the first object we saw. He advanced to meet us, and I could not help observing, that at sight of each other both he and Sir Clement changed colour.

We went into the parlour, where we found the same party we had left. Mrs. Selwyn presented Sir Clement to Mrs. Beaumont; Lady Louisa and Lord Merton he seemed well acquainted with already.

The conversation was upon the general subjects, of the weather, the company at the Wells, and the news of the day. But Sir Clement, drawing his chair next to mine, took every opportunity of addressing himself to me in particular.

I could not but remark the striking difference of *his* attention, and that of Lord Orville: the latter has such gentleness of manners, such delicacy of conduct, and an air so respectful, that, when he flatters most, he never distresses, and when he most confers honour, appears to receive it! The former *obtrudes* his attention, and *forces* mine; it is so pointed, that it always confuses me, and so public, that it attracts general notice. Indeed I have sometimes thought that he would rather *wish*, than dislike to have his partiality for me known, as he takes great care to prevent my being spoken to by any body but himself.

When, at length, he went away, Lord Orville took his seat, and said with a half-smile, "Shall *I* call Sir Clement, – or will *you* call me an usurper, for taking this place? – You make me no answer? – Must I then suppose that Sir Clement – "

"It is little worth your Lordship's while," said I, "to suppose any thing upon so insignificant an occasion."

"Pardon me," cried he, – "to *me* nothing is insignificant in which you are concerned."

To this I made no answer, neither did he say any thing more, till the ladies retired to dress; and then, when I would have followed them, he stopped me, saying, "One moment, I entreat you!"

I turned back, and he went on. "I greatly fear that I have

been so unfortunate as to offend you; yet so repugnant to my very soul is the idea, that I know not how to suppose it possible I can unwittingly have done the thing in the world that, designedly, I would most wish to avoid."

"No, indeed, my Lord, you have not!" said I.

"You sigh!" cried he, taking my hand, "would to Heaven I were the sharer of your uneasiness whencesoever it springs! with what earnestness would I not struggle to alleviate it! – Tell me, my dear Miss Anville, – my new-adopted sister, my sweet and most amiable friend! – tell me, I beseech you, if I can afford you any assistance?"

"None, none, my Lord!" cried I, withdrawing my hand, and moving towards the door.

"Is it then impossible I can serve you? – perhaps you wish to see Mr. Macartney again?"

"No, my Lord." And I held the door open.

"I am not, I own, sorry for that. Yet, oh, Miss Anville, there *is* a question, – there is a conjecture, – I know not how to mention, because I dread the result! – But I see you are in haste; – perhaps in the evening I may have the honour of a longer conversation. – Yet one thing will you have the goodness to allow me to ask? – Did you, this morning when you went to the Wells, – did you *know* who you should meet there?"

"Who, my Lord?"

"I beg your pardon a thousand times for a curiosity so unlicensed, – but I will say no more at present."

He bowed, expecting me to go, – and then, with quick steps, but a heavy heart, I came to my own room. His question, I am sure, meant Sir Clement Willoughby; and, had I not imposed upon myself the severe task of avoiding, flying Lord Orville with all my power, I would instantly have satisfied him of my ignorance of Sir Clement's journey. And yet more did I long to say something of the assembly, since I found he depended upon my spending the evening at home.

I did not go down stairs again till the family was assembled to dinner. My dress, I saw, struck Lord Orville with astonishment; and I was myself so much ashamed of appearing whimsical and unsteady, that I could not look up.

"I understood," said Mrs. Beaumont, "that Miss Anville did not go out this evening?"

"Her intention in the morning," said Mrs. Selwyn, "was to stay at home; but there is a fascinating power in an *assembly*, which, upon second thoughts, is not to be resisted."

"The assembly!" cried Lord Orville, "are you then going to the assembly?"

I made no answer; and we all took our places at table.

It was not without difficulty that I contrived to give up my usual seat; but I was determined to adhere to the promise in my yesterday's letter, though I saw that Lord Orville seemed quite confounded at my visible endeavours to avoid him.

After dinner, we all went into the drawing-room together, as there were no gentlemen to detain his Lordship; and then, before I could place myself out of his way, he said, "You are then really going to the assembly? — May I ask if you shall dance?"

"I believe not, – my Lord."

"If I did not fear," continued he, "that you would be tired of the same partner at two following assemblies, I would give up my letter-writing till to-morrow, and solicit the honour of your hand."

"If I *do* dance," said I, in great confusion, "I believe I am engaged."

"Engaged!" cried he, with earnestness, "May I ask to whom?"

"To – Sir Clement Willoughby, my Lord!"

He said nothing, but looked very little pleased, and did not address himself to me any more all the afternoon. Oh, Sir! – thus situated, how comfortless were the feelings of your Evelina!

Early in the evening, with his accustomed assiduity, Sir Clement came to conduct us to the assembly. He soon contrived to seat himself next me, and, in a low voice, paid me so many compliments, that I knew not which way to look.

Lord Orville hardly spoke a word, and his countenance was grave and thoughtful; yet, whenever I raised my eyes, his, I perceived, were directed towards me, though instantly, upon meeting mine, he looked another way.

In a short time, Sir Clement, taking from his pocket a folded paper, said, almost in a whisper, "Here, loveliest of women, you will see a faint, a successless attempt to paint the object of all my adoration! yet, weak as are the lines for the purpose, I envy beyond expression the happy mortal who has dared make the effort."

"I will look at them," said I, "some other time." For, conscious that I was observed by Lord Orville, I could not bear he should see me take a written paper, so privately offered, from Sir Clement. But Sir Clement is an impracticable man, and I never yet succeeded in any attempt to frustrate whatever he had planned.

"No," said he, still in a whisper, "you must take them now, while Lady Louisa is away;" for she and Mrs. Selwyn were gone up stairs to finish their dress, "as she must by no means see them."

"Indeed," said I, "I have no intention to shew them."

"But the only way," answered he, "to avoid suspicion, is to take them in her absence. I would have read them aloud myself, but that they are not proper to be seen by any body in this house, yourself and Mrs. Selwyn excepted."

Then again he presented me the paper, which I now was obliged to take, as I found declining it was vain. But I was sorry that this action should be seen, and the whispering remarked, though the purport of the conversation was left to conjecture.

As I held it in my hand, Sir Clement teazed me to look at it immediately; and told me, that the reason he could not produce the lines publicly, was, that, among the ladies who were mentioned, and supposed to be rejected, was Lady Louisa Larpent. I am much concerned at this circumstance, as I cannot doubt but that it will render me more disagreeable to her than ever, if she should hear of it.

I will now copy the verses, which Sir Clement would not let me rest till I had read.

SEE last advance, with bashful grace,
Downcast eye, and blushing cheek,
Timid air, and beauteous face,
Anville, – whom the Graces[1] seek.
Though ev'ry beauty is her own,
And though her mind each virtue fills,
Anville, – to her power unknown,
Artless strikes, – unconscious kills!

I am sure, my dear Sir, you will not wonder that a panegyric such as this, should, in reading, give me the greatest confusion; and, unfortunately, before I had finished it, the ladies returned.

"What have you there, my dear?" said Mrs. Selwyn.

"Nothing, Ma'am," said I, hastily folding, and putting it in my pocket.

"And has *nothing*," cried she, "the power of *rouge*?"

I made no answer; a deep sigh which escaped Lord Orville at that moment, reached my ears, and gave me sensations – which I dare not mention!

Lord Merton then handed Lady Louisa and Mrs. Beaumont to the latter's carriage. Mrs. Selwyn led the way to Sir Clement's, who handed me in after her.

During the ride, I did not once speak; but when I came to the assembly-room, Sir Clement took care that I should not preserve my silence. He asked me immediately to dance; I begged him to excuse me, and seek some other partner. But on the contrary, he told me he was very glad I would sit still, as he had a million of things to say to me.

He then began to tell me how much he had suffered from absence; how greatly he was alarmed when he heard I had left town, and how cruelly difficult he had found it to trace me; which, at last, he could only do by sacrificing another week to Captain Mirvan.

"And Howard Grove," continued he, "which, at my first visit, I thought the most delightful spot upon earth, now

---

1   The three Graces were Aglaia, Euphrosyne, and Thalia, daughters of Zeus and Eurynome, attendants of Venus: "young, beautiful, modest, personifications of gracefulness" (Zimmerman 58).

appeared to be the most dismal; the face of the country seemed altered: the walks which I had thought most pleasant, were now most stupid: Lady Howard, who had appeared a chearful and respectable old lady, now seemed in the common John Trot style[1] of other aged dames: Mrs. Mirvan, whom I had esteemed as an amiable piece of still-life,[2] now became so insipid, that I could hardly keep awake in her company: the daughter too, whom I had regarded as a good-humoured, pretty sort of girl, now seemed too insignificant for notice: and as to the Captain, I had always thought him a booby, – but now he appeared a savage!"

"Indeed, Sir Clement," cried I, angrily, "I will not hear you talk thus of my best friends."

"I beg your pardon," said he, "but the contrast of my two visits was too striking, not to be mentioned."

He then asked what I thought of the verses?

"Either," said I, "that they are written ironically, or by some madman."

Such a profusion of compliments ensued, that I was obliged to propose dancing, in my own defence. When we stood up, "I intended," said he, "to have discovered the author by his looks; but I find you so much the general loadstone of attention, that my suspicions change their objects every moment. Surely you must yourself have some knowledge who he is?"

I told him, no. Yet, my dear Sir, I must own to you, I have no doubt but that Mr. Macartney must be the author; no one else would speak of me so partially; and, indeed, his poetical turn puts it, with me, beyond dispute.

He asked me a thousand questions concerning Lord Orville; how long he had been at Bristol? – what time I had spent at Clifton? – whether he rode out every morning? – whether I ever trusted myself in a phaeton? and a multitude of other enquiries, all tending to discover if I was honoured with much of his Lordship's attention, and all made with his usual freedom and impetuosity.

Fortunately, as I much wished to retire early, Lady Louisa

---

1 "A man of slow, uncultured intellect, a bumpkin, a clown" (*OED*).
2 "Quiet, uneventful, dull" (*OED*).

makes a point of being among the first who quit the rooms, and therefore we got home in very tolerable time.

Lord Orville's reception of us was grave and cold: far from distinguishing me, as usual, by particular civilities, Lady Louisa herself could not have seen me enter the room with more frigid unconcern, nor have more scrupulously avoided honouring me with any notice. But chiefly I was struck to see, that he suffered Sir Clement, who stayed supper,[1] to sit between us, without any effort to prevent him, though till then, he had seemed to be even tenacious of a seat next mine.

This little circumstance affected me more than I can express: yet I endeavoured to *rejoice* at it, since neglect and indifference from him may be my best friends. – But, alas! – so suddenly, so abruptly to forfeit his attention! – to lose his friendship! – Oh Sir, these thoughts pierced my soul! – scarce could I keep my seat; for not all my efforts could restrain the tears from trickling down my cheeks: however, as Lord Orville saw them not, for Sir Clement's head was constantly between us, I tried to collect my spirits, and succeeded so far as to keep my place with decency, till Sir Clement took leave: and then, not daring to trust my eyes to meet those of Lord Orville, I retired.

I have been writing ever since; for, certain that I could not sleep, I would not go to bed. Tell me, my dearest Sir, if you possibly can, tell me that you approve my change of conduct, – tell me that my altered behaviour to Lord Orville is right, – that my flying his society, and avoiding his civilities, are actions which *you* would have dictated. – Tell me this, and the sacrifices I have made will comfort me in the midst of my regret, – for never, never can I cease to regret that I have lost the friendship of Lord Orville! – Oh Sir, I have slighted, have rejected, – have thrown it away! – No matter, it was an honour I merited not to preserve, and I now see, – that my mind was unequal to sustaining it without danger.

Yet so strong is the desire you have implanted in me to act with uprightness and propriety, that, however the weakness of my heart may distress and afflict me, it will never, I humbly

---

1  Sir Clement waited to have his supper – the last meal of the day – with them at Mrs. Beaumont's.

trust, render me wilfully culpable. The wish of doing well governs every other, as far as concerns my conduct, – for am I not *your* child? – the creature of your own forming? – Yet, oh Sir, friend, parent of my heart! – my feelings are all at war with my duties; and, while I most struggle to acquire self-approbation, my peace, my happiness, my hopes, – are lost!

'Tis you alone can compose a mind so cruelly agitated; you, I well know, can feel pity for the weakness to which you are a stranger; and, though you blame the affliction, soothe and comfort the afflicted.

## LETTER XII.

### Mr. Villars to Evelina.

Berry Hill, Oct. 3.

Your last communication, my dearest child, is indeed astonishing; that an acknowledged daughter and heiress of Sir John Belmont should be at Bristol, and still my Evelina bear the name of Anville, is to me inexplicable: yet the mystery of the letter to Lady Howard prepared me to expect something extraordinary upon Sir John Belmont's return to England.

Whoever this young lady may be, it is certain she now takes a place to which you have a right indisputable. An *after-marriage* I never heard of; yet, supposing such a one to have happened, Miss Evelyn was certainly the first wife, and therefore her daughter must, at least, be entitled to the name of Belmont.

Either there are circumstances in this affair at present utterly incomprehensible, or else some strange and most atrocious fraud has been practised; which of these two is the case, it now behoves us to enquire.

My reluctance to this step, gives way to my conviction of its propriety, since the reputation of your dear and much-injured mother must now either be fully cleared from blemish, or receive its final and indelible wound.

The public appearance of a daughter of Sir John Belmont

will revive the remembrance of Miss Evelyn's story in all who have heard it, – who the *mother* was, will be universally demanded, – and if any other Lady Belmont shall be named, – the birth of my Evelina will receive a stigma, against which honour, truth, and innocence may appeal in vain! a stigma which will eternally blast the fair fame of her virtuous mother, and cast upon her blameless self the odium of a title, which not all her purity can rescue from established shame and dishomour!

No, my dear child, no; I will not quietly suffer the ashes of your mother to be treated with ignominy! Her spotless character shall be justified to the world, – her marriage shall be acknowledged, and her child shall bear the name to which she is lawfully entitled.

It is true, that Mrs. Mirvan would conduct this affair with more delicacy than Mrs. Selwyn; yet, perhaps, to save time is, of all considerations, the most important, since the longer this mystery is suffered to continue, the more difficult may be rendered its explanation. The sooner, therefore, you can set out for town, the less formidable will be your task.

Let not your timidity, my dear love, depress your spirits: I shall, indeed, tremble for you at a meeting so singular, and so affecting, yet there can be no doubt of the success of your application: I enclose a letter from your unhappy mother, written, and reserved purposely for this occasion: Mrs. Clinton, too, who attended her in her last illness, must accompany you to town. – But, without any other certificate of your birth, that which you carry in your countenance, as it could not be effected by artifice, so it cannot admit of a doubt.

And now, my Evelina, committed, at length, to the care of your real parent, receive the fervent prayers, wishes, and blessings, of him who so fondly adopted you!

May'st thou, oh child of my bosom! may'st thou, in this change of situation, experience no change of disposition! but receive with humility, and support with meekness, the elevation to which thou art rising! May thy manners, language, and deportment, all evince that modest equanimity, and chearful gratitude, which not merely deserve, but dignify prosperity!

May'st thou, to the last moments of an unblemished life, retain thy genuine simplicity, thy singleness of heart, thy guileless sincerity! And may'st thou, stranger to ostentation, and superior to insolence, with true greatness of soul, shine forth conspicuous only in beneficence!

ARTHUR VILLARS.

## LETTER XIII.

[Inclosed in the preceding Letter.]

*Lady Belmont to Sir John Belmont.*

In the firm hope that the moment of anguish which approaches will prove the period of my sufferings, once more I address myself to Sir John Belmont, in behalf of the child, who, if it survives its mother, will hereafter be the bearer of this letter.

Yet in what terms, – oh most cruel of men! – can the lost Caroline address you, and not address you in vain? Oh deaf to the voice of compassion, – deaf to the sting of truth, – deaf to every tie of honour, – say, in what terms may the lost Caroline address you, and not address you in vain?

Shall I call you by the loved, the respected title of husband? – No, you disclaim it! – the father of my infant? – No, you doom it to infamy! – the lover who rescued me from a forced marriage? – No, you have yourself betrayed me! – the friend from whom I hoped succour and protection? – No, you have consigned me to misery and destruction!

Oh hardened against every plea of justice, remorse, or pity! how, and in what manner, may I hope to move thee? Is there one method I have left untried? remains there one resource unessayed? No; I have exhausted all the bitterness of reproach, and drained every sluice of compassion!

Hopeless, and almost desperate, twenty times have I flung away my pen; – but the feelings of a mother, a mother agonizing for the fate of her child, again animating my courage, as often I have resumed it.

Perhaps when I am no more, when the measure of my woes is compleated, and the still, silent, unreproaching dust has received my sad remains, – then, perhaps when accusation is no longer to be feared, nor detection to be dreaded, the voice of equity, and the cry of nature may be heard.

Listen, oh Belmont, to their dictates! reprobate not your child, though you have reprobated its mother. The evils that are past, perhaps, when too late, you may wish to recall; the young creature you have persecuted, perhaps, when too late you may regret that you have destroyed; – you may think with horror of the deceptions you have practised, and the pangs of remorse may follow me to the tomb: – oh Belmont, all my resentment softens into pity at the thought! what will become of thee, good Heaven, when with the eye of penitence, thou reviewest thy past conduct!

Hear, then, the solemn, the last address with which the unhappy Caroline will importune thee.

If, when the time of thy contrition arrives, – for arrive it must! – when the sense of thy treachery shall rob thee of almost every other, if then thy tortured heart shall sigh to expiate thy guilt, – mark the conditions upon which I leave thee my forgiveness.

Thou know'st I am thy wife! – clear, then, to the world the reputation thou hast sullied, and receive as thy lawful successor the child who will present thee this my dying request!

The worthiest, the most benevolent, the best of men, to whose consoling kindness I owe the little tranquillity I have been able to preserve, has plighted me his faith that, upon no other conditions, he will part with his helpless charge.

Should'st thou, in the features of this deserted innocent, trace the resemblance of the wretched Caroline, – should its face bear the marks of its birth, and revive in thy memory the image of its mother, wilt thou not, Belmont, wilt thou not therefore renounce it? – Oh babe of my fondest affection! for whom already I experience all the tenderness of maternal pity! – look not like thy unfortunate mother, – lest the parent whom the hand of death may spare, shall be snatched from thee by the more cruel means of unnatural antipathy!

I can write no more. The small share of serenity I have painfully acquired, will not bear the shock of the dreadful ideas that crowd upon me.

Adieu, – for ever! –

Yet oh! – shall I not, in this last farewell, which thou wilt not read till every stormy passion is extinct, – and the kind grave has embosomed all my sorrows, – shall I not offer to the man once so dear to me, a ray of consolation to those afflictions he has in reserve? Suffer me, then, to tell thee, that my pity far exceeds my indignation, – that I will pray for thee in my last moments, – and that the recollection of the love I once bore thee, shall swallow up every other!

Once more, adieu!

CAROLINE BELMONT.

## LETTER XIV.

*Evelina to the Rev. Mr. Villars.*

Clifton, Oct. 3d.

This morning I saw from my window, that Lord Orville was walking in the garden; but I would not go down stairs till breakfast was ready: and then, he paid me his compliments almost as coldly as Lady Louisa paid her's.

I took my usual place, and Mrs. Beaumont, Lady Louisa, and Mrs. Selwyn, entered into their usual conversation. – Not so your Evelina: disregarded, silent, and melancholy, she sat like a cypher,[1] whom to nobody belonging, by nobody was noticed.

Ill brooking such a situation, and unable to support the neglect of Lord Orville, the moment breakfast was over, I left the room; and was going up stairs, when, very unpleasantly, I was stopped by Sir Clement Willoughby, who, flying into the hall, prevented my proceeding.

He enquired very particularly after my health, and entreated

---

1 "A person who fills a place, but is of no importance or worth, a nonentity, a 'mere nothing'" (*OED*).

me to return into the parlour. Unwillingly I consented, but thought any thing preferable to continuing alone with him; and he would neither leave me, nor suffer me to pass on. Yet, in returning, I felt not a little ashamed of appearing thus to take the visit of Sir Clement to myself. And, indeed, he endeavoured, by his manner of addressing me, to give it that air.

He stayed, I believe, an hour; nor would he, perhaps, even then have gone, had not Mrs. Beaumont broken up the party, by proposing an airing in her coach. Lady Louisa consented to accompany her: but Mrs. Selwyn, when applied to, said, "If my Lord, or Sir Clement, will join us, I shall be happy to make one; – but really, a trio of females will be nervous to the last degree."

Sir Clement readily agreed to attend them; indeed, he makes it his evident study to court the favour of Mrs. Beaumont. Lord Orville excused himself from going out; and I retired to my own room. What he did with himself I know not, for I would not go down stairs till dinner was ready: his coldness, though my own change of behaviour has occasioned it, so cruelly depresses my spirits, that I know not how to support myself in his presence.

At dinner, I found Sir Clement again of the party. Indeed he manages every thing his own way; for Mrs. Beaumont, though by no means easy to please, seems quite at his disposal.

The dinner, the afternoon, and the evening, were to me the most irksome imaginable: I was tormented by the assiduity of Sir Clement, who not only *took*, but *made* opportunities of speaking to me, – and I was hurt, – oh how inexpressibly hurt! – that Lord Orville not only forbore, as hitherto, *seeking*, he even *neglected* all occasions of talking with me!

I begin to think, my dear Sir, that the sudden alteration in my behaviour was ill-judged and improper; for, as I had received no offence, as the cause of the change was upon *my* account, not *his*, I should not have assumed, so abruptly, a reserve for which I dared assign no reason, – nor have shunned his presence so obviously, without considering the strange appearance of such a conduct.

Alas, my dearest Sir, that my reflections should always be too late to serve me! dearly, indeed, do I purchase experience! and much I fear I shall suffer yet more severely, from the heedless indiscretion of my temper, ere I attain that prudence and consideration, which, by foreseeing distant consequences, may rule and direct in present exigencies.

Oct. 4<sup>th</sup>.

Yesterday morning, every body rode out, except Mrs. Selwyn and myself: and we two sat for some time together in her room; but, as soon as I could, I quitted her, to saunter in the garden; for she diverts herself so unmercifully with rallying me, either upon my gravity, – or concerning Lord Orville, – that I dread having any conversation with her.

Here I believe I spent an hour by myself; when, hearing the garden-gate open, I went into an arbour at the end of a long walk, where, ruminating, very unpleasantly, upon my future prospects, I remained quietly seated but a few minutes, before I was interrupted by the appearance of Sir Clement Willoughby.

I started; and would have left the arbour, but he prevented me. Indeed I am almost certain he had heard in the house where I was, as it is not, otherwise, probable he would have strolled down the garden alone.

"Stop, stop," cried he, "loveliest and most beloved of women, stop and hear me!"

Then, making me keep my place, he sat down by me, and would have taken my hand; but I drew it back, and said I could not stay.

"Can you, then," cried he, "refuse me even the smallest gratification, though, but yesterday, I almost suffered martyrdom for the pleasure of seeing you?"

"Martyrdom! Sir Clement."

"Yes, beauteous insensible! *martyrdom*: for did I not compel myself to be immured in a carriage, the tedious length of a whole morning, with the three most fatiguing women in England?"

"Upon my word the Ladies are extremely obliged to you."

"O," returned he, "they have, every one of them, so copious a share of their own personal esteem, that they have no right to repine at the failure of it in the world; and, indeed, they will themselves be the last to discover it."

"How little," cried I, "are those Ladies aware of such severity from *you*!"

"They are guarded," answered he, "so happily and so securely by their own conceit, that they are not aware of it from any body. Oh Miss Anville, to be torn away from *you*, in order to be shut up with *them*, – is there a human being, except your cruel self, could forbear to pity me?"

"I believe, Sir Clement, however hardly you may choose to judge of them, your situation, by the world in general, would rather have been envied, than pitied."

"The world in general," answered he, "has the same opinion of them that I have myself: Mrs. Beaumont is every where laughed at, Lady Louisa ridiculed, and Mrs. Selwyn hated."

"Good God, Sir Clement, what cruel strength of words do you use!"

"It is you, my angel, are to blame, since your perfections have rendered their faults so glaring. I protest to you, during our whole ride, I thought the carriage drawn by snails. The absurd pride of Mrs. Beaumont, and the respect she exacts, are at once insufferable and stupifying; had I never before been in her company, I should have concluded that this had been her first airing from the herald's-office,[1] – and wished her nothing worse than that it might also be the last. I assure you, that but for gaining the freedom of her house, I would fly her as I would plague, pestilence, and famine. Mrs. Selwyn, indeed, afforded some relief from this formality, but the unbounded licence of her tongue – "

"O Sir Clement, do *you* object to that?"

"Yes, my sweet reproacher, in a *woman*, I do; in a *woman* I think it intolerable. She has wit, I acknowledge, and more understanding than half her sex put together; but she keeps alive a perpetual expectation of satire, that spreads a general

---

1   "Heralds' College, or College of Arms; a royal corporation, founded 1483, consisting of the Earl Marshal, kings-of-arms, heralds, and pursuivants, exercising jurisdiction in matters armorial, and now recording proved pedigrees, and granting armorial bearings. Heralds' Office, the office of this corporation" (*OED*).

uneasiness among all who are in her presence; and she talks so much, that even the best things she says, weary the attention. As to the little Louisa, 'tis such a pretty piece of languor, that 'tis almost cruel to speak rationally about her, – else I should say, she is a mere compound of affectation, impertinence, and airs."

"I am quite amazed," said I, "that, with such opinions, you can behave to them all with so much attention and civility."

"Civility! my angel, – why I could worship, could adore them, only to procure myself a moment of your conversation? Have you not seen me pay my court to the gross Captain Mirvan, and the virago Madame Duval? Were it possible that a creature so horrid could be formed, as to partake of the worst qualities of all these characters, – a creature who should have the haughtiness of Mrs. Beaumont, the brutality of Captain Mirvan, the self-conceit of Mrs. Selwyn, the affectation of Lady Louisa, and the vulgarity of Madame Duval, – even to such a monster as that, I would pay homage, and pour forth adulation, only to obtain one word, one look from my adored Miss Anville!"

"Sir Clement," said I, "you are greatly mistaken if you suppose such duplicity of character recommends you to my good opinion. But I must take this opportunity of begging you never more to talk to me in this strain."

"Oh Miss Anville, your reproofs, your coldness, pierce me to the soul! look upon me with less rigour, and make me what you please; – you shall govern and direct all my actions, – you shall new-form, new-model me: – I will not have even a wish but of your suggestion; – only deign to look upon me with pity, – if not with favour!"

"Suffer me, Sir," said I very gravely, "to make use of this occasion to put a final conclusion to such expressions. I entreat you never again to address me in a language so flighty, and so unwelcome. You have already given me great uneasiness; and I must frankly assure you, that if you do not desire to banish me from wherever you are, you will adopt a very different style and conduct in future."

I then rose, and was going, but he flung himself at my feet to prevent me, exclaiming, in a most passionate manner, "Good

God! Miss Anville, what do you say? – is it, can it be possible, that so unmoved, that with such petrifying indifference, you can tear from me even the remotest hope!"

"I know not, Sir," said I, endeavouring to disengage myself from him, "what hope you mean, but I am sure that I never intended to give you any."

"You distract me!" cried he, "I cannot endure such scorn; – I beseech you to have some moderation in your cruelty, lest you make me desperate: – say, then, that you pity me, – O fairest inexorable! loveliest tyrant! – say, tell me, at least, that you pity me!"

Just then, who should come in sight, as if intending to pass by the arbour, but Lord Orville! Good Heaven, how did I start! and he, the moment he saw me, turned pale, and was hastily retiring; – but I called out, "Lord Orville! – Sir Clement, release me, – let go my hand!"

Sir Clement, in some confusion, suddenly rose, but still grasped my hand. Lord Orville, who had turned back, was again walking away; but, still struggling to disengage myself, I called out, "Pray, pray, my Lord, don't go! – Sir Clement, I *insist* upon your releasing me!"

Lord Orville then, hastily approaching us, said, with great spirit, "Sir Clement, you cannot wish to detain Miss Anville by force!"

"Neither, my Lord," cried Sir Clement, proudly, "do I request the honour of your Lordship's interference."

However, he let go my hand, and I immediately ran into the house.

I was now frightened to death lest Sir Clement's mortified pride should provoke him to affront Lord Orville: I therefore ran hastily to Mrs. Selwyn, and entreated her, in a manner hardly to be understood, to walk towards the arbour. She asked no questions, for she is quick as lightening in taking a hint, but instantly hastened into the garden.

Imagine, my dear Sir, how wretched I must be till I saw her return! scarce could I restrain myself from running back: however, I checked my impatience, and waited, though in agonies, till she came.

And, now, my dear Sir, I have a conversation to write, the most interesting to me, that I ever heard. The comments and questions with which Mrs. Selwyn interrupted her account, I shall not mention; for they are such as you may very easily suppose.

Lord Orville and Sir Clement were both seated very quietly in the arbour: and Mrs. Selwyn, standing still, as soon as she was within a few yards of them, heard Sir Clement say, "Your question, my Lord, alarms me, and I can by no means answer it, unless you will allow me to propose another?"

"Undoubtedly, Sir."

"You ask me, my Lord, what are my intentions? – I should be very happy to be satisfied as to your Lordship's."

"I have never, Sir, professed *any*."

Here they were both, for a few moments, silent; and then Sir Clement said, "To what, my Lord, must I, then, impute your desire of knowing mine?"

"To an unaffected interest in Miss Anville's welfare."

"Such an interest," said Sir Clement, drily, "is, indeed, very generous: but, except in a father, – a brother, – or a lover – "

"Sir Clement," interrupted his Lordship, "I know your inference; and I acknowledge I have not the right of enquiry which any of those three titles bestow, and yet I confess the warmest wishes to serve her, and to see her happy. Will you, then, excuse me, if I take the liberty to repeat my question?"

"Yes, if your Lordship will excuse my repeating that I think it a rather extraordinary one."

"It may be so," said Lord Orville; "but this young lady seems to be peculiarly situated; she is very young, very inexperienced, yet appears to be left totally to her own direction. She does not, I believe, see the dangers to which she is exposed, and I will own to you, I feel a strong desire to point them out."

"I don't rightly understand your Lordship, – but I think you cannot mean to prejudice her against me?"

"Her sentiments of *you*, Sir, are as much unknown to me as your intentions towards *her*. Perhaps, were I acquainted with either, my officiousness might be at an end: but I presume not to ask upon what terms – "

Here he stopped; and Sir Clement said, "You know, my Lord, I am not given to despair; I am by no means such a puppy as to tell you I am upon *sure ground*, however, perseverance – "

"You are, then, determined to persevere?"

"I am, my Lord."

"Pardon me, then, Sir Clement, if I speak to you with freedom. This young lady, though she seems alone, and, in some measure, unprotected, is not entirely without friends; she has been extremely well educated, and accustomed to good company; she has a natural love of virtue, and a mind that might adorn *any* station, however exalted: is such a young lady, Sir Clement, a proper object to trifle with? – for your principles, excuse me, Sir, are well known."

"As to that, my Lord, let Miss Anville look to herself; she has an excellent understanding, and needs no counsellor."

"Her understanding is, indeed, excellent; but she is too young for suspicion, and has an artlessness of disposition that I never saw equalled."

"My Lord," cried Sir Clement, warmly, "your praises make me doubt your disinterestedness, and there exists not the man who I would so unwillingly have for a rival as yourself. But you must give me leave to say, you have greatly deceived me in regard to this affair."

"How so, Sir," cried Lord Orville, with equal warmth.

"You were pleased, my Lord," answered Sir Clement, "upon our first conversation concerning this young lady, to speak of her in terms by no means suited to your present encomiums; you said she was a *poor, weak, ignorant girl,* and I had great reason to believe you had a most contemptuous opinion of her."

"It is very true," said Lord Orville, "that I did not, at our first acquaintance, do justice to the merit of Miss Anville; but I knew not, then, how new she was to the world; at present, however, I am convinced, that whatever might appear strange in her behaviour, was simply the effect of inexperience, timidity, and a retired education, for I find her informed, sensible, and intelligent. She is not, indeed, like most modern young ladies, to be known in half an hour; her modest worth, and fearful excellence, require both time and encouragement to shew themselves. She does not, beautiful as she is, seize the soul by surprise, but, with more dangerous fascination, she steals it almost imperceptibly."

"Enough, my Lord," cried Sir Clement, "your solicitude for her welfare is now sufficiently explained."

"My friendship and esteem," returned Lord Orville, "I do not wish to disguise; but assure yourself, Sir Clement, I should not have troubled *you* upon this subject, had Miss Anville and I ever conversed but as friends. However, since you do not chuse to avow your intentions, we must drop the subject."

"My intentions," cried he, "I will frankly own, are hardly known to myself. I think Miss Anville the loveliest of her sex, and, were I a *marrying man*, she, of all the women I have seen, I would fix upon for a wife: but I believe that not even the philosophy of your Lordship would recommend to me a connection of that sort, with a girl of obscure birth, whose only dowry is her beauty, and who is evidently in a state of dependency."

"Sir Clement," cried Lord Orville, with some heat, "we will discuss this point no further; we are both free agents, and must act for ourselves."

Here Mrs. Selwyn, fearing a surprise, and finding my apprehensions of danger were groundless, retired hastily into another walk, and soon after came to give me this account.

Good Heaven, what a man is this Sir Clement! so designing, though so easy; so deliberately artful, though so flighty! Greatly, however, is he mistaken, all confident as he seems; for the girl, obscure, poor, dependent as she is, far from wishing the honour of his alliance, would not only *now*, but *always* have rejected it.

As to Lord Orville, – but I will not trust my pen to mention him, – tell me, my dear Sir, what *you* think of him? – tell me if he is not the noblest of men? – and if you can either wonder at, or blame my admiration?

The idea of being seen by either party, immediately after so singular a conversation, was both awkward and distressing to me; but I was obliged to appear at dinner. Sir Clement, I saw, was absent and uneasy; he watched me, he watched Lord Orville, and was evidently disturbed in his mind. Whenever he spoke to me, I turned from him with undisguised disdain, for

I am too much irritated against him, to bear with his ill-meant assiduities any longer.

But, not once, – not a moment did I dare meet the eyes of Lord Orville! All consciousness myself, I dreaded his penetration, and directed mine every way – but towards his. The rest of the day, I never quitted Mrs. Selwyn.

Adieu, my dear Sir: to-morrow I expect your directions whether I am to return to Berry Hill, or once more to visit London.


## LETTER XV.

*Evelina in continuation.*

Oct. 6$^{th}$.

And now, my dearest Sir, if the perturbation of my spirits will allow me, I will finish my last letter from Clifton Hill.

This morning, though I did not go down stairs early, Lord Orville was the only person in the parlour when I entered it. I felt no small confusion at seeing him alone, after having so long and successfully avoided such a meeting. As soon as the usual compliments were over, I would have left the room, but he stopped me by saying, "If I disturb you, Miss Anville, I am gone."

"My Lord," said I, rather embarrassed, "I did not mean to stay."

"I flattered myself," cried he, "I should have had a moment's conversation with you."

I then turned back; and he seemed himself in some perplexity: but after a short pause, "You are very good," said he, "to indulge my request; I have, indeed, for some time past, most ardently desired an opportunity of speaking to you."

Again he paused; but I said nothing, so he went on.

"You allowed me, Madam, a few days since, you allowed me to lay claim to your friendship, – to interest myself in your affairs, – to call you by the affectionate title of sister; – and the honour you did me, no man could have been more sensible of; I am ignorant, therefore, how I have been so unfortunate as to forfeit it: – but, at present, all is changed! you fly me, – your averted eye shuns to meet mine, and you sedulously avoid my conversation."

I was extremely disconcerted at this grave, and but too just accusation, and I am sure I must look very simple; – but I made no answer.

"You will not, I hope," continued he, "condemn me unheard; if there is any thing I have done, – or any thing I have neglected, tell me, I beseech you, *what*, and it shall be the whole study of my thoughts how to deserve your pardon."

"Oh my Lord," cried I, penetrated at once with shame and gratitude, "your too, too great politeness oppresses me! – you have done nothing, – I have never dreamt of offence; – if there is any pardon to be asked, it is rather for *me*, than for *you*, to ask it."

"You are all sweetness and condescension!" cried he, "and I flatter myself you will again allow me to claim those titles which I find myself so unable to forego. Yet, occupied as I am with an idea which gives me the severest uneasiness, I hope you will not think me impertinent, if I still solicit, still entreat, nay implore you to tell me, to what cause your late sudden, and to me most painful, reserve was owing?"

"Indeed, my Lord," said I, stammering, "I don't, – I can't – indeed, my Lord, – "

"I am sorry to distress you," said he, "and ashamed to be so urgent, – yet I know not how to be satisfied while in ignorance, – and the *time* when the change happened, makes me apprehend – may I, Miss Anville, tell you *what* it makes me apprehend?"

"Certainly, my Lord."

"Tell me, then, – and pardon a question most essentially important to me; – Had, or had not, Sir Clement Willoughby, any share in causing your inquietude?"

"No, my Lord," answered I, with firmness, "none in the world."

"A thousand, thousand thanks!" cried he: "you have relieved

me from a weight of conjecture which I supported very painfully. But one thing more; is it, in any measure, to Sir Clement that I may attribute the alteration in your behaviour to myself, which, I could not but observe, began the very day of his arrival at the Hotwells?"

"To Sir Clement, my Lord," said I, "attribute nothing. He is the last man in the world who would have any influence over my conduct."

"And will you, then, restore to me that share of confidence and favour with which you honoured me before he came?"

Just then, to my great relief, – for I knew not what to say, – Mrs. Beaumont opened the door, and in a few minutes, we went to breakfast.

Lord Orville was all gaiety; never did I see him more lively or more agreeable. Very soon after, Sir Clement Willoughby called, to pay his respects, he said, to Mrs. Beaumont. I then came to my own room, where, indulging my reflections, which now soothed, and now alarmed me, I remained very quietly, till I received your most kind letter.

Oh Sir, how sweet are the prayers you offer for your Evelina! how grateful to her are the blessings you pour upon her head! – You *commit me to my real parent*, – Ah, Guardian, Friend, Protector of my youth! – by whom my helpless infancy was cherished, my mind formed, my very life preserved, – *you* are the Parent my heart acknowledges, and to you do I vow eternal duty, gratitude, and affection!

I look forward to the approaching interview with more fear than hope; but important as is this subject, I am, just now, wholly engrossed with another, which I must hasten to communicate.

I immediately acquainted Mrs. Selwyn with the purport of your letter. She was charmed to find your opinion agreed with her own, and settled that we should go to town to-morrow morning. And a chaise is actually ordered to be here by one o'clock.

She then desired me to pack up my cloaths; and said she must go, herself, to *make speeches*, and *tell lies* to Mrs. Beaumont.

When I went down stairs to dinner, Lord Orville, who was still in excellent spirits, reproached me for secluding myself so much from the company. He sat next me, – he *would* sit next me, – at table; and he might, I am sure, repeat what he once said of me before, *that he almost exhausted himself in fruitless endeavours to entertain me*; – for, indeed, I was not to be entertained: I was totally spiritless and dejected; the idea of the approaching meeting, – and oh Sir, the idea of the approaching parting, – gave a heaviness to my heart, that I could neither conquer nor repress. I even regretted the half explanation that had passed, and wished Lord Orville had supported his own reserve, and suffered me to support mine.

However, when, during dinner, Mrs. Beaumont spoke of our journey, my gravity was no longer singular; a cloud instantly overspread the countenance of Lord Orville, and he became nearly as thoughtful and as silent as myself.

We all went together to the drawing-room. After a short and unentertaining conversation, Mrs. Selwyn said she must prepare for her journey, and begged me to see for some books she had left in the parlour.

And here, while I was looking for them, I was followed by Lord Orville. He shut the door after he came in, and approaching me with a look of great anxiety, said, "Is this true, Miss Anville, are you going?"

"I believe so, my Lord," said I, still looking for the books.

"So suddenly, so unexpectedly, must I lose you?"

"No great loss, my Lord," cried I, endeavouring to speak chearfully.

"Is it possible," said he, gravely, "Miss Anville can doubt my sincerity?"

"I can't imagine," cried I, what Mrs. Selwyn has done with these books."

"Would to Heaven," continued he, "I might flatter myself you would allow me to prove it!"

"I must run up stairs," cried I, greatly confused, "and ask what she has done with them."

"You are going, then," cried he, taking my hand, "and you

give me not the smallest hope of your return! – will you not, then, my too lovely friend! – will you not, at least, teach me, with fortitude like your own, to support your absence?"

"My Lord," cried I, endeavouring to disengage my hand, "pray let me go!"

"I will;" cried he, to my inexpressible confusion, dropping on one knee, "if you wish to leave me!"

"Oh, my Lord," exclaimed I, "rise, I beseech you, rise! – such a posture to me! – surely your Lordship is not so cruel as to mock me!"

"Mock you!" repeated he earnestly, "no, I revere you! I esteem and I admire you above all human beings! you are the friend to whom my soul is attached as to its better half! you are the most amiable, the most perfect of women! and you are dearer to me than language has the power of telling!"

I attempt not to describe my sensations at that moment; I scarce breathed; I doubted if I existed, – the blood forsook my cheeks, and my feet refused to sustain me: Lord Orville, hastily rising, supported me to a chair, upon which I sunk, almost life-less.

For a few minutes, we neither of us spoke; and then, seeing me recover, Lord Orville, though in terms hardly articulate, entreated my pardon for his abruptness. The moment my strength returned, I attempted to rise, but he would not permit me.

I cannot write the scene that followed, though every word is engraven on my heart: but his protestations, his expressions, were too flattering for repetition: nor would he, in spite of my repeated efforts to leave him, suffer me to escape; – in short, my dear Sir, I was not proof against his solicitations – and he drew from me the most sacred secret of my heart!

I know not how long we were together, but Lord Orville was upon his knees, when the door was opened by Mrs. Sel-wyn! – To tell you, Sir, the shame with which I was over-whelmed, would be impossible; – I snatched my hand from Lord Orville, – he, too, started and rose, and Mrs. Selwyn, for some instants, stood facing us both in silence.

At last, "My Lord," said she, sarcastically, "have you been so good as to help Miss Anville to look for my books?"

"Yes, Madam," answered he, attempting to rally, "and I hope we shall soon be able to find them."

"Your Lordship is extremely kind," said she, drily, "but I can by no means consent to take up any more of your time." Then, looking on the window-seat, she presently found the books, and added, "Come, here are just three, and so, like the servants in the Drummer,[1] this important affair may give employment to us all." She then presented one of them to Lord Orville, another to me, and taking a third herself, with a most provoking look, she left the room.

I would instantly have followed her; but Lord Orville, who could not help laughing, begged me to stay a minute, as he had many important matters to discuss.

"No, indeed, my Lord, I cannot, – perhaps I have already stayed too long."

"Does Miss Anville so soon repent her goodness?"

"I scarce know what I do, my Lord, – I am quite bewildered!"

"One hour's conversation," cried he, "will I hope compose your spirits, and confirm my happiness. When, then, may I hope to see you alone? – shall you walk in the garden to-morrow before breakfast?"

"No, no, my Lord; you must not, a second time, reproach me with making an *appointment*."

"Do you then," said he, laughing, "reserve that honour only for Mr. Macartney?"

"Mr. Macartney," said I, "is poor, and thinks himself obliged to me; otherwise – "

"Poverty," cried he, "I will not plead; but if being *obliged* to you has any weight, who shall dispute *my* title to an appointment?"

"My Lord, I can stay no longer, – Mrs. Selwyn will lose all patience."

---

1  *The Drummer; or, The Haunted House* (1716) was a comedy by Joseph Addison (1672-1719). In Act V of the play, three servants are involved in locating writing implements.

"Deprive her not of the pleasure of her *conjectures*; – but, tell me, are you under Mrs. Selwyn's care?"

"Only for the present, my Lord."

"Not a few are the questions I have to ask Miss Anville: among them, the most important is, whether she depends wholly on herself, or whether there is any other person for whose interest I must solicit?"

"I hardly know, my Lord, I hardly know myself to whom I most belong."

"Suffer, suffer me, then," cried he, with warmth, "to hasten the time when that shall no longer admit a doubt! – when your grateful Orville may call you all his own!"

At length, but with difficulty, I broke from him. I went, however, to my own room, for I was too much agitated to follow Mrs. Selwyn. Good God, my dear Sir, what a scene! surely the meeting for which I shall prepare to-morrow, cannot so greatly affect me! To be loved by Lord Orville, – to be the honoured choice of his noble heart, – my happiness seemed too infinite to be borne, and I wept, even bitterly I wept, from the excess of joy which overpowered me.

In this state of almost painful felicity, I continued, till I was summoned to tea. When I re-entered the drawing-room, I rejoiced much to find it full of company, as the confusion with which I met Lord Orville was rendered the less observable.

Immediately after tea, most of the company played at cards, – and then, – and till supper-time, Lord Orville devoted himself wholly to me.

He saw that my eyes were red, and would not let me rest till he had made me confess the cause; and when, though most reluctantly, I had acknowledged my weakness, I could with difficulty refrain from weeping again at the gratitude he expressed.

He earnestly desired to know if my journey could not be postponed; and when I said no, entreated permission to attend me to town.

"Oh, my Lord," cried I, "what a request!"

"The sooner," answered he, "I make my devotion to you

public, the sooner I may expect, from your delicacy, you will convince the world you encourage no mere *danglers*."[1]

"You teach me, then, my Lord, the inference I might expect, if I complied."

"And can you wonder I should seek to hasten the happy time, when no scruples, no discretion will demand our separation? and when the most punctilious delicacy will rather promote, than oppose, my happiness in attending you?"

To this I was silent, and he re-urged his request.

"My Lord," said I, "you ask what I have no power to grant. This journey will deprive me of all right to act for myself."

"What does Miss Anville mean?"

"I cannot now explain myself; indeed, if I could, the task would be both painful and tedious."

"O Miss Anville," cried he, "when may I hope to date the period[2] of this mystery? when flatter myself that my promised friend will indeed honour me with her confidence?"

"My Lord," said I, "I mean not to affect any mystery, – but my affairs are so circumstanced, that a long and most unhappy story, can alone explain them. However, if a short suspense will give your Lordship any uneasiness, – "

"My beloved Miss Anville," cried he, eagerly, "pardon my impatience! – You shall tell me nothing you would wish to conceal, – I will wait your own time for information, and trust to your goodness for its speed."

"There is *nothing*, my Lord, I wish to conceal, – to *postpone* an explanation is all I desire."

He then requested, that, since I would not allow him to accompany me to town, I would permit him to write to me, and promise to answer his letters.

A sudden recollection of the two letters which had already passed between us occurring to me, I hastily answered, "No, indeed, my Lord! – "

"I am extremely sorry," said he, gravely, "that you think me too presumptuous. I must own I had flattered myself that to soften the inquietude of an absence which seems attended by

---

1   "One who hangs or hovers about a woman; a dallying follower" (*OED*).
2   See the end of this mystery.

so many inexplicable circumstances, would not have been to incur your displeasure."

This seriousness hurt me; and I could not forbear saying, "Can you indeed desire, my Lord, that I should, a second time, expose myself, by an unguarded readiness to write to you?"

"A *second time! unguarded readiness!*" repeated he; "you amaze me!"

"Has your Lordship then quite forgot the foolish letter I was so imprudent as to send you when in town?"

"I have not the least idea," cried he, "of what you mean."

"Why then, my Lord," said I, "we had better let the subject drop."

"Impossible!" cried he, "I cannot rest without an explanation!"

And then, he obliged me to speak very openly of both the letters; but, my dear Sir, imagine my surprise, when he assured me, in the most solemn manner, that far from having ever written me a single line, he had never received, seen, or heard of my letter!

This subject, which caused mutual astonishment and perplexity to us both, entirely engrossed us for the rest of the evening; and he made me promise to shew him the letter I had received in his name to-morrow morning, that he might endeavour to discover the author.

After supper, the conversation became general.

And now, my dearest Sir, may I not call for your congratulations upon the events of this day? a day never to be recollected by me but with the most grateful joy! I know how much you are inclined to think well of Lord Orville, I cannot, therefore, apprehend that my frankness to him will displease you. Perhaps the time is not very distant when your Evelina's choice may receive the sanction of her best friend's judgment and approbation, – which seems now all she has to wish!

In regard to the change in my situation which must first take place, surely I cannot be blamed for what has passed! the partiality of Lord Orville must not only reflect honour upon me, but upon all to whom I do, or may belong.

Adieu, most dear Sir. I will write again when I arrive at London.

# LETTER XVI.

*Evelina in continuation.*

Clifton, Oct. 7$^{th}$.

You will see, my dear Sir, that I was mistaken in supposing I should write no more from this place, where my residence, now, seems more uncertain than ever.

This morning, during breakfast, Lord Orville took an opportunity to beg me, in a low voice, to allow him a moment's conversation before I left Clifton; "May I hope," added he, "that you will strole into the garden after breakfast?"

I made no answer, but I believe my looks gave no denial; for, indeed, I much wished to be satisfied concerning the letter. The moment, therefore, that I could quit the parlour I ran up stairs for my calash;[1] but before I reached my room, Mrs. Selwyn called after me, "If you are going to walk, Miss Anville, be so good as to bid Jenny bring down my hat, and I'll accompany you."

Very much disconcerted, I turned into the drawing-room, without making any answer, and there I hoped to wait unseen, till she had otherwise disposed of herself. But, in a few minutes, the door opened, and Sir Clement Willoughby entered.

Starting at the sight of him, in rising hastily, I let drop the letter which I had brought for Lord Orville's inspection, and, before I could recover it, Sir Clement, springing forward, had it in his hand. He was just presenting it to me, and, at the same time, enquiring after my health, when the signature caught his eye, and he read aloud "Orville."

I endeavoured, eagerly, to snatch it from him, but he would not permit me, and, holding it fast, in a passionate manner exclaimed, "Good God, Miss Anville, is it possible you can value such a letter as this?"

The question surprised and confounded me, and I was too much ashamed to answer him; but finding he made an attempt

---

1 "A woman's hood made of silk, supported with whalebone or cane hoops, and projecting beyond the face" (*OED*).

to secure it, I prevented him, and vehemently demanded him to return it.

"Tell me first," said he, holding it above my reach, "tell me if you have, since, received any more letters from the same person?"

"No, indeed," cried I, "never!"

"And will you, also, sweetest of women, promise that you never *will* receive any more? Say that, and you will make me the happiest of men."

"Sir Clement," cried I, greatly confused, "pray give me the letter."

"And will you not first satisfy my doubts? – will you not relieve me from the torture of the most distracting suspence? – tell me but that the detested Orville has written to you no more!"

"Sir Clement," cried I, angrily, "you have no right to make any conditions, – so pray give me the letter directly."

"Why such solicitude about this hateful letter? can it possibly deserve your eagerness? tell me, with truth, with sincerity tell me; Does it really merit the least anxiety?"

"No matter, Sir," cried I, in great perplexity, "the letter is mine, and therefore – "

"I must conclude, then," said he, "that the letter deserves your utmost contempt, – but that the name of Orville is sufficient to make you prize it."

"Sir Clement," cried I, colouring, "you are quite – you are very much – the letter is not – "

"O Miss Anville," cried he, "you blush! – you stammer! – Great Heaven! it is then all as I feared!"

"I know not," cried I, half frightened, "what you mean; but I beseech you to give me the letter, and to compose yourself."

"The letter," cried he, gnashing his teeth, "you shall never see more! You ought to have burnt it the moment you had read it!" And, in an instant, he tore it into a thousand pieces.

Alarmed at a fury so indecently outrageous, I would have run out of the room; but he caught hold of my gown, and cried, "Not yet, not yet must you go! I am but half-mad yet, and you must stay to finish your work. Tell me, therefore, does

Orville know your fatal partiality? – Say *yes*," added he, trembling with passion, "and I will fly you for ever!"

"For Heaven's sake, Sir Clement," cried I, "release me! – if you do not, you will force me to call for help."

"Call then," cried he, "inexorable and most unfeeling girl; call, if you please, and bid all the world witness your triumph! – but could ten worlds obey your call, I would not part from you till you had answered me. Tell me, then, does Orville know you love him?"

At any other time, an enquiry so gross would have given me inexpressible confusion; but now, the wildness of his manner terrified me, and I only said, "Whatever you wish to know, Sir Clement, I will tell you another time; but for the present, I entreat you to let me go!"

"Enough," cried he, "I understand you! – the art of Orville has prevailed; – cold, inanimate, phlegmatic as he is, you have rendered him the most envied of men! – One thing more, and I have done: – Will he marry you?"

What a question! my cheeks glowed with indignation, and I felt too proud to make any answer.

"I see, I see how it is," cried he, after a short pause, "and I find I am undone for ever!" Then, letting loose my gown, he put his hand to his forehead, and walked up and down the room in a hasty and agitated manner.

Though now at liberty to go, I had not the courage to leave him: for his evident distress excited all my compassion. And this was our situation, when Lady Louisa, Mr. Coverley, and Mrs. Beaumont entered the room.

"Sir Clement Willoughby," said the latter, "I beg pardon for making you wait so long, but – "

She had not time for another word; Sir Clement, too much disordered to know or care what he did, snatched up his hat, and, brushing hastily past her, flew down stairs, and out of the house.

And with him went my sincerest pity, though I earnestly hope I shall see him no more. But what, my dear Sir, am I to conclude from his strange speeches concerning the letter? does it not seem as if he was himself the author of it? How else should he be so well acquainted with the contempt it merits? Neither do I know another human being who could serve any interest by such a deception. I remember, too, that just as I had given my own letter to the maid, Sir Clement came into the shop; probably he prevailed upon her, by some bribery, to give it to him, and afterwards, by the same means, to deliver to me an answer of his own writing. Indeed I can in no other manner account for this affair. Oh, Sir Clement, were you not yourself unhappy, I know not how I could pardon an artifice that has caused me so much uneasiness!

His abrupt departure occasioned a kind of general consternation.

"Very extraordinary behaviour this!" cried Mrs. Beaumont.

"Egad," said Mr. Coverley, "the Baronet has a mind to tip us a touch of the heroicks[1] this morning!"

"I declare," cried Lady Louisa, "I never saw any thing so monstrous in my life! it's quite abominable, – I fancy the man's mad; – I'm sure he has given me a shocking fright!"

Soon after, Mrs. Selwyn came up stairs, with Lord Merton. The former, advancing hastily to me, said, "Miss Anville, have you an almanack?"[2]

"Me! – no, Madam."

"Who has one, then?"

"Egad," cried Mr. Coverley, "I never bought one in my life; it would make me quite melancholy to have such a time-keeper in my pocket. I would as soon walk all day before an hour-glass."

"You are in the right," said Mrs. Selwyn, "not to *watch time*, lest you should be betrayed, unawares, into reflecting how you employ it."

"Egad, Ma'am," cried he, "if Time thought no more of me,

---

1   To "tip" is "to put on, present, or exhibit the character of" (*OED*); in this case, Mr. Coverley indicates rather sarcastically that Sir Clement has exhibited for his audience the "high-flown and bombastic ... sentiments" common for the hero of tragic dramas of the late seventeenth and the eighteenth centuries.

2   "An annual table, or (more usually) a book of tables, containing a calendar of months and days, with astronomical data and calculations, ecclesiastical and other anniversaries, besides other useful information, and, in former days, astrological and astrometeorlogical forecasts" (*OED*).

than I do of Time, I believe I should bid defiance, for one while, to old age and wrinkles, – for deuce take me if ever I think about it at all."

"Pray, Mr. Coverley," said Mrs. Selwyn, "why do you think it necessary to tell me this so often?"

"Often!" repeated he, "Egad, Madam, I don't know why I said it now, – but I'm sure I can't recollect that ever I owned as much before."

"Owned it before!" cried she, "why, my dear Sir, you own it all day long; for every word, every look, every action proclaims it."

I know not if he understood the full severity of her satire, but he only turned off with a laugh: and she then applied to Mr. Lovel, and asked if *he* had an almanack?

Mr. Lovel, who always looks alarmed when she addresses him, with some hesitation answered, "I assure you, Ma'am, I have no manner of antipathy to an almanack, – none in the least, I assure you; – I dare say I have four or five."

"Four or five! – pray may I ask what use you make of so many?"

"Use! – really, Ma'am, as to that, – I don't make any particular use of them, – but one must have them, to tell one the day of the month, – I'm sure, else, I should never keep it in my head."

"And does your time pass so smoothly unmarked, that, without an almanack, you could not distinguish one day from another?"

"Really, Ma'am," cried he, colouring, "I don't see any thing so very particular in having a few almanacks; other people have them, I believe, as well as me."

"Don't be offended," cried she, "I have but made a little digression. All I want to know, is the state of the moon,[1] – for if it is at the *full* I shall be saved a world of conjectures, and know at once to what cause to attribute the inconsistencies I have witnessed this morning. In the first place, I heard Lord Orville excuse himself from going out, because he had business of

---

1 A full moon was said to cause people to act strangely.

importance to transact at home, – yet have I seen him sauntering alone in the garden this half-hour. Miss Anville, on the
other hand, I invited to walk out with me; and, after seeking
her every where round the house, I find her quietly seated in
the drawing-room. And but a few minutes since, Sir Clement
Willoughby, with even more than his usual politeness, told me
he was come to spend the morning here, – when, just now, I
met him flying down stairs, as if pursued by the Furies;[1] and, far
from repeating his compliments, or making any excuse, he did
not even answer a question I asked him, but rushed past me,
with the rapidity of a thief from a bailiff!"

"I protest," said Miss Beaumont, "I can't think what he
meant; such rudeness from a man of any family is quite incomprehensible."

"My Lord," cried Lady Louisa to Lord Merton, "do you
know he did the same by *me*? – I was just going to ask him
what was the matter, but he ran past me so quick, that I declare
he quite dazzled my eyes. You can't think, my Lord, how he
frighted me; I dare say I look as pale – don't I look very pale,
my Lord?"

"Your Ladyship," said Mr. Lovel, "so well becomes the lilies,
that the roses might blush to see themselves so excelled."

"Pray, Mr. Lovel," said Mrs. Selwyn, "if the roses should
blush, how would you find it out?

"Egad," cried Mr. Coverley, "I suppose they must blush, as
the saying is, like a blue dog,[2] – for they are *red* already."

"Prithee, Jack," said Lord Merton, "don't you pretend to talk
about blushes, that never knew what they were in your life."

"My Lord," said Mrs. Selwyn, "if experience alone can justify mentioning them, what an admirable treatise upon the subject may we not expect from your Lordship!"

"O, pray, Ma'am," answered he, "stick to Jack Coverley, – he's
your only man; for my part, I confess I have a mortal aversion
to arguments."

"O fie, my Lord," cried Mrs. Selwyn, "a senator of the

---

1   The three Furies – Alecto, Magaera, and Tisiphone – were female "spirits of pun-
    ishment avenging wrongs done to kindred" (Cooke 298).
2   To blush like a blue dog is to not blush at all.

nation! a member of the noblest parliament in the world! – and yet neglect the art of oratory?"

"Why, faith, my Lord," said Mr. Lovel, "I think, in general, your house is not much addicted to study; we of the lower House[1] have indubitably most application; and, if I did not speak before a superior power," bowing low to Lord Merton, "I should presume to add, we have likewise the most able speakers."

"Mr. Lovel," said Mrs. Selwyn, "you deserve immortality for that discovery! But for this observation, and the confession of Lord Merton, I protest I should have supposed that a peer of the realm, and an able logician, were synonymous terms."

Lord Merton, turning upon his heel, asked Lady Louisa if she should *take the air* before dinner?

"Really," answered she, "I don't know; – I'm afraid it's monstrous hot; besides," (putting her hand to her forehead) "I a'n't half well; it's quite horrid to have such weak nerves! – the least thing in the world discomposes me: I declare, that man's oddness has given me such a shock, – I don't know when I shall recover from it. But I'm a sad weak creature, – don't you think I am, my Lord?"

"O, by no means," answered he, "your Ladyship is merely delicate, – and devil take me if ever I had the least passion for an Amazon."[2]

"I have the honour to be quite of your Lordship's opinion," said Mr. Lovel, looking maliciously at Mrs. Selwyn, "for I have an insuperable aversion to strength, either of body or mind, in a female."

"Faith, and so have I," said Mr. Coverley; "for egad I'd as soon see a woman chop wood, as hear her chop logic."[3]

---

1    Lord Merton is a member of the House of Lords (the "upper" House of the British Parliament) by virtue of his noble birth; Lovel was elected to the House of Commons (the "lower" House).

2    "Tribe of female warriors who lived east of the Greek regions of Asia Minor. They cut off their right breasts in order to use the bow more easily – 'Amazon' means breastless. They had no dealings with men except for breeding and as opponents in war; they reared only their female young" (Zimmerman 19).

3    One who chops logic is a "contentious, sophistical arguer" (*OED*), shrewd and aggressive in her arguing.

"So would every man in his senses," said Lord Merton; "for a woman wants nothing to recommend her but beauty and good-nature; in every thing else she is either impertinent or unnatural. For my part, deuce take me if ever I wish to hear a word of sense from a woman as long as I live!"

"It has always been agreed," said Mrs. Selwyn, looking round her with the utmost contempt, "that no man ought to be connected with a woman whose understanding is superior to his own. Now I very much fear, that to accommodate all this good company, according to such a rule, would be utterly impracticable, unless we should chuse subjects from Swift's hospital of idiots."[1]

How many enemies, my dear Sir, does this unbounded severity excite! Lord Merton, however, only whistled; Mr. Coverley sang; and Mr. Lovel, after biting his lips some time, said, "'Pon honour, that lady – if she was *not* a lady, – I should be half tempted to observe, – that there is something, – in such severity, – that is rather, I must say, – rather – *oddish.*"

Just then, a servant brought Lady Louisa a note, upon a *waiter,*[2] which is a ceremony always used to her Ladyship; and I took the opportunity of this interruption to the conversation, to steal out of the room.

I went immediately to the parlour, which I found quite empty; for I did not dare walk in the garden after what Mrs. Selwyn had said.

In a few minutes, a servant announced Mr. Macartney, saying, as he entered the room, that he would acquaint Lord Orville he was there.

Mr. Macartney rejoiced much at finding me alone. He told me he had taken the liberty to enquire for Lord Orville, by way of pretext for coming to the house.

I then very eagerly enquired if he had seen his father.

"I have, Madam," said he; "and the generous compassion you have shewn made me hasten to acquaint you, that upon reading

---

1   Jonathan Swift (1667-1745) wrote *A Serious and Useful Scheme to Make an Hospital for Incurables* (Dublin 1733) and describes a madhouse in *A Tale of a Tub* (1704); he left money in his will to St. Patrick's Hospital for the treatment of the mentally ill.
2   "A salver, small tray" (*OED*).

my unhappy mother's letter, he did not hesitate to acknowledge me."

"Good God," cried I, with no little emotion, "how similar
are our circumstances! And did he receive you kindly?"

"I could not, Madam, expect that he would: the cruel transaction which obliged me to fly Paris, was too recent in his
memory."

"And, – have you seen the young lady?"

"No, Madam," said he mournfully, "I was forbid her sight."

"Forbid her sight! – and why?"

"Partly, perhaps, from prudence, – and partly from the
remains of a resentment which will not easily subside. I only
requested leave to acquaint her with my relationship, and be
allowed to call her sister; – but it was denied me! – *You have no
sister*, said Sir John, *you must forget her existence*. Hard, and vain
command!"

"You have, you have a sister!" cried I, from an impulse of
pity which I could not repress, "a sister who is most warmly
interested in your welfare, and who only wants opportunity to
manifest her friendship and regard."

"Gracious Heaven!" cried he, "what does Miss Anville
mean?"

"Anville," said I, "is not my real name; Sir John Belmont is
my father, – he is your's, – and I am your sister! – You see,
therefore, the claim we mutually have to each other's regard; we
are not merely bound by the ties of friendship, but by those of
blood. I feel for you, already, all the affection of a sister, – I felt
it, indeed, before I knew I was one. – Why, my dear brother, do
you not speak? – do you hestitate to acknowledge me?"

"I am so lost in astonishment," cried he, "that I know not if I
hear right!" –

"I have then found a brother," cried I, holding out my hand,
"and he will not own me!"

"Own you! – Oh, Madam," cried he, accepting my offered
hand, "is it, indeed, possible *you* can own *me*? – a poor,
wretched adventurer! who so lately had no support but from
your generosity? – whom your benevolence snatched from
utter destruction? – Can *you*, – Oh Madam, can you indeed,

and without a blush, condescend to own such an outcast for a brother?"

"Oh, forbear, forbear," cried I, "is this language proper for a sister? are we not reciprocally bound to each other? – Will you not suffer me to expect from *you* all the good offices in your power? – But tell me, where is our father at present?"

"At the Hotwell, Madam; he arrived there yesterday morning."

I would have proceeded with further questions, but the entrance of Lord Orville prevented me. The moment he saw us, he started, and would have retreated; but, drawing my hand from Mr. Macartney's, I begged him to come in.

For a few moments we were all silent, and, I believe, all in equal confusion. Mr. Macartney, however, recollecting himself, said, "I hope your Lordship will forgive the liberty I have taken in making use of your name?"

Lord Orville, rather coldly, bowed, but said nothing.

Again we were all silent, and then Mr. Macartney took leave.

"I fancy," said Lord Orville, when he was gone, "I have shortened Mr. Macartney's visit?"

"No, my Lord, not at all."

"I had presumed," said he, with some hesitation, "I should have seen Miss Anville in the garden; – but I knew not she was so much better engaged."

Before I could answer, a servant came to tell me the chaise was ready, and that Mrs. Selwyn was enquiring for me.

"I will wait on her immediately," cried I, and away I was running; but Lord Orville, stopping me, said, with great emotion, "Is it thus, Miss Anville, you leave me?"

"My Lord," cried I, "how can I help it? – perhaps, soon, some better opportunity may offer – "

"Good Heaven!" cried he, "do you indeed take me for a Stoic?[1] What better opportunity may I hope for? – is not the chaise come? – are you not going? have you even deigned to tell me whither?"

---

1  "One who practices repression of emotion, indifference to pleasure or pain, and patient endurance" (*OED*). The Stoic philosophy developed under the Greek Zeno (fl. c. 300 B.C.).

"My journey, my Lord, will now be deferred. Mr. Macartney has brought me intelligence which renders it, at present, unnecessary."

"Mr. Macartney," said he, gravely, "seems to have great influence, – yet he is a very young counsellor."

"Is it possible, my Lord, Mr. Macartney can give you the least uneasiness?"

"My dearest Miss Anville," said he, taking my hand, "I see, and I adore the purity of your mind, superior as it is to all little arts, and all apprehensions of suspicion; and I should do myself, as well as you, injustice, if I were capable of harbouring the smallest doubts of that goodness which makes you mine for ever: nevertheless, pardon me, if I own myself surprised, – nay, alarmed, at these frequent meetings with so young a man as Mr. Macartney."

"My Lord," cried I, eager to clear myself, "Mr. Macartney is my brother!"

"Your brother! you amaze me! – What strange mystery, then, makes his relationship a secret?"

Just then, Mrs. Selwyn opened the door. "O, you are here!" cried she; "Pray is my Lord so kind as to assist you in *preparing* for your journey, – or in *retarding* it?"

"I should be most happy," said Lord Orville, smiling, "if it were in my power to do the *latter*."

I then acquainted her with Mr. Macartney's communication.

She immediately ordered the chaise away, and then took me into her own room, to consider what should be done.

A few minutes sufficed to determine her, and she wrote the following note.

*To Sir John Belmont, Bart.*[1]

Mrs. Selwyn presents her compliments to Sir John Belmont, and, if he is at leisure, will be glad to wait on him this morning, upon business of importance.

---

1  Baronet.

She then ordered her man to enquire at the pump-room for a direction; and went herself to Mrs. Beaumont to apologise for deferring her journey.

An answer was presently returned, that he would be glad to see her.

She would have had me immediately accompany her to the Hotwells; but I entreated her to spare me the distress of so abrupt an introduction, and to pave the way for my reception. She consented rather reluctantly, and, attended only by her servant, walked to the Wells.

She was not absent two hours, yet so miserably did time seem to linger, that I thought a thousand accidents had happened, and feared she would never return. I passed the whole time in my own room, for I was too much agitated even to converse with Lord Orville.

The instant that, from my window, I saw her returning, I flew down stairs, and met her in the garden.

We both walked to the arbour.

Her looks, in which disappointment and anger were expressed, presently announced to me the failure of her embassy. Finding that she did not speak, I asked her, in a faultering voice, Whether or not I had a father?

"You have *not*, my dear!" said she, abruptly.

"Very well, Madam," said I, with tolerable calmness, "let the chaise, then, be ordered again, – I will go to Berry Hill, – and there, I trust, I shall still find one!"

It was some time ere she could give, or I could hear, the account of her visit; and then she related it in a hasty manner; yet I believe I can recollect every word.

"I found Sir John alone. He received me with the utmost politeness. I did not keep him a moment in suspense as to the purport of my visit. But I had no sooner made it known, than, with a supercilious smile, he said, "And have you, Madam, been prevailed upon to revive that ridiculous old story?" Ridiculous, I told him, was a term which he would find no one else do him the favour to make use of, in speaking of the horrible actions belonging to the *old story* he made so light of; "actions," continued I, "which would dye still deeper the black annals of

Nero or Caligula."[1] He attempted in vain to rally, for I pursued him with all the severity in my power, and ceased not painting the enormity of his crime, till I stung him to the quick, and, in a voice of passion and impatience, he said, "No more, Madam, – this is not a subject upon which I need a monitor." "Make, then," cried I, "the only reparation in your power. – Your daughter is now at Clifton; send for her hither, and, in the face of the world, proclaim the legitimacy of her birth, and clear the reputation of your injured wife." "Madam," said he, "you are much mistaken, if you suppose I waited for the honour of this visit, before I did what little justice now depends upon me, to the memory of that unfortunate woman: her daughter has been my care from her infancy; I have taken her into my house; she bears my name, and she will be my sole heiress." For some time this assertion appeared so absurd, that I only laughed at it; but at last, he assured me, I had myself been imposed upon, for that the very woman who attended Lady Belmont in her last illness, conveyed the child to him while he was in London, before she was a year old. "Unwilling," he added, "at that time to confirm the rumour of my being married, I sent the woman with the child to France; as soon as she was old enough, I put her into a convent, where she has been properly educated; and now I have taken her home. I have acknowledged her for my lawful child, and paid, at length, to the memory of her unhappy mother, a tribute of fame,[2] which has made me wish to hide myself hereafter from all the world." This whole story sounded so improbable, that I did not scruple to tell him I discredited every word. He then rung his bell, and enquiring if his hair-dresser was come, said he was sorry to leave me, but that, if I would favour him with my company to-morrow, he would do himself the honour of introducing Miss Belmont to *me*, instead of troubling me to introduce her to *him*. I rose in great indig-

---

1  Caligula ruled Rome from 37-42 A.D.; Nero was Roman emperor from 54-68 A.D. Both were tyrannical, politically and personally ruthless, and unstable rulers who caused their subjects as well as friends and relatives much suffering.

2  Sir John believes that in publicly acknowledging his daughter and, thereby, his shameful behavior to her mother, his reputation has been ruined.

nation, and, assuring him I would make his conduct as public as it was infamous, I left the house."

Good Heaven, how strange the recital! how incomprehensible an affair! The Miss Belmont, then, who is actually at Bristol, passes for the daughter of my unhappy mother! – passes, in short, for your Evelina! Who she can be, or what this tale can mean, I have not any idea.

Mrs. Selwyn soon after left me to my own reflections. Indeed they were not very pleasant. Quietly as I had borne her relation, the moment I was alone I felt most bitterly both the disgrace and the sorrow of a rejection so cruelly inexplicable.

I know not how long I might have continued in this situation, had I not been awakened from my melancholy reverie by the voice of Lord Orville. "May I come in," cried he, "or shall I interrupt you?"

I was silent, and he seated himself next me.

"I fear," he continued, "Miss Anville will think I persecute her; yet so much as I have to say, and so much as I wish to hear, with so few opportunities for either, she cannot wonder, – and I hope she will not be offended, – that I seize with such avidity every moment in my power to converse with her. You are grave," added he, taking my hand; "I hope you do not regret the delay of your journey? – I hope the pleasure it gives to *me*, will not be a subject of pain to *you*? – You are silent? – Something, I am sure, has afflicted you: – Would to Heaven I were able to console you! – Would to Heaven I were worthy to participate in your sorrows!"

My heart was too full to bear this kindness, and I could openly answer by my tears. "Good Heaven," cried he, "how you alarm me! – My love, my sweet Miss Anville, deny me no longer to be the sharer of your griefs! – tell me, at least, that you have not withdrawn your esteem! – that you do not repent the goodness you have shewn me! – that you still think me the same grateful Orville whose heart you have deigned to accept!"

"Oh, my Lord," cried I, "your generosity overpowers me!" And I wept like an infant. For now that all my hopes of being acknowledged seemed finally crushed, I felt the nobleness of his disinterested regard so forcibly, that I could scarce breathe under the weight of gratitude which oppressed me.

He seemed greatly shocked, and in terms the most flattering, the most respectfully tender, he at once soothed my distress, and urged me to tell him its cause.

"My Lord," said I, when I was able to speak, "you little know what an outcast you have honoured with your choice! – a child of bounty, – an orphan from infancy, – dependent, even for subsistence dependent, upon the kindness of compassion! – Rejected by my natural friends, – disowned for ever by my nearest relation, – Oh, my Lord, so circumstanced, can I deserve the distinction with which you honour me? No, no, I feel the inequality too painfully; – you must leave me, my Lord, you must suffer me to return to obscurity, – and there, in the bosom of my first, best, – my only friend, – I will pour forth all the grief of my heart! – while you, my Lord, must seek elsewhere –"

I could not proceed; my whole soul recoiled against the charge I would have given, and my voice refused to utter it.

"Never!" cried he, warmly; "my heart is yours, and I swear to you an attachment eternal! – You prepare me, indeed, for a tale of horror, and I am almost breathless with expectation, – but so firm is my conviction, that, whatever are your misfortunes, to have merited them is not of the number, that I feel myself more strongly, more invincibly devoted to you than ever! – Tell me but where I may find this noble friend, whose virtues you have already taught me to reverence, – and I will fly to obtain his consent and intercession, that henceforward our fates may be indissolubly united, – and then shall it be the sole study of my life to endeavour to soften your past, – and guard you from future misfortunes!"

I had just raised my eyes, to answer this most generous of men, when the first object they met was Mrs. Selwyn!

"So, my dear," cried she, "what, still courting the rural shades! – I thought ere now you would have been satiated with this retired seat, and I have been seeking you all over the house.

But I find the only way to meet with *you*, – is to enquire for *Lord Orville*. However, don't let me disturb your meditations; you are possibly planning some pastoral dialogue."

And, with this provoking speech, she walked on.

In the greatest confusion, I was quitting the arbour, when Lord Orville said, "Permit *me* to follow Mrs. Selwyn, – it is time to put an end to all impertinent conjectures; will you allow me to speak to her openly?"

I assented in silence, and he left me.

I then went to my own room, where I continued till I was summoned to dinner; after which, Mrs. Selwyn invited me to her's.

The moment she had shut the door, "Your Ladyship," said she, "will, I hope, be seated."

"Ma'am!" cried I, staring.

"O the sweet innocent! So you don't know what I mean? – but, my dear, my sole view is to accustom you a little to your dignity elect, lest, when you are addressed by your title, you should look another way, from an apprehension of listening to a discourse not meant for you to hear."

Having, in this manner, diverted herself with my confusion, till her raillery was almost exhausted, she congratulated me very seriously upon the partiality of Lord Orville, and painted to me, in the strongest terms, his disinterested desire of being married to me immediately. She had told him, she said, my whole story; and yet he was willing, nay eager, that our union should take place of any further application to my family. "Now, my dear," continued she, "I advise you by all means to marry him directly; nothing can be more precarious than our success with Sir John; and the young men of this age are not to be trusted with too much time for deliberation, where their interests are concerned."

"Good God, Madam," cried I, "do you think I would *hurry* Lord Orville?"

"Well, do as you will," said she; "luckily you have an excellent subject for Quixotism;[1] – otherwise, this delay might prove

---

1    A reference to Cervantes' Don Quixote, "an enthusiastic visionary person ... inspired by lofty and chivalrous but false or unrealizable ideals" (*OED*). Mrs. Sel-

your ruin: but Lord Orville is almost as romantic as if he had been born and bred at Berry Hill."

She then proposed, as no better expedient seemed likely to be suggested, that I should accompany her at once in her visit to the Hotwells to-morrow morning.

The very idea made me tremble; yet she represented so strongly the necessity of pursuing this unhappy affair with spirit, or giving it totally up, that, wanting her force of argument, I was almost obliged to yield to her proposal.

In the evening, we all walked in the garden: and Lord Orville, who never quitted my side, told me he had been listening to a tale, which, though it had removed the perplexities that had so long tormented him, had penetrated him with sorrow and compassion. I acquainted him with Mrs. Selwyn's plan for to-morrow, and confessed the extreme terror it gave me. He then, in a manner almost unanswerable, besought me to leave to him the conduct of the affair, by consenting to be his before an interview took place.

I could not but acknowledge my sense of his generosity; but I told him I was wholly dependent upon you, and that I was certain your opinion would be the same as mine, which was, that it would be highly improper I should dispose of myself for ever, so very near the time which must finally decide by whose authority I ought to be guided. The subject of this dreaded meeting, with the thousand conjectures and apprehensions to which it gives birth, employed all our conversation then, as it has all my thoughts since.

Heaven only knows how I shall support myself, when the long-expected, – the wished, – yet terrible moment arrives, that will prostrate me at the feet of the nearest, the most reverenced of all relations, whom my heart yearns to know, and longs to love!

---

wyn finds Lord Orville's lack of concern for Evelina's parentage or prospects generous but also unusual and therefore somewhat suspect.

# LETTER XVII.

*Evelina in continuation.*

Oct. 9.

I could not write yesterday, so violent was the agitation of my mind, – but I will not, now, lose a moment till I have hastened to my best friend an account of the transactions of a day I can never recollect without emotion.

Mrs. Selwyn determined upon sending no message, "Lest," said she, "Sir John, fatigued with the very idea of my reproaches, should endeavour to avoid a meeting: all we have to do, is to take him by surprise. He cannot but see who you are, whether he will do you justice or not."

We went early, and in Mrs. Beaumont's chariot; into which, Lord Orville, uttering words of the kindest encouragement, handed us both.

My uneasiness, during the ride, was excessive, but, when we stopped at the door, I was almost senseless with terror! the meeting, at last, was not so dreadful as that moment! I believe I was carried into the house; but I scarce recollect what was done with me: however, I know we remained some time in the parlour, before Mrs. Selwyn could send any message up stairs.

When I was somewhat recovered, I entreated her to let me return home, assuring her I felt myself quite unequal to supporting the interview.

"No," said she, "you must stay now; your fears will but gain strength by delay, and we must not have such a shock as this repeated." Then, turning to the servant, she sent up her name.

An answer was brought, that he was going out in great haste, but would attend her immediately. I turned so sick, that Mrs. Selwyn was apprehensive I should have fainted; and opening a door which led to an inner apartment, she begged me to wait there till I was somewhat composed, and till she had prepared for my reception.

Glad of every moment's reprieve, I willingly agreed to the proposal, and Mrs. Selwyn had but just time to shut me in, before her presence was necessary.

The voice of a *father* – Oh dear and revered name! – which then, for the first time, struck my ears, affected me in a manner I cannot describe, though it was only employed in giving orders to a servant as he came down stairs.

Then, entering the parlour, I heard him say, "I am sorry, Madam, I made you wait, but I have an engagement which now calls me away: however, if you have any commands for me, I shall be glad of the honour of your company some other time."

"I am come, Sir," said Mrs. Selwyn, "to introduce your daughter to you."

"I am infinitely obliged to you," answered he, "but I have just had the satisfaction of breakfasting with her. Ma'am, your most obedient."

"You refuse, then, to see her?"

"I am much indebted to you, Madam, for this desire of encreasing my family, but you must excuse me if I decline taking advantage of it. I have already a daughter, to whom I owe every thing; and it is not three days since, that I had the pleasure of discovering a son; how many more sons and daughters may be brought to me, I am yet to learn, but I am, already, perfectly satisfied with the size of my family."

"Had you a thousand children, Sir John," said Mrs. Selwyn, warmly, "this only one, of which Lady Belmont was the mother, ought to be most distinguished; and, far from avoiding her sight, you should thank your stars, in humble gratitude, that there yet remains in your power the smallest opportunity of doing the injured wife you have destroyed, the poor justice of acknowledging her child!"

"I am very unwilling, Madam," answered he, "to enter into any discussion of this point; but you are determined to compel me to speak. There lives not, at this time, the human being who should talk to *me* of the regret due to the memory of that ill-fated woman; no one can feel it so severely as myself: but let me, nevertheless, assure you I have already done all that remained in my power to prove the respect she merited from me; her child I have educated and owned for my lawful heiress; if, Madam, you can suggest to me any other means by which I may more fully do her justice, and more clearly manifest her innocence, name them to me, and though they should wound my character still deeper, I will perform them readily."

"All this sounds vastly well," returned Mrs. Selwyn, "but I must own it is rather too enigmatical for *my* faculties of comprehension. You can, however, have no objection to seeing this young lady?"

"None in the world."

"Come forth, then, my dear," cried she, opening the door, "come forth, and see your father!" Then, taking my trembling hand, she led me forward. I would have withdrawn it, and retreated, but as he advanced instantly towards me, I found myself already before him.

What a moment for your Evelina! – an involuntary scream escaped me, and covering my face with my hands, I sunk on the floor.

He had, however, seen me first; for in a voice scarce articulate he exclaimed, "My God! does Caroline Evelyn still live!"

Mrs. Selwyn said something, but I could not listen to her; and, in a few minutes, he added, "Lift up thy head, – if my sight has not blasted thee, – lift up thy head, thou image of my long-lost Caroline!"

Affected beyond measure, I half arose, and embraced his knees, while yet on my own.

"Yes, yes," cried he, looking earnestly in my face, "I see, I see thou art her child! she lives – she breathes – she is present to my view! – Oh God, that she indeed lived! – Go, child, go," added he, wildly starting, and pushing me from him, "take her away, Madam, – I cannot bear to look at her!" And then, breaking hastily from me, he rushed out of the room.

Speechless, motionless myself, I attempted not to stop him: but Mrs. Selwyn, hastening after him, caught hold of his arm. "Leave me, Madam," cried he, with quickness, "and take care of the poor child; – bid her not think me unkind, tell her I would at this moment plunge a dagger in my heart to serve her, – but she has set my brain on fire, and I can see her no more!" Then, with a violence almost frantic, he ran up stairs.

Oh Sir, had I not indeed cause to dread this interview? – an interview so unspeakably painful and afflicting to us both! Mrs.

Selwyn would have immediately returned to Clifton; but I entreated her to wait some time, in the hope that my unhappy father, when his first emotion was over, would again bear me in his sight. However, he soon after sent his servant to enquire how I did, and to tell Mrs. Selwyn he was much indisposed, but would hope for the honour of seeing her to-morrow, at any time she would please to appoint.

She fixed upon ten o'clock in the morning, and then, with a heavy heart, I got into the chariot. Those afflicting words, *I can see her no more*, were never a moment absent from my mind.

Yet the sight of Lord Orville, who handed us from the carriage, gave some relief to the sadness of my thoughts. I could not, however, enter upon the painful subject, but begging Mrs. Selwyn to satisfy him, I went to my own room.

As soon as I communicated to the good Mrs. Clinton the present situation of my affairs, an idea occurred to her, which seemed to clear up all the mystery of my having been so long disowned.

The woman, she says, who attended my ever-to-be-regretted mother in her last illness, and who nursed me the first four months of my life, soon after being discharged from your house, left Berry Hill entirely, with her baby, who was but six weeks[1] older than myself. Mrs. Clinton remembers, that her quitting the place appeared, at the time, very extraordinary to the neighbours, but, as she was never heard of afterwards, she was, by degrees, quite forgotten.

The moment this was mentioned, it struck Mrs. Selwyn, as well as Mrs. Clinton herself, that my father had been imposed upon, and that the nurse who said she had brought his child to him, had, in fact, carried her own.

The name by which I was known, the secrecy observed in regard to my family, and the retirement in which I lived, all conspired to render this scheme, however daring and fraudulent, by no means impracticable, and, in short, the idea was no sooner started, than conviction seemed to follow it.

Mrs. Selwyn determined immediately to discover the truth

---

1  The *Errata* to the first edition indicates "weeks" should replace "months." This change was not made until the third edition.

or mistake of this conjecture; therefore, the moment she had dined, she walked to the Hotwells, attended by Mrs. Clinton.

I waited in my room till her return, and then heard the following account of her visit.

She found my poor father in great agitation. She immediately informed him of the occasion of her so speedy return, and of her suspicions of the woman who had pretended to convey to him his child. Interrupting her with quickness, he said he had just sent her from his presence: that the certainty I carried in my countenance, of my real birth, made him, the moment he had recovered from a surprise which had almost deprived him of reason, suspect, himself, the imposition she mentioned. He had, therefore, sent for the woman, and questioned her with the utmost austerity: she turned pale, and was extremely embarrassed, but still she persisted in affirming, that she had really brought him the daughter of Lady Belmont. His perplexity, he said, almost distracted him; he had *always* observed that his daughter bore no resemblance to either of her parents, but, as he had never doubted the veracity of the nurse, this circumstance did not give birth to any suspicion.

At Mrs. Selwyn's desire, the woman was again called, and interrogated with equal art and severity; her confusion was evident, and her answers often contradictory, yet she still declared she was no impostor. "We will see that in a minute," said Mrs. Selwyn, and then desired Mrs. Clinton might be called up stairs. The poor wretch, changing colour, would have escaped out of the room, but, being prevented, dropt on her knees, and implored forgiveness. A confession of the whole affair was then extorted from her.

Doubtless, my dear Sir, you must remember *Dame Green*, who was my first nurse. The deceit she has practised, was suggested, she says, by a conversation she overheard, in which my unhappy mother besought you, that, if her child survived her, you would take the sole care of its education; and, in particular, if it should be a female, you would by no means part with her early in life. You not only consented, she says, but assured her you would even retire abroad with me yourself, if my father should importunately demand me. Her own child, she said, was then in her arms, and she could not forbear wishing it were possible to give *her* the fortune which seemed so little valued for me. This wish once raised, was not easily suppressed; on the contrary, what at first appeared a mere idle desire, in a short time seemed a feasible scheme. Her husband was dead, and she had little regard for any body but her child; and, in short, having saved money for the journey, she contrived to enquire a direction to my father, and telling her neighbours she was going to settle in Devonshire, she set out on her expedition.

When Mrs. Selwyn asked her, how she dared perpetrate such a fraud,[1] she protested she had no ill designs, but that, as *Miss* would be never the worse for it, she thought it pity *nobody* should be the better.

Her success we are already acquainted with. Indeed every thing seemed to contribute towards it: my father had no correspondent at Berry Hill, the child was instantly sent to France, where being brought up in as much retirement as myself, nothing but accident could discover the fraud.

And here, let me indulge myself in observing, and rejoicing to observe, that the total neglect I thought I met with, was not the effect of insensibility or unkindness, but of imposition and error; and that at the very time, we concluded I was unnaturally rejected, my deluded father meant to shew me most favour and protection.

He acknowledges that Lady Howard's letter flung him into some perplexity; he immediately communicated it to Dame Green, who confessed it was the greatest shock she had ever received in her life; yet she had the art and boldness to assert, that Lady Howard must herself have been deceived: and as she had, from the beginning of her enterprize, declared she had stolen away the child without your knowledge, he concluded that some deceit was *then* intended him; and this thought occasioned his abrupt answer.

Dame Green owned, that from the moment the journey to England was settled, she gave herself up for lost. All her hope

---

1 Such imposture has resulted in Sir John's paying for Polly's education and has endangered Evelina's inheritance. This abuse of property would be deemed theft and would be punishable under law (if Sir John were to prosecute Dame Greene).

was to have had her daughter married before it took place, for which reason she had so much promoted Mr. Macartney's addresses: for though such a match was inadequate to the pretensions of *Miss Belmont*, she well knew it was far superior to those *her daughter* could form, after the discovery of her birth.

My first enquiry was, if this innocent daughter was yet acquainted with the affair? No, Mrs. Selwyn said, nor was any plan settled how to divulge it to her. Poor unfortunate girl! how hard is her fate! She is entitled to my kindest offices, and I shall always consider her as my sister.

I then asked whether my father would again allow me to see him?

"Why no, my dear, not yet," answered she; "he declares the sight of you is too much for him: however, we are to settle every thing concerning you to-morrow, for this woman took up all our time to-day."

This morning, therefore, she is again gone to the Hotwell. I am waiting in all impatience for her return; but as I know you will be anxious for the account this letter contains, I will not delay sending it.

## LETTER XVIII.

*Evelina in continuation.*

Oct. 9.

How agitated, my dear Sir, is the present life of your Evelina! every day seems important, and one event only a prelude to another.

Mrs. Selwyn, upon her return this morning from the Hotwell, entering my room very abruptly, said, "Oh my dear, I have terrible news for you!"

"For me, Ma'am! – Good God! what now?"

"Arm yourself," cried she, "with all your Berry Hill philosophy; – con over every lesson of fortitude or resignation you ever learnt in your life, – for know, – you are next week to be married to Lord Orville!"

Doubt, astonishment, and a kind of perturbation I cannot describe, made this abrupt communication alarm me extremely, and, almost breathless, I could only exclaim, "Good God, Madam, what do you tell me?"

"You may well be frightened, my dear," said she, ironically, "for really there is something mighty terrific, in becoming, at once, the wife of the man you adore, – and a Countess!"[1]

I entreated her to spare her raillery, and tell me her real meaning. She could not prevail with herself to grant the *first* request, though she readily complied with the second.

My poor father, she said, was still in the utmost uneasiness. He entered upon his affairs with great openness, and told her he was equally disturbed how to dispose either of the daughter he had discovered, or the daughter he was now to give up; the former he dreaded to trust himself with again beholding, and the latter he knew not how to shock with the intelligence of her disgrace. Mrs. Selwyn then acquainted him with my situation in regard to Lord Orville; this delighted him extremely, and, when he heard of his Lordship's eagerness, he said he was himself of opinion, the sooner the union took place the better: and, in return, he informed her of the affair of Mr. Macartney. "And, after a very long conversation," continued Mrs. Selwyn, "we agreed, that the most eligible scheme for all parties would be to have both the real and the fictitious daughter married without delay. Therefore, if either of you have any inclination to pull caps for the title of Miss Belmont, you must do it with all speed, as next week will take from both of you all pretensions to it."

"Next week! – dear Madam, what a strange plan! – without my being consulted – without applying to Mr. Villars, – without even the concurrence of Lord Orville!"

"As to consulting *you*, my dear, it was out of all question, because, you know, young ladies' hearts and hands are always to be given with reluctance; – as to Mr. Villars, it is sufficient we know him for your friend; – and as for Lord Orville, he is a party concerned."

---

1  "In the peerage of Great Britain and Ireland, the wife or widow of an Earl" (*OED*), which is the position held by Lord Orville.

"A party concerned! – you amaze me!"

"Why, yes; for as I found our consultation likely to redound to his advantage, I persuaded Sir John to send for him."

"Send for him! – Good God!"

"Yes, and Sir John agreed. I told the servant, that if he could not hear of his Lordship in the house, he might be pretty certain of encountering him in the arbour. – Why do you colour, my dear? – Well, he was with us in a moment; I introduced him to Sir John, and we proceeded to business."

"I am very, very sorry for it! – Lord Orville must, himself, think this conduct strangely precipitate."

"No, my dear, you are mistaken, Lord Orville has too much good sense. Every thing was then discussed in a rational manner. You are to be married privately, though not secretly, and then go to one of his Lordship's country seats: and poor little Miss Green and your brother, who have no house of their own, must go to one of Sir John's."

"But why, my dear Madam, why all this haste? why may we not be allowed a little longer time."

"I could give you a thousand reasons," answered she, "but that I am tolerably certain *two* or *three* will be more than you can controvert, even with all the logic of genuine coquetry. In the first place, you doubtless wish to quit the house of Mrs. Beaumont, – to whose, then, can you with such propriety remove, as to Lord Orville's?"

"Surely, Madam," cried I, "I am not more destitute now, than when I thought myself an orphan?"

"Your father, my dear," answered she, "is willing to save the little impostor as much of the mortification of her disgrace as is in his power: now if you immediately take her place, according to your right, as Miss Belmont, why not all that either of you can do for her, will prevent her being eternally stigmatized, as the Bantling[1] of Dame Green, wash-woman and wet nurse of Berry Hill, Dorsetshire. Now such a genealogy will not be very flattering, even to Mr. Macartney, who, all-dismal as he is, you will find by no means wanting in pride and self-consequence."

---

1    "A young or small child, a brat. (Often used depreciatively, and formerly as a synonym of 'bastard')" (*OED*).

"For the universe," interrupted I, "I would not be accessary to the degradation you mention; but, surely, Madam, I may return to Berry Hill?"

"By no means," said she; "for though compassion may make us wish to save the poor girl the confusion of an immediate and public fall, yet justice demands you should appear, henceforward, in no other light than that of Sir John Belmont's daughter. Besides, between friends, I, who know the world, can see that half this prodigious delicacy for the little usurper, is the mere result of self-interest; for while *her* affairs are husht up, Sir John's, you know, are kept from being brought further to light. Now the double marriage we have projected, obviates all rational objections. Sir John will give you, immediately, £30,000; all settlements,[1] and so forth, will be made for you in the name of Evelina Belmont; – Mr. Macartney will, at the same time, take poor Polly Green, – and yet, at first, it will only be generally known, that *a daughter of Sir John Belmont's* is married."

In this manner, though she did not convince me, yet the quickness of her arguments silenced and perplexed me. I enquired, however, if I might not be permitted to again see my father, or whether I must regard myself as banished his presence for ever?

"My dear," said she, "he does not know you; he concludes that you have been brought up to detest him, and therefore he is rather prepared to dread, than to love you."

This answer made me very unhappy; I wished, most impatiently, to remove his prejudice, and endeavour, by dutiful assiduity, to engage his kindness, yet knew not how to propose seeing him, while conscious he wished to avoid me.

This evening, as soon as the company was engaged with cards, Lord Orville exerted his utmost eloquence to reconcile me to this hasty plan: but how was I startled, when he told me that next *Tuesday* was the day appointed by my father to be the most important of my life!

"Next Tuesday!" repeated I, quite out of breath, "Oh my Lord! – "

---

1 Property a woman would receive upon marriage from her family.

"My sweet Evelina," said he, "the day which will make me the happiest of mortals, would probably appear awful to you, were it to be deferred a twelvemonth: Mrs Selwyn has, doubtless, acquainted you with the many motives which, independent of my eagerness, require it to be speedy; suffer, therefore, its acceleration, and generously complete my felicity, by endeavouring to suffer it without repugnance."

"Indeed, my Lord, I would not wilfully raise objections, nor do I desire to appear insensible of the honour of your good opinion; – but there is something in this plan, so very hasty, – so unreasonably precipitate, – besides, I shall have no time to hear from Berry Hill, – and believe me, my Lord, I should be for ever miserable, were I in an affair so important, to act without the sanction of Mr. Villars' advice."

He offered to wait on you himself; but I told him I had rather write to you. And then he proposed, that, instead of my immediately accompanying him to Lincolnshire, we should, first, pass a month *at my native Berry Hill.*

This was, indeed, a grateful proposal to me, and I listened to it with undisguised pleasure. And, – in short, I was obliged to consent to a compromise, in merely deferring the day till Thursday! He readily undertook to engage my father's concurrence in this little delay, and I besought him, at the same time, to make use of his influence to obtain me a second interview, and to represent the deep concern I felt in being thus banished his sight.

He would then have spoken of *settlements,* but I assured him, I was almost ignorant even of the word.

And now, my dearest Sir, what is your opinion of these hasty proceedings? believe me, I half regret the simple facility with which I have suffered myself to be hurried into compliance, and, should you start but the smallest objection, I will yet insist upon being allowed more time.

I must now write a concise account of the state of my affairs to Howard Grove, and to Madame Duval.

Adieu, dearest and most honoured Sir! every thing, at present, depends upon your single decision, to which, though I yield in trembling, I yield implicitly.

# LETTER XIX.

*Evelina in continuation.*

Oct. 11.

Yesterday morning, as soon as breakfast was over, Lord Orville went to the Hotwells, to wait upon my father with my double petition.

Mrs. Beaumont then, in general terms, proposed a walk in the garden. Mrs. Selwyn said she had letters to write, but Lady Louisa arose to accompany her.

I had had some reason to imagine, from the notice with which her Ladyship had honoured me during breakfast, that her brother had acquainted her with my present situation: and her behaviour now confirmed my conjecture; for, when I would have gone up stairs, instead of suffering me, as usual, to pass disregarded, she called after me with an affected surprise, "Miss Anville, don't you walk with us?"

There seemed something so little-minded in this sudden change of conduct, that, from an involuntary emotion of contempt, I thanked her, with a coldness like her own, and declined her offer. Yet, observing that she blushed extremely at my refusal, and recollecting she was sister to Lord Orville, my indignation subsided, and upon Mrs. Beaumont's repeating the invitation, I accepted it.

Our walk proved extremely dull; Mrs. Beaumont, who never says much, was more silent than usual; Lady Louisa strove in vain to lay aside the restraint and distance she has hitherto preserved; and as to me, I was too conscious of the circumstances to which I owed their attention, to feel either pride or pleasure from receiving it.

Lord Orville was not long absent; he joined us in the garden with a look of gaiety and good-humour that revived us all. "You are just the party," said he, "I wished to see together. Will you, Madam," taking my hand, "allow me the honour of introducing you, by your real name, to two of my nearest relations? Mrs. Beaumont, give me leave to present to you the daughter of Sir John Belmont; a young lady who, I am sure, must long since have engaged your esteem and admiration, though you were a stranger to her birth."

"My Lord," said Mrs. Beaumont, graciously saluting[1] me, "the young lady's rank in life, – your Lordship's recommendation, – or her own merit, would any one of them have been sufficient to have entitled her to my regard; and I hope she has always met with that respect in my house which is so much her due; though, had I been sooner made acquainted with her family, I should, doubtless, have better known how to have secured it."

"Miss Belmont," said Lord Orville, "can receive no lustre from family, whatever she may give to it. Louisa, you will, I am sure, be happy to make yourself an interest in the friendship of Miss Belmont, whom I hope shortly," kissing my hand, and joining it with her Ladyship's, "to have the happiness of presenting to you by yet another name, and by the most endearing of all titles."

I believe it would be difficult to say whose cheeks were, at that moment, of the deepest dye, Lady Louisa's or my own; for the conscious pride with which she has hitherto slighted me, gave to her an embarrassment which equalled the confusion that an introduction so unexpected gave to me. She saluted me, however, and, with a faint smile, said, "I shall esteem myself very happy to profit by the honour of Miss Belmont's acquaintance."

I only courtsied, and we walked on; but it was evident, from the little surprise they expressed, that they had been already informed of the state of the affair.

We were, soon after, joined by more company: and Lord Orville then, in a low voice, took an opportunity to tell me the success of his visit. In the first place, Thursday was agreed to; and, in the second, my father, he said, was much concerned to hear of my uneasiness, sent me his blessing, and complied with my request of seeing him, with the same readiness he should agree to any other I could make. Lord Orville, therefore, settled that I should wait upon him in the evening, and, at his particular request, unaccompanied by Mrs. Selwyn.

---

1   A gesture of greeting, a kiss.

This kind message, and the prospect of so soon seeing him, gave me sensations of mixed pleasure and pain, which wholly occupied my mind till the time of my going to the Hotwell.

Mrs. Beaumont lent me her chariot, and Lord Orville absolutely insisted upon attending me. "If you go alone," said he, "Mrs. Selwyn will certainly be offended; but, if you allow me to conduct you, though she may give the freer scope to her raillery, she cannot possibly be affronted: and we had much better suffer her laughter, than provoke her satire."

Indeed, I must own I had no reason to regret being so accompanied; for his conversation supported my spirits from drooping, and made the ride seem so short, that we actually stopt at my father's door, before I knew we had proceeded ten yards.

He handed me from the carriage, and conducted me to the parlour, at the door of which I was met by Mr. Macartney. "Ah, my dear brother," cried I, "how happy am I to see you here!"

He bowed and thanked me. Lord Orville, then, holding out his hand, said, "Mr. Macartney, I hope we shall be better acquainted; I promise myself much pleasure from cultivating your friendship."

"Your Lordship does me but too much honour," answered Mr. Macartney.

"But where," cried I, "is my sister? for so I must already call, and always consider her: – I am afraid she avoids me; – you must endeavour, my dear brother, to prepossess her in my favour, and reconcile her to owning me."

"Oh Madam," cried he, "you are all goodness and benevolence! but at present, I hope you will excuse her, for I fear she has hardly fortitude sufficient to see you: in a short time, perhaps — "

"In a *very* short time, then," said Lord Orville, "I hope you will yourself introduce her, and that we shall have the pleasure of wishing you both joy: allow me, my Evelina, to say *we*, and permit me, in your name as well as my own, to entreat that the first guests we shall have the happiness of receiving, may be Mr. and Mrs. Macartney."

A servant then came to beg I would walk up stairs.

I besought Lord Orville to accompany me; but he feared the displeasure of Sir John, who had desired to see me alone. He led me, however, to the foot of the stairs, and made the kindest efforts to give me courage; but indeed he did not succeed, for the interview appeared to me in all its terrors, and left me no feeling but apprehension.

The moment I reached the landing-place, the drawing-room door was opened, and my father, with a voice of kindness, called out, "My child, is it you?"

"Yes, Sir," cried I, springing forward, and kneeling at his feet, "it is your child, if you will own her!"

He knelt by my side, and folding me in his arms, "Own thee!" repeated he, "yes, my poor girl, and Heaven knows with what bitter contrition!" Then, raising both himself and me, he brought me into the drawing-room, shut the door, and took me to the window, where, looking at me with great earnestness, "Poor unhappy Caroline!" cried he, and, to my inexpressible concern, he burst into tears. Need I tell you, my dear Sir, how mine flowed at the sight?

I would again have embraced his knees; but, hurrying from me, he flung himself upon a sopha, and leaning his face on his arms, seemed, for some time, absorbed in bitterness of grief.

I ventured not to interrupt a sorrow I so much respected, but waited in silence, and at a distance, till he recovered from its violence. But then it seemed, in a moment, to give way to a kind of frantic fury; for, starting suddenly, with a sternness which at once surprised and frightened me. "Child," cried he, "hast thou yet sufficiently humbled thy father? – if thou hast, be contented with this proof of my weakness, and no longer force thyself into my presence!"

Thunderstruck by a command so unexpected, I stood still and speechless, and doubted whether my own ears did not deceive me.

"Oh, go, go!" cried he, passionately, "in pity – in compassion, – if thou valuest my senses, leave me, – and for ever!"

"I will, I will," cried I, greatly terrified; and I moved hastily towards the door: yet stopping when I reached it, and, almost involuntarily, dropping on my knees, "Vouchsafe," cried I, "oh, Sir, vouchsafe but once to bless your daughter, and her sight shall never more offend you!"

"Alas," cried he, in a softened voice, "I am not worthy to bless thee! – I am not worthy to call thee daughter! – I am not worthy that the fair light of heaven should visit my eyes! – Oh God! that I could but call back the time ere thou wast born, – or else bury its remembrance in eternal oblivion!"

"Would to Heaven," cried I, "that the sight of me were less terrible to you! that, instead of irritating, I could soothe your sorrows! – Oh Sir, how thankfully would I then prove my duty, even at the hazard of my life!"

"Are you so kind?" cried he, gently; "come hither, child, – rise, Evelina; – alas, it is for *me* to kneel, not you – and I *would* kneel, – I would crawl upon the earth, – I would kiss the dust, – could I, by such submission, obtain the forgiveness of the representative of the most injured of women!"

"Oh, Sir," exclaimed I, "that you could but read my heart! – that you could but see the filial tenderness and concern with which it overflows! – you would not then talk thus, – you would not then banish me your presence, and exclude me from your affection!"

"Good God," cried he, "is it then possible that you do not hate me? – Can the child of the wronged Caroline look at, – and not execrate me? Wast thou not born to abhor, and bred to curse me? did not thy mother bequeath thee her blessing, on condition that thou shouldst detest and avoid me?"

"Oh no, no, no!" cried I, "think not so unkindly of her, nor so hardly of me." I then took from my pocket-book her last letter, and, pressing it to my lips, with a trembling hand, and still upon my knees, I held it out to him.

Hastily snatching it from me, "Great Heaven!" cried he, "'tis her writing – Whence comes this? – who gave it you? – why had I it not sooner?"

I made no answer; his vehemence intimidated me, and I ventured not to move from the suppliant posture in which I had put myself.

He went from me to the window, where his eyes were for

some time rivetted upon the direction of the letter, though his hand shook so violently he could hardly hold it. Then, bringing it to me, "Open it," – cried he, – "for I cannot!"

I had, myself, hardly strength to obey him; but, when I had, he took it back, and walked hastily up and down the room, as if dreading to read it. At length, turning to me, "Do you know," cried he, "its contents?"

"No, Sir," answered I; "it has never been unsealed."

He then again went to the window, and began reading. Having hastily run it over, he cast up his eyes with a look of desperation; the letter fell from his hand, and he exclaimed, "Yes! thou art sainted! – thou art blessed! – and I am cursed for ever!" He continued some time fixed in this melancholy position; after which, casting himself with violence upon the ground, "Oh wretch," cried he, "unworthy life and light, in what dungeon canst thou hide thy head?"

I could restrain myself no longer; I rose and went to him; I did not dare speak, but with pity and concern unutterable, I wept and hung over him.

Soon after, starting up, he again seized the letter, exclaiming, "Acknowledge thee, Caroline! – yes, with my heart's best blood would I acknowledge thee! – Oh that thou couldst witness the agony of my soul! – Ten thousand daggers could not have wounded me like this letter!"

Then, after again reading it, "Evelina," he cried, "she charges me to receive thee; – wilt thou, in obedience to her will, own for thy father the destroyer of thy mother?"

What a dreadful question! I shuddered, but could not speak.

"To clear her fame, and receive her child," continued he, looking stedfastly at the letter, "are the conditions upon which she leaves me her forgiveness: her fame, I have already cleared; – and oh how willingly would I take her child to my bosom, – fold her to my heart, – call upon her to mitigate my anguish, and pour the balm of comfort on my wounds, were I not conscious I deserve not to receive it, and that all my affliction is the result of my own guilt!"

It was in vain I attempted to speak; horror and grief took from me all power of utterance.

He then read aloud from the letter, "*Look not like thy unfortunate mother!* – Sweet soul, with what bitterness of spirit hast thou written? – Come hither, Evelina: Gracious Heaven!" looking earnestly at me, "never was likeness more striking! – the eye, – the face, – the form, – Oh my child, my child!" Imagine, Sir, – for I can never describe my feelings, when I saw him sink upon his knees before me! "Oh dear resemblance of thy murdered mother! – Oh all that remains of the most-injured of women! behold thy father at thy feet! – bending thus lowly to implore you would not hate him; – Oh then, thou representative of my departed wife, speak to me in her name, and say that the remorse which tears my soul, tortures me not in vain!"

"Oh rise, rise, my beloved father," cried I, attempting to assist him, "I cannot bear to see you thus; – reverse not the law of nature, rise yourself, and bless your kneeling daughter!"

"May Heaven bless thee, my child! –" cried he, "for *I* dare not." He then rose, and embracing me most affectionately, added, "I see, I see that thou art all kindness, softness, and tenderness; I need not have feared thee, thou art all the fondest father could wish, and I will try to frame my mind to less painful sensations at thy sight. Perhaps the time may come when I may know the comfort of such a daughter, – at present, I am only fit to be alone: dreadful as are my reflections, they ought merely to torment myself. – Adieu, my child; – be not angry, – I cannot stay with thee, – oh Evelina! thy countenance is a dagger to my heart! – just so, thy mother looked, – just so –"

Tears and sighs seemed to choak him! – and waving his hand, he would have left me, – but, clinging to him, "Oh, Sir," cried I, "will you so soon abandon me? – am I again an orphan? – oh my dear, my long-lost father, leave me not, I beseech you! take pity on your child, and rob her not of the parent she so fondly hoped would cherish her!"

"You know not what you ask," cried he; "the emotions which now rend my soul are more than my reason can endure: suffer me, then, to leave you, – impute it not to unkindness, but think of me as well as thou canst. – Lord Orville has behaved nobly; – I believe he will make thee happy." Then, again embracing me, "God bless thee, my dear child," cried he, "God bless thee, my Evelina! – endeavour to love, – at least not to hate me, – and to make me an interest in thy filial bosom by thinking of me as thy father."

I could not speak; I kissed his hands on my knees; and then, with yet more emotion, he again blessed me, and hurried out of the room, – leaving me almost drowned in tears.

Oh Sir, all goodness as you are, how much will you feel for your Evelina, during a scene of such agitation! I pray Heaven to accept the tribute of his remorse, and restore him to tranquillity!

When I was sufficiently composed to return to the parlour, I found Lord Orville waiting for me with the utmost anxiety: – and then, a new scene of emotion, though of a far different nature, awaited me; for I learnt, by Mr. Macartney, that this noblest of men had insisted the so-long-supposed Miss Belmont should be considered *indeed* as my sister, and as the co-heiress of my father! though not in *law*, in *justice*, he says, she ought ever to be treated as the daughter of Sir John Belmont.

Oh Lord Orville! – it shall be the sole study of my happy life, to express, better than by words, the sense I have of your exalted benevolence, and greatness of mind!

## LETTER XX.

*Evelina in continuation.*

Clifton, Oct. 12.

This morning, early, I received the following letter from Sir Clement Willoughby.

*To Miss Anville.*

I have this moment received intelligence that preparations are actually making for your marriage with Lord Orville.

Imagine not that I write with the imbecile idea of rendering those preparations abortive. No, I am not so mad. My sole view is to explain the motive of my conduct in a particular instance, and to obviate the accusation of treachery which may be laid to my charge.

My unguarded behaviour when I last saw you, has, probably, already acquainted you, that the letter I then saw you reading was written by myself. For your further satisfaction, let me have the honour of informing you, that the letter you had designed for Lord Orville, had fallen into my hands.

However I may have been urged on by a passion the most violent that ever warmed the heart of man, I can by no means calmly submit to be stigmatised for an action seemingly so dishonourable; and it is for this reason that I trouble you with my justification.

Lord Orville, – the happy Orville, whom you are so ready to bless, – had made me believe he loved you not, – nay, that he held you in contempt.

Such were my thoughts of his sentiments of you, when I got possession of the letter you meant to send him; I pretend not to vindicate either the means I used to obtain it, or the action of breaking the seal; – but I was impelled by an impetuous curiosity to discover the terms upon which you wrote to him.

The letter, however, was wholly unintelligible to me, and the perusal of it only added to my perplexity.

A tame suspense I was not born to endure, and I determined to clear my doubts at all hazards and events.

I answered it, therefore, in Orville's name.

The views which I am now going to acknowledge, must, infallibly, incur your displeasure, – yet I scorn all palliation.

Briefly, then, – I concealed your letter to prevent a discovery of your capacity, – and I wrote you an answer which I hoped would prevent your wishing for any other.

I am well aware of every thing which can be said upon this subject. Lord Orville will, possibly, think himself ill used; – but I am extremely indifferent as to his opinion, nor do I now write by way of offering any apology to him, but merely to make known to yourself the reasons by which I have been governed.

I intend to set off next week for the Continent. Should his Lordship have any commands for me in the mean time, I shall be glad to receive them. I say not this by way of defiance, – I should blush to be suspected of so doing through an indirect channel, – but simply that, if you shew him this letter, he may know I dare defend, as well as excuse my conduct.

CLEMENT WILLOUGHBY.

What a strange letter! how proud and how piqued does its writer appear! To what alternate *meanness* and *rashness* do the passions lead, when reason and self-denial do not oppose them! Sir Clement is conscious he has acted dishonourably, yet the same unbridled vehemence which urged him to gratify a blameable curiosity, will sooner prompt him to risk his life, than confess his misconduct. The rudeness of his manner of writing to me springs from the same cause: the proof he has received of my indifference to him, has stung him to the soul, and he has neither the delicacy nor forbearance to disguise his displeasure.

I determined not to shew this letter to Lord Orville, and thought it most prudent to let Sir Clement[1] know I should not. I therefore wrote the following note.

*To Sir Clement Willoughby.*

Sir,

The letter you have been pleased to address to me, is so little calculated to afford Lord Orville any satisfaction, that you may depend upon my carefully keeping it from his sight. I will bear you no resentment for what is past; but I most earnestly entreat, nay implore, that you will not write again, while in your present frame of mind, by *any* channel, direct or indirect.

I hope you will have much pleasure in your purposed expedition, and I beg leave to assure you of my good wishes.

---

1   The *Errata* to the first edition indicates "Sir Clement" should replace "him." This change was not made to the second edition.

Not knowing by what name to sign, I was obliged to send it without any.

The *preparations* which Sir Clement mentions, go on just as if your consent were arrived: it is in vain that I expostulate; Lord Orville says, should any objections be raised, all shall be given up, but that, as his hopes forbid him to expect any, he must proceed as if already assured of your concurrence.

We have had, this afternoon, a most interesting conversation, in which we have traced our sentiments of each other from our first acquaintance. I have made him confess how ill he thought of me, upon my foolish giddiness at Mrs. Stanley's ball; but he flatters me with assurances, that every succeeding time he saw me, I appeared to something less and less disadvantage.

When I expressed my amazement that he could honour with his choice a girl who seemed so infinitely, in *every* respect, beneath his alliance, he frankly owned, that he had fully intended making more minute enquiries into my family and connections, and particularly concerning *those people* he saw me with at Marybone, before he acknowledged his prepossession in my favour: but the suddenness of my intended journey, and the uncertainty of seeing me again, put him quite off his guard, and "divesting him of prudence, left him nothing but love." These were his words; and yet, he has repeatedly assured me, that his partiality has known no bounds from the time of my residing at Clifton.

★    ★    ★    ★    ★

Mr. Macartney has just been with me, on an embassy from my father. He has sent me his kindest love, and assurances of favour, and desired to know if I am happy in the prospect of changing my situation, and if there is any thing I can name which he can do for me. And, at the same time, Mr. Macartney delivered to me a draught[1] on my father's banker for a thousand pounds, which he insisted that I should receive entirely for my own use, and expend in equipping myself properly for the new rank of life to which I seem destined.

I am sure I need not say how much I was penetrated by this

---

1    A bank draft, "a formal written order for the payment of money, 'drawn on,' or addressed to, a person holding funds available for this purpose" (*OED*).

goodness; I wrote my thanks, and acknowledged, frankly, that if I could see *him* restored to tranquillity, my heart would be without a wish.

## LETTER XXI.

*Evelina in continuation.*

Clifton, October 13.

The time approaches now, when I hope we shall meet, – yet I cannot sleep, – great joy is as restless as sorrow, – and therefore I will continue my journal.

As I had never had an opportunity of seeing Bath,[1] a party was formed last night for shewing me that celebrated city; and this morning, after breakfast, we set out in three phaetons. Lady Louisa and Mrs. Beaumont with Lord Merton; Mr. Coverley with Mr. Lovel; and Mrs. Selwyn and myself with Lord Orville.

We had hardly proceeded half a mile, when a gentleman from a post-chaise,[2] which came galloping after us, called out to the servants, "Holla, my Lads, – pray is one Miss Anville in any of them *thing-em-bobs*?"[3]

I immediately recollected the voice of Captain Mirvan, and Lord Orville stopt the phaeton. He was out of the chaise, and with us in a moment. "So, Miss Anville," cried he, "how do you do? so I hear you're Miss Belmont now; – pray how does old Madame French do?"

"Madame Duval," said I, "is, I believe, very well."

---

1   Bath, in the eighteenth century a fashionable resort town, is 12 miles southeast of Bristol, situated on the Avon River, and built on the remains of a Roman city. During the city's popularity as a spa in the eighteenth century, John Wood the Elder and his son, John Wood the Younger, designed distinctive and prestigious buildings there, including the Royal Crescent, a semicircle of town houses; the King's Circus, a circle of town houses; and Prior Park, just outside Bath and the country estate of Ralph Allen, which could be seen from the North and South Parades, streets of fashionable homes.
2   "A travelling carriage, either hired from stage to stage, or drawn by horses so hired" (*OED*).
3   Things.

"I hope she's in *good case*," said he, winking significantly, "and won't flinch at seeing service: she has laid by long enough to refit and be made tight.[1] And pray how does poor *Monseer* Doleful do? is he as lank-jawed as ever?"

"They are neither of them," said I, "in Bristol."

"No!" cried he, with a look of disappointment, "but surely the old dowager intends coming to the wedding! 'twill be a most excellent opportunity to shew off her best Lyons silk. Besides, I purpose to dance a new-fashioned jig[2] with her. Don't you know when she'll come?"

"I have no reason to expect her at all."

"No! – 'Fore George, this here's the worst news I'd wish to hear! – why I've thought of nothing all the way but what trick I should serve her!"

"You have been very obliging!" said I, laughing.

"O, I promise you," cried he, "our Moll would never have wheedled me into this jaunt, if I'd known she was not here; for, to let you into the secret, I fully intended to have treated the old buck with another frolic."

"Did Miss Mirvan, then, persuade you to this journey?"

"Yes, and we've been travelling all night."

"*We!*" cried I: "Is Miss Mirvan, then, with you?"

"What, Molly? – yes, she's in that there chaise."

"Good God, Sir, why did not you tell me sooner?" cried I; and immediately, with Lord Orville's assistance, I jumpt out of the phaeton, and ran to the dear girl. Lord Orville opened the chaise door, and I am sure I need not tell you what unfeigned joy accompanied our meeting.

We both begged we might not be parted during the ride, and Lord Orville was so good as to invite Captain Mirvan into his phaeton.

I think I was hardly ever more rejoiced than at this so seasonable visit from my dear Maria; who had no sooner heard the situation of my affairs, than with the assistance of Lady Howard

---

1   Captain Mirvan hopes Madame Duval is "well off" since she has had time to recuperate after his last assault on her, and ready to encounter him again. He likens her to a ship that has been repaired and is ready to be put to sea again.
2   Captain Mirvan intends to play new practical jokes on Madame Duval.

and her kind mother, she besought her father with such earnestness to consent to the journey, that he had not been able to withstand their united entreaties; though she owned that, had he not expected to have met with Madame Duval, she believes he would not so readily have yielded. They arrived at Mrs. Beaumont's but a few minutes after we were out of sight, and overtook us without much difficulty.

I say nothing of our conversation, because you may so well suppose both the subjects we chose, and our manner of discussing them.

We all stopped at a great hotel, where we were obliged to enquire for a room, as Lady Louisa, *fatigued to death*, desired to *take something* before we began our rambles.[1]

As soon as the party was assembled, the Captain, abruptly saluting me, said, "So, Miss Belmont, I wish you joy; so I hear you've quarrelled with your new name already?"

"Me! – no, indeed, Sir."

"Then please for to tell me the reason you're in such a hurry to change it."

"Miss Belmont!" cried Mr. Lovel, looking around him with the utmost astonishment, "I beg pardon, – but, if it is not impertinent, – I must beg leave to say, I always understood that Lady's name was Anville."

"'Fore George," cried the Captain, "it runs in my head, I've seen you somewhere before! and now I think on't, pray a'n't you the person I saw at the play one night, and who did n't know, all the time, whether it was a tragedy or a comedy, or a concert of fidlers?"

"I believe, Sir," said Mr. Lovel, stammering, "I had once, – I think – the pleasure of seeing you last spring."

"Ay, and if I live an hundred springs," answered he, "I shall never forget it; by Jingo, it has served me for a most excellent good joke ever since. Well, howsomever, I'm glad to see you still in the land of the living," shaking him roughly by the hand; "pray, if a body may be so bold, how much a night may you give at present to keep the undertakers aloof?"

---

1  They have rented a room at the hotel in which they can rest and eat before sight-seeing. Mackinnon identifies this hotel as the White Hart in Stall St. (540).

"Me, Sir!" said Mr. Lovel, very much discomposed; "I protest I never thought myself in such imminent danger as to – really, Sir, I don't understand you."

"O, you don't! – why then I'll make free for to explain myself. Gentlemen and Ladies, I'll tell you what; do you know this here gentleman, simple as he sits there, pays five shillings a night to let his friends know he's alive!"

"And very cheap too," said Mrs. Selwyn, "if we consider the value of the intelligence."

Lady Louisa, being now refreshed, we proceeded upon our expedition.

The charming city of Bath answered all my expectations. The Crescent, the prospect from it, and the elegant symmetry of the Circus, delighted me. The Parades, I own, rather disappointed me; one of them is scarce preferable to some of the best paved streets in London, and the other, though it affords a beautiful prospect, a charming view of Prior Park and of the Avon, yet wanted something in *itself* of more striking elegance than a mere broad pavement, to satisfy the ideas I had formed of it.

At the pump-room, I was amazed at the public exhibition of the ladies in the bath: it is true, their heads are covered with bonnets, but the very idea of being seen, in such a situation, by whoever pleases to look, is indelicate.

"'Fore George," said the Captain, looking into the bath, "this would be a most excellent place for old Madame French to dance a fandango[1] in! By Jingo, I would n't wish for better sport than to swing her round this here pond!"

"She would be very much obliged to you," said Lord Orville, "for so extraordinary a mark of your favour."

"Why, to let you know," answered the Captain, "she hit my fancy mightily; I never took so much to an old tabby[2] before."

"Really, now," cried Mr. Lovel, looking also into the bath, "I must confess it is, to me, very incomprehensible why the ladies

---

1   "A lively dance in ¾ time" (*OED*).
2   "An old or elderly maiden lady … Sometimes applied to any spiteful or ill-natured female gossip or tatler" (*OED*).

chuse that frightful unbecoming dress to bathe in![1] I have often pondered very seriously upon the subject, but could never hit upon the reason."

"Well, I declare," said Lady Louisa, "I should like of all things to set something new a going; I always hated bathing, because one can get no pretty dress for it; now do, there's a good creature, try to help me to something."

"Who? me! – O dear Ma'am," said he, simpering, "I can't pretend to assist a person of your Ladyship's taste; besides, I have not the least head for fashions. – I really don't think I ever invented above three in my life! – but I never had the least turn for dress, – never any notion of fancy or elegance."

"O fie, Mr. Lovel! how can you talk so? – don't we all know that you lead the *ton*[2] in the *beau monde*? I declare, I think you dress better than any body."

"O dear Ma'am, you confuse me to the last degree! *I* dress well! – I protest I don't think I'm ever fit to be seen! – I'm often shocked to death to think what a figure I go. If your Ladyship will believe me, I was full half an hour this morning thinking what I should put on!"

"Odds my life," cried the Captain, "I wish I'd been near you! I warrant I'd have quickened your motions a little! Half an hour thinking what you'd put on? and who the deuce, do you think, cares the snuff of a candle[3] whether you've any thing on or not?"

"O pray, Captain," cried Mrs. Selwyn, "don't be angry with the gentleman for *thinking*, whatever be the cause, for I assure you he makes no common practice of offending in that way."

"Really, Ma'am, you're prodigiously kind!" said Mr. Lovel, angrily.

---

1   Lydia Melford, in Smollett's *Humphry Clinker* (1771), describes one of the principal activities at Bath: "Right under the Pump-room windows is the King's Bath; a huge cistern, where you see the patients up to their necks in hot water. The ladies wear jackets and petticoats of brown linen, with chip hats, in which they fix their handkerchiefs to wipe the sweat from their faces ..." (Ed. Lewis Knapp, [New York: Oxford University Press, 1966], 39).

2   "Ton" is "the fashion, the vogue, the mode" (*OED*). Lady Louisa asserts that Mr. Lovel is at the forefront of the fashionable world in style.

3   "Used to denote something of no value" (*OED*).

"Pray, now," said the Captain, "did you ever get a ducking in that there place yourself?"

"A ducking, Sir!" repeated Mr. Lovel; "I protest I think that's rather an odd term! – but if you mean a *bathing*, it is an honour I have had many times."

"And pray, if a body may be so bold, what do you do with that frizle-frize top[1] of your own? Why I'll lay you what you will, there is fat and grease enough on your crown, to buoy you up, if you were to go in head downwards."

"And I don't know," cried Mrs. Selwyn, "but that might be the easiest way, for I'm sure it would be the lightest."

"For the matter of that there," said the Captain, "you must make him a soldier, before you can tell which is lightest, head or heels. Howsomever, I'd lay ten pounds to a shilling, I could whisk him so dexterously over into the pool, that he should light plump upon his foretop, and turn round like a tetotum."[2]

"Done!" cried Lord Merton; "I take your odds!"

"Will you?" returned he; "why then, 'fore George, I'd do it as soon as say Jack Robinson."[3]

"He, he!" faintly laughed Mr. Lovel, as he moved abruptly from the window, "'pon honour, this is pleasant enough; but I don't see what right any body has to lay wagers about one, without one's consent."

"There, Lovel, you are out;" cried Mr. Coverley; "any man may lay what wager about you he will; your consent is nothing to the purpose: he may lay that your nose is a sky-blue, if he pleases."

"Ay," said Mrs. Selwyn, "or that your mind is more adorned than your person; – or any absurdity whatsoever."

"I protest," said Mr. Lovel, "I think it's a very disagreeable

---

1  Frizzled hair; "short, crisp curls" (*OED*).

2  "A small 4-sided disk or die having an initial letter inscribed on each of its sides, and a spindle passing down through it by which it could be twirled or spun with the fingers like a small top, the letter which lay uppermost, when it fell, deciding the fortune of the player" (*OED*).

3  Mackinnon quotes Grose in *A Classical Dictionary of the Vulgar Tongue* (1796) who notes that this saying comes from a "very volatile gentleman of that appellation, who would call on his neighbors, and be gone before his name was announced" (542).

privilege, and I must beg that nobody may take such a liberty with *me.*"

"Like enough you may," cried the Captain; "but what's that to the purpose? suppose I've a mind to lay that you've never a tooth in your head? – pray, how will you hinder me?"

"You'll allow me, at least, Sir, to take the liberty of asking how you'll *prove* it?"

"How? – why, by knocking them all down your throat."

"Knocking them all down my throat, Sir!" repeated Mr. Lovel, with a look of horror, "I protest I never heard any thing so shocking in my life; and I must beg leave to observe, that no wager, in my opinion, could justify such a barbarous action."

Here Lord Orville interfered, and hurried us to our carriages.

We returned in the same order we came. Mrs. Beaumont invited all the party to dinner, and has been so obliging as to beg Miss Mirvan may continue at her house during her stay. The Captain will lodge at the Wells.

The first half-hour after our return, was devoted to hearing Mr. Lovel's apologies for dining in his riding-dress.

Mrs. Beaumont then, addressing herself to Miss Mirvan and me, enquired how we liked Bath?

"I hope," said Mr. Lovel, "the Ladies do not call this seeing Bath."

"No? – what should ail 'em?" cried the Captain; "do you suppose they put their eyes in their pockets?"

"No, Sir; but I fancy you will find no person, – that is, no person of any condition, – call going about a few places in a morning *seeing Bath.*"

"Mayhap, then," said the literal Captain, "you think we should see it better by going about at midnight?"

"No, Sir, no," said Mr. Lovel, with a supercilious smile, "I perceive you don't understand me, – *we* should never call it *seeing Bath*, without going at the right season."[1]

---

1 The "season" at Bath was both spring and fall, though Lovel here implies that only the spring is the true season; fashionable people would be present in Bath during the season; "seeing Bath" was not so much a matter of seeing the sights, but of seeing the right people and being seen by them.

"Why, what a plague, then," demanded he, "can you only see at one season of the year?"

Mr. Lovel again smiled; but seemed superior to making any answer.

"The Bath amusements," said Lord Orville, "have a sameness in them, which, after a short time, renders them rather insipid: but the greatest objection that can be made to the place, is the encouragement it gives to gamesters."[1]

"Why I hope, my Lord, you would not think of abolishing *gaming*," cried Lord Merton; "'tis the very *zest* of life! Devil take me if I could live without it!"

"I am sorry for it," said Lord Orville, gravely, and looking at Lady Louisa.

"Your Lordship is no judge of this subject," continued the other; – "but if once we could get you to a gaming-table, you'd never be happy away from it."

"I hope, my Lord," cried Lady Louisa, "that nobody *here* ever occasions your quitting it."

"Your Ladyship," said Lord Merton, recollecting himself, "has power to make me quit any thing."

"Except *herself*," said Mr. Coverley. "Egad, my Lord, I think I've helpt you out there."

"You men of wit, Jack," answered his Lordship, "are always ready; – for my part, I don't pretend to any talents that way."

"Really, my Lord?" asked the sarcastic Mrs. Selwyn; "well, that is wonderful, considering success would be so much in your power."

"Pray, Ma'am," said Mr. Lovel to Lady Louisa, "has your Ladyship heard the news?"

"News! – what news?"

"Why, the report circulating at the Wells concerning a certain person?"

"O Lord, no; pray tell me what it is!"

"O no, Ma'am, I beg your La'ship will excuse me; 'tis a profound secret, and I would not have mentioned it, if I had not thought you knew it."

---

1  Gamblers; gaming is gambling.

"Lord, now, how can you be so monstrous? – I declare, now, you're a provoking creature! But come, I know you'll tell me; – won't you, now?"

"Your La'ship knows I am but too happy to obey you; but 'pon honour, I can't speak a word, if you won't all promise me the most inviolable secrecy."

"I wish you'd wait for that from me," said the Captain, "and I'll give you my word you'd be dumb for one while. Secrecy, quoth a! – 'Fore George, I wonder you a'n't ashamed to mention such a word, when you talk of telling it to a woman. Though, for the matter of that, I'd as lieve blab it to the whole sex at once, as to go for to tell it to such a thing as you."

"Such a thing as me, Sir!" said Mr. Lovel, letting fall his knife and fork, and looking very important: "I really have not the honour to understand your expression."

"It's all one for that," said the Captain; "you may have it explained whenever you like it."

"'Pon honour, Sir," returned Mr. Lovel, "I must take the liberty to tell you, that I should be extremely offended, but that I suppose it to be some sea-phrase, and therefore I'll let it pass without further notice."

Lord Orville, then, to change the discourse, asked Miss Mirvan if she should spend the ensuing winter in London?

"No, to be sure," said the Captain, "what should she for? she saw all that was to be seen before."

"Is London, then," said Mr. Lovel, smiling at Lady Louisa, "only to be regarded as a *sight*?"

"Why pray, Mr. Wiseacre, how are you pleased for to regard it yourself? – Answer me to that?"

"O Sir, *my* opinion I fancy you would hardly find intelligible. I don't understand *sea-phrases* enough to define it to your comprehension. Does n't your La'ship think the task would be rather difficult?"

"O Lard, yes," cried Lady Louisa, "I declare I'd as soon teach my parrot to talk Welch."

"Ha! ha! ha! admirable! – 'Pon honour your La'ship's quite in luck to day; – but that, indeed, your La'ship is every day. Though, to be sure, it is but candid to acknowledge, that the gentlemen of the ocean have a set of ideas, as well as a dialect, so opposite to *ours*, that it is by no means surprising *they* should regard London as a mere *shew*, that may be seen by being *looked at*. Ha! ha! ha!"

"Ha! ha!" echoed Lady Louisa: "Well, I declare you are the drollest creature!"

"He! he! 'pon honour I can't help laughing at the conceit of *seeing London* in a few weeks!"

"And what a plague should hinder you?" cried the Captain; "do you want to spend a day in every street?"

Here again Lady Louisa and Mr. Lovel interchanged smiles.

"Why, I warrant you, if I had the shewing it, I'd haul you from St. James's to Wapping[1] the very first morning."

The smiles were now, with added contempt, repeated; which the Captain observing, looked very fiercely at Mr. Lovel, and said, "Hark'ee, my spark, none of your grinning! – 'tis a lingo I don't understand; and if you give me any more of it, I shall go near to lend you a box o' the ear."

"I protest, Sir," said Mr. Lovel, turning extremely pale, "I think it's taking a very particular liberty with a person, to talk to one in such a style as this!"

"It's like you may," returned the Captain; "but give a good gulp and I warrant you'll swallow it." Then, calling for a glass of ale, with a very provoking and significant nod, he drank to his easy digestion.

Mr. Lovel made no answer, but looked extremely sullen: and soon after, we left the gentlemen to themselves.

I had then two letters delivered to me; one from Lady Howard and Mrs. Mirvan, which contained the kindest congratulations; and the other from Madame Duval, – but not a word from *you*, – to my no small surprise and concern.

Madame Duval seems greatly rejoiced at my late intelligence: a violent cold, she says, prevents her coming to Bristol. The Branghtons, she tells me, are all well; Miss Polly is soon to be married to Mr. Brown, but Mr. Smith has changed his

---

1   From St. James's Palace in the fashionable West End of London to Wapping in the Eastern part of the city, where many seamen lived and the shipping industry was centered.

lodgings, "which," she adds, "has made the house extremely dull. However, that's not the worst news; *pardi*, I wish it was! but I've been used like nobody, – for Monsieur Du Bois has had the baseness to go back to France without me." In conclusion, she assures me, as you prognosticated she would, that I shall be sole heiress of all she is worth, when Lady Orville.

At tea-time, we were joined by all the gentlemen but Captain Mirvan, who went to the hotel where he was to sleep, and made his daughter accompany him, to separate her *trumpery*, as he called it, from his cloaths.

As soon as they were gone, Mr. Lovel, who still appeared extremely sulky, said, "I protest, I never saw such a vulgar, abusive fellow in my life, as that Captain: 'pon honour, I believe he came here for no purpose in the world but to pick a quarrel; however, for my part, I vow I won't humour him."

"I declare," cried Lady Louisa, "he put me in a monstrous fright, – I never heard any body talk so shocking in my life!"

"I think," said Mrs. Selwyn, with great solemnity, "he threatened to box your ears, Mr. Lovel, – did not he?"

"Really, Ma'am," said Mr. Lovel, colouring, "if one was to mind every thing those low kind of people say, – one should never be at rest for one impertinence or other, – so I think the best way is to be above taking any notice of them."

"What," said Mrs. Selwyn, with the same gravity, "and so receive the blow in silence!"

During this discourse, I heard the Captain's chaise stop at the door, and ran down stairs to meet Maria. She was alone, and told me that her father, who, she was sure, had some scheme in agitation against Mr. Lovel, had sent her on before him. We continued in the parlour till his return, and were joined by Lord Orville, who begged me not to insist on a patience so unnatural, as submitting to be excluded our society. And let me, my dear Sir, with a grateful heart let me own, I never before passed half an hour in such perfect felicity.

I believe we were all sorry when the Captain returned; yet his inward satisfaction, from however different a cause, did not seem inferior to what ours had been. He chucked Maria under the chin, rubbed his hands, and was scarce able to contain the fullness of his glee. We all attended him to the drawing-room, where, having composed his countenance, without any previous attention to Mrs. Beaumont, he marched up to Mr. Lovel, and abruptly said, "Pray have you e'er a brother in these here parts?"

"Me, Sir? – no, thank Heaven, I'm free from all incumbrances of that sort."

"Well," cried the Captain, "I met a person just now, so like you, I could have sworn he had been your twin-brother."

"It would have been a most singular pleasure to me," said Mr. Lovel, "if I also could have seen him; for, really, I have not the least notion what sort of a person I am, and I have a prodigious curiosity to know."

Just then, the Captain's servant opening the door, said, "a little gentleman below desires to see one Mr. Lovel."

"Beg him to walk up stairs," said Mrs. Beaumont. "But pray what is the reason William is out of the way?"

The man shut the door without any answer.

"I can't imagine who it is," said Mr. Lovel; "I recollect no little gentleman of my acquaintance now at Bristol, – except, indeed, the Marquis of Charlton, – but I don't much fancy it can be him. Let me see, who else is there so very little?" –

A confused noise among the servants now drew all eyes towards the door; the impatient Captain hastened to open it, and then, clapping his hands, called out, "'Fore George, 'tis the same person I took for your relation!"

And then, to the utter astonishment of every body but himself, he hauled into the room a monkey! full dressed, and extravagantly *à-la-mode*!

The dismay of the company was almost general. Poor Mr. Lovel seemed thunderstruck with indignation and surprise; Lady Louisa began a scream, which for some time was incessant; Miss Mirvan and I jumped involuntarily upon the seats of our chairs: Mrs. Beaumont herself followed our example; Lord Orville placed himself before me as a guard; and Mrs. Selwyn, Lord Merton, and Mr. Coverley, burst into a loud, immoderate, ungovernable fit of laughter, in which they were joined by the Captain, till, unable to support himself, he rolled on the floor.

The first voice which made its way through this general noise, was that of Lady Louisa, which her fright and screaming rendered extremely shrill. "Take it away!" cried she, "take the monster away, – I shall faint, I shall faint if you don't!"

Mr. Lovel, irritated beyond endurance, angrily demanded of the Captain what he meant?

"Mean?" cried the Captain, as soon as he was able to speak, "why only to shew you in your proper colours." Then rising, and pointing to the monkey, "Why now, Ladies and Gentlemen, I'll be judged by you all! – Did you ever see any thing more like? Odds my life, if it was n't for this here tail, you would n't know one from t'other."

"Sir," cried Mr. Lovel, stamping, "I shall take a time to make you feel my wrath."

"Come, now," continued the regardless Captain, "just for the fun's sake, duff your coat and waistcoat, and swop with Monsieur *Grinagain* here, and I'll warrant you'll not know yourself which is which."

"Not know myself from a monkey? – I assure you, Sir, I'm not to be used in this manner, and I won't bear it, – curse me if I will!"

"Why heyday," cried the Captain, "what, is Master in a passion? – well, don't be angry, – come, he sha'n't hurt you; – here, shake a paw with him, – why he'll do you no harm, man! – come, kiss and friends!" –

"Who I?" cried Mr. Lovel, almost mad with vexation, "as I'm a living creature, I would not touch him for a thousand worlds!"

"Send him a challenge," cried Mr. Coverley, "and I'll be your second."

"Ay, do," said the Captain, "and I'll be second to my friend Monsieur Clapperclaw[1] here. Come, to it at once! – tooth and nail!"

"God forbid!" cried Mr. Lovel, retreating, "I would sooner trust my person with a mad bull!"

---

1    "To claw or scratch with the open hand and nails; to beat, thrash, drub.... Figuratively, revile, abuse" (*OED*).

"I don't like the looks of him myself," said Lord Merton, "for he grins most horribly."

"Oh I'm frightened out of my senses!" cried Lady Louisa, "take him away, or I shall die!"

"Captain," said Lord Orville, "the ladies are alarmed, and I must beg you would send the monkey away."

"Why, where can be the mighty harm of one monkey more than another?" answered the Captain; "howsomever, if it's agreeable to the ladies, suppose we turn them out together?"

"What do you mean by that, Sir?" cried Mr. Lovel, lifting up his cane.

"What do *you* mean?" cried the Captain, fiercely: "be so good as to down with your cane."

Poor Mr. Lovel, too much intimidated to stand his ground, yet too much enraged to submit, turned hastily round, and, forgetful of consequences, vented his passion by giving a furious blow to the monkey.

The creature darting forwards, sprung instantly upon him, and clinging round his neck, fastened his teeth to one of his ears.

I was really sorry for the poor man, who, though an egregious fop, had committed no offence that merited such chastisement.

It was impossible, now, to distinguish whose screams were loudest, those of Mr. Lovel, or of the terrified Lady Louisa, who, I believe, thought her own turn was approaching: but the unrelenting Captain roared with joy.

Not so Lord Orville: ever humane, generous, and benevolent, he quitted his charge, who he saw was wholly out of danger, and seizing the monkey by the collar, made him loosen the ear, and then, with a sudden swing, flung him out of the room, and shut the door.

Poor Mr. Lovel, almost fainting with terror, sunk upon the floor, crying out, "Oh I shall die, I shall die! – Oh I'm bit to death!"

"Captain Mirvan," said Mrs. Beaumont, with no little indignation, "I must own I don't perceive the wit of this action; and I am sorry to have such cruelty practised in my house."

"Why, Lord, Ma'am," said the Captain, when his rapture abated sufficiently for speech, "how could I tell they'd fall out so? – by Jingo, I brought him to be a messmate for t'other."

"Egad," said Mr. Coverley, "I would not have been served so for a thousand pounds!"

"Why then there's the odds of it," said the Captain, "for you see he is served so for nothing. But come," (turning to Mr. Lovel,) "be of good heart, all may end well yet, and you and *Monseer* Longtail be as good friends as ever."

"I'm surprised, Mrs. Beaumont," cried Mr. Lovel, starting up, "that you can suffer a person under your roof to be treated so inhumanly."

"What argufies so many words?" said the unfeeling Captain, "it is but a slit of the ear; it only looks as if you had been in the pillory."[1]

"Very true," added Mrs. Selwyn, "and who knows but it may acquire you the credit of being an anti-ministerial writer?"[2]

"I protest," cried Mr. Lovel, looking ruefully at his dress, "my new riding-suit's all over blood!"

"Ha, ha, ha!" cried the Captain; "see what comes of studying for an hour what you shall put on."

Mr. Lovel then walked to the glass, and looking at the place, exclaimed, "Oh Heaven, what a monstrous wound! my ear will never be fit to be seen again!"

"Why then," said the Captain, "you must hide it; – 'tis but wearing a wig."

"A wig!" repeated the affrighted Mr. Lovel, "*I* wear a wig?[3] – no, not if you would give me a thousand pounds an hour!"

"I declare," said Lady Louisa, "I never heard such a shocking proposal in my life!"

---

1 "A contrivance for the punishment of offenders, consisting usually of a wooden framework erected on a post or pillar, and formed, like the stocks, of two movable boards which, when brought together at their edges, leave holes through which the head and hands of an offender were thrust, in which state he was exposed to public ridicule, insult, and molestation. In other forms, the culprit was fastened to a stake by a ring round his neck and wrists" (*OED*).

2 Writing critical of the government's policies was especially dangerous during a time of war; writers who wrote in this vein risked being put in the pillory.

3 It was no longer fashionable for a man to wear a wig.

Lord Orville then, seeing no prospect that the altercation would cease, proposed to the Captain to walk. He assented; and having given Mr. Lovel a nod of exultation, accompanied his Lordship down stairs.

"'Pon honour," said Mr. Lovel, the moment the door was shut, "that fellow is the greatest brute in nature! he ought not to be admitted into a civilized society."

"Lovel," said Mr. Coverley, affecting to whisper, "you must certainly pink him:[1] you must not put up with such an affront."

"Sir," said Mr. Lovel, "with any common person, I should not deliberate an instant; but, really, with a fellow who has done nothing but fight all his life, 'pon honour, Sir, I can't think of it!"

"Lovel," said Lord Merton, in the same voice, "you *must* call him to account."

"Every man," said he, pettishly, "is the best judge of his own affairs, and I don't ask the honour of any person's advice."

"Egad, Lovel," said Mr. Coverley, "you're in for it! – you can't possibly be off!"

"Sir," cried he, very impatiently, "upon any proper occasion, I should be as ready to shew my courage as any body; – but as to fighting for such a trifle as this, – I protest I should blush to think of it!"

"A trifle!" cried Mrs. Selwyn; "good Heaven! and have you made this astonishing riot about a *trifle*?"

"Ma'am," answered the poor wretch, in great confusion, "I did not know at first but that my cheek might have been bit: – but as 'tis no worse, why it does not a great deal signify. Mrs. Beaumont, I have the honour to wish you good evening; I'm sure my carriage must be waiting." And then, very abruptly, he left the room.

What a commotion has this mischief-loving Captain raised! Were I to remain here long, even the society of my dear Maria could scarce compensate for the disturbances which he excites.

When he returned, and heard of the quiet exit of Mr. Lovel, his triumph was intolerable. "I think, I think," cried he, "I have

---

1 "Pierce, prick, or stab with any pointed weapon or instrument" (*OED*).

peppered him well![1] I'll warrant he won't give an hour to-morrow morning to settling what he shall put on; why his coat," turning to me, "would be a most excellent match for old Madame Furbelow's[2] best Lyons silk! 'Fore George, I'd desire no better sport, than to have that there old cat here, to go her snacks!"

All the company then, Lord Orville, Miss Mirvan, and myself excepted, played at cards, and *we* – oh how much better did we pass our time!

While we were engaged in a most delightful conversation, a servant brought me a letter, which he told me had, by some accident, been mislaid. Judge of my feelings, when I saw, my dearest Sir, your revered hand-writing! My emotions soon betrayed to Lord Orville whom the letter was from; the importance of the contents he well knew, and, assuring me I should not be seen by the card-players, he besought me to open it without delay.

Open it, indeed, I did, – but read it I could not; – the willing, yet aweful consent you have granted, – the tenderness of your expressions, – the certainty that no obstacle remained to my eternal union with the loved owner of my heart, gave me sensations too various, and though joyful, too little placid for observation. Finding myself unable to proceed, and blinded by the tears of gratitude and delight which started into my eyes, I gave over the attempt of reading, till I retired to my own room: and, having no voice to answer the enquiries of Lord Orville, I put the letter into his hands, and left it to speak both for me and itself.

Lord Orville was himself affected by your kindness; he kissed the letter as he returned it, and, pressing my hand affectionately to his heart, "You are now," (said he, in a low voice) "all my own! Oh my Evelina, how will my soul find room for its happiness? – it seems already bursting!" I could make no reply; indeed I hardly spoke another word the rest of the evening; so little talkative is the fullness of contentment.

---

1   "To inflict severe punishment or suffering upon" (*OED*).
2   "A contemptuous term for showy ornaments or trimmings, especially in a lady's dress" (*OED*).

O my dearest Sir, the thankfulness of my heart I must pour forth at our meeting, when, at your feet, my happiness receives its confirmation from your blessing, and when my noble-minded, my beloved Lord Orville, presents to you the highly-honoured and thrice-happy Evelina.

A few lines I will endeavour to write on Thursday, which shall be sent off express, to give you, should nothing intervene, yet more certain assurance of our meeting.

Now then, therefore, for the first – and probably the last time I shall ever own the name, permit me to sign myself,

Most dear Sir,
Your gratefully affectionate,
EVELINA BELMONT.

Lady Louisa, at her own particular desire, will be present at the ceremony, as well as Miss Mirvan and Mrs. Selwyn: Mr. Macartney will, the same morning, be united to my foster-sister, and my father himself will give us both away.

## LETTER XXII.

### Mr. Villars to Evelina.

Every wish of my soul is now fulfilled – for the felicity of my Evelina is equal to her worthiness!

Yes, my child, thy happiness is engraved, in golden characters, upon the tablets of my heart! and their impression is indelible; for, should the rude and deep-searching hand of Misfortune attempt to pluck them from their repository, the fleeting fabric of life would give way, and in tearing from my vitals the nourishment by which they are supported, she would but grasp at a shadow insensible to her touch.

Give thee my consent? – Oh thou joy, comfort, and pride of my life, how cold is that word to express the fervency of my approbation! yes, I do indeed give thee my consent, and so thankfully, that, with the humblest gratitude to Providence, I would seal it with the remnant of my days.

Hasten, then, my love, to bless me with thy presence, and to receive the blessings with which my fond heart overflows! – And, oh my Evelina, hear and assist in one only, humble, but ardent prayer which yet animates my devotions: that the height of bliss to which thou art rising may not render thee giddy, but that the purity of thy mind may form the brightest splendor of thy prosperity! – and that the weak and aged frame of thy almost idolizing parent, nearly worn out by time, past afflictions, and infirmities, may yet be able to sustain a meeting with all its better part holds dear; and then, that all the wounds which the former severity of fortune inflicted, may be healed and purified by the ultimate consolation of pouring forth my dying words in blessings on my child! – closing these joy-streaming eyes in her presence, and breathing my last faint sighs in her loved arms!

Grieve not, oh child of my care, grieve not at the inevitable moment; but may thy own end be equally propitious! Oh may'st thou, when full of days, and full of honour, sink down as gently to rest, – be loved as kindly, watched as tenderly as thy happy father! And may'st thou, when thy glass is run, be sweetly but not bitterly mourned, by some remaining darling of thy affections, – some yet surviving Evelina!

ARTHUR VILLARS.

## LETTER XXIII.

*Evelina to the Rev. Mr. Villars.*

All is over, my dearest Sir, and the fate of your Evelina is decided! This morning, with fearful joy, and trembling gratitude, she united herself for ever with the object of her dearest, her eternal affection.

I have time for no more; the chaise now waits which is to conduct me to dear Berry Hill, and to the arms of the best of men.

EVELINA.

## FINIS.

# Introduction to Appendices

The focus of the appendices complements the introduction's focus on eighteenth-century family relations and comic theory. Some of the works that appear in Appendices B and C are alluded to in Burney's early journals and letters, in the years before she wrote *Evelina*; they are works she had read or was reading at the time that she was working on *Evelina*; often they are works she knew well enough to quote from. Others are seventeenth- or eighteenth-century texts whose subject matter informed social and familial interaction during Burney's day.

The texts of the excerpted works in Appendices B and C are reproductions of the first editions, when possible, or subsequent contemporary editions; occasionally, nineteenth- or early twentieth-century editions have been used as copy texts when no other earlier edition was available. Where no author is given, the work is anonymous. Edition information is given in the headnote for each work within the appendices; dates given in parentheses after the titles are initial publication dates of texts. The entries are arranged in chronological order. The texts have been emended minimally, treated along the lines of Burney's novel. The Appendices have been annotated in the same manner as the text of *Evelina* with an eye to clarifying those terms, allusions, and references whose obscurity would seriously compromise the reader's experience of the texts.

Appendix A provides the full text of the major contemporary reviews of *Evelina*, with the exception of the *Critical Review* article which reprinted the dedicatory poem at the beginning of the novel; I have deleted this poem from the review, since it is not commented upon by the reviewer and is used simply as a concluding note in the review. As the introduction notes, the contemporary reviews of Burney's first novel were generally short but positive. They did much to move the book along with the public, but, as Burney later noted, word of mouth did more, especially as the novel's fans included such influential literary, intellectual, and artistic figures as Johnson,

Burke, and Reynolds. The reviews tend to stress the didactic capacity of the novel and steer it toward youthful readers; they establish the comparative merit of the novel, given the present situation of novel-writing; and they place the novel firmly in the camp of one of the most respected of past novelists, Samuel Richardson, both in terms of its strengths and its weaknesses.

Appendix B contains excerpts from late seventeenth- and eighteenth-century works that discuss family and kin relations at all social levels; female education – practical, intellectual, and moral; the place of women – single, married, separated, or widowed – in society; courtship, especially with regard to the considerations a women must weigh in her choice of a mate; and inheritance practices, to name the most inclusive categories. These selections create a context within which the reader may consider the novel's treatment of kinship and family relations. The context is derived from works in a variety of genres which include fiction, as in Richardson's *Collection of the Moral and Instructive Sentiments ... Contained in the Histories of "Pamela," "Clarissa," and "Sir Charles Grandison"* and Haywood's *The Female Spectator*; educational works, including the conduct books of George Savile, Marquis of Halifax, and William Fleetwood as well as the more program-oriented works of Hester Mulso Chapone and the Edgeworths; and the more personal letters of Sarah Churchill, Duchess of Marlborough, and Lady Sarah Pennington. It is a context which underscores both the difficult nature of kin relations, and their necessity in the world of early modern England.

Appendix C contains selections from comic works and works of comic theory. Several of the jest books represented – the anonymous *Pasquil's Jests* and *Scoggin's Jests* – date from the early sixteenth century but were still current in the eighteenth century; also included in this appendix are selections from the most popular jest books of the eighteenth century, *Joe Miller's Jest Book*, written by John Mottley, and *Quin's Jests*, containing the jests of and stories about the contemporary actor James Quin. While these jest books celebrate the pithy pun and the witty comeback, they also bear witness to the verbal and physical brutality and coarseness of the age that lurked beneath the civilized veneer in the hostile practical jokes and denigrating verbal repartee they chronicle.

Also represented in Appendix C is a number of excerpts from contemporary comic works of fiction, verse, and essay. This offering includes Christopher Anstey's *The New Bath Guide*, an extremely popular work of comic verse which Burney herself had read and which she mentions in *Evelina*; certainly, aspects of the tone and content of these comic epistolary memoirs of the B—R—D family is clearly echoed in *Evelina*, especially with regard to the not-so-comic dysfunctionality of the B—R—D family relations revealed in the verse epistles. The excerpt from Jane Collier's *Essay on the Art of Ingeniously Tormenting* offers in its depiction of the cat stalking the mouse a vivid image of the joking relationship in all its cunning, cruelty, and exhuberance. And, finally, the selection from Eliza Haywood's *Female Spectator*, with its didactic practical joke – cruel, potentially dangerous, but (from the husband's perspective) all for the wife's good – rounds out the selections from comic works of the period.

Appendix C also contains excerpts from contemporary comic theory and criticism in order to make clear the age's treatment of comedy as a serious concern, and its efforts to articulate a theory of comedy. These theorists were building on the work of earlier classical and seventeenth-century British theoreticians, but their work is specifically alive to the eighteenth-century spirit of comedy: highly various in form and content, sly as well as brash, highly articulate and sensitive to nuances of word play while also resorting to coarse gestures or violent slapstick to get the laugh, politically charged as well as innocent and universal in its appeal. Addison's *Spectator* articles, Morris's *Essay towards Fixing the True Standards of Wit, Humour, Raillery, Satire, and Ridicule*, the anonymous *Essay on Laughter*, and Hazlitt's *Lectures on the English Comic Writers* are particularly concerned with analyzing the joking relationship in literature and society. These writers are especially sensitive to the potential power inherent in the joking relationship, within the larger public realm of society as well as the privacy of the family. Since both arenas figure in Burney's novel, the private and the public, the family and the society at large, these works offer a helpful way into a consideration of the significance of the intersection of comedy and family in Burney's *Evelina*.

# Appendix A: Contemporary Reviews

## 1. *London Review* 7 (February 1778): 151

The history of a young lady exposed to very critical situations. There is much more merit, as well respecting stile, character and incident, than is usually to be met with among our modern novels.

## 2. *Monthly Review* 58 (April 1778): 316

This novel has given us so much pleasure in the perusal, that we do not hesitate to pronounce it one of the most sprightly, entertaining, and agreeable productions of this kind, which has of late fallen under our notice. A great variety of natural incidents, some of the comic stamp, render the narrative extremely interesting. The characters, which are agreeably diversifyed, are conceived and drawn with propriety, and supported with spirit. The whole is written with great ease and command of language. From this commendation, however, we must except the character of a son of Neptune,[1] whose manners are rather those of a rough, uneducated country figure, than those of a genuine sea-captain.

## 3. *Westminster Magazine* 6 (June 1778): 325

May prove equally useful and entertaining to the younger part of our *male* as well as *female* Readers; to the latter of whom we particularly recommend it, as conveying many practical lessons both on morals and manners.

## 4. *Gentleman's Magazine* 48 (September 1778): 425

"To draw characters from nature, tho' not from life, and to mark the manners of the times, is the attempted plan of the fol-

---

1   Captain Mirvan.

lowing letters. For this purpose, a young female, educated in the most secluded retirement, makes, at the age of seventeen, her first appearance upon the great and busy stage of life: with a virtuous mind, a cultivated understanding, and a feeling heart, her ignorance of the forms, and inexperience of the manners of the world, occasion all the little incidents which these volumes record, and which form the natural progression of the life of a young woman of obscure birth, but conspicuous beauty, for the first six months after her *Entrance into the World*." – Such is the just account given of this work by the author; to which we shall only add that these volumes will afford a pleasing, inno- cent amusement, exhibiting, in an easy style, many such charac- ters as occur in the world, not raised so high as to be extravagant, nor sunk so low as to be disgusting.

### 5. *Critical Review* 46 (September 1778): 202-04

This performance deserves no common praise, whether we consider it in a moral or literary light. It would have disgraced neither the head nor the heart of Richardson.[1] The father of a family, observing the knowledge of the world and the lessons of experience which it contains, will recommend it to his daugh- ters; they will weep and (what is not so commonly the effect of novels) will laugh, and grow wiser, as they read; the experi- enced mother will derive pleasure and happiness from being present at its reading; even the sons of the family will forego the diversions of the town or the field to pursue the entertainment of Evelina's acquaintance, who will imperceptibly lead them, as well as their sisters, to improvement and to virtue.

If the author of this amusing and instructive novel possess any of Richardson's merits, he labours also under one of his principal faults. The gold is in some places beat out consider- ably too fine. The second volume deserves few of the solid praises which we with pleasure bestow on the first and the third. The Roman sibyl, after she had burnt part of her work,

---

1 Samuel Richardson (1689-1761), well-respected author of the popular novels *Pamela*, *Clarissa*, and *Sir Charles Grandison*, provided the standard throughout the century against which other novelists were judged.

still persisted in demanding the same price for what remained; we should set a higher value upon this performance had the writer made it shorter – but perhaps, as Swift[1] said of a long letter, he had not time.

The outline of Evelina's story is this. – The child of a mother who gave her existence at the expence of her own life; and of a brutal father who occasioned that mother's death, and refused, as it was supposed, to acknowledge her daughter; she is educated under the paternal care of Mr. Villars, a worthy clergyman. The novel opens when Evelina is of the age at which young ladies are, as the phrase is, introduced into the world. Mr. Villars trusts his accomplished ward with a family of fashion and fortune, that she may be brought upon the public stage in that great theatre of the world, London. Her simplicity, good sense, and inexperience, are productive of useful humour and diverting satire. The characters of her newly-discovered grandmother Madame Du Val, and of a captain Mirvan, the latter an honest, English sailor, the former a frenchified English waiting-woman, whose good stars had made her the widow of a man of rank and fortune, are well supported, finely drawn, and, in a great measure original. During the few months which Evelina spends at a distance from Mr. Villars, she commences an acquaintance, that ripens into love, with lord Orville. His lordship's rivals are painted from nature, the progress of the amour is traced by the hand of an artist. The winding up of the story is obvious – Evelina gets a husband, and discovers a father. We could wish her husband had not been a lord, and that her father had been less rich. Lords and ladies cannot afford to spend their *precious* time in reading novels, and, if they could, they bear no proportion to the commonality of the literary world. The purchasers of novels, the subscribers to circulating libraries, are seldom in more elevated situations than the middle ranks of life. – The subjects of novels are, with a dangerous uniformity, almost always taken from superior life. The satirists complain with injustice of the want of virtue in our modern

---

1   Jonathan Swift (1667-1745), writer of satiric poetry and prose, whose influence on subsequent writers of satire remained strong well into the decades in which FB was writing.

nobility; when the hero and the heroine of every novel hardly ever fail, sooner or later, to turn out a lady or a lord. What effect has this upon the readers? They are convinced that happiness is not to be found in the chilling climate of low life, nor even, where one of our poets so truly fixed it, in the temperate zone of middle life. – Rank alone contains this unknown good, wealth alone can bestow this coveted joy. – The title of Sir Charles Grandison, the fortune of Miss Byron,[1] are the least with which our young novel readers are determined to sit down satisfied. What is the consequence? Their fates have perhaps destined them to be a petty attorney or a silversmith's daughter, a grocer's son or a clergyman's heiress; fortune *positively* refuses to realize any of their romantic dreams; and a quarter of an hour's perusal of an unnatural novel has embittered all their lives.

We have heard of an advertisement for a house with a N. B. that it must not be within a mile of a lord: we wish, to see one novel in which there is no lord....

---

1    Harriet Byron, a character in Samuel Richardson's *Sir Charles Grandison*.

# Appendix B: Works on Family

### 1. George Savile, Marquis of Halifax, *The Lady's New-Year's-Gift; or, Advice to a Daughter* (1688), 6th ed. (London: M. Gillyflower, 1699).

from "Behaviour and Conversation"

It is time now to lead you out of your *House* into the *World*. A Dangerous step; where your Vertue alone will not secure you except it is attended with a great deal of *Prudence*. You must have *both* for your *Guard*, and not stir without them. The Enemy is abroad, and you are sure to be taken, if you are found stragling. Your *Behaviour* is therefore to incline strongly towards the *Reserved part*; your *Character* is to be immoveably fixed upon that Bottom, not excluding a mixture of greater freedom, as far as it may be innocent and well-timed. The *Extravagancies* of the Age have made *Caution* more necessary; and by the same reason that the too great Licence of ill Men hath by Consequence in many things restrained the Lawful Liberty of those who did not abuse it, the unjustifiable Freedoms of some of your Sex have involved the rest in the Penalty of being reduced. And though this cannot so alter the Nature of things, as to make that *Criminal*, which in it self is *Indifferent*; yet if it maketh it *dangerous*, that alone is sufficient to justifie the *Restraint*. A *close behaviour* is the fittest to receive *Vertue* for its constant *Guest*, because there, and there only, it can be secure. Proper *Reserves* are the Outworks, and must never be deserted by those who intend to keep the Place; they keep off the possibilities not only of being *taken*, but of being *attempted*; and if a Woman seeth Danger tho at never so remote a Distance, she is for that time to shorten her *Line of Liberty*. She who will allow her self to go to the *utmost Extent* of every thing that is *Lawful*, is so very near going farther, that those who lie at watch, will begin to count upon her.

    *Mankind*, from the double temptation of *Vanity* and *Desire*, is apt to turn every thing a *Woman* doth to the *hopeful side*; and there are few who dare make an impudent Application, till they discern something which they are willing to take for an *Encouragement*. It is safer therefore to prevent such *Forwardness*, than to go about to *cure* it. It gathereth Strength by the first *allowances*, and claimeth a Right from having been at any time suffered with Impunity. Therefore nothing is with more care to be avoided, than such a kind of *Civility* as may be mistaken for *Invitation*; and it will not be enough for you to keep your self free from any criminal *Engagements*; for if you do that which either raiseth *Hopes* or createth *Discourse*, there is a Spot thrown upon your Good Name; and those kinds of Stains are the harder to be taken out, being dropped upon you by the *Man's Vanity*, as well as by the *Woman's Malice*.

*    *    *    *

To the *Men* you are to have a *Behaviour* which may secure you, without offending them. No ill-bred affected *Shyness*, nor a *Roughness*, unsuitable to your *Sex*, and unnecessary to your *Vertue*; but a way of Living that may prevent all coarse *Railleries* or *unmannerly Freedoms*; *Looks* that forbid without *Rudeness*, and oblige without *Invitation*, or leaving room for the sawcy Inferences Men's Vanity suggesteth to them upon the least Encouragements. This is so very nice, that it must engage you to have a perpetual *Watch* upon your *Eyes*, and to remember, that one careless *Glance* giveth more advantage than a *hundred Words* not enough considered; the *Language* of the *Eyes* being very much the most *significant*, and the most *observed*.

Your *Civility*, which is always to be preserved, must not be carried to a *Compliance*, which may betray you into irrecoverable Mistakes. This *French* ambiguous word *Complaisance* hath led your Sex into more blame, than all other things put together. It carrieth them by degrees into a certain thing called a *good kind of woman*, an easie *Idle Creature*, that doth neither *Good* nor *Ill* but by *chance*, hath no *Choice*, but leaveth that to the Company she keepeth. *Time*, which by degrees addeth to the signification of *Words*, hath made her, according to the Modern Stile, little better than one who thinketh it a *Rudeness* to deny when civilly required, either her *Service in Person*, or her *friendly Assistance*, to those who would have a *meeting*, or want a *Confident*.

She is a certain thing always at hand, an easie *Companion*, who hath ever great *Compassion* for *distressed Lovers*: She censureth nothing but *Rigor*, and is never without a *Plaister*[1] for a *wounded Reputation*, in which chiefly lieth her skill in *Chirurgery*;[2] She seldom hath the Propriety of any *particular Gallant*, but liveth upon *Brokage*, and waiteth for the Scraps her Friends are content to leave her.

There is another *Character* not quite so *Criminal*, yet not less *Ridiculous*; which is that of a *good-humour'd Woman,* one who thinketh she must always be in a *Laugh*, or a broad *Smile*, because *Good-humour* is an obliging Quality; thinketh it less ill manners to talk *Impertinently*, than to be silent in Company. When such a prating *Engine* rideth *Admiral*, and carrieth the *Lantern*, in a *Circle of Fools*, a *cheerful Coxcomb* coming in for a *Recruit*, the *Chattering* of *Monkeys* is a better noise than such a *Concert* of *senceless Merriment*. If she is applauded in it, she is so encouraged, that, like a *Ballad singer*, who if commended, breaketh his Lungs, she letteth her self loose, and overfloweth upon the Company. She conceiveth that Mirth is to have no intermission, and therefore she will carry it about with her, though it be to a *Funeral*; and if a Man should put a familiar Question, she doth not know very well how to be angry, for then she would be no more that pretty thing called a *Good-humour'd Woman*. This necessity of appearing at all times to be so infinitely pleased is a grievous mistake; since in a *handsom Woman* that *Invitation* is unnecessary; and in one who is not so, *ridiculous*. It is not intended by this, that you should forswear *Laughing*; but remember, that Fools being always painted in that posture, it may fright those who are wise from doing it too frequently, and going too near a Copy which is so little inviting, and much more from doing it *loud*, which is an unnatural Sound and looketh so much like another Sex, that few things are more offensive. That *boisterous* kind of *Jollity* is as contrary to *Wit* and *Good Manners*, as it is to *Modesty* and *Vertue*. Besides, it is a course kind of quality, that throweth a Woman into a lower Form, and degradeth her from the Rank of those who

---

1   Bandage.
2   Surgery.

are more refined. Some *Ladies* speak *loud* and make a *noise* to be the more minded, which looketh as if they beat their *Drums* for *Volunteers*, and if by misfortune none come in to them, they may, not without reason, be a good deal out of Countenance.

*    *    *    *

I will add one *Advice* to conclude this head, which is that you will let every seven years make some alteration in you towards the *Graver* side, and not be like the *Girls* of Fifty, who resolve to be always *Young*, whatever *Time* with his Iron Teeth hath determined to the contrary. Unnatural things carry a *Deformity* in them never to be *Disguised*; the *Liveliness* of *Youth* in a riper Age, looketh like a *new patch* upon an *old Gown*; so that a *Gay Matron*, a cheerful *old Fool* may be reasonably put into the List of the *Tamer* kind of *Monsters*. There is a certain Creature call'd a *Grave Hobby-Horse*, a kind of a she *Numps*,[1] that pretendeth to be pulled to a Play, and must needs go to *Bartholomew Fair*, to look after the young Folks, whom she only seemeth to make her care, in reality she taketh them for her excuse. Such an old *Butterfly* is of all *Creatures*, the most ridiculous, and the soonest found out. It is good to be early in your Caution, to avoid any thing that cometh within distance of such despicable Patterns, and not like some *Ladies*, who defer their *Conversion*, till they have been so long in possession of being laughed at, that the World doth not know how to change their style, even when they are reclaimed from that which gave the first occasion for it.

The advantages of being *reserved* are too many to be set down, I will only say, that it is a *Guard* to a *good Woman*, and a *Disguise* to an *ill one*. It is of so much use to both, that those ought to use it as an *Artifice*, who refuse to practise it as a *Vertue*.

from "Censure"

I will come next to the Consideration, how you are to manage your *Censure*; in which both Care and skill will be a good deal required. To distinguish is not only *natural* but *necessary*; and the

---

1    "A silly or stupid person" (*OED*).

Effect of it is, That we cannot avoid giving Judgment in our Minds, either to *absolve or to condemn* as the Case requireth. The *Difficulty* is, to know when and where it is fit to *proclaim* the *Sentence*. An *Aversion* to what is *Criminal*, a *Contempt* of what is *ridiculous*, are the *inseparable Companions* of Understanding and Vertue; but the letting them go farther than our own *Thoughts*, hath so much danger in it, that though it is neither possible nor fit to *suppress* them intirely, yet it is necessary they should be kept under very great *Restraints*. An *unlimited Liberty* of this kind is little less than sending a *Herald* and proclaiming War to the World, which is an *angry Beast* when so provoked. The Contest will be *unequal*, though you are never so much in the right; and if you begin against such an Adversary, it will tear you in pieces, with this Justification, That it is done in its own defence. You must therefore take heed of *Laughing*, except in Company that is very sure. It is throwing Snow-balls against Bullets; and it is the *disadvantage* of a Woman, that the Malice of the World will help the Brutality of those who will throw a *slovenly Untruth* upon her. You are for this Reason to suppress your *Impatience* for Fools; who besides that they are too strong a Party to be unnecessarily provoked, are of all others, the most dangerous in this Case. A *Blockhead* in his *Rage* will return a *dull Jest* that will lie heavy, though there is not a *Grain* of *Wit* in it. Others will do it with more Art, and you must not think your self secure because your *Reputation* may perhaps be out of the reach of *Ill will*; for if it findeth that part *guarded*, it will seek one which is more *exposed*. It flieth, like a corrupt Humour in the Body, to the *weakest* Part. If you have a *tender Side*, the World will be sure to find it, and to put the worst *Colour* upon all you say or do, give an *Aggravation* to every thing that may lessen you, and a *spiteful turn* to every thing that might recommend you. *Anger* laieth open those Defects which *Friendship* would not see, and *Civility* might be willing to forget. *Malice* needeth no such *Invitation* to encourage it, neither are any *Pains* more superfluous than those we take to be ill spoken of. If *Envy*, which never dyeth, and seldom sleepeth, is content sometimes to be in a *Slumber*, it is very unskilful to make a noise to *awake* it.

Besides, your *Wit* will be misapplied if it is wholly directed to discern the *Faults* of *others*, when it is so necessary to be often used to *mend* and *prevent your own*. The sending our *Thoughts* too much abroad, hath the same Effect, as when a *Family* never stayeth at home; *Neglect* and *Disorder* naturally followeth; as it must do within our selves, if we do not frequently turn our Eyes inwards, to see what is amiss with us, where it is a sign we have an *unwelcome Prospect*, when we do not care to *look* upon it, but rather seek our *Consolations* in the *Faults* of those we converse with.

Avoid being the first in fixing a *hard Censure*, let it be confirmed by the *general Voice*, before you give into it; Neither are you then to give Sentence like a *Magistrate*, or as if you had a *special Authority* to bestow a *good* or *ill Name* at your discretion. Do not dwell too long upon a *weak Side*, touch and go away; take pleasure to stay longer where you can commend, like Bees that fix only upon those Herbs out of which they may extract the Juice of which their Honey is composed. A *Vertue* stuck with *Bristles* is too rough for this Age; it must be adorned with some *Flowers*, or else it will be unwillingly entertained; so that even where it may be fit to strike, do it like a *Lady*, gently; and assure your self, that where you care to do it, you will wound others more, and hurt your self less, by *soft Strokes*, than by being *harsh* or *violent*.

The Triumph of *Wit* is to make your *good Nature* subdue your *Censure*; to be quick in *seeing Faults*, and slow in *exposing* them. You are to consider, that the invisible thing called a *Good Name*, is made up of the Breath of Numbers that speak well of you; so that if by a *disobliging Word* you silence the *meanest*, the *Gale* will be less strong which is to bear up your *Esteem*. And though nothing is so vain as the eager pursuit of *empty Applause*, yet to be well thought of, and to be kindly used by the World, is like a *Glory* about a Woman's *Head*; 'tis a Perfume she carrieth about with her, and leaveth where-ever she goeth; 'tis a Charm against *Ill-will*. *Malice* may empty her Quiver, but cannot wound; the Dirt will not stick, the Jests will not take; Without the consent of the World a *Scandal* doth not go deep;

it is only a slight stroak upon the injured Party and returneth with the greater force upon those that gave it.

**2. William Fleetwood,** *The Relative Duties of Parents and Children, Husbands and Wives, Masters and Servants* **(London: Charles Harper, 1705).**

from "Discourse. III."
Exod. xx. Verse 12.

*Duty of Children to Parents*
Having shewn the necessity there is, that Children should be obedient *to*, and govern'd *by* their Parents, in all things, where they are at liberty by the Laws of God, and of their Country, and in common sense and reason ought to be at liberty; I am, before I leave this Head, to speak a little to the Authority of *Mothers*, and to the Obedience that is due to them, both whilst the Fathers are alive, and after they are dead. The Scriptures make no manner of difference betwixt the Obedience, Fear, or Honour, due to Parents; the *Mother* is still included, still expressed, with the Father. *Honour thy Father and Mother. He that smiteth his Father or Mother, shall surely be put to Death,* Exod. 21. 15. *He that curseth his Father or Mother, shall surely be put to Death,* Verse 17. *Ye shall fear every Man his Mother and Father. If a Man hath a Rebellious Son, which will not obey the voice of his Father, or the voice of his Mother, then shall his Father and his Mother lay hold on him, and say, this our Son is stubborn and rebellious, he will not obey our voice,* Deut. 21. 18. And, *Cursed be he that setteth light by his Father or his Mother,* 28. 16. And, *My Son, hear the Instructions of thy Father, and forsake not the Law of thy Mother;* and so in many other places, where the same Duty is requir'd to be paid the Mother, with the Father; and in truth, there is equal reason in most cases, why we should do so, and in some, greater. The Mothers undergo most pain and sorrow for them, bear all the trouble of their Infancy and Childhood, do all they can for them, and intend them much more; have at least the same, but generally a much greater affection to them, and the same inter-

est and concern for their good and welfare. And therefore in Nature, and true Reason, and Gratitude, the Children are obliged to make no difference betwixt the Father and Mother, in their Observance and Obedience of, and to them.

But because the Father is also superiour to the Mother, both in Natural Strength, in Wisdom, and by God's appointment, and that there is no obeying contrary commands, therefore the Children are especially to obey the Fathers, in cases where they have power to command, and where they cannot obey both Parents together: They must never obey one Parent to the prejudice of the other: The Father has no right to command the Children any thing undutiful, disrespectful, or injurious to the Mother; but if it happen that the inclinations or desires of Mothers, should differ from those of the Fathers, in the choice of Trade, or Calling, or in Matches for the Children, or other things of moment; so that the Children must displease one Parent by complying with the other; the Father is the Superiour Authority, and must be obeyed, because both the Laws of God and Man have subjected the Wife to the Husband; she is not presum'd to have a *Will* contrary to her Husband's, and therefore the Child disobeys not his Mother, who obeys his Father's command, because the Mother is to be obedient also: And the case is not very much altered, although the Father do not lay express command upon the Child, but is passive and content, likes and approves the choice he makes, although the Mother be wholly averse to it, in such a case the Father is to be regarded, for he is the proper Superiour.

But when the Mother is the *only* Parent, then her Authority increases, and she is then solely to be regarded; But the Civil Laws do generally free the Sons at such an Age, supposing them the Masters of the Family, and by the advantage of their Sex and Education, fit to govern, and dispose of themselves and their Affairs. The Daughters are indeed kept longer in Subjection, suppos'd to want the Care and Wisdom of the Parents longer, but growing up to liberty, as they advance in Years and Understanding. There can indeed be no exact Rules in any such Cases, for the Wisdom of either, Parent, or Children, must necessarily make some alteration in the measures of Obedience, in respect to some Commands which relate so nearly to the Children, as Marriage especially does.

And even in Cases where the Sons and Daughters may be reasonably presum'd at liberty, and would otherwise take and use that liberty, yet unless it be a matter of great moment, it should not easily be ventur'd on, to the Mother's great sorrow; for the grief of Parents is not to be occasion'd cheaply and lightly; much will be suffered by a dutiful good-natur'd Child, before he will afflict and grieve his Parent; and since this is especially the infirmity and feebleness of Mothers, the Children are oblig'd to greater care and circumspection in their behaviour towards them, to prevent their sorrows; for every thing that gives them grief, is a sort of disobedience. I will end this whole matter, with forewarning Children, of what will certainly come to pass; and that is, that they will never be able to remember any act of disobedience to their Parents, without much trouble and remorse, without great sorrow and concern of mind, it will dwell continually upon them, and haunt them like an Evil Spirit; they will wish a thousand times, they had behav'd themselves more dutifully, kindly, and obediently, and rather gone without their desires than have occasion'd any trouble or sorrow to their Parents.

★      ★      ★      ★

These are the Duties Children owe their Parents; *Love, Respect*, or *Honour, Obedience*, and *Support* of all kinds, whenever they stand in need of it; and all of them comprehended under *Honouring* them, all of them enjoyn'd to Children in this Command – *Honour thy Father and thy Mother*.

But because the Case of *going to Law with Parents*, is what does sometimes happen, and yet would not properly fall under any of the fore-mentioned Heads, and yet deserves to be considered, it may not be unseasonable to speak a little to it, before I go on to the Promise and Encouragement annex'd by God, to the honouring of our Father, and Mother.

If therefore the Enquiry be, whether it be lawful at any time, *for any Cause*, for Children to call their Parents into question before the Civil Magistrate or Judge; it is to be answered, *affir-*

*matively*, but with many Restrictions. It is certain that Parents have a great Authority, but 'tis as certain that they may abuse it: They are not incapable of *doing* Injury. It is also certain that Children are to be very *subject* to their Parents, but as sure also that they are not *Slaves*, but may *receive* injury. And whoever can suffer wrong, may also be righted: The Laws of God do no where forbid this; and the Laws of the Land are free and impartial, they make no difference of Persons, and know no Relation; Justice is in this respect to be blind: And therefore it is certain, that in some Cases, a Son or Daughter may, without offence of God's Law, appeal to the Laws of the Land, against their Parents.

In case of *alimony*,[1] if the Parent be so unnatural, as to deny the Child its Food and Rayment,[2] the remedy at Law may be justly implor'd, and no one would charge with undutiful and disobedient Carriage, a Child that should implore assistance in such case. So if a Parent should so cruelly use a Child, as to dismember it, or make it lame, or do it any other lasting mischief, the Child might very justly make the Case known to the Magistrate, and beg his favour and assistance. In these and such like Cases, the Common Sense and Pity of Mankind, would teach us, that such complaint were not a breach of Children's Duty to Parents, but very consistent with it. And yet this is one way of Children's going to Law with their Parents. But here, the occasion must be, we see, exceeding great and pressing, and visibly, to wise impartial People, reasonable and just. It is not allowed to make even these Complaints, upon any slight mischief; it must be sharp, and very near intollerable, before the Children must appeal to Magistrates. For tho' there are no positive Laws, yet Reason, Custom, and Consent of People, give such Power of Castigation and Correction to Parents, that the Laws forbid to any one besides; presuming always that the occasion will be very just, and the provocation very great, when the Parents proceed to much severity; the Laws still trust, as well they may, a great deal to the Parental kindness and affection. And yet they see sometimes that there is need of interposing their Authority, and hindring Passion from proceeding to Extremities. And in

---

1  Child support.
2  Clothing.

all such Cases, the Children are to ask for nothing but relief and ease to themselves; no hardship, penalty, or punishment, is to be sought for, to the Parent, by them; that would be impious cruelty indeed; no thought of revenge must come into their minds: They will be miserable enough in having such Parents as will provoke them to fly from *them*, for succour, to a *stranger*, without the trouble and uneasiness of seeing them miserable and suffering any Evil.

And as for matters of Contract, Estate, Inheritance, or Money, it must not be for any small matter, nor for a light injury, nor any thing easy to be born, that a Child can implead[1] his Parent; the hardship must be near intollerable; the injustice great and pressing, when a wise indifferent Man, or a Man's own Conscience can permit him to go to Law with his Father or Mother. We are oblig'd, as Christians, to bear *somewhat* at every one's Hands, and little injuries are the least we can forgive to one another. And common Sense and Reason will tell one, he is certainly oblig'd to bear more from a Parent, than from any other: And therefore the provocation and necessity must be exceeding Great and Violent, when it is not to be passed over with patience and submission by the Children. It should therefore be plain and visible to all considering People, that the Parent is very much in the wrong, doing a manifest injustice, violating the Laws of Nature, and putting off the parental love and tenderness, before a Child should publickly contest at Law: the Neighbourhood, and world around, should be convinc'd of the Parent's iniquity, and see the injury intended or done, to be intollerable, and see withal the necessity of seeking redress at the hands of Publick Justice, before the Children do it. Publick fame should go before, and prepare the minds and ears of all that shall hear it, so that every one should pitty the Children's case, in having to deal with so injurious Parents, and be concern'd to wish them success: By all which I mean to say, that the justice of the Children's Cause must be notorious, and the injury done them manifestly great, and grievous to them, before they are permitted, by their Duty, Decency, and Religion, to go to Law with their Parents.

---

1 "To sue (a person, etc.) in a court of justice" (*OED*).

The Duty indeed is somewhat altered in the case of Mothers, when they hasten to second Marriages, apparently prejudicial to their Children. The necessity of going to Law with *them*, is more frequent and more urgent than with Fathers, or with Mothers still continuing in the state of Widdowhood; because they seem to have translated their Affection and interest to another Family; and most of the comforts and conveniencies arising from such contested Money or Estate, go to *strange* People, to whom the Children have no Obligation; and therefore that Piety in Children that would permit the Mother to enjoy in peace and quiet, what was perhaps in justice none of hers, need not sometimes be scrupulous of recovering it from her, since she her self would have the least advantage by it, but it would go to utter Strangers.

While she continues in a state of Widowhood, she is their Mother still, and they are all of one piece and Family, she is presum'd to intend nothing but their Advantage, and all she has is look'd upon as theirs; and therefore if she, through covetous desire, or through mistake, or peevishness, will needs retain, what does not properly belong to her, the Children, if it can consist with their welfare by any means, will be content to bear with so much loss, or disappointment for the present, since it will certainly be theirs at last, rather than give their Parent an unnecessary grief and trouble, by going to Law. But when a new affection, and a new engagement intervene, then all the prospect is disturb'd, they see new interests rising, and the new Wife is supposed to make her self as acceptable as she can to her new choice, by bearing with her all the advantages of fortune she can get together, and in such cases does, too oft, forget her Children, and her former Love. In this case the Children are much more at liberty, to persue their just rights than otherwise they would be, because, as I said, the advantages of forbearing, would not accrue so much to the Parent, as to an utter Stranger, to whom the Children have little or no Obligation.

And yet in this case, the Children must consider well, and take good care, that they be not overbyass'd by this common prejudice, that *second Marriages are always prejudicial to the Children's Rights and Interests*, for it is not always so, though it is too often; and therefore the injury must be great and sure, as before, that will justifie the Children in their contending with their Mother, though she has now forgot their Father's House and Family. But both in this and all other cases, when the Reason is great and manifest, and the Occasion just and unavoidable, the Suit is to be manag'd with all the care and tenderness imaginable. Contests at Law, are very seldom manag'd with ordinary and common Charity; they are full of Reproach, and full of Scandal; few People think of any thing but vexing and afflicting their Adversaries, and therefore have their Eyes and Ears continually open to the faults and aspersions of their Enemies, glad to hear them represented ill, and willing to believe them so, as if they were themselves advantag'd by it. They are perpetually contriving and inventing how to lessen one another, and gain to themselves credit, at the other's expence; this makes the Law very hazardous, few People go out so innocent as they enter; they begin with desire of *Justice*, and end with a desire of *Mischief*: They begin with calmness and a tender regard to their Adversary, but proceed with Anger, and increase to Malice, and end, too often, with impatient longings for Revenge. Thus it is most commonly, when People that are Strangers, or little known to each the other go to Law together. One would hope that it should not be so with Friends and Relations, but that their natural ties of Love, should lay restraint upon their Passions, and keep them in better order. But 'tis rather all the contrary, they try at first, it may be, to moderate and keep themselves in good temper, but they quickly fly out into excess, recriminate, complain of, and reproach each other, with more sharpeness and ill-will, than other People; and knowing more of each other, they are apt to proclaim more Secrets, and consequently meet with much more Credit and Belief, and consequently do each other much more Mischief. And 'tis still worse, the nearer these Relations are to each the other; when *Children* and their *Parents* strive, there is a world of danger of ill consequences.

It must needs be uneasie to the Parents, to be suspected of Injustice, and ill design against their own Children, and to be charg'd in publick of being so: And it must needs be uneasie to the Child, to think of striving with the Parent, and to believe the Parent ill-intentioned towards him; but this Contention does too frequently betray the Child into unkind, undutiful and hard expressions; and oftentimes the Parent, to angry Curses, and fearful Imprecations, which both good Children and good Parents would by all means avoid. The fear of Injury and hope of Victory, do so exasperate People's Minds, that 'tis the sense of these ill consequences, makes the going to Law of Children with their Parents so affrightful: And makes it so much more eligible to endure a great hardship, and considerable injury, than seek for remedy at Law, to the hazarding so much mischief as does frequently ensue in such unkind contentions. What joy of Victory can be to either side, when *they* must be asham'd, confounded, and, it may be, much prejudic'd, whom we are tied, of all folks living, to honour most, and do the best service to.

But after all, let one be never so much inclin'd to favour, and secure the rights and the respects of Parents, as Nature, Reason, Decency, the Laws of God and Man require, yet when the Parents put off natural affection, and have no regard to Honesty and Justice, but follow blindly and perversely their own humour, and will not be advis'd by wise and sober and impartial People, to do that right to Children, which both the Laws of God and Man require and call for at their hands, no one can reasonably condemn the Children that implore the assistance of the Laws and Magistrates, to get themselves redress'd: Provided they do it by necessity, with tenderness, and all the respect an honour possible, never aggravating any thing done, any farther than there is need to their own vindication, of which they must not yet be over-tender, to the disparagement and great blame of their Parents: They ought to be exceeding careful to conceal the faults and the miscarriages of them: I do not see, but the same piety would have endeavour'd to cover *Noah's Cruelty*, or *Injustice*, or *Perverseness*, had he been guilty of them, that was so careful to conceal his *nakedness* and folly, for they are also the shame and nakedness of the understanding; and such infirmities of the mind no less dishonourable than those of the body, which no one likes to discover in their Parents and Relations.

★     ★     ★     ★

from "Discourse IV."
Ephesians vi. Verse 4.
*And ye Fathers provoke not your Children to wrath, but bring them up in the Nurture, and Admonition of the Lord.*

Having already treated of the Duty of Children to their Parents, and considered some of the most proper Cases, in that Relation; I am now to speak a little to the advice that St. *Paul* here gives to Parents, how to behave themselves towards their Children. He had spoken to Children, in the verse before, *Children obey your Parents in the Lord, for this is right; Honour thy Father and Mother, that it may be well with thee, and thou mayest live long on the Earth*; and then he applies himself to Parents, *And ye Fathers, & c.*

I take if for a Rule, and granted, that there is no Relation in the World, either Natural, or Civil and agreed upon, but there is a Reciprocal duty obliging each Party. There is no such thing as one Man's requiring Love, Respect, Honour, Service, or Obedience, from another, without being, at the same time, oblig'd to do him some good turn for it, or for having already done it. God is not indeed a Debtor to any Man, but the thing at the bottom is the same; it is for our Creation, Preservation, for all the blessings of this Life, and for the promises and hopes of a better, that we owe him, and are call'd upon to pay him, Honour and Service, Praise and Thanksgiving. Without *those*, he would have no right to *these*; we need not fear to say so. We should not *praise* him, but for the good we have receiv'd, nor *pray* to him, but for the good we expect to receive *from* him. Now though he does not antecedently owe these favours and blessings to Mankind, yet it is necessary that he do them, before any Obligation can be laid on Mankind, to pay him Prayer or Praise, Honour, Service or Thanksgiving. There is therefore nothing more certain than this, that as all Duties and Relations are at first founded upon Benefits hoped for, or already receiv'd, so no one can require any thing, as a Duty, at another's hands, without having oblig'd him, or intending to oblige him, by something answerable to what he asks. And therefore though the Parental Relation, may seem, of all others, to be most at liberty, yet the truth is this, that all the Right and Claim they have to the Love, Respect, the Service, and Obedience of their Children, is founded on the love they shew them, and the good they do them, according to their Understanding and Ability. And therefore if Parents, out of cruelty or wantonness, should expose their Newborn-Infants to the rage of wild Beasts, or throw them into Rivers, and they should afterwards escape by good Providence, they might account those People for their Parents, if they would, and they might *pay* them, but they would not *owe* them, Love, or Honour, or Obedience: Their barbarous usage cancell'd the bond of Nature, and left them under no other Obligation to their Parents, than to Strangers. No body can assign a Reason why these Parents should require or expect any Duty, at these Children's Hands: For as for the *being* they may be said to give them, they took it away, as soon, and cruelly, as they could.

I only mention this, to make it very evident, that the Obligation of Children to love, honour, respect, and obey their Parents, is founded originally upon the Parents' love and care of *them*, and to shew that no one can require any thing from another as a Duty, to whom he does not also *owe* something, by way of Duty. This is necessarily to be premis'd, not only when we are considering the Duty of Parents to their Children, but to be kept in mind, in considering the duties of all Relations else, whether Natural or Civil; for, in all Relations, each Party is mutually, though differently oblig'd to each the other.

★　　★　　★　　★

And though Children (by which I understand those of years and discretion, but under the tutelage of their Parents) though Children, I say, will be the last, in whom this ill usage begets hatred, yet it will surely enough beget it in them at last; and that is a fearful consequence, of provoking Children to wrath, both to the Parents and the Children. A Man can hardly be easie under the known ill-will of any Relation, or one he has much to do withal; but this uneasiness grows up to pain and great trouble, when the Relation is very near; it is impossible for either Parents to hate their Children, or Children their Parents, or to think they are hated by each the other, without great grief and trouble; it sits so hard upon their minds, that they are never quiet under it; if they are otherwise never so happy, yet the remembrance of this enmity interrupts their content, and spoils all; *All this availeth me nothing*, saith *Haman* to his Wife recounting his felicities, *whilst I see* Mordechai *the* Jew *sitting at the Gate*. It is not what we have, that makes us happy, if we think we want something besides; that which a restless Envy, and unmeasurable Ambition spake by *him*, is spoken inwardly by Love or Grief, when near Relations quarrel with each other; all things besides afford no setled Peace or Pleasure, whilst that great breach continues.

Even where the mind of one Party, (and that the injur'd and offended one) is satisfied with the reasonableness and justice of his being at variance, and sees the necessity there is of continuing his displeasure, and that great mischiefs would arise from a Compliance and Reconciliation (and such cases may very well happen, and that between Parents and Children) yet is not the mind at perfect quiet, for all this; the voice of Nature is louder than that of Reason, and strict Justice, and beats importunately at the Heart, and there will be no lasting rest, till all is over, and a thorough Reconciliation bring back each Party to their natural Affections, and place them in the state they were at first, and always should be.

This sore and uneasie condition the mind is in, during a state of enmity, should be one motive to the keeping and preserving love and friendship betwixt Relations; and since the Hearts of Parents do so naturally incline to Children, and *love*, they say, *descends*, it ought to move them to the greater care, not to irritate them too far by a cruel usage; that they put it not past the power of Reconciliation; for when hatred is once taken up, and begins to fix and settle in People's minds, it is very hard to root it out again.

\*　　\*　　\*　　\*

And, after all that can be said, it were much better for the World, and more reasonable, all things considered, that more Children should suffer from the rigours of their Parents, than do, (or ever will do) than that Parents out of fear of offending on this side, should be restrain'd from using such severities, as they (who know their Children's Humours and Inclinations best) shall think convenient, and most proper; or that Children should dispute, contest and quarrel their right, or should withdraw themselves from their Obedience, upon any such pretence: Of the two evils, this, beyond Comparison, would be the greater; and therefore, however hard and heavy the dominion of some Parents may be, I know no remedy or way to ease the Children, whilst they continue under them, but a submissive, meek, and dutiful Deportment towards them; patience, and quiet undergoing what is laid upon them, will soonest bring the Parents to Consideration and Reason, and mollifie and break their fury, and sometimes their Hearts; when a perverse and contumacious obstinacy will but exasperate to greater anger and severity: And time at length will either vanquish their Austerity, or set the Children at their liberty, so that they have not long, or much to suffer. And therefore tho' the Text is, *Fathers provoke not your Children to Wrath*; Yet I will make an end with the Command foregoing, *Children obey your Parents in the Lord, for this is right.*

### 3. Sarah, Duchess of Marlborough,[1] "Correspondence with her Granddaughter, Diana, Duchess of Bedford, 1732-35," in *Letters of a Grandmother 1732-35*, ed. Gladys Scott Thomson (London: Jonathan Cape, 1943).

November 18, 1732

I will come to you this afternoon, my dear Duchess of Bedford since you desire it of me. But I must at the same time own to you, that I think it would be more for your own satisfaction if you would live with me as I proposed; that is with all the outward appearance that is usual between such near relations who

---

1   Sarah, Duchess of Marlborough (1660-1744). Born Sarah Jennings, she secretly married John Churchill, First Duke of Marlborough (1650-1722), a prominent English general, in 1678. In 1683 she became a Lady of the Bedchamber for Anne, influencing the future queen to support the overthrow of her father, James II, in the Glorious Revolution of 1688, and subsequently, to privilege the Whig party in the awarding of political offices. She was dismissed from Anne's service after losing favor with the queen.

have been so long good friends and that would prevent any new discourses in the world, for whatever you do I shall always wish your happiness and think it of more consequence than my own, but I can't do impossibilities. Any person that ever loved another must needs be sensible that there can be no great joy in the conversation of those that come to one from one's greatest enemies and such as have used me in so shameful a manner. Something of this kind I have intended to say to you ever since the monstrous treatment which I had from the rest of your family, which I do believe you were very sorry for, though I have often observed you were very partial to them, and I was unwilling to give you uneasiness in the condition you were in and therefore deferred it. But now I must tell you that you must choose one of two things: which is to live with me as I have proposed, or to distinguish yourself by shewing how far you are from having any of Lady Bateman's principles.[1] I don't mean by this that you should not see your brothers, but she is a disgrace to be anybody's sister.

It has been the custom of all times to put a mark upon the contriver of any great mischief, and as to my two grandsons, they cannot help their weakness, nor is there any reason to apprehend any deep plot from them, they have only given a great wound to their characters. Since John Spencer[2] likes it better to depend upon a vain extravagant brother than to have had a great estate from me, by only acting like a man of sense and true principles, he may please himself, for I shall concern myself no more about him. But for Lady Bateman I must declare that I never can have any satisfaction in the conversation of anybody that has any commerce with her, I mean as to my own relations, for as to common acquaintances, I don't concern myself with what they do.

I desire, my dear, that you will consider very well before you take your resolution, for, as I have already said, your happiness is what I most desire in everything that is in nature possible for

---

1   Lady Bateman, formerly Anne Spencer, was Diana's sister and Sarah's granddaughter. Sarah distrusted Lady Bateman, believing that she worked against her in all family concerns.

2   John Spencer, Sarah's grandson and Diana's older brother.

me to comply with and whatever you do must be with the approbation of the Duke of Bedford,[1] for without doing everything that is agreeable to him you cannot be happy. If you determine upon the way that the two ladies you sent told me you were inclined, (that is) not to take away those few comforts I have left, (then) you must be very plain with Lady Bateman – for there is no acting in a thing of this kind by halves or by trimming – in letting her know that you can have no commerce with her; that you are very sorry that she did not reflect upon the very ill consequences of what she has done; that all people that are either good or reasonable are and must be sensible that there is no precedent of such a treatment to a grandmother that for thirty years has been labouring to assist and serve the whole family, and has done it with great success; and that you cannot live with any quiet or ease if you do anything that is grievous to me.

I think I am not in my nature at all partial, and I am the more persuaded my notions are right in this, because I do know that those of the most cool temper can't help saying that nothing was ever so scandalous as all that Lady Bateman has done, but I do again protest to you that I wish to have you do as you judge best and right, and all I desire is that I may be as easy as I can make myself in such melancholy circumstances, and whatever you do, I shall always be most affectionately yours.

S. Marlborough

Tunbridge Wells[2]<br>August 24th, 1733

I have received yours, dear Di, of the 20th from Thorney, and since I find by it that my former letter has found you, I will thank you likewise for that of the 11th from Woburn,[3] and send mine to Southampton House,[4] where I suppose, somebody always knows where you are.

---

1  Diana's husband, previously Lord John Russell.
2  Sarah was visiting this fashionable spa, known for its health-giving mineral springs.
3  Woburn Abbey, residence of John Russell and his wife Diana Spencer Russell.
4  Southampton House, in Bloomsbury Square, London, was the family home of the Dukes of Bedford, though Lady Rachel Russell, the grandmother of John and his

I am not yet determined when I shall leave this place, because, though the weather, I believe, is a little too cold for waters, I take them in bed and by putting them into a very hot cup, which takes off the great coldness of them, I hope they will do me some good, for hitherto they have agreed very well with me.

*     *     *     *

When I came here first, my Lady Bristol[1] bragged mightily how many votes she had got for the Duke of Dorset.[2] I wish he had nothing to serve him better than her interest, for she is a mighty ridiculous woman, entirely wicked in all things. But though her actions are so bad, I can't think her what one calls a fool. She is worthless, but there is a mixture of cunning and sometimes a good deal of wit and sharpness in her answers.

Now I will tell you a thing that may perhaps make you laugh. She came to me and reproached me much for not coming to her at London, nor letting her come to me. I answered her civilly, but extremely coldly. But at last she prevailed with me to make a party to play[3] at my house (for I never play abroad, nor go out but to take the air) and we agreed upon articles, how it should be, and one of the chief preliminaries of this peace was, that she should stake. For her method is that sometimes a mark goes for a guinea and sometimes for five, and it is extreme puzzling and troublesome to watch her. But at last she agreed to all the conditions I proposed and we played two or three days. But at last it was so uneasy to her to be kept in order, that when she sat down to play, she put her hand in her pocket and said she had lost her purse. There was no remedy for that: so we played as well as we could. She sent several mes-

---

brother Wriothesley, had continued to live there until her death in 1723. At Wriothesley's death, his brother John, Diana's husband, became Duke of Bedford.

1   Lady Bristol was the second wife of John Hervey, Earl of Bristol, and a Lady of the
Bedchamber to Queen Caroline. She was fifty-seven years old at this time (compared to Sarah's seventy-three years).

2   Lionel Cranfield Sackville, first Duke of Dorset (1688-1765). He was Lord Lieutenant of Ireland from 1730-37. In 1735, Sir Robert Walpole tried to have him
removed from office by advising the Queen to offer his post to Lord Scarlborough.
Scarlborough refused the position, and Dorset continued as Lord Lieutenant.

3   To play cards.

sages about for this purse and acted the part pretty well. But I observed that she was not really angry, nor troubled at the disappointment of all her enquiries. And yet she said, there was eight or ten guineas in it and a double moidore.[1] Notwithstanding, she was in a sweet temper all the night, which made me conclude this losing the purse was only a stratagem to save staking, in order to make her mark sometimes forgot. When the play was over, I told her, that I had often looked into my pockets for things and have not found them at first, having four little pockets in one great one. And I desired her to search again all her pockets, which are made the same as mine. She said she was sure, and had not it. Then I desired the Duchess of Manchester, and I might search all the pockets. And so we went to romps. But she struggled with us and got the better, for I would not carry the jest too far....

The post is just going and I have time only to desire that you will present my humble service to the Duke of Bedford.

**4. Samuel Richardson, *Letters Written To and For Particular Friends, on the Most Important Occasions* (1741), in *Familiar Letters on Important Occasions*, ed. Brian W. Downs (New York: Dodd, Mead & Co., 1928).**

LETTER XLIX

*To a Brother too captious[2] to bear himself the Ridicule he practices upon others.*

*Dear* Jack,

I am glad to find you improve both in *thought* and *speech*. You know I am no witch at either: But, so as we have some wit in our family, no matter who is at the trouble of carrying it, for what he'll get by it. I suppose you thought to give no small pleasure to the company last night by your facetious flings at all

---

1  A moidore was "a gold coin of Portugal, current in England in the first half of the eighteenth century ..." (*OED*).
2  Liable to find fault in others.

around you, not excepting the Parson himself: But should you not have considered, that every one in the room had a right to return the freedom you took, in the best manner he was able? Was it therefore well in you to resent so warmly as you did, a smart remark made by Mr. Crispe, on a palpable blunder of your own, when you had taken so much liberty with him, as well as every body else, just before? Indeed, brother, you must either lay aside ridicule, or learn to bear it better; and, in the present case, you should have remembered, that, in the manner you began with that gentleman, it was not possible for him to say any thing it would have been to your credit to resent. A retort on these occasions must be excused, tho' fraught with resentment; for a man is not always in a humour to be jested with, and it is the duty of him who begins, to take what follows. Your failing in this known rule, whatever you may think, has made you appear in so mean a light to the whole company, that all your acuteness will not in haste atone for it.

If I judge rightly, nothing is more delicate than ridicule: Where it is conducted with prudence and humour, it is sure to please even the man who is the subject of it, if he is not of a morose temper: but when, instead of that, personal failings, or private indiscretions, are exposed for the entertainment of a company, tho' you may think to raise a laugh by it in the unreflecting, it will bring upon you the censure of the considerate. It is our duty to consult what we can *bear* ourselves, as well as what we can *inflict* on others. For my own part, I know I cannot bear what is called a *close rub*,[1] as many men can; and for that reason I never jest with any body, unless by way of reprisal; and that I shorten all I can, lest my temper should not hold out.

No doubt but you have more humour than I; but if you do not blend in it a quantity of temper sufficient to carry it off, you will be no gainer by the qualification. The philosopher says, That to *bear* and *forbear*, are the highest points of wisdom: If so, where is his wisdom, who will neither do the one nor the

---

1   A joke that comes too close to home.

other? You may not like the freedom I have here taken; but I respect you too well to pass over your foibles without some observation; being

Your truly affectionate Brother.

## LETTER XCIV

*To a rich Widow Lady, with Children, dissuading her from marrying a Widower of meaner Degree who has Children also.*

*Dear Madam,*
It is with some reluctance, and great respect, that I prevail on myself to give you this trouble. The frequent visits Mr. Clarkson makes you, and the airs that gentleman assumes, have given birth to a report, that a treaty of marriage between you is on foot; and that, in all probability, it will be soon brought to effect.

To be sure Mr. Clarkson is not to be blam'd, to endeavour to procure for his wife a lady of your prudence, good character, and fortune; but whether you will be able to avoid the censure of the world, if you choose *him* for an husband, is another point, which greatly concerns you to consider of, and affects me, and all who wish you well.

His fortune, madam, is not equal to yours, supposing it to be better than the world reports it: He has children: So have you. What inconveniences may not arise from hence! Especially, as he is not thought to be one of the best and smoothest temper'd men in the world. – His character is not equal, in any respect, to say the least (for I would not detract from any man's merit), to that of your late good spouse, my dear friend; who would have been much grieved, if he had had but the least apprehension, that the man he would not have accompany'd with, should succeed him in his bed.

Far be it from me, dear madam, if you are so disposed, as to wish to hinder you from a change of condition with a suitable person! But as your late spouse left *his* and *your* children so much in your power, methinks you should take especial care how and to whom you communicate any part of that power, and thereby give a *right* to controul not only *them,* but yourself. Must *he* not be partial to *his own* children? And will he not expect, that your complaisance to him should make *you* so too; or, at least, be his children's behaviour what it will, that it shall induce you to put them upon a *par* with your own? His daughters will be spies upon your conduct, and, be you ever so kind to them, will always suspect your partiality to your own, and treat you as their *mother-in-law*; and their father will believe all they shall suggest, for *that* very reason, and because he will *judge,* tho' perhaps not *allow for,* that you *ought* to prefer *your own* to *his*: And this will be the source of perpetual uneasiness between you. Consider, dear madam, whether your late affectionate spouse deserved from you, that *his* children and *your own* should be put upon such difficulties, in favour of those of *any other* person whatever.

No doubt but you may make your own conditions with Mr. Clarkson. He will be glad to call you and your fortune *his,* upon any terms: But consider, madam, how difficult it may be, whatever articles you make, for a good wife, who has been accustomed to think her *interest* the *same* with that of her *husband,* to refuse to his *importunities,* and perhaps to his *conveniency,* if not *necessities,* those communications of fortune, which you may reserve in your own power, when they will make him *easier* in circumstance, and *more complaisant* in temper: And how hard it will be to deny a man *any thing,* to whom you have given your *person,* and to whom you have vowed *duty* and *obedience.* But if you should have the resolution to *refuse* him, what he may not be backward to *ask,* do you think yourself so well able to bear that *indifference,* if not *worse,* which such a refusal may occasion? And would you choose to have advantage taken of your *tenderest hours,* either to induce you to acquiesce with importunities, which, comply'd with, may hurt your *children*; or to have those tender moments dash'd with suspicions of *selfishness* and *design*? For prudence will oblige you to be on your guard, that even the *highest acts of kindness,* and the *strongest professions* of *affection,* may not be preparative arts to obtain from you concessions you *ought* not to make. And how will the pure joys which flow from an *unsuspected* union of minds and interests, the want whereof will make *any* matrimony unhappy, be found in a state thus circumstantiated?

If, madam, you are bent upon a change of condition, your friends would wish first, that you will be pleased absolutely to ascertain the fortunes of your children, according to the *design* and *will* of their *dear father*, as far as may *legally* be done, either by choosing trustees for them, or by such other way as shall put it out of a *new* husband's power to hurt them: and when he shall know this *is done*, you will have a better testimony of his affection, as he will know what *is*, and what *is not* yours, and can hope for no more, because it is not in your power to give more. But how much more is it to be wished, for your own sake, as well as your children's, that if you do change, it may be with a person who has *no* children! And then what *other* children may be the results of your *new marriage*, they will be *your own* as well as *his*, and so be *more properly* intitled to your *care*, and your *kindness*, than any man's children by *another wife* can be.

By this means, madam, most of the uneasinesses we every day see in families, where are *two sorts* of children, will be prevented; or perhaps your present children will be grown up, and out of the way, before the other can *interfere* essentially with them; or if *not,* they will be *naturalized*, as one may say, to each *other*; and, having the *same* mother, who has an *equal* interest in them *all*, will *expect* and *allow* for an *equal* exertion of tenderness and favour to *all*.

I will trouble you with no more at present on this head; and am confident, that when you consider maturely what I have written, and the respectful manner in which I have ventured to give my opinion, and my own disinterestedness besides, and that I might still have urged other powerful motives, which I forbear in *honour* to you, you will have the goodness to excuse the liberty I have taken, which is so suitable to the laws of *friendship*, by which I am bound to be, dear madam,

*Your zealous Well wisher, and humble Servant.*

# LETTER CXXVIII

*A Sea Officer to his Wife.*

Port-Mahon,[1] October 31.

*My dear Life,*

I take the opportunity afforded me by Captain Copythorne, who is returning to England, to let you know, that I am in perfect health at present, God be praised; tho' I have, with many of the crew, been down of the *bloody-flux*,[2] occasioned by being a little too free with the new wines and fruit of these countries; and yet I thought I was very moderate in both. Our captain continues very civil and kind, and places his principal confidence in me; and I endeavour so to behave on the occasion, as to avoid incurring the envy of every one; and indeed, have the good fortune to be generally respected.

Captain Copythorne is so kind as to carry to you a token of my affection; which is a small parcel of Cyprus wine, that I believe will be agreeable to your best friend Mrs. Simpson, to whom therefore you may present half, and keep the other for your own use. The Captain has also fifty dollars to present you with, from me, only paying out of them the *duty for the wine*; for it is but *just*, that it should be so, if he cannot meet with favour in so small parcel; for what the law of the land, which protects us all, gives to the King, is as much *his* due (however other people act), as any part of my private property, which is secured to me by the *same law*, is *mine*: and I am convinc'd, that if every one acted up to this just principle, there need not be so many taxes as there are; and the fair trader, and all honest men, would be the better for it.

I hope my dear Jacky and Nancy continue in good health, and dutiful, and come on in their *schooling*; for that will stand them in stead, perhaps, when the poor matters we are enabled to do for them, may not be worth trusting to.

I long to see my dear Betty. God give us a happy meeting, if it be his blessed will. But, I believe, it will hardly be till we have

---

1  Seaport capital of the Spanish island Menorca, off the east coast of Spain.
2  Dysentery.

humbled the proud Jack Spaniard:[1] Which God also grant. For that nation has been very vile and base to us honest Englishmen. This concludes me at present.

*Your ever-loving Husband.*

Love and service to all friends.

## LETTER CXXIX

*A Wife to her Husband at Sea.*

*My Dear,*
I think it a long time since I have had the comfort and satisfaction of hearing of your welfare. Often and often do I reflect on the unhappiness of us poor women, who are married to seafaring men. Every *wind* that blows, every *pyrate*[2] we hear of, and now, in *time of war,*[3] every hour of our lives, the dread of *enemies* alarms us. God's providence is our reliance, and so it ought; for nothing else can sustain us thro' our different apprehensions every day we live. But to be sure the unhappiness is still greater to such as love one another, as we always did. I hope, when it shall please God to return you safe to my wishes, that you will take no more of these very long voyages, if you can help it. The trips to Holland or France are so pretty, that they rather add to, than diminish one's comforts: But, oh, these long, long voyages! Yet, in time of war, people cannot do as they will. And I must be contented; and the more, when I see, that the fine ladies of Captains, Commodores, and Admirals, are no better off than your poor Jenny.

We have had the misfortune to lose Uncle James since you went: He was a *landman,* out of the dangers *you* run; yet, as I hope, God has preserved *you,* while *he* is dead and *gone.* So we see there is nothing to be said for it, when our time is come.

---

1     Britain was at war with Spain over the War of the Austrian Succession (1740–48). "Jack Spaniard" was a derogatory name for the country's naval forces.
2     Pirate.
3     The War of the Austrian Succession (1740–48), in which the British, with Hessian and Hannovarian armies, fought the French and Spanish to determine the successor to the Austrian throne.

They talk of my aunt's marrying again; and she has a courtier comes to her, because she is aforehand in the world; and yet Uncle James has not yet been dead three months. Fie upon her, I say, tho' she is my aunt! for she had a good husband of him. As to you and me, my dear, I hope God will spare us to one another; for you are my *first* love, and shall be my *last*. Cousin Barns had the misfortune to break his leg, but is in a good way. Jenny Adams is to be married next week to John Lascells. This is all the news among our acquaintance; for I am sure it is none to tell you, that I am

*Your faithful and loving Wife.*

## LETTER CXLVII

*A Lady to her Friend, a young Widow Lady, who, having bury'd a polite and excellent Husband, inclines to marry a less deserving Gentleman, and of unequal Fortune.*

Dear Madam,
Were I to lay it down for a maxim, that *maids* often mend their circumstances by marriage, *widows* very rarely, I believe I might be justified by every one's experience. To what can the truth of this observation be owing? Is it to be supposed, that widows have stronger passions than maids? Shall the proud lordly sex have it to boast, that they are such estimable creatures, that when once one of them has had the fortune to be chosen by a lady, and has been taken from her by death, she cannot live without taking another, and finds herself obliged to accept of the next that offers, thro' all disadvantages, and every degree of inequality? Surely this cannot be the case! Surely a prudent, a modest lady, will not say this, in *so many words*! – Much less, then, ought she to confess it by her *actions*, which are much stronger than *words*. For I believe no woman who ever enter'd the pale of matrimony with sprightly hopes about her, found the possession (*sex only* consider'd) equal to her expectations. The maid may hope, may fansy much, in the commerce between the sexes, from her meditating on the heighten'd scenes which pernicious novels, and idle romances, the poison

of female minds, abound with.[1] But the widow *knows* 'tis all *free-masonry*,[2] all empty hope, flashy, foolish, unworthy, unpermanent, and, but for the law of nature, despicable. —— Whence is it then, that the *wishing*, expecting maid, should be more prudent than the *knowing*, experienced widow? Should be better proof, with raised imaginations, against courtship or persuasion, than one who well knows the transitory vanity and unsatisfactoriness of the end to which that courtship or persuasion tends?

If it be said, That *this* point is not so much the case, as the *settled* life of matrimony, which has been once so satisfactorily experienced; let the circumstances of a lady who abounds in every thing, answer this poor, but common excuse; and let the choice she makes of the person and fortune of her second husband (which is generally, as I have observed above in both cases, far short of her former choice) acquit or convict her, as her conduct shall deserve.

If a young widow, indeed, advantages *herself*, and worsts not her *children* (if she has any), in her second adventure, let her proceed: She is justified to worldly prudence. But this, as I have said, is so seldom the case, even with widow ladies of modesty, and *discretion* in other respects, that I must own I have been often puzzled and confounded how to account for the motives of such an one, reputably; especially when she appears to me and all the world, neither to have done honour to the memory of her late spouse, to her family, to herself, nor, as sometimes has been the case, paid any regard to common decency. How, I say, shall this be accounted for, in a lady of prudence and virtue? Is it, that, as one extreme is said to border on another, *extreme joy* treads on the heels of *extreme sorrow*? It cannot be; for as, on one

---

1 Richardson is writing at a time – the early 1740s – when novel-writing was in its infancy. The novel as a genre was somewhat primitive, blending together in various combinations such earlier prose forms as the romance, the travel narrative, the scandal chronicle, and the rogue biography, as well as others, to create a hybrid form that in its newness and its mixed nature made readers somewhat uncomfortable and suspicious. Young girls, especially, were advised not to read novels by many conduct books of the day.

2 The masons' guilds in medieval England were originally set up as professional organizations for stonecutters, but by the eighteenth century the organizations had opened up to men of prominence in the community and embraced the ideals of religious toleration, equality, and fraternity, as well as a spirit of liberalism.

hand, I am sure there can be no *extreme joy* in the matrimonial commerce; so, I fear, where a woman can soon forget her departed spouse, she cannot be sensible of *extreme grief* for his loss. And if she will take upon her this latter part of the character, and own the first was thus indifferent to her, she shall have my consent to do any thing she has a mind to do, and I will exempt her willingly from the observation of every other rule of prudence and decency.

But in a case the direct reverse of this, how shall we account for such a behaviour? How, in particular, if the charming the blooming Miss Bendish, who was so coy a maiden, and with so much difficulty won by the late amiable and conversable Mr. Brookes, with a fortune superior to her own, should, within a few months after his decease, when blest with an affluence left her by his generosity and affection for her, be won by Mr. Fownes, a man less accomplish'd as to knowledge, less amiable in his person, less polite in his conversation, and of a fortune so much beneath what was even her maiden one, that her friends then would never have thought him worthy of her? – How, I say, shall we account for this, if it should be so? Is there a secret sympathy in tempers and dispositions, that attracts each its like by motives imperceptible and unaccountable? It cannot be in *this* case, surely. For can the polite Mrs. Brookes be less polite for having been marry'd to one of the best bred and best–behav'd gentlemen in *England*? And can she so soon get over forms as a *widow*, for such a suitor as Mr. Fownes, which as a *maid* were so long before they could be dispensed with in favour of *such* a lover as Mr. Brookes? – Is her soft and delicate mind, as we all think it, after *all*, more on a level with that of the one gentleman, than that of the other *far more* excellent one? Has she, will the licentious ask, stronger incentives to a married state as a widow, than she had as a maid? – It cannot be! – What then shall we say to all this? – For, after all, two years won not Miss Bendish, to a gentleman of exalted worth; and two months seem to have made a great progress with Mrs. Brookes! – And that in favour of a gentleman, whom we all think unworthy of her at all.

My dear bosom-friend, my schoolfellow, my companion, as

well in the *maiden* as in the *matrimonial*, tho', I bless God, not in the *vidual*[1] state, resolve me these questions; answer to me for this conduct; account to me for these seemingly unaccountable motives; and thereby justify yourself to your *reputation*, to the *memory* of the *dear departed*, to your *own sex*, to the *other sex* (so attentive as they *both* are to your conduct in this particular), and, lastly, which will for ever oblige me, to

> *Your affectionate and Faithful Friend and Servant.*

## LETTER CXLVIII

*From a Gentleman, strenuously expostulating with an old rich Widow, about to marry a very young gay Gentleman.*

*Madam,*

I am very sorry to hear of the encouragement you give to the visits of young Mr. Barnes, because of the great difference in years between you. I cannot help giving you the trouble of this expostulation, tho' I am told (and much affected I am with the news, if it be true), that the matter between you is so far gone, that all I can say may too probably prove ineffectual.

Our sex, madam, in all your late husband's time, has received an advantage and a credit from your conduct in the married state; and now, I wish it may not receive as great a disparagement, since the prudent Mrs. Bates thinks fit to countenance the addresses of one who was born after she was marry'd, and a mother, and who can possibly have no other inducement than your fortune. I believe, madam, you never knew one happy marriage of this sort in all your life: And you will reflect, that you will not be intitled to pity, nor the young man to censure, if he should prove the worst and most profligate of husbands to you. For every one will censure *you*, and acquit *him*, should he even treat you with personal abuse and barbarity.

Besides, it is well known, that Mr. Barnes is a young man of no very promising inclinations. Some young gentlemen are as grave and discreet at twenty-five, as others at thirty-five: But he

---

1   "Of or belonging to, befitting, a widow or widowhood" (*OED*).

has all the vanity, the gaiety, the affectation, of any one at his time of life: And can you expect, that he will treat *you* well, that was never noted for treating his *own mother* very dutifully, who, by the way, is *younger* than yourself? Advanced years are the constant subject of ridicule with such wild young fellows, to their shame be it spoken! And what can you expect, when the very motives by which you shall be supposed to be activated in such a match, will involve you in the deepest censure, will make you the contempt of persons of all ages, and both sexes, and expose you to the low buffoonery even of the man you have chosen, who, instead of being your protector, as an hus-band ought to be, will probably be the person who will *lead the jest* that all will join in upon you, in order to excuse his own sordid choice?

You owe it, madam, give me leave to say, to the *memory* of your late worthy *husband*; you owe it to your *sex*; you owe it to *yourself*, and your *own interest*, and *future good*; nay, to *decency*, I will venture to add; to proceed no further in this affair. It seems to me, to be next to a degree of incest for a woman all hoary and grey-goosed over by time, or who will be soon so, to expose herself to the embraces of a young fellow, who is not so old as her first son would have been, had he lived. Forgive me, madam; but I cannot help this plain-dealing on the occasion. If you proceed in giving encouragement to the boy's address, I expect not, nor can I desire, to be forgiven, or to stand upon common terms with you: If otherwise, I am ready to ask your pardon. But I cannot with patience think, that Mrs. Bates, who has passed thro' every station *hitherto* with so much applause, as well that of the prudent *widow*, and exemplary *matron*, as the affectionate *wife*, should give so great a wound to her sex as she will do, if she makes such a boy as Mr. Barnes the successor to her late worthy husband, and the master of her person and for-tune: By which act she will vow obedience to one who was in the cradle, when she had children of her own who were rising from it; and who would undoubtedly despise her in this light, were it not for her wealth; all of which that he can get at, by force, or fair means (if he act by you as others generally have done in the same circumstances), will be squandered away upon rival objects more suitable to his youth, while you will be the laughing-stock and scorn of such as will revel in *your* spoils, and triumph over you by the help of your own *fortune*. Meantime you will be so far from engaging the pity of your sex, that the more considerate of them will shun and contemn you, as one who has brought a disgrace upon it: The men will despise and flout you, and you will have nothing to do but to hide in a contemn'd obscurity that grey-green head which has so inconsiderately involved you in so much distress, and to turn penitent for it, and pray for an end to a miserable life; which, come when it will, will give cause of joy and triumph to your young husband, and very little sorrow to any other person.

But I hope still for better things; and I hope for pardon for this freedom; for fain would I be thought by Mrs. Bates,

*Her affectionate and faithful Friend, and humble Servant.*

## LETTER CLIV

[*From a Young Lady in Town to her Aunt in the Country.*]
*Diversions of* Vaux-hall *described.*

*Honoured Madam,*

I went on Monday last to Vaux-hall Gardens;[1] whither everybody must go, or appear a sort of monster in polite company. For the convenience of waterage, as well as of conversation, we were a pretty large company, and the evening proved serene and clear.

The passage from Somerset Stairs,[2] where we took water, was pleasant enough; the Thames[3] at high-water being a most beautiful river, especially above Westminster,[4] where the green banks, and the open country, afford a very agreeable prospect. The place we landed at was crouded with boats, and from the water-side to the gardens we walked through a double line of gaping watermen, footmen, old beggar women, and children.

---

1  Vauxhall Gardens, a popular pleasure garden.
2  Stairs down to the river, at Somerset.
3  River that runs through London.
4  The City of Westminster, on the north bank of the Thames.

As soon as we entered the walks, I was pleased with a sort of stage, or scaffold, raised at the entrance, for the servants of the company to sit out of their masters' way, and yet within call of the waiters.

The music-gallery and organ look perfectly polite; and their being raised one story from the ground has a good effect upon the music. The walks are well enough, but environ'd with paltry wooden boards, where I expected at least a good brick-wall. One part of the whole is thrown into walks only; the other is on the sides filled with seats or arbours, with painted backs; on each of which is represented some scene of our most common plays, or the youthful representation of the infant games, &c. I happened to have at my back honest Hob, come dripping wet out of the well;[1] and the young fellows, under colour of shewing their taste in observing the beauties of the piece, were so perpetually staring in our faces, that Cousin Bet and I had little pleasure in our supper. Perhaps you will wonder at our supping in so open a place; but I assure you, madam, no lady is too tender for so fashionable a repast. My uncle treated us very chearfully; but I could not help grudging the expence he was at; for when the reckoning was paid, it amounted to no less than ten shillings a head; which I think too dear, as the entrance-money must be sufficient to defray the house and music. But as the whole is devoted to pleasure, the expence seems rather to create satisfaction, than distaste, as it gives an opportunity to gallant people to oblige those they love, or pretend to love, in order, most of them, to pay themselves again with large interest.

The figure of Mr. Handel,[2] a great master of music, stands on one side the gardens, and looks pretty enough: The music plays from five to ten, about three tunes (I believe I should have said pieces) in an hour. They are all reported to be the best

---

1   "Hob" is "a familiar or rustic variation of the Christian name 'Robert' or 'Robin.' Hence formerly a generic name for: A rustic, a clown" (*OED*). The scene represented on the back of the young lady's seat is of the representative uncouth rural youth playing a game.

2   Georg Friedrich Handel (1685-1759), German composer who moved to England in 1712 and remained there for the rest of his life. Known for his *Water Music* (1717), *Messiah* (1742) and over 40 operas.

performers who assist here: But my rough ears cannot distinguish.

About ten o'clock, many people think of home: But the votaries of Cupid, I am told, about that time, visit the remotest walks, and sigh out the soft passion in accents that may possibly be improved by the melting sweetness of the music – I would not have you from hence conclude any rudeness can be offered; for at the termination of every walk, through the whole garden, is placed a man to protect the company from all manner of insult. But when the place grows thin of company, the lovers have a better chance to escape being laugh'd at, on the appearance of any amorous symptom.

Soon after ten, we returned to our boat; and I found the passage extremely cold, notwithstanding a covering over us: I must own, I wish'd to be at home, long before I reached it; for I was taken with such a shivering, as did not leave me for two days.

Thus, madam, have I been at Vaux-hall, with the croud of fashion-hunters. But if nobody had a greater inclination than I have to go thither again that amusement would soon be given up – for I see more and more, that, do what I will, Nature never designed me to be polite; and I can sincerely declare, that I take more satisfaction in an evening-walk with you up the West-grove, where I am so often benefited by your good instructions, than in the inchanting shades of the so much celebrated Vaux-hall. I am, honoured madam,

*Your most dutiful Niece.*


LETTER CLVIII

*From the same.*
*On the Diversions of the Playhouse.*

*Honoured Madam,*
Now I have, by your indulgence, tarry'd in town till the approach of winter, you will expect, that I should give you a little account of the diversions of the stage. To begin then: My cousin William and his two sisters conducted me last night to

the playhouse, and we took places in the pit.[1]

You may believe I was agreeably surprised at the magnificence of the stage, and its elegant ornaments; and I was mightily pleased to see such a prodigious number of people seated with ease, and conveniently placed to hear the natural pitch of a common voice. I did not expect to find the music so near the audience; but believe *that* the most proper situation to convey the sound over the whole theatre.

The play I saw was a comedy, in which the parts acted by women had several speeches that I thought not quite consistent with the modesty of the sex. And the freedom of their voice and gestures, tho', perhaps, suitable enough to the characters they represented, were not so pleasing to a mind bent upon innocent amusement (if not wholly upon instruction), as speeches that put us not to the expence of a blush. What hardship must it be to the minds of these women, to enter first upon this employment! How must their virtue (and sure no woman is without virtue at her entrance into the world) be shock'd, to offer themselves for the entertainment of six hundred men, and to utter words which convey ideas too gross for a modest ear, and such as would be difficult to hear in private company without confusion! How hard, then, must the utterance of them be to a numerous and gay assembly! And yet, I am assured, several women, who get their bread upon the stage, are strictly virtuous. If such there are, how great must be their merit, when compared with that of the wicked ones of our sex, who are liable to none of their certain and numerous temptations! But yet, where it can be avoided, why should women expose themselves to certain dangers, if there is a possibility of obtaining a tolerable subsistence without it! And those who can live by performance upon the stage, certainly possess qualifications more than sufficient to subsist in safer and less dependent stations.

The behaviour of the men I did not so much wonder at; for a becoming assurance in them is rather pleasing than disobliging: Nor did I perceive, that so many expressions, which are oftener miscalled *arch*, than more truly named *obscene*, were put

---

1 Fashionable seats in the theater.

into the mouths of the men as of the women; though the reason that poets have for this I cannot guess.

The conduct of the company I thought, to the highest degree, commendable: The utmost decency was observed, and I saw nothing disagreeable to the strictest politeness, or good manners; the awe given by so great an audience of persons of taste, being too much to admit any thing but what is decent and obliging: Not that I think it adviseable for women to go alone to the playhouse; for the *complaisance*, so fashionable at present, affords a sort of *occasion* for laying them under such seeming obligations as cannot be returned, and ought therefore not to be accepted.

These, dear madam, are the rough thoughts, on this occasion, of

*Your dutiful Niece.*

**5. [John Hill], *On the Management and Education of Children, A Series of Letters Written to a Neice; By the Honourable Juliana-Susannah Seymour* (London: R. Baldwin, 1754).**

from Letter VII of the Forming of Childrens' Tempers

I must confess that I have never thought Wit a very desirable Quality in a Man, and I doubt whether it have not in general done much more Harm than Good to all who have been possessed of it: In Women I am sure it is always to be feared: I never knew one of my own Sex, who had ever so small a Share of it, that did not make a very bad Use of that. The Fear when a Woman has a little Wit, is, that she should think she has a great deal; and when she has an Opinion of this she will stick at no Occasion of exerting it. Men have been condemned sometimes for sacrificing their Friend to their Joke; a Woman never made any Scruple of this. Ill-nature and Wit are commonly joined in Men; in Women, whenever there is but the smallest Portion of the latter, the former is always abundant. Ill-nature, indeed, will sometimes stand in the Place of Wit; especially when they are People of bad Dispositions with whom we converse; and this is an Accessary a Woman who would be called a Wit will never fail to take in to her Assistance. Indeed, I do not know so despicable a Character as that of a Woman who supposes she must support that of a Wit; and I wish I could not say, that, from this constant Recourse to Severity, it is in general more hateful than contemptible.

I have given you, my Dear, a frightful Character of a Woman of Wit; but look among your Acquaintance and examine those who are ambitious to be called so, and you will not say I have exaggerated any thing. My Dear, Wit, in itself, is not this hateful Thing, but it is the Associations that make it so. Wit with Candour and Good-humour is as pleasing, as with this other Mixture it is disgustful: It is thus with the Men; and certainly with the Women the Observation must hold doubly. I do not know so agreeable a Character in the World as that of a Woman who should have one of these common Acquaintance without the other; and I must confess, that if you had not too much favoured the Severity of this little Lady when her tender Years made every thing become her, she would now have been the exact Model that I would wish to propose to her Sex in that Respect. Her Wit would have been all Pleasantry, and Good-humour would have communicated an irresistible Grace to her Vivacity.

## 6. Samuel Richardson, *A Collection of the Moral and Instructive Sentiments, Maxims, Cautions, and Reflexions, Contained in the Histories of* PAMELA, CLARISSA, *and* SIR CHARLES GRANDISON (London: S. Richardson, 1755).[1]

*A Collection of the Moral and Instructive Sentiments Contained in the History of* PAMELA

Relations.

*Pamela reasons as follows with her father, who consulted her on the offer made him by several of their relations, to serve him in cultivating the farm and estate committed to his care by Mr. B.*

---

1 Richardson compiled these passages from his three novels – *Pamela* (1740), *Clarissa* (1747-48), and *Sir Charles Grandison* (1753-54) – and printed the book himself, having continued in his profession as a printer even after his success as a novelist.

We are apt to expect more regard from relations, they more indulgence from us, than strangers can have reason for...

If you bear with their faults, there will be no end of impositions; if you dismiss them, you will have their ill-will; they will impute to pride and unnaturalness, your very justice. Your prosperous lot will raise you enemies, who will believe them rather than you...

The world, moreover, will be apt to think, you are crouding upon our benefactor a numerous family of low and indigent people, tho' they should be ever so deserving....

One would not therefore, for *their* sakes, accept of their services; especially as they may serve others with equal benefit to themselves...

For I would not that any of them should be lifted out of his station, and made independent at Mr. B's expence, if their own industry would not make them so; tho' I would never scruple, reasonably, to reward their industry in the way of their callings...

If you receive some of them, will not others expect to be equally favoured? And may not this sow the seeds of envy among *them*, and occasion ill will to you?...

Mr. B. himself will perhaps, when he visits you for a month or two, as he proposes, be under some polite difficulty how to avoid taking notice of people who are your relations, tho' were they not so, their offices would not intitle them to it...

And, if they are modest and worthy, would not his more than common notice of them, lay *them* under equal difficulty?...

As for myself, believe me, I could sit down and rejoice with the meanest and remotest relation I have: But to the world's eye, I must, if I have ever so much reluctance to appear superior in theirs, endeavour to behave so properly as not to give additional discredit to his choice...

And will you not have it in your power, without injuring in the least our common benefactor, and without incurring censure for your partiality, to do kinder things by any of our relations, when *not* with you, than you can do, were they to live with you?...

There are undoubtedly more happy persons in low than in high life; one would not, therefore, encourage in any of our relations, such a proud spirit, as should make them want to raise themselves by favour, rather than merit...

I am sure, tho' four or five years of different life had passed with me in my old lady's[1] days, I had, at a certain time, a pleasure which I cannot express, in the thought of working for my living with you...

*A Collection of the Moral and Instructive Sentiments contained in the history of* CLARISSA.

"Parents. Children."

SEVERITY in some cases is clemency...

Needless watchfulness, and undue restraint, often produce artifice and contrivance...

Parents, by violently fighting against a Lover, frequently fight for him...

Daughters, *says James Harlowe*, are chickens brought up for a stranger's table...

Most unhappy is the situation of that *worthy* Child, who is obliged, in her own defence, to expose a Parent's failings...

It is impolitic in Parents to join two people in one interest, whom they wish for ever to keep asunder...

Tho' the parental authority should be deemed sacred, yet Parents should have reason in what they do...

Where the heart of a Child is sought to be engaged, the eye ought not to be disgusted...

A worthy Daughter would rather wish to appear amiable in the eyes of her own Friends and Relations, than in those of all the world besides...

Disgraceful treatment will often bring about the very end which it is intended to frustrate...

In family contentions, when every expedient to bring about

---

1 Pamela is here referring to her former mistress, Lady B, for whom she worked as a lady's maid until Lady B died, after which her son, Mr. B, pursued Pamela and eventually married her.

a reconciliation is tried, whatever be the event, the person so trying has the less to blame herself for...

How much greater must be the comfort of that young woman in an unhappy marriage, who can reflect, that she followed the advice of her Friends, and owes not her unhappiness to her own headstrong will!...

The difference between the hard usage a Child receives from a severe Parent, and the obsequious regard paid to her by a flattering Lover, is enough to make her run all risks with the latter, in order to get out of the hands of the former...

Parents sometimes make not those allowances for Youth, which, when young, they wish'd to be made for themselves...

Parents must not always expect, that *advice* should have the same force upon their Children, as *experience* has upon themselves...

In giving advice, and remonstrating, Parents and Guardians should proceed by patient reasoning and gentleness, that they may not harden where they wish to convince...

Unkind circumstances on the Parent's part, and heedless ones on the Child's, in a debate where both mean well, will make small differences great ones...

A Parent, by forcing a Child to marry the man she hates, may occasion an utter dissipation of the Child's morals, and, of consequence, her everlasting perdition...

Aversion in a Child should be distinguished from willfulness...

Strings that are overstrained must either be relaxed or break...

The time may come for a Child to consider, as the highest benefit to herself, those measures of a Parent which at present she may think grievous...

The more obstinate a Child is in her opposition to a Parent's will, the more will a Parent be apt to think his authority concerned to carry his point...

Harsh and cruel treatment humbles a Child, and makes her seem *cheap* in her own eyes...

*Is she not then in the way to become the easy prey of a man whom otherwise she would have despised?*

If Parents, by appeals or otherwise, needlessly expose a Child, she will be apt to think, that, do what she will, she cannot incur more disgrace than she already labours under...

To endeavour to force a free mind, is to dishonour it...

It is better for a good Child to be able to say, her Parents were unkind to *her*, than that she was undutiful to *them*...

The exertion of a seasonable lenity may save a penitent Child from utter destruction...

The Father and Mother who would secure to themselves the undivided love of their Children, should avoid such durable contentions with each other, as would distress their Children which side to take, when they would be glad to reverence both...

A good Parent must have greater pain in the *necessary* restraint of a headstrong Daughter, than she can give to such a Daughter...

At every age on this side matrimony it will be found, that a Parent's wings are the most effectual safeguards of Daughters, from the villainous birds of prey that hover round them...

A Parent, for a failure in her own duty, is *not* answerable to her Child...

Reverence is too apt to be forgot by Children, when Parents forget what belongs to their own characters...

Parents and Children, when separated, and seeing each other but seldom, like other lovers, shew their best sides to each other...

The bad qualities in which fond Parents too often indulge their Children when infants, not seldom, at riper years, prove the plague of their hearts...

It is as necessary to direct Daughters in the choice of their female companions, and to watch against the intrigues of women-servants, as it is to guard them against the designs of men...

Parents the most indulgent in their own natures, often, from the errors of a Child, incur the censure of hard-heartedness...

Doubly faulty is that Child, therefore, who, by a rash action, not only disgraces herself, but depreciates the most revered characters...

What confusion of mind must attend the reflexions of a Child, who, from the most promising outsetting, has brought ruin on herself, and distress on her Friends!...

The voice of nature must at last be heard in favour of a Child truly penitent...

When a Daughter is strongly set upon a point; it is better for a Mother (if the point be of no high consequence) to make herself of her party, than violently to oppose her...

Parents should take care that they do not weaken their authority, by a needless exertion of it...

What an enormity is there in that crime of a Child, which can turn the hearts of Parents, before indulgent, against her!...

The resentment which Children, and even the world, may ascribe to cruelty in an offended Parent, may be owing to excess of love, and disappointed hopes...

It is to be hoped, *says Miss Howe*, that unforgiving Parents were always good, dutiful, and passive Children to *their* Parents...

Parents who would cure a Child's impatience of spirit, should not betray a want of temper in themselves...

Children, depending on the weakness of their Parents tempers, too often harden their own hearts...

While Parents *think* a Child in fault, as they have a right to judge for themselves, they ought to have great allowances made for them; especially if, till their displeasure took place, they had always been kind and indulgent...

Good Children make *both* their Parents happy in *each other*, as well as in *them*; bad Children unhappy in both...

When the nearest Friends give up an unhappy Child, every one is ready to propagate slander against her...

A good Child will be careful of making a party against even harsh and severe Parents...

It requires a high degree of understanding and discretion in a Daughter, when grown up, to let it be seen that she mingles reverence with her love to a Parent, who has talents visibly inferior to her own...

Parents, in order to preserve their Children's veneration for them, should take great care not to let them see any thing in their own conduct, behaviour, or principles, which they themselves would not approve of in others...

Such Parents as have a visible narrowness of heart, must needs weaken their own authority with Children of spirit...

*A Collection of Moral and Instructive Sentiments contained in the History of* Sir Charles Grandison.

"Kindred."

Kindred minds will soon recognize one another...

Two sisters agreed to manage a love-affair, have advantages over a lady and her woman...

Sisters are sometimes convenient to each other in a bashful or beginning love...

Brothers and sisters, when they are deprived of one or both parents, should endeavour to supply to each other the irreparable loss...

Relations have a right to expect to be made easy and happy, by such of their Kindred as can make them so, without hurting themselves...

Men of rank, if men of merit, must be of Kindred, and recognize the relation the moment they meet...

What is the relation of body to that of mind?...

True brotherly love will ever hold the principal seat in the heart of a good man, when he sits in judgment upon a sister's conduct...

Why, taking advantage of the defencelessness of her sex is a sister to be treated by her brothers in a love case (not disgracefully circumstanced) as if she had not a will of her own, when, perhaps, she is not inferior to them, either in discretion or understanding?...

from "Public Places. Modern *fine Ladies and Gentlemen. Depravity of Times and Manners.*
Racketing."

Many persons of low genius among the gentry, have such a taste for foreign diversions, that they think not tolerably of those of their own country, however preferable...

★　　★　　★　　★

The taste of the men of the present age is dress, equipage, and foppery: Must a woman, who is addressed by a man of inferior talents to her own, hide hers, to keep him in countenance?...

A woman cannot pick and choose as a man can; what can she do, if her lot be cast only among such foplings?...

★　　★　　★　　★

Young women should be indulged [once or twice in a season] at the innocent Public Diversions, that they may not add expectation (which runs very high in young minds, and is seldom answered) to the ideal scenes...

By this indulgence a bound is set to the imagination...

What knowlege a young person will gain by her introduction to Public places, if the diversions engage her attention, she had better be without...

★　　★　　★　　★

Yet the number of single women that croud to Ranelagh and Vaux hall markets, to be *cheapened*, will convince us, *she says*, that maids will be as soon above shame and controul, as wives...

But were not the *fathers, proceeds she*, willing to get the drugs off their hands, those freedoms would not be permitted...

As for *mothers, concludes this free-speaking Lady*, many of them are for escorting their daughters to Public places, in order to take their share of the Racketing...

from "Single *Women.*"
To what evils may a sole and independent woman be exposed?…

Many men are to be looked upon as wild beasts of the desart; a Single, an independent woman they hunt after as their proper prey…

★    ★    ★    ★

The age of fancy is a dangerous time in a young woman's life…

How unworthy of encouragement must he be, who, for selfish considerations, seeks to involve a young woman in difficulties which she never knew in her father's house?…

Young women who encourage the first man that offers, frequently sacrifice their future preferment to their want of patience…

★    ★    ★    ★

Young women should refuse a libertine man, if not for their own sakes, for the sake of their posterity…

★    ★    ★    ★

Experience therefore, engaging with inexperience, and perhaps to a great difference in years, the combat must be unequal…

Most young women who begin a correspondence with men, find themselves mistaken, if they think they can stop when they will…

"Wit. Witty *Men.* Witty *Women.*"
It may perhaps be some degree of merit, to be able to repeat and apply other men's Wit with some tolerable propriety…

Wit and Wisdom are different qualities, and are rarely seen together…

Women who despise their own sex, are as deservedly, as generally, laughed at by both…

Persons of quick parts frequently, by their improvidence, lay themselves under obligation to those of slower, whom they have been accustomed to despise…

A man of understanding is greatly to be preferred to a man of Wit...

Sprightly persons often make it necessary for them to ask two forgivenesses instead of one...

That species of Wit, which cannot shine without a foil, is not a Wit to be proud of...

A Witty Woman should not think of marrying a man of inferior understanding, if she cannot resolve to shield him, not only against her own, but every other person's ridicule...

Such a one should confine her vivacities to time and place...

The lively woman, who has not the offer of a man of understanding superior to her own, should encourage the addresses of one who will be likely to allow the superiority of hers...

A Witty Woman's vivacity may less become the wife, than the single woman...

Vivacity should never carry us beyond the bounds of prudence and discretion...

Witty people seem to think they cannot shew their own consequence, but by putting a fool's coat on the back of a friend...

Sterling Wit requires not a foil to set it off...

It is sometimes the misfortune of a Witty Woman herself, sometimes that of her companions, that she cannot *help* being Witty...

Witlings study for their pleasantries, and hunt for occasions to be smart...

There can be no firm friendship, where there is a rivalry in Wit...

Mere Wit is a foolish thing...

That ought not to be called Wit, in the good sense of the word, that has not justice in its sallies; nor humour, that preserves not decorum...

Wicked Wit, *says Miss Byron*, what a foe art thou to decent chearfulness!...

**7. James Nelson, *An Essay on the Government of Children*, 2nd ed. (London: R. and J. Dodsley, 1756).**

from "Manners."

At the same time that Parents are industrious to make Children obedient to themselves, they must teach them to consider every one as an Individual of Society, and give them a deep Sense of the Necessity of good Behaviour to all, whatever be their Circumstances or Condition. In every Family there are particular Obligations which Children must be taught to distinguish, and to reduce to Practice. Next to their Parents, Children owe to all senior Relations, Respect and Duty; to their Brothers and Sisters they owe not only a tender but an unalterable Affection; and all of more distant Kin have a Claim of Respect which cannot be refused them. Yet all this is but little, if compared with the universal Demand Mankind have on one another. We cannot without Injustice deny Virtue and Merit our Esteem; old Age is venerable, and to refuse the Honours due to it, is a Degree of Impiety; Obligations demand Gratitude; Misfortunes call for Friendship and Compassion; and even Vice and Folly demand our Pity and Concern, nay more, demand our Endeavours to remove them. But among the various Situations in Life, that which most requires the Care and Attention of Parents is, the teaching Children a due Regard to People in Poverty and Distress. It does not cost much pains to give Children a proper and becoming Behaviour to their Betters and Equals; but to persuade them to maintain a considerable Degree of Respect to Inferiors, or to those in disadvantageous Circumstances, is an arduous Task; still it may and ought to be done. Nothing so humanizes the Soul, nothing so strongly proves the Man, as sympathizing with, and relieving the Distresses of our Fellow Creatures: 'tis then the Duty of Parents never to let their Children speak or act with the least Degree of Rudeness to the lowest among Mankind; never to let them divert themselves with their Rags or Misfortunes; but on the contrary, they should sometimes furnish them with Money or other Things, that the Relief they design to give the Needy may pass through their Hands: and at the same time imprint this Truth on their Minds; that he who is thus reduced to ask, is often far more deserving than he who bestows.

Another indispensable Duty of Parents to their Children is, that they teach them never to dare to sport with the natural Defects of others. As an ingenious Author says, "This Practice, though levelled at the Creature, reflects on the Creator; it mocks the Architect, and burlesques the Creation." 'Tis strange that Persons of the best Understanding so seldom reflect on this Point. What can be more absurd than to ridicule one Man for being too tall, and another for being too short? one for having too little Nose, another for having too much? The Degrees of Beauty and Deformity are infinite; and to be perfectly free from natural Defects and Blemishes is the Lot of very few: nor is it easy to fix the Standard of Beauty. We know by Anatomy, Sculpture and Painting, the general Rules of Symmetry and Proportion, and thus easily distinguish the gross Defects; but Beauty in the superlative Degree, in it's ultimate Perfection, is not so readily determined. But farther; what is beautiful in the Eye of one is not so in the Eye of another; what was accounted Beauty in some former Age or distant Country, is not esteemed such at present. Since then we see that 'tis our general Lot to be more or less defective, and that All are made by one Almighty Hand, how inhuman must it be to insult or despise another for what, if an Imperfection, it is not in his Power to avoid; and that perhaps while the Insulter himself is not free from other Blemishes, full as obvious and offensive to many.

But the Defects of the Body are not alone the Subject of our Ridicule; we sport too with those of the Mind. Providence for wise Reasons does not give to all alike; are we therefore to hold another in contempt for not knowing so much as ourselves? Are we to laugh at a Man for not knowing what he has had no opportunity to learn? no surely. A Neglect to improve, and the Abuse of natural Talents, are the only things that deserve the Scourge; and even here it often happens, that he who exercises the Rod, deserves it more than he who feels it. Such however is the Partiality, such the false Practice of Mankind. Can Parents then be too careful to obviate these Errors in their Children? Can they take too much Pains to imprint on their Souls the Meanness and Folly of such Mistakes? surely they cannot.

## 8. Eliza Haywood, *The Female Spectator* (1744-46), 5th ed. (London: T. Gardner, 1755). Volume I.

Book 3.

*Leolin*, a gentleman descended from one of the best families in *Wales*, and born to a considerable estate, had, from his very early years, been attached by the most tender passion to a young lady called *Elmira*, an heiress of 1600*l.* a year. – His vows had all the success he could desire; and if he thought that all the charms of the whole sex were united in his *Elmira*, she could find nothing worthy of her affection but her *Leolin*. Their fathers, who had been long intimate friends, approved their mutual flame; and when *Leolin* arrived at his twentieth year, and *Elmira* to that of sixteen, they resolved to join the hands of two persons, whose hearts had been united even before they knew either the nature, or the aim of the passion they were inspired with.

Accordingly the marriage-articles were drawn, and great preparations were making to solemnize the nuptials, when within two or three days of that which was intended to compleat it, the father of *Elmira* had the misfortune to fall off his horse and break his leg, which turning to a mortification, was obliged to be cut off. – Either want of skill in the surgeons, or his own obstinacy in not suffering the amputation to be above the knee, proved fatal to him, and he died in twenty-four hours after the operation.

This occasioned a melancholy delay of our lover's happiness. – The virtuous and discreet *Elmira* could not think of devoting herself to the joys and gaiety of a bridal state immediately after the loss of a parent to whom she had been extremely dear, and whose indulgence she had always repaid with the most sincere filial duty and affection. – *Leolin* himself, who shared in all her sorrows, durst not presume to press it; and his father was too great an observer of decency, as well as too much concerned for the death of his good old friend, to urge the completion of an affair, which though he very much desired, yet he thought might be more agreeable to all the parties concerned, when time had a little worn off the present poignancy of grief.

The first mourning being over, and the white garments accompanied with somewhat of a more chearful aspect, the passionate *Leolin* began by degrees to remind his charming mistress of her engagement; and she was half-consenting to put an end to all his languishments, when a second, and, in its consequences, more fatal disappointment than the former, came between them and the felicity they expected.

The father of *Leolin* was taken suddenly ill: – His indisposition terminated in a violent fever, which in a very few days took him from the world; but even this event, afflicting as it was to the son, proved a slight misfortune to that which immediately ensued. – The funeral obsequies were no sooner over, than the house of the young gentleman was forcibly entered by officers, who came to seize on all he had, by virtue of a deed of gift made, as they said, by his father, some years before, to his brother's son. *Leolin*, impetuous by nature, opposed their passage all he could; but the number they brought with them by far exceeded those of his servants, and they took possession: – on which he went to the house of a neighbouring gentleman, who had been an intimate acquaintance of his father, complained to him of his wrongs, and intreated his advice.

Not only this person, but the chief gentleman of the county, persuaded him to have recourse to law, – it seeming highly improbable, that any father should give away the inheritance of an only son, and such a son as *Leolin*, who had never done any thing to disoblige him, and of whom he had always seemed extremely fond.

The kinsman, however, had his pretences, which, for the better understanding this mysterious affair, I must not pass over in silence. – The mother of *Leolin*, when he was not above four or five years old, eloped from her husband, and took refuge in *France* with a gentleman who had formerly courted her, and whom she continued to love, to the eternal ruin of all that ought to be dear to womankind.

So manifest a proof of her unchastity, it is certain, made him disregard the young *Leolin* for a time, as dubious if he were really of his blood; – and witnesses were produced, who swore they had heard him say, *The bastard should never inherit an acre of his land*; and when they answered, *that it would not be in his power to cut him off,* he rejoined, *No matter, there were other courses to be taken.*

This they deposed that they understood as meant by the deed of gift now produced; and that tho' since then he had treated *Leolin* as his son, and seemed to use him well, it was only to avoid any farther noise being made in the world of his dishonour while he lived, referring to shew his resentment to the mother on the son, till after his decease.

In fine, after a long process, the trial came on, and the kinsman had so well concerted his measures, that, in spite of all the probabilities that were against him, he got the better of *Leolin*; – the judge only, in consideration of his having been bred a gentleman, and in the expectation of so large an estate, ordering he should be allowed 200*l. per annum* out of so many thousands.

Few there were, however, who did not believe him greatly wronged; nor could the jury themselves reconcile, to their own reason, the verdict they were obliged to give on the evidence, who swore so positively, and corroborated their depositions with so many circumstances, that, in law, there was no possibility for the court to act otherwise than it did on this occasion.

*Leolin*, who, for his many good qualities, had always been highly esteemed and beloved in the country where he was born, had many friendly offers made him, and continual invitations from one house to another, but he would accept of none, avoided all conversation with those he was once intimate with, and shut himself up in a little farmhouse, ordering the people belonging to it to suffer no person whatever to come to him.

But his behaviour with regard to *Elmira* was the most astonishing, and what indeed excited me to give this melancholy detail of his adventures, – During the continuance of the lawsuit, and while he had hope of overcoming his adversary, he was scarce ever from her; and, in spite of the vexation this cruel invasion of his birthright had involved him in, found always a satisfaction in her unaltered and endearing conversation, which more than compensated for all the frowns of fortune. – But the moment he was cast, that he was certain his ruin was completed, he shunned her even more than all the world beside; and though her love, and the engagements between them, made her not to look upon it as a breach of modesty to write to him, to conjure him in the most pressing terms to come to her, and assured him the change in his circumstances had wrought no change in her affection; and that she was ready to make him a present of that with herself; yet could she not prevail on him to see her.

In fine, from the most affable and obliging of mankind, he was now become the most stern, morose, and ill-tempered; according to the poet,

> *Great souls grow always haughty in distress.*

In vain a mistress so lately loved, admired, almost adored, now condescended to solicit him to accept all in her power to give: – all the proofs she gave him of her tenderness, her constancy, her disinterested passion, served but to add new matter for his discontent; and, to get rid of her importunities, he at last sent one letter in answer to the many obliging ones he had received from her. – A friend of mine, happening to be with her when it arrived, assured me it contained these lines:

Madam,

*I believe there is no occasion for any asservations that no man has ever loved with greater sincerity than I have done, or more passionately desired to be united to you for ever, while there remained the least hope of being so without rendering both of us the subject of ridicule. – In fine, I have still too much regard for you to have it said you bought a husband, and for myself to think of submitting to the slavish dependance on a wife's fortune. – Were the ballance on my side, I should not act in this manner; but, as things are now circumstanced between us, I beg you will give neither yourself or me any further trou-*

*ble on this score: — the most prudent step you can take for the peace of both is to think of me no more, since I never can be, in the manner I once flattered myself with being,*

Yours, &c.

Leolin.

P.S. *I quit the place I am in this very moment, nor shall make any person in the world the confidante of my retirement; so that no letters can possibly come to my hands; but have ordered the honest man who has been my host for some time, to pay you* 300l. *which you may remember I borrowed of you while my unhappy law-affair was in agitation, and the interest due upon the loan. — Adieu for ever; be assured I wish you much better than you do yourself.*

Poor *Elmira* read the letter with tears in her eyes, and cried out, *O what a noble mind is here perverted! — Quite changed from what he was, by an ill-judging and injurious world!* But when she came to the postscript, and the man counted the money to her on the table, she grew beyond all patience. — *How meanly must he think of me!* said she. — *How little does he know of* Elmira! — And then again, *What! am I turn'd usurer*[1] *then!* This little indignation, however, soon subsided, and gave way to the softer dictates of love and friendship: she asked the farmer a thousand questions concerning his behaviour; — conjured him to deal sincerely with her, and to inform her whether he had really left his house or not, and if he had, what road he took.

To all this he replied with a great deal of truth, that he had never seen a man so changed as to his humour, but that he did not think his brain was any way disordered: — that some time past he sent for a money-scrivener, and sold the annuity ordered him for life for 1000l. part of which he had disposed of in paying all the little debts he had contracted since his misfortune, and had taken the remainder with him: — that he went on horseback, but could not say what road, because he was forbid accompanying him even to the lane's end that led to his house.

In the present emotions of her various passions, she would certainly have followed him herself, could she have known

---

1   Lender of money at high interest rates.

what route to take, and either brought him back, or gone with him; but as this was impossible, she dispatched men and horses every where she could think of, to each of whom she gave little billets, beseeching him by all he ever did or could love, to return to her, and not make them both miserable by a foolish punctilio, which the sense of the injuries he had sustained alone had put into his head.

The servants knowing their mistress's attachment, and besides having a very great respect for *Leolin*, who had been always extremely affable and liberal to them, spared no pains to execute their commission.

But all their endeavours were fruitless; *Leolin*, doubtless, suspecting what would be the consequence of his letter, and obstinate in his resolution, to suffer any thing rather than be under the least obligation even to the woman he loved, passed through such bye-ways as eluded all their search.

He came up to *London*, where, having furnished himself with all things necessary for a campaign, he went a volunteer into the army. – The little regard he had for life, joined to his natural impetuosity, hurried him into the thickest dangers, and he fell among many other gallant men at the battle of *Dettingen*.[1]

An old officer, who had been an acquaintance of his father's, saw and knew him on his first coming into the camp; and, having heard the story of his misfortunes, offered him all the services in his power; but *Leolin* rejected every thing that might afford him any advantage, and continued determined to the last not to be obliged to any one.

It was this gentleman, who, on the account of his great age and many wounds, returning to *England* after the campaign was over, brought the account of him, who else perhaps might to this moment have been vainly sought by the disconsolate *Elmira*.

So anxious, so unhappy had she been from the time of his

---

1 The Battle of Dettingen am Main in Bavaria on June 27, 1743, in which an army of Hessian, Hannovarian, and British troups under George II routed the French, was an early conflict in the War of the Austrian Succession (1740-48).

departure, that to hear he was no more could scarce add to it. – The news, however, encouraged several gentlemen to make their addresses to her, which, while he was living, in any circumstances, they knew would have been in vain; but they found his death of no service to their suit: – his memory was still a rival, which all their efforts were too weak to surmount; – to *that* she assures them she is wedded, and to *that* will to her last breath continue constant.

What now can we say of this *Leolin*, but that he was an honest, brave, and worthy man! Can we help admiring him, at the same time that we condemn him! – And had not that unhappy obstinacy, to which he fell a martyr, wounded at the same time the breast of the generous, the sweet *Elmira*, should we not have greatly compassionated a foible, which, if we examine to the bottom, we shall find had its rise from a virtue in excess!

The love of freedom and independency, it seems, was his darling propensity; and though he had nothing in reality to fear from the excellence of *Elmira's* nature, yet to know himself obliged, and that there was even a possibility for her some time or other to think he was so, had somewhat in it which the greatness of his spirit could not submit to bear. I am apt to believe, that had she been reduced in the manner he was, and he been possessed of as many millions as he was born to thousands, he would, with the utmost pleasure, have thrown them at her feet, and found his greatest felicity in her acceptance.

Such a man must certainly have made a very great figure in the senate, had he ever arrived at being a member of it; and for the good of my country, I sincerely wish there were five hundred of the same way of thinking. – What in *private* life was his greatest misfortune, would in a *public* one have rendered him of the highest service to the present age, and endeared his name to late posterity. – No caresses, – no pensions, – no ribbands, – no preferments, would have had any influence over a person of his principles: – resolute to support the native freedom of an *Englishman*, he would have uttered his mind without reserve; and the more he had been offered by a court parasite for his silence, the more warmly had he spoke in the cause of liberty. – Perhaps, indeed, he might have been too bold, and, for his particular mortification, have occasioned the *Habeas Corpus* act[1] to be suspended; but what of that! it might have hurt some individuals, but must have been of general service, and have opened the eyes of those, who, more through *indolence* and *luxury*, than *corruption*, were made blind.

So far I blame him, in refusing a fine woman whom he loved, and who had an estate which would have put it in his power to be of use to his country, which, heaven knows, and he could not have been ignorant of, stands in need of such supports; but as he was very young, and the consideration of these things had not time to make the impression it ought, I cannot but pity him, and lament the loss which the public have in a friend so qualified to serve the common interest.

All the young and gay of both sexes, who are advocates for the tender passion, I know, cannot find in their hearts to forgive him: – as to the considerations I have mentioned, they will have indeed but very little weight with them. – The griefs of *Elmira* will be accounted of infinite more consequence, and he will be looked upon as a man of a savage and barbarous soul, who, to gratify his pride, could forsake a lady that so truly loved and had made him such condescensions. I grant that there was something cruel in the *effects* of his behaviour to her, yet I cannot help vindicating the cause; and I think I cannot do it more effectually, than by setting a character of a quite opposite nature in the same point of light with him. – *White* is best illustrated by being near to *Black*; and the rough diamond, which at present appears of so little value, will rise in a more just estimation when placed near a common pebble.

---

1   The English Parliament passed the *Habeas Corpus* Act in 1679 to penalize those judges who refused to issue a Writ of *Habeas Corpus*, and those officers who refused to comply with the Writ. The Writ of *Habeas Corpus* was an order issued by a court to a person having custody of another, requiring that he/she produce the detained person to determine the legality of the detention.

## 9. Lady Sarah Pennington, *An Unfortunate Mother's Advice to Her Absent Daughters; In a Letter to Miss Pennington* (London: S. Chandler, 1761).

Thus much I thought it necessary to premise concerning myself, tho' foreign to the Design of this Epistle,[1] which is only to remind you that you have still an affectionate Mother, anxious for your Welfare, to give you some Advice with regard to your Conduct in Life, – and to lay down a few Precepts that, if attended to, will in the best Manner in my Power supply the Deprivation of a constant tender maternal Care: The Address is to you in particular, your Sisters being yet too young to receive it, but my Intention for the equal Service of you all.

You are just entering, my dear Girl, into a World full of Deceit and Falshood, where few Persons or Things appear as they really are: Vice hides her Deformity with the borrowed Garb of Virtue; and though discernable, by the unbecoming Aukwardness of her Deportment under it, passes on Thousands undetected: Every present Pleasure usurps the Name of Happiness, and as such deceives the unwary Pursuer; thus one general Mask disguises the Whole, and it requires a long Experience, and a penetrating Judgment to discover the Truth. – Thrice happy those whose docile Tempers improve the Instructions of maturer Age, and thereby attain some Degree of this necessary Knowledge while it may be chiefly useful in directing their Conduct!

The Turn your Mind now takes, fixes the Happiness or Misery of your whole future Life, and I am too nearly concerned for your Welfare not to be most solicitously anxious that you may early be led into so just a way of Thinking as will be productive of a prudent, rational Behaviour, and secure to yourself a lasting Felicity. You was old enough, before our Separation,[2] to convince me that Heaven had not denied you a good natural Understanding, which, properly cultivated, will set you above that trifling Disposition too common among the Female

---

1  Letter.
2  Pennington's husband left her and took her children from her, accusing her of improper behavior.

World, that makes Youth ridiculous, Maturity insignificant, and old Age contemptible; 'tis therefore needless to enlarge on that Head, since good Sense is there the best Adviser, and without it all Admonitions or Directions on the Subject would be as fruitless as to lay down Rules for an Idiot not to act foolishly.

There is no room to doubt but that sufficient Care will be taken to give you a polite Education;[1] but a religious one is of still greater Consequence; necessary as the former is toward your making a proper Figure in the World, and being well accepted in it, the latter is yet more so, as that only can secure to you the Approbation of the greatest and best of Beings, on whose Favour depends your everlasting Happiness: Let, therefore, your Duty to God be ever the first and principal Object of your Care; as your Creator and Governor, he claims Adoration and Obedience; as your Father and Friend, submissive Duty and Affection: Remember that from this common Parent of the Universe you received your Life, that to His general Providence you owe the Continuance of it, and to his Bounty, all the Health, Ease, Advantages, or Enjoyments which help to make that Life agreeable. A sense of Benefits received naturally inspires a grateful Disposition, with a Desire of making some suitable Returns; all that can here be made, for innumerable Favours every Moment bestowed, is a thankful Acknowledgment, and a willing Obedience; in These be never wanting: Make it an invariable Rule to begin and End the Day with a solemn Address to the Deity; I mean not by this, what is commonly with too much Propriety called saying of Prayers, viz. a customary Repetition of a few good Words without either Devotion or Attention, than which, nothing is more inexcusable and affrontive; 'tis the Homage of the Heart that can alone be accepted. Expressions of our absolute Dependence and entire Resignation, Thanksgiving for the Mercies already received, Petitions for those Blessings it is fit for us to pray for, and Intercessions for all our Fellow-Creatures, compose the principal Parts of this Duty; which may be comprized in very few Words, or more enlarged upon as the Circumstances of

---

1   That is, an education in which she would learn French, enough Mathematics for keeping the household accounts, Dancing, Embroidery.

Time and Disposition may render most suitable; for it is not the Length, but the Sincerity and Attention of our Prayers that will make them efficacious: A good heart, joined to a tolerable Understanding, will seldom be at a Loss for proper Words with which to cloath these Sentiments, and all Persons being best acquainted with their own particular Circumstances, may reasonably be supposed best qualified for adapting their Petitions and Acknowledgments to them....

★    ★    ★    ★

The sincere Practice of these religious Duties naturally leads to the proper Discharge of the social ones, which may be all comprehended in that one great general Rule of doing unto others as you would they should do unto you....

★    ★    ★    ★

With persons for whom you can have no Esteem, Good-breeding may oblige you to keep up an Intercourse of ceremonious Visits, but Politeness enjoins not the Length or Frequency of them; here Inclination may be followed without a Breach of Civility; there is no Tax upon Intimacy, but from Choice, and that Choice should ever be founded on Merit, the Certainty whereof you cannot be too careful in previously examining; great Caution is necessary not to be deceived by specious Appearances; a plausible Behaviour, often, upon a superficial Knowledge, creates a Prepossession in favour of Persons, whom, upon a nearer View, may be found to have no Claim to Esteem; the forming a precipitant Judgment sometimes leads into an unwary Intimacy, which it may prove absolutely necessary to break off, and yet that Breach be attended with innumerable Inconveniencies, nay, perhaps, with very material and lasting ill Consequences: Prudence, therefore, here enjoins the greatest Circumspection. Few People are capable of Friendship, and still fewer have all the Qualifications one would choose in a Friend; the fundamental Point is a virtuous Disposition; but to that should be added, a good Understanding, solid Judgment, Sweetness of Temper, Steadiness of Mind, Freedom of Behaviour, and Sincerity of Heart....

★    ★    ★    ★

Happy is her Lot, who in an Husband finds this invaluable
Friend! yet so great is the Hazard, so disproportioned the
Chances, that I could almost wish the dangerous Die was never
to be thrown for any of you! but as most probably it may, let me
conjure ye all, my dear Girls, if ever any of you take this most
important Step in Life, to proceed with the utmost Care, and
deliberate Circumspection. Fortune and Family it is the sole
Province of your Pappa to direct in, who certainly has always
an undoubted Right to a Negative Voice, though not to a
Compulsive One; as a Child is very justifiable in the Refusal of
her Hand, even to the absolute Command of a Father, where
her heart cannot go with it; so is she extremely culpable, by
giving it contrary to his Approbation. – Here I must take
Shame to myself! and for this unpardonable Fault, do justly
acknowledge the subsequent ill Consequences of a most
unhappy Marriage were the proper Punishment: this and every
other Error in my own Conduct, I do, and shall, with the
utmost Candour, lay open to you, sincerely praying, that you
may reap the Benefit of my Experience, and avoid those Rocks
I have, either by Carelessness, or sometimes, alas! by too much
Caution split against.

But to return. – The chief Point to be regarded in the
Choice of a Companion for Life, is a real virtuous Principle, an
unaffected Goodness of Heart; without this you will be continually shocked by Indecency, and pained by Impiety. So numerous have been the unhappy Victims to the ridiculous Opinion,
that a reformed Libertine[1] makes the best Husband; that, did
not Experience daily evince the contrary, one would believe it
impossible for a Girl, who has a tolerable Degree of common
Understanding, to be made the Dupe of so erroneous a Position, that has not the least Shadow of Reason for its Founda-
tion, and which a small Share of Observation will prove to be
false in Fact. A Man who has been long conversant with the
worst Sort of Women, is very apt to contract a bad Opinion of,

---

1  "A man who is not restrained by moral law, esp. in his relations with the female
   sex" (*OED*).

and a Contempt for the Sex in general; incapable of esteeming any, he is suspicious of all; jealous without Cause, angry without Provocation, and his own disturbed Imagination is a continual Source of ill Humour; to this is frequently joined a bad Habit of Body, the natural Consequence of an irregular Life, which gives an additional Sourness to the Temper. What rational Prospect of Happiness can there be with such a Companion?

★    ★    ★    ★

Most sincerely do I pray this may never be your Lot! and hope your prudent Circumspection will be sufficient to guard you from the Danger: but the bare Possibility of such an Event, makes it not unnecessary to lay down a few Rules, for the maintaining some Degree of Ease, under the Deprivation of Happiness. This is by far the most difficult Part of my present Undertaking; it is hard to advise here, and still harder to practise the Advice: the Subject also is too extensive to be minutely treated within the Compass of a Letter, which must confine me to the most material Points only; in these, shall give you the best Directions in my Power, ardently wishing you may never have Occasion to make use of them.

The being united to a Man of Irreligious Principles makes it impossible to discharge a great Part of the proper Duty of a Wife; to name but one Instance; that of Obedience will be rendered impracticable, by frequent Injunctions inconsistent with and contrary to, the higher Obligations of Morality. This is not mere Supposition, but spoke from Facts I have often seen, and can attest. Where this happens, the Reasons for non-compliance ought to be offered in a plain, strong, good-natured Manner; there is at least the Chance of Success from being heard; but should those Reasons be rejected, or the hearing of them be refused, and Silence on the Subject enjoined (which is most probable, few People caring to hear what they know to be right, when determined not to appear convinced by it) in this obey, nor farther urge the Argument; but keep steady to your Principles, and neither by Persuasion or Threats be prevailed with to act contrary to them; all Commands repugnant to the Laws of Christianity it is your indispensible Duty to disobey; all Requests that are inconsistent with Prudence, incompatible with that Rank and Character you ought to maintain in Life, 'tis your Interest to refuse; a Compliance with the former would be Criminal, a Consent to the latter highly Indiscreet, and subject you to general Censure; for a Man capable of requiring from his Wife what he knows to be in itself wrong, is equally capable of throwing the whole Blame of such Misconduct on her, and afterwards upbraiding her for a Behaviour he will, upon the same Principle, disown his having been accessary to. Many similar Instances have come within the Compass of my own Observation. In Things of a less material Nature, that are neither Criminal in themselves, nor pernicious in their Consequences, always acquiesce, if insisted on, however disagreeable they may be to your own Temper and Inclination; such a Compliance will evidently prove that your Refusal in the other Case proceeds not from a Spirit of Contradiction, but merely from a just Regard to that superior Duty which can never be infringed with Impunity: Passion may resent, but Reason must approve this Conduct; and therefore, it is the most likely Method, in Time, to make a favourable Impression; but failing there, you will at least enjoy that satisfactory Self-Approbation, which is the inseparable Attendant of a truly religious and rational Deportment.

Should the painful Task of dealing with a morose tyrannical Temper be assigned you, there is little more to be recommended than a patient Submission to an Evil which admits not of a Remedy. Ill Nature is encreased, Obstinacy confirmed by Opposition; the less such a Temper is contradicted, the more supportable will it be to those who are under its baneful Influence. When all Endeavours to please are ineffectual, and a Man seems determined to find Fault with every Thing, as if his chief Pleasure consisted in tormenting those about him, it requires a more than common Degree of Patience, and Resolution, to forbear uttering those Reproaches which such a Behaviour may be justly allowed to deserve; yet is it absolutely necessary to the maintaining any tolerable Degree of Ease, not only to restrain all Expressions of Resentment, but even those disdainful Looks which are apt to accompany a contemptuous

Silence, both equally tending to encrease the Malady. This dia-bolical Delight, in giving Pain, is most unwearied in the Search of Matter for its Gratification, and can either find, or unac-countably form it in almost all the Occurrences of Life; but, when suffered unobstructed, unregarded to run its malicious Course, will quickly vent its blunted Arrows, and die of Disap-pointment; whilst all Endeavours to appease, all Complaints of Unkindness, sharpens against yourself the Weapon's Edge, and by proving your Sensibility of the Wound, gives the wished Satisfaction to him who inflicts it. Prudence here directs more than ordinary Circumspection; that every Part of your Behav-iour may be as blameless as possible, even to the abstaining from the least Appearance of Evil; and after having, to the utmost of your Power, strove to merit Approbation, expect not to meet with it; by this Means you will escape the Mortifica-tion of being disappointed, which, often repeated, is apt to give a gloomy Sourness to the Temper incompatible with any Degree of Contentment: you must also learn to be satisfied with the Consciousness of acting Right, according to your best Ability, and look with an unconcerned Indifference on the Reception every successless Attempt to please may meet with.

This, it must be owned, is a hard Lesson of Philosophy; it requires no less than an absolute Command over the Passions; but let it be remembered, that such a Command, will itself most amply recompence every Difficulty, every Pain the obtaining it may cost; besides, 'tis, I believe, the only Way to preserve any Tranquillity of Mind under so disagreeable a Connection.

10. "Portia" [pseud.], *The Polite Lady; or, A Course of Female Education. In a Series of Letters, from a Mother to her Daughter,* 2nd ed. (London: Newbery and Carnan, 1769).

LETTER XVIII.

My dear Sophy,
As the happiness of our lives depends so much on the prudent choice of our friends, and as you are resolved to take no step in this important affair without the advice and directions of your

mother, I now sit down to continue and finish the subject, which I have treated pretty largely in my two last letters.

★   ★   ★   ★

Nor would there be less danger, my Dear, in the other case; I mean, in contracting a friendship with a person greatly beneath you in family and fortune. Your mind would be debased by her low conversation; your pride would be inflamed by her servile and cringing behaviour: for such only could you expect from her. As she courts you, not for your personal merit, but for your rank, your wealth and interest, she would take care never to forfeit your good graces by doing any disagreeable action, or telling any unpleasing truth, how much soever the doing the one, or telling the other might be for your real interest and advantage. Your faults she would either conceal or extenuate; your virtues she would magnify and exaggerate; nay, perhaps, praise you for virtues you never possessed. She might, indeed, be your flattering sycophant, but she could not possibly be your faithful friend, one of whose principal duties it is to inform you of your faults, and to assist you in correcting them.

But, my Dear, not only is our pride encreased by cultivating a friendship with persons in low life; what is more, the very act of forming such a friendship is a certain proof of our original pride and vanity: for, if we had not been naturally proud, we never would have formed it. This, you will imagine, is a very strange way of thinking. What? can it ever be a sign of pride and vanity to cultivate a friendship with our inferiors? Is it not rather a mark of humility and condescension? Such, my Dear, will be your opinion; and such, I believe, is the opinion of half the world: but either they or I must be mistaken, or it is a very false opinion. For, where is the humility in keeping company with those who are perpetually flattering us? who, we are sure, will never venture to contradict us, but will commend and applaud every thing we say or do, however foolish or ridiculous? If this be humility, 'tis a very strange kind of it, and quite above my comprehension. The truth is, persons of this character are, of all others, the most proud, vain, and conceited. They don't like the company of their superiors, because they scorn to fawn or flatter; they don't like the company of their equals, because they cannot bear contradiction: and, therefore, they fly to the company of their inferiors, where they are free from contradiction, and, instead of offering, are sure of receiving the incense of flattery and adulation.

Of this kind of pride, (for, it must be confessed, it has something very particular in it) lady Lambton is a remarkable instance. I went to visit her a few days ago, and found her surrounded with a large company of ladies, who, in every thing but sense, were certainly her inferiors. What the subject of conversation was before I enter'd, I know not; but the usual compliments were hardly over, when she took occasion to commend her daughter, who was settled at a country boarding-school, for her great improvement in writing; and, as a specimen of her abilities, produced a letter she had lately received from her. All the rest of the company agreed in praising it, tho' one half of them had not so much as seen it: – there was flattery for you with a witness. But I, who scorn to flatter any one, took the freedom to observe, that I thought it was very indifferent, and that my Sophy, tho' younger, could write much better; and as a proof, shew'd them a letter of yours, which I happened to have in my pocket. Upon a comparison, they could not refuse giving the preference to you, tho' with apparent reluctance. After this, lady Lambton was extremely grave and demure, and the rest looked very silly and foolish. In any other company I would not have behaved in this manner; it would have been ill-manners; but such a conceited fool, and a parcel of such servile flatterers, deserved no better treatment. Her vanity and their meanness of spirit were equally the object of contempt and disdain.

Thus have I finished what I had to say on the subject of friendship.

★    ★    ★    ★

Farewell, my dear Sophy. May God Almighty bless you with every comfort of life, and, particularly, with a true friend. I am
　　Your affectionate mother,
Portia.

## 11. Hester Mulso Chapone, *Letters on the Improvement of the Mind. Addressed to a Young Lady* (1773) (Boston: William Green, n.d.). Volume II.[1]

from "On Politeness and Accomplishments. Letter VIII."

In your father's house it is certainly proper for you to pay civility to the guests, and talk to them in your turn – with modesty and respect – if they encourage you to it. Young ladies of near your own age, who visit there, fall of course to your share to entertain. But whilst you exert yourself to make their visit agreeable to them, you must not forget what is due to the elder part of the company – nor by whispering and laughing apart, give them cause to suspect what is too often true, that they themselves are the subjects of your mirth. It is so shocking an outrage against society to talk of, or laugh at any person in his own presence, that one would think it could only be committed by the vulgar. I am sorry however, to say, that I have too often observed it amongst young ladies, who little deserved that title whilst they indulge their overflowing spirits, in defiance of decency and good nature. The desire of laughing will make such inconsiderate young persons find a subject of ridicule, even in the most respectable characters. Old age, which, if not disgraced by vice or affectation – has the justest title to reverence, will be mimicked and insulted; and even personal defects and infirmities will too often excite contempt and abuse, instead of compassion. If you have ever been led into such an action, my dear girl, call it seriously to mind, when you are confessing your faults to Almighty God; and, be fully persuaded that it is not the least which you have to repent of. You will be immediately convinced of this, by comparing it with the great rule of justice, that of doing to all as you would they should do unto you. No person living is insensible to the injury of contempt, nor is there any talent so invidious, or so certain to create ill-will, as that of ridicule. The natural effects of years, which all hope to attain, and the infirmities of the body, which

---

1   The National Union Catalogue lists three editions of the work published in Boston and printed by Robert Hodge for William Green; no definitive publication dates are given for any of the three, though [1782] and [1783] appear.

none can prevent, are surely of all others the most improper objects of mirth. There are subjects enough that are innocent, and on which you may freely indulge the vivacity of your spirits; for I would not condemn you to a perpetual seriousness – on the contrary, I delight in a joyous temper, at all ages, and particularly at yours. Delicate and good-natured raillery amongst equal friends, if pointed only against such trifling errors as the owner can heartily join to laugh at, or such qualities as they do not pique themselves upon, is both agreeable and useful; but then it must be offered in perfect kindness and sincere good humour; – if tinctured with the least degree of malice, its sting becomes venomous and detestable. The person rallied should have liberty and ability to return the jest, which must be dropped upon the first appearance of its affecting the temper.

You will wonder perhaps, when I tell you that there are some characters in the world, which I would freely allow you to laugh at – though not in their presence. Extravagant vanity, and affectation, are the natural subjects of ridicule, which is their proper punishment. When you see old people, instead of maintaining the dignity of their years, struggling against nature to conceal them, affecting the graces, and imitating the follies of youth. Or a young person assuming the importance and solemnity of old age – I do not wish you to be insensible to the ridicule of such absurd deviations from truth and nature. You are welcome to laugh, when you leave the company, provided you lay up a lesson for yourself at the same time, and remember, that unless you improve your mind whilst you are young, you also will be an insignificant fool in old age – and that, if you are presuming and arrogant in youth, you are as ridiculous as an old woman with a head-dress of flowers.

## 12. Clara Reeve, *Plans of Education* (London: T. Hookham and J. Carpenter, 1792).

from "Letter IV. Mrs. Danford to Lady A—."

In the morning of life, when youth are first engaged in worldly pursuits and expectations, in the warmth of their hearts they find every thing around them in the right place.

All they see is beautiful, all they hear is delightful; the society they mix with is the most agreeable, the country they were born in is the first in the world; its government and manners the most perfect. – As they advance in their progress, experience draws back the veil that blinded them, and shews them the defects of all those things they once admired. When they have reached the top of the hill, they stand still and reflect upon them; they compare things past with the present, and look forward to the future with doubt and suspicion; but in this state they are most likely to judge truly and impartially.

As they descend the hill, they grow more dissatisfied and querulous; they grow partial to the time of their youth, when their passions were most awakened, and their enjoyments the most lively and engaging.

Thus the young and the old throw contempt upon each other, and each of them have enough to say in justification of their own opinions. The affected wisdom and garrulity of age, is a constant subject of ridicule to youth; and serves them as a touchstone to sharpen their wit upon.

> "My grand-mother told me, what her grand-mother
> told her,
> The times grow worser child, as they grow older.
> Oh, God-a-mercy times! – If this were true,
> What would another century dwindle to? –
> I dare maintain this time as good as any,
> In spite of whiners, grumblers, or my granny."
>
> *Epilogue to a Dramatic Caricature,*
> *called, Taste and Feeling.*[1]

This is the constant language of ignorance, pertness, and folly; but to the many it may seem like wit, poetry, and even truth. This false idea is the source of a thousand errors and vices. If things stand still, and grow neither better nor worse, why should we give ourselves any concern about times or manners?

---

1  Possibly *Taste and Feeling*, a "dramatic caricature in one act," first produced Aug. 13, 1790, at the Little Theatre (or Theatre Royal), Haymarket, by George Colman the Younger.

A second inference is, that if all things are right, they can have nothing to reform; we are then as good as we need to be, and it is only peevish, melancholy, and querulous people who find fault; because it gives vent to their spleen and ill-nature. Neither times nor people want any amendment, and we resolve neither to amend the times, nor ourselves.

But let us listen to the man of reason and reflection, who stands at the top of the hill, and attend to his observations and inferences:

> "Let me not live," (says he,)
> "After my flame lacks oil, to be the snuff
> Of younger spirits, whose apprehensive sense
> All but new things disdain: – whose judgments are
> Mere fathers of their garments, – whose constancies
> Expire before their fashions."
>
> Shakespeare.[1]

Let us examine into the truth of these opinions respectively. History and experience inform us that all sublunary things are in an eternal rotation: states and kingdoms, arts and sciences, languages and manners, all are subject to perpetual vicissitudes. Who dares affirm that any thing stands still, when the world itself, and all that it contains, are in continual motion?

When a nation is in a state of civilization, there is a gradation by which it ascends to the highest degree of cultivation; when the language and manners, arts and sciences, are in the greatest perfection – refinement upon these succeeds; refinement becomes fastidious, wanton, effeminate. False taste and affectation succeed relaxation in manners and discipline; all these descend and decline, till in process of time, they return to ignorance and barbarism.

★    ★    ★    ★

Nothing is of equal consequence to the health of a state, as the education of youth. When the manners are chaste and virtu-

---

1  Shakespeare's *All's Well That Ends Well* I.ii.55-63, slightly misquoted: "says" should be "quoth" and "sense" should be "senses."

ous, we cannot doubt that education was so; when there is a general relaxation of manners and discipline, there must be great defects in the methods of education.

★ ★ ★ ★

Let us then enquire into one great point, upon which all our reasoning must depend. – Ought children to be governed by discipline, or left to educate themselves? – Are they to be restrained very strongly, – very gently, – or not at all? – I am not going to set up for a system-maker, I shall only remark upon the systems of others, according to my own judgment.

from "Letter V. Mrs. Darnford to Lady A—."

Since the disciplinarian method has been exploded, we have gone by rapid steps to the other extreme, and become advocates for all kinds of relaxation. – In Milton's[1] time, his system of education might have been practicable, but in our days, men are not virtuous enough to follow it.

Locke's System of Education[2] was admired by all wise and virtuous parents: it was admired but not followed. Madame de Genlis[3] has accounted for this with her usual penetration and sagacity:

"Locke's work was translated into all languages. It was in every body's hand's when Rousseau's Emilius[4] appeared; – but had not brought about any change in the systems adopted. Wisdom has less influence than enthusiasm, because it is always simple in its expressions, and scarce ever assumes an imposing or authoritative tone. – The English philosopher only seemed to give his advice; Rousseau repeated the same things, but he did not advise; he commanded, and was obeyed."

---

1  John Milton (1608-74), English poet, essayist, educated his two nephews.
2  John Locke (1632-1704), English philosopher; his *Thoughts on Education* (1693) greatly influenced educational theory in the eighteenth century.
3  Stephanie Félicité Ducrest de St. Aubin, Comtesse de Genlis (1746-1830), French dramatist, essayist; she wrote *Théâtre d'education* (1779) for the royal children in her charge, one of whom was the future King Louis Phillippe.
4  Jean Jacques Rousseau (1712-78), political and educational philosopher and essayist, born in Geneva. His novel *Emile* is his controversial and influential work on education.

She likewise observes, that Rousseau follows the system of Mr. Locke in almost every respect; he copies him literally, but without quoting him, or acknowledging his obligations to him. It is thus that many other French writers have imitated our best authors on most subjects.

Rousseau has done much harm by encouraging a general relaxation of discipline, and he has uttered many false dogmas, that would have been laughed at from any other man; particularly that *one man* can only educate *one pupil*; which experience proves to be false and absurd; nevertheless, in his writings are many excellent and admirable things, and it is much to be wished that the grain could be separated from the chaff.

That children are to be restrained without cruelty, and instructed without severity, can never be too strongly inculcated. That there is no necessity of scourging them through a course of learning, which they cannot attain by a gentle and moderate course of instruction.

The points mistaken and too strongly urged, have seemed to countenance the opinions of those who oppose all manner of subjection; but the truth is, that people ought to study the capacities and dispositions of their children, not only before they destine them to any particular calling or profession, but before they resolve on the course of education they are to go through.

Those youths who cannot profit by a learned education, may yet do so by an useful one, and may be better members of the community, than those who spend so large a portion of their time in the study of the dead languages, or in other kinds of learning, of more credit than utility.

But above all other kinds of learning, the first principles of religion and virtue should be early sown and strongly inculcated, they are not to be left to their own vague opinions, but the great outlines are to be written upon their hearts in strong and indelible characters. Here we turn aside from the sceptical Rousseau, and follow the instructions of a greater master.[1]

---

1  God.

Train up a child in the way he should go, and when he is old he will not depart from it.[1]

Precept must be laid upon precept, and line upon line; here a little and there a little.[2]

I shall here conclude this letter, but shall soon send another; in the interim, I remain your ladyship's most humble servant,

Frances Darnford.

from "LETTER XXII. Mrs. Darnford to Mrs. Strictland."

*London, Feb. 28.*

Captain Maurice has called here almost every day since my last. He converses with ease and freedom; and though not a man of polished manners, he has a general kind of knowledge, and is by no means disagreeable. He has signed the instrument[3] which I prepared for him, trusting in me, that I would make no ill use of it; he did it in a very handsome manner.

He has since done a generous action; for the first was only an act of justice. – He has added to Charlotte's fortune, in presents; it is now full three thousand pounds. He makes me her guardian; and she is to receive her fortune when she comes of age; or if she marries sooner, with my consent, (upon which, he says, his depends) upon the day of her marriage.

After this was accepted, he took another paper out of his pocket, and bowing very low, offered it to me. I desired to know the contents, otherwise I could not accept it. – He blushed – hesitated – and looked as if soliciting a favour, rather than confering one. This is the criterion of true generosity; it is not confined to pecuniary matters; it is modest, diffident, humble – in short – it is greatness of soul! Monsieur St. Evremond[4] says, that most of those people who complain of ingratitude, ought rather to be complained of. – They know not how to

---

1   *Proverbs* 22:6.
2   *Isaiah* 28:10. "For precept must be upon precept, precept upon precept; line upon line; line upon line; here a little, and there a little."
3   Legal document.
4   Charles Saint-Evremond (1613-1703), French historian, writer, social critic.

confer favours; they humble the receiver to dust, and then complain of ingratitude. – If people knew how to confer them, there would be few persons ungrateful. Maurice declined opening the paper; I returned it to him. He then spoke with some confusion, as follows: –

My obligations to you, Madam, are such as I can never repay. First, you have restored my mind to peace with itself, by recovering Donna Isabella to health of mind and body; and secondly, you have been a mother to my child, and you will continue your cares for her, till she is of an age to act for herself. – I humbly beg your acceptance of my best acknowledgements, and of an act and deed which proves my gratitude for your great and real services to me and mine. This paper is an act of settlement of my farm at D––, upon my Charlotte, irrevocably; and the income of it to you, Madam, during your life.

I was astonished and confounded. – I declined accepting it. He kneeled to me, and with tears in his eyes besought me, for his own peace and happiness, to accept his honest and sincere gratitude. – I was distressed; he was resolute; and he gained the victory.

Charlotte ran into my arms, and thanked me for obliging her father; in short, we were all so much affected, that we did not soon recover it; as soon as Mr. Maurice was composed, he left us.

The next day he called again; he looked more chearful than I ever saw him. – "Madam," said he, "I slept well last night, and am happier than I have been for many years past; I thank God, and I thank you!" – "I rejoice to hear you say so, Sir; may the remainder of your days be easy and happy!" – "Thank you again and again, Madam; and may you be rewarded for all your goodness!"

★     ★     ★     ★

As Charlotte Brady will have so handsome a fortune, I will give her some of the ornamental accomplishments. She has already an eminent dancing master to attend her; and she shall learn music and drawing, beside; I will show her all that is worth seeing in town, and carry her once or twice to each of the public places; teaching her, at the same time, to distinguish between the tinsel ornaments, and things of intrinsic value.

Lady A— is just come to town, she desires to see me as soon as possible; I will give you an account of my visit.

Accept and distribute my regards among all my friends at Woodlands. I write to Madame di Soranzo under the same cover. For this time I bid you adieu!

F. Darnford.

### 13. Mrs. Bonhote, *The Parental Monitor*, 3rd ed. (London: William Lane, 1796). Volume II.

The Family Fire-side.

"Home's home, however homely," wisdom says,
And certain is the fact, though coarse the phrase;
To prove it, if it needed proof at all,
Mark what a train attends the muse's call;
And, as she leads th' ideal group along,
Let your own feelings realize her song.
Clear then the stage; no scen'ry we require,
Save the snug circle round the parlour-fire;
And enter, marshall'd in procession fair,
Each happier influence that governs there: –
First, love, by friendship mellow'd into bliss,
Lights the warm glow, and sanctifies the kiss!
When, fondly welcom'd to th'accustom'd seat,
In sweet complacence wife and husband meet,
Look mutual pleasure, mutual purpose share,
Repose from labours to unite in care.
Ambition! – does ambition there reside?
Yes, when the boy, in manly mood, astride,
(Of headstrong prowess innocently vain,)
Canters, – the jockey of his father's cane.
While emulation, in the daughter's heart,
Bears a more mild, though not less pow'rful part;
With zeal to shine her flutt'ring bosom warms,

And in the romp the future housewife forms.
Or both, perchance, to graver sport incline,
And art and genius in their pastime join; –
This the cramp riddle's puzzling knot invents,
That rears aloft the card-built tenements.
Think how joy animates, intense, tho' meek,
The fading roses on their grandame's cheek;
When, proud the frolic progeny to survey,
She feels and owns an int'rest in their play;
Adopts each with their wayward whims unfold,
And tells, at every call, the story ten times told.

14. Thomas Gisborne, *An Enquiry into the Duties of the Female Sex* (London: T. Cadell jun. and W. Davis, 1797).

from "Chap. VIII. On Amusements in General. – Masquerades. – The Efficacy of Individual Example Considered."

Amusements, private as well as public, form another province over which custom and fashion are generally allowed to preside. The claim is, under due limitations, not unreasonable. But that propensity to imitation in the female sex, which has already been explained, concurs with the high spirits and inexperience of youth occasionally to lead women to venture in this province, on ground that is manifestly inauspicious, and sometimes on ground which ought to be deemed forbidden. In former ages, when the barbarous combats of gladiators were exhibited in the Roman Circus; and exhibited in so many cities and with such frequency, as in some instances to cost Europe from twenty to thirty thousand lives within the space of a month; the wives and daughters of the citizens of all ranks are represented as having been passionately addicted to these spectacles (f).[1] To our own countrywomen, whose eyes have not been polluted nor their hearts hardened by cruel and sanguinary entertainments, this recital may scarcely appear credi-

---

1  TG's note: "(f) Lipsius, Sat. b.i.c. 12." Justus Lipsius (1547-1606), Flemish humanist, born near Brussels, a classical scholar whose *I. LipsI Satvrnalium sermonvm libri dvo* (1582) TG refers to here.

ble. But the fact is confirmed by similar examples. I mean not to dwell on the concurrent accounts given by different writers, of the extreme delight which the women among the North American Indians experience, when vying with each other in embittering the tortures inflicted on the captive enemy: partly because a large share of the pleasure is derived from the triumphant spirit of revenge; and partly because parallels drawn from the untamed ferocity of savage life, cannot fairly be applied to illustrate the influence of custom on modern periods of refinement. But a fact, too nearly corresponding to that which has been alleged from the annals of Rome, was very recently to be witnessed, I believe that it is even yet to be witnessed, in one of the cultivated nations of the South of Europe. I allude to the Spanish Bull-feasts. Persons of credit, who have lately visited Spain, unite in describing the Spanish ladies as beyond measure fond of this barbarous species of entertainment (g);[1] and as most vehement in their applause when the scene of danger is at the height. I state these facts as affording an impressive example of the force of custom; and a warning of the firmness with which the despotism of fashion may in many cases require to be withstood, even when it is aspiring to jurisdiction merely over amusements. If in the present age, in a christian country, among a people which lays claim to considerable refinement, fashion has power to benumb the sympathetic emotions of humanity which characterise the female heart; to render exhibitions of cruelty and bloodshed, the miseries of

---

1 TG's note: "(g) See *Townsend's Journey through Spain, in the year 1786 and 1787*, second edition, vol. i. p. 342, &c. According to his statement, the Bull-feasts at Madrid are regularly held one day in every week, and often two days, throughout the summer. On each of these days six bulls are slaughtered in the morning, and twelve in the evening. Of the men who engage the furious animal, some maintain the combat on foot, some on horseback. The danger of the employment may be estimated from two circumstances, mentioned with another view by the author whom I quote. First, that *seventeen horses* on an average are killed by the bulls each day; and that *sixty* horses have been known to perish in a day. Secondly, that among the official attendants on the Bull-feasts, is a priest appointed to administer the sacrament to persons mortally wounded in the conflict. He concludes his account in the following terms: 'The fondness of the Spaniards for this diversion is scarcely to be conceived. Men, women, and children, rich and poor, all give the preference to it beyond all other public spectacles.' His testimony might receive confirmation, were it necessary, from other authorities." Joseph Townsend (1739-1816), *A Journey through Spain, in the Years 1786 and 1787* (London: C. Dilly, 1791).

tortured animals (h)[1] and the dangers of their wretched assailants, not merely tolerable to female eyes, but a spectacle gratifying beyond every other in the way of amusement; let it not be thought very improbable, that in our own country fashion may, on some occasions, prove herself able to attach women to amusements, which, though neither stained with blood, nor derived from the infliction of pain, may be such as for other reasons ought to be universally reprobated and exploded. And whenever such occasions may arise, let every woman remember, that modes of amusement intrinsically wrong, or in any respect unbecoming the female sex, are not transformed into innocent recreations by the countenance of numbers, nor by the sanction, if they should obtain the sanction, of nobility, or of a court.

from "Chap. XIX. On Parental Duties."

There is a medium which is not always easy to be observed, with respect to daughters being allowed to accept invitations to pass some time in other families. Such intercourse on proper occasions is improving as well as pleasant. But if a young woman is accustomed to be frequently absent from home, roving from house to house and accumulating visit upon visit; she is in no small danger of acquiring an unsettled and dissipated spirit; of becoming dissatisfied with the calm occupations and enjoyments of the family fireside; and even of losing some portion of the warm affection which she felt for her parents and near relations, while she was in the habit of placing her chief delight in their society. If the parent would guard her daughters

---

1  TG's note: "(h) In the former part of the sixteenth century, Bearbaiting is affirmed to have been 'a favourite diversion exhibited as a suitable amusement for a Princess.' Henry's History of England, vol. vi. p. 671. An amusement thus countenanced was probably acceptable to English ladies in general. It appears, at a later period, to have still maintained a place among the recreations of women of rank. Among the spectacles displayed for the diversion of Queen Elizabeth, when she was entertained at Kenilworth Castle by the Earl of Leicester, bear-baitings and boxing-matches are enumerated by the historian of the festivity." Possibly referring to Henry Hallam's *Constitutional History of England from the Accession of Henry VII to the Death of George II* (1827), if Gisbourne added this note to a later edition of the work.

from all propensity to this extreme, let her aid the sobriety of disposition and sedateness of character, already instilled into them, by the charms of never-failing and affectionate good humour on her own part, which are essential to the comfort of domestic life, and particularly attractive in the eye of youth. There are fashionable mothers who, at the same time that they introduce their daughters into a general and free acquaintance with others of their age, sex, and station, carefully instil into them the prudential maxim, to contract friendship with none. The scheme either fails to succeed, or breeds up a character of determined selfishness. Let the parent encourage her daughters in friendly attachment to young women, in whom amiable manners and virtuous principles are exemplified. With the society of such friends let her willingly gratify them; sometimes abroad; more frequently under her own roof. But let her not consent to their residence in families where they will be conversant with ensnaring company of either sex; where boldness of demeanour will be communicated by example, an extravagant fondness for amusements inspired, habits of serious reflection discouraged, and the rational employment of time disregarded. Let her not be flattered by the solicitations, imprudent, however well intended, of ladies of superior rank, desirous to introduce her daughters into circles in which they are not destined to move. If ambition be once kindled by introduction into a higher sphere, is it likely that it will descend contentedly from its elevation? Is it likely that the modest retirement of private life will remain as engaging as before?

**15. Maria Edgeworth and Richard Lovell Edgeworth,** *Practical Education*, **2 vols. (London: J. Johnston, 1798).**

Volume 1. from "Truth"

Ridicule certainly is not the test of truth; but it is a test which truth sometimes find it difficult to stand. Vice never "bolts her arguments" with more success, than when she assumes the air of raillery, and the tone of gaiety. All vivacious young people are fond of wit; we do not mean children, for they do not understand it; those who have the best capacities, and the strictest habits of veracity, often appear to common observers absolutely stupid, from their aversion to any play upon words, and from the literal simplicity with which they believe every thing that is asserted. A remarkably intelligent little girl of four years old, but who had never in her own family been used to the common phrases which sometimes pass for humour, happened to hear a gentleman say, as he looked out of the window one rainy morning, "It rains cats and dogs to day:" the child with a surprised, but believing look, immediately went to look out of the window to see the phænomenon. This extreme simplicity in childhood is sometimes succeeded in youth by a strong taste for wit and humour: young people are, in the first place, proud to shew that they understand them, and they are gratified by the perception of a new intellectual pleasure. At this period of their education great attention must be paid to them, lest their admiration for wit and frolic should diminish their reverence and their love for sober truth. In many engaging characters in society, and in many entertaining books, deceit and dishonesty are associated with superior abilities, with ease and gaiety of manners, and with a certain air of frank carelessness which can scarcely fail to please. Gil Blas,[1]* Tom Jones, Lovelace, Count Fathom,[2] are all of this class of characters; they should not be introduced to our pupils till their habits of integrity are thoroughly formed, and till they are sufficiently skilful in analysing their own feelings, to distinguish whence their approbation and pleasure in reading of these characters arise. In books we do not actually suffer by the tricks of rogues, or by the lies they tell; hence their truth is to us a quality of no value; but their wit, humour, and the ingenuity of their contrivances, are of great value to us, because they afford us entertainment....

---

1    *ME/RLE note: See Mrs. Macaulay's Letters on Education.
2    Gil Blas, picaresque hero of the four-volume novel of the same title written by Alain Rene Le Sage (1668-1747) and published between 1715 and 1735; Tom Jones, the titular hero of the comic novel, published in 1749, by Henry Fielding (1707-54); Lovelace, the libertine seducer of the heroine of English novelist Samuel Richardson's (1689-1761) *Clarissa* (1748); and Count Fathom, the villain of Scottish novelist Tobias Smollett's (1721-71) *Ferdinand, Count Fathom* (1753).

**16. Frances Burney D'Arblay,** *Memoirs of Doctor Burney*, **3 vols. (London: Edward Moxon, 1832).**

Volume I. from "Esther."

From this period, to that of their exquisitely happy union,

> "Gallopp'd apace the fiery-footed steeds,"[1]

that urged on Time with as much gay delight as prancing rapidity; for if they had not, in their matrimonial preparations, the luxuries of wealth, neither had they its fatiguing ceremonies; if they had not the security of future advantage, they avoided the torment of present procrastination; and if they had but little to bestow upon one another, they were saved, at least, the impatiency of waiting for the seals, signatures, and etiquettes of lawyers, to bind down a lucrative prosperity to survivorship.

To the mother of the bride, alone of her family, was confided, on the instant, this spontaneous, this sudden felicity. Little formality was requisite, before the passing of the marriage act, for presenting at the hymeneal altar its destined votaries; and contracts the most sacred could be rendered indissoluble almost at the very moment of their projection: a strange dearth of foresight in those legislators who could so little weigh the chances of a minor's judgment upon what, eventually, may either suit his taste or form his happiness, for the larger portion of existence that commonly follows his majority.

This mother of the bride was of a nature so free from stain, so elementally white, that it would scarcely seem an hyperbole to denominate her an angel upon earth – if purity of mind that breathed to late old age the innocence of infancy, and sustained the whole intervening period in the constant practice of self-sacrificing virtue, with piety for its sole stimulus, and holy hope for its sole reward, can make pardonable the hazard of such an anticipating appellation, – from which, however, she, her humble self, would have shrunk as from sacrilege.

---

1   Shakespeare, *Romeo and Juliet* III.ii.1.

She was originally of French extraction, from a family of the name of Dubois; but though her father was one of the conscientious victims of the Edict of Nantz,[1] she, from some unknown cause – probably of maternal education – had been brought up a Roman Catholic. The inborn religion of her mind, however, counteracted all that was hostile to her fellow-creatures, in the doctrine of the religion of her ancestors; and her gentle hopes and fervent prayers were offered up as devoutly for those whom she feared were wrong, as they were vented enthusiastically for those whom she was bred to believe were right.

Her bridal daughter, who had been educated a Protestant, and who to that faith adhered steadily and piously through life, loved her with that devoted love which could not but emanate from sympathy of excellence. She was the first pride of her mother, – or, rather, the first delight; for pride, under any form, or through any avenue, direct or collateral, by which that subtle passion works or swells its way to the human breast, her mother knew not; though she was endued with an innate sense of dignity that seemed to exhale around her a sentiment of reverence that, notwithstanding her genuine and invariable humility, guarded her from every species and every approach of disrespect.

She could not but be gratified by an alliance so productive, rather than promising, of happiness to her favourite child; and Mr. Burney – as the married man must now be called – soon imbibed the filial veneration felt by his wife, and loved his mother-in-law as sincerely as if she had been his mother-in-blood.

---

1   The Edict of Nantes, decreed in 1598 by Henry IV in order to end fighting between Catholics and Protestants in France, gave some religious freedom to the French Protestants, or Huguenots. It was revoked in 1685 by Louis XIV.

Volume II.

*Copied from a Memorandum-book of Dr. Burney's, written in the year* 1808, *at* Bath.

"The literary history of my second daughter, Fanny, now Madame d'Arblay, is singular. She was wholly unnoticed in the nursery for any talents, or quickness of study: indeed, at eight years old she did not know her letters; and her brother, the tar,[1] who in his boyhood had a natural genius for hoaxing, used to pretend to teach her to read; and gave her a book topsy-turvy, which he said she never found out! She had, however, a great deal of invention and humour in her childish sports; and used, after having seen a play in Mrs. Garrick's box,[2] to take the actors off, and compose speeches for their characters; for she could not read them. But in company, or before strangers, she was silent, backward, and timid, even to sheepishness: and, from her shyness, had such profound gravity and composure of features, that those of my friends who came often to my house, and entered into the different humours of the children, never called Fanny by any other name, from the time she had reached her eleventh year, than The Old Lady.

Her first work, Evelina, was written by stealth, in a closet up two pair of stairs, that was appropriated to the younger children as a play room. No one was let into the secret but my third daughter, afterwards Mrs. Phillips; though even to her it was never read till printed, from want of private opportunity. To me, nevertheless, she confidentially owned that she was going, through her brother Charles, to print a little work, but she besought me never to ask to see it. I laughed at her plan, but promised silent acquiescence; and the book had been six months published before I even heard its name; which I learnt at last without her knowledge. But great, indeed, was then my surprise, to find that it was in general reading, and commended in no common manner in the several

---

1   Seaman.
2   Mrs. Garrick, wife of actor David Garrick, would have had private, reserved seating in the theater her husband managed.

Reviews of the times. Of this she was unacquainted herself, as she was then ill, and in the country. When I knew its title, I commissioned one of her sisters to procure it for me privately. I opened the first volume with fear and trembling; not having the least idea that, without the use of the press, or any practical knowledge of the world, she could write a book worth reading. The dedication to myself, however, brought tears into my eyes; and before I had read half the first volume I was much surprised, and, I confess, delighted; and most especially with the letters of Mr. Villars. She had always had a great affection for me; had an excellent heart, and a natural simplicity and probity about her that wanted no teaching. In her plays with her sisters, and some neighbour's children, this straightforward morality operated to an uncommon degree in one so young. There lived next door to me, at that time, in Poland street, and in a private house, a capital hair merchant, who furnished peruques[1] to the judges, and gentlemen of the law. The merchant's female children and mine, used to play together in the little garden behind the house; and, unfortunately, one day, the door of the wig magazine being left open, they each of them put on one of those dignified ornaments of the head, and danced and jumped about in a thousand antics, laughing till they screamed at their own ridiculous figures. Unfortunately, in their vagaries, one of the flaxen wigs, said by the proprietor to be worth upwards of ten guineas – in those days a price enormous – fell into a tub of water, placed for the shrubs in the little garden, and lost all its gorgon buckle, and was declared by the owner to be totally spoilt. He was extremely angry, and chid very severely his own children; when my little daughter, the old lady, then ten years of age, advancing to him, as I was informed, with great gravity and composure, sedately says; "What signifies talking so much about an accident? The wig is wet, to be sure; and the wig was a good wig, to be sure; but its of no use to speak of it any more; because what's done can't be undone."

"Whether these stoical sentiments appeased the enraged

---

1   Wigs.

peruquier, I know not, but the younkers[1] were stript of their honours, and my little monkies were obliged to retreat without beat of drum, or colours flying."

1    "A young nobleman or gentleman" (*OED*).

# Appendix C: Works on Comedy

**1. Anon.,** *Pasquil's Jests, Mixed with Mother Bunches Merriments* **(1604), ed. W. Carew Hazlitt (London: Willis and Sotheran, 1866).**

*How a woman served a Glutton, but yet he was too good for her.*

Not unlike to Mother Bunch our Hostesse, an olde woman in Sussex, that brewed good Ale, there dwelt, that had every weeke a lusty eater, and as tall a drinker, [who] used to her house; but when he had served himselfe, he would not pay any thing at all. The Woman, grieving to be thus used still, knew not what remedy to have, for with his swaggering hee domineerd, because hee had bene a souldier. One Tuesday morning he comes thither, saying: Hostesse, what shall we have to breakefast? I have nothing of your price (quoth she) at this time. Whereupon he began to sweare so pityfully, that he so feared the woman that she set a dish of sweet butter before him, that shee had kept for others that were to come thither, whereof he began to eate so greedily, that she feared he would eate up all. And thereupon she stept to the dore, as though one had knockt, and came in agayne, and sayd to him: Sir, there is one at the dore would speake with you. Whereupon hee went to the doore. In the meane space she thrust his knife in the fire, and heat it almost red hote. In comes hee againe, saying, there was nobody there. Then belike he is gone, quoth she. Hee, taking his knife againe, would haue cut the butter, but it fell still from the knife; whereat he wondring sayd: Hostesse, I marvaile what ailes my knife? Truely, sir, your knife blushes to see his master so unreasonable. In faith, sayd he, if this knife blush, his fellow here yet looketh pale; and so drawes out his other knife, and eates up the rest of the butter cleane.

*A witty answere of a Magistrate to a malicious accuser of an offender.*

A malicious fellow, willing to bring a neighbour of his unto all the disgrace he could devise, and shrewdly suspecting him to have more then a moneths mind to a fine mistres neere unto him, oftentimes watching his going in and comming out of her house: one day, among other, in the evening, noting his long stay, suspected that there was somewhat to doe more then all the Parish was acquainted with, and therefore seeing the maide gone foorth upon some errand, beeing very earely in the morning, suddenly stept in with a companion of his, and tooke them together at their exercise; which, being glad of, and that he had witnesse to make his matter good, runnes to the Magistrate of the Citie, who had to deale with such persons and such cases, and told him as much as he had seene, with: oh, Sir, I assure you he is a perillous man for a woman; and, to tell you the troth, we tooke him in bed with her: what say you to such a fellow? The Magistrate, some what allyed unto the young man, and wishing rather a secret amendment then an open reprehension, gave him this answere: Truely, for the matter, it is not well; but for being taken in bed with her, in truth I can thinke no otherwise, but hee was a sluggard: I know not what to say to him. The accuser, seeing the people smile, and himselfe mocked with this speech, did no further aggravate the matter, but, with a flea in his eare, went away with his malicious humor.

**2. Joseph Addison, *The Spectator* (1711), in *The British Essayists*, 2nd ed., ed. James Ferguson (London: J. Richardson, et al., 1823).**

*No. 35. Tuesday, April 10, 1711.*

> *Risu inepto res ineptior nulla est.*[1]
> > Mart.
> Nothing so foolish as the laugh of fools.

Among all kinds of writing, there is none in which authors are more apt to miscarry than in works of humour, as there is none in which they are more ambitious to excel. It is not an imagi-

---

1    Catullus, *Carmina* XXXIX: "Untimely grinning is the silliest sin" (*The Oxford Dictionary of Quotations*, 2nd ed. [New York: Oxford University Press], 1955).

nation that teems with monsters, an head that is filled with extravagant conceptions, which is capable of furnishing the world with diversions of this nature: and yet if we look into our productions of several writers, who set up for men of humour, what wild irregular fancies, what unnatural distortions of thought do we meet with? If they speak nonsense, they believe they are talking humour; and when they have drawn together a scheme of absurd, inconsistent ideas, they are not able to read it over to themselves without laughing. The poor gentlemen endeavour to gain themselves the reputation of wits and humorists, by such monstrous conceits as almost qualify them for Bedlam; not considering that humour should always lie under the check of reason, and that it requires the direction of the nicest judgment, by so much the more as it indulges itself in the most boundless freedoms. There is a kind of nature that is to be observed in this sort of compositions, as well as in all other; and a certain regularity of thought which must discover the writer to be a man of sense, at the same time that he appears altogether given up to caprice. For my part, when I read the delirious mirth of an unskilful author, I cannot be so barbarous as to divert myself with it, but am rather apt to pity the man, than laugh at any thing he writes.

The deceased Mr. Shadwell,[1] who had himself a great deal of the talent which I am treating of, represents an empty rake, in one of his plays, as very much surprised to hear one say that breaking of windows was not humour; and I question not but several English readers will be as much startled to hear me affirm, that many of those raving incoherent pieces, which are often spread among us, under odd chimerical titles, are rather the offsprings of a distempered brain, than works of humour.

It is indeed much easier to describe what is not humour, than what is; and very difficult to define it otherwise than as Cowley[2] has done wit, by negatives. Were I to give my own notions of it, I would deliver them after Plato's manner, in a

---

1   Thomas Shadwell (c. 1642–92), English dramatist, author of thirteen comedies, three tragedies. Appointed Poet Laureate 1689.
2   Abraham Cowley (1618–67), English poet of great contemporary reknown.

kind of allegory,[1] and by supposing Humour to be a person, deduce to him all his qualifications, according to the following genealogy. Truth was the founder of the family, and the father of Good Sense. Good Sense was the father of Wit, who married a lady of collateral line[2] called Mirth, by whom he had issue Humour. Humour therefore being the youngest of this illustrious family, and descended from parents of such different dispositions, is very various and unequal in his temper; sometimes you see him putting on grave looks and a solemn habit, sometimes airy in his behaviour and fantastic in his dress; insomuch that at different times he appears as serious as a judge, and as jocular as a merry andrew. But as he has a great deal of the mother in his constitution, whatever mood he is in, he never fails to make his company laugh.

But since there is an impostor abroad, who takes upon him the name of the young gentleman, and would willingly pass for him in the world; to the end that well-meaning persons may not be imposed upon by cheats, I would desire my readers, when they meet with this pretender, to look into his parentage, and to examine him strictly, whether or no he be remotely allied to Truth, and lineally descended from Good Sense; if not, they may conclude him a counterfeit. They may likewise distinguish him by a loud and excessive laughter, in which he seldom gets his company to join with him. For as True Humour generally looks serious, while every body laughs about him; False Humour is always laughing, whilst every body about him looks serious. I shall only add, if he has not in him a mixture of both parents, that is, if he would pass for the offspring of Wit without Mirth, or Mirth without Wit, you may conclude him to be altogether spurious and a cheat.

The impostor of whom I am speaking, descends originally from Falsehood, who was the mother of Nonsense, who was brought to bed of a son called Frenzy, who married one of the daughters of Folly, commonly known by the name of Laughter,

---

1   Plato (c. 428–c. 347 B.C.), Greek philosopher, wrote *The Republic*, at the center of which is the allegory of the cave (Book 7) in which Plato distinguishes between knowledge based on reality and belief based on appearances.

2   "Situated or placed side by side (with one another)" (*OED*).

on whom he begot that monstrous infant of which I have here been speaking. I shall set down at length the genealogical table of False Humour, and, at the same time, place under it the genealogy of True Humour, that the reader may at one view behold their different pedigrees and relations:

Falsehood.
Nonsense.
Frenzy – Laughter.
False Humour.
Truth.
Good Sense.
Wit – Mirth.
Humour.

I might extend the allegory, by mentioning several of the children of False Humour, who are more in number than the sands of the sea, and might in particular enumerate the many sons and daughters which he has begot in this island. But as this would be a very invidious task, I shall only observe in general, that False Humour differs from the True, as a monkey does from a man.

First of all, He is exceedingly given to little apish tricks and buffooneries.

Secondly, He so much delights in mimicry, that it is all one to him, whether he exposes by it vice and folly, luxury and avarice; or, on the contrary, virtue and wisdom, pain and poverty.

Thirdly, He is wonderfully unlucky insomuch that he will bite the hand that feeds him, and endeavour to ridicule both friends and foes indifferently. For having but small talents, he must be merry where he can, not where he should.

Fourthly, Being entirely void of reason, he pursues no point either of morality or instruction, but is ludicrous only for the sake of being so.

Fifthly, Being incapable of any thing but mock representations, his ridicule is always personal, and aimed at the vicious man or the writer; not at the vice, or the writing.

I have here only pointed at the whole species of false humourists; but as one of my principal designs in this paper is to beat down that malignant spirit, which discovers itself in the writings of the present age, I shall not scruple, for the future, to single out any of the small wits, that infest the world with such compositions as are ill-natured, immoral, and absurd. This is the only exception which I shall make to the general rule I have prescribed myself, of attacking multitudes, since every honest man ought to look upon himself as in a natural state of war with the libeller and lampooner, and to annoy them wherever they fall in his way. This is but retaliating upon them, and treating them as they treat others.

*No. 47. Tuesday, April 24, 1711.*

Ride si sapis —<br>Mart.<br>Laugh, if you are wise.

Mr. Hobbs, in his Discourse of Human Nature,[1] which, in my humble opinion, is much the best of all his works, after some very curious observations upon laughter, concludes thus: "The passion of laughter is nothing else but sudden glory arising from some sudden conception of some eminency in ourselves, by comparison with the infirmity of others, or with our own formerly: for men laugh at the follies of themselves past, when they come suddenly to remembrance, except they bring with them any present dishonour."

According to this author therefore, when we hear a man laugh excessively, instead of saying he is very merry, we ought to tell him he is very proud. And indeed, if we look into the bottom of this matter, we shall meet with many observations to confirm us in this opinion. Every one laughs at somebody that is in an inferior state of folly to himself. It was formerly the custom for every great house in England to keep a tame fool dressed in petticoats, that the heir of the family might have an

---

1    Thomas Hobbes (1588-1679), English philosopher, political theorist.

opportunity of joking upon him, and diverting himself with his absurdities. For the same reason, idiots are still in request in most of the courts of Germany, where there is not a prince of any great magnificence, who has not two or three dressed, distinguished, undisputed fools in his retinue, whom the rest of the courtiers are always breaking their jests upon.

The Dutch, who are more famous for their industry and application than for wit and humour, hang up in several of their streets what they call the sign of the Gaper, that is, the head of an idiot dressed in a cap and bells, and gaping in a most immoderate manner. This is a standing jest at Amsterdam.

Thus every one diverts himself with some person or other that is below him in point of understanding, and triumphs in the superiority of his genius, whilst he has such objects of derision before his eyes. Mr. Dennis[1] has very well expressed this in a couple of humorous lines, which are part of a translation of a satire in monsieur Boileau:[2]

"Thus one fool lolls his tongue out at another,
And shakes his empty noddle at his brother."

Mr. Hobbs's reflection gives us the reason why the insignificant people above mentioned are stirrers up of laughter among men of a gross taste: but as the more understanding part of mankind do not find their risibility affected by such ordinary objects, it may be worth the while to examine into the several provocatives of laughter, in men of superior sense and knowledge.

In the first place I must observe, that there is a set of merry drolls, whom the common people of all countries admire, and seem to love so well, "that they could eat them," according to the old proverb: I mean those circumforaneous wits whom every nation calls by the name of that dish of meat which it loves best: in Holland they are termed Pickled Herrings; in France, Jean Pottages; in Italy, Macaronies; and in Great Britain, Jack Puddings. These merry wags, from whatsoever food they

---

1  John Dennis (1657-1734), English critic, wit, author of nine uncelebrated plays.
2  Nicolas Boileau (1636-1711), French critic, satirist.

receive their titles, that they may make their audiences laugh, always appear in a fool's coat, and commit such blunders and mistakes in every step they take, and every word they utter, as those who listen to them would be ashamed of.

But this little triumph of the understanding, under the disguise of laughter, is no where more visible than in that custom which prevails every where among us on the first day of the present month, when every body takes it into his head to make as many fools as he can. In proportion as there are more follies discovered, so there is more laughter raised on this day than on any other in the whole year. A neighbour of mine, who is a haberdasher by trade, and a very shallow conceited fellow, makes his boast that for these ten years successively he has not made less than an hundred April fools. My landlady had a falling out with him about a fortnight ago, for sending every one of her children upon some sleeveless errand, as she terms it. Her eldest son went to buy an halfpennyworth of inkle at a shoemaker's; the eldest daughter was dispatched half a mile to see a monster; and, in short, the whole family of innocent children made April fools. Nay, my landlady herself did not escape him. This empty fellow has laughed upon these conceits ever since.

This art of wit is well enough, when confined to one day in a twelvemonth; but there is an ingenious tribe of men sprung up of late years, who are for making April fools every day in the year. These gentlemen are commonly distinguished by the name of Biters: a race of men that are perpetually employed in laughing at those mistakes which are of their own production.

Thus we see, in proportion as one man is more refined than another, he chooses his fool out of a lower or higher class of mankind, or to speak in a more philosophical language, that secret elation or pride of heart, which is generally called laughter, arises in him, from his comparing himself with an object below him, whether it so happens that it be a natural or an artificial fool. It is, indeed, very possible, that the persons we laugh at may in the main of their characters be much wiser men than ourselves; but if they would have us laugh at them, they must fall short of us in those respects which stir up this passion.

I am afraid I shall appear too abstracted in my speculations, if I shew, that when a man of wit makes us laugh, it is by betraying some oddness or infirmity in his own character, or in the representation which he makes of others; and that when we laugh at a brute, or even at an inanimate thing, it is at some action or incident that bears a remote analogy to any blunder or absurdity in reasonable creatures.

But to come into common life: I shall pass by the consideration of those state coxcombs that are able to shake a whole audience, and take notice of a particular sort of men who are such provokers of mirth in conversation, that it is impossible for a club or merry meeting to subsist without them; I mean those honest gentlemen that are always exposed to the wit and raillery of their well-wishers and companions; that are pelted by men, women, and children, friends and foes, and in a word, stand as butts in conversation, for every one to shoot at that pleases. I know several of these butts who are men of wit and sense, though by some odd turn of humour, some unlucky cast in their person or behaviour, they have always the misfortune to make the company merry. The truth of it is, a man is not qualified for a butt, who has not a good deal of wit and vivacity, even in the ridiculous side of his character. A stupid butt is only fit for the conversation of ordinary people: men of wit require one that will give them play, and bestir himself in the absurd part of his behaviour. A butt with these accomplishments frequently gets the laugh of his side, and turns the ridicule upon him that attacks him. Sir John Falstaff[1] was an hero of this species, and gives a good description of himself in his capacity of a butt, after the following manner: "Men of all sorts," says that merry knight, "take a pride to gird at me. The brain of man is not able to invent any thing that tends to laughter more than I invent, or is invented on me. I am not only witty in myself, but the cause that wit is in other men."[2]

---

1 Falstaff appears in Shakespeare's *Henry IV, Part 1*; *Henry IV, Part II*; and *The Merry Wives of Windsor*.
2 From *Henry IV, Part II* I.ii.10.

### 3. Anon., *Scoggin's Jests* (1626), ed. W. Carew Hazlitt (London: Willis & Sotheran, 1866).

[How] *Scogin* told his wife he had parbraked[1] a crow.

After a while that Scogin came to London, hee married a yong woman, taking her for a maid, as other men doe. At last he thought to prove his wife, and fained himselfe sicke. Oh! good wife, saies he, I will shew you a thing, and if you will promise me to conceale it. His wife said: sir, you may tell mee what you will; I were worse than accursed, if I should disclose your counsell. O! wife, said Scogin, I had a great pang to day in my sicknesse, for I did parbrake and cast out a crow. A crow, said shee. Yea, said Scogin, God helpe me! Be of good comfort, said she, you shall recover and doe well. Well, wife, said Scogin, goe to church and pray for me. She went to the church, and by and by one of her gossips[2] met with her, and asked how her husband did. I wis, said she, a sore sick man he is, and like to die: for there is an evill signe and token in him. What is that, gossip? said she. Nay, by gisse,[3] I will not tell it to any man alive. What, said the woman, you may tell me, for I will never bewray your counsell. By gisse, said Scogin's wife, if I wist that you wold keep my counsel, I wold tel you. Then said the woman: whatsoever you doe tell, I will lay it dead under my feet. Oh, said Scogin's wife, my husband parbraked two crows. Jesus! said the woman, I never heard of such a thing. This woman, as she did meet with another gossip of hers, shewed that Scogin had parbraked three crowes. So it went from one gossip to another that, ere mattens were finished, all the parish knew that Scogin had parbraked twenty crowes; and when the priest was ready to goe into the pulpit, one came to request him and all the parish to pray for Scogin, for hee had parbraked twenty crowes. The priest blessed him, and said to the parishioners: I doe pray you pray for Scogin, for he is in perill of his life, and hath parbraked twenty one crowes. By and by, one went to Scogin, and said: sir,

---

1    *WCH's note:* "Vomited."
2    Women friends.
3    *WCH's note:* "By Jesus."

is it as it is spoken in the Church of you? What is that? said Scogin. The priest said in the Pulpit, that you parbraked twenty one crows. Said Scogin: what a lie is this! By and by, the bels were told for sacring, and Scogin hied him to church lustily and merry, and when the men and women did see him in the church, they looked one upon another, and marvelled of this matter. After Masse, Scogin asked what were they that should bring up such a tale upon him. At last the matter was so boulted out,[1] that the original of the cause began at Scogin's wife. Here a man may see, that it is hard to trust a woman with a man's secrets; wherefore it is good to prove a friend, ere one have need.

How *Scogin* caused his wife to be let blood.

After that Scogin's wife had played this aforesaid pranke, she used so long to go a gossipping, that if her husband had spoken any word contrary to her minde, she would crow against him, that all the street should ring of it. Scogin thought it was time to breake his wife of such matters, and said to her: I would you would take other wayes, or else I will displease you. Displease me! said shee, beware that you doe not displease yourselfe. Yea, said Scogin, I wil see that one day, how you will displease me. She still continued in opprobrious words; at last Scogin called her into a chamber, and tooke one of his servants with him, and said to her: dame, you have a little hot and proud blood about your heart and in your stomacke, and if it be not let out, it will infect you and many more; therefore be content, there is no remedy but that blood must bee let out.[2] I defie thee, said Scogin's wife (and was up in the house top). Yea? said he; come, said Scogin to his servant, and let us bind her to this forme.[3] Shee scratched and clawed them by the faces, and spurned with her feet so long, that shee was weary; so at the last she was bound hand and foot to the forme. Now said Scogin to his servant: goe fetch mee a surgeon, or a barbor[4] that can let

---

1    *WCH's note:* "Sifted."
2    Blood-letting, or phlebotomy, was a common medical practice during this period.
3    "A long seat without a back, a bench" (*OED*).
4    *WCH's note:* "What was formerly known as a 'barber-surgeon'."

blood. The servant went and brought a surgeon. Scogin said to him: sir, it is so that my wife is mad and doth rave, and I have been with physicians, and they have counselled me to let her blood: she hath infectious blood about the hart, and I wold have it out. Sir, said the surgeon, it shall be done. Scogin said: shee is so mad, that she is bound to a forme. The better for that, said the surgeon. When Scogin and the surgeon entred into the chamber, shee made an exclamation upon Scogin. Then said Scogin: you may see that my wife is mad; I pray you let her blood both in the arme and the foot, and under the tongue. Scogin and his man held out her arme, and they did open a veine named Cardica. When shee had bled well: now stop that veine, said Scogin, and let her blood under the foot. When shee saw that: sir, said she, forgive me, and I will never displease you hereafter. Well, said Scogin, if you do so, then I do thinke it shall be best for us both. By this tale it proveth, that it is a shrewd hurt that maketh the body fare the worse, and an unhappy house where the woman is master.

**4. [John Mottley], *Joe Miller's Jest Book* (1739), 70th ed. (Philadelphia: Crawford & Co., 1884).**

## DCXL. – A PROMISE TO PAY.

Joe Haines was more remarkable for his practical jokes than for his acting. He was seized one morning by two bailiffs, for a debt of 20*l*., as the Bishop of Ely was passing by in his coach. "Gentlemen," said Joe, "here's my cousin the Bishop of Ely going by his house; let me but speak to him, and he'll pay the debt and charges." The bailiffs[1] thought they might venture this, as they were within three or four yards of him. Joe went boldly up to the coach, and pulled his hat off to the bishop. His lordship ordered the coach to stop, when Joe whispered him gently, "My lord, here are two men who have such great *scruples of conscience*, that I fear they'll hang themselves." – "Very well," said the bishop; so, calling to the bailiffs, he said, "You two men

---

1 "An officer of justice under a sheriff, who executes writs and processes, distrains and arrests ... " (*OED*).

come to me to-morrow morning, and *I will satisfy you.*" The men bowed, and went away pleased. Early on the following day, the bailiffs, expecting the debt and charges, paid a visit to the bishop; when, being introduced, his lordship addressed them. "Well, my men, what are your scruples of conscience?" – "Scruples!" echoed the bailiff; "we have *no scruples.* We are bailiffs, my lord, who yesterday arrested your cousin, Joe Haines, for a debt of 20*l.*; and your lordship kindly promised to satisfy us to-day." The bishop, reflecting that his honor and name would be exposed were he not to comply, paid the debt and charges.

## MXLVIII. – NOT NECESSARY.

"You flatter me," said a thin exquisite the other day to a young lady who was praising the beauties of his moustache. "For heaven's sake, ma'am," interposed an old skipper, "don't make that *monkey any flatter* than he is!"

## MXLIX. – ASSURANCE AND INSURANCE.

Sterne,[1] the author of the "Sentimental Journey," who had the credit of treating his wife very ill, was one day talking to Garrick[2] in a fine sentimental manner in praise of conjugal love and fidelity: "The husband," said he, with amazing assurance, "who behaves unkindly to his wife, deserves to have his house burnt over his head." – "If you think so," replied Garrick, "I hope *your* house is insured."

## MCCVI. – SEVERE.

A lady asked a sailor whom she met, why a ship was called "*she.*" The son of Neptune replied that it was "because the *rigging* cost more than the hull."

---

1   Lawrence Sterne (1713-68), English novelist. His *Sentimental Journey through France and Italy* was published in 1768.
2   David Garrick (1717-79), English actor, theater manager, dramatist.

# MCCXIV. – THE RICHMOND HOAX.

One of the best practical jokes in Theodore Hook's[1] clever "Gilbert Gurney," is Daly's hoax upon the lady who had never been at Richmond before, or, at least, knew none of the peculiarities of the place. Daly desired the waiter, after dinner, to bring some "maids of honor" – those cheesecakes for which the place has, time out of mind, been celebrated. The lady stared, then laughed, and asked, "What do you mean by 'maids of honor?'" – "Dear me!" said Daly, "don't you know that this is so courtly a place, and so completely under the influence of state etiquette, that everything in Richmond is called after the functionaries of the palace? What are called cheesecakes elsewhere, are here called maids of honor; a capon is called a lord chamberlain; a goose is a lord steward; a roast pig is a master of the horse; a pair of ducks, grooms of the bedchamber; a gooseberry-tart, a gentleman usher of the black rod; and so on." The unsophisticated lady was taken in, when she actually saw the maids of honor make their appearance in the shape of cheesecakes; she convulsed the whole party by turning to the waiter, and desiring him, in a sweet but decided tone, to bring her a *gentleman usher of the black rod*, if they had one in the house quite cold!

**5. [Corbyn Morris], *An Essay Towards Fixing the True Standards of Wit, Humour, Raillery, Satire, and Ridicule* (London: J. Roberts, 1744).**

Raillery *is a genteel poignant Atttack of a* Person *upon any* slight Foibles, Oddities, *or* Embarrassments *of his, in which he is tender, or may be supposed to be tender, and unwilling to come to a free Explunation.*

Satire *is a witty and severe Attack of* mischievous Habits *or* Vices;

Ridicule *is a free* Attack *of any* Motly[2] Composition, *wherein*

---

1   Theodore Hook (1788-1841), English playwright, punster, practical joker.
2   "Composed of elements of diverse or varied character" (*OED*).

*a real or affected* Excellence *and* Defect *both jointly appear,* glaring *together, and* mocking *each other, in the same* Subject.

Hence the Aim of *Raillery,* is to please you, by some little *Embarrassment* of a *Person;* Of *Satire,* to scourge *Vice,* and to deliver it up to your just *Detestation;* And of *Ridicule,* to set an Object in a mean ludicrous Light, so as to expose it to your *Derision* and *Contempt.*

It appears therefore that *Raillery* and *Ridicule* differ in several Circumstances.

1. *Raillery* can only be employ'd in relation to *Persons,* but *Ridicule* may be employ'd in what relates either to *Persons,* or other *Objects.*

2. *Raillery* is us'd only upon *slight* Subjects, where no real Abilities or Merit are questioned, in order to avoid degrading the Person you attack, or rendering him contemptible; Whereas *Ridicule* observes no such Decency, but endeavours really to degrade the person attack'd, and to render him contemptible.

3. *Raillery* may be pointed at a whimsical Circumstance, only because a Person is known to be tender upon it; and your Pleasure will arise from the *Embarrassment* he suffers, in being put to an Explanation; – Thus a young Gentleman may be *rallied* upon his Passion for a Lady; – At the same Time there may be no Ground for *Ridicule* in this Circumstance, as it may no way deserve your *Derision* or *Contempt.*

4. As it thus appears that there are Subjects of *Raillery,* into which *Ridicule* cannot justly be admitted; So there are Subjects of *Ridicule,* wherein your Derision and Contempt are so strongly excited, that they are too gross for *Raillery;* – As a person tossed in a Blanket; or the unfortunate Attack which another has made upon a Windmill.

5. In short, *Raillery,* if the Adventures it is turn'd upon are too *gross* and *luscious,* becomes *Ridicule;* And therefore, in Comparison together, *Raillery* appears like *Wine* of a thin Body, and delicate poignant Flavour; *Ridicule,* like a *Wine* which is fuller, and more rich, and luscious.

## 6. Eliza Haywood, *The Female Spectator* (1744-46), ed. Mary Priestley (London: John Lane, 1929).

*The Innocent Stratagem of a Husband*

An acquaintance of mine, who is accounted a very good husband, and in effect is so, took somewhat an extraordinary method to cure his wife of a too great passion she had expressed on their first marriage, for going to these nocturnal revels. Notice was no sooner given of a masquerade,[1] than her eyes sparkled with joy, the habit-maker[2] was immediately sent for, and nothing was either talked or thought on, but the dress she should wear on the approaching happy night. Not but what he was convinced her intentions were perfectly innocent, as she never desired to go without him, and even testified an eagerness that he would participate of a pleasure which had so many charms for herself: but he was a man who knew the town, and the dangers to which many women had been exposed in these assemblies; besides, the expense was what he could by no means relish, and fearing to draw on himself the character of a churlish, or a jealous husband if he gave either of these reasons for restraining her, he bethought himself of a stratagem which should render her avoiding going for the future entirely her own act and deed.

He caused, unknown to her, one of his intimate friends to put on a habit so exactly the same with what he wore himself, that being of a pretty equal stature, they could not be distinguished from each other when the masks were on. This gentleman, in the midst of a dance, slipped into the husband's place, who immediately withdrew and absconded till the ball was over. The poor lady, little suspecting the deception, kept close to her supposed spouse the whole time, and when the company broke up, was put by him into a hackney coach, which had orders to drive to a tavern in *Pall Mall*. She was a little surprised at finding where she was; but thinking it a whim of him, whom

---

1  "An assembly of people wearing masks and other disguises ... and diverting themselves with dancing and other amusements; a masked ball" (*OED*).

2  Dress-maker.

it was her duty to comply with, suffered herself to be conducted into a room, where he, plucking off his mask, the sight of his face, and his desiring she would do the same, with some of expressions not very becoming the person she had taken him for, so alarmed and terrified her that she gave a great shriek. The husband, who had followed them in another coach, came in that moment and found her ringing the bell, calling for the people of the house and for a chair, the gentleman struggling with her and endeavouring all he could to prevail on her to unmask. He so well acted his part that the person who employed him was highly diverted, and had suffered the farce to go on some time longer, had not the excessive fright his wife was in obliged him to put an end to it, which he did by plucking off his vizard[1] and, taking her in his arms, conjured her to compose herself; this accident, said he, might have proved of ill consequence indeed had it not happened with my particular friend. I saw and followed you with a resolution to avenge the affront I imagined offered to me; I am now convinced it was all a mistake on his side, as well as yours. See here, continued he, taking off his wife's mask, who it is you have gallanted and were about to be so free with.

The gentleman affected to start and be very much amazed and ashamed of what he had done, begged his friend's pardon and the lady's, who he said he accosted, as thinking her a fine woman, and meeting with no manner of repulse, but on the contrary, that she was very desirous of keeping as near to him as possible; and shunning all other conversation, he had all the reason in the world to flatter himself she would be no less satisfied with his company in another place. But, said he, I now perceive that the likeness of habits deceived her, and that while I was gaining a mistress, she doubted not but she was following a husband. This adventure occasioned a good deal of merriment among them, but it had all the effect my friend wished it should have on his wife, and she resolved never more to set her foot within a place where virtue and reputation were liable to such hazards ...

---

1   Mask.

**7.** Jane Collier, *An Essay on the Art of Ingeniously Tormenting;
with Proper Rules for the Exercise of that Pleasant Art. Humbly
addressed, in the First Part, to the Master, Husband, etc.; in the
Second Part, to the Wife, Friend, etc. With some General Instructions for Plaguing all Your Acquaintance* (1753), 2nd ed. (London: A. Millar, 1757).

CONCLUSION *of the* ESSAY.

That great emperor Marcus Antoninus,[1] in those excellent reflexions which he has left to the world, declares, that he learnt
such a precept from one person, and such a precept from
another: Give me leave so far to follow his example, as modest-
ly to disclaim the honour of invention in most of the foregoing
rules, especially in those which appear the most exquisite and
refined; for nothing but experience and observation could have
convinced me, that the practice of some of them was possible.

So very delicate is this ingenious art of Tormenting, that it is
not obvious to vulgar eyes, in what manner it is most feelingly
inflicted. For this reason it is, that rustic Jobson, when his wife
offends him, takes the strap; and where the strength of arm is
with the wife, she generally uses it in a manner to excite her
neighbours to lampoon her by a Skimmington.[2] But I have
done my endeavour to set this matter in a clear light, throughout every chapter of my second division.

I once heard a lady declare, that she carefully concealed from
her *friends* every thing she disliked, as she knew that to be the
only chance she had for not being teazed and plagued with
every little thing that was disagreeable to her. And can any one,
from experience, contradict her prudence, founded, no doubt,
on just observation? How have I seen a whole company made
uneasy from the screeching of a cork between some person's
fingers! the constant drumming upon the table, or shaking of
the knee, of another! the hawking and spawlting of a third!

---

1    Marcus Aurelius Antoninus, (188–217) nicknamed Caracalla, Roman Emperor.
2    "A ludicrous procession, formerly common in villages and country districts, usually
     intended to bring ridicule or odium upon a woman or her husband in cases where
     the one was unfaithful to, or ill-treated, the other" (*OED*).

with various inventions of disagreeableness for offending some or all of the senses! To rise a little higher – It is not your violent quarrels, or downright brutal sayings, which sometimes pass in company, that you have reason to fear; it is your sly, malicious reflexions, and invidious turns, that may be given to well-meant words, that makes company frequently very disagreeable. The lion and the tiger come not often in our way; or if they did, we should be aware of their teeth and claws; but it is your gnats, your wasps, and, in some countries, your musketo flies,[1] that are your constant and true tormentors.

I know that many learned and good men have taken great pains to undermine this our noble art, by laying down rules, and giving exemplars, in order to teach mankind to give no offence to any one, and, instead of being a torment, to be as great a help and comfort to their friends, as it is in their power to be. But with infinite pleasure do I perceive, either that they are not much read, or, at least, that they have not the power of rooting from the human breast, that growing sprig of mischief there implanted with our birth; and generally, as we come to years of discretion, flourishing like a green palm-tree: yet, to shew my great candour and generosity to these my mortal (or rather moral) foes, I will endeavour, as far as my poor recommendation will go, to forward the sale of their books, even among my own pupils. For if, my good scholars, you will guard your minds against the doctrines they intend to teach; if you will consider them as mere amusements; you have my leave to peruse them. Or rather, if you will only remember to observe my orders, in acting in direct opposition to all that a Swift, an Addison, a Richardson, a Fielding,[2] or any other good ethical writer intended to teach, you may (by referring sometimes to these my rules, as helps to your memory) become as profound adepts in this Art, as any of the readers of Mr. Hoyle[3] are in the science of whist.

---

1 Mosquito.
2 Jonathan Swift (1667-1745), English poet and prose satirist; Joseph Addison (1672-1719), English dramatist and essayist; Samuel Richardson (1689-1761), English novelist, printer; Henry Fielding (1707-54), English novelist and dramatist.
3 Edmund Hoyle (1672-1769), British writer on card games, especially known for his *A Short Treatise on the Game of Whist* (1742).

Great are the disputes amongst the learned, whether man, as an animal, be a savage and ferocious, or a gentle and social beast. Swift's picture, in his Yahoes,[1] gives us not a very favourable view of the natural disposition of the animal man; yet I remember not, that he supposes him naturally to delight in tormenting; or does he make him guilty of any vices, but following his brutish appetites. Must not this love of Tormenting therefore be cultivated and cherished? There are many tastes, as that of the olive, the oyster, with several high sauces, cooked up with assa ffitida[2] and the like, which at first are disgustful to the palate, but when once a man has so far depraved his natural taste, as to get a relish for those dainties, there is nothing he is half so fond of.

I can recollect but one kind of brute, that seems to have any notion of this pleasant practice of Tormenting; and that is the cat, when she has got a mouse. – She delays the gratification of her hunger, which prompted her to seek for food, and triumphs in her power over her wretched captive. – She not only sticks her claws into it, making it feel the sharpness of her teeth (without touching the vitals enough to render it insensible to her tricks), but she tosses it over her head in sport, seems in the highest joy imaginable, and is also, to all appearance, at that very time, the sweetest best-humoured animal in the world. Yet should any thing approach her, that she fears will rob her of her play-thing (holding her prey fast in her teeth), she swears, she growls, and shews all the savage motions of her heart. As soon as her fears are over, she again resumes her sport; and is, in this one instance only, kinder to her victim, than her imitators men, that by death she at last puts a final end to the poor wretch's torments.

Was I to rack my invention and memory for ever, I could not find a more adequate picture of the true lovers of Tormenting than this sportive cat: nor will I tire my reader's patience longer, than to add this farther precept:

---

1  In Swift's *Gulliver's Travels* (1726), the yahoos are savage beasts, faintly resembling humans, whom Gulliver meets and shuns in Book IV, in favor of the civilized race of horses, the Houyhnhnms.
2  A pungent spice used in cooking.

REMEMBER ALWAYS TO DO UNTO EVERY ONE, WHAT YOU WOULD LEAST WISH TO HAVE DONE UNTO YOURSELF; for in this is contained the whole of our excellent SCIENCE.

**8. Christopher Anstey, *The New Bath Guide: or, Memoirs of the B–R–D Family* (London: J. Dodsley, 1766).**

LETTER I.
Containing,
Miss JENNY W—D—R to Lady ELIZ. M—D—SS,
at —— Castle, North.[1]

*A View from the Parades at* Bath,[2] *with some Account of the* Dramatis Personae.

Sweet are yon Hills, that crown this fertile Vale!
    Ye genial Springs! Pierian Waters,[3] hail!

Hail, Woods and Lawns! Yes – oft I'll tread
    Yon' Pine-clad Mountain's Side,
Oft trace the gay enamel'd Mead,
    Where Avon[4] rolls his Pride.

Sure, next to fair CASTALIA's Streams,[5]
    And Pindus'[6] flow'ry Path,
Apollo[7] most the Springs esteems,
    And verdant Meads of *Bath*.

---

1  Northumberland.
2  As noted in the annotations to the text of *Evelina*, Bath, a city in the southwest of England, was a fashionable resort in the eighteenth century. The Parades were the central pedestrian thoroughfares of the city.
3  Refers to the spring on Mt. Olympus where the Muses and Orpheus were born.
4  River that runs through Bath.
5  The nymph Castalia was turned into a spring on Mr. Parnassus while being pursued by Apollo. Afterward, the spring was held sacred to the Muses and Apollo.
6  Pindar (522-443 B.C.), Greek lyric poet.
7  Apollo was one of the 12 Greek gods, son to Zeus and Leto. He was known as the Sun god, as well as the god of fine arts.

The Muses[1] haunt these hallow'd Groves,
 And here their Vigils keep,
Here teach fond Swains[2] their hapless Loves
 In gentle Strains to weep.

From Water sprung like Flow'rs from Dew,
 What Troops of Bards appear!
The God of Verse, and Physic too,
 Inspires them twice a year.

Take then, my Friend, the sprightly Rhyme,
While you inglorious waste your Prime,
At Home in cruel Durance pent,
On dull domestic Cares intent,
Forbid, by Parent's harsh Decree,
To share the Joys of *Bath* with me.
Ill-judging Parent! blind to Merit,
Thus to confine a Nymph of Spirit!
With all thy Talents doom'd to fade
And wither in th' unconscious Shade!
I vow, my Dear, it moves my Spleen,
Such frequent Instances I've seen
Of Fathers, cruel and unkind,
To all paternal Duty blind.
What Wretches do we meet with often,
Whose Hearts no Tenderness can soften!
Sure all good Authors should expose
Such Parents, both in Verse and Prose,
And Nymphs inspire with Resolution,
Ne'er to submit to Persecution.
This wholesome Satyr[3] much enhances
The Merit of our best Romances;
And modern Plays, that I could mention,
With Judgment fraught, and rare Invention
Are wrote with much the same intention;

---

1  The Nine Muses, daughters of Zeus and Mnemosyne.
2  Shepherds.
3  Satire.

But, thank my Stars! that worthy Pair
Who undertook a Guardian's Care,
My Spirit never have confin'd:
(An Instance of their gen'rous Mind)
For Lady B—N—R—D, my Aunt,
Herself propos'd this charming Jaunt,
All from Redundancy of Care
For SIM, her fav'rite Son and Heir;
To him the joyous Hours I owe
That *Bath's* enchanting Scenes bestow;
Thanks to her Book of choice Receipts,[1]
That pamper'd Him with sav'ry[2] Meats;
Nor less that Day deserves a Blessing
She cramm'd his Sister to Excess in:
For now she sends both Son and Daughter
For Crudities to drink the Water.
And here they are, all Bile and Spleen,
The strangest Fish that e'er were seen;
With TABBY RUNT their Maid, poor Creature,
The queerest Animal in Nature:
I'm certain none of HOGARTH's[3] Sketches
E'er form'd a Set of stranger Wretches.
I own, my Dear, it hurts my Pride,
To see them blund'ring by my Side;
My Spirits flag, my Life and Fire
Is mortify'd *au Desespoir*,[4]
When SIM, unfashionable Ninny,
In Public calls me *Cousin Jenny*;
And yet, to give the Wight his Due,
He has some Share of Humour too,
A comic Vein of pedant Learning
His Conversation you'll discern in,
The oddest Compound you can see
Of Shrewdness and Simplicity,

---

1 Recipes.
2 Savory.
3 William Hogarth (1697-1764), English engraver, painter, caricaturist.
4 To despair.

With nat'ral Strokes of aukward Wit,
That oft, like Parthian Arrows[1] hit,
For when He seems to dread the Foe
He always strikes the hardest Blow;
And when you'd think He means to flatter,
His Panegyrics turn to Satire:
But then no Creature you can find
Knows half so little of Mankind,
Seems always blund'ring in the dark,
And always making some Remark;
Remarks, that so provoke one's Laughter,
One can't imagine what he's after:
And sure you'll thank me for exciting
In SIM a wondrous itch for Writing;
With all his serious Grimace
To give Descriptions of the Place.
No Doubt his Mother will produce
His poetry for gen'ral Use,
And if his Bluntness does not fright you,
His Observations must delight you;
For truly the good Creature's Mind
Is honest, generous, and kind:
If unprovok'd, will ne'er displease ye,
Or ever make one Soul uneasy. –
I'll try to make his Sister PRUE
Take a small Trip to *Pindus* too.

And me the Nine[2] shall all inspire
To tune for Thee the warbling Lyre:
For Thee, the Muse shall ev'ry Day
Speed, by the post, her rapid Way.
For Thee, my Friend, I'll oft explore
Deep Treasures of Romantic Lore,
Nor wonder, if I Gods create,

---

1  In 250 B.C., the Parthians, of Parthia, a country in Asia, near the Caspian Sea, founded the Parthian empire. While they defeated the Romans in 53 B.C., they were in turn conquered by the Persians in A.D. 226.
2  Muses.

As all good Bards have done of late;
'Twill make my Verse run smooth and even,
To call new Deities from Heaven:
Come then, thou Goddess I adore,
But soft – my Chairman's¹ at the Door,
The Ball's begun – my Friend, no more.

BATH, 1766. J— W— D— R.

LETTER V.

S— B—N—R—D,

*Mr. SIMKIN B—N—R—D to Lady B—N—R—D,*

*at ——— Hall, North.*

*Salutations of Bath, and an Adventure of*

*Mr. B—N—R—D's in Consequence thereof.*

No City, dear Mother, this City excels
For charming sweet Sounds both of Fiddles and Bells;
I thought, like a Fool, that they only would ring
For a Wedding, or Judge, or the Birth of a King;
But I found 'twas for *Me*, that the good-natur'd People
Rung so hard that I thought they would pull
down the Steeple,
So I took out my Purse, as I hate to be shabby,
And paid all the Men when they came from the Abbey;
Yet some think it strange they should make such a Riot
In a Place where sick Folk would be glad to be quiet,
But I hear 'tis the Business of this Corporation²
To welcome in all the *Great* Men of the Nation,
For you know there is nothing diverts or employs
The Minds of *Great* People like making a Noise:
So with Bells they contrive all as much as they can
To tell the Arrival of any such Man.
If a Broker, or Statesman, a Gamester,³ or Peer,⁴

---

1  Man who carried the chair in which she would ride through the streets to her destination.
2  Chamber of Commerce for the city of Bath.
3  Gambler.
4  Lord, member of the aristocracy.

A nat'raliz'd Jew, or a Bishop comes here;
Or *an eminent Trader in Cheese* should retire
Just to think of the Bus'ness the State may require,
With Horns and with Trumpets, with Fiddles and Drums,
They'll strive to divert him as soon as he comes.
'Tis amazing they find such a Number of Ways
Of employing his Thoughts all the Time that he stays;
If by chance the *Great* Man at his Lodging alone is,
He may view from his Window the Colliers Ponies
On both the Parades, where they tumble and kick,
To the great Entertainment of those that are sick:
What a Number of Turnspits[1] and Builders he'll find
For relaxing his Cares, and unbending his Mind,
While Notes of sweet Music contend with the Cries
Of *fine potted Laver,*[2] *fresh Oysters*, and *Pies!*
And Music's a Thing I shall truly revere,
Since the City-Musicians so tickled my Ear;
For when we arriv'd here at *Bath* t'other Day,
They came to our Lodgings on Purpose to play:
And I thought it was right, as the Music was come,
To foot it a little in TABITHA's Room,
For Practice makes perfect, as often I've read,
And to Heels is of Service as well as the Head;
But the Lodgers were shock'd such a Noise we should make,
And the Ladies declar'd that we kept them awake;
Lord RINGBONE, who lay in the Parlour below,
On Account of the Gout[3] he had got in his Toe,
Began on a sudden to curse and to swear,
I protest, my dear Mother, 'twas shocking to hear,
The Oaths of that reprobate gouty old Peer:
"All the Devils in Hell sure at once have concurr'd
To make such a Noise here as never was heard,
Some blundering Blockhead, while I am in Bed,

---

1   "A dog kept to turn the roasting-spit by running within a kind of tread-wheel connected with it" (*OED*).
2   Dulse (*Porphyra*) is a purple seaweed served as food or condiment in many countries, including Scotland and England.
3   Arthritis, caused by a metabolic imbalance, occurring primarily in men.

Treads as hard as a Coach-Horse just over my Head;
I cannot conceive what a Plague he's about,
Are the Fidlers come hither to make all this Rout
With their d——mn'd squeaking Catgut[1] that's worse than
                                            the Gout?
If the Aldermen bad 'em come hither, I swear
I wish they were broiling in Hell with the May'r;[2]
May Flames be my Portion if ever I give
Those Rascals one Farthing as long as I live!" –
So while they were playing their musical Airs,
And I was just dancing the Hay round the Chairs,
He roar'd to his Frenchman to kick them down Stairs.
The Frenchman came forth with his outlandish Lingo,
Just the same as a Monkey, and made all the Men go:
I could not make out what he said, not a Word,
And his Lordship declar'd I was very absurd.
Says I, "Master RINGBONE, I've nothing to fear,
Tho' you be a Lord, and your Man a Mounseer,[3]
For the May'r and the Aldermen bad them come here:
                — As absurd as I am,
                I don't care a Damn
                For you, nor your *Valee de Sham*:[4]
                For a Lord, do you see,
                Is nothing to me,
                Any more than a Flea;
                And your Frenchman so eager,
                With all his soup Meagre,[5]
                Is no more than a Mouse,
                Or a Bug, or a Louse,
And I'll do as I please while I stay in the House:
For the B——N——R——D Family all can afford
To part with their Money as free as a Lord. – "

---

1   Used to make bow strings.
2   Mayor.
3   A derogatory form of the French "Monsieur"; Captain Mirvan uses this title when
    speaking of M. Du Bois and of any Frenchman.
4   *Valet de chambre*, or man-servant.
5   "Thin soup, made chiefly from vegetables or fish" (*OED*).

So I thank'd the Musicians, and gave them a Guinea,
Tho' the Ladies and Gentlemen call'd me a Ninny;
And I'll give them another the next Time they play,
For Men of good Fortune encourage, they say,
All Arts and all Sciences too in their Way;
And the Men were so kind as to hallow and bawl
"G—d bless you, Sir, thank you, good Fortune befall
Yourself, and the B—N—R—D Family all. – "

Excuse any more, – for I very well know
Both my Subject and Verse – *is exceedingly low*;
But if any great Critic finds Fault with my Letter,
He has nothing to do but to send you a better.
And now, my dear Mother, &c. &c. &c.
Bath, 1766. S—— B—N—R—D.

### 9. [James Quin], *Quin's Jests; or, The Facetious Man's Pocket-Companion* (London: S. Bladon, 1766).

Quin being greatly teazed in the company of some frisky girls, by a number of frivolous and impertinent questions, was at length asked by one of them, "Whether his mother had *longed* for any thing, and if he was *marked*?" "Yes, Miss, he replied, my mother had *a very great longing* for what I am pretty much *marked* with; and what is more, if she had not *longed* for it, perhaps, I should not have been here."

★   ★   ★   ★

Some years before Quin left the stage, he had laid a wager with Gissard, that, before the season was out, he would tell all the audience to kiss his a—e; and that, so far from being offended, they would applaud him for it. An opportunity offered one night when some of the royal family was expected, and when the curtain could not be drawn up till their arrival. Quin went upon the stage, after the repeated clamours of the galleries for the last music, when he told the audience they could not possibly begin yet; but that, if they pleased, he would, in the mean time, attempt to divert them with a west country story. "Hear him, hear him," re-echoed from every quarter. "An honest working man in Somersetshire took for better for worse a strapping wench, whose name was Jane: she, in due time, proved, that she was neither barren, nor her husband impotent. – Their first issue was called after his father Jeremiah. – A whimsical esquire in the neighbourhood, who stood godfather to the second, and whom they therefore thought would make a comfortable provision for him in due time, had the liberty to name him as he pleased. – He called him *Kiss my A—e*! When they grew up, John was intended for his father's profession – *Kiss my A—e for nothing*! However, the 'squire dying, and no provision being made for his godson, he soon took up his father's trade, which was neither more nor less than *Trencher-maker. – Jere* made *square Trenchers – Kiss my A—e all round.* Their father died some time after; and having been a sober, industrious man, had saved a small matter, which he fairly divided between his two sons. Flushed with this acquisition, they came up to London to see the world, got dressed, and came to the play. – *Jere* was of a more prudent turn than his brother, and went into the gallery – *Kiss my A—e in the Pit.* They were so fond of what they had seen, that they returned the next night, the house was crammed, and – *Kiss my A—e in the Boxes.*" Quin had got thus far in his story, with repeated acclamations, when the regal part of the audience arrived, and prevented the sequel.

★    ★    ★    ★

Quin was strongly importuned by a lady, who was greatly suspected of having just had a lucky-begotten,[1] to make grimaces; telling him, she had heard he was very facetious that way. – "And, Madam, said he, as I have been told, you have a much better nack at *making faces* than me: I beg you'll begin first."

★    ★    ★    ★

An elderly lady, who was past her grand climacteric, having taken, "for better for worse," a young fellow whose shoulders bore a promising appearance, was severely chid by a near rela-

---

1 A child out of wedlock.

tion for what the latter imagined so striking a piece of folly; and being asked what felicity she could expect from such a disproportionate match, the bride answered, she was still able to lay the great *groundwork* of happiness, if her husband could but raise the *superstructure*.

*     *     *     *

A lady, who was none of the most virtuous, either in disposition or conduct, had, nevertheless, prevailed upon a nobleman to make a very handsome settlement upon her, and to believe he was the only happy man. To corroborate this opinion in some measure, she had ordered her jeweller to make her a locket in the form of a heart, which she proposed presenting her inamorato with; and having wrote a motto, which she intended inscribing, it was left upon her toilet,[1] when one of her acquaintance, who was paying her a morning visit, perceiving *Un me suffit*, added *à la fois*. The jeweller, ignorant of the language, inserted the whole; and she, having no suspicion of the improvement, presented it to her lover, who was so enraged at the imaginary insult, that he would never after see her. – What reparation could the wit make for the injury he had done her? He wrote a ballad in her praise, which is sung in all public places.

*     *     *     *

A certain couple of amorous lovers who had lived upon very good terms for about six years, began to think at last they were going on in a wrong course, and the swain, of his own accord, proposed that they should be lawfully married; but upon the lady's enquiring what would be the price of a licence, to avoid the publication of banns, she swore she would rather *die a maid*, than pay so much money to *change her name* and *be exposed*.

*     *     *     *

The following story would not be a bad one, if it did not look too much like an imitation of that of the Ephesian Matron. An amorous wife, who had pined herself almost to death for her

---

1   Dressing table.

sick husband, was not comforted by her father, though he took every opportunity to administer consolation to her. He would say, "My dear girl, consider our fragile state – death is a debt we must all pay upon demand – the tyrant is inexorable, and we must submit to fate. – Have courage, my girl, for suppose even your husband should go off this bout, have not I another in my eye for you that is younger, more vigorous, and richer than this?" But she, tender creature, could listen to no such remonstrances: – she lived but in her husband; their hearts were so intwined, that wound but one, the other must feel the deadly blow. – The thoughts of a second husband did but aggravate her misery. – Such was her language, when, lo! her better half departs: – what rage! what phrenzy! what transports! what anguish! she tears her hair, beats her bosom, casts herself upon his corpse, and swears to embrace for ever the dear and only image of her love. The funeral tears and sighs take place, her eyes begin to dry, her bosom less to heave. – "Heaven's will be done, says she, I see 'tis in vain to moan, it will not bring him back. – Pray, Sir (continues she to her father) methinks I heard you mention something of *another* husband: does he live far off?"

★    ★    ★    ★

A certain vain, supercilious man of fashion, who comes constantly to Bath once a year, told Quin one day very seriously, "I do believe, says he, I am one or other the most facetious fellow in the world, for I never go into any company, but what I set them all a laughing. "Are you sure, said Quin, that they don't laugh at you, instead of your wit." "I don't care if they do, said he, for I am pretty certain there is no man laughs at me, but what I laugh at him again." "Then, said Quin, you lead the merriest life of any man in Europe."

**10. Anon., *An Essay on Laughter* (London: T. Davies and L. Davis, 1769).**

The following objection may be started on this occasion: "Although it be pride that makes us *laugh* at our own droll jokes and conceptions, are we thence to conclude, that we are instigated by the same principle when we *laugh* at the *bons mots* of *others*? Our *Laughter* is a manifest approbation of such sayings, and a suffrage of this nature seems to be less the effect of a partial presumption for ourselves, than of candidly sacrificing one's *self-love*, by such a tribute of applause paid to another's merit."

However specious the assigning of such a cause may appear, yet it is not the true one; which must be sought for in another source: and thus, by our adopting the facetious sallies, and approving the *bons mots* or witty sayings of others, we, by the rebound, arrogate to ourselves, as it were, the glory of them. For then a secret vanity makes us turn such approbation to our own advantage, and becomes the flattering handmaid of our *pride*, for not letting them have escaped our encouraging notice.

This appearing homage on our side, when duely scrutinized, will be found to be but an indirect tribute at best, and that the applause, however just, which we express at the ingenious sallies of others, and the happy invention of other authors, is kindly reflected in part on ourselves, by way of complimentary incense to our own judgment. The praise due for a happy hit-off, a brilliancy of imagination and expression, we freely resign to the author's ready invention; but the merit of adequately feeling, discerning, and judging, we claim as our own right. – Who then will dare to dissent from my assertion, that it is overweening *pride* which compels us to *laugh* at the wit and pleasantry of others?

Why were you so pleased at that comic exhibition, during which, *Laughter* almost incessantly flowed from you, till you began to discover that your own character was struck out? Your notes were then soon altered; and why pray? – Because *self-love* gratified delights in *laughing*, but when offended, loseth all relish for such grating raillery; and this too is an incontestable proof that *pride* is the true principle of the *laughing convulsion*, peculiar to the human frame; which it has an equal power of exciting or stopping. At the display of any comic portraitures, we are alike interested in the cause of our friends, who if we find to be attacked therein, our *Laughter* immediately ceases.

> You count me mad in fashion, you forbear
> To *laugh*, nor think I need a doctor's care,

Or guardian from the *prætor*, tho' my friend
On whom my fortune and my life depend,
My chief support, in short, my only guard;
And who art vex'd to see my nails ill par'd.

Creech.[1]

Now either take off a person's manner of *laughing*, or rebuke him for *laughing* mal-a-propos, rely upon it, you sting him most sensibly ... Why? Because you interrupt him in the secret enjoyment of his pride; you cruelly surprize him in, and expose him for the shameful abuse of his self-love – whereof the glaring reason occurs – *that pride is the source of Laughter.*

What fathers we have seen with enraptured tenderness, and mothers with almost idolatrous fondness, caress a darling babe, and chear its infancy with continued smiles; why? because while in this helpless condition, it appears in a natural state of subordination to them; which inferiority was not displeasing to their vanity – but when the child has reached the age of thirteen or fourteen years, and begins to reason in consequence of daily expanding ideas, that bring him in new recruits of knowledge, it remains no longer implicitly obedient to the will of parents, but frequently rises in opposition to it, nay, demands more convincing arguments from their side, who, from that epoch of a child's resistance to their mandates, begin to abate gradually of their parental affection, which not rarely on such occasions becomes totally extinguished: for from that moment their self-love is chagrined, their pride is piqued. Then the fathers, in order to recover their lost authority, substitute harshness and severity in the place of their late fondness and complacency. Such is the supreme, universal, and invariable law established by nature. The bear fondles its nursling cubs but while they cannot help themselves. The eagles turn away from their young progeny as soon as they are able to fly and procure sustenance for themselves.

But if a child so circumstanced as we have hinted above, come to distinguish himself in society by his eminent qualities,

---

1  Either Thomas Creech (1659-1700), translator of Lucretius, or William Creech (1745-1815), Edinburgh publisher.

or any lucky occurrence, tending to flatter the vanity of his parents, their love is kindled anew; and this revival of affection for their child, is but the returning complaisance of their own *self-love*, that re-plumes itself for the flattering acquisition of a long forgotten object, now no longer beheld without a smile of conscious pride.

## 11. William Hazlitt, *Lectures on the English Comic Writers* (London: Taylor and Hessy, 1819).

from "On Wit and Humour"

The essence of the laughable then is the incongruous, the disconnecting one idea from another, or the jostling of one feeling against another. The first and most obvious cause of laughter is to be found in the simple succession of events, as in the sudden shifting of a disguise, or some unlooked-for accident, without any absurdity of character or situation. The accidental contradiction between our expectations and the event can hardly be said, however, to amount to the ludicrous: it is merely laughable. The ludicrous is where there is the same contradiction between the object and our expectations, heightened by some deformity or inconvenience, that is, by its being contrary to what is customary or desirable; as the ridiculous, which is the highest degree of the laughable, is that which is contrary not only to custom but to sense and reason, or is a voluntary departure from what we have a right to expect from those who are conscious of absurdity and propriety in words, looks, and actions.

Of these different kinds or degrees of the laughable, the first is the most shallow and short-lived; for the instant the immediate surprise of a thing's merely happening one way or another is over, there is nothing to throw us back upon our former expectation, and renew our wonder at the event a second time. The second sort, that is, the ludicrous arising out of the improbable or distressing, is more deep and lasting, either because the painful catastrophe excites a greater curiosity, or because the old impression, from its habitual hold on the imagination, still recurs mechanically, so that it is longer before we can seriously make up our minds to the unaccountable deviation from it. The third sort, or the ridiculous arising out of absurdity as well as improbability, that is, where the defect or weakness is of a man's own seeking, is the most refined of all, but not always so pleasant as the last, because the same contempt and disapprobation which sharpens and subtilises our sense of the impropriety, adds a severity to it inconsistent with perfect ease and enjoyment. This last species is properly the province of satire. The principle of contrast is, however, the same in all the stages, in the simply laughable, the ludicrous, the ridiculous; and the effect is only the more complete, the more durably and pointedly this principle operates.

To give some examples in these different kinds. We laugh, when children, at the sudden removing of a pasteboard mask: we laugh, when grown up, more gravely at the tearing off the mask of deceit. We laugh at absurdity; we laugh at deformity. We laugh at a bottle-nose in a caricature; at a stuffed figure of an alderman in a pantomime, and at the tale of Slaukenbergius.[1] A giant standing by a dwarf makes a contemptible figure enough. Rosinante[2] and Dapple[3] are laughable from contrast, as their masters from the same principle make two for a pair. We laugh at the dress of foreigners, and they at ours. Three chimney-sweepers meeting three Chinese in Lincoln's-inn Fields, they laughed at one other till they were ready to drop down. Country people laugh at a person because they never saw him before. Any one dressed in the height of the fashion, or quite out of it, is equally an object of ridicule. One rich source of the ludicrous is distress with which we cannot sympathise from its absurdity or insignificance. Women laugh at their lovers. We laugh at a damned author, in spite of our teeth, and though he may be our friend. "There is something in the misfortunes of our best friends that pleases us." We laugh at people on the top of a stage-coach, or in it, if they seem in great extremity. It is

---

1  In Laurence Sterne's *Tristram Shandy* (1759-61), the "Tale of Slaukenbergius" concerns the adventures of a man with a very large nose.
2  Rosinante is Don Quixote's horse in Cervantes' *Don Quixote* (1605); though it is an old, broken-down horse, Don Quixote sees it as a gallant steed.
3  Dapple is the name given to Sancho Panza's donkey in Smollett's translation of *Don Quixote*.

hard to hinder children from laughing at a stammerer, at a negro, at a drunken man, or even at a madman. We laugh at mischief. We laugh at what we do not believe. We say that an argument or an assertion that is very absurd, is quite ludicrous. We laugh to shew our satisfaction with ourselves, or our contempt for those about us, or to conceal our envy or our ignorance. We laugh at fools, and at those who pretend to be wise – at extreme simplicity, awkwardness, hypocrisy, and affectation. "They were talking of me," says Scrub,[1] "for they laughed consumedly." Lord Foppington's[2] insensibility to ridicule, and airs of ineffable self-conceit, are no less admirable; and Joseph Surface's[3] cant maxims of morality, when once disarmed of their power to do hurt, become sufficiently ludicrous. – We laugh at that in others which is a serious matter to ourselves; because our self-love is stronger than our sympathy, sooner takes the alarm, and instantly turns our heedless mirth into gravity, which only enhances the jest to others. Some one is generally sure to be the sufferer by a joke. What is sport to one, is death to another. It is only very sensible or very honest people, who laugh as freely at their own absurdities as at those of their neighbours. In general the contrary rule holds, and we only laugh at those misfortunes in which we are spectators, not sharers. The injury, the disappointment, shame, and vexation that we feel, put a stop to our mirth; while the disasters that come home to us, and excite our repugnance and dismay, are an amusing spectacle to others. The greater resistance we make, and the greater the perplexity into which we are thrown, the more lively and *piquant* is the intellectual display of cross-purposes to the by-standers. Our humiliation is their triumph. We are occupied with the disgreeableness of the result instead of its oddity or unexpectedness. Others see only the conflict of motives, and the sudden alternation of events; we feel the pain as well, which more than counterbalances the speculative entertainment we might receive from the contemplation of our abstract situation.

---

1  Scrub is a witty valet in Farquhar's play *The Beaux' Strategem* (1707).
2  Lord Foppington is a silly, arrogant gentleman in Vanbrugh's comedy *The Relapse* (1696).
3  Joseph Surface is a mean-spirited, two-faced character in Richard Brinsley Sheridan's *The School for Scandal*.